V.E. SCHWAB

TITAN BOOKS

The Fragile Threads of Power

The Fragile Threads of Power

V.E. SCHWAB

TITAN BOOKS

THE FRAGILE THREADS OF POWER
Trade hardback edition ISBN: 9781785652462
E-book edition ISBN: 9781785652479
Signed trade hardback edition ISBN: 9781803368368
Waterstones edition ISBN: 9781803368412
Illumicrate edition ISBN: 9781803368382
Forbidden Planet edition ISBN: 9781803368399
Export paperback edition ISBN: 9781803367392
Signed export paperback edition ISBN: 9781803368375

Published by Titan Books
A division of Titan Publishing Group Ltd
144 Southwark Street, London SE1 0UP
www.titanbooks.com

First edition: September 2023
10 9 8 7 6 5 4 3 2 1

A CIP catalogue record for this title is available from
the British Library.

Printed and bound by CPI Group (UK) Ltd,
Croydon CR0 4YY

For the ones who still believe in magic

Magic is the river that waters all things.
It lends itself to life, and in death calls it back,
and so the stream appears to rise and fall,
when in truth, it never loses a single drop.

—TIEREN SERENSE,
ninth *Aven Essen* of the London Sanctuary

WHITE LONDON, *seven years ago*

It came in handy, being small.

People talked of growing up like it was some grand accomplishment, but small bodies could slip through narrow gaps, and hide in tight corners, and get in and out of places other bodies wouldn't fit.

Like a chimney.

Kosika shimmied down the last few feet and dropped into the hearth, sending up a plume of soot. She held her breath, half to keep from inhaling ash and half to make sure no one was home. Lark had said the place was empty, that no one had come or gone in more than a week, but Kosika figured it was better to be silent than sorry, so she stayed crouched in the fireplace a few moments, waiting, listening until she was sure she was alone.

Then she scooted onto the edge of the hearth and slipped off her boots, tying the laces and hanging them around her neck. She hopped down, bare feet kissing the wooden floor, and set off.

It was a nice house. The boards were even, and the walls were straight, and though the shutters were all latched, there were a lot of windows, and thin bits of light got in around the edges, giving her just enough to see by. She didn't mind robbing nice houses, especially when people just up and left them unattended.

She went to the pantry first. She always did. People who lived in houses this nice didn't think of things like jam and cheese and dried meat as precious, never got hungry enough to worry about running out.

But Kosika was always hungry.

Sadly, the pantry shelves were sparse. A sack of flour. A pouch of salt. A single jar of compote that turned out to be bitter orange (she hated bitter orange). But there, in the back, behind a tin of loose tea, she found a waxy paper bag of sugar cubes. More than a dozen of them, small and brown and shining like crystals. She'd always had a sweet tooth, and her mouth began to water even as she tucked one in her cheek. She knew she should only take one or two and leave the rest, but she broke her own rules and shoved the whole bag in her pocket, sucking on the cube as she went off in search of treasure.

The trick was not to take too much. People who had *enough* didn't notice when one or two of their things went missing. They figured they'd simply misplaced them, put them down and forgotten where.

Maybe, she told herself, the person who'd lived here was dead. Or maybe they had simply gone on a trip. Maybe they were rich, rich enough to have a second home in the country, or a really big ship.

She tried to imagine what they were doing as she padded through the darkened rooms, opening cupboards and drawers, looking for the glint of coins, or metal, or magic.

Something twitched at the edge of her sight, and Kosika jumped, dropping into a crouch before she realized it was only a mirror. A large, silvered looking glass, propped on a table. Too big to steal, but still she drifted toward it, had to stand on her toes to see her face reflected back. Kosika didn't know how old she was. Somewhere between six and seven. Closer to seven, she guessed, because the days were just starting to get shorter, and she knew she was born right at the point where summer gave way to fall. Her mother said that was why she looked like she was caught between, neither here nor there. Her hair, which was neither blond nor brown. Her eyes, which were neither green nor grey nor blue.

(Kosika didn't see why a person's looks even mattered. They weren't like coin. They didn't spend.)

Her gaze dipped. Below the mirror, on the table, there was a drawer.

It didn't have a knob or a handle, but she could see the groove of one thing set into another, and when she pressed against the wood, it gave, a hidden clasp released. The drawer sprang out, revealing a shallow tray, and two amulets, made of glass or pale stone, one bound in leather and the other in thin strands of copper.

Amplifiers.

She couldn't read the symbols scratched into the edges, but she knew that's what they were. Talismans designed to capture power, and bind it to you.

Most people couldn't afford magic-catchers—they just carved the spells straight into their skin. But marks faded, and skin sagged, and spells turned with time, like rotten fruit, while a piece of jewelry could be taken off, exchanged, refilled.

Kosika lifted one of the amulets, and wondered if the amplifiers were worth less, or even more, now that the world was waking up. That's what people called the *change*. As if the magic had just been sleeping all these years, and the latest king, Holland, had somehow shaken it awake.

She hadn't seen him yet, now with her own eyes, but she'd seen the old ones, once, the pale twins who rode through the streets, their mouths stained dark with other people's blood. She'd felt only a pang of relief when she heard they were dead, and if she was honest, she hadn't cared much at first about the new king, either. But it turned out Holland was different. Right after he took the throne, the river began to thaw, and the fog began to thin, and everything in the city got a little brighter, a little warmer. And all at once, the magic began to flow again. Not much of it, sure, but it was there, and people didn't even have to bind it to their bodies using scars or spellwork.

Her best friend, Lark, woke up one morning with his palms prickling, the way skin did sometimes after it went numb, and you had to rub the feeling back. A few days later, he had a fever, sweat shining on his face, and it scared Kosika to see him so sick. She tried to swallow up the fear, but it made her stomach hurt, and all night she lay awake, convinced that he would die and she'd be even more alone. But then, the next day, there he was, looking fine. He ran toward her, pulled her into an alley, and held

11

out his hands, cupped together like he had a secret inside. And when he opened his fingers, Kosika gasped.

There, floating in his palms, was a small blue flame.

And Lark wasn't the only one. Over the last few months, the magic had sprouted up like weeds. Only it never really grew inside the grown-ups—at least, not in the ones who wanted it most. Maybe they'd spent too long trying to force magic to do what they wanted, and it was angry.

Kosika didn't care if it skipped them, so long as it found *her*.

It hadn't, not yet.

She told herself that was okay. It had only been a few months since the new king took the throne and brought the magic with him. But every day, she checked her body, hoping to find some hint of change, studied her hands and waited for a spark.

Now Kosika shoved the amplifiers in her pocket with the sugar cubes, and slid the secret drawer shut, and headed for the front door. Her hand was just reaching for the lock when the light caught on the wooden threshold and she jerked to a stop. It was spelled. She couldn't read the marks, but Lark had taught her what to look for. She looked balefully back at the chimney—it was a lot harder going up than down. But that's exactly what she did, climbing into the hearth, and shoving her boots back on, and shimmying up. By the time Kosika got back onto the roof, she was breathless, and soot-stained, and she popped another sugar cube into her mouth as a reward.

She crept to the edge of the roof and peered down, spotting Lark's silver-blond head below, hand outstretched as he pretended to sell charms to anyone who passed, even though the charms were just stones painted with fake spells and he was really standing there to make sure no one came home while she was still inside.

Kosika whistled, and he looked up, head cocked in question. She made an X with her arms, the sign for a spell she couldn't cross, and he jerked his head toward the corner, and she liked that they had a language that didn't need words.

She went to the other side of the roof and lowered herself down the gutter, dropping to a crouch on the paving stones below. She straightened and looked around, but Lark wasn't there. Kosika frowned, and started down the alley.

A pair of hands shot out and grabbed her, hauling her into the gap between houses. She thrashed, was about to bite one of the hands when it shoved her away.

"Kings, Kosika," said Lark, shaking his fingers. "Are you a girl or a beast?"

"Whichever one I need to be," she shot back. But he was smiling. Lark had a wonderful smile, the kind that took over his whole face and made you want to smile, too. He was eleven, gangly in that way boys got when they were growing, and even though his hair was as pale as the Sijlt before it thawed, his eyes were warm and dark, the color of wet earth.

He reached out and patted the soot off her clothes. "Find anything good?"

Kosika took out the amplifiers. He turned them over in his hands, and she knew he could read the spells, knew they were a good find by the way he studied them, nodding to himself.

She didn't tell Lark about the sugar, and she felt a little bad about it, but she told herself he didn't like sweet things, not as much as she did, and it was her reward for doing the hard work, the kind that got you caught. And if she'd learned anything from her mother, it was that you had to look out for yourself.

Her mother, who had always treated her like a burden, a small thief squatting in her house, eating her food and sleeping in her bed and stealing her heat. And for a long time, Kosika would have given anything to be noticed, to feel wanted, by someone else. But then children started waking up with fire in their hands, or wind beneath their feet, or water tipping toward them like they were downhill, and Kosika's mother started noticing her, studying her, a hunger in her eyes. These days, she did her best to stay out of the way.

Lark pocketed the amulets—she knew whatever he got for them, he'd give her half, he always did. They were a team. He ruffled her in-between hair, and she pretended not to like the way it felt, the weight of his hand on her head. She didn't have a big brother, but he made her feel like she did.

And then he gave her a gentle push, and they broke apart, Lark toward wherever it was he went, and Kosika toward home.

She slowed as the house came into sight.

It was small and thin, like a book on a shelf, squeezed between two others on a road barely large enough for a cart, let alone a carriage. But there *was* a carriage parked in front, and a short man standing by the front door. The stranger wasn't knocking, just standing there, smoking a taper, thin white smoke pluming around his head. His skin was covered in tattoos, the kind the grown-ups used to bind magic to them. He had even more than her mother. The marks ran over his hands and up his arms, disappearing under his shirt and reappearing at his throat. She wondered if that meant he was strong, or weak.

As if the man could feel her thinking, his head swiveled toward her, and Kosika darted back into the shadow of the nearest alley. She went around to the back of the house, climbed the crates beneath the window. She slid the frame up, even though it was stiff and she'd always had a fear that it would swing back down and cut her head right off as she was climbing through. But it didn't, and she shimmied over the sill, and dropped to the floor, holding her breath.

She heard voices in the kitchen.

One was her mother's, but she didn't recognize the other. There was a sound, too. The *clink clink clink* of metal. Kosika crept down the hall, and peered around the doorway, and saw her mother and another man sitting at the table. Kosika's mother looked like she always did—tired and thin, like a piece of dried fruit, all the softness sucked away.

But the man, she'd never seen before. He was stringy, like gristle, his hair tied back off his face. A black tattoo that looked like knots of rope traced the bones on his left hand, which hovered over a stack of coins.

He lifted a few and let them fall, one by one, back onto the stack. That was the sound she'd heard.

Clink clink clink.
Clink clink clink.
Clink clink clink.
"Kosika."

She jumped, startled by her mother's voice, and by the kindness in it.

"Come here," said her mother, holding out her hand. Black brands ringed each of her fingers and circled her wrist, and Kosika resisted the urge to back away, because she didn't want to make her mother mad. She took a cautious step forward, and her mother smiled, and Kosika should have known then, to stop out of reach, but she took another slow step toward the table.

"Don't be rude," snapped her mother, and there, at least, was the tone she knew. "Her magic hasn't come in yet," her mother added, addressing the man, "but it will. She's a strong girl."

Kosika smiled at that. Her mother didn't often say nice things.

The man smiled, too. And then he jerked forward. Not with his whole body, just his tattooed hand. One second it was there on the coins and the next it was around her wrist, pulling her close. Kosika stumbled, but he didn't let go. He twisted her palm up, exposing the underside of her forearm, and the blue veins at her wrist.

"Hmm," he said. "Awfully pale."

His voice was wrong, like rocks were stuck inside his throat, and his hand felt like a shackle, heavy and cold around her wrist. She tried to twist free, but his fingers only tightened.

"She does have some fight," he said, and panic rose in Kosika, because her mother was just sitting there, watching. Only she wasn't watching *her*. Her eyes were on the coins, and Kosika didn't want to be there anymore. Because she knew who this man was.

Or at least, *what* he was.

Lark had warned her about men and women like him. Collectors who traded not in objects, but in people, anyone with a bit of magic in their veins.

Kosika *wished* she had magic, so she could light the man on fire, scare him away, make him let go. She didn't have any power, but she did at least remember what Lark told her, about where to hit a man to make him hurt, so she wrenched backward with all her weight, forcing the stranger to his feet, and then she kicked him, hard, as hard as she could, right between his legs. The man made a sound like a bellows, all the air whooshing out, and the hand around her wrist let go as he crashed into the table, toppling the stack of coins as she shot toward the door.

Her mother tried to grab her as she passed, but her limbs were too slow, her body worn out from all those years of stealing magic, and Kosika was out the door before she remembered the other man, and the carriage. He came at her in a wreath of smoke, but she ducked beneath the circle of his arms, and took off down the narrow road.

Kosika didn't know what they'd do if they caught her.

It didn't matter.

She wouldn't let them.

They were big but she was fast, and even if they knew the streets, she knew the alleys and the steps and all nine walls and the narrow gaps in the world—the ones that even Lark couldn't fit through anymore. Her legs started to hurt and her lungs were burning, but Kosika kept running, cutting between market stalls and shops until the buildings staggered and the path climbed into steps and gave way onto the Silver Wood.

And even then, she didn't stop.

None of the other children would go into the wood. They said it was dead, said it was haunted, said there were faces in the trees, eyes watching from the peeling grey bark. But Kosika wasn't scared, or at least, not as scared of the dead forest as she was of those men, with their hungry eyes and shackle hands. She crossed the first line of trees, straight as bars on a cage, and kept going one row, two, three, before pressing herself back against a narrow trunk.

She closed her eyes, and held her breath, and tried to listen past the hammer of her heart. Listen for voices. Listen for footsteps. But the world was suddenly quiet, and all she heard was the murmur of wind through the mostly bare branches. The rustle of it on brittle leaves.

Slowly, she opened her eyes. A dozen wooden eyes stared back from the trees ahead. She waited for one of them to blink, but none of them did.

Kosika could have turned back then, but she didn't. She'd crossed the edge of the woods, and it had made her bold. So she went deeper, walking until she couldn't see the rooftops, or the streets, or the castle anymore, until it felt like she wasn't in the city at all, but somewhere else. Somewhere calm. Somewhere quiet.

And then she saw him.

The man was sitting on the ground, his back against a tree, his legs out and his chin dropped against his chest, limp as a rag doll, but the sight of him still made her gasp, the sound loud as a snapping stick in the silent woods. She clapped a hand over her mouth and ducked behind the nearest tree, expecting the man's head to jerk up, his hand to reach for a weapon. But he didn't move. He must have been asleep.

Kosika chewed her lip.

She couldn't leave—it wasn't safe to go home, not yet—and she didn't want to put her back to the man on the ground, in case he tried to surprise her, so she sank down against another tree, legs crossed, making sure she could see the sleeping stranger. She dug in her pockets, came up with the waxy bag of sugar.

She sucked on the cubes one at a time, eyes darting now and then to the man against the tree. She decided to save one of the sugar cubes for him, as thanks for keeping her company, but an hour passed, and the sun sank low enough to scrape the branches, and the air went from cool to cold, and the man still didn't move.

She had a bad feeling, then.

"*Os?*" she called out, wincing as the sound of her voice broke the silence of the Silver Wood, the word bouncing off the hard trees.

Hello? Hello? Hello?

Kosika got to her feet and made her way toward the man. He didn't look very old, but his hair was silver white, his clothes finely made, too nice to be sitting on the ground. He wore a silver half-cloak, and she knew, as soon as she got close enough, that he wasn't sleeping.

He was dead.

Kosika had seen a dead body before, but it had been much different, limbs askew and insides spilled out onto the cobblestones. There was no blood on the man beneath the tree. He looked like he'd just gotten tired, and decided to sit down and rest, and never managed to get back up. One arm was draped in his lap. The other hung at his side. Kosika's gaze followed it down to his hand where it touched the ground. There was something beneath his fingers.

She leaned closer, and saw that it was grass.

17

Not the hard, brittle blades that coated the rest of the Silver Wood, but soft, new shoots, small and green and spreading out beneath him like a cushion.

She ran her fingers over it, recoiling when her hand accidentally grazed his skin. The man was cold. Her eyes went to his half-cloak. It looked nice, and warm, and she thought of taking it, but she couldn't bring herself to touch him again. And yet, she didn't want to leave him, either. She took the last of the sugar cubes from the waxy bag and set it in his palm, just as a sound shattered the quiet.

The scrape of metal and the thud of boots.

Kosika leapt up, darting into the trees for cover. But they weren't coming after her. She heard the steps slow, then stop, and she stopped, too, peering around a narrow trunk. From there, she couldn't see the man on the ground, but she saw the soldiers standing over him. There were three of them, their silver armor glinting in the thin light. Royal guards.

Kosika couldn't hear what they were saying, but she saw one kneel, heard another let out a ragged sob. A sound that splintered the woods, and made her wince, and turn her back, and run.

I

CLOCKS,
LOCKS,
AND
CLEARLY
STOLEN
THINGS

I

RED LONDON, *now*

Master Haskin had a knack for fixing broken things.

The sign on his shop door said as much.

ES HAL VIR, HIS HAL NASVIR, it declared in neat gold font.

Once broken, soon repaired.

Ostensibly, his business was devoted to the mending of clocks, locks, and household trinkets. Objects guided by simple magic, the minor cogs that turned in so many London homes. And of course, Master Haskin *could* fix a clock, but so could anyone with a decent ear and a basic understanding of the language of spells.

No, most of the patrons that came through the black door of Haskin's shop brought stranger things. Items "salvaged" from ships at sea, or lifted from London streets, or claimed abroad. Objects that arrived damaged, or were broken in the course of acquisition, their spellwork having rattled loose, unraveled, or been ruined entirely.

People brought all manner of things to Haskin's shop. And when they did, they invariably encountered his apprentice.

She was usually perched, cross-legged, on a rickety stool behind the counter, a tangle of brown curls piled like a hat on her head, the unruly mass bound up with twine, or netting, or whatever she could find in a pinch. She might have been thirteen, or twenty-three, depending on the light. She sat like a child and swore like a sailor, and dressed as if no one had ever taught her how. She had thin quick fingers that were always moving, and keen dark eyes that twitched over whatever broken thing lay gutted on the counter, and she talked as she worked, but only to the skeleton of the owl that sat nearby.

It had no feathers, no flesh, just bones held together by silver thread. She had named the bird Vares—*prince*—after Kell Maresh, to whom it bore little resemblance, save for its two stone eyes, one of which was blue, the other black, and the unsettling effect it had on those it met—the result of a spell that spurred it now and then to click its beak or cock its head, startling unsuspecting customers.

Sure enough, the woman currently waiting across the counter jumped.

"Oh," she said, ruffling as if she had feathers of her own. "I didn't know it was *alive*."

"It's not," said the apprentice, "strictly speaking." In truth, she often wondered where the line was. After all, the owl had only been spelled to mimic basic movements, but now and then she'd catch him picking at a wing where the feathers would be, or notice him staring out the window with those flat rock eyes, and she swore that he was thinking *something* of his own.

The apprentice returned her attention to the waiting woman. She fetched a glass jar from beneath the counter. It was roughly the size of her hand, and shaped like a lantern with six glass sides.

"Here you are then," she said as she set it on the table.

The customer lifted the object carefully, brought it to her lips, and whispered something. As she did, the lantern lit, the glass sides frosting a milky white. The apprentice watched, and saw what the woman couldn't— the filaments of light around the object rippled and smoothed, the spellwork flowing seamlessly as the woman brought it to her ear. The message whispered itself back, and the glass went clear again, the vessel empty.

The woman smiled. "Marvelous," she said, bundling the mended secret-keeper away inside her coat. She set the coins down in a neat stack, one silver lish and four red lin.

"Give Master Haskin my thanks," she added, already turning away.

"I will," called the apprentice as the door swung shut.

She swept the coins from the counter, and hopped down from her stool, rolling her head on her shoulders to stretch.

There was no Master Haskin, of course.

Once or twice when the shop was new, she'd dragged an old man from the nearest tavern, paid him a lin or two to come and sit in the back with his head bent over a book, just so she could point him out to customers and say, "The master is busy working now," since apparently a man half in his cups still inspired more faith than a sharp-eyed girl who looked even younger than her age, which was fifteen.

Then she got tired of spending the coin, so she propped a few boxes and a pillow behind a mottled glass door and pointed to that instead.

These days she didn't bother, just flicked her fingers toward the back of the shop and said, "He's busy." It turned out, no one really cared, so long as the fixing got done.

Now, alone in the shop, the apprentice—whose name, not that anyone knew it, was Tesali—rubbed her eyes, cheekbones bruised from the blotters she wore all day, to focus her gaze. She took a long swig of black tea, bitter and over-steeped, just the way she liked it—and still hot, thanks to the mug, one of the first things she'd ever spelled.

The day was thinning out beyond the windows, and the lanterns around the shop began to glow, warming the room with a buttery light that glanced off the shelves and cases and worktops, all of them well stocked, but not cluttered, toeing the line between a welcome fullness and a mess.

It was a balance Tes had learned from her father.

Shops like this had to be careful—too clean, and it looked like you were lacking business. Too messy, and customers would take that business elsewhere. If everything they saw was broken, they'd think you were no good at fixing. If everything they saw was fixed, they'd wonder why no one had come to claim it.

Haskin's shop—*her* shop—struck the perfect balance.

There were shelves with spools of cable—copper and silver, mostly, the best conduits for magic—and jars full of cogs and pencils and tacks, and piles of scrap paper covered in the scrawls of half-worked spells. All the things she guessed a repair shop might keep on hand. In truth, the cogs, the papers, the coils, they were all for show. A bit of set dressing to put the audience at ease. A little sleight of hand, to distract them from the truth.

Tes didn't need any of these things to fix a bit of broken magic.

All she needed were her eyes.

Her eyes, which for some reason saw the world not just in shape and color, but in threads.

Everywhere she looked, she saw them.

A glowing ribbon curled in the water of her tea. A dozen more ran through the wood of her table. A hundred delicate lines wove through the bones of her pet owl. They twisted and coiled through the air around and above everyone and everything. Some were dull, and others bright. Some were single strands and others braided filaments, some drifted, feather light, and others rushed like a current. It was a dizzying maelstrom.

But Tes couldn't just see the threads of power. She could touch them. Pluck a string as if it were an instrument and not the fabric of the world. Find the frayed ends of a fractured spell, trace the lines of broken magic and mend them.

She didn't speak the language of spellwork, didn't need to. She knew the language of magic itself. Knew it was a rare gift, and knew what people did to get their hands on rare things, which was exactly why she maintained the illusion of the shop.

Vares clicked his beak, and fluttered his featherless wings. She glanced at the little owl, and he stared back, then swiveled his head to the darkening streets beyond the glass.

"Not yet," she said, finishing her tea. Better to wait a bit and see if any more business wandered in. A shop like Haskin's had a different kind of client, once darkness fell.

Tes reached beneath the counter and pulled out a bundle of burlap, unfolding the cloth to reveal a sword, then took up the pair of blotters. They looked like spectacles, though the gift lay not in the lens, but in the frames, heavy and black, the edges extending to either side like the blinders on a horse. Which is exactly what they were, blotting out the rest of the room, narrowing her world to just the space of the counter, and the sword atop it.

She settled them over her eyes.

"See this?" She spoke to Vares, pointing to the steel. A spell had originally been etched into the flat side, but a portion of it had scraped away in a fight, reducing the blade from an unbreakable weapon to a scrap of flimsy metal. To Tes's eyes, the filaments of magic around the weapon were similarly frayed.

"Spells are like bodies," she explained. "They go stiff, and break down, either from wear or neglect. Reset a bone wrong, and you might have a limp. Put a spell back in the wrong way, and the whole thing might splinter, or shatter, or worse."

Lessons she'd learned the hard way.

Tes flexed her fingers, and ran them through the air just over the steel.

"A spell exists in two places," she continued. "On the metal, and in the magic."

Another fixer would simply etch the spell into the blade again. But the metal would keep getting damaged. No, better to take the spell and weave it into the magic itself. That way, no matter what happened to the sigils on the steel, the power would hold.

Carefully, she reached into the web of magic and began to mend the threads, drawing the frayed ends together, tying tiny knots that then fell away, leaving the ribbons smooth, intact. She got so lost in the work, she didn't hear the shop door open.

Didn't notice, not until Vares perked up, beak clicking in alarm.

Tes looked up, her hands still buried in the spell.

With the blotters on, she couldn't see more than a hand's width, so it took her a moment to find the customer. He was large, with a hard face, and a nose that had been broken more than once, but her attention went, as it always did, to the magic around him. Or the lack of it. It wasn't common to see a person without any power, and the utter absence of threads made him a dark spot in the room.

"Looking for Haskin," he grunted, scanning the shop.

Tes carefully withdrew her fingers, and tugged the goggles off, flicking the burlap back over the sword. "He's busy," she said, tipping her head toward the rear of the shop, as if he were back there. "But I can help."

The man gave her a look that made her hackles rise. She only got two kinds of looks: appraising, and skeptical. Those who saw her as a woman, and those who saw her as a girl. Both looks made her feel like a sack of grain being weighed, but she hated the latter more, that way it was meant to make her feel small. The fact, sometimes, it *did*.

The man's hard eyes dropped to the sword, its hilt poking out from beneath the burlap. "You even old enough to handle magic?"

Tes forced herself to smile. With teeth. "Why don't you show me what you have?"

He grunted, and reached into his coat pocket, withdrawing a leather cuff and setting it on the table. She knew exactly what it was, or rather, what it was meant to be. Would have known, even if she hadn't glimpsed the black brand circling his left wrist as he set it down. That explained the lack of threads, the darkness in the air around him. He wasn't magicless by nature—he'd been marked with a limiter, which meant the crown had seen fit to strip him of his power.

Tes took up the cuff, and turned it over in her hands.

Limiters were the highest price a criminal could pay, shy of execution, and many considered it a harsher punishment, to live without access to one's magic. It was forbidden, of course, to bypass one. To negate the limiter's spell. But forbidden didn't mean impossible. Only expensive. The cuff, she guessed, had been sold to him as a negater. She wondered if he knew that he'd been ripped off, that the cuff was faulty, the spellwork unfinished, a clumsy snarl in the air. It was never designed to work.

But it *could*.

"Well?" he asked, impatient.

She held the cuff between them. "Tell me," she said, "is this a clock, a lock, or a household trinket?"

The man frowned. "*Kers?* No, it's a—"

"This shop," she explained, "is licensed to repair clocks, locks, and household trinkets."

He looked pointedly down at the sword sticking out of the burlap. "I was told—"

"It looks like a clock to me," she cut in.

He stared at her. "But it's not a clock . . . ?" His voice went up at the end, as if no longer certain. Tes sighed, and gave him a weighted look. It took far too long for him to catch it.

"Oh. Yes." His eyes flicked down to the leather cuff, and then to the dead owl, which he'd just realized was watching him, before returning to the strange girl across the counter. "Well then, it's a clock."

"Excellent," she said, pulling a box from beneath the counter and dropping the forbidden object inside.

"So he can fix it?"

"Of course," Tes said with a cheerful grin. "Master Haskin can fix anything." She tore off a small black ticket with the shop's sigil and a number printed in gold. "It'll be ready in a week."

She watched the man go, muttering about clocks as the door swung shut behind him. She started to wonder what he'd done to earn that limiter, but caught herself. Curiosity was more danger than a curse. She didn't survive by asking questions.

It was late enough now, the tide of foot traffic beyond the shop retreating as the residents of the *shal* turned their attention toward darker pursuits. It got a bad reputation, the *shal*, and sure, it could be a rough place. The taverns catered to those who'd rather not cross paths with the crown, half the coin used in the shops had come from someone else's pocket, and residents turned their backs at the sound of a cry or a fight instead of running in to stop it. But people relied on Haskin's shop to fix and fence and not ask questions, and everyone knew that she was his apprentice, so Tes felt safe—as safe as she could ever be.

She put away the unfinished sword, downed the last of her tea, and went about the business of locking up.

Halfway to the door, the headache started.

Tes knew it was only a matter of time before it made itself at home inside her skull, made it hard to see, to think, to do anything but sleep. The pain no longer took her by surprise, but that didn't make it any less a thief. Stealing in behind her eyes. Ransacking everything.

"*Avenoche,* Haskin," she murmured to the empty shop, fishing the day's coin from the drawer with one hand and sweeping up Vares with the other, heading past the shelves and through the heavy curtain into the back. She'd made a nest there, a corner for a kitchen, a loft with a bed.

She kicked off her shoes, and put the money in a metal tin behind the stove before heating up a bowl of soup. As it warmed, she freed her hair from the pile on her head, but it didn't come down so much as rise around her in a cloud of nut-brown curls. She shook her head and a pencil tumbled out onto the table. She didn't remember sticking it there. Vares bent his skull to peck at the stick as she ate, soaking up broth with hunks of bread.

If anyone had seen her then, it would have been easy to guess that the apprentice was young. Her bony elbows and sharp knees folded up on the chair, the roundness of her face, the way she shoveled soup into her mouth and kept up a one-sided conversation with the dead owl, talking out how she'd finish the negater, until the headache sharpened and she sighed, and pressed her palms against her eyes, light ghosting on the inside of the lids. It was the only time Tes longed for home. For her mother's cool hands on her brow, and the white noise of the tide, the salt air like a salve.

She pushed the want away with the empty bowl, and climbed the ladder up into the little loft, setting Vares on a makeshift shelf. She pulled the curtain, plunging the cubby into darkness—as close to dark as she could get, considering the glow of threads that hovered over her skin, and ran through the little owl, and the music box beside him. It was shaped like a cliff, small metal waves crashing up against shining rocks. She plucked a blue thread, setting the little box in motion. A soft whoosh filled the loft, the breathlike rhythm of the sea.

"*Vas ir,* Vares," Tes whispered as she tied a thick cloth over her eyes, erasing the last of the light, and then curled up in the little bed at the back of Haskin's shop, letting the sound of waves draw her down to sleep.

II

The merchant's son sat in the Gilded Fish, pretending to read about pirates.

Pretending to read, because the light was too low, and even if it weren't, he could hardly be expected to focus on the book in front of him—which he knew by heart—or the half-drunk pint of ale—which was too bitter and too thick—or anything but the waiting.

The truth was, the young man wasn't sure who—or what—he was waiting for, only that he was supposed to sit and wait, and it would find him. It was an act of faith—not the first, and certainly not the last, that would be asked of him.

But the merchant's son was ready.

A small satchel rested on the ground between his feet, hidden in the shadow of the table, and a black cap was pulled low on his brow. He'd chosen a table against the wall, and put his back to it. Every time the tavern door swung open, he looked up, careful not to be too obvious, to lift only his eyes and not his whole head, which he'd learned from a book.

The merchant's son was short on experience, but he had been raised on a steady diet of books. Not histories, or spell guides, though his tutors made him read those, too. No, his true education had come from *novels*. Epic tales of rakes and rogues, nobles and thieves, but most of all, of *heroes*.

His favorite was *The Legends of Olik,* a saga about a penniless orphan who grows up to be the world's greatest magician/sailor/spy. In the third book, he discovers he's actually of *ostra* blood, and is welcomed into court, only to learn that the nobles are all rotten, worse than the scoundrels he faces at sea.

In the fourth book—which was the best one, in his opinion—the hero Olik meets Vera, a beautiful woman being held hostage on a pirate ship—or so he *thinks,* but then discovers she's actually the captain, and the whole thing was a ruse to capture him and sell him to the highest bidder. He escapes, and after that, Vera becomes his greatest foe, but never quite his equal, because *Olik* is the hero.

The merchant's son feasted on those stories, supped on the details, gorged himself on the mystery, the magic, and the danger. He read them until the ink had faded and the spines cracked, and the paper was foxed at the edges from being thumbed, or from being shoved into pockets hastily when his father came around to the docks to check his work.

His father, who didn't—couldn't—understand.

His father, who thought he was making a terrible mistake.

The tavern door swung open, and the merchant's son tensed as a pair of men ambled in. But they didn't look around, didn't notice him, or the black cap he was told to wear. Still, he watched them cross the room to a table on the other side, watched them flag the barkeep, watched them settle in. He'd only been in London a few weeks, and everything still felt new, from the accents—which were sharper than he'd grown up with—to the gestures, to the clothes and the current fashion of wearing them in layers, so that each outfit could be peeled apart to reveal another, depending on the weather, or the company.

The merchant's son searched their faces. He was a wind magician by birth but those were common. He had a second, more valuable skill: a keen eye for details, and with it, a knack for spotting lies. His father appreciated the talent because it came in handy when asking sailors about their inventory, how a crate was lost, why a purchase had fallen through, or vanished en route.

He didn't know why or how he could so quickly parse a person's features. The flickering tension between the eyes, the quick clench of teeth, the dozen tiny tugs and twitches that made up their expression. It was its own language. One that the merchant's son had always been able to read.

He turned his attention back to the book on the table, tried to focus on the words he'd consumed a hundred times, but his mind slipped uselessly across the page.

His knee bounced beneath the table.

He shifted in his chair, and flinched, the skin at the base of his spine still raw from the brand that bound him to his chosen path. If he focused, he could feel the lines of it, the splayed fingers like spokes running out from the palm. That hand was a symbol of progress, of change, of—

Treason.

That was the word the merchant had shouted as he'd followed his son through the house.

"You only call it that," the younger man countered, "because you do not understand."

"Oh, I understand," snapped the merchant, face flushing red. "I understand that my son is a child. I understand that Rhy Maresh was a

30

brave prince, and now he is a valiant king. Seven years he's ruled, and in that time, he has avoided a war with Vesk, opened new trade channels, channels that help *us,* and—"

"—and none of that changes the fact that the empire's magic is failing."

The merchant threw up his hands. "*That* is nothing but a rumor."

"It's not," said the son, adjusting the satchel on his shoulder. He had already packed, because a ship to London was leaving that day, and he would be on it. "A new *Antari* hasn't emerged since Kell Maresh, a quarter century ago. Fewer magicians are showing an affinity for multiple elements, and more are being born with none at all. My friend's niece—"

"Oh, your friend's niece—" sniped the merchant, but his son persisted.

"She's seven now, born a month after your king was crowned. She has no power. Another friend has a cousin, born within the year. Another, a son."

The merchant only shook his head. "There have always been those without—"

"Not this many, or this close together. It is a warning. A *reckoning.* Something is broken in the world. And it's been broken for a while. There is a sickness spreading through Arnes. A rot at the heart of the empire. If we do not cut it out, we cannot heal. It is a small sacrifice to make for the greater good."

"A small sacrifice? You want to kill the king!"

The merchant's son flinched. "No, we'll motivate the people, and build their voices loud enough, and if the king is so noble as he claims, then he will understand that if he truly wants what is best for his kingdom, he will step aside and—"

"If you believe this will end without blood, then you are a traitor *and* a fool."

The merchant's son turned to go, and for the first time, his father reached out and caught his arm. Held him there. "I should turn you in."

Anger burned in his father's eyes, and for a moment, the merchant's son thought that he would resort to violence. Panic bloomed behind his ribs, but he held the older man's gaze. "You must follow your heart," he said. "Just as I follow mine."

31

The father looked at his son as if he were a stranger. "Who put this idea into your head?"

"No one."

But of course that wasn't true.

After all, most ideas came from somewhere. Or someone.

This one had come from *her*.

She had hair so dark, it ate the light. That was the first thing the merchant's son had noticed. Black as midnight, and skin the warm brown that came with life at sea. Eyes the same shade, and shot through with flecks of gold, though he wouldn't be close enough to see them until later. He'd been on the docks counting inventory when she arrived, cut like a blade through the boredom of his day.

One moment he was holding a bolt of silver lace up to the sun, and the next, there she was, peering at him through the pattern, and soon they were turning through the bolts together, and then the cloth was forgotten and she was leading him up the ramp of her ship, and laughing, not a delicate wind-chime laugh like the girls his age put on, but something raw, and wild, and they climbed down into the warm, dark hold, and he was undoing the buttons of her shirt, and he must have seen it then, the brand, like a shadow on her ribs, as if a lover had grabbed her there, burned their hand into her skin, but it wasn't until after, when they lay flushed and happy, that he brought his own palm and fingers to the mark and asked her what it was.

And in the darkened hold, she'd told him. About the movement that had started, how fast and strong it had grown. The Hand, she'd said, would take the weakness in the world and make it right.

"The Hand holds the weight that balances the scale," she said, stroking his bare skin. "The Hand holds the blade that carves the path of change."

He devoured her words, as if they belonged to a novel, but they didn't. This was better. This was real. An adventure he could be a part of, a chance to be a hero.

He would have sailed away with her that night, but by the time he returned to the docks, the ship was gone. Not that it mattered, in the end. She hadn't been Vera to his Olik but she *was* a catalyst, something to turn the hero toward his purpose.

"I know you do not understand," he'd said to his father. "But the scales have fallen out of balance, and someone must set them right."

The merchant was still gripping his son's arm, searching his face for answers, even though he wasn't ready to hear them.

"But why must it be *you*?"

Because, thought the merchant's son.

Because he had lived twenty-two years, and had yet to do anything of consequence. Because he lay awake at night and longed for an adventure. Because he wanted a chance to matter, to make a difference in the world—and this was it.

But he knew he couldn't say any of that, not to his father, so he simply met the merchant's eye and said, "Because I can."

The merchant pulled him closer, cupped his son's face in shaking hands. This close, he could see that his father's eyes were glassy with tears. Something in him slipped and faltered, then. Doubt began creeping in.

But then his father spoke.

"Then you are a fool, and you will die."

The son staggered, as if struck. He read the lines of the merchant's face, and knew the man believed the words were true. Knew, then, too, that he'd never be able to convince his father otherwise.

The woman's voice drifted back to him, then, up from the darkened hold.

Some people cannot see the need for change until it's done.

His nerves hardened, and so did his resolve.

"You're wrong," he said quietly. "And I will show you."

With that, the merchant's son pulled free of his father's hands, and walked out. This time, no one stopped him.

That had been a month ago.

A month, so little time, and yet, so much had changed. He had the brand, and now, he had the *mission*.

The door to the Gilded Fish swung open, and a man strolled in. His gaze swept over the tables before landing on the merchant's son.

He broke into a smile, as if they were old friends, and even if the look had been leveled at someone else, the merchant's son would have known it was a lie.

"There you are," called the stranger as he strolled over to the table. He had the gait of a sailor, the bearing of a guard. "Sorry I'm late."

"That's all right," said the merchant's son, even as a nervous energy rolled through him, half excitement and half fear. The other man carried no satchel, and weren't there supposed to be two of them? But before he could say more, the stranger cut in.

"Come on, then," he said cheerfully. "Boat's already at the dock."

He tucked the book in his back pocket and rose, dropped a coin on the table, and threw back the last of his ale, forgetting that the reason he'd left it to warm was because it was too bitter and too thick. It stuck now to the sides of his throat instead of going down. He tried not to cough. Failed. Forced a smile, one that the other man didn't catch because he'd already turned toward the door.

As soon as they were outside, the other man's good humor fell away. The smile bled from his face, leaving something stern and hollow in its wake.

It occurred to the merchant's son, then, that he didn't actually know the nature of their mission. He asked, assuming the other man would ignore him, or go out of his way to speak in code. He didn't. "We're going to liberate something from a ship."

Liberate, he knew, was just another word for *steal.*

The merchant's son had never stolen anything before, and the other man's answer only bred more questions. What thing? Which ship? He opened his mouth to ask, but the words stuck like the ale in his throat as they passed a pair of royal guards. The merchant's son tensed at the sight of them, even though he'd committed no crime, not yet, unless you counted the mark smuggled under his clothes.

Which they would.

Treason, echoed his father's voice, in time with his own heart.

But then the other man raised a hand to the soldiers, as if he knew them, and they nodded back, and the merchant's son wondered if they knew the truth, or if the rebellion was simply that good at hiding in plain sight.

The Gilded Fish sat less than a ship's length from the start of the London docks, so it was a short trip, one that ended at a narrow, nameless boat. Light enough to be sailed by a single wind magician, like himself, a fleet-bottomed skiff, the kind used for brief, fast trips, where speed was of more worth than comfort.

He followed the man up onto a short ramp onto the deck. As their boots sounded on the wood, his heart pounded just as loud. The moment felt vital, charged with power and portent.

The merchant's son smiled, and put his hands on his hips.

If he were a character in a book, this was how his story would start. Perhaps, one day, he'd even write it.

Behind them, someone cleared their throat, and he turned to find a second man, a wiry figure who didn't even bother to feign recognition.

"Well," said the newest man, gaze scraping over the merchant's son. The latter waited for him to go on, and when he didn't, he held out a hand, was about to introduce himself, but the word was still on his tongue when the first man shook his head. The second stepped forward, poked him in the chest, and said, "No names."

The merchant's son frowned. Olik always introduced himself. "What will we call each other?"

The other men shrugged, as if this weren't a crucial detail.

"There are three of us," said the one who'd collected him from the Gilded Fish.

"You can count that high, can't you?" said the other dryly. "He's the first. I'm the second. Guess that makes you the third."

The merchant's son frowned. But then, he reminded himself, numbers were often symbolic. In the stories he had read, things often came in threes, and when they did, the third was always the one that mattered. The same must be true of people.

And so, as the lines were soon thrown off, and the boat drifted in the crimson current, and turned, the royal palace looming in their wake, the merchant's son—now the third man—smiled, because he knew, from the crown of his head to the bottoms of his boots, that he was about to be the hero of this story.

And he couldn't wait.

III

Alucard Emery was used to turning heads.

He liked to think it was his dashing looks—the sun-kissed hair, the storm-blue eyes, the warm brown skin—or perhaps his impeccable taste—he'd always had a flair for well-trimmed clothes and the occasional gem, though the sapphire no longer winked above his brow. Then, of course, it might be his reputation. A noble by birth, a *privateer* by trade, once captain of the infamous *Night Spire,* reigning victor of the final *Essen Tasch* (they hadn't held another tournament since Vesk used the last to assassinate the queen), survivor of the Tide, and consort to the king.

Each on its own would have made him interesting.

Together, they made him infamous.

And yet, that night, as he ambled through the Silken Thread, no heads turned, no gazes lingered. The pleasure garden smelled of burnt sugar and fresh lilies, a perfume that wafted through the halls and drifted up the stairs, curling like smoke around the guests. It was a stately establishment, close enough to the Isle that the river's red light tinted the windows on the southern side, and named for the white ribbons the hosts wore around their wrists to mark them from the patrons. And like all upscale brothels, its tenants were skilled in the art of *un*noticing. The hosts could be counted on for their discretion, and if any patrons knew him, as they surely did, they had the good taste not to stare, or worse, to make a sce—

"Alucard Emery!"

He flinched at the volume of the voice, the brazenness of being called by name, turned to find a young man ambling toward him, already well into his cups. A single blue thread curled through the air around the youth, though only Alucard could see it. He was dressed in fine silk, the collar open to reveal a trail of smooth, tan skin. His golden hair was rumpled, and his eyes were *black*. Not edge to edge, like Kell's, but perfect drops of ink that pooled in the center of the white, and swallowed up the pupils, so he couldn't tell if they were shrunk to pinpricks, or blown wide with pleasure.

Alucard searched his memory until it produced a name. *Oren.*

"Master Rosec," he said, as cordially as he could muster, since Oren was the son of a noble house.

"You remember!" Oren clapped him on the shoulder as if they were old friends. In truth, the Rosecs had long kept their residence up north, and the two had met only once, five years before, at the royal wedding. At the time, Alucard had thought the boy a spoiled brat. Now, he was certain. Oh, there was no doubt that Oren Rosec was handsome. But the effect was tarnished by the fact the young man clearly knew it, and carried himself with an arrogance that eroded his looks and left Alucard with only the impression of a very punchable face.

"I'm surprised to see a Rosec so far south," he said. "How is London suiting you?"

"Wonderfully," said Oren with a sloppy grin and an insufferable wink. "I find myself quite at home."

"And your sister?" asked Alucard, glancing around in hopes of finding his host, and with her, an escape.

"Oh, Hanara?" Oren waved his hand. "She stayed with the estate. She was the oldest, after all."

Alucard's attention snagged on that word. *Was.* But before he could ask, Oren leaned in, far too close, and said, far too loud, "But I am surprised to see *you* here, Master Emery, and not at the king's side."

Alucard smiled thinly. "Last I checked, I am not tethered to the crown. And thus, free to amuse myself."

Oren laughed. "I don't blame you," he said, fingers tightening on Alucard's arm. "After all, these days the king's bed must be so crowded."

Alucard clenched his teeth, and wondered what he might have said next if Oren had not suddenly seen a host he fancied across the room.

"If you'll excuse me," said the younger noble, already propelling himself forward.

"Happily," muttered Alucard, glad to see him go.

Just then, a ribboned hand settled on his shoulder, and Alucard turned to find a woman in a white dress, though the words did little justice to the woman or the dress. She was exquisite, long-limbed and pale, her ash-blond hair swept up atop her head, held in place with a dozen long silver pins, their handles sculpted into thornlike tips. The dress was a single length of white silk bound around her body like a ribbon round a parcel, cinching here and there until every vital curve was drawn in sharp detail.

Most knew her as the White Rose.

Few also knew her as the owner of the Silken Thread, its proprietor as well as its most desired host.

Alucard knew her as Ciara.

"Master Emery," she purred, smooth as the silk itself. "It has been too long."

The air around her warmed a little as she spoke, and he knew it was only her magic—could see the yellow threads of it dancing just over her skin—and yet he flushed and felt himself lean in toward her, like a flower to the sun.

"It has," he said, taking her hand, and pressing the knuckles to his lips. "And yet, somehow, I doubt your bed is ever cold."

She shrugged. "All bodies warm, but few have truly burned my sheets."

Alucard stifled a laugh as she led him through the salon to the bar, whose marble surface curled like a single piece of ribbon through the room. She tapped one perfect nail on the counter and soon two short crystal glasses appeared, their contents amber. They each took up the glass—the brothel's way of sealing a deal between a patron and their chosen host.

"*Vas ir,*" she said in Arnesian.

"*Glad'och,*" he replied in Veskan.

A shadow crossed Ciara's face—the briefest cloud—before she tapped his drink with her own and downed the contents. Alucard followed. The liquor tasted of sunlight and sugar, but he knew it was strong enough to make an unsuspecting patron feel as if they'd gone to bed on land, and woken up at sea. Thankfully his years captaining the *Spire* had given him steady legs and a very high tolerance for spirits.

He took the empty glasses in one hand, and let her lead him with the other, up the stairs, and down a corridor, and into a room that smelled less like the brothel's careful perfume and more like the woods at night. Wild.

By the time the door closed, and locked, she was already guiding him up against the wall, pressing playful kisses to his collar.

"Ciara," he said gently, and then, when she did not withdraw, more firmly. "*Ciara.*"

Her lips drew into a perfect pout. "You really are no fun," she said, rapping her nails against his chest. "Does the king alone still hold your heart?"

Alucard smiled. "He does."

"What a waste," she said, retreating. As she did, she pulled the end of the white silk that wrapped around her, and it unraveled, and fell away. She stood there, naked, the full length of her body shining like moonlight, but his eyes were drawn less to her curves, and more to her scars. Silver traced the hollow of her throat, the curves of her breasts, the crooks of her elbows, the insides of her wrists. A relic of the Tide that fell on London seven years before. The cursed magic that spilled the Isle's banks.

Few people knew that the magic had a name, and it was Osaron.

Osaron, the destroyer of Black London.

Osaron, the darkness that believed itself a god.

Osaron, who corrupted everything and everyone he touched.

Most who survived did so by succumbing to his will. Those who fought largely perished, burned alive by the fever raging in their veins. The few who did not fall, who fought the magic and the fever and lived, they alone were marked by the battle, their veins scorched silver in the curse's wake.

Alucard handed Ciara a lush white robe, his gaze flicking briefly to his own hand, and the molten silver mottling his wrist.

He shed his rich blue coat and cast it over a chair, unbuttoning the clasp at his throat, the closest he would come to undressing. They left the bed untouched, as they always did, and turned instead to the small table that held the Rasch board.

It was already laid, pieces huddled on the six-sided board, black gathered on one side, white on the other. Three taller figures—priest, king, and queen—surrounded by twelve soldiers. Ciara's board had been a gift from a generous patron who happened to prefer her insight to her body, and the pieces were carved from marble instead of wood, ribbons of gold ore running through the stone.

"May I?" he asked, nodding to the bottle on the sill.

"This night is costing you a fortune. You might as well enjoy it."

"I always do," he said, pouring them each a second glass of the golden liquor. He lifted his, dragging an old saying up from memory. *"Och ans, is farr—"*

"Don't," she snapped, as if the sound offended her.

Alucard hesitated. He knew he lacked the king's fluency. He spoke Arnesian and High Royal, what Lila Bard called English, and could recite a handful of sayings in other tongues, enough to manage niceties at court. But his Veskan was stilted and gruff, learned from a sailor on his ship. That said, he didn't think it was the accent that bothered Ciara.

"You know," he said, "it is not a bad thing, to be from more than one place."

"It is," she countered, "when those places are at war."

Alucard raised a brow. "I didn't know we *were*," he said, taking his seat. "Do you know something I don't?"

"I'd wager I know many things." She poured herself into the opposite chair as if she too were liquid. "But we both know that Arnes and Vesk are wolves snapping at each other's throats. It's only a matter of time before one of them draws blood."

But of course, one of them already *had*.

Seven years ago, two of Vesk's heirs had arrived at the palace, ostensibly to celebrate the *Essen Tasch* and solidify the bonds between empires. But they'd come with their own plans—to cripple the crown, and seed the ground for war. They'd succeeded, in part, slaughtering Rhy's mother, Emira. They would have succeeded in killing Rhy too, if such a thing were still possible. The only thing that kept Arnes from declaring outright war was the more immediate danger of Osaron's attack and then, in its wake, the Veskans' disavowal of the offending son and daughter.

They'd gone so far as to offer up their youngest heir, Hok, as penance, but Rhy had seen too much blood in too short a time, had lost his mother to another prince's ambition and his father to the darkness at the palace doors, had watched the Tide sweep through his capital, and been forced to fight against the darkness that ended an entire world. In a matter of days, he had been orphaned and crowned, left to pick up the pieces of London. And if he sought retribution, it wouldn't be with the life of a child.

And so what *should* have been the first trumpets of war had been allowed to quiet once again back into the whispers of strategy.

Still, seven years later, tensions remained high, the veil of diplomacy shroud-thin, and Alucard didn't blame Ciara for downplaying her heritage when she made her livelihood in the shadow of the royal palace. Perhaps she was right. Perhaps it was only a matter of time before war came to London, in one form or another.

They drained their glasses, and took their seats, and the game began.

Alucard moved three of his soldiers, a bold opening.

Unlike Sanct, there was no way to cheat in Rasch. It was pure strategy. When a player swept a piece from the other side, they could take it off the board, or turn it into one of theirs, depending on the endgame. Some played to eviscerate their enemies. Others to make them allies. As long as one of the prime three pieces was still standing, there was a chance to win.

"*Anesh*," he said as he waited for her to make her move. "Have you had any interesting guests?"

Ciara considered. "All of my guests are interesting." She moved her priest to the back of the board, where it would be safe. "They sometimes talk in their sleep."

"Do they?" asked Alucard, waiving his turn.

When it came to Rasch, she was *far* better than him, so he rarely bothered trying to win, preferring instead to find new ways to vex his opponent.

"There are rumors," Ciara went on, having finished her next move, "of a pirate fleet off the coast of Hal. One almost as big as the Rebel Army."

"Funny," said Alucard, "*my* spies say it is only four ships, and they cannot seem to settle on a course of sail, let alone a captain." He pushed a soldier forward. "And in Vesk?"

"The crown prince has not been seen at court in weeks. Some think he is at sea. Others, that he has docked somewhere in Arnes, and travels southward in disguise to save his youngest brother, Hok."

41

Alucard drew the soldier back again. "Save him from what? Stiff beds and long-winded metaphors?" Rhy had placed the Veskan heir in the hands of the priests at the London Sanctuary, and all reports were that he was proving a bright and exceedingly polite pupil.

As Ciara considered her move, he sat back, rubbing absently at one wrist.

It was a habit born years before the Tide, when the worst scar he wore came from the iron he'd been forced into as a prisoner, the metal heated until it burned a cuff into his skin. A painful reminder of a life he'd left behind. Now the darkened band was little more than a backdrop to the molten silver running up his arms, tracing his collar, his throat, his temples.

Most, like Ciara, saw the silver as a badge of honor, a sign of strength, but for a long time, he'd hated the marks. They hadn't been a reminder of his might, only a testament to his weakness.

For months, every time he caught the glint of silver, he saw was his little sister, Anisa, hollowed out in death, felt his own body collapsing to his cabin floor, remembered the fever, burning his worst memories into his mind as Osaron turned his whole spirit from a fire to a candle flame. And Alucard knew that his life would have been snuffed out if Rhy Maresh hadn't found him there, dying on the floor of his ship. If Rhy hadn't lain down beside him on the sweat-stained board, and tangled his hands through his, and refused to let go.

For months, every time he crossed a mirror, he'd stop and stare, unable to look at himself. Unable to look away.

It was only a matter of time before Rhy caught him staring.

"You know," said the king, "I've heard humility is an attractive trait."

Alucard had managed a smile, and parried, with a shadow of his usual charm. "I know," he'd said, "but it's hard when you're this striking." And Rhy must have heard the sadness in his voice, because he'd draped himself over Alucard, and pressed a kiss into the silver-creased hollow of his throat.

"Your scars are my favorite part of you," said the king, running a finger from the molten lines all the way to the brands at his wrists. "I love them all. Do you know why?"

"Because you were jealous of my looks?" he quipped.

For once, Rhy didn't laugh. He brought his hand to Alucard's cheek, and turned his gaze away from the mirror. "Because they brought you back to me."

"Your move," said Ciara. Alucard forced his attention back to the board.

"What of Faro?" he asked, moving the same soldier. "They claim to be our ally."

"Ambassadors have silver tongues. You and I both know that Faro wants a war with Vesk."

"They do not stand to win."

"They might, if Arnes goes to battle with them first."

Alucard sacrificed his pieces one by one as she spoke.

"You're not even trying," she hissed, but he was. Just not trying to win.

Sadly, Ciara could not seem to play for pretense, cutting a swathe through his pieces. In three more moves, it was done. She flicked her fingers, and a tiny gust of air swept through, tipping over the last of his pieces.

"Again?" she asked, and he nodded.

As she reset the board, he refilled their glasses.

"Well then?" he said. "What about the Hand?"

At the mention of the rebels, Ciara leaned back in her chair. "You pay me to listen for valid threats. The Hand are nothing but a petty nuisance."

"So are moths," he said. "Until they eat your finest coat."

Ciara drew out a pipe and lit it with her fingers. A thin tendril of blue-grey smoke curled around her. "The crown is truly worried, then?"

"The crown is watchful. Especially when a group roams the city, calling for its head."

Ciara hummed, running a finger around her glass. "Well, either its members are very chaste, or very good at holding their tongues. As far as I know, I've never had one in my bed."

"You're sure?"

"Is it true they all bear the mark somewhere on their skin?"

"So I've heard."

"Then I'm quite sure," she said with a small, wicked grin. Alucard rose, suddenly restless. It had been several years since the first appearance of the

Hand, and at the time, the sect had seemed merely an annoyance, a pebble in the kingdom's shoe. But over the course of the past year, they'd grown into something more. There was no obvious leader, no mouthpiece, no face to the movement, nothing but a symbol, and a message: magic was failing, and it was Rhy Maresh's fault.

It was ridiculous. Unfounded. A battle cry for the discontent, an excuse to cause chaos and call it change. But there were people—bitter, angry, powerless people—who were beginning to listen.

Alucard stretched, and went to the windowsill. The Silken Thread sat on the northern bank of the city. Beyond the glass, he could see the crimson glow of the Isle, and the vaulting palace, doubled gold against the river's surface in the dark.

He didn't hear Ciara stand, but he saw her in the glass, felt her arms drape lazily around him.

"I should go," he said, weariness leaking into his voice.

"So soon?" she asked. "We haven't finished playing."

"You've already won."

"Perhaps. But still, I wouldn't want anyone to doubt your . . . capacity."

He turned in her embrace. "Is it my reputation you're worried about, or your own?"

She laughed, and he plucked the pipe from her fingers, and inhaled, letting the heady smoke coil in his chest. Then he leaned in and kissed her lightly, sighing the smoke into her lungs.

"Goodnight, Ciara," he said, smiling against her lips.

Her eyelids fluttered, and drifted open. "Tease," she said, blowing out the word in a puff of smoke.

Alucard only laughed, and slipped past her, shrugging on his coat.

He stepped out into the dark and started down the street.

Only the roads nearest the river were lined with pubs and gaming halls and inns. Beyond those, the northern bank gave way to pleasure gardens and galleries, and then to walled estates with well-groomed land, where most of the city's nobles made their homes.

It had been a fair and sun-warm day, but now, as he left the Silken Thread, the night hovered on a knife's edge between cool and cold. Winter was on its way. Alucard had always been partial to the winter months, with their hearth fires and spiced wines and endless parties meant to rage against the chill and lack of light.

But tonight, he found the sudden cold disconcerting.

As he walked, he turned over Ciara's words, wearing them smooth.

The rumors of Faro and Vesk were disturbing, but not unexpected. It was the lack of intel on the rebels he found maddening. He had been counting on the White Rose's intelligence, her capacity to gather threads of gossip and spin them into more. She was a popular and beautiful host, with the kind of liquid grace that loosened tongues. It wasn't only the patrons who spoke to her. The other hosts did, too, carrying her secrets and confidences the way a blackbird carried offerings, unable to tell the difference between crystal and glass.

A cold rain started to fall. Alucard turned one hand palm up, the air over his head arcing into a canopy, sheltering him from the downpour. It would be a bad look, he reasoned, the victor of the final *Essen Tasch,* trudging through London like a sodden cat. Around him, people rushed through the bad weather, heads down as they hurried for the nearest awning.

It didn't take Alucard long to realize he was being followed.

They were good, he'd give them that. They blended into the surrounding night, and if he were anyone else, he wouldn't have seen them at all, but as his eyes scanned the lamp-stained air and rain-slicked streets, the world reduced to gold and grey, their magic shone like firelight, tracing their edges in crimson and emerald and blue.

A thrill ran through him; not panic, exactly, but something more akin to glee. Part of him thrilled, the same part that had first been drawn to Lila Bard, the part that led him to compete in, and win, the world's greatest tournament of magic. The part of him that was always a little eager for a fight.

But then one of the shadows moved, and he caught the faintest gleam of gold beneath their cloak, and his hopes died with it. They were not thieves, or killers, or rebels.

These particular shadows belonged to the palace. The *res in cal*, they were called. The *crown's crows*.

Alucard rolled his eyes, and wiggled his fingers in a wave, and the shadows reluctantly slunk back, folding deeper into the night, no doubt carrying word of his exploits back to the palace.

He walked on, slowing only when he reached a crossing he knew all too well. To his left, the palace bridge, and at its center, the *soner rast*, as the palace was called, the *beating heart*, rising above the Isle.

To his right, the road that led up to the abandoned Emery estate.

It should have been easy enough, to turn away. But it wasn't. There was a tug behind his ribs, like an anchor at the end of a rope. The saying came to him, then, the one he'd tried to summon in Ciara's room.

Och ans, is farr, ins ol'ach, regh narr.

There was no easy way to translate Veskan. It was the kind of language where every word could mean a dozen things, depending on their order and their context. It's why he'd never managed more than a frail grasp on a handful of phrases. But this one he'd held on to. This one Alucard understood.

A head gets lost, but a heart knows home.

If he turned up that road, Alucard knew what he'd find.

He closed his eyes, imagined walking through the open gate, climbing the steps, and pushing open the door, imagined Anisa throwing her arms around his neck, imagined his father, not a shadow in the doorway but a proud hand on his shoulder, his brother Berras standing by the fire, holding out a glass, saying it was about time he found his way back. Alucard stood there, imagining a life that was not, and had never been, and would never be.

The house had been a ruin in the wake of his battle with Berras, his brother poisoned by Osaron's power. The whole thing should have been torn down—that's what he thought every time his feet carried him there, to the open gate, every time he saw the cracked façade, the sagging walls. It should have been erased. It was another scar, only this one he didn't *need* to live with. Alucard knew that all he had to do was ask, and Rhy would see it razed.

But he couldn't bring himself to give the order. It had not just been his brother's home, his father's. It had been his mother's once, his sister's, his own. And on some level, he wanted to believe it could be his again. He must have said as much to Rhy one night, after too many drinks, because the next time he'd made the weary trek to the Emery estate, he'd found it standing proud, the house repaired in loving detail, every stone and pillar and pane of glass in its place.

Alucard knew, as soon as he saw it, that he'd made a terrible mistake. He hated it. Hated the way the house sat, stately but sleeping, the doors locked and the windows dark.

It was a monument. It was a crypt.

There was nothing waiting for him but the dead.

Alucard blew out a breath, and turned left, toward the bridge.

And the palace.

And home.

IV

The White Rose stood at the window, watching Emery go.

Then she took up the length of silk that had been her dress and began the careful work of winding it back around her limbs, her chest, her waist, moving with expert fingers as she tied the one and only knot in a bow at her wrist, despite the fact she had no intention of being unwrapped again that night.

If she had, Ciara would have gone down the stairs, returning to the salon and the bar, and the waiting patrons below. Instead, she went up, past the various chambers, most already in use, and stopped only when she reached the door at the last level. Behind it lay the private quarters that served as her office, the place where the famed White Rose shed the role of host, and stepped back into that of businesswoman. She was, after all, the brothel's owner.

The door was locked—or at least, it should have been. But as Ciara reached the landing, she was surprised to find the door ajar. If she had touched the handle, she would have found it cold—frozen, even—to the touch.

Instead, she reached into her hair and drew out one of the thin silver pins, letting it hang from her fingers as she stepped inside.

The room was just as she'd left it, with one noticeable exception. A man now sat behind the pale wood desk—*her* desk—as if it were his own. She flicked her fingers, and several candles sprang to life, casting the room and the intruder in a soft yellow glow. His face brightened, or rather, the mask he wore did, reflecting the light. It was an ornate thing, the surface like poured gold, the top curling upward like the spokes of a sun.

Ciara's shoulders loosened in recognition. She painted on a smile, but didn't let go of the pin.

"The Master of the Veil," she said. "What brings you here?"

The Veil was another pleasure garden, one of dozens in the city. But unlike the others, it didn't stay in one place, and only opened at the whims of its master. That was the gimmick, an invitation-only club that descended like a cloud-shadow, sweeping over a building for a single night.

The man behind the desk spread his hands and said in Veskan, "I was waiting for you."

She stiffened a little, answered in Arnesian. "There are far more comfortable rooms in which to wait."

"I'm sure," he said, lifting a glass orb from the desk. Inside, a white rose hung suspended, preserved in perpetual bloom. A gift from one of her patrons. "But none are quite so private."

Ciara lifted her chin. "You should know, more than most, the discretion of my hosts."

He began to roll the orb across the table, from one hand to another. "Indeed. They have certainly been . . . accommodating."

As the glass ball whispered on the table, Ciara studied the Master of the Veil.

She'd never seen his face, but then, she didn't need to. She'd dealt with enough patrons to read the kinds of truth only a body tells. She noticed the way he draped himself across the chair—*her* chair. The way he took up space, even in a private office, as if entitled to it. *Ostra,* she thought. Maybe even *vestra.* It was there, in his posture, and in the languidness of his Arnesian, and the formality of his Veskan, which spoke more to education than experience. It was there, in the shape of his hands, and the crescents of his nails. It was there, in the taunt that tugged at the corner of his voice, as if they too were seated at a Rasch board. Though she guessed he didn't play games, not unless he already knew that he would win.

The man pushed the glass ball again, but this time, as his left hand flung the orb away, his right made no motion to catch it. It rolled, briskly, across the desk, and straight over the edge.

Ciara lunged forward, caught the sphere just before it shattered on the floor. She sighed, and straightened, and when she did, the Master of the Veil was right there, no longer behind the desk but in front of it, in front of *her*, so close that she could *almost* see the eyes behind the mask.

A single lock of dark hair curled around the corner of the golden mask. She reached up, as if to tuck it behind his ear, her fingers ready to pull the mask aside, but his hand closed around her wrist, his fingers burning cold. She flinched, but his grip tightened, seeming to enjoy her discomfort. She'd handled enough patrons to recognize the ones who took pleasure in another's pain. She fought the urge to drive the silver pin into his side, and smiled through the biting cold.

"There are other rooms for that," she said evenly. "And other hosts."

"Speaking of hosts—" He let go, returned to his seat—her seat—at the table. "I've come to hire three, for my next opening. It will be a larger crowd."

"Perhaps you should hire more of your own, instead of borrowing mine."

"The beauty of the Veil is that it's always changing. Never the same garden—"

"Never the same flowers."

"Precisely," he said.

Ciara looked down at her wrist, the skin there red from the lingering cold. "It will cost double. Because of the risk."

"Risk?" She couldn't *see* him arch a brow, but she could hear it in his voice.

"Businesses like ours cater to a diverse clientele, but my consorts have noticed that many of your patrons share the same mark." She looked down at the glass ball in her hand. "Now, they are of course discreet. But I think you will agree, in this case, that discretion is worth the extra cost."

As she spoke, she saw the frost spread across the window, felt the air go cold around her, cold enough that if she exhaled, she might see her breath. It left an awful, eerie feeling, like his fingers sliding over her skin. Ciara flexed, and the warmth returned. She would not be made to shiver in her own house.

The Master of the Veil leaned back in the chair. "Perhaps what you say is true," he mused, "perhaps not. We are paid to overlook the details of our patrons."

"Discretion isn't the same as ignorance," she countered. "Nothing happens in my brothel without my knowing. And I'm willing to bet nothing happens in the Veil without yours."

She studied the golden mask, and the man behind it.

"I was just with the king's consort."

The Master of the Veil inclined his head. "Here? Has the royal bed gone cold?"

"He came searching for information. The palace is worried. He suspects I've heard something. He would have paid me handsomely. Yet I gave him nothing."

"And instead, you tip your hand to me."

Ciara shrugged. "It's not tipping if you mean to show it. I want you to know exactly where I stand."

"You support the cause, then?" Surprise rang through his voice, and for the first time, she wondered if the Master of the Veil did more than simply *host* the Hand at his establishment.

Ciara considered. "I have nothing against the crown. And no love for your cause. But business is business, and our business is better in times of . . . upheaval." She returned the glass orb with its rose to the cradle on the desk—her desk. "Still, my consorts' discretion may be free. But mine will cost you."

He rose to his feet, one hand slipping into his pocket.

"Three hosts should be sufficient," he said, setting a stack of silver lish on the edge of the desk. To these, he added a single cheap red lin. "For your time," he said, and despite the mask, she could hear the corner of his mouth twitch up in amusement before he slipped past her, and out the office door, leaving a chill breeze in his wake.

Ciara watched him descend the stairs, but she didn't move, not until she was *certain* the Master of the Veil was gone.

V

SOMEWHERE AT SEA

A few hours after they set sail, the first two men explained the plan.

They were going to rob the *Ferase Stras*.

The third man listened, his excitement dissolving into horror.

He'd heard tales about the floating market, back when he was still just the merchant's son, and not a hero in the making.

Not much was known about the legendary ship, which dealt in the empire's most dangerous goods. Despite its name, the vessel wasn't a market so much as a vault, a place to store forbidden magic. Few things aboard were actually for sale, and those went only to the right buyers, chosen by the captain, Maris Patrol.

Some said she was a phantom, bound to the boards of her ship for all time. Others claimed she was just an old woman—though she'd been an old woman as long as there had been the *Ferase Stras*.

It was impossible to *find* the market without a map, and the only maps that led there seemed to lead nowhere at all—unless you knew how to read them. And if you did manage to find your way by water, the ship could not be taken, since no guest could set foot on deck without an invitation. And even then, it could not be robbed, since the wards laid upon it were as thick as lacquer, and not only stifled any magic, but would turn a thief's body to ash before it reached the rail.

It was a doomed endeavor, an impossible quest, and yet, two days later, here they were, huddled on the platform outside the *Ferase Stras,* waiting to be invited in.

It was a narrow ledge high above the water, little more than a plank fixed to the side of the ship, too small for three men and a trunk, and so as the first man knocked, the third clung to the back edge, close enough to feel the place where the platform fell away beneath his heels. His heart was pounding, bobbing on the line between excitement and terror. He thought of Olik, the hero who walked right onto enemy ships, and

51

made himself at home. Olik, who had put his fear in a metal box, and sunk it in the sea. The third man pictured himself bottling up everything he felt and letting it drop over the edge behind them, leaving him steady, and sure.

Still, he wished he had a mask, like Olik's friend Jesar, the ghostly terror. The hero never wore one, but the third man knew too well how much faces gave away. Unfortunately, he also knew they'd never be allowed on board with such concealments, so there he was, trying to keep his features smooth, his brow steady, and his mouth set. Trying to make a mask of his own face.

The first man knocked again on the simple wooden door.

"Maybe they're dead," mused the second, when still no one came.

"Better not be," growled the first, resting his boot on the trunk. "We don't know if the wards are bound to the ship or the bodies aboard."

The third man said nothing, only stared at the floating market, and wondered how many of the stories were true. If there really were talismans aboard that could split mountains, or plunge thousands into sleep. Blades that drew out secrets instead of blood, and mirrors that showed a person's future, and metal cages that trapped and stored a person's magic, their mind, their soul.

"Should we just go in?" asked the second.

"Be my guest," said the first. "I told them we didn't need *three* men for this mission."

The second man rubbed his fingers, calling up a flame. It flickered to life but as he brought it to the door, the fire guttered, snuffed out by the force of the market's wards.

The third man tugged nervously at his tunic.

He was dressed, like the others, in the rough-spun black common to pirates. It was scratchier than he thought it would be. Olik never mentioned that. Nor how the constant rocking of a boat could turn one's stomach.

Finally, the door rattled open.

He looked up, expecting to see the infamous Maris Patrol, but found a middle-aged man instead, dressed in a crisp white cowl.

The captain's oldest nephew, Katros. The steward of the ship.

52

He was broad-shouldered and dark-skinned, a sheen of sweat on his brow, as though he'd been ill. But he wasn't ill, strictly speaking. He was drugged. That was part of the plan. Katros's younger brother, Valick, took a skiff to shore twice a month, and came back laden with food and drink, the latest shipment of which had been laced with savarin, an odorless powder that weakened the body and clouded the mind. The bulk of the toxin had been put in the wine that Maris favored, from a vintner who now served the Hand.

She must have been in a generous mood.

It wasn't *poison*, he reminded himself, as Katros swayed on his feet, his skin taking on a greyish hue. Olik wasn't in the business of murder—went out of his way to avoid needless death, and so would he. Besides, there was too good a chance the spellwork aboard would catch it. But some people took savarin for pleasure. The danger was only in the dosage, and that was in the drinker's hands.

Katros Patrol cleared his throat, and steadied himself.

"Tokens," he said, holding out a hand.

The first man toed their trunk. "We're selling, not buying."

But the steward of the ship only shrugged. "Doesn't matter."

The third man understood. This wasn't just a doorway. The entrance to the *Ferase Stras* was a threshold, and all good thresholds demanded a price. A cost to board the market, a payment for simply setting foot among its wares. And according to the tales, nothing so common as coin would do. You had to part with something special, to add to Maris's collection.

They'd docked earlier at Sasenroche for just that purpose.

The first man held out a piece of paper, bound with ribbon. It was a page from a book that once belonged in Black London.

The second man produced a pencil, its core filled with powdered blood instead of charcoal, and spelled to write only truths.

When it was his turn, the third man reached into his pocket, fingers tracing the cool rim of the glass before drawing it out. It was a disc, roughly the size of his palm. He'd spent the last hours of the trip, from the black market to this one, staring into its surface.

It was spelled to answer only one question: *Am I going to die today?*

When the glass turned black, the answer was yes.

He didn't want to part with the token—felt deeply that it was meant to be his—but told himself if that was true, it would find its way back.

Powerful objects had a way of doing that.

As he held it up one last time, he asked the question in his mind, and sighed in relief when the glass stayed clear.

Of course he wouldn't die, he thought.

This was his story, after all.

He watched as the three tokens vanished in Katros Patrol's white linen sleeve. And then the door to the floating market was swinging wide, ushering them into their fate.

The room was dim, and cluttered with cabinets. Items gleamed from every shelf, the only clean surface a broad wooden desk, beside which stood a large black sphere, though whether it was made of glass or stone he couldn't tell. It sat in its stand like a globe, but its surface was as smooth and blank as the maps that led to the *Ferase Stras*.

The third man glimpsed a mask, a lovely piece of molten silver, on a mantle, and his fingers twitched with longing.

"Where is the captain?" asked the first man, eyeing the empty desk.

"She will come when she is needed," said Katros, leading them through the office door, and out onto the decks. There they found Maris's other nephew, Valick, leaning against the mast, dressed in the same unblemished white—so out of place amid the salt and grime of the sea—and either he did not drink or he had a stronger constitution, because he seemed hale and steady, untouched by the savarin.

The other two men carried the trunk, its contents rattling, but the third gazed around, in awe, at the maze of corridors and rooms, stairs and tents, that rose like a miniature city around the deck. He drifted to an alcove, where a cane lay within a glass case, its polished bronze head in the shape of a crow. There was no spellwork written on its surface, but its beauty was hypnotic.

"What does it do?"

He didn't realize he'd spoken aloud, not until the faces turned.

"If you don't know," said Valick, "then it isn't meant for you." He turned back to the other two men. "Have you come to trade, or sell?"

"That depends," said the first man, "whether you have what we're looking for."

"And what would that be?" asked Katros, stepping forward.

The second man produced a folded slip of paper, on which the object was drawn. It was roughly the size of a child's element set, and did not look like much, but then, neither did a fruit knife, and it could still cut deep enough to kill.

Katros studied the drawing a moment, then shook his head. "We do not have this here."

He was lying.

The young man who had been the merchant's son cracked his knuckles, the agreed-upon signal, and the other two heard.

"Then I suppose," said the first, who had styled himself the leader, "we're only here to sell."

"That assumes we want to buy," said Katros, nodding at the trunk. "Show us what you have."

"Of course." He knelt before the trunk and freed the lock.

The second man slid aside the clasps, and lifted the lid.

The third watched as the trunk fell open to reveal a pile of fabric. Not silk or velvet but heavy cloth, the color of a forest canopy at dusk. A cloak. It did not look like much, but then, of course, all stories were full of powerful artifacts and objects that had been disguised as common fare.

"It's designed to shield the wearer against magic," said the first, drawing the cloth from the trunk, and settling it around his own shoulders. "Let me show you how it works."

Valick frowned. "The ship is spelled."

"Ah," countered the man, "but there's one kind of spell that still works, even here." A cool smile. "The wards."

The words landed like a fuse. It burned across Valick's face, lit in Katros's still-drugged eyes as the two stewards of the *Ferase Stras* realized what they meant to do next.

The second man had already reached down into the trunk, fingers curling around the blade he'd hidden beneath the cloak. He sent the weapon flying. It sliced through the air, burying itself in Valick Patrol's chest. Katros roared and flung himself at the attacker, and the two went down on the deck, while the first of the thieves took off, vanishing into the maze of rooms.

The third one scrambled over to the open trunk, but a hand caught his foot and he fell to the deck.

Valick lay gasping, blood spilling between his fingers and his teeth, the white of his tunic stained red around the blade buried in his ribs, but his free hand was a vise around the young man's ankle.

"You will die," snarled the steward.

"Not today," he said, channeling the voice of a pirate, and kicking free. But Katros had gained the upper hand in his own fight, and slammed the second thief back into the mast. The whole ship shook with the force of it, and as his attacker slumped to the deck, Katros turned on *him*.

The third man threw out his hand, intending to call a gust of wind— forgetting the ship would not allow it. No wall of air rose up to stop the advancing storm of Katros Patrol. If the steward had been well, if there had been no gash to his temple, no savarin coursing through his veins, the glass disk would surely have turned black when he had asked if he would die that day. But Katros was unsteady on his feet, and he was sober and quick, and desperate to be a hero.

He danced backward, drawing a sword from the trunk's depths and slashing out, too wide. He swung again, and this time Katros's arm came up to block the blow. The blade slashed down, and he expected to feel the meaty give of flesh, but steel rang against steel as the white linen parted to reveal a metal bracer.

The third man turned the blade and slashed again, up toward Katros's face, and to his horror, the steward of the *Ferase Stras caught* the sword. A thick palm clapped against the flat side of the blade, and a second later it was torn from the third man's grip, and turned against him.

He twisted out of its path, or tried, but he felt the edge bite through his shirt, carving a shallow line across his ribs, and he had just enough time to register the searing heat, the fact *Olik* never seemed to feel pain in the throes of battle—

And then Katros hit him. Hard.

His vision went white, then red, blood pouring from his nose as he fell back to the deck. Pain rang through his head and blurred his sight, and despite the chaos breaking out aboard the floating market, the former merchant's son found himself *insulted*.

There were rules, he wanted to say. It was an affront to use one's hands, to strike someone with bare flesh instead of fire or water or earth.

Instead, he spit blood onto the deck and rolled onto his back in time to see Katros Patrol looming over him, one boot raised to crush his skull.

The world seemed to slow down, then. It was not the work of a spell. There was no magic to it. It was simply the moment someone turned the last card in Sanct when you've bet your whole pot. The sinking feeling you get when you realize you've gambled. And lost.

But the boot never came down.

Just then the second man, shaking off his stupor, threw himself once more at Katros, fist closing around his cowl as he hauled him back. The third's head was still ringing, but he saw a slash of steel, heard the crack of bodies against a wooden rail, and then the two men vanished over the side of the ship, crashing into the sea below.

The third man didn't remember getting to his feet, but he was there now, stumbling toward the sound, when he saw the flash of a green cloak, and the first man appeared, racing across the deck with a parcel under his arm.

He'd done it. They'd done it.

The first man headed straight for the rail, clearly meant to jump the narrow gap between the *Ferase Stras* and their own skiff. And he might have, if not for Valick Patrol. The young man had somehow gotten to his knees, then his feet, and despite the blood turning his tunic red, he summoned the strength to reach for the thief as he surged past, caught the tail of the other man's cloak, bloody fingers gripping the precious cloth. The clasp broke free right as the thief lunged for the side of the ship. The cloak slipped off in the moment just before he reached the edge of the rail.

And the world flashed blue.

Like a bolt of lightning in reverse, it seemed to travel out from the man's body as it made contact with the ship's wards. A clap of thunder, like a door slamming shut, rolled across the air, and then the first man was flung back, his body only a burnt shell by the time it hit the deck.

And the object—the thing they'd come all this way for, the prize that would help them change the world—bounced roughly against the deck, a mess of bending metal and splintering wood, a handful of pieces breaking off entirely as it rolled.

The first man was a smoldering ruin, the second had gone overboard with Katros Patrol, Valick had finally succumbed to his wounds, and in the brief but crushing stillness, the third man realized he was the only one left.

But not for long.

He could hear the sound of people struggling below, their bodies slamming against the hull, and a door opening somewhere above, and so he scrambled forward, boots slipping in blood as he gathered up the broken object, which looked even smaller now that it was in several singed and smoking pieces.

All that work, thought the third man, *for* this.

He grabbed the green cloak from where it lay, slung it around his shoulders and clutched the folds against his chest as he ran to the ship's edge, and leapt. This time, there was no terrible blue lightning, no thunderous crack. He felt only a brief, lurching resistance, as if a hook had lodged inside him, a line drawn taut as it tried to reel him back. But then the line snapped, and the thief was falling.

He landed hard on the deck of the waiting skiff, and rolled upright, the remains of the object still pressed to his chest. It was broken, but broken things could be fixed. He bundled the fragments into the cloak and got to his feet. He reached for a gust of wind, hoping his magic and nerve wouldn't fail—and free of the *Ferase Stras*'s wards, the air rushed up to meet him, filling the sail. Moments later, the skiff had turned, and was cutting swiftly through the waves, carrying him away from the floating market.

The third man, who was now the *last* man, let out a small whoop of victory.

They said it couldn't be done, but he'd done it.

He'd robbed the *Ferase Stras*.

He rubbed at his chest, where a small pain had formed. But it was one among a dozen hurts, so he paid it no mind.

The glass disk had been right.

He would not die today.

VI

Maris Patrol had very few vices.

She liked jewel figs and silk sheets, pure silver and secrets. And fine spirits, which she allowed herself to sample most nights, but always in moderation. A short glass of amberlow before bed, to ease the ache in her old bones and rest her mind. Never enough to upset her balance or muddy her thoughts.

So she knew, when she woke with ash in her mouth and her head like the shallows after a storm, that she'd been drugged.

Light spilled thinly through the curtains of her cabin. She sat up, limbs shaking with the effort. She was old—older than most—wrinkles gouged like grooves into her brown skin, but her ringed hands were still steady, her bony spine straight. Sweat broke out as she tried to stand, and failed, sagging back onto the edge of the bed.

"*Sanct,*" she swore under her breath, and the pile of bones and fur that called itself a dog looked up from the rug nearby at the unexpected sound of his name.

Voices reached her from across the ship. They weren't raised, but this was the *Ferase Stras,* and its walls kept no secrets, not from her. Two of the voices belonged to her nephews, but the rest were foreign. A small voice in the back of her own mind told her to lie back, to rest, to let Valick and Katros handle the customers. One day, they would have to run the market themselves. One day—but Maris was still the captain of this ship, and they might be grown men, but they were still young, still—

A shout went up, a pained cry slicing through the air, and Maris was on her feet. Her knees nearly gave way at the suddenness, but she made it to the cabinet by the door, dragged open a heavy drawer and shuffled through until she found the vial, the liquid inside like melted pearl. She tipped it back, swallowing the contents, which tasted of metal and left ice in their wake. Unpleasant, yes, but in seconds, her limbs had stopped shaking. Her breath steadied. Fresh sweat slicked her skin, but it had the pearl shine of the concoction, and as she wiped it from her brow, she felt her senses return to her in full.

She swept her robe from the nearby hook, and was still pulling it around her bony shoulders when the wards of the *Ferase Stras* shattered.

The force of it rocked through the ship, and Maris swore out loud again. Only a fool would try to rob the floating market. But she'd been alive long enough to know the world was full of fools.

She surged across the cabin, Sanct unfolding from his place and rising to follow, a pale ghost in her wake. She snatched her dagger from the desk, threw open the cabin door, and stepped out onto an upper deck, her silver hair loose and wild in the wind.

"*Venskal,*" she told the dog. *Wait.*

Maris silently crossed the maze of halls, checking for broken cabinets as she passed, signs of theft. The sounds of a struggle wafted up from the main deck, followed by a splash, the sound of boots shuffling over wood. She pulled a blade from its sheath and descended the stairs.

But by the time she reached the main deck, the scene was oddly still.

The ship swayed gently from the force of the blown ward, and Maris could smell the stain of blood and magic. A chest sat open and empty on the deck, and the body of a thief lay halfway to the rail, little more than a blackened shell. There was no sign of Katros, but several strides away she found her youngest nephew, Valick, his once-white tunic dark with blood. It pooled beneath him, a shadow creeping across the deck. His face was turned up, his eyes on the sky, open and unseeing.

Maris knelt beside him, ran a ringed hand over Valick's black hair. Not a single strand of grey.

"*Venskal,*" she whispered again, this time to her nephew's corpse.

She knew there was an order to the world, a give and take, a season for all things. She knew it was forbidden to wade into the stream of magic and try to change its course. But Maris Patrol was the captain of a ship that traded in forbidden things.

And she would have used every single one to bring her nephew back to life.

Maris slid a ring from her right hand. It was a heavy silver band, but when she closed her fist around it, the metal shattered, the shell crumbling away to reveal the thinnest length of golden thread.

She was still wrapping one end around her narrow wrist when Katros hauled himself over the side of the ship, boots sloshing as he landed on the deck.

Red ran into one eye, and his ruined tunic clung to his body, fresh blood blooming here and there against the once-white cloth. But the wounds were shallow, and he was upright, and dragging another body in his wake.

He dropped the second thief onto the deck, where the man shuddered and retched, seawater rattling in his chest. His head fell back, the strength going out of his limbs.

Maris's mind raced. She should keep him alive, question him, find answers.

But Valick.

Her older nephew must have seen the struggle in her eyes, because he squeezed the sea from his shirt and said, "I broke his jaw. Doubt he can speak."

She shot Katros a grateful look, then began to wind the golden thread around the man's limp wrist instead of her own. It looked as brittle as a strand of hair, but it held firm, even biting into the skin. She twisted the other end around Valick's palm, curling his dead fingers over it.

Katros watched, eyes dark, and if he judged her for using such illicit magic, he said nothing. He knew she would have done the same for him.

Maris squeezed her youngest nephew's hand and said a single word, the one that had been carved onto the inside of the heavy silver ring. The spell lit like a fuse, began to burn its way across the gold thread, moving from the thief's body to Valick's.

From the living to the dead.

"What happened?" asked Maris, watching as the light traveled down the golden thread, turning it black in its wake.

"Thieves," said Katros. "They came aboard as patrons, claimed they had something to sell." He nodded to the empty chest. "It was a cloak, designed to shield against wards."

Maris looked to the charred body on the deck. Its clothes burned black against its skin. "Little good it did him."

"It was a ruse," said Katros, but Maris wasn't listening. In that moment, the light reached Valick's hand, and winked out. As it vanished, the thief went still, and Valick inhaled sharply. The thread crumbled to ash between the two men. The thief sagged in death, and Valick's chest rose and fell, and Maris herself finally exhaled.

She felt tired, as if she'd paid for the life herself after all.

"Fools," she muttered, rising to her feet. "Two lone men thought they could rob *my* ship?"

And that's when Valick opened his eyes, and said a word that sent a shiver down Maris's ancient spine. "Three."

Maris's head snapped toward his face. "What?"

Valick sat up, wincing even as the wound between his ribs began to knit. "There were three of them," he coughed, blood still staining his teeth. "One got away."

Maris straightened, scanning the horizon. It was nearly dusk, the line between sea and sky smudged with fog, but in the distance, she could just make out the retreating shape of a small boat. She gauged the distance, but the *Ferase Stras* was not a vessel meant to move with any speed. Someone had robbed her ship. And he was getting away. But no cloak could save him from the many protections she'd laid upon the market.

"Fast or slow," she said, half to herself. "The other wards will do their work."

"They were after something," said Katros.

"And they got it," said Valick.

Maris's mood darkened as Katros drew a piece of paper from his sodden clothes. The ink had bled and the parchment was barely holding together, but she knew every piece in her collection.

Including this one.

There were a great many objects aboard the *Ferase Stras,* all of them forbidden. But *forbidden* could mean a number of things. There were talismans like the ring she'd just used, forbidden because they went against the law of nature. There were others that bound mind and will, forbidden because they went against the law of control. There were things forbidden for the potency of their power, or the scale of their magic, or the volatility of their spellwork, and things forbidden because in the wrong hands they could raze kingdoms, or splinter worlds.

This was none of those.

Maris frowned.

It wasn't the most powerful object on her ship, not by far. And yet, these men had gone to all this trouble to steal it. Worse, they hadn't just known what they were looking for. They'd known where it was aboard the ship. The market's cluttered impression was a ruse; there was in fact an order to it, a logic to the placement of every piece in her collection. And at least one of them must have known where to look. He'd seen a map, not *to* the *Ferase Stras* but *of* it—its rooms, its hoard. And that was just as dangerous as half the things aboard.

Maris shook her head. A problem for another day.

First things first.

She dropped the slip of paper and turned, abandoning the deck, the ship's contents unfolding in her mind as she wove through crowded corridors, past cabinets and cases and alcoves that to anyone else would have seemed cluttered. But she knew where she was going, and found what she was looking for.

A black box, a gold eye carved into the top.

Inside, half a dozen grooves in a velvet-lined tray. Four of the slots were empty. The remaining two held panes of colored glass, each the size of Sanct cards.

Her nephews were sharp. Chances were they had not forgotten anything important.

But Maris wasn't in the habit of taking chances.

She drew a glass card from the case and returned topside, held the brittle pane up and spoke.

"*Enis*," she said.

Begin.

The glass pane fogged momentarily between her fingers, and when it cleared, the deck beyond began to draw itself back, and back, and back, retreating through the minutes until the thieves were there again, having just set foot aboard her ship.

"*Skar.*"

Stop.

The image shuddered, held, the figures frozen as they set the trunk down on the deck in front of her nephews.

Maris strode forward, putting herself in the center of the scene, her back to the image of Valick and Katros so she could better see the thieves.

"*Enis.*"

The scene rolled forward, just as it had. She turned in a circle as she watched it all play out, saw Valick's death and the thieves' attack, the first broken by the wards, the second gone with Katros over the side, saw the parcel break against the deck, only to be salvaged by the third.

And as he stumbled, dazed and bleeding toward the ship's edge, she saw it, through the tear in his shirt—a tattoo, or perhaps a brand, across his ribs. And though she couldn't see the entire image, she knew what she was looking for, and there it was: a hand.

Then the thief was gone, over the side, and Maris was there once more, kneeling over Valick as the past caught up to the present, and the glass splintered in her hand, and turned to sand, and blew away.

Maris sighed, and felt every one of her many, many years, and then she turned to Katros.

"Search the bodies," she said. "And throw them over."

"And then?" asked Valick.

Maris glanced at the horizon. The other ship was gone. Her aching fingers cracked as they closed into a fist. No one stole from the *Ferase Stras.*

"Clean yourself up," she told him. "I have a favor to call in."

II

THE CAPTAIN AND THE GHOST

I

Delilah Bard leaned against the rail of the *Grey Barron,* watching the prow split the sea.

The wind was up, propelling the ship with enough force to send up a spray of mist that shimmered where it caught the light.

The sails snapped in the breeze, and Lila tipped her head back, brown eyes squinting at the sky. A stranger would never know that one of those eyes was real and one was fake. Would never know that the one she'd lost hadn't been brown at all, but black as pitch, carved out by a two-bit doctor back in London, England—the only London she'd known of, then—when she was just a child. As if it had been a poisoned thing, a spreading rot, and not a sign of strength, a marker of extraordinary power, once-in-a-generation magic.

If only she'd been born in *this* world, the one that worshipped magic, instead of the one that had forgotten it. But she was here now.

She held out her hand, calling the water to her.

"Tyger, tyger," she murmured, even though she no longer needed words to focus her power. She simply curled her fingers, and the water answered, drew itself around her wrist and hardened there into an icy bangle. Easy, effortless. As natural as breathing.

Lila smiled.

Over the years, she had been many things.

A con artist. A captain. A traveler. A mage.

Once upon a time—and a world away—she'd been nothing but an orphan, a pickpocket, a thief with dreams of stealing a ship and sailing away. Dreams of becoming a pirate, laying claim to foreign seas. Dreams of fine knives and good coins, and more than anything, of *freedom*.

It had been hard-won, bought and paid for in years and battle and blood—not always her own—but at last, she had it all.

She flicked her fingers, and the icy bangle shattered with enough force that a few bits of ice drove into the rail. She plucked them out, and dropped them over the side. In her head, she heard Alucard muttering about his ship. But of course, it wasn't his ship, not anymore.

She had rechristened it, much to the old captain's displeasure, but the *Night Spire* had had its time at sea; now it was the *Grey Barron*'s turn.

The *Barron* had spent its first few years as an independent vessel, under no flag but its own. It had been pleasant enough, to sail for the sake of sailing, to discover new ports, new markets, new seas. But Lila had spent the first nineteen years of her life with one goal, and in its wake, she found herself coveting a new purpose. She was almost relieved when the rumors began to spread, first of more trouble with the empire's reluctant allies, Faro and Vesk, and then, worse still, of trouble at home. So Alucard had asked her to put the ship to use. To go where no royal vessel could, and do what no royal vessel would.

To spy. To sack. To sabotage. To plunder, and sink, and fight, and steal.

To plunge in like a knife, and disappear again before anyone knew they had been cut, let alone that they were bleeding out.

Now and then, when it suited, the *Grey Barron* would still don the *Spire*'s black sails, become the shadow on the sea again, but today, its sails were white, its hull a nondescript grey. With luck, they would blend right in with all the other smugglers and thieves traveling down the Blood Coast.

Some places earned their names by dint of nature—they had black sands, perhaps, red silt, green tides—but the Blood Coast was not one of them. No, when the powers carved up Arnes and Faro and Vesk centuries before, there was a seam, a single juncture where all three empires met. No one could agree on the exact boundary, and so, after decades of discontent, of sabotage and sunken ships, the stretch had earned its moniker.

And they were bound for the capital, the infamous port of Verose.

Lila scanned the horizon, waiting for the jagged line of the city's pale cliffs to take shape on the horizon. The Arnesian guard had done their best to clean up Verose decades before, to drive out the worst of the violence and impose a kind of order—the old king, Rhy's father, Maxim Maresh, had even served a stint as captain of its base. But Verose had proved a lawless place, by nature or by choice.

And Lila loved it.

It was the kind of place where blood spilled often, every gathering was always one drawn blade away from a brawl, and—

A bottle shattered somewhere behind her on the deck, followed by a raucous cheer. Lila sighed, and turned toward her crew. Tav and Vasry were jostling, while the usually stern-faced Stross barked in laughter, all three faces red. The only one missing was Vasry's wife, Raya. Lila craned her head and scanned the rigging until she found the woman, black-haired and pale as marble, perched on the masthead. The sun was high, and hot, but the woman didn't seem to mind. Her gaze dropped to Lila, her eyes the same icy blue as the glacier she'd come from.

"Didn't think I could do it, did you?" Vasry was whooping in Arnesian, and it was clear from the volume of his voice and the way he swayed that he had emptied the bottle before breaking it. "But I've been practicing."

Lila looked down at the shards of glass littering her deck. "Practicing what, exactly?" she asked.

Tav made a small explosive gesture with both hands, and mouthed the word *boom*. Lila raised a brow. Vasry was a wind mage by nature, though he had never been a very good one. As far as she could tell, he'd gotten far more use out of his looks than his magic. His hair was a tawny gold, his eyes fringed thick with lashes, and, obnoxiously, he seemed to be getting more handsome with age instead of less, which came in handy when someone needed charming, less so when their ship could use a strong gust.

"Here, here," he said, handing Stross another bottle. "Give this one some air."

"That better be empty," said Lila the second before her first mate hurled the bottle up over the side of the ship. Vasry's hand shot out, eyes narrowed and lips moving. Clearly he meant to hit the glass with some concussive force, but he missed, and the bottle simply arced, and fell, untouched, landing with a quiet plop in the surf below.

"Oops," he said, and after a moment of silence, all three men broke out laughing again. Vasry hiccupped. Lila shook her head.

"I think you've all had enough."

Tav spread his arms. "But Captain," he said, with mock sincerity, "this is meant to be a *pleasure* vessel."

"Charted for a lark," added Vasry.

"That's right," grumbled Stross, suddenly defensive. "We're just being thorough."

In that moment, she regretted letting them pick the *Barron*'s cover for this particular mission, even as she took up the last of the bottles waiting on the crate. She went to take a swig, only to find it empty.

Lila gritted her teeth. "Tell me there's still liquor somewhere on this ship."

The three men had the decency to look at least a little guilty. "Should still be some in the hold."

She sighed, then turned and tossed the empty bottle up into the air.

Instead of splaying her hand, she closed it, not into a fist but a pistol. Thumb up, finger pointed. She followed the bottle's arc with her finger, and squeezed the imaginary trigger.

The bottle shattered with a bang. The crew whooped and cheered, and the captain stifled a small smile as she strode away, the sounds following her down into the hold.

II

Lila hummed as she moved between the crates, her voice echoing faintly against the hull.

The *Grey Barron*'s hold was home to many things. There were stores, of course, enough supplies that they could stay at sea for weeks without calling into port. But there was also plenty to trade, or keep—bolts of fine cloth and scrying stones; Veskan masks and Faroan mantles; books of poetry, histories, and spells; and of course, a fair number of weapons stashed among the crates, since her burgeoning collection had long overflowed her private quarters. Everyone deserved a hobby, and just because Lila sailed for the crown didn't mean she couldn't serve herself.

The hold was also home to a handsome collection of spirits, skimmed from private stashes or lifted from the captain's cabins of the ships they crossed, the ones left sinking in their wake.

"*How do you know that the Sarows is coming . . .*" she sang, pulling open the wine cage. Her fingers danced across the bottles on the rack, tracing the empty spaces like missing teeth.

Just being thorough, Stross had said.

"Bastards," she muttered, just before an arm closed around her throat.

It wrenched her back with sudden force, lifting her off her feet. Her hand went to the dagger at her hip, but the attacker's hand went there, too, pinning her fingers against the hilt before she could draw the blade. His grip was solid stone, but she still had another hand, and she used it, dragging free a second blade and driving it blindly back into his chest.

It should have found flesh. It didn't.

Instead, the attacker let go, flinging her forward into the rack with clattering force. A bottle of summer wine went crashing to the floor, and shattered.

"Oh, you'll pay for that," she hissed, turning just in time to block the blade that came slicing toward her throat. Beyond the scraping steel, she saw him—the flash of a black mask, the ripple of a coat, a pair of lips twitching into a smile. But her attacker made no sound. Not when she spoke, and not when he struck, and not when he leapt back from the boot she tried to slam into his chest. By the time he landed, her dagger was already flying. It sliced through the air, embedded itself in a beam as the attacker twisted out of the way, vanishing behind a stack of crates.

Lila called the dagger back into her fingers. She held her breath, listened for the sound of steps in the hold. Bodies took up space. They made noise.

71

Overhead, the crew were singing a shanty, oblivious.

Down here, the only sounds were the slosh of sea against the hull, and the heartbeat thudding in her chest.

Lila didn't call for help. Instead, she forced herself to close her eyes. Block out the cluttered hold, the tip and sway of the boat, and stretch her senses, feeling for the other body as if it were just another element for her to touch. Not wood or water but blood and bone.

There.

She blinked, her hand cutting sideways at one of the crates. It slammed back, wood scraping over the floor, and she readied her blade, expecting the attacker to dive out of the way. Instead, he vaulted over the top, weight slamming into her, both of them crashing down to the floor. They rolled, and when they stopped, he was on top, but her blade was at his throat.

His chest rose and fell.

Her steel kissed his skin, but didn't draw blood.

"You're lucky," she said, "that I have such a steady hand."

The hood of his coat had fallen back, and even in the dull light of the hold, his copper hair shone, a single silver streak glinting at his temple. Lila tugged on the mask that hid the top half of his face, and it came away, revealing a pair of mismatched eyes, one blue, the other black.

"Admit it," said Kell Maresh. "I caught you off guard."

Lila shrugged. "I still would have killed you, in the end."

He raised a brow. "Are you sure?"

She turned the fight over in her mind. If he had used a blade instead of his arm. If he had gone for the kill right then and there, instead of the game, would she have been able to feel the intent? Would the knife have sung in his fingers, that tune she knew so well?

"Fine," she said, still beneath him on the floor. "In my own hold, on my own ship, you caught me off guard. Now get off me," she said, "unless you'd rather stay down here and have a tumble."

It was worth it, just to see the color rising in Kell's cheeks.

"You could put the mask back on," she added, and his blush only deepened.

He tried to hide it with a frown as he rose off her, offering a hand to help her to her feet. Lila ignored it, stood, and pushed past him, returning to the open wine cage. She fetched up the bottom half of the broken bottle, studying the shallow pool of ruined summer wine.

"I was saving that," she muttered, looking back over her shoulder.

Kell wasn't listening. He was too busy fumbling with his coat, turning it inside out, trading the black he'd worn when he'd attacked her for red, then red for blue, and finally blue for grey. Each side of the peculiar coat was a different one entirely, from the color to the cut to the buttons and clasps, to the contents of the pockets, and each had a story. She recognized most of them by now—here was the one he'd been wearing the night they'd met; here was the royal crimson with gold buttons down the front, the one he wore as prince; here, the pale grey he'd donned in the *Essen Tasch,* when he first became Kamerov Loste—but every now and then she'd see one she'd never noticed, tucked like secrets in a life she knew so well.

He found the one he was looking for—the charcoal coat he'd come to favor in their years at sea—and he shrugged it on just as a voice rang out from the deck above.

Not Vasry or Tav calling down for wine, but Stross, his deep tones booming across the ship.

"*Hals!*"

Land.

III

THE SOUTHERN POINT, *seven years ago*

"*Hals!*"

Stross's voice rang through the ship a moment *after* something scraped against the hull. One second Lila was asleep beneath a mound of quilts, and the next she was lurching out of bed, balance thrown by the steadiness of the floor beneath her legs.

She swore, shoving her socked feet into the boots she kept beside the bed, and sliding into her coat as she flung open the cabin door. Kell was already there, his own coat in his hands, his face taut with alarm, and moments later Vasry and Tav spilled into the hall, the former disheveled but dressed, the latter wearing far less but clutching a sword.

Lila opened her mouth to speak, but she was cut off by the sound that a captain never, ever wanted to hear: the splintering of wood.

She surged up the steps onto the deck. A pale mist surrounded the ship, and the sun sat somewhere below the horizon, the sky promising a dawn that hadn't yet arrived, but in the soft light, she saw Stross gripping the rail, and staring down over the side.

"You're supposed to call land *before* we hit it!" she snarled, breath pluming in the frigid air.

"It's not land," said Kell, from the upper deck.

She stomped over to the nearest rail, looked down, and swore even louder when she saw that he was right. The ship hadn't struck land.

It had struck *ice*.

Three weeks before, Lila had decided to point the ship south, and sail until something stopped them. And now, at last, something had.

She should have seen it coming, should have turned back days before, when she'd first woken to find frozen slivers floating on the surface of the water. When the cold turned sharp enough to drag its blade across her skin. When Kell's coat started offering him warmer and warmer sides, cowls and hoods and collars lined with fleece, gloves already waiting in the pockets.

They should have turned back, but the world was vast, and she was hungry.

And now they were stuck.

This wasn't an icy plinth they'd struck against, a cap floating in the sea. There *was* no sea anymore. It had frozen solid. Which meant she would have to unfreeze it. She sighed, and swung her leg over the side.

"Captain," called Stross, but she waved him away.

"Lila," warned Kell, but she ignored him.

She was an *Antari,* the strongest magician in the world. She could move a ship.

She jumped, held her breath on instinct, expecting the ice to shatter when she landed on it, expecting to feel the bone-jarring cold of the water closing over her head. But her boots hit the ice with a slap, and the world beneath didn't so much as shiver.

Lila squinted into the distance, but it was like staring into an empty scrying glass. Her good eye played tricks, tried to conjure *something* in the absence—a port, a dock, another ship—but the images all dissolved back into the fog.

She circled the ship, hoping to find a path of water in its wake, but in the short time they'd been stuck, the ice had somehow already frozen around the hull. Lila rolled her neck and cracked her knuckles, the cold wind latching on to her bare hands. She rubbed them together.

"Put wind in the sails," she called up, her voice echoing across the vast expanse of ice.

Moments later, Tav had the canvas drawn taut and Vasry conjured a gust of air. The whole ship groaned in protest, and Lila thrust both hands out in front of her, taking hold of the surrounding ice, wrapping her will over it like fingers as she ordered the mass to *melt*.

The scene before her shone, and shimmered. The ice seemed to thin in places, but beyond that, it did not heed. Annoyance bloomed into anger, and anger was powerful. She tightened her grip, forced her will into the surrounding ice, told it to be water.

The sound of it rushed in her ears, along with the crack of the topmost layers of ice.

The world tipped, but it wasn't the frozen mass giving way. It was her sight. Lila's good eye blurred, her head suddenly heavy, and Alucard's voice echoed a warning in her ears, from those first days when he began to teach her magic. The larger the element, he'd said, the harder it was to wield. A magician could only manipulate what they could hold. A current from the air, a few inches from the soil, a wave from the sea.

No one can stretch their mind around an ocean.

"Yeah, yeah, yeah," she muttered now, as something warm and wet grazed her lip. She touched her hand to it, and it came away red. Lila rubbed the blood between her fingers.

Perhaps she couldn't wrap her will around the ice. But there were other ways to break it. She was *Antari,* after all.

75

"Hey Captain," called Vasry, "maybe we should—"

She didn't hear him after that. She pressed both hands to the ice, hissing at the brutal cold. Her teeth chattered as she said the words.

"As Staro."

Break.

As soon as the sound left her lips, a deep vibration rang through the ice. A deafening clap, and cracks ran out to every side. And beneath her feet. Lila braced herself, balanced on the bobbing floe as her ship swayed, the wind in the sails dragging it free. One pace, then two.

And then, to her horror, the ice *re-formed*, not at a natural rate, but as if her magic had been a spool of yarn, unwound, and now another hand was drawing it just as swiftly back. In seconds, her work was undone.

"Son of a bitch," she hissed, bowing her head.

Boots thudded onto the ice nearby, and the next thing she knew Kell was there beside her, wrapped in the hooded grey coat that had appeared like a warning the night before.

"Lila, stop," he said, holding out a gloved hand to steady her. "It isn't working."

She knocked the hand away. "It will. With enough force."

Kell studied the ship, and she could see the shadow cross his face, the way it did sometimes when he stared down at his own hands, studying them as if they were useless now, as if they couldn't still hold a rope, or wield a sword. As if magic was the only thing that mattered.

He cleared his throat. "Maybe it's been long enough."

Lila grimaced, but said nothing. It had been three months since they left London. Three months since the battle with Osaron had shattered Kell's magic. Three months in which he had not reached for his power, convinced it simply needed time to *heal*. As if it were a broken limb.

Maybe he was right.

Maybe—but she doubted it. She knew what it was like, to have a piece of yourself torn away without your accord. Remembered well still those first few weeks after she'd lost her eye, the impotence, the denial, the rage. It hadn't come for Kell yet, but it would.

Until then, she resolved to give him space.

"Don't bother," she said, brushing off her hands. "It's stuck."

She shoved her numb fingers in her pockets and looked around. The sun should have broken free by now, but it still hung in the same way, just beneath the horizon. As if they were trapped inside a snow globe, stuck in time as well as ice.

"Have you noticed—" she started, then stopped. Kell's attention had cut past her. His eyes narrowed. "What is it?"

He frowned, voice dropping to a whisper. "Someone's coming."

Lila started to point out how ridiculous that was, the idea of a stranger finding them out here, in the middle of a frozen sea. But then she turned, and saw that he was right. A figure was indeed shuffling toward them. At first, she thought it might be a *bear*. It was massive, and shaggy, its clawed steps cracking heavily against the ice. But then it drew near, and the shape resolved into a large man wearing a hooded coat. He had no claws, but boots with spikes that gripped the frozen surface.

Lila's cold fingers drifted to her nearest knife. The man was smiling at them as he approached, but that meant nothing. Plenty of pirates and murderers smiled before they struck.

Stross, Vasry, and Tav stood watching from the bow above, and she didn't have to see the glint of steel to know that they were armed. She tipped her head to one side, a silent order to hold.

"*Skalsa!*" the man called out in a musical voice, in a language she didn't know. He was even bigger up close, his hair and beard pitch black beneath the fur-lined hood, his skin so pale it looked the same shade as the ice in the eerie light. His gaze was a startling blue, and as it swept over them, Lila was grateful she'd worn her brown glass eye to bed, grateful that Kell's hood was up, his black eye hidden in the thin predawn light.

The man was still talking in a fluid stream, the sounds little more than highs and lows in her ears. It sounded like a speech, something formal and rehearsed. When he reached the end, he stopped, and stared, clearly waiting for their answer.

Lila looked from the man to Kell and back again, was about to explain that she had absolutely no idea what he was saying, when Vasry leaned over the side of the ship and said, "Is he speaking Fresan? I was with a Fresan girl once. Great fun. Cold hands, but—"

"Is there a point to this?" muttered Kell.

"The point," said Vasry, descending the ladder, "is that I learned a bit. Maybe I can help." He dropped onto the ice beside them, slipped, steadied himself. "*Skalsa!*" he said, addressing the man in that same musical tone. The man nodded, and started his speech again.

Within seconds, Vasry waved his hands, urging him to slow down. He stammered his way through a few phrases. The man frowned. And then drew out a large knife.

"What did you *say* to him?" demanded Lila.

Vasry was fumbling through an answer, but she was no longer listening. Instead, she watched as the man knelt, turning the blade in his hand and using the hilt to scratch something into the ice. A few moments later, he straightened, and said something under his breath. The marks on the ice began to twist and coil, then rose into the air, rippling between them like a curtain. This time, when he spoke, his voice crossed the line of the spell, and became Arnesian. He seemed surprised to hear it. She wondered how often sailors from Arnes ventured this far south.

"I heard the ice break," he said, the words echoing as the spell translated. "Is something wrong?"

Lila gestured to the ice gripping the hull, surprised the problem needed words. "Our ship is stuck."

The man shook his head. "Not stuck. No. *Spelled.*"

Well, thought Lila, that explained the strange nature of the ice, the way it kept closing like a hand around her ship.

"Well then," she said, "if you wouldn't mind *un*-spelling it—"

"Ah," he cut in, "I'm afraid only the dock master can unlock a ship once it has entered port."

Lila looked around at the surrounding ice, as if to point out that there was nothing resembling a port. Seeing her confusion, the man swept a mittened hand over the scene.

"This is an *ice* port," he explained. "You crossed the wharf line some ways back. If you wish to leave, you will have to wait for the dock master."

"And you are *not* the dock master?" asked Kell, sounding vaguely amused.

The man shook his head and chuckled. "No, no, I am just looking after the ships, while she is at the fair. But don't worry, she should be back by the end of the day."

At the mention of *day*, Lila found her gaze returning to the line of dull light still hugging the horizon. "When does the sun come up?"

The man laughed. "Ah, that depends! Certain months, it never sets. Other times, it never rises. We are at the end of the lightless season now, so it should break through sometime in the next few days. I've never been good at keeping track, but I don't mind. It makes the day of light a nice surprise. Come, you can wait in the port house, if you like."

He turned, and began to walk away, boots biting into the ice. Kell and Lila exchanged a glance, and then followed, Vasry at their heels. She turned and signaled to Stross and Tav to stay and wait with the ship. She would have felt bad about that, but Stross could rarely be parted from the vessel, and Tav had a nasty habit of getting drunk in foreign ports and picking fights he couldn't always win.

As they walked, the mist clinging to the cold air began to ripple and thin, revealing dozens of other ships scattered across the frozen port, dipping in and out of sight like ghosts in the weak light. The farther they traveled into port, the more of them she saw. Lila glimpsed figures here and there, but for the most part, the vessels all looked empty.

The language spell, luckily, had followed their guide, which was helpful since he kept up a steady stream of conversation.

"You are very far from home," he said. "What is the purpose of your trip?"

Lila met Kell's eye. "We're mapmakers," she said after a moment. That was the story they'd agreed on when they set out months ago. It was a gamble. Most places saw mapmakers as artists, creating an independent survey. A few thought they were spies, charting foreign coasts for conquer.

But the port man seemed pleased by the answer.

"Excellent. It's about time the northern empires grasped that the world goes on beyond their borders. Plenty to appreciate down here. Take the lightless fair. Started as a way to pass the darkest days, but good things have a way of growing. Now people come from all around. These days, we look forward to the dark! Here we are. . . ."

They'd reached the edge of the port. Lila expected the ice to give way to land, but it didn't. Instead, it simply sloped up, first into a set of steps, and then, into a shelter. She had expected to find something rough-hewn, but this was large, the ice as smooth and thick as polished stone. The man clapped his mittens together, shedding frost as he led them into a magnificent room. Tapestries hung from the frozen walls, and a fire roared in an icy hearth without melting it, and a long table ran through the center of the room, its benches draped with wool and fur.

Vasry let out a contented sigh and crossed to the hearth as their guide vanished into another room. He returned moments later, carrying three mugs of something sweet and steaming.

"So you run the port house, then," said Vasry, taking a cup.

"No, no," said the man. "I'm just looking after it, while the clerk is at the fair."

He gestured to the long table. Like everything in the room, she realized, it was made of ice, several skeins of thick cloth draped over the top. As they took their seats, Lila looked around the hall. The whole place reminded her of a fairy tale: quaint, and welcoming, and too good to be true.

The man drifted off to tend the fire. Lila watched him go, and felt Kell watching her.

"What?" she said, without meeting his eye.

"Not everything is a trap." The words made something tug behind her ribs. At being watched, but more so, at being seen.

"Am I that easy to read?"

"No," he said simply. "But I like to think I'm learning."

Lila forced herself to relax and take up the drink. The cup was warm against her bare hands, the wine—if that's what it was—hot and sweet. She downed it in a few short gulps, and rapped her fingers on the table, rising to her feet.

The light outside had not changed. She didn't know what time it was, or how long it would be until the dock master returned.

But she did know one thing: she had not sailed to the edge of the world just to stop there.

She made her way to the fire, and the man now tending it.

"Well then," she said. "Which way to the lightless fair?"

IV

Now

"*L*and!"

Stross bellowed again as Lila vaulted out of the hold, still holding the broken bottle of summer wine. Kell followed, frowning, in her wake.

Dusk was falling over the coastline. Back in the capital, he mused, the setting sun would have cast everything in red and gold, infusing the city with a warm and constant glow. But here, the light landed with a tinny glare, glinting off the serrated sprawl of buildings that spilled down from the rocks and into the bay below.

So this was Verose.

He tried not to think too often about London, or what his brother and family might be doing at this moment (he'd followed Lila to the end of the world and back, and it had been worth it). Seven years with the *Grey Barron,* and most days, he felt at ease on the ship, if not among the crew.

But places like Verose were a reminder of how far he was from home. Even at a distance, the city looked sharp enough to cut their sails.

The crew assembled now, all hands on deck.

There was Stross, the first mate of the *Barron,* stocky and sober, scratching at a black beard that had started to show grey, his temporary cheer settling back into sterner stuff as they approached their destination.

And Vasry, standing beneath the sails and looking, as he always did, like he was posing for a portrait, his chin up and his blond hair pulled back as he put his meager wind skills to good use and guided them to port.

Then there was Tav, small and scrappy, and currently heaving his guts up over the side of the ship after having a little too much fun this afternoon, even for a ship pretending to be a pleasure vessel staffed with rowdy pirates.

And last of all, Raya, dropping like a sparrow to the deck, black braids fluttering behind her.

Raya, who'd come aboard the ship after the lightless fair, and never disembarked, despite Lila's vocal aversion to new blood.

"I think I'm in love," Vasry had said the next morning, and at the time, none of them had paid it much attention, because, frankly, Vasry fell in love the way other people fell down after too much wine, so Lila probably assumed it would sort itself, and they'd put the girl ashore at the next port. But then Raya turned out to be a decent water worker and an even better cook, and Vasry surprised everyone by staying smitten, and Lila grudgingly let the girl stay.

Nearly seven years on, she still didn't speak a word of Arnesian, seemed to take pride in the fact, but she had as many expressions as Kell had frowns, and was good at saying everything that needed saying with a look.

And on top of it all, she could fight, a fact they'd discovered when the *Barron* ran into trouble with a raiding ship, and the girl had swiftly conjured a pair of swords out of ice and driven one through the nearest pirate as he tried to come aboard.

Lila liked her more after that.

And Kell liked not being the newest person on the crew.

Now, as the *Grey Barron* pulled into Verose, he scanned the line of ships already there, and found the one they wanted mooring three vessels out from the leftmost side of the dock. A Veskan craft with bloodred flags and wings scorched into the pale hull. *Eh Craen,* it was called.

The Crow.

If Alucard Emery's intelligence was good, then this ship was on its way south, ready to pass cargo off to an Arnesian smuggler bound for London. Alucard wanted to know what it was carrying.

And Kell wanted what he always did these days.

To prove that even now, without the power that had once defined his life, marked him as *Antari* and made him the strongest magician in the world, he was still worth something to the *Grey Barron,* and Lila Bard, to the palace and the empire, and himself.

V

THE SOUTHERN POINT OF FRESA, *seven years ago*

Kell Maresh had never been this cold.

For years, if he felt so much as a chill, he could conjure flame into his hands, or warm the air against his skin, the gesture as natural as breathing. Effortless. Simple.

But nothing was simple anymore.

The wine's welcoming warmth had dwindled as the crew made their way down the port house path, as instructed, which led not into a town, but a massive tunnel carved straight into the glacier. A vicious wind whistled through it, singing against the ice, and sinking its teeth into every inch of skin.

And yet, for all the discomfort, there was something extraordinary about this place.

He had seen ice before, but the word did no justice to the scale.

He had stood in the king's map room when he was young, and studied the empire modeled on the table, the drawings on the wall, wondered how a map could have edges when the world went on beyond it. *Where is the rest?* he'd asked, and the king had told him, *This is the part that matters.*

But Maxim Maresh was wrong.

Kell shook himself, not wanting to think about the man who'd raised him, and yet had never seen him as a son. The king who'd fallen, along with so many, at Osaron's hands, and forced Rhy, too soon, onto the throne.

Ahead, Lila ran her bare fingers along the tunnel wall, and began to hum a sea shanty, the melody ricocheting around them, a song carrying its own chorus. Their footsteps echoed.

Without the eerie dawn haze, the tunnel should have been pitch black. But it wasn't. In fact, the ice to every side seemed to glow with its own internal light, a pale blue Kell swore was growing brighter as they walked. He slowed, approaching the tunnel wall, a warped reflection taking shape in the ice. A long, pale face. Red hair parted by a single line of silver. The only outward mark of the battle that had changed his life.

He rested one gloved hand against the surface of the ice. And felt it. There was an energy to the ice, like a current in a stream. The water had frozen, but something inside it was undeniably alive.

He realized then what it must be. A *source*.

Kell knew, of course, that the Isle river back in London was not the only one, that sources of magic were scattered all over the world. But it was still a strange and wonderful thing to find another. To stand inside it. To bathe in the glow as if it were a healing thing. Perhaps, he thought—and hoped—it was.

He closed his eyes, imagined the light curling over him. Stitching back the parts that had torn.

A tremor ran through the tunnel, and Kell recoiled, half expecting to see cracks lacing the wall around his fingers. Vasry turned in a circle, and a knife had appeared in Lila's hand, and for a single, horrible moment, Kell thought he'd done something to damage the source. But then the crash came again, and this time, he could tell, it wasn't coming from *behind* or around them, but just ahead. It was followed by another sound, a tide of voices. Cheers.

They quickened their pace, rounded a bend, and reached the mouth of the tunnel. It yawned open to reveal a city carved in and out of ice.

And in the center stood the lightless fair.

Of course, it was not really lightless. The source's blue shine met the twilight haze, giving everything a frosted glow. A dreamy, dusk-like illumination.

A hundred stalls rose straight out of the frozen ground, every ice-made shop draped in long, bright lengths of silk, adorned with lanterns and flags. A hundred patrons shuffled through, bundled in their coats, as merchants called out in Fresan, their voices reduced to music in his ears as they offered meat and tea, games and magic. There was laughter, and music, and more people than Kell had seen in months.

They passed through an ornate archway, icicles rising from its top like crown points, moon-like spheres balanced on each. A crowd had gathered just beyond, forming a wide circle around a pale woman in a silver coat.

She stood in the center of a small platform, bare hands raised before her as if holding puppet strings. For a long moment, she stood still, and then, as they watched, her arms began to move, fingers dancing through the air.

And the ice around her grew.

It rose, and drew together, delicately shaping itself into the curved bones of a ship. It spread like frost across the air, around her body, over her head, until the sculptor vanished inside her work.

The ship grew until it was the size of a house, details fashioned down to the bolts and the sails. And that would have been marvel enough, but then, it began to move. Rolling slightly as if caught on the waves. It went still again, but this time, there was a kind of menace to that stillness. An eerie calm. A child gasped, and soon Kell saw why. A single, icy tendril had appeared, curling itself around the ship. And then another. And another. The crowd held its breath as the limbs of a sea beast wrapped themselves around the hull, and the mast, and the sails, and began to squeeze.

The ship groaned, as if it were wood. It began to crack beneath the force.

Kell watched, awestruck.

It was one thing to sculpt an object from an element. It was another thing entirely to give it movement, to put wind into ice-made sails and tension into ice-made limbs. It was a feat of magic, a craft unlike anything he'd ever seen. To re-create the world in such detail, and then—

All at once, the ship *shattered* with a sound that shook the fair.

The whole scene burst apart, the ice dissolving into glittering flakes that drifted down over the spectators, dusting their shoulders and hoods with snow. The woman stood at the center of her platform, alone again.

The crowd erupted in applause.

Vasry whooped, and Kell clapped, and beside him, Lila's face lit up, the way it had that first day in Red London, when everything was new. She took it all in, not with a wicked glee, but a hungry kind of wonder. And then she looked at him, and smiled, and started to walk on, but Kell caught her bare hand, and pulled her back to him, and kissed her.

Heat poured through him, and he didn't know if it was her magic sparking on the air or his own body flushing, but either way it was welcome.

85

Lila pulled back, just enough to meet his gaze, her breath a plume of white between their lips. "What was that for?" she asked.

"For warmth," he said, and they both smiled at the words, the memory drawn like thread between them, between now and that first night when she had done the same to him, and claimed it was for luck. She kissed him again, deeper, hands sliding beneath his coat. Kell leaned in. He loved her. It scared him, but frankly, so did Lila. She always had.

Delilah Bard wasn't a soft bed on a summer morning. She was a blade in the dark, dazzling, and dangerous, and sharp. Even now, he half expected to feel her teeth against his lip, the bright prick of pain, the taste of his own blood.

But all Kell felt was her.

Nearby, Vasry cleared his throat. "I think I'll find my own warmth," he said, slipping away into the fair.

And then Lila was pulling away, too, drawn to the many stalls and their offerings. She looked back only once, lips twitching in a grin.

And then she was gone.

Kell was about to follow when a small weight collided with his side and bounced off. He turned to see a child stumbling back, landing hard on the ice. A girl, so bundled up against the cold that he could only see the tops of her flushed cheeks, and her blazing blue eyes.

She hiccupped, sounded about to cry, when a woman arrived and swept the child up into her arms, turning to Kell to apologize. She looked at him, and as she did, cold raked its fingers over his scalp, and he realized his hood had fallen back, revealing his red hair. His black eye.

Kell flinched, bracing himself for the weight of recognition. For fear, or awe, and the scene it would bring. But there was no scene. His appearance meant nothing to her. Of course it meant nothing. He was a thousand leagues from home. He wasn't a prince, not in this land, and as for an *Antari*, perhaps she didn't even know what an *Antari* was. Perhaps she didn't care.

To her, he was just a stranger at the lightless fair.

She carried the child off, and Kell watched them go, a small laugh escaping in a cloud of fog.

"*Hassa,*" called a voice, and it took Kell a moment to realize it was calling to *him.* He turned, and saw a man in one of the stalls, a scarf wrapped tight over the lower half of his face.

"*Hassa!*" he called again, waving Kell over. He wasn't sure what the man was selling—the table before him was full of figurines—but it was the back wall that caught Kell's eye.

The entire space was taken up by a single sculpture, a large and impossibly delicate thing that might have been a palace, or simply a very ornate house, its façade interrupted by a series of windows.

And unlike the stall itself, whose ice was several inches thick, the sculpted house was made of frost-thin panes, and looked like it might crumble at the slightest push. That, Kell realized, was the point.

As he approached, the man running the stall started talking quickly. Rhy had always been the one with a gift for language. Kell had picked up pieces on his travels, but Fresan was new to him, a breathy melodic thing that broke down against his ears, especially when the speaker's mouth was hidden behind a scarf.

"I'm sorry," Kell cut in, backing away. "I don't understand."

He started to leave, but the man smiled, eyes crinkling in delight. "Ah. Arnesian!" he said, sliding into a broken version of the tongue. "Come. Is *game.*"

As he said it, he turned to the ornate house, and pointed to its many windows. In each, there was a sphere of colored ice, just large enough to touch the frame on either side.

"You break one," he said, circling the target with a mittened hand. "But not house. Touch house. You lose."

It was, of course, a game of magic.

Not a terribly challenging one, either—a very careful child would be able to do it. To summon an element and control it enough to melt or move one of the spheres without disrupting the fragile house. To a skilled magician, it should be simple. To an *Antari,* nothing at all.

"You won't lose," said the man, "you touch ball, just ball, you win. . . ."

He gestured at the prizes on the table, small figures sculpted not from ice, but a delicate translucent stone. There were animals—birds and bears, dogs

87

and whales—but also tiny shops, fair stalls, even a replica of the archway they'd passed through. And there, at the edge, a single ship. It made Kell think of the *Grey Barron*. It made him think of Lila.

"You play," said the man.

Kell swallowed. He flexed his fingers, half-frozen despite the gloves his coat had given him.

It had been three months.

Three months since the battle in Osaron's makeshift palace. Three months since Holland and Lila and Kell combined their power to fight the dark god back. Three months since Holland had used an Inheritor to contain the demon's power, and Kell had been caught between the two, and nearly torn apart.

Three months, and he told himself, the longer he waited, the better it would heal. But he could feel the magic pooling just beneath his skin. Waiting to be summoned. Waiting to be used.

That was the hardest part. He knew it was there, an untapped well, and every day, he found himself reaching for it, the way he had all his life, only to stop short as he remembered. Remembered the pain, the wrenching, rending agony that had torn through him when he first tried to use his power after they'd won.

But it had been three months.

Three months, he was sure, was long enough.

"How much does it cost to play?" he asked.

The man shrugged. Kell dug a hand in his pocket, hoping the coat would provide. He withdrew a handful of coins, none of them Fresan. The man surveyed the small pile, and selected an Arnesian lin, crimson with a small gold star at its center. The coin vanished into his coat.

"Good," he said, clapping his hands. "Now, you play."

Kell swallowed, and drew off his gloves as he decided which element he'd use. Flame was the easiest to summon, but the most likely to damage the rest of the house. Earth would be useless; there was none of it here. He could call on the water in the sphere itself, but the rest of the frame was made of the same stuff. No, it would be wind. A single breath, to knock it from its perch.

His pulse quickened in anticipation. It had been so hard to wait this long, and he felt like a starving man about to eat his first meal.

Kell took a deep breath, and raised his hand, and called his magic back.

And it came.

Rushing up to meet him like a long-lost friend.

It came, so eager, and so quick.

It came.

But so did the pain.

Not the stiffness of a muscle after too much rest, of a bone that's been left to set, but the fresh agony of an open wound. As the wind rolled out from his fingers toward the ice-made house, the pain unspooled, tore through his chest, squeezing the air from his lungs and the strength from his limbs.

And the entire house shattered.

Kell didn't see it happen. He was already doubled over on the icy ground, heaving, sweat slicking his skin beneath the coat, horror rising with the bile in his throat.

He struggled to stand as people turned to stare, and the man in the stall looked sadly at the broken house. "You lost," he said, as if that wasn't obvious.

Kell scrambled backward, desperate to get away, to escape the stalls, and the crowd, and the lightless fair. He made it through the archway before sagging to his knees and retching. It was wrong. Everything was wrong. Once upon a time, Kell Maresh had been the best magician in the world. Now, he could not even best a children's game.

He didn't hear Lila walking up behind him, but then she was there, a hand on his shoulder.

"Kell," she said, and there was something in her voice, something he'd never heard before, something that sounded almost like pity. He wrenched away from her touch.

"Three months," he gasped. He was still struggling to breathe, though now it was as much from panic as lingering pain. "Three months, and it meant *nothing*. It should have healed. It should have *helped*. But it's still broken." He raked his hands through his hair. "I'm still broken."

He shook his head. "It's not fair."

Lila met his gaze, her glass eye shining in the strange light. "It never is."

His throat tightened. "I'm an *Antari,* Lila." The words clawed as they came out. "I am nothing without my power."

She scowled. "Was I nothing, without mine?"

And before he could say that this was different, and she knew it, Vasry strolled up, his gold lashes thick with frost, a young woman on his arm. "Look," he said cheerfully, "I found my own warmth!"

Kell shoved past them both, heading for the tunnel and the port and the ship.

Vasry's voice trailed after. "Where's he going?"

"To wallow," said Lila.

But she was wrong. Kell was done wallowing, done waiting for his power to mend. He'd been wrong to wait. Wrong to think his magic was a thing that had to heal. If his power wouldn't return on its own, he would bring it back by force.

One month later

Kell was coming undone.

That's how it felt, as he stood in the center of the cabin, shirt open and sleeves rolled, sweat dripping down his skin. His coat had been flung over a chair, and a wine bottle lay empty on the floor nearby. A candle sat on the table, the small flame staring at him, steady and waiting.

Kell kept his own quarters on the ship. Unlike the captain's chamber, this one was small and sparse, little more than a bed and a chest and a basin. But it was his, as the upstairs room in the Setting Sun had been, a place to be alone. With his thoughts. With his power.

He took a deep breath, held his hand out, and dragged the fire toward him.

The moment it answered, so did the pain. As bright and brutal as a white-hot knife, slicing into his skin. Carving a path behind his ribs. Telling him to stop.

He might have, if not for himself, then for his brother, Rhy, whose life was bound to his, who felt every ounce of hurt as if it were his own. Their suffering was a shared cord. Wound one of them, and the other suffered, too, and Kell could never bring himself to cause his brother hurt.

But he had quickly learned that this particular pain belonged to him alone. It was not a physical thing. It did not live in his body, but the fabric of his soul. And so, he pressed on, as he had every night since they'd visited Fresa and the lightless fair.

He held the fire in his palm, teeth gritted in pain as he reached out with his other hand, toward a glass, calling the water inside it. It rose, drifting in a ribbon toward him, but Kell's limbs had begun to shake, his copper hair plastered to his skin with sweat.

He could do this.

He had to do this.

He was Kell Maresh. *Antari* magician and adopted prince. He had traveled across worlds, been known and feared by the rulers of Grey London, and Red, and White. He had faced Vitari and the darkness it tried to breed inside him, had bested all but Lila in the *Essen Tasch,* had fought against Holland, and then beside him, had watched the other *Antari* sacrifice everything he had, everything he *was,* to save their cities. Holland, who had not survived the battle. But Kell had.

He had survived all those horrors.

And he would survive this. He—

He staggered and lost his hold. The flame extinguished, the water fell in drops like rain, and his legs buckled beneath him, one knee cracking against the wooden floor.

"Get up," he hissed through gritted teeth.

His muscles trembled, but after a moment, he rose, bracing himself against the table. He reached for the empty glass, but instead of taking it up, he swept it from the table. Watched it shatter as it hit the floor.

"Pick it up," he told himself, wrapping his will around the shards.

The pieces shivered.

"Pick it up," he growled as they rose, slowly, haltingly, into the air. Kell's chest hitched. His hands trembled.

Put it back together, he thought.

Put yourself back together.

The shards floated toward each other, rattling like chimes when they knocked together, drifted apart. The white-hot knife drove between his ribs, and Kell's hold faltered. He overcorrected, flinging all his will at the shards of glass. They crashed together, crumbling to sand, and Kell sagged, gasping, to the floor.

He let out a ragged sob, and bowed his head against the wood.

He told himself he would grow accustomed to the pain. That its edges would eventually wear smooth. That at some point, the pain would fade—it *had* to fade. It was a wound, and all wounds healed. Skin knitted and scarred, and yet, every time *this* wound felt fresh. It was not a tear in his flesh. Something at the very heart of him had splintered, frayed, and he was beginning to suspect—to fear—that it would never heal. Never get easier. Never hurt less.

If it were a ruined limb he would have cut it off, but there was no faulty limb. The ruin was everywhere. In his darkest moments, when he could not see a life without magic, or a future without pain, he thought, *I cannot live like this*. But he had to. This pain may be his own, but his life was not. Never would be.

And so he dragged his broken spirit forward, felt it shred again with every step, waited for the moment when his magic failed entirely, knowing it would be a mercy when it did.

But for now, it was still there. Frayed, and torn, and waiting to be called.

He forced himself back up onto his hands and knees as a drop of red hit the ground. Blood was dripping from his nose, his body pleading with him to stop. Instead, he wiped his hand across his face and pressed his stained palm to the damp floor, and summoned his *Antari* power.

"As Isera," he said, bracing for what happened next. Magic bloomed between the blood and the command. A sheen of ice spread beneath his hand, coating the wooden planks, and Kell felt a bright, brief flare of relief that the power still worked. And then his vision dropped away, and his world went black as the white-hot horror carved beneath his skin.

He fought the urge to scream, and failed, the sound tearing free as he collapsed, his burning cheek against the icy patch of floor, and sobbed in pain, and anger, and grief.

Who was he without magic?

What was he worth?

His sight flickered back, but the room was spinning now, and he squeezed his eyes shut, and tried to force air back into his aching lungs. He was still lying there when he heard the door open, boots stomping across the wooden floor. The world darkened behind his eyes as a shadow fell across his face.

"Enough," said Lila, and he could hear the anger in her voice.

But it wasn't enough. He couldn't stop, not until the magic spoke to him again. Not until it remembered who and what he was. Not until he was strong enough to take it back.

"You're scaring the crew."

"My apologies," he murmured.

If she were someone else, she might have stroked his hair, might have even lain down there beside him on the cabin floor, tangled her fingers with his, and told him it would be all right, they would get through this, they would find a way, he would be whole again.

Instead, she took out a knife.

He heard the scrape of the weapon sliding free from its sheath, and a moment later, the steel dropped to the floor beside him, the edge within reach. The message seemed rather clear.

"If I could put myself out of my misery, I would," he muttered, and in that moment, it felt true. But Lila only hissed through her teeth.

"Idiot," she said, dropping into a nearby chair. "Do you know what else you are, Kell?"

"Tired?"

"Spoiled," she said. "And lazy."

"I'm already down," he said with a wince. "You don't have to kick me."

Lila sighed and leaned back in the chair. "There was a sellsword, back in London."

She never called it Grey London, but he knew that's what she meant. Her voice took on a different quality whenever she spoke of her other life, the one before.

Kell took a questing breath. The pain had faded, leaving exhaustion in its wake. He tried to sit up, but couldn't manage yet, so he summoned the strength to roll onto his back, and looked at the ceiling instead of her. "What was his name?"

"Jack? Jones?" Lila shrugged. "It doesn't matter. He was the best at what he did. A genius with a blade. Could fight three at once, or slit a man's throat before he even felt the kiss of the knife. And then they caught him."

"Who?" asked Kell.

He could feel her annoyance. "What? It doesn't matter who. Someone that good is always in danger of being caught. So they caught him. Didn't kill him, but they did take his life. You know how?" She didn't wait for Kell to answer. "They took his sword hand. Cut it off right at the wrist. Even burned the wound so he wouldn't bleed out. They thought that living like that was a fate worse than death. And do you know what he did?"

Lila sat forward in the chair, and Kell looked at her. He couldn't help it.

"He found those men, and he used his sword to cut their throats. Every single one."

"How?" asked Kell, and Lila flashed him a wicked smile, and rose to her feet again.

"Isn't it obvious?" she said, walking past Kell, and the blade she'd left beside him. "He learned to use his other hand."

VI

Now

It was fully dark by the time the *Barron* had docked at Verose.

Stross and Vasry, who'd sobered a bit in the intervening hour, stumbled off the ship as if they were still drunk, and made their laughing way down the docks. They returned an hour later with a few more bottles of wine, and a count.

Nine.

That was the number of sailors aboard the *Crow*.

"You're sure?" asked Lila. Vasry bobbed his head, and nearly lost his balance. Not so sober, then. She turned to Stross, who confirmed the tally.

"Nine," he said, and she nodded, was already trying to decide how to dispatch them all, when Kell shot her a warning look. Lila sighed. Of course, he'd insist on keeping them alive.

"Nine *were* aboard the ship," clarified Vasry. "But two set off for the cliffs."

"And four left for the Red Robes," added Stross. "I paid the hosts there to take their time."

"That leaves three," said Vasry.

"Yes," said Lila dryly, "I can count." She tapped her fingers on her sleeve as she played it out. Killing three men was easy enough. *Not* killing them was harder. Alucard's orders weren't to *stop* the ship, only to find out what it was carrying, which meant she needed time to search the hold. Stross would serve as watch, and diversion if need be. Tav was good for blunt force, and always game for a fight. And Kell, well, what was the point of sharpening a knife if you never let it cut?

"Vasry, Raya, you stay put," she said.

"If you insist," said Vasry, palming his wife's waist. "This is meant to be a pleasure vessel. We'll keep up appearances."

"You keep wind in the sails," she warned. "In case we need a quick break. And you," she added, nodding at Raya. "Don't let anyone touch my ship."

She looked at Kell, then, who was tightening the holsters beneath his black coat. He met her gaze, and straightened, pulling the hood up until it hid his copper hair. Tav and Stross stood waiting, ready.

"Well then," she said, spreading her arms. "Let's go and say hello."

Four people ambled down the Verose dock.

They looked like they'd come from a good time, and were on their way to find a better one. Lila smiled and tipped her head back, as if savoring the night. A few steps ahead, Tav laughed softly, as if Stross had just told a joke, though she didn't think Stross had *ever* told a joke. Wasn't sure he even knew one.

Beside her, Kell smelled like summer wine.

Before they'd left, she'd tipped the last of the ruined bottle into her palm and run it through his hair.

"At least it won't be wasted," she'd said, splashing him with the dregs.

Now his arm was slung around her shoulders and hers was wrapped around his waist, her narrow body tucked against him, and he half sang, half hummed a sea song into her hair.

"Who knew you were such an actor," she said when he swayed, leaning his weight into hers. "Where did you learn this art?"

"You forget my brother's reputation," he said, lips brushing her temple. "I had plenty of time to study his form while I was dragging him home at dawn."

"Always the keeper," she mused with a sigh. "Never the kept."

"Believe it or not," he said, "I am *capable* of having a good time."

She laughed, a buoyant sound that carried down the dock. "Capable, perhaps. Willing? Never."

Their steps slowed as they neared the *Crow*.

Stross reached out to brace himself against the pale, wing-painted hull, as if he didn't trust his legs to carry him on, simply needed a moment to rest. Tav slipped into the shadow along the ship and hauled himself up, dropping silently over the side onto the deck.

"We get in, we get out," Kell reminded her. "We don't cause a scene."

Lila rolled her eyes. "Next you'll say you want them unscathed."

"Preferably, yes."

She sighed. "So much for a good time." As she said it, she pulled him into the shadow of the ship. Kell reached back to brace himself against the hull as Lila ran her hands down his front. Even in the dark, she could see him blush, before her fingers dipped into the pocket of his coat and drew out the small black shape. She leaned close enough to kiss him, and instead placed the mask on his face. It settled like a cool hand against his skin, and he smiled, a stranger's smile, as Kell Maresh fell away like a coat.

VII

SOMEWHERE AT SEA, *six years ago*

"Any day now," said Lila, picking at her nails.

They were on the ship's deck, the sails down and the tide still.

The sun was just rising, and the night's chill had yet to burn off, and the only mercy, as far as Kell could tell, was that she'd told the crew to make themselves scarce, though he assumed that they were watching from whatever perch they could find.

"Pointy end toward me," she teased.

He glared, fingers tightening on the short sword in his hand.

Kell *knew* how to wield a blade.

He had been raised within the palace walls, with all the pretexts of a prince, but he was also raised to guard the royal family. More specifically, he'd been charged with Rhy's protection. Rhy, who had no magic to arm himself, no power of his own to shield him. Rhy, who'd insisted on learning the sword, and so Kell had joined him as a sparring partner, until the prince was good enough to practice on the royal guards.

Kell knew how to hold a blade, and how to use it, and yet the weight of the steel in his hand felt odd, clunky. Far less elegant than the weapons he'd conjured out of wind and stone and ice.

Lila hopped down from the crate and spread her arms. "Come on, then."

"You're not armed."

"Kell," she said with a pitying grin. "I think you know me better than that." Her fingers twitched in invitation. She had fought him once, back in Grey London, when he'd known her only as a thief, and she hadn't known what magic was, let alone that she possessed it, and it had been her steel versus his spells. They had sparred more fiercely in the *Essen Tasch,* when he was pretending to be Kamerov Loste and she pretending to be Stasion Elsor, but that had been a game of magic, of fire and water and earth. A competition bound by rules.

Kell had never faced Delilah Bard like this.

He scanned the deck, taking in the ropes and boxes, the nets and nails, all the things he would have used as weapons once.

Now, all he had was the sword in his hand.

He marched toward Lila, expecting her to dodge back, retreat, but her boots stayed planted and her hands stayed wide, and the only part of her that moved was the corner of her mouth, which twitched in pleasure, right before he swung the blade at her head.

Steel against steel, the sound rang out across the deck.

Her hands had been empty the second before, but now a dagger flashed in one fist. His sword scraped free and he swung again, low and fast, a blow that should have carved a line across her ribs. But a second dagger appeared in her other hand, and she pinned the sword between her knives.

He freed himself and swung again, thinking she should have picked a longer blade, but instead of dodging back she lunged *in,* twisting around his sword and tucking herself against him like a lover as she brought one dagger up beneath his chin.

"Dead," she whispered.

And then she danced backward, out of the embrace, and said, "Again."

He ran a hand through his hair, slicking it out of his face, and readied himself, this time studying the way she balanced, turned her head to compensate for the lack of sight. If he could just—

But this time she didn't wait.

She struck first, vicious and quick, forcing him to retreat.

He dodged backward, and slashed again. And again. And somehow, despite the fact he had the longer blade, the better reach, she was always there to block, to parry. She wasn't a graceful fighter, but she moved with all the speed of a whip, and no matter how Kell searched, there was no way past, no opening.

He danced back, or tried to, but he'd lost track of his surroundings, and instead of open deck, he slammed into the mast. The force knocked the wind out of his lungs, and the sword slipped from his hand, but Lila was still coming, daggers glinting, and there was no time to think, so he didn't, simply flung out his fingers and called a nearby coil of rope. It rose, flying toward Lila's wrist, even as the pain tore through him, jagged and deep, and in the end, it was for nothing, because her blade sliced through the rope before it came to rest against his throat.

"Dead," she whispered. Her hand dropped. "What happened?"

The words slid like a gasp between his teeth. "I forgot."

Lila studied the edge of her knife. "I forgot, too, at first. Ran into doors, fell down steps. It took me months to find my balance, to gauge distance. It was hard, but I learned. So will you."

Anger bloomed inside him. He wanted to tell her it was different, that her eye was gone, and his magic was still there. A limb he felt but couldn't use. A weapon he was forced to hold but couldn't wield.

He wanted to lash out at her. To scream.

Instead he knelt and picked up his sword, and said, "Again."

Five years ago

The sun bled into the sea, turning the world around them red.

The *Barron* had dropped anchor off a Faroan port. The air held on to the day's heat like a clay oven after the fire's gone out. Kell's lungs burned, his limbs ached.

"You're too quick," he said, gasping for breath.

"So catch up," said Lila as she ducked, and dodged, and danced out of reach.

They sparred until the sun vanished and the red dusk gave way to night, until Stross went about lighting the lanterns across the deck. By the light, Kell could see the rest of the crew, perched like birds around the *Barron*, watching the match. Even the newest member, Raya, the woman from the south that Vasry had brought back to the ship. She sat up in the netting, pale eyes burning the dark.

Kell ignored them. He had to. Staying alive took all of his focus.

"You're too good," he said, narrowly dodging Lila's latest cut.

"So get better," she answered. There was a ruthless focus to her movements, a precision he couldn't seem to crack. No wonder she had made it here, he thought. Delilah Bard was a force of nature. The world hadn't simply opened for her. It had been cleaved, parted like skin beneath her knife.

She was incredible.

"Has anyone told you," he said, "that you're gorgeous when you fight?"

The words knocked her off-balance, like a boot catching on uneven ground. She stumbled, for just a second, and in that second, he swung. Her dagger came up at the last moment, but it was close, beautifully close, the two blades shivering against her throat.

For once, Lila scowled.

For once, Kell smiled.

And then she kicked him in the chest.

He hadn't seen it coming, and he went down hard on the deck, gasping for breath.

Rhy would feel that one, he thought, imagining his brother, leagues away, in the middle of some gala or feast, wincing at the force of Lila's boot against his brother's ribs. Kell said a silent apology as he lay there, exhausted, staring up at the sky. It was a moonless night, black and full of stars.

And then Lila was there, holding out her hand, and helping him back onto his feet.

He fell into bed that night, limbs aching and leaden.

Everything hurt, but for the first time in months, he welcomed the pain.

Four years ago

Kell's coat lay cast aside, his shirt soaked through with sweat and rain. As Lila circled, he ran a hand through his damp hair, slicking it back—he'd cut it shorter, but somehow it still ended up in his face. A storm had swept through in the middle of the last match. It had passed, replaced by a scorching summer sun, but the deck was still damp beneath his feet, water dripping from the sails as Kell twisted out of the way of Lila's blade.

He dodged another blow, and a cheer went up.

They were no longer alone on the deck. The *Barron*'s crew watched with giddy interest, whooping and hollering and making bets, though Kell doubted they ever bet on *him*. Even though he did win.

Sometimes.

Rarely.

More often than not, it was only a question of how long he could hold her off, his victories measured in minutes. He'd gotten better in the last few months. He'd had to. But Lila always found a way to keep him on his toes. Dragging him out to spar at dawn, at midday, in the middle of the night,

100

so he could learn how to see a weapon's movement in sun and shade, noon glare and moonlight and full dark.

Now and then, he still slipped, found himself reaching for his magic, and every time, he paid for the mistake. But his sword hand was getting stronger, and the steel began to feel, if not a part of him, then at least like something he could wield, not just competently, but *well*.

As soon as he grew comfortable with the short sword, Lila gave Kell two, and by the time he could hold his own with those, the crew had stopped feigning indifference and gotten involved in the fights. The first mate, Stross, was the one who'd suggested the lottery.

"A way to make things interesting," he'd said, presenting the box in the galley one night as Raya spooned out helpings of stew. Kell suspected they were just tired of him losing, and were hoping to spice things up. Inside the box, scribbled out on scraps of paper, was the name of every weapon they had on board the ship.

Lila had always possessed a fondness for sharp things, and since becoming captain of the *Barron,* her collection had only grown, expanding in impressive ways beyond the usual steel.

Which was why, as they circled each other now, Kell found himself holding a pair of small scythes, their edges curved, while Lila hefted a broadsword. Vasry and Tav exchanged a look, and Kell suspected they must have added that one to the lot more recently. Maybe they were betting on him after all.

Tired of holding the blade up, Lila attacked, and despite the weapon's size, she still managed to move with unnatural speed. She swung and Kell lunged back, expecting the sword's weight to carry her forward. But somehow, impossibly, she pivoted, reversing the weapon's arc.

He got one of the scythes up and blocked, the force ringing up his arm as they crashed together, but his second blade was already carving through the air toward her chest. Her eyes widened, and he thought, *I have you,* right before she let go of the broadsword entirely and ducked beneath his scythe. She sprang back, falling in a crouch as the hulking sword crashed to the deck between them.

It was the first time Lila Bard had ever lost her blade.

Around the deck, the voices had stopped. The crew held its breath.

Lila looked up at Kell, a grin spreading across her face.

She had so many different smiles. Some happy and some cruel and some positively wicked, ones full of humor and ones full of hate, and he was still learning how to read them all. But this one he knew, not because it was common, but because it was rare.

It was pride.

But the match wasn't over. She hadn't surrendered yet. Lila rose, eyes going to the blade she'd abandoned on the deck between them. She dove for it, and so did he. But as soon as Kell tried to lunge forward, something forced him to a stop. He looked down to see a sheen of ice running up over his feet. His boots were frozen to the deck.

Lila caught up the sword, and raised it, letting its weight come to rest against his chest.

"I win," she said simply, and he stared in shock at the blood dripping from her free hand. She'd used magic. Not even elemental, but *Antari*.

"You *cheated*," he said, indignant, but Lila only shrugged.

"*I'm* not the one who can't use magic."

And with that she dropped the sword and strode away, leaving him to break the ice from his boots. From that day on, there were no rules.

Kell only fought to win.

Three years ago

It took three tries to get the straps on right.

Kell cursed softly, adjusting the buckles over his chest.

"What in god's name is taking so long?" demanded Lila.

Beyond the screen, she wasn't so much sitting in the chair as sprawling across it, one leg thrown over the side, the horned Sarows mask twirling lazily around her finger.

"Unless there are corsets and skirts involved, you're taking too long. If you need a hand—"

"Be still," growled Kell, lacing up his boots. "This was your idea."

In truth, it had been Alucard's.

After all, he was the one who'd written, asking them to put the *Barron* to good use. Lila had been more than ready. The trouble, of course, was Kell.

Thanks to Lila's ruthless sparring, he no longer *fought* like a prince, but he couldn't change the fact that he still looked like one. Everywhere they docked, heads turned toward him. Clocked his eye, his hair, his bearing. If he was ever going to be someone other than Kell Maresh, *Antari* prince, he needed a disguise.

Lila had pointed at the coat, with its infinite number of sides, and asked if there was one tucked in there, something that made him look less a noble and more like a pirate. Less like the fire and more like the dark.

Kell took up the mask, and settled it onto his face.

It had been a month since her suggestion, and in the intervening time, neither had brought it up again, until tonight, when he told her to come with him into the captain's quarters, told her to sit there in the chair facing the wall, and wait.

"Are you almost done?" Lila called out, but this time, he did not answer. She glanced over her shoulder. "Kell?"

Her leg slipped from the arm of the chair and came to rest against the floor. She was about to stand when his hand came down on her shoulder.

Lila *almost* startled.

He smiled. It was hard to get the jump on her, but she clearly hadn't heard his boots ringing on the cabin floor. Hadn't heard the sigh of fabric, or the shift of weight. She rose and turned toward him, and he braced for some snide remark, but for once in her life, she seemed to be speechless.

Lila stared at the stranger in her room.

Once upon a time, he would have shifted his weight beneath the scrutiny, tugged at his clothes as if they did not fit. But tonight, he did not. Tonight, he stood perfectly still, letting her study him.

He was dressed in a black coat, with matte black buttons that disappeared instead of catching the light, and a hood, which he'd drawn up over his hair. The entire top half of his face was concealed by a black mask, one that shielded both eyes behind a piece of gossamer.

Slowly, he reached up and pushed back the hood. It slumped onto his shoulders, revealing his copper hair, no longer loose and messy but slicked back against his head. His hands slid down his front, and as he unfastened the buttons, the coat fell open onto more of that light-swallowing fabric. He shrugged out of the coat, letting it pool on the floor, revealing black trousers and a black tunic that hugged his chest, the collar wrapping like a hand around his throat. Thin ropes of black leather crossed over his ribs. Holsters.

Lila reached out and ran her hands along the straps. He'd grown stronger with their sparring, and he tensed, muscle corded beneath her touch.

"I must admit, Kell," she said, letting out a soft, breathy laugh. "I am impressed."

"Are you?" he asked. His voice came out different. Lower. Smoother. Not stone but silk. He leaned a little closer, as if sharing a secret, and said, "And my name isn't Kell."

"Oh?" asked Lila, intrigued. "What is it, then?"

Below the mask, his mouth twitched, one corner drawing up into a grin. "You can call me Kay."

"Kay," she mused, turning the sound over in her mouth as she made a slow, appraising circle. He heard the small hum of pleasure when she discovered the pair of short swords holstered against his back. They'd become his weapon of choice over the months of training, but these were special. Purchased from the forbidden market in Sasenroche. He knew she would like them, felt her fingers graze one of the leather sheaths before drifting to the hilt.

"Not every blade belongs to you," he said.

"It does if I can take it." Her hand nearly closed around the hilt, but he turned suddenly, catching her wrist.

"I wouldn't," he warned, but he knew she wouldn't be able to resist. Sure enough, Lila twisted out of his grip, knocking him off-balance. He was fast, but she was faster, and in an instant she was behind him again, drawing one of the swords, holding it aloft like a prize for half a second, before she let out a yelp, and dropped the blade as if burned.

It clattered to the floor, and he clicked his tongue, and knelt, and took it up again. He turned the blade so it caught the light, revealing the spellwork etched into the steel.

"See?" he said. "I can still use magic, too."

He slid the sword back into its sheath and straightened, lifting his chin. In the end, he'd realized something. He didn't have to shed all his princely airs. He could double down on them, cultivate a kind of menace, an arrogance that read as danger.

"You let me take that sword," she snapped, shaking the sting from her palm.

"Pain is a quick teacher," he said, catching her hand and bringing her burned fingers to his lips. "And I did warn you."

Lila's heart quickened—he felt it through her skin.

"I like this new you," she said, and there was something in her voice, a naked want that made him stiffen.

"Do you?" he purred.

She grinned, and reached out to pull him toward her, but he beat her to it, stepping forward and pressing his body into hers. He guided her back one stride, then two, until her boots met the edge of the bed.

With a quick, almost playful shove, he pushed her down, and she let herself fall, fingers tangling in the leather straps as she pulled him with her onto the bed. He braced himself over her, reached up to draw away the mask, but this time it was Lila who stopped him, fingers wrapped around his wrist.

"Not yet," she said, with a wicked grin. "I want to see what *Kay* can do."

VIII
PORT OF VEROSE, *now*

He dropped onto the *Crow*'s deck in silence.

Against his face, the black metal molded to his skin. It had taken time to grow accustomed to its weight, the faint shadow it carved at the edge of his vision, the ghost of the gossamer over his eyes, but now, he clung to its presence, the way he felt when he was wearing it. Like someone else entirely.

No longer Kell, but Kay.

Lila landed into a crouch beside him, the familiar Sarows mask fitted over her own face.

Tav pressed himself against the mast of the unfamiliar ship, a finger to his lips. Across the deck, a Veskan sailor sat on a crate, whittling a stick with a short, sharp blade. After a moment he raised the object to his mouth, and it gave up a soft, sweet tune. In the cover of that sound, they crept forward. As it ended, Tav's shadow crossed into the man's light.

"*Och vel?*" he asked, rising to his feet. He must have taken them for shipmates, but his face fell as Lila stepped forward, the horns of her mask curling to points above her head.

"Nice ship," she said, running her hand along the rail, and the man was so surprised, he didn't notice Kay behind him, not until the arm wrapped around his throat.

He could have cut the man down—these days he knew exactly where to drive the blade, how to end a life—but instead he forced the cloth against the man's nose and mouth, held his own breath as the plume of dreamsquick clouded the air with the force of the struggle before all the fight went out of him.

The body slumped in Kay's arms, and he lowered it to the deck as a second Veskan spilled out of the doorway and came to an abrupt halt, taking in the scene: the two masked figures and the legs of the man they'd drugged jutting out from behind a crate. But he *didn't* see Tav, in the shadow by the door, not until he was on him, slamming the cloth over the Veskan's mouth. He should have gone down in seconds, but he didn't. He thrashed, and struggled, clawing at Tav, who was half his size and having trouble staying on. More than once he nearly flung Tav off, even as one knee finally buckled, and then the other, the fight only going out of him when his head pitched forward onto the deck.

For a moment, no one moved.

Tav rocked back on his heels, chest heaving from the effort. Lila cocked her head, and Kay held his breath as they waited for the third Veskan. But there was no sign of them. With any luck, they'd left the others to stand guard and gone to bed, would never know that they were there.

Tav rolled up to his feet. "Could've helped," he muttered, dusting himself off.

"Oh, I would've," whispered Lila, as she turned toward the hold, "but it was too much fun to watch."

As they went down into the hold, light bloomed in Lila's palm, and his own hand prickled, a phantom longing in his fingers. He tried to put it from his mind as Tav tossed him an iron bar, and he used it to pry open the nearest crate. The nails groaned, and the wood gave with a crack, and Kay paused, listening for sounds above. None came. He shifted the lid off the box. Inside, he found spirits in thin stoppered bottles, amber vials of tark, a liquor that went down like honey but landed like stone. He had tried it once, at Rhy's behest, and woken the next morning with no memory and wet hair, only to learn he'd gone swimming in the Isle. In winter. Without any clothes. Now he cringed at the sight of the tark, but Tav swiped a vial and pocketed it before he could put the lid back on the box.

Nearby, Lila let out a small whistle. He turned and saw her elbows-deep in a carton, and a moment later, she emerged holding her prize aloft: a blade. Kay rolled his eyes. He knew there was no point in telling her to put it back. It had already disappeared inside her coat.

Tav snapped his fingers, calling them over to a third crate.

It was full of paper lanterns. They were folded almost flat, but when he held one up, it bloomed open into a pale white moon. Kay frowned, the sight of it tugging on something in his mind. A memory he couldn't place. He held the lantern up in the hold's thin light, and saw the ghost of spellwork on the inside of the paper shell. It was small, and tight, and he was still trying to read it when a voice rang out overhead.

"Oster? *Han'ag val rach?* Oster?"

Oster, he guessed, was one of the men now napping on the deck, lungs full of dreamsquick.

Metal glinted at the edge of Kay's sight. Lila had drawn one of her knives. He shook his head, and swept past her, up the steps.

"*Ag'ral vek,*" he called out in Veskan as he reached the deck. *I'm right here.*

It was a poor impression, but it wasn't meant to hold, only to make the man on deck hesitate, which he did, right until he saw the masked figure standing there, swathed in black. The man squinted at Kay, as if trying to make sense of the stranger on his ship.

107

"You're not Oster," he grumbled, the words muffled by drink.

"No," said Kay. "I'm not."

For a moment, nothing happened. And then—everything did.

The man flung out his hand and Kay felt the *Crow*'s deck slant drastically, the water shifting beneath the boat. But a blade, he'd learned, had one distinct advantage over relying on the elements: it was far quicker to summon. His sword sang free of its sheath before the wave crested the side of the ship. He surged forward while the Veskan was still calling the water to him.

He spun and slammed the hilt of his sword into the Veskan's temple as the water rose over their heads. The light went out of the man's eyes, and he folded, hitting the deck with a thud. As he collapsed, so did his hold on the wave. Kay dropped to one knee, bracing himself as the torrent crashed down on top of him, sudden and shockingly cold.

He rose to his feet, soaked through and shivering, but victorious. Beneath him, the ship bobbed once, violently, as the water settled, but it had been a large wave, and he watched as a ripple carried down the docks, setting all the other ships rocking in their berths.

Sanct, he thought as lanterns lit on half of the surrounding boats, and a handful of sailors took to their decks to see who'd been foolish enough to mess with the tide in the bay.

"*Really?*" hissed Lila, halfway out of the hold. "You couldn't have just—"

But then she cut off, head whipping to the right. He heard it at the same time. Stross, too loud, on the dock below, asking someone if they knew the way to the Merry Host. Too loud, and too late, as boots came thudding up the ramp. *Several pairs* of boots.

The crew of the *Crow* had come back.

He flicked his fingers, a silent signal, and Lila and Tav retreated a step, back into the shadow of the hold. Kay turned and pressed himself against the mast as three more Veskans stomped onto the deck.

"Oster?" they called out. "Aroc? Esken?"

They began to mutter amongst themselves, and they might have thought the two they'd left behind had gotten bored, or bitter, had gone to entertain themselves.

They might have. If not for the body lying in the center of the waterlogged deck.

Kay swore to himself as he heard them rush to the fallen sailor. He drew his second sword and stepped out from behind the mast to face the new arrivals.

Two men and a woman, tall as houses, their hair ranging from blond to white. Their gazes were steady and sober. Either they hadn't been drinking, or they knew how to hold their liquor. The two men drew weapons—one a hatchet, the other a broadsword—while the third spread out her arms, the air filling with the scent of magic. The water on the deck rose up, freezing to ice around her hands. She flicked her wrist, and a shard shot like an arrow across the deck.

At him.

Kay's blade came up just in time, and the ice shattered against the steel. The sound rang out like a starting bell, and the bodies on the deck surged into motion.

He danced back, cutting down the next three shards, then ducked as the hatchet buried itself in the mast where his head had been. It freed itself from the wood, returning to the Veskan's hand. Two magicians, then.

The deck froze beneath his feet as he leapt up onto the nearest crate, landed on dry wood, and found himself face-to-face with the largest man, who was easily a head taller, and three times as wide, the broadsword raised over his head.

Kay twisted out of the way just before the sword cleaved a trench in the ship's deck. It lodged, buried a foot into the wood, and he swept his blade across the man's bare throat—or meant to. The Veskan's arm came up to block the blow, and the steel met armor instead, hard enough to make the blade ring in Kay's grip.

Tav and Lila were on the deck now—out of the corner of his eye, he saw them, going head-to-head with the other two sailors, Tav quick on his feet, slicing the ropes that bound the sails so they fell in heavy sheets, covering the icy deck, and Lila, fire licking down her knives as she melted a path through an ice-made shield, and kicked the wielder back into the rail hard enough to make it splinter.

She was grinning.

Of course she was grinning.

The woman sagged onto the deck, and—

"Look out," shouted Kay as the hatchet whistled through the air, straight toward Lila's back. But she was already dropping to the deck. She landed like a cat to her hands and knees as the ax sailed past, and then she was up again, her daggers in one hand, and this time, when the hatchet flew back toward the Veskan's hand, she *caught* it. Plucked the weapon out of the air as if it were her own, and turned and buried it in the man's chest.

So much for letting them live, he thought, just as his attacker's broadsword came free with a scrape. He jumped back as the massive blade swung toward him. He twisted out of the Veskan's reach, or tried, but the man's mouth began to move and he had just enough time to curse that there were *three* magicians, wielding magic as well as weapons, before a wall of wind slammed into him from behind, knocking the breath from his body as he fell to the deck, one of his blades skating from his grip and vanishing under the crumpled sail.

The broadsword came down and Kay rolled onto his back, got his one remaining sword up in time to block the blow, or rather, redirect its force, up and away from his chest. If it had been any other sword, it would have met only the air over his shoulder, but it was two hands wide, and the bottom edge scraped along his collar, steel skating against bone.

Pain turned his vision white.

Kay gasped, and rolled, spinning up onto his feet, one hand clutching his blade and the other pressed to his bloody shoulder. But before he could dodge again, put any space between him and the wall of a man, he was thrown back into the mast, not by wind, but flesh, the Veskan's hand closing around his throat like steel, like stone. He hacked at the man's wrist, but the blade glanced off an armored cuff until a gust of air whipped the weapon from his grip. There was another blade, in his boot, but before he could reach it, the Veskan hauled him up until he was no longer standing on the deck, his boots skimming uselessly as the hand crushed his windpipe, the other still clenching the massive sword.

The man drew back, ready to bury the blade in his chest, and Kay did the only thing his mind could conjure to save him from certain death.

He reached out and wrapped his bloody hand around the Veskan's forearm, and said, in a gasping breath, "*As Staro.*"

The man's eyes went wide. The magic rolled over his skin, and through his bones, turning every inch of him from flesh and blood to stone. His fingers loosened at the last instant, and Kay dropped to the deck, gasping, but free.

For an instant, power rippled through him, as welcome as a warm hearth in winter.

And then, all he felt was pain.

IX

Lila Bard had taken to playing a game.

Every time she fought, she gave herself a challenge.

Tonight, she'd think, *I will only use fire.*

Tonight, I will only use ice.

Tonight, I will let them strike first.

Tonight, I will fight as if I have no magic, as if I am back in London, my London, and I have nothing to lose but my life.

The man with the hatchet was dead, but she was having a fine time with the ice-wielding woman, watching her conjure shards, a shield, letting her leave a sheen of frost on Lila's skin, letting her freeze the deck, letting her think she had a chance. It felt good, to fight. Like stretching stiff limbs.

Until Kay screamed.

Kay, who would always be *Kell* in her mind, no matter which coat he was wearing, or how he slicked his hair, or how he'd learned to fight. Kell was the one screaming now, and the sound tore through her like a dull blade, the kind that took its time to kill you, and left a ragged tear in its wake. Lila knew what that sound meant. She wasted no more time, but spun behind the Veskan and slit her throat. The woman fell, and the frost began to melt from Lila's coat as she strode across the deck, past Tav—who was dispatching one of the men who'd had the misfortune of coming-to in the midst of the fight—to Kell.

The largest of the Veskans stood in the moonlight, his massive sword drawn back, but both he and the blade were now made of solid stone.

Beyond the statue, Kell was on his knees, head bowed. His hood had fallen back, his chest heaving as he dragged in ragged breaths, sweat sliding down his face beneath the mask.

Lila leaned against the statue of the man. "Well," she said, tapping a bloody knife against the stone. "So much for leaving them alive."

Kell's breathing steadied. Slowly, jaw clenched, he rose to his feet. Behind his mask, she knew, his eyes would be glassy with pain. But all she could see was black. He looked around, as if wondering what to do about the mess, but Lila had an idea. She brought her hands to the stone figure, and *pushed*. It was massive, but the wind leaned with her, and the stone leaned, too, and the statue fell, crashing straight through the wooden deck, and the hold below, cracking open the ship's hull like cannon shot.

The other boats had all lost interest as soon as they realized the fight wouldn't spill onto their ships, so there was no one on the docks but Stross to see the three shadows disembark, or free the ropes that bound the *Crow* to its berth. They watched as the boat drifted backward, the one sail Tav hadn't cut catching a sudden, carefully directed breeze.

It had already begun to take on water.

Wouldn't be long until it sank.

"Well," said Tav cheerfully. "I for one am far too sober."

Stross cleared his throat. "I could use a drink. Captain?"

Lila shrugged. They would be gone by daybreak, and Verose sat waiting like an untouched mark. She wanted to search its pockets, skim her fingers down its coat, see if it had anything worth taking. And she could do with a drink. "Why not?"

Kell's voice, when he spoke, was little more than a murmur. "I fear I'm not good company right now."

Lila cocked a brow. "Who said you were invited?"

He made a sound that died short of a laugh. He was clearly still in pain, and trying to hide it, but he couldn't. Not from her. To Lila, Kell had always been a pane of glass tilted toward her just so, so that where others saw only colors and streaks, she saw the truth of it. Of him.

And in that moment, she knew he wanted to be alone.

"I won't be long," she said, plucking off the Sarows mask and tossing it his way. He caught it, and she saw him wince, his body stiff with pain. Her fingers twitched with the urge to heal him, though she knew he wouldn't let her.

Stubborn ass, she thought as he turned back toward the *Barron,* and she turned to join Stross and Tav. The pain was his, and so she let him have it. But she did look back, more than once, watching his black coat ripple in the cold breeze until he was just another shadow in the dark.

X

This, thought Lila sometime later, was the worst drink she'd ever had. She'd never considered herself picky when it came to ale, but whatever was in her glass tasted like whoever owned the Black Tide had spilled cheap spirits into piss and called it a pint. It was strong, she had to give it that, but every time she took a sip, it tried to fight its way back up.

Tav and Stross didn't seem to mind. At least, not enough to stop drinking.

"The trick," offered Tav, "is to hold your breath."

"S'not that bad," grumbled Stross, but then, it was a well-known fact aboard the ship that her first mate had no sense of taste, a truth discovered during his brief stint as cook.

Lila abandoned the drink and reached instead into her coat, retrieving the blade she'd lifted from the *Crow*'s hold. She hadn't used it back on the ship, hadn't needed to, and it was still in its sheath. It was deceptively small—Veskans tended to favor broadswords, but this was closer to a dagger in shape, and roughly the length of her hand. When she drew the blade free, it was as thin as a ribbon, and shone the color of pearl. A cool breeze wafted off the metal, and when she tipped it toward the nearest light, she could just make out a string of spellwork etched along the edge, though she couldn't read it.

"Now that's a lovely piece of work," said Tav, who, not having any magic of his own, shared her fondness for sharp things.

"It is," she mused. The edge was dazzlingly sharp, but she resisted the urge to test it against her thumb. She sheathed the blade again, and set it down on the table.

Around them, the Black Tide was brimming with bodies.

In one corner, a trio of women with a small fortune of silver in their hair leaned forward, heads together over a map. In another, a ship's crew was getting blindingly drunk over a game of Sanct. There were even a pair of Arnesian soldiers—not dressed as such, of course, but they might as well be branded with the cup and sun and decked in red and gold.

Between the crowd, the planked walls, and the dark curtains, the place felt less like a tavern and more like the hull of a ship. Or, given the stale air, the belly of a whale.

She let her gaze drift over the room, though in truth, she wasn't looking. She was *listening*.

Verose was a thieves' haven, a place where the rule of the empire gave way to the will of the people, most of them criminals, pirates, and exiled magicians. It was the kind of place that fostered grudges, and turned them into bad ideas. The kind of place that could easily have produced the rebels that called themselves the Hand.

So Lila listened. Or tried—most of the patrons in the Tide were speaking a version of Arnesian, but some handled the language like a pen, while others used it like a hammer. Add to that the staccato bursts of laughter, the scrape of chairs, the way the voices rose and fell, and it was like fighting with a wave. Easier to relax, and let the words wash over her.

Tav, meanwhile, had produced a set of cards, and he and Stross were now engaged in an intense drinking game, one that had something to do with throwing down cards at rapid speed, and shouting loudly when you saw a king or queen. The loser drank. Or maybe the winner. Honestly, Lila wasn't sure. But she watched them bicker like old maids as they played, and marveled at the easy way they were together, the way they were with her, the space between them all worn smooth. She found herself wishing Kell was there. And Vasry, and Raya.

How strange.

Ask her at nineteen the definition of freedom, and it would have been *one*. One person. One ship. One big wide world. And yet here she was, seven years on, free, but far from alone.

She liked being alone. She was good at it. Had never trusted or taken to people.

But these weren't people, not really. They were something else. Allies. Friends. Family.

Once upon a time, the thought would have been enough to send her heart lurching in a seasick way, her pulse hitting that old familiar drum, telling her to run, run, run. As if it were a snaring trap, a snake of chain around her legs. As if people were just anchors, dead weight designed to hold you fast, drag you down.

Caring could drown you, if you let it.

But it could also help you float.

Not that she'd ever let the bastards know.

"Another round?" asked Tav, scraping the cards back into a pile.

Stross shook his head. "I'm tired," he said, rising to his feet, and finishing his drink.

"Tired of losing, you mean," said Tav, even as he stood and dropped a handful of coins on the table. They looked to Lila. "You coming, Captain?"

She looked around, shook her head. "Not yet."

Tav hesitated, and Stross weighed her with a look, and seemed about to sit down again when she waved them both away. "Oh, fuck off," she said, "and let me have a drink in peace."

If Kell were there, he'd make a fuss, insist on sticking around until she was done, trail her like a moody shadow back to the boat. But Kell wasn't there, and Stross knew better than to tell her to be safe, or careful. They all knew she could take care of herself.

"Your orders," said Tav, tipping an invisible cap.

Lila watched the two men go, and flagged down another drink.

The coat slumped to the cabin floor.

The mask, he flung against the wall. The swords came next, the leather holsters stiff beneath his bloodstained hands, but piece by piece, Kay fell

115

away, leaving only Kell.

Vasry and Raya had parted like a tide when he swept past. They didn't bother making small talk, or asking how the mission went. The evidence was right there, sinking in the bay. Right there, in the bloodstained steps he left on the *Barron*'s deck.

Seven years of practice, and still he slipped. No matter how long or hard Kell trained, there were times when his body still forgot.

He dragged the sodden shirt over his head, wincing at the pain that lanced across his shoulder, the wound left by the broadsword's bite. He made his way to the basin, gaze sliding to the large mirror propped behind it. In the glass, his hair fell into his face, a single streak of silver cutting through the red. In the glass, his bare skin was a tapestry of scars. Blood welled from the fresh cut along his collarbone, sliding in a narrow ribbon down his chest. It followed the line of his necklace until it reached the three coins that still hung at the end of the chain. Tokens that had once carried him to other Londons. Other worlds.

As Travars, he thought grimly, as blood dripped from the coins into the basin, staining the water pink, then red.

Kell's hand drifted up, almost absently, toward the tokens, and then past them, to the angry sword wound, which he knew his brother must have felt.

It was a marvel he hadn't heard from Rhy—or worse, from *Alucard*.

He glanced down at the red ring on his right hand, as if expecting the thought to summon the king of Arnes or his consort, but the band stayed dark and cold. As did the black one beside it. The red ring bore the royal seal—the chalice and rising sun. The black one bore a ship.

They were rare and precious things, these rings, not one of a kind, but *two*. Each had a twin, a perfect replica designed to rest on another finger.

It was a clever piece of magic, gifted to him by the queen four years before, a way to link two people, no matter where they were. One simply had to touch the surface of the ring and say the words *as vera tan—I need you*—and its twin would burn with light and heat. Place both rings upon a scrying board, and the distance between them disappeared, the flat black surface turned to glass; not a door, but at least a window, a way to see and speak.

116

His brother had married well, Kell thought, not for the first time.

The red ring that he wore belonged of course to Rhy Maresh, who said he'd only wear it if it matched his other finery. The black one, Kell had given to Lila. Or rather, he'd tried. It hadn't gone well. She'd paled when he'd offered her the charm, recoiled as if it were a serpent, or a bottle of poison he was asking her to drink, and too late, he remembered the customs of her world, the meaning of such a ring to someone in Grey London.

He'd shown her the one on his own hand, tried to explain how the bands were linked, how in case of trouble, she could call on him, but her gaze had gone flat and mocking.

"If I'm in trouble," she'd said, "I'll get myself out."

He had shouted, then, and so had she. He had called her stubborn and she had called him selfish, he had called her frightened and she had called him a fool, and in the end, she had stormed out, and he had slammed the door, and the waves had sloshed angrily against the ship, and he knew she'd cast her ring into the sea.

They did not talk about it after that.

And yet, he didn't take his off. Not that day, or the next, or the next. It was silly, he knew—after all, the ring was useless on its own, nothing but a sentimental trinket, but he wore it, still, to spite her. To say that in his mind they were still linked, that they would always be, that she was one of only two he loved so much, that he would let himself be bound to them like this.

Kell ran his thumb over the black band, then thrust his hands into the basin, rinsing them clean, before he set to work on his wounds.

Antari magic was an incredible thing.

It was the only kind of power that was both element and spell. Chaos and order. A drop of blood, a pair of words, and you could turn a man to stone, open a door into another world, mend almost any injury.

As Hasari.

Two words he had said a hundred times, to heal the sick, undo a mortal wound. What a simple thing it would have been, to mend a shoulder.

Lila would have done it, of course, if he had asked.

Instead, Kell drew two bottles from the cabinet beneath.

The first he brought to his lips, drinking long and deep. The second he used to douse a cloth. The sharp smell filled his head, and then the narrow room. As he pressed the cloth to his shoulder, the pain flared, bright enough to steal his breath, and he clenched his teeth against it, but in moments, the bleeding had stopped, and he said a silent apology to his brother as he threaded a needle, and adjusted the light, and leaned toward the mirror.

As the barb bit into his skin, he forced his mind back to the fight on the *Crow*. With every pierce, every tug, every tightened stitch, he counted his missteps, his mistakes, reliving every motion until the fight was burned into his memory, and he was certain that next time, he wouldn't forget.

XI

Somehow, the second drink Lila ordered looked even worse than the first.

It was the color of oil and the texture of silt, and when she lifted the glass to the low tavern light, it was like staring at paint. She brought the glass absently to her lips, was even about to take a questing sip when a nearby voice interrupted.

"Wouldn't do that."

Lila glanced up to find a woman on the other side of her table, dark hair bundled up into a crown. Her eyes glittered in the tavern light, and when she smiled, only her lips moved, drawing taut over her teeth.

"Let me guess," said Lila dryly. "It's poisoned."

"Might as well be," said the woman, dropping down into a chair as if invited. Her gaze went, almost immediately, to the weapon Lila had left out on the wood.

"That," said the stranger, "is a very nice knife."

"I know," said Lila. "Worth the ship I sank to get it."

"Ah, a pirate, then."

"A captain."

The woman glanced around. "And your crew?"

Lila didn't know if she was being threatened or wooed. "Minding their own business."

The woman didn't take the hint.

"Tanis," she said, by way of introduction. She waited for Lila to give her name. Lila didn't.

"What do you want, Tanis?"

The woman leaned back in her chair, studying Lila. "You're not from here." Lila said nothing, and Tanis went on. "Most people aren't. They're just passing through, they don't know how the city works." Tanis spread her hands. "Sometimes, they need a guide."

"Let me guess," said Lila. "You're a guide."

Tanis smiled again. All lips, no teeth. "That's me. So, what brings you to Verose?"

Lila tipped her head as if considering. "I'm on holiday."

Tanis let out a barking laugh. "And you came here?"

"I wanted to see where the Rebel Army made their stand."

It had been forty years since the makeshift army, led by magicians from each of the three empires, had sailed up the Blood Coast, on their way toward London, determined to overthrow Arnes.

It was a gamble. A baited hook.

Tanis tipped her head. "Not a fan of the crown?"

The bait, taken. The line drew taut. Lila let her face slide from bland amusement into anger. She looked down at the blade on the table, deciding on her next words.

"Priests talk about balance. They say magic follows the laws of nature. But nature *changes*. So why doesn't power?" She looked up when she said this last bit, met Tanis's gaze. Fire bloomed in Lila's hand, and she turned it, pressing her palm down against the table, burning the handprint into the wood. "Verose strikes me as the kind of place where sparks grow into flames."

Lila did not say the word *menas—hand—*she didn't have to. A look of recognition had already crossed Tanis's face. Her eyes darkened, but her smile never fell. And then she leaned forward, and pressed her own hand over the mark.

"I'm afraid you're mistaken," she said, drawing her palm in a smoothing gesture over the table, erasing the burn from the wood. "If you're looking

119

for a helping *hand*," she said, "Verose really isn't the place." She stood. "But if you find yourself in London, I hear the gardens are lovely." Her gaze flicked once more to the blade on the table. "And I'd put that away, if I were you," she added. "I'd hate for you to lose it." Tanis tipped her head toward the barkeep.

"Oli," she called out, "get the captain a real drink."

And then she was gone.

A pint of ale arrived, and this time the contents were not entirely sludge, though a far cry from amber. Still, Lila drank, and sank back in her seat, turning over the woman's words. Lost in her thoughts, the ale fizzing through her head, Lila took a moment to realize the air in the tavern had changed.

As if Tanis had shined a light on her and left it there.

She was suddenly glad she'd worn the brown eye instead of the black. The last thing she needed was word of an *Antari* here. Knowing Verose, someone would try to cut the eye from her head—lot of good it would do them—or take her as a prize to ransom, sell her to the highest bidder, and if that happened, she'd have to *make a scene,* and Kell would never let her hear the end of it.

But Tanis was right about one thing: she should have put the knife away. She'd left it on the table, that pearl sheath shining strangely, and at some point, the Tide's patrons had begun to notice.

At some point, she'd gone from being the thief to being the mark.

Lila felt studied as she drained her drink. As she dug in her pocket for a coin. As she turned up the collar of her coat. As her fingers closed around the Veskan dagger and she rose from her seat. So she wasn't surprised when she looked up and found a man standing on the table's other side. He was tall, and thin as a pole, his eyes dark knots in the hollow of his face. His eyes slouched toward the blade.

"Careful," he said. "Don't want to cut yourself."

"Fuck off," she said, which, it turned out, was not a welcome answer. She was about to round the table when he shoved it forward, into Lila's stomach, pinning her back against the wall.

"Give it up," he said, hands splayed on the wood as he leaned forward.

"Fine," Lila growled. She drew the blade from its sheath.

And drove it down into his hand.

The man gaped at her, his face a mask of rage and pain, but before he could pull back, or howl, or draw a weapon of his own, a change rolled over him. He went rigid, mouth open, as his veins blackened, and his skin curled, and he *burned*, charring from the inside out in the time it took Lila to suck in a breath and blow it out.

And then he simply *fell apart*.

Nothing but an ashy streak on the table, the floor.

The blade stayed upright, unscathed.

And the patrons, who had carried on despite brawls and broken glass, and the sight of drawn steel, turned to see Lila standing there, her blade driven down into the table, surrounded only by a mound of dust.

Lila decided it was time to go. She retrieved the blade and dropped a coin onto the wood, sending up a tiny plume of ash as she slid the dagger back into its sheath and walked away. No one followed. She stepped out into the night, which had gone cold.

The top button of her shirt had come undone at some point, and her necklace swung free. A black ring hung at the end of the leather cord, its face printed with a ship. She closed her hand over the band and tucked it back beneath her shirt as she set off toward the docks.

She made it exactly ten feet before she realized she wasn't alone.

"Fair warning," she said, "I'm not in a sparing mood tonight."

"I can see that," said a voice, smooth and deep. She turned and saw a dark-skinned man, dressed head to toe in white, and her first thought was how strange it was, that choice of white, so out of place among sailors. She'd thought as much the first time she'd seen the outfit, on Maris's ship.

Valick, she thought. That was his name.

"You're a long way from the floating market." His gaze dropped to the blade in her hand, and her fingers tightened. "Finders keepers," she added.

And he couldn't have known what it was, but he obviously did, because he said, "A weapon like that belongs on the *Ferase Stras*, not on the street."

Lila cocked a brow. "You came all this way for a knife?"

"No," said Valick. "I came all this way for you."

Lila's gaze narrowed. "If you plan to add *me* to your collection—"

"You owe Maris a favor," he cut in. "She's calling it in."

A favor. Lila should have known, when Maris offered her the glass black eye, should have paid then and there, given up a year or two of her life and called it even instead of trading for a favor. A favor was just a nice word for a debt, and Lila hated owing. She had been waiting for the old bat to call it in, had begun to wonder, over the years, if she'd forgotten.

Obviously not.

"Well? What does she want?"

Valick held out his other hand. "She'll tell you herself." In his palm was a ring. Not black, like the one around her neck, but silver, a small hourglass stamped into its surface. Still, she recognized the queen's handiwork, and was willing to bet there was a twin ring, on the old woman's hand.

"We'll need to find a scrying board," he began, but Lila was already stepping toward him.

"Nonsense," she said, nicking her palm with one of her knives. "Waste of perfectly good magic."

She reached out, closing her fingers over the ring, and Valick's hand, pinning the metal between their palms. And before he could pull back, she whispered the words into the air, and the whole world shivered and came apart.

XII

Lila Bard stepped out of the darkened road, and into a ship's cabin, dragging Valick Patrol behind her. The floor rocked a little beneath her boots, the air rumbling with something like thunder. The room was narrow, lantern light spilling over cabinets and chests and across a desk, behind which sat Maris Patrol, captain of the floating market.

The old woman was dressed in a white silk robe, her silver hair loose and flowing down her back. She had a glass of wine in one hand, a book in the other, and a moment before she had obviously been enjoying both. Now, however, she was looking up, and Lila had the rare pleasure of seeing surprise scrawled across the captain's face, right before it—and the book—snapped shut.

"You absolute fool," said Maris in Arnesian, as the thunder trailed off. "You *do* know this ship is warded against magical intrusion." So that was the source of the crackling air.

"I had a feeling it would work."

"A *feeling*," said the old woman dryly. "You risked my nephew's life for a *feeling*."

"An educated guess, then." Lila twirled Valick's ring on her finger. "The palace wards are bound to blood, so the royal family can come and go without a dozen stuffy spells. I figured the *Ferase Stras* would be the same. And as you can see, your nephew is fine." She glanced at Valick, whose brown skin had taken on a grey pallor. He looked like he was about to be sick.

"More or less," she added.

"Not in my room," snarled Maris, and Valick nodded and bolted, stumbling out into the dark. A gust of cold sea air blew in before the door swung shut. Lila turned to survey the contents of the cabinets. It had been seven years since she'd stood in this very room, seven years since she'd come aboard this ship in search of a way to beat Osaron. She'd been waiting for a chance to come back.

"What are you doing here?" demanded Maris.

"I was invited," said Lila, holding out the silver ring. Its twin glinted, one of several on the woman's bony hand.

"That was an invitation to talk," she said without reaching for the band. "Not *visit*. I'm sure Valick made that clear."

"Must have slipped his mind," said Lila, letting the ring fall onto the table. "I suppose I could ask how you got your hands on a piece of the queen's craft, but . . ." She trailed off, gesturing at the ship, whose very purpose was to trade in, and store, risky magic.

"She is a clever thing, isn't she?" mused Maris. "Of course, Her Majesty did not *invent* paired magic, but still, an elegant execution of the principle. A mind like that can be a dangerous thing."

"By all means, take her. Store her in one of the crates on your ship."

Maris inclined her head. "You don't like her."

"I don't trust her," said Lila, sinking into the chair opposite the desk.

A pale sack lay beside her boot, and it took her a moment to realize it was, in fact, an ancient-looking dog. It was suspiciously still. She toed it gently with her boot, just to make sure that it was breathing. It sighed, and she turned her attention back to Maris. "You look old."

"I feel older," she shot back, adding, "what have you done with your eye?"

They both knew she wasn't talking about the ones currently in Lila's face, but the one currently back in her cabin, stored in its velvet box, its surface neither brown nor blue but black as pitch. Black as the eye she'd lost to a doctor's scalpel back in her London, before she'd known about other worlds, or the magic they possessed, let alone the term *Antari*.

The eye she'd traded for a favor.

"I do wear it, now and then," she said. "But I've found that people are fools. Showing them your power is like showing them your hand at cards. Make them *guess* at it instead, and they'll almost always guess wrong."

The door opened, and Valick returned, looking steadier on his feet. He crossed the room and set the spelled blade on the desk.

"That's still mine," said Lila as Maris took up the dagger and eased it from its sheath, studying the pearl surface. She frowned, wrinkles cracking like ice across her skin.

"Do you know what this does?"

"It kills people."

Maris rolled her eyes. "Ordinary knives kill people. *This* uses a person's own magic to destroy them. It taps into the power in their blood and turns it against their body. . . ."

Lila straightened, interest piqued. She remembered the way the man in the tavern seemed to catch fire from the inside out, just before he turned to ash. She wondered what it might do to a bone magician. Would they come apart like a string of pearls, or collapse like a sack of boneless meat? And what would happen if it skewered an *Antari*?

". . . with a single cut," finished Maris.

"Right," said Lila. "So . . . it's a knife. And it kills people."

Maris shook her head. "What a shame that all your power doesn't come with sense." She tugged open a drawer in her desk.

"Still mine," muttered Lila as the blade vanished inside.

124

"Consider it payment for boarding my ship. Now get out."

"But I just got here. And you haven't even said why you called. Unless it was simply to catch up. I know it must get lonely—"

"Out of my *chambers*. Valick, show Captain Bard to the lower deck. Don't let her touch anything."

Lila rose, hands splayed. "Come now. Even I wouldn't be foolish enough to steal from *your* ship."

"Someone was," said Maris, and before Lila could ask, she emptied her glass and nodded at the door.

Lila made to leave, but halfway out, she glanced back. There was something she had been wanting to ask. Something she had to know. "The strongest magic in the world is on this ship. If there were anything here that could help Kell . . ." Her voice tightened, betraying her need.

Over the last seven years, they had searched, tried tinctures, tried spells, tried every fucking thing under the sun. And nothing they'd found in the three empires, or any markets, black or hidden or otherwise, had been able to fix what was broken in him.

Eventually, Kell had stopped looking.

But she hadn't.

"I would pay the price," she added.

Maris pursed her lips. "Clear one debt before you take another."

Venom rose like bile in her throat, but the captain held up a hand to cut her off. She looked suddenly tired. "If I had anything that could restore Kell Maresh's power, or ease his suffering, I would give it . . ." She almost said *freely*—Lila saw her shaping the word—but Maris had more sense than that.

Instead, the old woman shook her head, and said, "But I don't."

The words landed like a heavy door swung shut by the wind. And this time, when Maris waved her away, Lila turned and followed Valick out.

If Red London's night market had been scraped off the avenue beside the Isle and piled onto a boat, tents and stalls crowding every inch of space, it still wouldn't have held a candle to the *Ferase Stras*.

The ship was twice the size of her *Barron,* a maze of halls and decks and cabins, spaces piled like a stack of books on a too-small table.

Lila had always been good at making maps. Not the kind on paper, but the ones that lived in her head, maps of town alleys and city streets, multiple worlds consigned entirely to memory. She could walk a road and learn it with her feet, and never get turned around a second time—and yet, there was no point aboard the *Ferase Stras.* Maybe it was magic, a spell designed to alter memory, or maybe it was simply the chaos and clutter, the dazzling distraction of a hundred powerful things.

But Valick clearly knew his way.

She followed him down the stairs and through a corridor packed tight with rooms. More than once her steps slowed before a curtained alcove, hoping to steal a look at the contents within, but Valick's voice called her on, around a corner, up one set of stairs and down another until they finally reached the only stretch of open space on board, the lower deck. The captain's other nephew, Katros, leaned against the mainmast, carving a bit of wood into a Rasch piece. At the sight of Lila Bard, he straightened, eyes flicking once from the platform on the side of the ship where visitors were *meant* to board to the way from which she'd clearly come. But *Lila's* gaze went straight to the deck.

Even in the lantern glow, she could see the damage. The stain of blood on the wooden boards, the fractal scorch of magic.

"What happened here?" she asked, following the tendrils of the shattered ward to a section of splintered rail. Katros and Valick both opened their mouths, but it was Maris who answered.

"I was robbed."

She had clearly taken another route, and dressed on the way, trading the robe for a white linen tunic and pants, her silver hair pulled back into a braid. The old white dog trailed silently behind.

"Robbed?" Lila's hand fell away from the rail. "I didn't think that was possible."

"It shouldn't be," said Maris, crossing her arms.

Lila wanted to ask how they'd done it, but questions were like coins to people like Maris, you had to be careful how you spent them. So instead, she asked the more pertinent question. "What does this have to do with me?"

"Three thieves came aboard my ship. One got away."

Lila scuffed her shoe over the bloodstained deck. "And you want me to track them down?"

"The thief matters far less than the object they took—or who might have wanted to collect it."

Katros held out a slip of paper with a drawing on it.

"It was damaged in the attack," said Maris. "But it could still work."

Lila studied the drawing. It looked like a detailed sketch of a box, its only decoration an iron ring set into its front. It looked simple enough, but when Lila was young, she'd stolen something that reminded her of it—a puzzle box, the kind designed to hide its own key. It was small and made of wood and brass, with pieces that slid and turned, hinges that shifted and clasps that would only come free if you moved all the bits in the right way and the right order.

It had taken her three hours to open that box.

The first two to try and solve the puzzle, the third to crush it with a rock.

This one looked basic enough, but then again, it was on the *Ferase Stras*. Not just that, but Maris cared enough for her to track it down, when it might not even work. Which meant the chance it *did* was enough to make the old woman call in her favor.

"What does it do?" asked Lila.

Maris sighed and gazed out past the ship, into the dark. It was a moonless night, the sea so black that they seemed to be floating in the sky. The old woman had a faraway shine in her eyes, and Lila had a feeling she was about to hear a story, whether she wanted one or not.

"*Antari* have always been rare. But there was a time when you could count them on more than one hand. A time when most people hadn't only heard tell of their power, but seen it up close. Seen it, and wanted it for themselves. It's hardly surprising. A drop of blood, a single phrase, and you can turn flesh to stone, can shatter walls, or seal them up, heal a mortal wound, or open doors within the world, and between them."

127

"I'm well aware what *I* can do," said Lila.

Maris shot her a warning look. "Everything *you* do can be done with a spell. That was the theory. So fabricators set out to design spellwork that could emulate your gifts."

A bad feeling was beginning to curl in Lila's gut, but this time, she didn't interrupt.

"*Antari* magic," continued Maris, "is the place where spell and element meet. It is simple, and elegant, and the craft needed to replicate it was none of those things. It was volatile, and complicated, and required devices to contain the magic, to keep the spells from falling apart, or unraveling in horrible ways."

"But it worked," guessed Lila.

"But it worked," said Maris. "The object they stole is called a *persalis*. A doormaker."

Lila's bad feeling turned to horror. "Tell me this doesn't make doors between worlds."

"Thankfully, no," said Maris. "Only *Antari* were ever able to manage that. But it does make doors *within* them. The iron ring in the front comes free and is used to mark the destination. The box creates a portal."

Just like *As Tascen*, thought Lila. The spell that had allowed her to make a shortcut into the world, step from the street onto the ship.

"*Unlike* your magic," continued Maris, "this portal stays open, no matter how many people pass through. As long as the spell is active, an entire army could move from one location into another."

Horror hardened into anger. Lila's jaw clenched. "Do you ever think," she said, "that instead of storing the world's most dangerous magic, you might simply destroy it, and save us all the headache?"

"If I had done that, there would have been no rings to share *Antari* power, and the three of you would have lost to Osaron, after which London would have fallen to his plague, followed swiftly, I imagine, by everywhere else. If you only think of the wrong hands magic can fall into, you forget that now and then there are right ones."

Lila raked a hand through her hair. "So one thief made it off the ship. And the other two . . . ?"

128

"Didn't," said Maris simply. She flicked her fingers at Katros, who produced a small pouch.

"Everything that was in their pockets," he explained, passing it to Lila. She pulled the string and tipped the contents out into her palm. Nothing but a few red lin. Barely enough to pay for a meal.

"Tell me you have more than this," she said, returning the coins to the pouch.

Maris cleared her throat. "He also had a mark burned into his skin. A handprint."

At that, Lila muttered a quiet "Fuck."

"Ever the poet," said the captain of the *Ferase Stras,* and Lila thought, not for the first time, that she should have paid for the damned glass eye some other way.

"I suggest you find the box quickly," added Maris. "Before *someone* puts it to use."

"And here I thought I'd take my time." Lila shoved the pouch of coins into her pocket. "Anything else?"

Maris drew something from her pocket. A card-sized piece of glass. "This might help."

Lila took the object, turned it over in her hands. It looked ordinary enough, but since it was here on Maris's ship, chances were it wasn't. She held it up. "Are you going to make me guess?"

The old woman let out a sound that might have been a laugh. It came out dry as paper.

"Think of it as a backward glance," she said. "In case, like me, you find yourself a step behind." She explained how to activate the spell, but when Lila lifted the glass to her eye to test it, the word already on her tongue, Maris's hand shot out, old fingers closing around her wrist.

"Use it wisely," she warned. "It only works once."

"Of course," the *Antari* sighed, slipping the fragile pane into her coat. "Well, if there's nothing else . . ." She unsheathed a small blade from her hip, but as she brought the steel to her skin, Maris cleared her throat.

"I wouldn't. The wards bent for my nephew. I doubt they'll be so kind to you." She nodded at the boarding platform, which jutted like a narrow tongue out over the sea. It reminded Lila of a plank, the kind mutinous sailors were forced to walk in penny dreadfuls. "Better safe than sorry."

Lila stepped up onto the plank. The ship bobbed in the current, the wooden board dipping beneath her boots, but she didn't stumble. She took one step, and then another, past the body of the ship and the wards that shielded it until she was safely out over the sea.

She could have stopped there, but something urged her forward, to the very edge of the plank. Lila looked down at the black water as she drew a sliver of wood from her pocket. A piece of the bird at the bow of her ship. Alucard had had a fit when he noticed the missing feather, chiseled from the sculpture's wing. But Lila had good reason.

The *persalis* may be an impostor's magic tool, but it understood one thing.

Never open a door unless you know where it leads.

She pressed her thumb to the edge of her knife, felt the bite of metal, the well of blood.

"Delilah," called Maris.

Lila looked back. "Let me guess, you want me to be careful."

Again, that dry laugh. "Careful is for old bodies crossing wet floors," said Maris, breeze tugging at her silver braid. "I want you to get me back that fucking box."

Lila smiled, and pressed her bloody thumb to the wooden feather.

"Aye aye, Captain," she said, stepping off the ship as the spell left her lips.

She never hit the waves.

A heartbeat later, Lila landed on the *Barron*'s deck.

A short drop, a lurch in her chest, and then her boots hit the wood, half a stride from Vasry and Raya, whose heads were bent over a game of Sanct. Vasry yelped and fell backward off his stool. Raya's mouth twitched in amusement.

"Never get used to that," said Vasry, getting back to his feet.

Lila rolled her head on her shoulders as she strolled away across the deck, tucking the wooden feather back in her pocket. The thrill of the night had worn away, and she felt suddenly tired, her bones aching from the fight on the *Crow,* her thoughts churning from Maris's mission, her skin stained with blood and power. She peeled off her coat and tossed it aside, rinsing her hands and face with a jug of water.

"Stross and Tav?"

"*Hesassa,*" answered Raya.

"Out cold," translated Vasry, whose Fresan had gotten understandably better over the years.

"What about our neighbors?" she asked, nodding down the docks to the empty berth where the *Crow* had been. "Any trouble?"

"Oh, plenty," said Vasry. "The other four came back, looking for their ship."

"And?"

"It's Verose," he said with an amiable shrug. "If they didn't want to lose it, they shouldn't have left it. They did come around," he added, "asking if we'd seen anything. But it was clear we were rather *occupied.*" Raya flicked her fingers, and a tiny curl of water splashed his face.

Lila scanned the deck.

"We haven't seen him," said Vasry, reading her thoughts. "Not since he came back. Went straight down to his room, and we thought, best to leave him be."

She nodded. All these years, and the crew still kept Kell at a distance. She couldn't exactly blame them. Stross wasn't happy to have a royal prince on board, said it drew too much attention. Tav and Vasry treated him like a piece of precious cargo. Raya acted like he was a cannon that might go off at any moment.

In short, they were afraid of him.

They were afraid of Lila, too, of course. But it was different. They were afraid of what she could *do.* They were afraid of what Kell *was.* Even if they were both *Antari,* the crew managed to forget about Bard's eye, until she did something like step out of thin air onto the ship.

Lila bid them goodnight, and went down the short flight of stairs into the body of the *Barron.* She wanted a bath. Wanted a hot meal. Wanted a bed. But when she reached her cabin, it was only to shed her coat, and slip the glass card Maris had given her into the top drawer of her desk.

After that, she continued down the narrow hall to the closed door at the end.

She didn't bother knocking.

Kell lay on his side in the dark, his hair making small waves across the pillow. His eyes were shut, but she knew he wasn't sleeping. He never slept, not when she was out. Lila sank down beside him, stretched out long in the narrow bed, and he pretended to stir, rolling first onto his back and then toward her.

"Hello," he said in English. His voice was soft and low, but she felt herself leaning into the word as much as the sound. All her life, she'd taken the language for granted, but here in this world, English was a royal tongue, reserved for Arnesian nobles and the crown at court, an ostentation born from centuries of *Antari* magicians carrying missives between London kings and queens. But here, at sea, it was something private. The language they slipped into only when they were alone.

Kell reached out and brushed a clump of hair behind her ear. These days his hands were rougher, but his touch was just as light, as if she were the one who might break.

"Where have you been?" he asked, and she told him. Of Tanis's warning, of Valick's arrival, of Maris, and the robbery aboard the floating market, and the mission that she'd been given.

Soon Kell was sitting up, chin resting on his knotted hands as he listened to the story of the *persalis,* the three thieves who came to steal it, and the one who got away. And when she finished, he did not tell her it was too dangerous, did not say that it was a fool's errand, a needle in a haystack when you couldn't find the hay. He did not even ask where they would start. He knew as well as she did. If this was the work of the Hand, it was to only one end. The palace. The crown. The king.

Lila stretched out long beside him, felt her limbs loosen at last.

"To London, then," he said in the dark.

She nodded, and whispered back.

"To London."

III

THE
KING'S
HEART

I

RED LONDON

The city was full of broken things, though few, Tes found, were truly beyond repair.

She spent her day off as she always did, combing through stalls and trinket shops, salvaging anything that struck her fancy. Some trinkets she would simply fix, but others she would take apart, pry the threads of magic loose and use them somewhere else. Take something that was and make it *better*. Other workers focused on inventions, but she preferred improvements.

A bag of the day's spoils rattled on her shoulder as Tes made her way through the crowded market. As she went, she murmured softly; not to herself, but to the owl tucked in the front pocket of her coat.

". . . still looking for an iron key. And I need a bit more copper, don't you think?"

Vares rattled his bones in agreement, the feeling like a second heart against her shirt.

It helped, having someone to talk to, even if that someone was more of a something and that something was technically dead. Tes felt on edge, her nerves jangling as they always did when she'd left the safety of the shop. It was probably the pot of bitter tea she'd downed before setting out, or the sugar bun she'd eaten in two gulping bites at the last market.

She reached the end of the stalls, but instead of continuing on, she turned, and slipped through a curtained fold between the tents, into a second, hidden line of tents.

One of the first things she learned was this: most good markets have two faces.

The first face was bland and unassuming, filled with the ordinary fare, but the second, the second loomed just behind it, back-to-back, like a coin turned edgewise, or the high priest in Sanct—the only card that had two sides.

Here, the magic shone a little brighter. Here, the cost could be sorted out in trade as well as coin. Here, you never knew what you might find.

The second side wasn't a *forbidden* market—Tes always avoided those out of her usual caution—simply one that preferred to conduct its own business, unbothered by the royal guard. Like the back room in an antiques shop, reserved for those who knew where to look, and also knew better than to ask any questions.

Tes slowed as she reached a table covered in different element sets, their lids yawning open to reveal their contents.

Five elements: water, fire, earth, wind, bone; the last included even though the use of it was strictly forbidden. Some of the sets were large, ornate chests, each of the elements contained in glass orbs the size of summer melons. Others were small enough to fit into a child's hand, the elements trapped inside glass beads.

Pouches crowded the front of the table, each filled with spare beads, the elements pooling in the bottom, as if resting. They sat like a dark spot in her vision, the power dormant, the magic unconjured.

There was no sign of the seller, but Tes let her fingers drift to one of the sets, a small, gold-edged box, the elements in a single row. But as she did, the bag on her shoulder slipped, and caught the nearest sack of beads, spilling the contents across the table.

"No, no, no," she hissed. She lunged, caught the pouch in time to right it, but not before a handful of glass beads had gone clattering over the side, hitting the cobblestones like hail. Tes flinched as heads turned toward her, and dropped to her knees, collecting the fallen beads, drops of tinted water sloshing inside each.

She grabbed two as they tried to roll away, missed the third as it disappeared beneath the table. She knelt to retrieve it, but as her fingers skimmed the glass, it rolled farther out of reach. At the same time, she saw the shift of boots behind the stall, heard the voices of two men.

". . . days are numbered."

"You know something I don't?"

A low chuckle. "Let's just say, I wouldn't invest in crimson and gold."

Tes went very still. They were talking about the crown.

"Does it really matter, which royal ass sits on the throne?"

"It does, when the body in question has no power."

Tes frowned. Everyone said that King Rhy had no magic to speak of, but she didn't see how that had anything to do with ruling Arnes, until the voice went on.

"It matters when the magic's drying up."

It wasn't the first time Tes had heard talk about the shortage of power, the tide of magic pulling back, but if the threads were dimming, she didn't see it. And if they were, well, who was to say it was the king's fault? The *Antari* were supposed to be the pinnacle of magic, and they'd been dwindling for centuries, while Rhy Maresh had only taken the throne in the wake of the Tide. The Tide, which spread like a plague through the London streets, infecting those who didn't fight, and killing most who did. If the power really *was* ebbing now, why not blame *that*? Didn't it seem more likely that the empire's magic had been damaged by *that* chaotic event, and not a magicless king on a man-made throne?

Not that it mattered.

When people wanted to make trouble, all they needed was a good excuse. For months, she'd been able to taste the trouble brewing. It was like smoke, or bitter tea, and every day it seemed a little stronger.

"Do you know what Faro and Vesk do to those without power?" one was saying as she held her breath and tried to reach the water bead.

"They sure as saints don't hand them a crown."

"Exactly. Makes us look weak. The way I see it, a mistake was made. The Hand is going to fix it."

"And if it doesn't?"

"Well, then, what's one less pampered royal in the world?"

At last, Tes's fingers closed around the lost bead. She scrambled back, and rose, dropping her quarry in the cloth pouch and hurrying away from the stall before the men stepped through the curtain and realized someone had heard them discussing treason.

She didn't look back, didn't slow, even when Vares pecked her through her shirt, as if the dead owl was nudging her to do something. And there *was* something she could do. Every citizen had seen the gold writing on the city's scrying boards, the orders that sounded more like pleas, instructing the people of London to report any signs of rebellion.

There was a scrying board at the market's edge. She knew if she pressed her palm to the mark, soldiers would come.

But she didn't.

Tes had nothing against the king.

She'd been only eight years old, and a hundred miles north, when the Tide hit London, and Rhy Maresh was forced onto the throne. She hadn't been there, to see the city fall, or rise again, to witness the rakish young prince suddenly orphaned and just as suddenly crowned king. But she remembered her first winter in the city, three years ago. The dazzling parade that filled the grand avenue with icy light on *Sel Fera Noche,* the royal family floating on a gilded platform, as if the road were a frozen lake. For a moment—only a moment—Tes had been close enough to see the king's face, his proud chin, his dazzling smile, the crown nestled in his glossy black curls, but she'd been drawn to his gold eyes, which, despite their molten brightness, struck her as sad.

No, she had nothing against Rhy Maresh. He seemed a good enough king. But Tes had enough problems on her own, so she made a point of staying clear of other people's trouble.

Besides, everyone thought the king powerless, but that day, during the parade, she'd seen the silver light that bloomed from his chest, spreading less threads than flames, burning the air around his crown.

Rhy Maresh wasn't nearly as helpless as he seemed.

"Well, if it isn't my favorite apprentice!"

She'd reached the last stall, where Lorn, a wiry old man with glasses perched on his nose, was waiting for her. He had a face like a weathered stump, lines cracking at the corners of his eyes and mouth whenever he spoke. "How is Master Haskin this week?"

She pushed the king from her mind, and managed a smile. "Busy," she said. "Believe it or not, things keep breaking."

Lorn shot her a shrewd look. "Hard to believe there are any clocks and locks and household trinkets left in London that need fixing."

Tes shrugged. "People must be clumsy."

Lorn had a bald spot on the crown of his head. Tes saw it every time she paid the stall a visit, because mirrors lined the back of his shop. They filled the small space, a dozen different shapes and sizes, some hung at odd angles so they reflected the world back in mismatched fragments. Spellwork wove in glowing lines around the frames, promising the future, the past, a memory, a wish.

As Lorn bent to fetch something from beneath the table, Tes caught sight of herself—her wild curls wrested into a plume at the base of her neck, instead of piled on her head, the bulge of Vares in her coat pocket, her own magic, which didn't curl in threads, like everyone else's, but frizzed into an aura, like light behind a fogged-up glass. She had tried to reach into that cloud so many times, but the light bent around her fingers, the only power she couldn't seem to catch.

"Let's see, let's see . . . ah."

The merchant straightened, and held out a small bag. They had an agreement, he and Haskin (at least, so Lorn assumed), that the former would collect any scraps a fixer might find useful, and in exchange, he could bring anything that might need fixing to the shop, free of charge.

Tes pulled the cord on the bag and peered down into the medley of parts. To anyone else, the contents might have looked like nothing but debris, but as she took in the glint of metal and the glow of magic, her mind was already whirring, racing ahead of her, back to the shop and the waiting worktable. She looked up to thank Lorn, but as she did, she caught the reflection of a woman in the mirrors, slipping between stalls.

Tes went rigid. It was like someone had driven a spike of ice straight through her, pinning her to the street. Her heart stuttered in her chest as the woman appeared, vanished, reappeared, flickering across the angled glass in pieces.

A sharp cheek.

A dark braid.

An emerald cloak.

The same one their father had given her oldest sister, Serival.

"For hunting," he'd said, his mouth twitching in a tight-lipped way— the closest thing it ever managed to a smile. And she'd been too young, then, to understand the nature of her sister's gift, or that it had nothing to do with animals.

"*Kers la?*" asked Lorn, but another voice was folding over it, low, and smooth, as it filled her ears, her head, her heart.

What's wrong, little rabbit?

Tes recoiled, spun around, expecting her sister to be right there, expression triumphant as those cold fingers closed around her throat.

Caught you.

But Serival wasn't there.

There was no sign of her, or the emerald cloak that had set Tes's pulse racing, just the usual stalls, and Lorn's face, splintering with worry. But Serival's voice played on in her head.

Where have you run to, little rabbit?

Tes backed away, the sack under one arm.

How long can you hide?

She mumbled something to Lorn—an apology, or maybe a thanks, she hoped—she couldn't hear the words over the sound of her pulse—then turned and darted through the nearest break in the tents, back into the safety of the crowded market.

Green flashed at the corner of her sight. The woman in the emerald cloak was standing feet away, her back turned as she ran her hand through bolts of cloth. Tes backed away, too fast, too hard, felt herself collide with someone—and something—felt the object slip, and fall, heard the man's cry of dismay and the hard sound of wood hitting the stone street.

The woman in green heard it, too, and turned, and for the first time, Tes saw her face. All the air went rushing out of her lungs. It wasn't Serival. Of course it wasn't.

Her sister hadn't found her.

Tes was still safe.

The owl fluttered in her coat pocket, and she knew he was trying to calm her.

"I'm all right," she whispered to Vares and herself. "I'm all right."

The man, meanwhile, was chirping in annoyance as he bent to fetch the box he'd dropped.

"Better not be broken," he snapped, and Tes could see it wasn't, but she still pulled a black-and-gold card from her pocket and shoved it at him.

"If it is," she said, "take it to Haskin. He'll fix it for free."

And before the man could make more of a fuss, before anyone else could turn and notice the strange girl with the sack of scraps and the wide, frightened eyes, Tes turned and fled, back to the four walls and the cluttered shelves and the safety of her shop.

II

Rhy Maresh cast off his crown.

The heavy gold circlet landed on top of his clothes, which he had left piled on the floor nearby, along with his shoes and his cloak, a messy heap of finery at the edge of the baths.

That is what it looks like, thought Rhy, *when the king sheds his skin.*

One of the servants would have surely rushed forward, stripped the clothes right off his body, and hung them neatly on the wall—as if it were a sin for a king's garments to touch the tiled floor, let alone be left to wrinkle there—but Rhy had banished both servants from the royal bath and the guards from the hall beyond, claiming that, as king, he wanted only to be left alone.

"But Your Majesty," protested the servants.

"*Mas res,*" urged the guards.

"Master Emery warned us . . ." began both, and at that point, Rhy had scowled, hardening his gold eyes, and snapped that last time he checked,

Master Emery had never been crowned king. He used his father's tone when he said it—seven years and it still felt like a borrowed voice, an air put on instead of owned—and rose to his full height the way his mother did when she wanted to command a room, but part of him had still been surprised when the guards and servants both apologized. When they obeyed.

Rhy sighed, and lowered himself into the steaming water.

The bath was the size of a grotto, forged in tile and gold instead of damp rock. Light shimmered on every surface, making the room feel like the inside of a gemstone. He ran a hand through his black hair and sagged back against the sunken wall, savoring the heat. His shoulder still ached, a dull throb along his collarbone from whatever Kell had done the night before. Or rather, whatever had been done *to* him. It had been a fairly shallow cut, he could tell; not by the amount of blood—his phantom wounds shed none—but by the way the pain had skated over his collarbone, instead of ringing through it. Still, he wondered about the circumstance, as he always did, when his brother's suffering became his own.

Rhy's hand dropped to his chest. He didn't have to look down, didn't have to see the scar on his dark skin, the elaborate tracery of spellwork that circled his heart. He had long memorized the whorls, the same pattern branded into Kell's pale skin.

Alucard hated to see Rhy hurt, but the truth was, he welcomed his brother's pain. He would have taken it entirely, if he could, stripped it away from Kell, and held it all himself, but that wasn't how the spell worked. Kell had dragged Rhy out of death, used his own life to keep him there, and now all he could do was share the burden of that living. If Kell died, so would he. Until then, they were bound—whatever harm came to one, the other felt as well.

But the bond, it turned out, only went so far. These days, he knew, Kell's pain ran deeper, a taproot to a source Rhy couldn't—had never been able to—reach. So he welcomed the dull ache in his shoulder as he sank deeper into the bath. Perhaps, he thought, the water would ease his brother's limbs as well. But even as he thought it, he knew better. It was a strange thing, their connection, and pleasure never seemed to carry half as well as pain.

Tendrils of steam rose off the water, and Rhy held out a ringed hand and watched the pale curls bend around his fingers. When he was young, he'd pretended it was magic, would squint at the steam and try to guide it into patterns. But the air never so much as stirred.

He flexed his hand, and the three rings caught the light.

The first was red, its surface stamped with the chalice and sun, and tethered him to Kell. The second, gold and marked with a crown and heart, belonged to Alucard. The third, marble white, embossed with a tree, bound him to the *Aven Essen,* the high priest assigned to comfort and advise the throne.

He'd worn a fourth ring, once, a lovely silver band, whose twin belonged to the queen, but Nadiya had taken it back, claiming he used the thing too often, and without proper respect for her work.

His wife, the inventor. He wasn't threatened by Nadiya's genius—on the contrary, he'd long accepted his lot in life as the handsome ruler, rather than the brilliant one. Of course, the queen was lovely, too, but with any luck, Rhy would age well, and she would not, and then his place would be secured. He had told her as much, before their wedding, savoring the way her left brow quirked.

"Oh, don't worry," she'd said, "I plan to be a hag."

Rhy smiled at the memory, and let his hand sink below the water as he tipped his head back against the tiled rim of the bath. He let his mind wander, thoughts drifting past the merchant guild he'd seen that afternoon, and the head of the city guard with her list of offenses and offenders, and the missives from Faro, explaining why they were forgoing their visit, and the plans for *Sel Fera Noche.*

The *Long Dark Night.*

It was the city's most important festival, the one that marked the passing of the coldest season, but also the years since the gates between the worlds were sealed, making it a celebration of the Maresh as well. It was, after all, the first Maresh king who saw the strange magic spilling from Black London, and used the *Antari*'s collective power to drive the cursed magic back, sealing the worlds off from the dark, and from each other, leaving Black London to consume itself behind its walls like a fire in a room with no windows, left to burn and then to die away to ash and nothing.

It had not died, of course. A fire needs only an ember to regain its heat, and embers had indeed survived. Embers like Vitari, a sliver of magic pressed into a stone. And Osaron, which was not an ember at all but the spark that started it all, waiting in Black London for a single breath to come and coax it back to life. Osaron, which had indeed burned again, hot enough to raze the world, and nearly had, before Kell and Lila and Holland had conquered it.

Not that the public knew. As far as they were concerned, Black London remained safely bound behind its wall and *Sel Fera Noche* was nothing but a time to celebrate. And with the three-hundred-year anniversary, the celebration would be even bigger. The entire city would be draped in red and gold, the chalice and sun of the royal seal, and in the streets and in the palace halls, all would toast to the Maresh.

And Alucard wanted to *cancel* it—not that Rhy could, not that he *would*—all because of the Hand.

The Hand, who claimed that magic was failing.

The Hand, who claimed that it was his fault.

Rhy Maresh, the king without magic. Poisoning the well.

Anger tightened around his ribs. Anger—and the fear that they were right.

Alucard claimed there was no truth to their words. Nadiya said there was no proof to be found. But the disquiet was only growing louder. They had to be stopped.

To do that, they had to be *caught*.

So Rhy spread his arms, and closed his eyes, and waited, until his thoughts finally quieted, and his mind floated away.

Seven years ago

R hy couldn't sleep, so he'd decided to get drunk instead.

It took some effort—his tolerance built over years of drinking Kell under the table—but he approached the task with dedication. He could picture his brother's disapproving scowl, and it brought him a brief flicker of joy, dulled by the knowledge that Kell would start to feel unsteady, too, and that they would both suffer for it in the morning.

"Sorry," Rhy murmured to his brother's door as he went by. His hand drifted out, as if to knock, before he remembered Kell wasn't actually there. Hadn't been in weeks. No, he was off, sailing to saints knew where with Lila Bard. Shedding his old life and savoring his newfound freedom, as Rhy sank beneath the weight of his father's crown.

Rhy took a long swig, to punish him for leaving.

He passed a gilded mirror and paused.

What a picture he made.

The new ruler of Arnes, barefoot and shirtless beneath his robe, his gold eyes glassy, his hair a mess of curls beneath the mourning crown. A starburst scar over his heart and a bottle of winter wine hanging from one hand.

He managed a weary smile, lifting his drink to the figure in the glass. At least he was still handsome.

His gaze dropped to the bottle. Summer wines were sweet and light, meant for sun-warmed days. But winter wines were bold and dark, spiced, and strong enough to stave off cold. They were usually kept in the cellars until the first night of the fall festival, which wasn't for another month. He pulled the cork from the bottle with his teeth. A perk of being king.

King.

The word hung like an ill-fitting shirt. Rhy knew how to be a *prince,* a *rogue,* a *brother,* a *son.* He had no idea how to be a *king.*

The guards stood still as statues as he passed, their gazes down, and he knew they only meant to grant him privacy, to let him grieve, and yet, their averted eyes made him feel like a specter. A ghost haunting the palace. Arnesians didn't believe in ghosts, but Veskans did. Faroans, too. They spoke of restless spirits who haunted the ground where they fell, or lingered in the shadow of the living. He found himself wondering about the other worlds as well. In Lila's city, they seemed obsessed with the idea of being haunted, devoted whole novels to the idea, even tried to summon the dead back into the room, as if they stood forever

145

waiting, just beyond the door. He wondered whether Holland's ghost was out there, too, walking its London, or finally at peace. And his own parents? Were they the weight he felt on his shoulders? Were they trailing in his wake?

He kept moving, past the royal chambers he couldn't bring himself to look at, let alone open, down the carpeted stairs. It was so quiet, so hollow. He felt the sudden urge to scream.

Beyond the palace windows, the Isle glowed its steady red, but the banks were studded with yellow-white flames.

In the weeks since Osaron's assault on the city, the pyres still burned day and night, returning bodies to the air and the earth, their life force to the current. Thousands dead. Souls who fought the darkness, and lost to it, their lives burned out like oil. Hundreds left scarred, veins scorched silver from having fought the poison in their blood. And countless more who survived the night *unscathed,* not because they were deserving, but because they chose not to fight at all. Untold masses who felt the darkness at their door and simply let it in.

"Do not hate them for living," Alucard had said.

But Rhy did. Because in the end, they were cowards and they were rewarded for it. They were weak in the face of evil, and they *lived.*

They survived while Maxim Maresh had not. Emira Maresh had not.

His family was dead, their home was a tomb, and Rhy was buried alive inside it while Alucard, who had just lost his sister, was out there with half the royal guard helping with the repairs, putting their magic to good use. And Rhy knew he should be with them. Useless as he was, he should be with them.

"You are the sun of Arnes," Alucard had said, kissing his forehead. "There is a time to rise, and a time to rest."

But Alucard was wrong. Rhy couldn't rest. He couldn't—

"My king," said a voice behind him, and he cringed at the title, as if cut, turned to find a young servant, his head bowed. "Is there anything I can get you?"

He let his head fall back, staring up at the vaulted ceilings of his tomb.

"My horse."

So what if he had no magic. Rhy Maresh was now king. He would ride through the streets as he had that horrible night, and let the people of the city know that he was with them.

Worry clouded the servant's face. "Your Majes—" he began, but Rhy's gold eyes narrowed.

"Ready my horse," he ordered, trying to summon a ghost of his father's strength.

"Sir," said the servant. "I have been told it is not safe."

And Rhy let out a mirthless laugh. "I promise you, there is no one less in danger."

The servant hesitated, then bowed deeper and withdrew. Rhy closed his eyes, felt himself sway. He kept walking, legs carrying him across the palace to the throne room.

He had spent most of the day here, in the Rose Hall, listening to a constant stream of citizens and supplicants, layering their suffering on top of his own, but now the massive room lay silent and empty. The bolts of red and gold between the pillars hung still. He made his way up the chamber, the marble cold beneath his bare feet.

He reached the base of the dais and stared up at the twin thrones. One of them was draped in black, the sigil of sun and chalice stitched in gold. Two crowns sat together on the shrouded seat. When it was time, they would be fused and melted, reforged into a new crown. It would sit twice as heavy on his head.

Rhy climbed the stone steps and sank onto the empty throne. He brought his hand to rest on the arm of the chair, felt the slight grooves made by Maxim Maresh's palm. Rhy wasn't a small man, by any measure, but his father had been a giant. Or at least, he'd always seemed that way, to his son.

The bottle slipped from Rhy's fingers. It hit the ground but did not break, only rolled impotently across the floor, leaving a trail of dark wine like drops of blood on the pale marble. Rhy stared at it until his vision swam with tears.

He heard the sigh of the throne room doors, and looked up, expecting to find the servant.

Instead, he saw the *Aven Essen*.

147

Tieren Serense, head priest of the London Sanctuary, advisor first to Nokil Maresh, and then to his son Maxim. And now, to Rhy, the only Maresh left.

"You're not my horse," he said dryly.

"No," answered the priest. "I'm not."

Tieren made his way up the hall, his white robes whispering over the marble.

There was no need to ask who had sent for him. "How did you get here so fast?"

"I have a room in the eastern wing."

"Is that allowed?"

Tieren raised a white brow. "We do not cease to be priests if we sleep outside the Sanctuary walls."

"Well," said Rhy, "I hope the room is sufficiently sparse. I wouldn't want to offend your modest sensibilities."

"Oh yes," assured Tieren. "Hardly any gold at all."

The *Aven Essen* stopped at the foot of the dais. He looked old, but then again, Rhy couldn't remember a time when the priest had not. Wrinkles ran like deep cracks across Tieren's face, but his back was still straight, his blue eyes bright.

"Master Rhy," he said gently, "how long has it been since you slept?"

"I no longer care for sleep," answered Rhy. "When I sleep—" He swallowed, his throat suddenly tight. He pressed on. "When I sleep, I dream."

He did not go on, did not say that most nights he woke screaming. That the first few times, the guards came rushing in, blades drawn, sure that he had been attacked. But that it happened so often now that they knew better, simply held their ground, and looked away, and somehow that was worse.

Rhy did not say any of those things. Instead, he folded forward, running his hands up his face, raking his fingers through his hair. They snagged on the mourning crown and he tore it off, flung the cursed thing away, the sound of it ringing as it struck the marble. Bounced. Rolled. Fetched up against a pillar.

He slouched back into the throne, let his gaze escape to the ceiling far above. "You know," he mused, "if the king and queen had been allowed to have a second heir, then we could have fought over the crown. I could have lost, and lived my days out as a vain, indulgent prince." Rhy closed his eyes. "Instead, I am alone."

Tieren's voice, when he spoke, was closer. "You will never be alone."

Rhy forced his attention down, and found the priest at his shoulder. He rubbed his eyes. When he spoke, the words came out a whisper. "I don't know how to rule."

The old man simply shrugged. "No one ever does." He looked out at the throne room. "Your mother, Emira, came to the palace when she was twenty-three. She was the second daughter of a noble house, with no real desire to be queen. Maxim had been banished to the Blood Coast for being a reckless youth. He returned a soldier prince and hero, and yet, when it came time for him to rule, your father sat exactly as you do now, on this very throne, and said to me, 'I know how to lead men to war. How can I lead them to peace?' No one is born knowing how to lead."

Rhy felt small and scared. "How do they do it, then?"

"They learn. They err. They try again. They fail. The worst rulers see their country as a game of Rasch, the men and women only pieces on their board. But you—" His hand came to rest on Rhy's shoulder. "—you will love them. You will bleed with them. You will hurt with them. A piece of you will die with them. The rest of you will live. I do not know if you will be a great king, Rhy Maresh. Only time will tell. But I believe with all my heart that you will be a good one."

Tieren's hand fell away.

"We all don clothes that do not fit, and hope we will grow into them. Or at least, grow used to them."

Rhy studied the *Aven Essen*. "Even you?"

Tieren surprised him with a smile. "Believe it or not, I wasn't *born* a priest."

He paused, seemed about to say more, when the throne room doors came crashing open. They both turned as Alucard Emery strode across the hall, his boots muddy and his shoulders damp. Something in Rhy loosened at the sight of him. The fingers of gold in his brown hair, the tracery of silver on his skin.

"My king," he said cheerfully, and in his mouth, the word felt less like a hammer, and more like a kiss. If Alucard read the meaning of Tieren's presence at this hour, or saw the strain in Rhy's face, he made no mention of it, simply swept up the mourning circlet as he approached the dais.

"My heart," answered Rhy, rising to his feet. His limbs felt leaden. His body longed for sleep. His pulse thrummed in fear of it, but then Alucard was there, one hand on his arm to steady him. Rhy leaned into the weight.

"Tell me," said Alucard, "is it too late to request an audience?" His blue eyes danced with mischief. "I have favors to ask of the crown."

Rhy managed the ghost of a smile. The grief lifted, like a curtain.

He turned to tell Tieren he could retire, but there was no need.

The priest was already gone.

III

Now

Steel rang against steel on the palace grounds.

Alucard leaned his elbows on the courtyard wall and watched as two dozen new recruits squared off below, swords ringing as they moved through the motions of combat. As if combat could be reduced to rules, refined to order. Someone dropped their sword. Someone made a sloppy swing, and their opponent swore.

He groaned inwardly. "Where did you find this batch?"

Isra stood beside him, her arms crossed, her short silver hair glinting in the late-day sun. She had served with Maxim Maresh at Verose, had returned to be the captain of his guard, and now, of Rhy's. "It wasn't the bottom of the barrel," she said, "but it was close."

She didn't have to say what Alucard already knew. For years, Arnesians had clamored to join the royal guard. But ever since Rhy Maresh had taken the throne, the numbers had begun to dwindle. The Hand's rumors didn't help.

"Well," mused Alucard. "If anyone can do it, you can."

He meant it, but Isra only rolled her eyes. "Flattery will get you nowhere. As for this lot—"

As if on cue, a fight broke out below. A shoving match that quickly escalated, threatened to tumble from disorder into revolt until Isra stepped to the wall and spoke, voice booming over the training ground, amplified by the wind magic that traced the air over her skin. *"Tarso!"*

Order.

One word, strong enough to rattle their armor, and recover their attention. Isra had that effect on people. As she descended the steps to the training ground, Alucard followed in her wake. The recruits fell into lines, or something like them, as Isra and Alucard passed through.

He felt the eyes on him, taking in his fine clothes, the fact that he was dressed in Rhy's colors, not his own. He knew what they called him.

Res in Rast.

King's Heart.

Alucard ran his thumb absently over his gold ring. It was a habit, feeling the heart and crown pressed into the face.

Of course, it was not the *only* name people used. There was *Res in Fera—King's Shadow—*and *Res in Stol—King's Blade.*

And then, there was *Sitaro.*

Consort.

If they had been common lovers, he and Rhy, few people would have cared. If Alucard had not been born to a rival royal house. If his arrival had not coincided with the *Antari*'s absence (as if it was his fault Kell had chosen to leave). If Alucard had been content to lie in the king's bed, without also insisting on a place at his side.

Sitaro was not a bad word, in and of itself—the trouble was the way it could be wielded. Words had two kinds of power—the first in their meaning, the second in how they were said. *Sitaro* was a title, and could be said with reverence, or at least respect. But it could also be spat, or cut down—drop the final note and turn *sitaro* into *sita*, *consort* into *whore.*

They all knew better than to say it in his earshot, but sometimes a thing didn't need to be said to be heard, loud and clear, in someone's posture, their expression, their gaze.

They forgot, that he was not just the king's consort, and a royal in his own right, but also a *triad*. If anyone else could have seen the magic twining

151

around Alucard now, they'd count not one strand, or even two, but three. Earth. Wind. Water.

Alucard Emery may not be an *Antari,* but he was still one of the strongest magicians in the world.

And he was happy to remind them.

He raised his voice. "These sparring drills are good enough for stamina," he said, "but they are no substitute for practical experience. Which is why it's important to spar as well. You never know who you'll be up against. You'll never know what they can do."

He let his gaze drift over the recruits, noting the magic on the air around them. Few knew about Alucard's peculiar sight, and he preferred to keep it that way. But it came in handy, when sizing up opponents. The soldiers gathered here were earth and water mostly, one or two wind, a handful of fire. No sight of bone, with its strange violet light, but that was hardly a surprise. The talent wasn't just rare, but *forbidden.* It went against the rules of magic and the laws of nature to control another body, and when a child did show an early affinity, they were quickly dissuaded from pursuing it. If they were smart, they listened. If they weren't—well, there were spells to sever a body from its magic.

"*Tac,*" said Alucard, spreading his hands. "Who wants to spar with *me?*"

Murmurs ran through the recruits. Alucard smiled. He raised the offer at least once a week, and in truth, it was for him as much as them. He missed the tournaments and the life at sea, the hundred ways to keep his magic keen. He held back, of course. He always held back. But now and then, for a moment at least, he found what he was looking for, the pulse-quickening thrill.

Some stepped forward, eager for the challenge. Others fell back, happy to watch. Alucard shrugged off his coat and tossed it onto a nearby post, unfastened his cuffs, rolled up his sleeves, and considered the options. He was no longer looking at their powers. He was studying their faces, searching for the shadows, the darkness, the disdain.

He found it quickly, on the face of a young man, his black hair swept back off his face.

"You," he said. "What's your name?"

The recruit straightened. "Yarosev."

"Yarosev," snapped Isra. "Is that how you address a member of the royal family?"

And there it was. His lips tightened in a sneer. His fire magic danced red on the air around his shoulders. "My name is Yarosev, *Your Highness*."

Alucard smiled. "Well, Yarosev," he said, drawing a blade. "Whenever you're—"

The recruit was fast, he had to give him that.

Yarosev drew his own sword, and at the same time, his hand shot out, his lips already forming the words he'd need to call forth magic. But words needed air.

Alucard's free hand vised shut, trapping the air in the soldier's chest.

Yarosev gasped, or tried, his mouth flapping like a fish flung onto land, as Alucard surged forward, blade slicing toward his chest.

His eyes widened as he lunged back, knocking the steel away. Alucard struck again, and again, none of the blows meant to land, let alone wound. No, he was taking his time, watching as the young soldier's face turned red, then purple, then blue. Yarosev stumbled, fell, was on the ground now, but didn't quit. He kept his sword up, the point shaking with the effort. The anger in his eyes had changed, twisted into a different kind of fire. He had fight in him. Alucard would give him that.

He flicked his free hand, let go of the air in Yarosev's lungs. The recruit gasped, and heaved. His sword hand fell.

Alucard sheathed his own weapon, and held out his hand to help the young recruit up, but Yarosev fisted a handful of dirt and flung it up into Alucard's face, in a last, desperate attempt to gain an upper hand. It might have worked, if Alucard hadn't seen it coming. It might have worked, if he were a lesser magician. But he wasn't. Alucard flicked his fingers, and the dirt stopped, and hung suspended, inches from where it left Yarosev's fist.

The recruit slumped onto his back, gasping for breath. He rapped the ground with his knuckles, signaling surrender.

Alucard let the dirt rain back to the ground and then leaned over and held out his hand again.

This time, Yarosev took it.

"Well done, soldier," he said, hauling the recruit to his feet.

"I lost," he muttered. As if that was all that mattered. As if, in all the years Alucard had been sparring with his soldiers, any of them had ever *won*.

He thumped Yarosev on the back, sending up plumes of dirt. "You kept fighting. Even when you were down."

Isra stood watching from beyond the circle. Their eyes met as Yarosev returned to the other recruits. She nodded. Alucard dusted off his palms. It had been a nice way to warm up.

He turned back to the gathered soldiers. Spread his hands again, gave a little flourish.

"All right," he said. "Who's next?"

When Alucard left the training ground an hour later, his shirt was singed, his trousers streaked with dirt, his hair coming loose from its braid. And yet, climbing the steps back into the courtyard, he felt better than he had in weeks. Now all he needed was a good strong drink and a hot bath, both of which the palace would afford.

There were several ways into the *soner rast*. He had learned half of them when he was a young noble, courting Rhy in secret, and the rest since joining the royal house. There was the main entrance on the southern bank, with its pale stone steps and grand gold doors; and the northern gates, accessed from the courtyard where the soldiers trained. Then there were the secret doorways built into the bridge's base; a balcony two stories up, reached only by the royal orchard; and a variety of bolder climbs one could take, back before the place was warded to the teeth. Alucard remembered one perilous night when he climbed the northern façade in moonlight, and nearly plummeted into the Isle.

These days, there was no such need for secrecy.

As Alucard approached the northern gates, the guards sank into low bows, their armor gleaming and their gazes down, red capes pooling like blood beneath them on the stone. He pressed his hand flat against the doors, letting the spell carved in the gilded surface read the memory of his touch. A lock turned somewhere inside the wood, and it swung open, welcoming him home.

The sun had dropped low, and with it, the palace had slipped into its evening rhythms, softer, quieter than it was during the day, when servants bustled and voices rang, and every room played host to something.

Alucard rolled his neck as he climbed the stairs to the royal wing, slowing when he reached the top of the steps and saw a *rabbit*.

It sat, nose twitching as it nibbled on the edge of a rug.

Alucard stared down at the animal. The animal stared up at him. This continued until he heard the swift padding of bare feet, and the rabbit bounced away as a small girl rounded the corner.

"Luca!" she shouted before flinging herself into Alucard's arms.

Tieren Maresh, who went by Ren, was barefoot, and half-dressed, her tunic unbuttoned and her black curls mussed.

Alucard set the child down, attempting to straighten her nightclothes. "Now, what did we say about letting animals roam?"

"But I can't keep him trapped in my rooms," said Ren, horrified. "Cages are for things you own, and the *Aven Essen* says you cannot *own* a living thing. . . ."

Exactly, thought Alucard, as the rabbit hopped out of reach and began to munch unmolested on the tassels of a cushion. It was not generally custom in Arnes to keep animals as pets, for just that reason. Hawks and crows and other such birds were meant to fly without restraint. Bears and big cats to roam wild as any other creature, hunting as nature allowed. There were exceptions—foundling kittens or pups, the occasional injured beast, and the horses they rode or used in work; even those were treated with as much reverence as possible. But in general, to collar a beast and put it in a cage ran counter to the cardinal rule of Arnesian magic: to never bind a mind or body, to never control a living thing. It was a reverence that set them apart from the other Londons, allowed their magic to thrive where theirs wasted, or withdrew.

But Ren's love of animals seemed to circumvent the laws of nature, and led to a host of unusual royal companions.

Rhy liked to remind Alucard that it was his fault.

155

After all, it had begun with Esa, the pampered cat who'd stalked the decks of the *Spire* alongside him. He might have left her to spend her remaining years at sea, too, but Lila Bard refused to keep the beast aboard the *Spire* when she took it over, citing a mutual distaste. Alucard suspected they were just too similar in nature, but regardless, Esa had come to live at the palace, left to wander as she pleased. And when Ren was born, the cat had feigned disinterest, but those amethyst eyes were always watching, and wherever the child toddled, the cat was somehow there.

Next had come the owl, when Ren was two. A massive snow-white bird that had landed on the balcony outside her rooms. She had coaxed the thing inside, and by the time a servant noticed the massive owl perched on a chair, and tried to set it free, the bird had refused to leave. For a year it had stayed there, in the princess's rooms, fed on whatever she managed to pocket at dinner, and when at last one spring, it flew away, Ren had let it go.

"It will come back," she'd said, with a child's confidence.

And to everyone's surprise but hers, it had. Things simply chose Ren's company. Even at four, she had a steady nature that put living things at ease, and while some at the palace had been wary of the princess's steadily growing menagerie, Rhy was charmed, and Alucard was certain that the animals in the palace lived better lives than most of the city's nobles, and did even less work to earn their keep.

Ren poked his cheek with her finger. "Luca."

"Yes?"

"Did you bring me a gift?"

Alucard sighed. He had made the terrible mistake of going on a trip the year before and returning with a small carved ship that sang whenever it was put on water. Now, every time he so much as returned from a walk, the princess expected some reward.

He was still searching his pockets for an offering when the child's nurse, Sasha, rounded the corner, a robe slung over her arm, a pair of slippers in one hand, and a golden circlet in the other. Without missing a step, she scooped up the rabbit as if it were another fallen toy.

Sasha was old enough to be a mother twice, but she moved with the sturdiness of a soldier. Her silver hair was up, but so much had escaped its braided crown that it formed a storm cloud around her head, marked by tiny streaks of lightning.

"There you are," she said matter-of-factly. "The water's getting cold."

Ren cast a forlorn look back at Alucard. "I wanted to take a bath with *Father*," she said, shoulders slumping. "But he said he wanted to be alone."

Alucard knelt face-to-face with the young royal. He met Ren's eyes, and wondered when the girl had grown so tall, when he'd stopped needing to look down.

"You don't want to share a bath with your father," he said. "He takes up too much space, and hoards *all* the bubbles."

"But the bubbles are my favorite part!" said Ren, aghast.

"I know!" said Alucard. "But when you take a bath with someone else, you have to share."

Ren looked to Sasha then, for confirmation. She nodded soberly. The princess chewed her lip, as if considering. And then she cleared his throat. "Tonight," she said with all the diplomacy a four-year-old could muster, "I will take my bath alone." She held out her hand, and Sasha took it.

"Very well, *mas vares*," she said, leading Ren away.

Alucard watched them go, and then turned, and went to find Rhy, certain that *he* could convince the king to share his bubbles.

IV

Rhy sighed and sank deeper in the bath.

He lay perfectly still, until his thoughts emptied, until the surface of the water turned to glass, until the only sounds were the quiet rush of his breath, the faint rustle of fabric.

And the whisper of steel.

The king's eyes shot open as the blade came down.

He twisted out of the way of the assassin's thrust just in time, the sword grazing his cheek instead of burying itself in his throat. The metal rang against the tile as he surged around and under, grabbing the attacker's arm and hauling him into the bath—where Rhy had hidden his knife beneath the tiled lip.

157

His hand closed around the hilt, the metal hot against his palm as he turned to face his attacker. The other man was on his feet again, the water sloshing around his chest.

He was young. Younger than Rhy. He didn't look like a murderer, or a rebel, or a rogue. He looked like a member of the palace staff, which was exactly what he was. Rhy recognized him, behind the red that ran in ribbons down the young man's face. At first glance it looked like blood, but Rhy knew it was paint, had glimpsed the handprint pressed against his brow and cheeks the instant before the man's blade came singing down.

Rhy touched his own face, and his fingers came away red. *That* was blood. He clicked his tongue.

"It is a crime," he said, "to wound a king." Not that it would last. He could feel his skin already knitting. His body, held together by Kell's magic.

For so long it had haunted him, the way he healed, made him wonder if he was still a person, or just the illusion of one. But here and now, he was grateful.

"The Hand gives and the Hand takes," recited the man, stalking toward him through the water.

"Oh, now you have a speech," muttered Rhy.

"The Hand builds and the Hand tears down."

He slashed out with his sword, and Rhy's blade came up to block the blow.

"I've always wondered . . ." mused the king. "Does that make you a finger? A knuckle? A hangnail?"

"The Hand holds the blade," growled the man, "that carves the path of change."

He surged forward as he said it. Rhy moved to block the blow, but this time something held his sword. He glanced down and saw the tip shivering where it was pinned on the water's surface, stilled by the attacker's magic.

Fuck, thought Rhy, right before the force wrenched the weapon from his grip. It vanished, sucked down beneath the surface, and then the attacker was there, his blade driving straight through Rhy's chest.

He let out a ragged gasp as the sword scraped his ribs, drove up and through, the tip coming out between his shoulder and his spine.

The pain was a rod of searing heat.

All this time, and he still hadn't gotten used to dying.

It stole his breath as blood dripped into the water, blooming like roses around them. His body betrayed him, sagging into the attacker's arms.

"This is the end of the Maresh," said the Hand.

Rhy laughed, blood spilling through gritted teeth. "Haven't you heard?" he said softly, dragging himself upright. "I'm the Unkillable King."

The other man's eyes widened in shock, then horror, as Rhy took a step back, and then another, drawing his body off the blade. It hurt—*saints,* it hurt—but it wouldn't be the end of him. Blood was pooling in one lung, but Rhy drew in a shaky breath, and then another, as the wound between his ribs begins to heal.

The attacker scrambled backward, slashing blindly with his sword as he tried to reach the other side of the bath. Rhy waded toward him, the pain receding in his chest, dulling into something he could stand.

The attacker dropped his sword, the blade disappearing into the bloody water as he raised his hands in surrender. Or at least, that's what Rhy assumed he was doing. Until the man's lips began to move.

The sound that came out had the whisper of magic, and as he spoke, something wrapped around Rhy's legs, and pulled, forcing him down, beneath the surface. He thrashed, but the reddened water twisted around him like rope, holding him against the bottom of the pool. Beyond the roiling surface, he could just make out the assassin, fingers splayed as he held the magic, and the magic held him, the way it had his sword.

And Rhy realized, as his lungs burned and his vision blurred, that he was going to drown.

Kell was eating dinner when he began to die.

Lila was leaning against the galley counter, peeling an apple, and he'd just taken a mouthful of Raya's latest stew when the pain erupted in his chest. The spoon fell from his fingers and he bowed his head, clutching the table as a white-hot blade drove between his ribs.

"Oh, come on," said Lila, "I know it's not her best, but—Kell?"

He sucked in a breath, and tasted the ghost of blood. Lila jabbed the paring knife into the fruit and set it down, starting toward him. He felt the phantom scrape of the blade dragging free, clutched at his chest even though he knew the wound wasn't there. Wasn't his.

Rhy.

The pain began to ebb from a sharp and violent thing into a vicious ache, and Kell drew in a ragged breath, and straightened, thinking the worst of it was over. He pulled the red ring from his finger, was about to utter the spell that connected the band to his brother's.

But when he opened his mouth, nothing came out.

He tried again, but his lungs tightened, unwilling to part with their air. He couldn't breathe. A visceral panic seized him, coiled around his limbs. His head began to swim, and a terrible pressure formed in his chest as something changed, the terrible sensation that his lungs were filling up with water. He made it out of the galley and into the narrow hall before he swayed, and retched, half expecting the water to spill onto the wooden floor.

Nothing came up, but his lungs vised again under the strain. He tried to stand, but his body buckled, his brother's ring falling from his fingers. His vision blurred, and then he was on his back, and Lila was kneeling over him, her face dark with worry, her mouth moving, but her voice was drowned by the pounding in his ears.

And the encroaching wall of black.

Rhy remembered wondering if they should ward the royal baths.

But magic kept the water hot, and it seemed like such a nuisance, such a waste of time and energy, so he'd opted to leave the room unwarded, and now here he was, pinned to the bottom of the bath by someone else's power.

Something glinted on the floor nearby. The sword he'd lost. Rhy strained, trying to reach toward it, but the water only tightened, squeezing the last of the air from his chest.

His lungs burned.

His vision began to blur.

Above, the surface of the water smoothed into a pane of tinted glass. Beyond it, the man's face contorted into a feral grin.

And then, suddenly, it changed. The amusement sloughed away, leaving only a slack horror. A few fresh drops of blood dripped and bloomed on the surface before Rhy's failing sight, and then the man tipped forward, falling facedown into the bath. As he did, the hold on Rhy's limbs disappeared, and he surged up out of the water, gasping for air.

He looked down at the body now floating beside him, saw the knife buried in his back, and then looked up to find Alucard Emery, who stood at the edge of the bath, wearing nothing but an open robe.

"What in the absolute fuck," said the king's shadow, the king's heart, blazing with anger. Rhy only sighed, and waded to the edge of the bath, and climbed out.

Alucard marched over to the pile of clothes and flung him his robe.

"Where were your servants?" he snapped as Rhy pulled the fabric around his shoulders. Blood still wept from the wound in his chest, but it was already healing.

"I wanted to be alone," said Rhy, sinking onto a bench at the edge of the room.

"And the guards?" demanded Alucard. "Why the saints would you banish *them*?"

He said nothing, only met Alucard's gaze. Alucard, the one person who never looked away just because he was king, who had always been able to read him like a book.

"Dammit, Rhy—"

"I didn't want them to get hurt."

"That's what they're *for*!" roared Alucard.

Rhy shot him a dark look, and gestured down at the weeping cut between his ribs, the one that would have killed any other man. "I will not have them die when I cannot."

Alucard let out an exhausted breath. It was an argument they'd had a dozen times over the last few years. He looked down at the body in the water, and frowned. "He looks familiar."

"He is. I hired him last week."

Alucard threw up his hands. "Of course you did. Never mind the protocols. You know, the ones put in place for the sole purpose of keeping this family safe."

As if that wasn't exactly what Rhy was trying to do. He looked at the killer's body and sighed. The whole idea had been to take the Hand alive, for questioning. He drew a deep breath, and winced. He spit a mouthful of blood onto the tile. He was beginning to think his night couldn't get much worse. Then, one of the rings on his right hand began to glow. The red one. Of course.

"Damn," muttered Rhy.

"Oh, you thought he wouldn't notice?" chided Alucard.

The king stared at the ring for a long moment, watching it grow brighter, until the light of the magic filled the room, casting the killer's body and the bloody bath in grim relief.

"Go on," insisted Alucard with troubling glee. "I can't wait to see Kell's face."

Rhy didn't need to see it. He could picture the expression well enough. He was still looking at the ring, wondering if he really had to answer, when Alucard walked up, snatched the red band off his finger, and stormed out into the hall.

One minute Kell had felt like he was drowning, and the next, the grip on his lungs was gone, the air flooding back into his chest. By the time he was on his feet, Lila was holding out the crimson ring. Kell grabbed it, and stormed past her.

There was only one scrying table aboard the *Barron,* a polished black basin in the captain's quarters.

"*As vera tan,*" he said, activating the spell as he surged into Lila's room.

The scrying table sat in the corner. Lila had clearly been using it as a hamper, several articles of clothing piled on top. He swept them all away and pressed the ring to the black stone table, and waited. For several agonizing moments, no answer came. Kell saw only his own mottled reflection, face pale, eyes wide in pain and worry and anger, in the darkened surface.

Then the black pane flickered and was replaced by a face Kell knew, and loathed.

Alucard Emery stood in the palace war room, wearing nothing but an open velvet robe, and Kell was very glad the image ended at the table.

"Where is he?" he demanded, and for once, the royal consort wasn't oozing his usual self-pleasure. He looked exasperated. Annoyed.

"Oh, your brother? I left him with the body of the assassin he invited into the bath."

Kell stared at Alucard in horror. "What do you mean, *invited*?"

"Apparently, His Royal Highness was eager to catch a Hand, and decided to use himself as bait." His blue eyes flicked past Kell. "Hello, Bard. How's my ship?"

Lila had appeared just behind him. "Still in one piece. And the crew wants you to know they like me better."

Alucard's mouth twitched in a smile, but Kell's ears were still ringing. He dug his fingers into the edge of the table. "How could you let this happen?"

The amusement flickered and died on the consort's face. "Me?"

"You have one job."

Alucard leaned forward. "Believe it or not, I have *many*. We can't all be off playing pirate. Tell me, do you still dress up? I heard you even have a fancy name."

"Oh, stop flirting," said Rhy, drifting into the frame. His robe was drawn tight, hiding the damage, but red water dripped from his black hair, staining the collar.

And Kell wanted to throttle his brother for being reckless, wanted to point out that while Rhy would not die as long as he lived, Kell did indeed require air to do that, and if he'd drowned for long enough, who knew what might happen to the spell that held them both together. But the apology was already written all over Rhy's face, so Kell resisted the urge to shout and asked only, "Are you all right?"

Rhy managed a smile, but it was thin. "Thanks to you, I think I'll live." He noticed Lila and rallied. "Ah, how's my favorite captain?"

Alucard shot Rhy an insulted look, then turned his ire back on Kell. "As you can see, your brother is in one piece, but I've got quite a mess to clean up here, so if you'll excuse us—"

Kell closed his eyes and took a steadying breath. "We're on our way."

"Oh no, that won't be necessary," said the consort, and before he could explain that it had nothing to do with the latest attempt on Rhy's life, Alucard Emery lifted the ring from the scrying board, and the image went dark.

"Bastard," muttered Kell, taking back his own ring. He pushed off the table and made his way back into the galley, sinking onto the bench even though his appetite was thoroughly ruined. Lila took up her apple, and returned to peeling it.

"You know," she said, "it's not a terrible idea." Kell dragged his head up. "I mean," she went on, carving a piece of apple from the core, "he does make good bait."

"He's the *king*," said Kell.

"He can't die," she shot back, jabbing the air with her knife.

"I'd rather not test the limits of that theory," he said, remembering the water in his lungs, the pressing dark. "Just because he's prone to self-destruction—"

Lila snorted. "Have you ever heard the saying about the kettle and the pot?"

Kell scowled, but she just shrugged and popped the slice of apple in her mouth.

V

A lucard drew the dropper from the vial, and watched three dark beads fall and bloom in the glass of pale wine. Behind him, Rhy sat on the edge of their bed, reading the day's reports as if he hadn't been stabbed an hour before. He wore only a pair of silk trousers, and his chest was smooth and dark, the signs of his encounter with the Hand already smoothed away like dust instead of mortal wounds.

Alucard turned from the cart, and crossed to the bed, holding out the glass.

"Drink," he said, less an offer than an order. He was still mad—mad that Rhy had not confided in him. Mad that after all this time, there were

164

moments he could not read the king's face, did not know the workings of his mind.

Rhy set his work down and took the glass, staring down into the contents. A tonic, meant to ease the body and quiet the mind.

"My nightly poisoner," he mused, setting the laced wine on the table by the bed. Alucard started to turn away, but Rhy caught his sleeve.

"Alucard." Just that name, on those lips. It had always been enough to undo him. Or at least to loosen his anger. Rhy saw it, and smiled, pulled him close, ringed fingers tangling in the sides of his robe as he dragged Alucard down into bed. He caught himself, hands sinking into the lush fabric on either side of Rhy's head.

Rhy reached up, tracing the line of his jaw.

"My heart," he said softly, gold eyes bright, and Alucard bent to kiss his king, but Rhy's nose crinkled in distaste. "You smell like the training ground."

"I planned to wash," he said, "but a king was busy drowning in the bath."

"How rude of him," teased Rhy, fingers splaying across his chest.

"Very rude," growled Alucard. "He tries my patience every day, the king."

"He sounds maddening." Rhy's hand drifted lower, tracing the muscles of Alucard's stomach. "And yet you stay. You must love him very much."

Alucard met the king's gaze. "I do." He let his weight sink onto Rhy, brought his mouth to his ear. "And he's very good in bed."

Rhy chuckled beneath him. "Is that so?" His teeth grazed Alucard's shoulder as his hand found the front of his trousers. Alucard's breath caught. He bowed his head as Rhy's hand slipped beneath the fabric.

Just then, the door burst open.

Alucard didn't stop, didn't think. By the time the light from the hall spilled in, he was on his feet, one hand flung out toward the drugged wine on the table, the contents rushing up out of the glass and hardening into an icy blade against his palm. Where were the guards? Why had there been no warning? No ringing steel? His thoughts rushed ahead. Someone had killed the palace guards. They had made it to the king's chamber.

But there was no assassin.

Only a small girl in red-and-gold pajamas, who should have been asleep.

"Saints," hissed Alucard, letting out a ragged breath. He hid the blade behind his back as the princess tumbled into the king's chamber like a prisoner who'd just escaped her cell.

There was no sign of the rabbit, but Esa padded in behind Ren and hopped onto a nearby chair, violet eyes surveying everything.

"What's this?" asked Rhy, retying his robe as their daughter climbed onto the giant bed and flung her small body down among the pillows. Alucard let go of the ice-made blade and it melted back into a ribbon of laced wine, then poured itself back into its glass.

"Ren Maresh," said Alucard, who was used to being the stern one, since Rhy refused to do it. "It's very late. You should be asleep."

"I need a story," said Ren, thrusting out her hands.

She was holding a book of Faroan myths. Tales of animals who could speak, but only tell the truth, or dream other people's dreams, or hatch new worlds from eggs. The illustrations were gilded works of art, the ink worn faintly where Ren could not help but stroke a feather or pet an ear.

"Ren," started Alucard, who was *certain* the girl had already had a story, or three, courtesy of her nurse, who was nowhere to be seen.

"Luca," pleaded Ren, employing the nickname like a well-honed spell as she patted the pillows beside her.

The youngest royal had her father's eyes—a molten gold, ringed with dark lashes—and her mother's mouth, though it smiled far more often.

"And she has nothing of me," Alucard had said one night, after too much wine.

But Rhy had placed his hands around his lover's face and said, "She has your heart."

Alucard sighed and rounded the bed, climbing in beside his daughter to study the page.

The stories in the book were all in Faroan, of course—not yet five, and Ren was already showing the king's gift for languages, an ability to slip between them as if they were rooms in the same house, with all the

166

doors flung open. If diplomacy failed, thought Alucard grimly, at least she would be able to speak to their enemies.

The book fell open to her current favorite, a story of a crow who could see the past and future, but had no way of knowing which was which.

The child curled between them, fingers tangling with Alucard's hair, and he marveled at how much he loved her. Rhy took the book and began to read, was just about to turn the page when someone cleared their throat.

Alucard looked up, expecting to see a weary Sasha trailing in the princess's wake. Instead, he found Ren's mother. The queen.

Nadiya Loreni stood in the doorway, a tiny smile tugging at the corner of her mouth. That's where her amusement always seemed to stop, balanced, as if about to spill. Despite her curves, there was little softness in the queen, not in her keen hazel eyes or the glossy black hair that she wore chopped short and tucked behind her ears, as if it were a nuisance.

The moment she appeared, Ren dove beneath the massive covers. Alucard cast a few pillows on top for good measure.

"My queen," said Rhy warmly.

"My king," she answered, drifting into the chamber. Not as if it were her own—it wasn't—but with the measured ease of a frequent guest. There had been a question, when Rhy first married. A question of where his queen would live, and sleep, whether or not the royal bed was meant to hold two, or three. But Nadiya showed no desire to share the king's chamber, aside from the task of conceiving the princess, and even that she'd approached less with passion than focused intent. A puzzle to be solved. A means to the end that they all desired.

"I must say, Rhy," mused Nadiya when she reached the bedpost, "I am relieved to see that you are well." Her voice was light, but the look in her eyes made it perfectly clear she knew what had happened in the baths. She cast a glance at Alucard, her face a mirror of his own exasperation.

"Tell me," said Rhy, with a knowing glance down at the covers, "have you, by chance, misplaced a child?"

"That depends," said Nadiya, leaning on the bedpost, "what does she look like?"

167

"This high," said Rhy, holding up a hand, "dark curls, rather adorable. Takes after her father, obviously."

"Hm," said Nadiya, "that does sound familiar. But *my* child is good, and knows how to behave."

A twitch of movement, beneath the covers.

"And *my* child is smart and knows it's time for bed."

The body wriggled, but did not emerge.

"And *my* child is brave, and wouldn't *hide* from sleep."

At that, Ren's small head popped up from the pillow. "I'm not *hiding*," she said defiantly. "I just wanted a story."

Rhy stared down at his daughter. "Where did *you* come from?" he asked in mock surprise. Ren giggled, and Alucard felt his heart twist, at the girl's joy and the love in Rhy's eyes.

"Is *this* the child you lost?" asked the king, holding Ren aloft like an offering.

The queen leaned in to study her daughter. "You know, I'm not sure."

"It's me," protested Ren, and Nadiya smiled, and reached to take her.

"Well, that's a relief," she said, swinging the girl onto her hip. Ren's head immediately began to loll, dark curls resting on her mother's shoulder. The queen kissed the top of the girl's head. "Say goodnight to your fathers." And Ren's voice was soft and small, murmuring her good nights first in High Royal and then Arnesian before Nadiya carried her from the room.

When they were gone, Rhy reached again for the glass, studying the tonic as if it were new to him, as if he did not take it every night, to keep his dreams at bay. Dreams of his mother dying in his arms. His father impaled on the palace steps. His own body tortured and torn apart, unable to die, unable to do anything but watch and suffer. Dreams from which Rhy woke screaming, and Alucard could do nothing but hold him back, hold him down, hold him close.

The tonic was a kindness, a mercy.

One Rhy seemed to think he didn't deserve.

"Rest is not a weakness," said Alucard gently. The king flashed him a wan smile, and downed the tonic in a single swallow.

The heat of earlier had melted away between them, leaving a pleasant warmth. Rhy sank back against the pillows, and Alucard flexed his fingers and summoned a small breeze, snuffing the candles and plunging the bedchamber into a darkness eased only by the Isle's red glow through the curtains. Or at least, that is how it must have looked to any other pair of eyes. To Alucard, the threads of magic still burned around their bodies. His own, the blue-green-white of a shallow surf, and Rhy's, a galaxy of silver against the dark silk sheets.

Alucard lay on his side, one arm draped across the king's stomach, and watched the rise and fall of his lover's chest, the fine tendrils that flowed in and out of his spelled heart. The threads were the moonlit shine peculiar to *Antari* magic, and yet, they did not look like Kell's or Lila's, did not move in the same steady way, tracing the lines of every limb and vein. Instead, all of them began and ended at the black sigil, the one Kell burned there with dark magic, binding their bodies, their pulse, and their pain.

Rhy glanced over and caught his stare. "What are you thinking about?"

"Your brother," said Alucard, regretting the words as soon as they were out.

Rhy raised a brow. "Should I be jealous?"

He rolled his eyes. "Go to sleep."

"I knew all that loathing was a farce."

"Be *still*," Alucard muttered, rolling onto his back.

The king chuckled, his voice trailing off as the tonic began to take effect. He sighed, and quieted, his limbs loosening as sleep dropped like a curtain. Alucard lay beside him in the dark, thumbing the gold band on his right hand. Feeling the impression of the heart and crown over and over as he rolled it around his finger. He was sure Rhy was asleep until his voice broke the quiet.

"Why do they hate me?" the king whispered.

The edges of his words were foxed, softened by the drug, but even in its grip, his mind had drifted back to the bath, the Hand.

"Many love you," said Alucard gently. "A few do not."

Rhy's eyes drifted open, gold slivers in the dark. "Am I such a terrible king?"

Alucard sighed. "All kings are terrible, to those looking for someone to blame."

Rhy's brow furrowed. Not the answer he'd expected. Alucard pressed on.

"You are the face for their ills. You are power and they have none. You have wealth and they are wanting. It is not Rhy Maresh those people hate. It is the throne itself."

A long pause, and then, "Would you wear the crown?"

Alucard laughed. Not a merry sound, but pointed, withering. "Not for all the gold in Arnes."

"It would look good on you."

"Oh, I have no doubt of *that*."

"Not as good as it looks on me, of course," murmured Rhy sleepily.

"Of course."

Rhy said nothing after that. His breathing slowed, the only motion now the pulse of silver, rising and falling with the current of his heart. Alucard lay beside him until he was sure the king was asleep.

And then, carefully, he rose, and tied his robe, and went to find the queen.

VI

Alucard considered himself a man with very few fears.

He was not afraid of death, having faced it several times. He was not afraid of pain, or darkness, spiders, or the open sea. But he maintained a healthy discomfort for the idea of being buried alive, and that was how it felt, descending into the Queen's Hall. Lamps burned on the walls, and spellwork caused their light to carry and meet, creating an unbroken ribbon of pale gold, but every downward step carried him farther from the surface. His footsteps echoed on the wide stone stairs, the sound like a whisper dropped down a well.

The palace was a dazzling spectacle, suspended on a bridge over the river Isle. But there was no magic to the feat. The bulk of its weight was held aloft by four large pillars, sunk into the river floor. Two of those pillars were solid stone, but the other two were hollow. One contained the royal prisons, cells that had once held Cora Taskon, one of the Veskan heirs who'd tried to end the Maresh line, and even once, briefly, Kell Maresh, when the old king jailed him in a fit of pique (Alucard couldn't blame him).

The other hollow pillar had been given to the queen as a wedding present.

There was a rumor, in some of the London pubs, that the queen of Arnes was in fact a prisoner, held in the sunken chamber against her will. But Nadiya Loreni was no one's prisoner, and while she did spend most of her nights entombed in the bowels of the *soner rast,* it was entirely by choice. She had been given splendid rooms in the royal wing—a luxurious bed she rarely slept in, a glittering lounge in which she never entertained—but the various servants and guards had taken to calling *this* her private chamber.

The hall bore no resemblance to the prisons in the other pillar, nor did it retain any trace of its own past, as a hidden training ground for the *Antari* prince.

Now it was a series of interconnected chambers, each as wide and open as the great halls above, and filled with just as much treasure. It was an impressive feat, all the size and grandeur of a royal estate, if that estate were windowless and housed at the bottom of the Isle.

Alucard hummed softly as he reached the bottom of the stairs, to let the queen know he was coming. She had scolded him once for sneaking up on her in the middle of a half-formed spell, warned him that if her hands had been less steady, she might have brought the entire palace down on their heads. To this day, he wasn't sure if she'd been joking.

He made a lazy circle around the chamber. She'd been busy. She was always busy.

There were a dozen surfaces, and every one of them was covered in something; the beginnings of a new device, or the remains of an old one. On one table he even saw a pistol—a weapon he'd recognized only because of Lila Bard's devotion. Its chamber was open, unloaded, but gilded spellwork was now laced along the barrel. Alucard left it, as he left everything in Nadiya's workshop, untouched.

In the next room he found her, head bowed over a table, a glass of wine at her elbow and her crown cast off, the golden circlet hanging from a nearby lamp as if it were a tunic, shed in the midst of passion. She was studying her work as if it were a Rasch board in the final motions of the game. The only movement was a ribbon of fire that circled around her fingers, as thin and precise as a healer's blade.

Her dark hair hung loose, and ended just above her shoulders. She'd come to court with a mane of it, cascading down her back, the kind of locks that men loved and women envied, and her first act as queen had been to hack it off. People gossiped, of course (not that it stopped them from trimming theirs to match). The same ones who shouted that she was a prisoner said that Rhy had cut it in a fit of pique, because he was jealous of her beauty. Others claimed he'd done it because he wanted her and Alucard to be a matching set.

The truth was much simpler—it got in the way of her work.

For Nadiya Loreni, that was reason enough to be rid of it.

Alucard was still humming as he traced the edge of the room, but if the queen heard him, she didn't bother to look up. He raised his voice a little, adding words to the song.

"I had a love, when I was young, he went to sea, I thought him gone . . ."

Still Nadiya didn't stir, and Alucard found himself hoping, not for the first time, that no one ever tried to assassinate the queen. He doubted she would even notice.

"But he came back, when I was grown," he sang, passing a shelf piled with rejected tokens, earlier versions of the twinned coins that she'd designed to turn a scrying board into a form of long-distance communication. Another held a collection of stoppered bottles, a mortar and pestle, a jar of herbs—the ingredients for the tonic that helped Rhy sleep without rendering his brother useless.

"I had waited, he had known . . ."

Alucard trailed his fingers through the air above the disembodied pieces of something that looked dangerously like an Inheritor, the device used to contain and pass down a person's magic. Those were outlawed a century before. The last in existence had been used to capture Osaron. Or so he thought.

"The day he sailed away from me . . ."

Next to it, a table covered in slivers of metal and sheafs of parchment, each filled with the queen's tight scrawl, a mixture of notation and spellwork. And there, in an open glass case, sat three silver rings.

"*. . . he took my heart and soul to sea . . .*"

Alucard trailed off. He knew those rings.

They were the same ones worn by the three *Antari* in their battle against the dark. The rings had bound Holland and Lila and Kell to one another, allowed their magic to be shared between them. But they had also shattered Kell's power when he didn't get his off in time. Even now, the magic that wove around them was strange, iridescent light shot through with shadow.

Alucard reached out, and shut the case's lid.

Then he switched to a louder, bawdier song as he drifted toward the queen.

"*The king was made of fire, and the queen was made of ice, and when they went to bed that night, he made her melt not once but twice—*"

"So that's where Ren heard it," said the queen at last. She blinked, as if drawn from a reverie, and looked up at him, a pair of magnifying glasses balanced on her nose. Behind them, her hazel eyes looked even larger than usual, flecked with gold and green.

"You, Alucard Emery, are a terrible influence."

"Believe it or not," he said, pouring himself a drink, "I've heard that before."

He had the glass halfway to his lips when Nadiya made to stop him.

"That's for cleaning metals."

Alucard sniffed, and set the glass aside, snagging the glass of wine from her elbow instead. He sank into a plush green chair, utterly at odds with its surroundings. Her sole concession to his frequent visits.

"Do you ever sleep?" he asked.

"And miss these golden hours? No, the night is made for work."

"Dreamers," he said, "might disagree."

"This is how I dream," she said, gesturing at the table, covered in half-formed spells. "And I could point out that you are also here, awake."

"I couldn't sleep."

"So you came to bother me?" But there was no annoyance in her voice.

"What can I say?" he teased. "You're such good company."

Nadiya laughed, the sound rare and bright, and Alucard leaned back in the emerald chair and tucked his hands behind his head, and she returned to her work, ignoring him completely.

VII

Five years ago

On the day that Rhy Maresh married Nadiya Loreni, Alucard Emery got very drunk.

He resolved not to be messy about it—he'd long learned to hold his liquor, and to maintain an appearance of charm and ease, despite whatever tumult was roiling within.

The ceremony was held in the Rose Hall, hundreds of *ostra* and *vestra* filing in to see their king and his chosen queen.

Alucard had offered to absent himself—had even hoped, perhaps, that the king would spare him—but Rhy insisted he be there. He was, after all, the king's shadow. His personal guard. So Alucard stood at the bottom of the dais, his face a mask of pleasant cheer as the *Aven Essen* bound a length of gold rope around their hands.

It shouldn't have been hard to watch, but it was.

Even though Rhy had done the same in their room the night before, when no one else was there to see. Had dragged Alucard from the bed, and taken the gold sash from his robe, and laced their fingers—Rhy's hand dark and studded with rings, Alucard's lighter, the veins scarred silver.

"I bind my life to yours," Rhy had said, wrapping the sash around their hands, and Alucard had chuckled, but Rhy's face was set, his voice sober. "I bind my life to yours," he said again, his gold eyes bright, searching, waiting.

"I bind my life to yours," answered Alucard.

Rhy wrapped the sash a second time.

"I bind my heart to yours," he said, only this time his voice carried so much farther, because he was no longer speaking to Alucard. He was standing at the front of the Rose Hall, before the *Aven Essen* and the gathered crowd.

"I bind my heart to yours," answered Nadiya Loreni.

Alucard swallowed.

"I bind my fate to yours," said the king.

"I bind my fate to yours," said the queen.

Tieren drew the gold rope from their hands with a flourish.

"*Is fir on,*" he said, the oath ringing through the hall. *It is done.*

The words landed on Alucard like a door slamming shut. Cheers went up. Voices rang out in celebration. The king and queen turned to face their court, their hands still joined.

Alucard smiled and clapped with the rest of the crowd, and then went to find himself another drink.

And why not? After all, the whole city was celebrating.

The port was full of ships, and the streets outside the palace were crowded with vendors, their stalls grown up like mushrooms overnight, and Alucard hadn't seen the *soner rast* so alive since before Maxim and Emira died.

The city's *ostra* were dressed in white, a sea of cream-draped bodies gathered in the Great Hall, where music rang against the gilded walls, and the tables were heaped with food and drink, and the marble pillars were draped in the colors of the newly twined houses. According to Rhy, the four colors would have clashed terribly—the red and gold of the Maresh, the dark purple and pale grey of the Loreni—so he had decided on two, purple and gold. He'd offered to add a streak of blue, for Emery, for *Alucard*, but he declined.

That was not his family anymore. And yet, when he had dressed that morning, he'd worn his family colors. Not because he missed the sight of silver and blue, the memories they conjured, but so that all who gathered here would see that the house of Emery stood with that of Maresh.

As if to drive the point home, in place of his own family's sigil, he wore the chalice and sun, forged in silver and sapphire instead of garnet and gold.

A servant came by and he held out his glass, watched as the golden wine rose like a tide inside the goblet. Rhy's laugh, full and bright, spilled toward him, and he turned, and saw the king across the hall, dark skin luminous beneath the gold. The queen smiled, and bowed her head, and jealousy coiled around his heart as he wondered what she could have said to make Rhy laugh like that.

He had just decided to retreat to the balcony when someone called out his name.

"Alucard Emery! How much you've grown." A woman strode toward him, her dress a lush forest green. The *ostra* were expected to wear white, but the *vestra* came draped in their own colors, another reminder that they too were royal families.

"Mirella Nasaro," he said, painting a smile on his face.

The sigil of the stallion hung around her neck in emerald and white, and her long hair was pulled back, revealing a widow's peak, the point made bolder by the pearls that traced her hairline. The largest fell in a crystal drop just over her brows. As he bowed to kiss her hand, his memory caught up, supplying the most relevant details.

The Nasaros were the farthest from the throne, scattered as they were across the countryside. Mirella was shrewd, but her husband was weak-minded and soft-willed, his only ambition for swaths of land and heads of cattle.

"Always the charmer," she said, reclaiming her hand and promptly using it to gesture out at the hall. "What a splendid affair this is. I wish my sister were still alive to see it. You may recall my niece, Ezril—you would have made a lovely couple, you know, if she hadn't gone off and become a priest."

"A pity, then," said Alucard, "that we both are spoken for."

Mirella nodded vaguely, scanning the crowd. "I cannot seem to find my son, though. He should be here by now. I wanted him to meet the king."

"And the queen, I'm sure."

"Oh yes, her too," said Mirella, clearly distracted, and Alucard backed away, planning to escape, when another voice said his name.

"Master Emery."

He sighed and turned to find Sol Rosec, draped in black and gold, their sigil—a blade and crown—shining at his throat. Behind him stood a boy and a girl, just shy of adulthood, and clearly siblings. Though when it came to Rosecs, it was sometimes hard to tell. It was often said that Rosecs were so proud, they wore their colors on their skin, and sure enough, all three had the same gold hair, albeit different shades, and the same black eyes, like drips of ink on white linen.

"Master Rosec," said Alucard, with a bow. "It has been too long."

"Indeed," said the *vestra*. The truth was, the Rosecs were the only royal family who did not keep a permanent home in London. Instead they held their own court in the north, though they knew better than to call it that.

Master Rosec gestured to his children. "My son, Oren. My daughter, Hanara."

The boy, Oren, gave a nearly perfect bow, but there was a mocking flourish to it, his mouth twisted in a private grin. The girl, Hanara, bowed her limbs, but not her head, those black eyes hanging on Alucard as she sank and rose again.

"You know, I was a good friend of your father's," said Sol Rosec.

Ten years dead, but the mention of Reson Emery still made Alucard stiffen.

"I was sorry to hear of his passing—"

"That makes one of us." The words came sloshing out before Alucard could stop them.

Behind his father, Oren snorted. Hanara arched a brow. Sol only frowned. He made a show of scanning the crowded hall. "And where is your older brother, Berras?"

Alucard flinched at the name. "I fear you have missed much of recent events," he said, "in your time away from London." He made sure to lean on the last word. "My brother is no longer welcome at court."

Rosec's black eyes raked over Alucard. "Pity. To see a great house fall into such . . . disrepair."

Alucard's fingers tightened on his glass. He imagined squeezing the air from the old man's lungs. It wouldn't be hard—Sol Rosec's own magic had once been a burnished red; now it was little more than a pale pink thread around his shoulders. He was dying. Alucard wondered if he knew it yet.

"Father." Oren was leaning forward. "Shouldn't we give our blessings to the king and queen?"

"Of course," said Rosec, and with that, the three departed, and were soon mercifully swallowed by the crowd.

Alucard did not abandon the hall at once. No, he endured another hour, smiled and joked and made pleasantries until his face hurt, and then at last he escaped to the gallery above, told himself it was not an escape at all, simply a chance to get a better view.

From here, the bodies below became a tapestry, one he could read as easily as the threads of magic in the air around them.

The king and queen, ablaze in gold.

The royal guards and servants, dressed head to toe in crimson.

The *ostra* and the Faroan emissaries both in white, though the latter's clothing was cut differently, wrapped close against their skin.

A single Veskan moved through the crowd—not a representative from the foreign court, but the youngest prince, Hok, now being raised by the London Sanctuary. He apparently spoke Arnesian well enough to pass for London-born, but the shock of the young man's fair skin and white-blond hair stood out easily in the crowd.

The green pool that must be Mirella Nasaro skirted the room, still looking for her son.

The three black-clad Rosecs grouped together like drops of ink.

The new queen's family, the Loreni, dressed in violet, grey collars shaped like crescent moons around their necks.

Alucard took in them all, but even once he scanned the entire hall, he found himself still searching. For a slash of silver. A swath of blue.

For any sign of his brother.

Of course, he wasn't there. Berras Emery had not shown his face in almost three years, not since the night Osaron's poison swept through the city. The night their sister Anisa died, and Alucard had burned fighting the magic that Berras let pour into him like drink.

Not that there had been much love before that.

Theirs was a wreckage tallied in years. In split knuckles and broken bones, in venomous words and exile plots. In their mother's absence, and

178

their father's shadow, in everything Alucard was and Berras wasn't.

And yet, despite it all, he had still expected Berras to come, if for no other reason than to make a scene. If he closed his eyes, he could see his older brother, dark hair swept back and head held high, wearing the family colors with a pride that Alucard had never been allowed to feel. He could see Berras's eyes, a blue so dark it read as black when he was mad. Could hear the scrape of his voice as he took in the chalice and sun at Alucard's throat and said, "Well, at least he put a collar on his bitch."

Alucard clutched the sigil until the silver bit into his palm. His vision blurred and he closed his eyes against the sudden threat of tears. Sound wafted up from the hall below, and yet, somehow, he still heard the priest's white robes whisper toward him on the balcony. Felt his presence before he turned and saw the tendrils of the *Aven Essen*'s magic, pale threads dancing in the air.

"Master Emery," Tieren said gently. He still stood straight, but in the last year, his cheeks had begun to hollow, his skin drooping on his frame, as if being pulled slowly back to the earth. Even the threads of his magic had begun to dim.

Alucard eyed the glass of wine in the older man's hand. "Is that allowed?"

The *Aven Essen* raised a white brow. "I am a priest, not a saint. Besides, it is a question of balance." He took a long sip, and closed his eyes, as if savoring. "All good things in quiet measure."

"I don't know," said Alucard, draining his glass. "I prefer my vices loud."

Tieren's eyes drifted open. They were pale, a winter-morning blue, and they studied him, seemed to peel away the varnish and the pride. "Alucard," he began softly.

Alucard felt his throat tighten. He turned away from the priest, leaned his elbows on the balcony. His gaze fell like a stone over the crowd. It could have landed anywhere, but of course, it landed on Rhy. The king smiled, that dazzling smile, and flung his arm wide, gesturing at the hall, or perhaps telling a story. Alucard wondered which, wished that he could read his lips from here. He should have been there, at Rhy's side. Instead, there was the queen, one hand resting on his shoulder, as if laying claim, as if the crown shining in her dark hair wasn't enough, as if anyone needed reminding that he was hers.

"It had to be done," said Tieren, and that was the worst part. Alucard knew the priest was right. He had sworn not only to love the king, but to protect him, and when it came to keeping the throne, a child was stronger than any sword or shield.

It was the one thing Alucard alone could not give Rhy.

And the one thing he needed to remain king.

The mandate of magic stated that a ruling king or queen could have only *one* heir—to keep their family from growing too vast, too strong— but if they had *none,* it was taken as a sign that their time to rule was at an end. The throne would pass to one of the other royal families—Rosec, Nasaro, Loreni, Emery. All of them had ruled before, and all would be too happy to rule again, if given the chance.

No, the Maresh had held the throne for three hundred years.

Alucard would not be the reason they lost it.

"It had to be done," he said, lifting the glass to his lips, only to find it empty.

Below, the new queen had left Rhy's side, and the king stood alone. He turned in a slow, searching circle, and Alucard told himself that Rhy was looking for him, until he saw that shock of crimson hair, and knew that it was Kell who held the king's attention.

Alucard gritted his teeth. He had promised he wouldn't rile the *Antari* prince, not today, but his resolve was weakening with every drink. He had just decided to go down and amuse himself, perhaps find Lila Bard, wherever she might be, when someone cleared their throat.

He turned, hoping it was his favorite captain.

It wasn't.

The first thing he saw was the crown, the twin of Rhy's own, which sat nestled in her black hair.

"Well," Alucard had said when Nadiya Loreni first came to court, "at least I'm still the pretty one." It was, of course, a joke—Nadiya was stunning. Most nobles could drape themselves in enough finery to seem attractive, but the oldest of the Loreni heirs was simply, undeniably beautiful. Her face was heart-shaped and her body curved with a softness that belied the cutting sharpness of her mind. Like her mother, and grandfather, and so many Loreni before, she was an inventor as well as a noble.

And now, she was also a queen.

Alucard looked around for the *Aven Essen,* but the priest had retreated, leaving him alone to face Rhy's bride. *Traitor,* he thought, as the queen drew near.

"Alucard," she said, and he resented her anew for the way she said his name, as if they were allies, or old friends.

"My queen," he said, bowing deeply. He thought he saw her roll her eyes.

He hadn't noticed that her hands were hidden behind her skirts until she produced them, revealing an open bottle of wine.

"You have no glass," he said as she filled his.

"No." She shrugged. "I suppose we'll have to share."

He downed the contents of the glass, and thrust it back, then turned from her, to the safety of the gallery's view. "Surely you should be down there, greeting your guests?"

"Somehow I think they'll survive my absence." She filled the glass, and sipping it, said, "And what about you?"

"What about me?" he asked, arching a brow.

"You are the king's shadow. Should you not be at his side?"

"Today I am the pet bird," he said dryly, "and so I prefer to perch."

Nadiya joined him at the marble rail. "I know for a fact you are his heart."

"Who told you that?"

"He did. The day we met. And every day since." Alucard's gaze slid toward her, and Nadiya surprised him, for the first of many times, by laughing. "Honestly, you think I don't know that I'm wedding you both?"

"Do you resent me?" he asked, bit the question off before he added *as I do you.*

"Why should I?" She downed the contents of the glass and studied it, as if it were a problem, a puzzle. "I have never understood why one person must be all things. I want to be a mother, not a wife."

"Then why be queen?"

"Power," she said, without hesitation, and Alucard must have failed to hide his reaction, because she went on. "Oh, not as you think it. I do not mean the power to command citizens or start wars. I simply mean the power to do as I please. To think and work and live as I like, with no one in my way." Her eyes shone as she spoke with a hungry kind of light.

"So you do not love him, then?"

"Am I meant to?" she teased, but seeing the shadow in his face, she sobered. "I am quite fond of our king." And Alucard liked the way she said *our* instead of *my,* and liked it even more when she added, "But I will never love him as you do, Master Emery. And that, I think, is fine with you. As it is fine with me."

The queen looked down over the rail at the celebration below, as Rhy held court in the center of it all.

"We will each love him," she said, "in our own way. I will give him what you cannot. And you will give him what I cannot. And together, we shall be a better kind of family."

His chest tightened, but for the first time that day, it was not in anger, or envy, or grief. It was hope.

"Now come down from your perch," said Nadiya, striding away, "and help me survive this party."

Alucard straightened, and said, with a ghost of a smile, "If you insist, my queen."

VIII

Now

Nadiya set her tools aside and straightened, massaging her neck, and Alucard knew it was safe to speak again.

"The king was nearly killed tonight."

"So I heard," said the queen, as if they were discussing dinner courses instead of regicide. And someone else might have thought she was being flippant. But Alucard knew her better. Nadiya turned and walked away, disappearing into the next chamber. She didn't tell him to follow her, didn't have to. When he reached the second room, the iron tang of blood hit his nose, followed by the scent of citrus and mint, thin streams of smoke rising from tapers.

The assassin's body lay naked on a stone block, the killing wound a bloodless tear in his chest.

"My queen, if you longed for company, you could have simply asked."

"Oh, Alucard," she said, rounding the body, "is that an invitation? You know you're not my type."

"Is it the manhood or the pulse?"

"Neither." She plucked the glasses from her face. "Or maybe both."

It was nothing but banter, as worn as a good pair of boots. Much to his dismay, Nadiya Loreni seemed perfectly content alone.

"But I am not alone," she'd told him, more than once. "I have a husband, and a daughter, and a friend who haunts me while I work. I have all the freedom of a wife, the wealth of a mother, and the indisputable power of a queen. In short, I have everything I need."

"And everything you want?" he'd pressed, knowing how it felt to be denied a dream, even when surrounded by riches. But Nadiya had only looked at him, amused, and said, "If I wanted a woman in my bed, Alucard, I'd have her. Believe it or not, I prefer to sleep alone."

And so he believed her—because if Nadiya Loreni wanted something, she would not stop until it was hers.

Alucard approached the block, studying Rhy's would-be killer. In death, the assassin looked young. A tinge of red streaked his cheeks, all that remained of the paint he'd worn.

Alucard's gaze dropped until he found what he was looking for. There, against his ribs, just below the killing blow. Fingers branded into skin.

The Hand.

Anger bloomed in his chest at the sight of the mark. He dug his nails into the block. The air shivered, lanterns flickering around the room. Rhy's voice came back to him, then, soft and sad and thick with sleep.

Why do they hate me?

Alucard looked up, past the body, to the chart that spanned the wall beyond. It had grown, like weeds in wet weather, spreading tendrils over stone.

Six months ago, when the whispers became rumors and the rumors showed no signs of dying out, he'd come to the queen, the sharpest mind he'd ever met, and the only one he trusted, and forced himself to ask.

"Is there truth to their claim that magic is failing? Is there any way to know?"

He hated the words before they left his lips. They tasted wrong, rancid with doubt, and he was scared to see the queen's reaction, the horror on her face.

But he should have known better. Nadiya was Nadiya, after all. She had not recoiled at the question, because she had already asked, and sought the answer herself. She'd led him here, and showed him the beginnings of her map. What would become a sprawling diagram of magic, as she attempted to chart its presence and its strength, from the sealing of the doors between worlds three centuries before—she lacked the data to go further back—to Rhy's time on the throne. That day, he'd seen the downward curve, his heart sinking with the angle.

"So there's truth then, to the rumor?"

The queen had only shrugged. "All things in nature ebb and flow. The tide rises and falls. The seasons come and go and come again."

"When will it come again?" he'd asked, trying to keep the panic from his voice. "When will the tide rise back?"

Nadiya had hesitated, her brow furrowing. She didn't answer, which meant she didn't know, and that was unnerving.

Alucard had stared at the chart until his vision blurred, the points and the lines between them smoothing into a shape that made the rise and fall less damning.

Maybe Nadiya was right.

But their enemies wouldn't care.

A blunt blade was still a weapon in the wrong hands.

He'd stared at the chart for what felt like hours. And then, at last, he'd said, "Don't tell the king."

"It's not Rhy's doing," she'd said. "The tide curves down before he takes the throne."

"It doesn't matter," said Alucard. "He will make himself a martyr."

Nadiya's fingers had come to rest on his shoulder, and he welcomed their steady weight.

"Then we protect him," she'd said. "From the Hand, *and* from himself."
They stayed like that for a long time. And then her hand fell away, and she
said, "I'm still missing a key piece of information."

And Alucard knew that she meant Ren.

Ren, who was not yet five. Too young to manifest her power. Or fail to.
He knew that was Rhy's worst fear. That his daughter would be like him,
born without magic. And if that happened, the Hand would use it as the
spark to light the fire, and burn the kingdom down.

But Nadiya had an arsenal of magic. She would destroy anyone who
came for her daughter.

And no one would. Because Alucard had no intention of waiting for
Ren to come of age. No intention of letting the Hand grow any stronger.

A glint of metal caught his eye, and Alucard dragged his attention away
from the wall and back to the body on the table, and the queen beyond, who
was rolling up her sleeves, a sharp knife in one hand.

"Do you intend to harvest him for parts?"

He meant it as a joke. He should have known better.

Nadiya had the kind of face that seemed always about to smile. Full lips,
and wide hazel eyes, and one eyebrow set ever so slightly above the other,
giving her a look of mischief, which she'd passed on to Ren. There was
no malice to it, only curiosity and wonder. The difference being that Ren
liked to draw birds, and Nadiya would prefer to take their wings apart one
feather at a time to understand exactly how they navigated currents. More
than one of Ren's pets had found their way down here . . . after meeting a
natural end. He hoped.

He watched as the queen slid the knife across the dead assassin's chest,
the skin parting waxily beneath the steel.

"What happens to a life when the body dies?" she mused aloud.
"Arnesians believe the body is a shell, a vessel for the life that animates it.
That as long as we're alive, we are full, and when we die, the vessel empties,
and the power is poured back into the stream, leaving nothing but the
empty shell. No memories. No mind. No spirit. If that is true, we can learn
nothing from the dead."

She took up a serrated knife, and began to saw open his ribs.

Alucard swallowed and looked away.

Nadiya chuckled. "Surely you saw worse when you were a pirate."

"Privateer," he corrected, "and even then, I never made a habit of butchering the dead. Care to tell me why you're . . ."

He trailed off as she set the saw aside and began to pry open the man's rib cage with her bare hands. Alucard felt bile rising in his throat. He took a step closer to the mint and citrus taper as Nadiya withdrew her bloodstained fingers long enough to retrieve a narrower blade, then resumed her work.

"Now, the Faroans also believe that the body is a vessel for the spirit," she continued, "but that, in the time the two are fused, they mark each other, like a hand in wet clay. The body is shaped by power. The flesh retains memories. . . ."

Her tone was casual, as if they were in the gallery, having tea and toast and—

Alucard tried to put the thought of food from his mind as her hands made a sucking sound inside the man's chest, and finally came free.

Holding his heart.

"The Hand plagues us because we know so little of them. We have yet to learn what they *want*."

"What all enemies want," he said. "To cause chaos, and call it change. To see the end of the Maresh rule."

"Those are ideals, not answers," she said, weighing the heart. "The Hand is a mantle, a mask, but masks are worn by *people*. And people all want different things." She looked at the bloody organ in her hand, eyes bright. "What did he want?"

She carried the heart to an altar, the surface of which was covered in a delicate tracery of spellwork, written out not in ink but sand. No, not sand. Sulfur. As Alucard approached, she set the heart in the very center of the pattern. She tipped out a vial of oil onto the heart, and snapped her fingers, and a small spark dropped from her hand onto the organ. It didn't ignite so much as consume itself, a blue-black flame swallowing the heart before sending slow fingers out along the lines of the sulfur spell.

Alucard had never had a gift for writing spells. He could read a basic one, and use it well enough, but he'd always favored elemental magic, the simple clarity of wind or earth or water in his hands over the more abstracted application of someone else's power.

Because of that, he never really thought of spellcraft as magic. But watching a new spell, one he'd never seen before, it felt, well, like the sorcery Bard sometimes spoke of, the strange, fanciful stuff relegated to stories back in her world, things dreamed up without being understood.

It felt to Alucard like watching the impossible made real, and realizing the only thing that separated one from the other was talent.

He couldn't imagine how Nadiya's mind worked, how she constructed her spells, but he could see the threads, woven as carefully as any garment. Here was earth, and water, to simulate the movement of blood in the veins. Here was fire, to emulate the spark of life.

"What I would give," said the queen, "to see the world as you do."

Alucard looked up, rubbing his brow. He was so used to blocking out the strings of light, to seeing past them, that apparently when he focused on the threads themselves, he squinted slightly, a furrow forming like a groove between his brows. It had given him away—the keen-eyed queen had noticed the squint years before, and he'd made the terrible mistake of telling her the truth of it.

"Do you think it's your mind, or your eyes?" Nadiya asked, as the spell continued to burn. "Eyes are, I believe, the seat of perception. Look at *Antari* magicians, the way the magic claims their ocular nerves. But then again, the mind makes sense of the world and processes its sights."

"Does this matter?"

"Of course," she said, affronted. But there was a fervor in her voice, and her pupils were as large and dark as a lover's in the throes of passion.

"I don't like it when you look at me like that," said Alucard.

"Like what?"

"Like one of your projects. Like something you'd like to take apart."

"I'd put you back when I was done. I do hope it's your eyes," she added with a smirk. "They are much easier to study. And such a lovely shade of blue."

"You cannot have my eyes."

"No bother," she said with a shrug. "I'll take them when you're dead."

The soft sizzle of magic died between them. The heart had stopped burning and now lay, a blackened lump, in the center of the sulfur diagram. The spell was done. Nadiya held her breath, and Alucard approached, and together, they looked down at the altar.

The lines had rearranged themselves, no longer an intricate circle around the heart. Now they branched out in every direction, like spokes on a wheel. Or spikes on a star. Or branches on a tree.

A memory came to him. Lila Bard, leaning her elbows on the *Spire*'s rail, staring down into a tin cup of awful black tea. She was telling him of a fair that had come to London—her London—once, of a woman there who claimed to see the future in the leaves.

"What did she say?" he'd asked.

Lila had looked out at the vast expanse of sea. "That I'd cause a lot of trouble, and die a long way from home."

Alucard had snorted. "I could have told you that, Bard."

She'd flicked him one of those smiles, sharp as a knife. "Yeah, well, I looked into the cup, and do you know what I saw?" He shook his head. She dumped the last of the black sludge into the water. "Nothing but tea."

Now Alucard stole a glance at Nadiya, who was staring down at the table, much as she'd been when he first found her, her eyes flat, unreadable, the current of her mind no doubt rushing past beneath the surface.

He cleared his throat. "Well? Did it work?"

Nadiya frowned, as if trying to make sense of the image. After several long seconds, disappointment flickered across her face.

"Not all spells work," she said, drawing her hand through the ashes and scattering the lines. She turned on her heel and returned to the ruined corpse, staring down into his open eyes. For a moment, he wondered if she meant to pry them out, and try again, but then she brought her hand to a lever on the table's side. The body vanished, falling through the surface and into the hollowed stone below. She flicked her wrist, and fire overtook the corpse.

"Do me a favor, Alucard," she said, as the body burned.

"What's that?"

"Next time, try to take the man alive."

IX

The last thief was starting to feel unwell.

It began as a pain, just below his ribs, a twisting in his gut.

At first, he blamed it on the boat—even as a merchant's son, he'd never had the strongest stomach, and as he'd sped away from the *Ferase Stras,* the little skiff had rocked and canted heavily on the night-rough swells. He blamed it on the energy he'd had to expel propelling the vessel alone, which left him sweaty and shaking by the time he reached the port, and the waiting ship, which had been hired to ferry the three men—now only him—back to London.

As he collapsed onto the cot in the little cabin, the stolen *persalis* bundled in the cloak and the whole thing pressed against his chest, he blamed the swelling sickness on the aftermath of his adventure, though it hadn't been nearly as much fun as he'd hoped.

The last thief never thought to blame the wards back on the *Ferase Stras,* or the fact he hadn't had time to throw the protective cloak over his shoulders as he flung himself over the side of the floating market.

He drifted, feverishly, turning the events over and over in his mind, until it read like one of the legends of Olik. Until he was, of course, the hero.

A rough hand shook him awake sometime before dawn. He was hot and cold, shivering with sweat, and it took him a moment to realize the ship was docked.

"London?" he asked hoarsely, but the man shook his head.

"Tanek."

He had to drag his thoughts together, retrace the plans. Yes, that was right. He remembered the other two talking about it, in the hours before the robbery. They would sail the skiff to the nearest port, and then board a merchant ship, which would take them as far as the mouth of the Isle, docking just before the checkpoint, where a horse and cart was waiting. The ports kept track of ships and passengers and cargo, but no one counted carriages.

The two more experienced thieves hadn't included the third man in the talks, but he had lurked and listened, and now he felt a bitter glee, because they were dead, and he was the only one left to carry out the mission.

But as he left the ship, his pride quickly faltered. The ground felt like it was still bobbing beneath his feet, and he was distressed to find that the ache had spread to his temples and his chest. He forced fresh air into his lungs as he tucked the wrapped parcel under his arm and went to meet his driver.

It was a nice carriage, big enough for three, and he had it to himself.

He tried to savor that as the wheels lurched and jolted on the road. Thin morning light streamed in through the carriage windows, and as London came into sight, he forced himself to unwrap the knotted cloak, and confront the glaring problem.

Their bounty—the *persalis*—was broken.

The doormaker had been in one piece aboard the *Ferase Stras,* and now it was in several. The last thief tried to recall the drawing he'd seen, the way the object had been meant to look when it was whole. Like a neat little box, a black-and-gold ring set into its front. That one piece was *supposed* to come away, he knew that much, and knew that when the *persalis* worked, it would open a kind of door that led to that ring, wherever it was placed.

The last thief had no idea what the Hand wanted the doormaker *for,* but he was pretty sure their plan relied on it working.

He studied the wreckage closer.

The pieces seemed to be all there, and he tried to fit them back together, thinking perhaps it was *meant* to fully come apart, but no—some of the metal was obviously warped, and the wood was splintered, and the one time he thought he might have it back together, the carriage hit a nasty bump and immediately the whole thing crumbled in his lap.

He sighed, letting his head fall back. His eyes slipped shut.

It was an adventure, he told himself.

It was an adventure, and he was Olik. He was the chosen one. He was—

—going to be sick.

He pounded on the roof of the carriage, and tumbled out before it had even stopped, retching in the street. There was nothing in his stomach—

he'd been too nervous to eat before the job, and too ill after—but something still came up, a red-black sludge that left the taste of metal in its wake.

He straightened, steadying himself against the carriage as his legs went shaky and his head went light. He looked around. They were in the *shal*. It was a part of London that the merchant's son had been taught to avoid when he was young and his parents brought him to the capital, a cluster of streets on the outskirts of the city that catered to all sorts of unsavory clientele. From here, the Isle's red glow was barely a tint on the low clouds, the palace spires a glint of gold in the distance.

And yet, it didn't seem so bad. This block, at least, had a baker, and a handful of carts, a tavern with its windows intact, a seamstress, and a shop with a gold *H* printed on the door. A sign was mounted just below, and he took a shaky step toward it until the words came into focus.

ONCE BROKEN, SOON REPAIRED.

And just like that, the last thief had an idea. It was a terrible idea, and if he hadn't been so sick, he might have stopped long enough to see the folly in it. Instead, he returned to the carriage, and told the driver to wait as he gathered up the broken pieces of the *persalis*. He had the sense at least to take out the keypiece, the black-and-gold ring, and tuck it in the breast pocket of his coat, before he bundled up the rest and stumbled toward the shop.

He flung his weight against the door, only to realize it was locked.

He tried the handle, hissing through his teeth before he saw the little CLOSED sign in the window. His vision was beginning to blur. He rested his forehead against the wooden door, fought to catch his breath.

Then he hauled himself back to the carriage, and sank into the welcome dark, to wait.

X

Tes had gone to bed craving dumplings.

Sometime in her sleep, the want had lodged like a splinter, and worried there, so that by the time she woke it was no longer a want, but a need. She hadn't even bothered with her first pot of tea, had simply shoved her feet into her boots, and thrown on her coat, and gone to find breakfast, telling herself the work would hold.

The shop could open late.

Over the last three years, Tes had made it a mission to sample all the dumplings London had to offer, from the dozen different street carts scattered across the city's many squares, to the large stall in the night market, to the fancy storefront on the northern banks that specialized in fish, to that one kind of dodgy cart there in the middle of the *shal*. It was an ongoing search, but so far the best by far came from a little white stall tucked between a butcher and a baker on Hera Vas, on the other side of the docks.

It was a long walk, but it was worth it, and half an hour later, Tes was on her way back to the shop, clutching the steaming satchel as if it were full of gold coins instead of pillowed dough.

Morning had broken like an egg over the city, a yellow light that looked warmer than it felt as it touched the rooftops and glinted on store windows. All around her, London was coming to life, and though Tes still missed the cliffs where she was born, the constant hush of the sea, she had grown fond of the capital, the way it sprawled and grew, like a garden in full bloom, every day a little different, a little bigger. She liked the way it brimmed with magic, even if it was sometimes so tangled and so bright it hurt her eyes. She liked the markets that sprang up like mushrooms, and the fact that no matter how often she explored, she always found something new. She liked the constant rattle of horses and the ramble of voices in the street, the melody that rose and fell but never fell away. She liked knowing she was in a place so big and full of noise that she could shout, and no one would turn. That she could hide, and no one would find her.

Where are you, little rabbit?

Tes shivered, told herself it was just the cold breeze that had kicked up, finding the holes in her coat.

"I should really mend those," she remarked to Vares, tucked in his usual pocket. The dead owl made no reply. She didn't blame him. They both knew she wasn't nearly as good with needle and string as she was with a thread of magic. Her mother always—But there Tes caught herself, and drew her thoughts another way. Perhaps it was time to buy new clothes, instead.

Fifteen was such a disconcerting age. Her body insisted on growing in fits and starts so that nothing seemed to fit, not even her skin.

She resolved to start looking for a new coat. Nothing magical, though. Most of the coats had something woven through them—a spell to keep the water off, a spell to make them warm in winter or cool in summer. All she wanted was good sturdy wool.

Her stomach growled, and she opened the sack and popped a dumpling in her mouth, savoring the scented steam that filled her senses as she bit down, the fine-diced onion, the spiced meat. She smiled.

"Worth it," she said, mouth full.

From her coat pocket, Vares clicked his beak as if he wanted a bite.

"You don't have a stomach," she pointed out. "You'll just make a mess."

The dead owl seemed to sigh. Tes swallowed, resisting the urge to reach for another until she was back in her shop with a cup of tea.

Tes sagged with relief as she reached the *shal,* her eyes welcoming the shadows that fell over the narrower streets, the river's light breaking like a surf against the buildings. She slowed only when she passed a shuttered store, and saw something drawn on the wall. The white paint was still wet against the stone.

Up close, it looked like massive strokes, but when she took a few steps back, she saw what it was meant to be.

A hand.

She hurried on, quickening her pace until she reached the shop, the gold *H* welcoming her back. She ran her fingers over the words on the sign—*once broken, soon repaired*—tugging on the threads she'd woven through them in protection, and loosening the spell that kept the place locked up.

But as Tes let herself in, she saw, too late, that the shop wasn't empty.

Someone stood at the counter, rummaging around, their back to the door. Fear prickled through Tes, her fingers reaching for the nearest weapon (which was unfortunately a small metal lantern, designed to magnify light) as she cleared her throat and said, in her most intimidating voice, "What do you think you are you doing?"

"Looking for sugar," said a familiar voice, and then the reed-thin body straightened, revealing black hair, and long limbs in a fraying grey coat. "Honestly, Tes, how can you drink it like this?" He turned his cheek as he said this, and his face caught the light, exposing a fox-sharp jaw and a playful grin.

Nero.

Tes felt her fear uncoil, her limbs relaxing until she saw that he had poured himself a cup of her finest tea.

"You know," she said, "people put locks on doors for a reason."

Nero leaned his elbows back on the counter and blew a lock of hair out of his eyes. "To make things more interesting?"

She set down the satchel of dumplings and fished the dead owl from her coat, returning him to his perch on the counter.

"Who's a good dead bird?" cooed Nero, digging a few fried seeds from his pocket.

"Don't do that," she said as he fed them to the owl. "You know he can't eat."

Sure enough, the seeds clacked and clattered through Vares's bones, and landed in a pile between his feet.

"Aw," said Nero, patting the bird's skull. "But look at how happy it makes him."

Vares clicked his beak in delight and ruffled his featherless wings.

Tes rolled her eyes. Even the damn bird was charmed. That was the trouble with Nero. He was *charming*. His black hair had a life of its own, from the widow's peak it made over his brow to the tendrils that curled against his cheeks, and the rest rose like a cloud over his head. As if that weren't enough, he had eyes that were gold at the edges and green at the center, and the kind of smile that made Tes blush, even though she didn't fancy him.

Charming wasn't the *only* word that came to mind, not by a long shot, but it was usually the first, followed by *criminal, con artist,* and *ne'er-do-well,* though those words conjured images of scowling brutes, and he was always surprisingly cheerful.

194

And then, there was *friend*. That one was a warm stone in her hand, and she was torn between the urge to hold it close, and cast it away. Friends were dangerous, and she'd never planned on making one, certainly not with someone like him.

Nero pushed off the counter and looked around. "How is Master Haskin today?" he asked, knowing there was no such person, and never had been.

"Hungry." Tes took the bag of dumplings with her as she rounded the counter, putting the boundary between them, if for no other reason than to remind Nero that there was one. "How did you even get in?"

"There are two doors," he said lightly, though she'd never shown him the second one, tucked like a secret in the back of the shop. "You only spelled the first."

She swore softly. "Aren't you clever."

"If only I had magic," he mused, "I wouldn't have to be."

Nero's mouth gave a bitter twitch as he said it, as if the world had marked him as lesser for his lack of power. And it would have, if he'd truly been born without an element.

But they both knew he was lying. Tes could see it written in the air around him, the shocking violet of his power, a color so rare it stood out, even against the cluttered threads of the shop. And even if she hadn't been able to read it there, in his threads, she had seen it once, and only once, in action. He had helped her out of a scrape when she first came to London, and used his power to do it. So she knew, and he knew that she knew, and they both knew well enough to lean into the lie.

"What are you doing here?" she asked, setting the kettle back on the stove and snatching up the mug he'd left on the counter.

Nero spread his arms. "I'm a customer."

"And you couldn't wait outside?"

"It was cold in the street."

"It's still summer," she said, lifting Vares to sweep away the mound of seeds.

"It looked like it might rain?" he ventured.

She looked around with a sigh. "Did you steal anything?"

Nero recoiled. "From you? I'd *never*." He then proceeded to pluck a dumpling out of the bag, and pop it into his mouth. "Honestly," he said around the mouthful. "Wow—that's good—I'm hurt that you'd even ask. But since we're both here now, I *could* use your help."

The trouble with Nero was that she knew he was trouble. He wore it like a brand, from that hapless grin to those green-gold eyes. It was like seeing a trap, and stepping into it anyway.

She just couldn't help but like him.

Perhaps it was the way he treated her: not like a mark, but a little sister.

She *was* a little sister—but not his. And if he ever asked, she would have lied and said she was an only child, and her parents had died horrible deaths at sea, so there was no one to miss her and no one who might come looking and that was that.

But Nero didn't ask. He never asked, because they had an understanding. They were allowed to know each other as they were now, not as they'd been sometime before. Pasts belonged right where they were, so he didn't ask what a girl her age (not that he knew it) was doing alone in the city, running an often-illegal repair shop, and she didn't ask him about the magic he pretended not to have, or why he always looked like he'd been on the wrong end of a fight.

Sure, over time, they'd traded small, and largely useless, details. He had a sweet tooth. She lived on strong tea. He had a smile that could charm a shadow into the light. She had a glare that could send it back. They both had a habit of talking to things that weren't really there, Nero to himself, and Tes to her owl. But the only reason Nero even knew her name was because he made her bet it in a round of Sanct, one letter for every losing hand, and by the time she realized the entire point of the game was to cheat, he had those first three letters, the only ones she used.

"Don't be cross," he'd said with a laugh. "It's only a name."

But he was wrong. A name was like a strand of hair or a hangnail—something people shed too easily, no concern for where it went. But since opening the shop, she'd seen spells woven with names at the center, curses spun out around syllables, charms folded over letters.

She'd seen names used to bribe, and to threaten.

Seen a man knifed for the name he'd given.

A woman arrested for spitting on the name of the king.

Names had value. And her father taught her never to give a thing away for less than it was worth. Especially something you couldn't buy back.

On some level, even Nero knew it. After all, he'd given her his first name, or at least, those four letters, N-E-R-O, tossed them out like bits of burning paper on *Sel Fera Noche*. But he'd never parted with the rest. If there was more, he'd cut it off, cast it away.

He was just Nero.

And she was just Tes.

He was just a thief.

And she was just a fixer.

"Show me."

Nero grinned, and pulled a necklace from his pocket. A gaudy, gilded thing, set with stones. He held it out to Tes. "Not really my color, is it?"

"I suppose thieves can't be picky." She plucked it from his hand, but as she did, her eyes went to his fingers. There was white paint on them. Her stomach clenched. She told herself she shouldn't care. It was none of her business.

Nero followed her gaze, and recoiled, wiping his hand on his trousers. "I didn't," he started.

"I don't want to know," she said.

"I touched the wall," he insisted. "I didn't realize it was wet."

"I don't care," she said. And she meant it. That was a kind of trouble she didn't need or want. The Hand was faceless. Nobody knew how many there were, or who had joined. If anyone knew a Hand, they didn't live to tell anyone, and if a Hand did go around bragging about being one, they didn't live long enough to do it twice.

"Let me guess," she said, turning her attention to the necklace. "You liberated this from a ship, or it fell off a merchant cart, or the wind just *blew* it into your hands."

Nero crossed his arms. "For your information, I won it fair and square in a game of Sanct."

"There's nothing fair or square about that game." Tes cleared a place on the counter and set the necklace down on a piece of black cloth.

"Well, I won it. Though perhaps a little too easily." He leaned forward, into her space. "I just want to make sure it's not cursed."

She reached for her blotters. "This is a shop for broken things," she began.

"Clocks, and locks, and household trinkets," he finished, "I know the line. Well, this is a household trinket, and I think it might be faulty, so maybe you could do whatever it is you do—" He made a little flourish. "—and check?"

Tes shook her head, even as she tugged the blotters on. The rest of the room disappeared, and Nero with it, the chaos of strings smoothed to a flat and empty black. She looked down at the necklace on its cloth, now the only magic in her vision. It was easy, then, to see the problem. She didn't need to touch it, but she did, made a show of lifting the necklace, and turning it over.

"It's not cursed," she said, "but it *is* tethered." Somewhere to her left, Nero groaned. "No wonder they let you win it," she went on. "Knowing they can hunt you down and take it back."

He slumped forward, into her line of sight. With the blotters on, all she could see was his face, too close, and the ominous purple of his magic as it twisted through the air around his green-gold eyes. Which were wide, and pleading.

"Unless you untether it."

Tes sighed. "Unless I untether it," she said. "Which I'm only going to do so the owner—"

"—*previous* owner—"

"—doesn't come looking for it in *my* shop."

Nero smiled that dazzling smile. "Have I told you you're the best?"

"Only when I'm doing you favors."

"I'll try to say it more often," he said, disappearing into the darkness beyond her sight.

"I don't need your flattery," she said, ignoring the heat that flooded stubbornly into her cheeks. "Now let me work." Tes took up a tool, pretending to prod at the spellwork written on the metal instead of the threads running through the air above it. Tools wouldn't work on the magic itself—she'd tried. Only her hands seemed able to catch and hold, to braid and fray, to knot and tear.

As she picked apart the spell, Nero wandered the shop.

"Don't touch anything," she said, and she could practically hear his fingers stop halfway to a shelf.

"How long will this take?"

"That depends," she said, "on how often you distract me."

She could have worked a lot faster, but it would have been too obvious what she was—and wasn't—doing. She heard the crackle of waxy paper as Nero stole another dumpling, and swore, picking at the threads.

Each time she pulled one free of the spell, and set it aside, the light instantly began to fade. Without being bound to something, the magic slipped away, diffused back into the world. In moments, the thread itself was gone. She worked, minutes sliding by, until the necklace sat on the counter, as lightless as the square of cloth beneath it. Nothing but a gaudy bauble. She was still staring at it, resting her eyes in the dark, when something large and metal crashed to the floor behind her.

Tes tore off the blotters and the world rushed in, too messy, too bright.

Nero was behind the counter, one hand still resting on her personal workshelf—her *stash*, he called it—the wall lined with baskets of half-fixed trinkets and half-formed spells. Things she toyed with between jobs. He knelt to fetch the fallen object.

"Don't touch that!" she shouted, and he proceeded to drop it again. Tes cringed as it struck the floor, hollow metal ringing as it bounced.

"Is it dangerous?" he asked as it rolled away.

"What do you think?"

"I think it looks like a kettle."

"It *is* a kettle," she said, rubbing her tired eyes. "You put the water in cold and it comes out hot. Or it will, when I fix it."

"Could you make it come out wine?"

She started to say no, then hesitated. That would be a much more complicated bit of spellwork, since one was simply heating water and the other involved a transmutation, the twisting of earth and mineral into—no; she stopped herself before her mind could race ahead, get lost in the potential.

"Here," she said, holding out the necklace. "No more tether. Just bad taste and a quick sale."

Nero took the jewelry, and turned it over in his hands.

"How does she do it?" he asked, directing the question to the owl instead of her.

The truth was, Tes didn't know. At least, not how to put it into words, ones that would make sense to anyone but her. Most people experienced magic one of two ways: as a raw element, or a constructed spell. Spells were designed to bind the elements into shape, they were instructions for those elements, but few elemental magicians handled spells, and few spellcrafters handled raw elements. One was yarn, and the other a tapestry, which meant that both were made of thread. People assumed that when Tes worked on an object, she read the spellwork, but honestly the marks meant nothing to her. She read the pattern itself, a language no one else could see or speak. One that existed between her, and the magic.

She wondered, sometimes, if there were others who could see the world the way she did, who could reach out and change it. If there were, she'd never heard of them. Which meant, if they did exist, they were smart enough to keep the talent to themselves.

So when Nero asked, as he always did, Tes simply said, "Magic," and left it at that.

"How much do I owe you?" he asked, pocketing the necklace.

Tes snatched up the bag of dumplings from the counter's edge. It felt suspiciously light. "Five lin."

Nero winced at the cost, and she felt herself relenting. It hadn't been that much work. "How about the three—" She checked the bag. "*Four* dumplings you ate."

He brightened. "I'll bring six."

"So you can eat half?" she countered.

He winked, and ambled backward, lazily unspooling himself toward the door.

"I want the *good* ones," she added, "from the shop on Hera Vas."

"Only the best," he said, tugging up the collar on his coat, which looked even rattier than hers.

"Use the money you're *not* paying me to get a better coat."

"Can't," he said. "This one's lucky."

"It's full of holes."

"And yet, nothing falls out, only in." Nero turned away. "Tell Master Haskin I said hello!" he called back, reaching for the door just as it swung open, and a young man stumbled in.

Nero could have jumped out of the man's path, but he didn't, and the two collided in a way that made Tes suspect something had just fallen out of the stranger's pocket, and into Nero's.

"Sorry," said Nero, slowing long enough to steady the new customer, and then he was gone, and the man was barreling toward her, something bundled against his chest.

"Haskin—" he started.

"—isn't here," she said. "But I can help you." Tes was about to go into her speech, about the clocks and locks and household trinkets, but the words died on her lips when she saw the threads in the air around the man.

They were . . . decaying.

The man couldn't be much older than Nero, but he looked awful. At first she thought he must be sick, but she'd seen sick people before, the light in their threads dimming with their health. This was different. Like poison spreading through roots. Or a *curse*.

She recoiled as he dumped the bundle onto the counter between them.

"Need you—to fix." He stumbled over the words, his hands shaking as he unwrapped the parcel on the counter, revealing splintered wood and warped metal, not so much an object as a collection of parts. Whatever it was—or had been once—it was very broken.

Tes hesitated. She didn't want to touch it, in case it was the source of the man's sickness. She had seen cursed objects before, threads dripping with the oily sheen of tainted magic, the air around them bruised, the strings crumbling with rot. But the threads above the broken thing were splintered, not rotten.

Unlike the customer, who seemed to be getting worse by the moment. Sweat ran down the bridge of his nose, and there were bruised hollows beneath his eyes.

201

"What is it?" she asked, but he wouldn't say, only muttered the words on her shop door.

"Once broken, soon repaired."

Tes folded her arms. "You want me to fix a thing, without knowing what it is or what it was meant to do?"

"It's broken," he wheezed. "That's what it is. It's meant to be whole. Can you fix it or not?"

That was a good question. She'd yet to find something she *couldn't* fix, but then, she usually knew how it was meant to work. And yet, in theory at least, the threads would tell her. If she could read the pattern. If she could reconstruct it.

It would be a challenge. But Tes loved a challenge.

She gestured at the mound of parts. "Is this everything?" she asked, and the stranger hesitated.

"Everything you need," he said, which wasn't the same thing, but he clearly wasn't well, and she didn't need him fainting in her shop.

"I'll do it," Tes said. "Eight lin. Half up front."

The man didn't argue. He fumbled in his pockets, pulled out a handful of loose coins. They were all lin, red metal printed with a small gold star, and yet he plucked them out of his palm one at a time, holding each coin to the light as if to check its value before setting it on the counter.

Tes produced a black ticket, a gold *H* on one side and a number on the other, and slid it across the table so she didn't have to touch him. In case it was the kind of curse that spread.

Her eyes were already drifting back to the parcel, the pieces, her mind racing ahead when he asked, "When will it be ready?"

"When it's ready," she said, and then, seeing the fear and panic that swept across his sickly face, she added, "Come back in three days."

She would know by then if she could fix it, or not.

His head jerked like a puppet's. "Three—days." He seemed loath to leave the bundle, broken as it was. He backed away from her, as Nero had done, but there was no ease, no charm, only a cord drawn taut. And then it snapped, and he was gone.

Tes got up and followed in his wake, turning the sign to CLOSED and

202

locking the door, despite the early hour. She scarfed down the remaining dumplings, and brewed a pot of strong black tea, and sat down before the stack of broken parts. She cracked her knuckles, and rolled her neck, and bundled the curls on top of her head.

"Well," she said to the dead owl at her elbow. "Let's see what we've got."

IV

THE OPEN DOOR

I

Lila's luggage hit the floor with a heavy thud.

"You know what I love?" she said, looking around. "You can change the name on the sign and the number of stairs. You can change the color of the walls and the view beyond the window. But no matter how many worlds you cross, a tavern inn is still a tavern inn." She took a deep breath. "Sawdust and stale ale. Always makes me feel at home."

Kell turned in a slow circle, taking in their room at the Setting Sun.

"*Ir cas il casor,*" he said. *To each their own.*

But in truth, he understood the point.

He had kept a room of his own here once, years before. It had been a respite—from palace life, and the weight of the king's attention—but also a place to keep the things he'd picked up on his travels.

And no wonder it felt familiar to Lila as well. After all, nearly a decade ago, Lila had lived in a room on this very spot, albeit in another world. The Setting Sun stood in the same place as the Stone's Throw in Grey London, the Scorched Bone in White.

Fixed points. That's how Kell had always thought of them, those rare places where the worlds perfectly lined up, so that what existed physically in one also existed in another, as if called into being by the echo. A bridge at the same bend in the river. A well on the same hill. A tavern on the same corner.

In those places, the walls between the worlds were thin—at least they had always felt that way to him—and as Kell stood in the center of the floor, he imagined that if he looked up, he would see the pale ribs of the Scorched Bone; that if he took a step, the boards would groan over Ned Tuttle's head; imagined he could feel those other places, the rain beyond the windows, the chill beneath the door, the shadow of something at the edge of his senses. Kell shivered, sure that he could feel—

A latch scraped free, dragging his attention back to the little room.

Lila had flung the window open. Beyond the peaked rooftops and carriage-filled roads, the Isle's red glow reflected up against the low clouds as day faded into night. Somewhere in the port, the *Grey Barron* rocked in the gentle tide, tethered in its berth.

Kell fell back onto the bed, wincing as his body struck the stiff pallet. "And to think," he muttered, "we chose this over the palace."

Lila rested her boot on the wooden chest. "*You* could stay in the palace."

"I could," he said. Then, tucking his hands behind his head, "You could stay on the ship."

"I could," she said.

"So why don't you?"

Lila looked up at the ceiling, and he thought she would tell the truth, then, spill the words she hated to say, the ones he needed to hear, that her place was with him as his was with her. But she only shrugged and said, "I can't stand to be on a stationary ship, chained like a beast to the dock. Makes me feel trapped." She turned toward the bed, cocking her head as her gaze raked over him.

"This reminds me," she said, "of the night we met. Do you remember?"

"When you robbed me, and then used the stolen magic to conjure a double who tried to kill you?" Kell crossed his ankles. "How could I forget?"

She waved her hand. "I meant after the robbery, and before the spell. When I bound you to a bed." A glint in her eye. "Just like this one."

"Lila, don't," he said, but it was too late. The wood was already peeling away from the frame. He tried to sit up, but it wrapped around his wrists like fingers, and forced him back against the narrow cot.

Lila Bard smiled, and sank onto the edge of the bed.

"Let me go," warned Kell, but her hand settled on his chest, the gesture firm, fingers splayed, as if laying claim to the body beneath. She met his gaze, and he couldn't believe he'd ever thought those eyes a matching set. One was vivid, alive, the other flat. The difference between an open window and a locked door.

She leaned down until her hair grazed his cheek. Until her mouth hovered over his. His chest rose and fell beneath her palm.

"Let me go," he said again, his voice dropping low. And this time, she did. But when the binds crumbled from his wrists, Kell didn't pull away. He reached up, threading his fingers through her hair.

"Why didn't you stay on the ship?" he asked again, because now and then, it was not enough to dance around the truth. He wanted to hear her say it. Even if she did not wear the ring. He wanted to know that she chose to be here, with him.

Lila held his gaze so long he could have counted the shards of light in her good eye. And then, at last, almost grudgingly, she said, "Because the bed would feel empty. Without you in it."

Kell felt his mouth tug into a smile. But before he could savor the words, she was up again, and across the narrow room, a knife in one hand and a slip of paper in the other.

"Get changed," she said. "I doubt *Kay* would be welcome at court."

Kell rolled up to his feet. He went to the basin and filled it from a pitcher. The water came out warm, thanks to a spell etched into the spout, and Kell washed his face, and ran a wet hand through his copper hair. He smelled strongly of salt and sea, and had no doubt Rhy would comment on it.

He shrugged out of his coat, and turned it inside out, from left to right, and so Kay's black mantle fell away, replaced by one Kell hadn't worn in months—an elegant red coat, gold buttons running down the front. The edges were trimmed in gold thread and the inside was lined with gold silk, and the whole thing smelled of palace candles and sweet floral soap. It was a coat that belonged to Kell Maresh, famed *Antari*, prince of Arnes, brother to the king.

It was a coat that no longer felt like it fit.

209

Technically, of course, it always would. Every one of the coat's many sides were perfectly tailored to his body. It was in the magic threaded through the garment so that even when Kell's body broadened at sea, new muscles winding over lean limbs thanks to hours of training with his swords, the coat had let itself out across the back, and drawn in at the waist, shaping itself easily to his new form.

And yet, as the crimson mantle settled on Kell's shoulders, it felt all wrong.

He felt wrong within it.

In the mirror over the basin, a ghost stared back. Eyes mismatched, and haunted. Jaw hardened and cheeks hollowed. A single pale streak, like a scar, through his copper hair.

Across the room, Lila drove the dagger she was holding into the wall, pinning the slip of paper there. On it was a symbol, one of the first he'd ever done, a simple circle cut through by a cross. A shortcut. *Antari* magic could take a person to the same place in different worlds, or different places in the same one. But the latter required a marker.

"Remind me again," said Lila, "why we couldn't use your brother's ring?"

A marker—or a token. The first would take you to a place, the other to a person.

"Because," said Kell, "I know better than to walk in on Rhy unannounced." It had been nearly a year since their last visit, and they'd made the mistake that time of traveling directly to the king. They had ended up standing in his private chambers, and Kell had seen far more of Alucard Emery than he'd ever wanted to.

Lila shrugged, and set to work, drawing her thumb along the knife's edge, just deep enough to cut. She used the blood to copy the symbol onto the wall, but he could tell her mind was elsewhere.

"Still thinking of the night we met?"

He'd been joking, but she didn't laugh. "I think about it often," she said as her touch whispered against the wall. "When Holland found me, you already had the stone. There was no reason for you to come back."

"It wasn't your fight," said Kell. "He was using you to get to me."

"Still," she said. "It only worked because you let it."

"Yes. I did." And then, "Good thing you came back for me, too."

Lila tilted her head, examining her work. "Indeed."

He paused, leaning on the basin. It must be the room, or the red light of the Isle, but he was feeling nostalgic. "Why did you?"

"Well, I had so much fun with Holland the first time, I thought—"

"Lila."

She tugged the knife from the wall. "I supposed I owed you. I got away that night because you took my place. I had lost the fight. You know how I hate losing. Turns out I hate it even more when someone else is losing for me. Now," she said, glancing over her shoulder. "Are you ready?"

"No."

Lila smiled. "Good."

He joined her at the wall. She tugged at the collar of his coat, then reached up and ruffled his copper hair so it fell in messy curls around his face. Then she took his hand, and placed her other on the symbol.

"*As Tascen.*"

The world didn't tear open.

It simply fell away.

It didn't hurt, not as it did when Kell performed a spell himself, but it felt *wrong*, as if he were a passenger, dragged along in the wake of someone else's magic.

Then the world took shape again, and the Setting Sun was gone, replaced by the royal palace. Kell reached out and steadied himself against a tapestried wall, waiting for the shallow wave of dizziness to pass before he followed Lila out of the alcove and into his royal chambers. He looked around, at the bed heaped high with pillows, the golden tray balanced on the sofa's edge, the balcony giving way to crimson dusk.

Home.

The word rose up like bile. He forced it down.

This room belonged to a different Kell, the one whose coat no longer fit. The one who had sat at a gilded table downstairs, trying to teach Rhy magic, the one for whom it came as easily as air. And standing there, amid the memories, he flinched, because of how badly he wanted to be that Kell again. To have that life back. But it was gone.

211

He had become someone else. By necessity, not choice.

And yet, this place called him back. Wrapped its arms around him in a strange embrace, and made promises it couldn't keep.

Kell went to the bed, ran a hand over the silk pillows. It had been nearly a year since he'd last set foot in this room, and yet, it looked as though he'd only just left. The hearth was clean, and waiting to be lit. Books sat exactly where he'd left them, their covers free of dust. A pitcher of clean water waited by a marble basin. He imagined Rhy giving the orders, imagined servants drawing the curtains back each day, and returning them each night, going through the motions as if his brother might arrive at any moment.

Kell heard the bedroom doors swing open, and turned in time to see Lila vanish into the hall, followed moments later by the sound of armor as bodies scrambled into motion.

"*Sanct,*" he muttered, hurrying after. He reached the hall, and found three soldiers squaring off, blocking Lila's way. At the sight of Kell they dropped their swords and sank into a bow, three plated knees striking the floor like bells.

"Well, that's just rude," muttered Lila, crossing her arms.

"*Mas vares,*" said the oldest guard, without looking up.

"Welcome back," added the second, who looked to be his age.

The youngest of the three had clearly never seen Kell Maresh in the flesh, because he paled, and instead of bowing his head, looked straight at Kell's eyes, his expression a rigid mix of awe and fear.

"*Aven,*" the young guard whispered under his breath, a blessing that might as well have been a curse.

Kell gestured for them all to rise, and said, "Where is the king?"

"In his rooms," said the oldest, before turning to Lila. "Apologies, *mas arna,*" he added as they stood aside, and Kell could almost hear Lila's teeth clenching at the term. *My lady.* The lights in the hall flared brighter.

Kell made it to the door first, knocking before Lila could barge in. Moments later, it swung open, and there stood Alucard Emery, slouched like a cat in the doorway, shirt open and brassy hair hanging loose around his face.

His dark blue eyes raked over Kell, and his mouth twitched into an arrogant smirk.

"I didn't order this!" he called to the guards over Kell's shoulder. "Send it back."

Kell scowled, and it was a good thing then, that magic no longer rushed to meet his mood. Instead, his hand drifted to the blade at his hip as Alucard looked to Lila, the smirk blooming into a genuine smile. "Bard. *You* can come in."

And then Rhy was there, pushing his lover aside, and flinging his arms around Kell's shoulders.

"Brother," said Rhy, holding him tight. And unlike the coat, and all the other trappings of Kell's old life, this one, at least, still fit.

II

Rhy Maresh was on top of the world.

At least, that's how it felt. In truth, he was perched on the sloping roof over his rooms, one leg drawn up, a bottle of silver wine balanced on his knee, and his brother at his side.

If he leaned forward far enough to look down over the edge, he'd be able to see his balcony below, the light spilling out his bedroom doors. If he looked straight out, he could see the entire city, a sprawling sea of glass and wood and stone divided by the brilliant crimson light of the Isle. And if he looked up, he saw only sky. Low clouds stained red, or the orb of the moon, or, on a dark night, the scattered light of stars.

Ask anyone in London, and they would tell you the best views of the city were those that looked onto the arching palace—but that was because they would never see this one.

A spire rose into a gleaming golden peak at his back, and beneath him, the roof splayed out like the bottom of a too-long cloak. It sloped, but gently—a bottle might roll off, but a body wouldn't—and it was wide enough for two grown men to stretch out, side by side, without their heads touching the spire or their heels grazing air.

One night, when Rhy had been eleven or twelve, he'd persuaded Kell to modify his balcony's wall, to draw grips out of the stone, handholds that could be hidden by the ivy that flowered on the wall. After that, this spot became their secret, their hidden escape.

Or so they thought, until Maxim Maresh's voice boomed up from the balcony one night, promising that if the brothers valued their heads, they would climb down at once.

"I told you it was a bad idea," Kell had muttered after, cheeks still burning from the king's rebuke.

"Then why did you come?" Rhy had shot back.

"To make sure you didn't break your neck."

"You could have stopped me," he'd said.

Kell had looked at him then with bald surprise. "Have you *met* you?"

But Rhy knew that secretly his brother liked their rooftop hideaway as much as he did. He saw the way Kell's shoulders loosened and his hands relaxed whenever they were up here, that constant frown softening to something thoughtful.

He glanced at Kell now, and was surprised to find his brother staring back.

"*Kers la?*" he asked, slipping into Arnesian. They'd always spoken it, when they were alone, to keep their tongues fluent, their accents smooth. At least, that had been Rhy's reason. Kell, he knew, preferred the common tongue.

"*Nas ir,*" said his brother, shaking his head. *Nothing.* "It's just, you look well."

"Of course I do," quipped Rhy, adding, "So do you."

Kell snorted. "Liar."

Was it a lie? Rhy didn't know. He studied his brother. He had always been able to read Kell, but he was starting to wonder if it was just that, growing up, Kell had always allowed himself to be read. But in their years apart, he'd changed, his face, once a pane of glass, now turned until the light bounced off instead of passing through. There was a coiled confidence in the way he held himself, even leaning back on one elbow, an edge that belonged more to a pirate than a prince. Not Kell, but Kay. As if he had to bury his past, *their* past, to live as he did now.

214

He'd managed to put on weight, his shoulders broadened from the months at sea. His pale skin, where it showed at his open collar and his wrists, had become a tapestry of scars. Rhy had felt every one, though his body never held the marks for more than a day or two. But those scars were nothing against the deeper wound. Even in the dark, Rhy could see the bruises beneath Kell's eyes, the long-term toll of so much suffering.

And he knew better than to ask, but he must have been drunker than he thought, because the words came out anyway. "What does it feel like?"

And Kell must have been drunker than he seemed, because he answered honestly. "It feels like my heart is breaking in my chest. Like I'm coming undone."

Rhy looked down at the bottle. "I would take it from you, if I could."

"I know."

"It isn't right," he muttered. "We are bound together. Everything that hurts you, should hurt me."

"This pain lives somewhere else," said Kell. "And I wouldn't wish it on you. Besides," he added with a grim smile, "someone once told me that pain is a reminder that we are alive."

Rhy shook his head at the memory of those words, spoken at a time when he was trying to convince himself. "Sounds like a fool."

"Or an optimist."

"An arrogant prince," said Rhy.

"Don't sell yourself short," said Kell with a smirk. "You were also stubborn. And vexing."

Rhy felt the laughter bubble up inside his chest. And with it, the air between them loosened.

"Well," said Kell, lifting the bottle of summer wine to his lips. "What have I missed?"

And so they traded stories, of the queen's inventions, and the *Grey Barron,* and of Lila, and Alucard. Kell regaled Rhy with tales of life at sea, and Rhy told him of Ren's animal menagerie and Kell smiled, and Rhy laughed, and for a little while, at least, it was easy to ignore the things they left unsaid. For a little while, at least, Kay was gone, and so was the king, and the two brothers drank and spoke of everything, and nothing.

Lila Bard stood over the world.

She ran her fingers down the coast of Arnes, skated her nails across the sea, splayed her hand over London, the tiny points of the palace spire pricking her palm. The model was massive, the land carved from a block of marble, the water made of stained glass. It was a wondrous thing, cities and port towns sculpted from colored stone. Tiny boats floated on panes of blue, or sat like matchsticks in their ports, and the glass of the Isle even turned red as it wound its way upriver from Tanek into London.

Lila took up a miniature ship and balanced it on the end of her finger, as across the room, Alucard drew two short glasses from a gilded cabinet, along with a bottle of wine.

The chamber was nearly as large as the king's, or Kell's, but where theirs were pale marble interrupted by gold silk and polished wood, Alucard's retained the spirit of the *Night Spire,* dark-walled and cluttered with finery. There was no bed—no need, she supposed—but there was a large wooden desk, like the one he'd left in the captain's quarters of his ship—now hers.

Only the ceiling belonged to the palace. Skeins of fabric billowed high overhead, unraveling into a gossamer sky, as they did in every chamber—only it was not sunrise, like Rhy's, or dusk, like Kell's, but the kind of night you found on open water, the blue almost black, the clouds lit by moon.

"I thought you didn't miss your life at sea," she mused, setting the tiny ship down in a port.

"It's not that I don't miss it," explained Alucard, pouring the wine. "I've simply found something worth staying put for." He joined her at the model's edge and handed her a glass. "Compliments of the royal cellar."

The wine inside was the color of pearls, and littered with little flecks of light, and when Lila drank, it tasted like moonlight. If moonlight could get you drunk. She held the glass up, studying the tiny bubbles that rose to the top.

"Tell me," said Alucard, rounding the model, stopping on the other side so the empire lay between them. "What brings the captain back to London?"

"Oh, you didn't hear? I need a ship."

The color drained from his face. "What happened to the *Spire*?"

"You mean the *Barron*?" She shrugged. "Afraid I sunk it."

He choked on his wine, looked at her in horror. "You didn't."

She shrugged, said nothing. The silence drew thick enough to cut. Until, at last, she cut him free. Her lips twitched, and Alucard collapsed back in his chair, the air rushing from his lungs.

"You're not funny," he muttered. "Why have you come back, then? Planning to go abroad?" He wasn't referring to Faro or Vesk. He knew that whenever Lila returned to this London, she made a point of visiting the others.

The first time she went *abroad,* as Alucard put it, it was only because Kell had asked her to. It was in those early months, when he still thought his magic simply needed time to rest. She had gone in his stead, the last *Antari* with working power, first to Grey London, to make sure Osaron's remains were still secure in the cellar of the Five Points (they were), and then to White London, to see what had grown in Holland's wake (imagine her surprise to discover, of all things, a child queen).

As far as Kell knew, those had been her last excursions. But they weren't. Over the last seven years, Lila had gone back again and again, despite having little love for one world, and a wealth of loathing for the other. Call it curiosity. Call it a desire to stretch her legs. Call it twenty-something years of living on guard. But Lila couldn't seem to choose ignorance, didn't believe it would ever equal bliss.

She'd only confided in Alucard when one day he'd broached the subject himself, asking if she would keep an eye on the other worlds. Arnes had enough enemies in its own, he'd said. The last thing it needed was another, knocking at the doors.

Now Lila shook her head.

"If you're not here for the other worlds," he said, "then what?"

She looked down into her glass. "Fair wine and decent company."

"I knew it," said her old captain with a grin. "I'm far more fun than Kell."

"Without a doubt," she said, but the humor was bleeding already from her voice.

Alucard leaned forward, bracing himself against the model cliffs. "What is it?"

Lila drained her glass, and set it down on a stretch of open sea. "Have you ever heard of a *persalis*?"

The look on his face said he hadn't. So she told him: of Maris, and the thieves who made it aboard her ship, of the two who died, and the one who got away. And the prize that went with him.

Alucard listened, eyes storm-dark, chin resting on his palm, until she was done. "And you think this thief was bound for London?"

Lila chewed her cheek. "He was branded, beneath his clothes. Can you guess the mark?" She fluttered her fingers, and Alucard let out an oath.

"A hand."

She nodded. "Since they're intent on tearing down the throne, London seemed the likely place to start." She rose, and rounded the model. "I don't suppose you've found them yet."

Alucard shook his head. "And if they have a *persalis,* it will only make it harder."

"According to Maris, it was damaged in the taking." As if damaged things could not be fixed. As if damaged did not still mean dangerous.

Alucard said nothing, his expression clouded with worry. Lila knew those thoughts. She'd had them, too. A weapon that could cut through space, the way *Antari* did. Only this door could be held open, and let a hundred killers through.

She reached out and rested a finger on one of the palace spires, its tip sharp enough to prick. "The palace is still warded, yes?"

"It is," he said. "But I don't know if those wards would hold against a door made *inside* the walls."

"According to Maris," she said, "there's a ring-shaped key at the core of the *persalis*. Something that has to be placed, to show the door exactly where to open."

If Alucard took heart from that news, he didn't show it. He didn't even seem to be listening. "I should have found them by now," he muttered. "I have eyes all over the city."

"And now you have mine, too," she said, starting toward the door.

He looked up. "Where are you going?"

"To put them to good use."

III

The last thief woke to the smell of something *burning*.

He didn't remember getting back to the room he'd rented, didn't remember collapsing, fully dressed, onto the bed, didn't remember sinking through delirium into the dream.

That beautiful dream.

In it, he'd gone home, and his father hadn't been mad, had simply folded him into his strong arms and agreed that youth was full of folly, said that he was forgiven; that he was, would always be, the merchant's son.

And it was going so well, until the world shuddered back, and he was dragged into waking by the acrid scent of smoke. His mouth tasted like ash, and there was a horrible heat beneath his skin, and he had the disconcerting sense that he was burning alive, being eaten from the inside out by some unseen flame, and that, he thought, must be the source of the smell. Until he heard voices, low and muttering, and accompanied by the all-too-real crackle of flame chewing through wood. He dragged his eyes open, wishing still that he was somewhere else, and saw that he wasn't alone, and his table was on fire.

It wasn't a large fire, not yet, contained to the surface of the table, but a block of a man with lank pale hair and a face covered in scars was slowly feeding the merchant's son's few possessions to the hungry flame.

"See?" said the stranger, crunching the word between his teeth. "Told you that would wake him up."

"A knife would have been faster," said a second voice. It came from the woman who was balanced on the back of his chair, her hair shaved short on the sides and braided long on top. She wore a metal bracer on one forearm, and it caught the light of the growing blaze.

"Left your door open," she said. "Someone could walk right in."

Of course, *someone* had.

219

He didn't know their names, but he knew what they were, and who they worked for. He'd seen them there, lurking like shadows against the wall, on the night he had been given his mission.

Now the woman tapped her fingers absently against the bracer, and as she did, the metal rippled like the surface of a pond. Across the room the pale-haired man tossed a shoe into the fire, which bellowed with unhappy smoke.

The merchant's son tried to rise from his bed, only to feel his body refuse, his limbs leaden. "Put it out," he croaked, wincing as the words raked his burning throat.

The man raised a scarred brow, and tossed the other shoe in.

"We waited," said the woman, unbothered by the growing flame. "Down at the docks. You three were supposed to come to us. But you didn't. We know, because we had to wait."

"Not a nice night for waiting," muttered the man, who was now tearing the pages from a journal.

"Please stop," said the merchant's son, head swimming as he forced himself to sit up. He tried to stand, but the bed was no longer a bed but a boat at sea, rocking beneath him. He sank down again, fought back the urge to retch.

"I hate waiting," continued the woman. "It's boring as shit. And I have to look at Calin there. Which is punishment enough. So I say to him, let's go find them. And turns out, the other two never made it back. And here you are, having a nap."

"If you ask me, Bex," said Calin, "that's pretty inconsiderate."

The woman—Bex—stared at the man, eyes wide, and he frowned. "What?"

"I honestly didn't think you knew any words that big."

Calin turned on her, fists clenched, and for a second, he thought the two might kill each other instead of him. But she waved him away, her eyes still on the merchant's son. They were the flat grey of unpolished steel.

"Where is it?" she asked. He didn't answer. She leaned forward. "You came all the way back to London," she said. "So you must have it."

"I don't—" he tried, and her expression darkened.

"Wrong answer."

"No, I—" he started again, but his stomach heaved, and bile rose in his throat. He retched over the side of the bed. Whatever came up left his mouth tasting like ash and rot. He swallowed. "I don't have it," he managed, "but I did, and I will. It got broken, back on the ship. So I took it somewhere, to get fixed. She'll have to bring it to me. I kept the key." He clawed at his pockets, searching for the metal ring.

But it wasn't there. It should have been. It had been.

Panic rolled through him, but he couldn't think, not with the sickness and the fever and the fire, which was spreading now, licking up one wall, smoke clouding the ceiling. He coughed, searching for something, anything. All he found was the little black ticket, with the gold *H* printed on one side, and the number on the other. He held it out, hoping it would be enough. The woman sat forward and plucked it from his shaking fingers.

"Well, Bex," said Calin, as he splashed the oil from a lantern into the growing blaze. "What do you think?"

"I think this is a fucking mess," she said, pocketing the ticket and getting to her feet. She turned toward the door. "And you can have him."

The merchant's son squeezed his eyes shut.

He didn't want to be a hero anymore.

He didn't want to be a Hand.

He just wanted to go home.

"Nah," said the man. "Waste of a good weapon."

"Since when do you have standards?"

Black smoke plumed across the ceiling, and the two strangers chatted on about who was going to kill him. The man drew a coin, and told the woman to call it. He won, and she rolled her eyes, and the merchant's son decided that he must be still asleep. This was all a horrible dream. He would wake up back at sea, sailing for the floating market. Or in the hull of a docked ship, in bed with a beautiful woman, their limbs still tangled, her fingers running through his hair. He must have drifted off. But he'd wake up.

He'd wake up.

The merchant's son didn't realize he was smiling until Bex shot him a strange look.

"What are you grinning at?" she said, as she turned her hand up, and the metal unfolded from her skin, re-forming into a shining spike.

"I'm still asleep," he said, closing his eyes, sinking back against the pillow.

Her voice, when it reached him, was soft, and far away.

"Sure you are," it said, and then he heard the metal whistle through the air, felt the brief, cold kiss of it against his throat.

He never woke up.

IV

There was a side to Kell few people ever saw.

It was like one of his coats, not the red one or the black one or any of the other sides he favored, but a shiny frock kept tucked away beneath so many turns that no one ever found it.

Except for Rhy.

It had always been a challenge, unwinding his brother.

Before—that was how Rhy thought of twenty-one years of life, as simply *before*; before Black London leaked into their world, before his parents died, before he became king—before, he'd drag Kell out into the city, under cover of night and common clothes, and ply him with drink until he found that rare and precious side. Until he stopped fighting so hard to hold on, and loosened his grip on the world. Until he let go. When that happened, the lines around Kell's eyes—lines that had nothing to do with age, lines he'd had since he was five—would soften, and he would smile, and laugh, and Rhy would marvel at this other version of his brother, and mourn the fact it was so hard to draw him out.

Now, on the roof, that side was shining through.

The bottle in Rhy's hand was long empty, and only a finger sloshed in the bottom of Kell's, and though pain had always traveled louder than pleasure, they'd drunk enough that one's light-headedness added to the other's. Kell's blue eye was bright, his free hand gesturing broadly as he recounted a story involving Lila Bard and a stolen ship that turned out to be carrying nothing but chickens. Which was made funnier by the fact that the Arnesian word for chicken—*corsa*—was so close to the word for swords—*orsa*: the only reason Bard had wanted aboard in the first place.

"You should have seen her face," said Kell. He straightened, just a little, injecting a Lila-esque edge in his voice. "What the fuck am I supposed to do with these?" Kell shook his head, remembering. "Vasry wanted to set them free. He even opened a crate, tried to shoo them over the side before he realized—"

"Chickens can't fly," said Rhy.

"No, they cannot," said Kell.

They met each other's eyes, and laughter bubbled up between them. After a moment, Rhy said, "The pirate life clearly suits you."

Kell raised a brow. "Excuse me," he said with feigned indignance, "I'm a *privateer*," and it was such an eerily perfect impression of Alucard, from the quirk of his mouth to the lift of his chin and the tone of his voice, that Rhy lost the last dregs of his composure, and threw back his head and laughed, and then he was on his back, the night sky sliding in and out of focus.

"I'm going to roll off," he said, gasping for breath.

"I'll catch you," said Kell without so much as a pause.

Rhy's laughter died away. "I know."

Kell lay down beside him, looking up. Silence settled over them again, but it was like a silk sheet on a summer night, cool and welcome. And as his heart slowed in his chest, Rhy realized he was happy. For a breath, it was the loudest thing. But then the guilt rushed in. How could he be happy, when the empire stood on a knife's edge, and the specter of violence hung over his head? How, when his parents were gone, and his brother was broken? And then, right on the heels of that guilt—fear.

Fear, not for his own life—that was an abstract thing, death impossible, and pain endurable—but the lives of those he loved. Fear that he could not shelter their flames as Kell had sheltered his. Fear that beat inside his chest, wrapped itself around his heart and lungs until he could not breathe. Fear that fed on his happiness, grew strong because of it. And that was the madness, the cruelty, that life was fragile, and he had so much to love, and spent all his time mourning the loss before he suffered it.

"Love and loss," he murmured.

"Are like a ship and the sea," finished Kell. It was one of Tieren's favorite sayings. The thought of the *Aven Essen* made Rhy's eyes burn.

Above, the moon was almost full, and when his vision blurred, it looked like one of the paper lamps they launched during *Sel Fera Noche*.

Rhy smiled. "Do you remember the year we hauled all those lanterns up here . . ." Kell had lit the wicks, and Rhy had set them free, and together they had watched the lights float away like newborn stars.

Beside him, Kell lurched upright. "*Sanct,*" he hissed. "I'm such a fool."

"Hm?" asked Rhy sleepily.

"I saw them. In the hold of the ship. I saw them, and I couldn't for the life of me remember what they were for."

"I haven't the faintest idea what you're talking about," said Rhy, the wine weighing down his limbs in a pleasant way. He wanted to hold on to that feeling, but the furrow was back in Kell's brow, and he seemed suddenly, painfully sober.

"We raided a Veskan smuggler. They had weapons, and bottles of tark—"

"I do love tark—"

"—and a crate of white lanterns, the kind we use on the Long Dark Night." Kell's head fell into his hands. "I should have thought to take one, but we were ambushed."

"Is it so strange?" asked Rhy. "Smugglers trade in whatever they can sell, and the lanterns are always in demand. Besides, every crate will be searched when it docks for the festival."

Kell stared at him, aghast. "You can't intend to celebrate this year."

Rhy stared back. "Of course I do," he said defensively.

"You are on the brink of war with Vesk, and a group of faceless rebels is plotting to overthrow you."

"Oh really?" said Rhy, sitting up. "I had no idea—"

"And you would hand them the perfect chance, a night when the city is overrun with strangers and magic, and you are on display."

"I have to do it."

"Don't be a fool," snapped Kell. "You don't have enough guards, and even if you did, you could not predict where an attack—"

"Kell," he said, the name cutting through the air. "I have to."

Rhy didn't look at his brother when he said it, but he could feel the weight of his gaze. A long moment passed. Then, a sharp intake of breath. "Tell me you aren't planning to use this to draw out the Hand."

Rhy rolled the empty wine bottle between his palms. "Fine, I won't."

He did not say that it had crossed his mind, did not say that he had spent the last few months as a prisoner in his own palace, caged by other people's threats and fears, did not say that he was sick of feeling terrified, and powerless.

"Three hundred years," he said instead. "This winter marks three hundred years since the darkness was defeated. By my family. The Maresh." He met Kell's gaze. "How will it look if I *don't*?"

Kell's jaw clenched, but he said nothing.

Rhy stared out at the sprawl of the city, bathed in crimson, the buildings jewel-lit in the dark.

"I am the king," he said quietly. "There will always be someone trying to kill me. Of course, I know it's not me—I'm just a crown, a name, a mantle in a fancy chair. But I admit, it's hard not to take it personally. Especially after the Shadows."

The Shadows—not a terribly inventive name for a rebellion, but then, the Hand wasn't much better. He'd been twelve when the Shadows abducted him from the palace grounds, left him bleeding to death in the bottom of a boat. If Kell hadn't found him—but of course, he had.

"I don't even know why they did it."

"Taxes, I think," said Kell, sipping his wine.

Rhy sighed. "How horribly mundane." But then, what drove the Hand? "I've wondered, you know, if it could be them. The Shadows, going by a different name."

"It's not," said Kell stiffly.

"How do you know?"

"Because I killed them all."

Rhy said nothing. He hadn't known. But he'd suspected. Not because the Shadows had suddenly vanished, though they had. No, there had been a moment the night after the attack. He'd woken up safe in the palace, buzzing with fear in the aftermath, and gone to find Kell. He'd snuck down the secret passage that joined their rooms, expected to see his brother asleep in bed. Instead he'd found him sitting in the copper-plated bath, his head tipped back against the rim. His clothes lay piled on the floor, and the only light was the crimson of the Isle spilling in from the balcony. And in that glow, it was hard to tell, but Rhy swore that the water was red.

His brother hadn't heard him, and Rhy had crept back down the hidden hall, and into bed. Now, Kell's voice dragged him back to the roof.

"The Long Dark Night is still weeks away," he said, emptying the bottle. "If you insist on celebrating, we better find the Hand."

Rhy swung his arm out, gesturing at the sprawling city and the untold thousands who filled its buildings and flooded its streets. "How hard could it be?"

Their footsteps echoed on the stairs.

"I don't suppose you could ask every citizen to strip," mused Lila, "so you can search their skin for brands."

The guards bowed as she and Alucard passed. Not as deeply as they did to Kell, she noticed, but at least none pulled a weapon on her.

"And drive a hundred more to their cause?" Alucard shook his head. "I think not."

"They have a leader," she said. "They must. All hands need arms, and all arms need a head. Do you have no suspicions?"

"I have many—but that is all they are."

"Care to share your strongest angle?"

"That for all their talk, they're not Arnesian at all."

Lila's steps didn't slow. It had occurred to her already, of course. "You think they're being funded by a foreign power."

"The best war is the one your enemy fights with itself."

They walked in silence to the bottom of the stairs. There, Lila rounded on him.

"Don't make the Hand more than they are. They are still bodies, and bodies can be found. They can be stopped."

Alucard gave a thoughtful hum. In this light, he didn't just look tired—he looked ill. Hollowed out. Drawn far past taut, a bowstring on the edge of breaking.

"If you were wound any tighter, you would snap," she said. "When's the last time you slept?"

"Lately, I've found it hard to rest." He flashed his teeth, more a grimace than a grin. "I can't imagine why."

Lila flicked her fingers, felt the cool steel of a blade skate into her palm. "I could try to kill you, if you like."

Alucard managed a thin, startled laugh. "And that would help me how?"

She shrugged. "It gets the blood flowing," she said. "How long has it been since you had a proper fight?"

"I spar with the soldiers every day," he said, a little indignant. "And if *that* is the only way you unwind before bed, I pity Kell."

He started down the hall again, and Lila fell in step beside him, the knife vanishing back into her sleeve. "I suppose there are other ways to burn off energy."

Alucard raised a brow. "Is that an offer?"

"Sadly, I have no desire to bed you. But I'm sure the king would happily oblige if—"

Just then, a small shape darted out from under a chair into their path. Lila stopped, and looked down. It was, of all things, a rabbit. Floppy and golden-hued, with large black eyes and a twitching nose.

"Looks like dinner got out of the kitchen," she said, but Alucard only sighed and hoisted the little beast under one arm.

"Miros," he said grimly. "And where there's a pet, there's—"

As if on cue, a child came bounding around the corner, singing a bedtime song.

"*Gentle, gentle, hissed the snake,*" she sang, dancing between the patterned lines of the lush hall rug. "*Quiet, quiet, barked the dog. Careful, careful, purred the cat, right before it pounced!*" On these last words, she leapt as far as she could, landing in a crouch on one of the rug's golden circles. Right in front of them.

Ren had grown since Lila last saw her, morphed from a stumbling toddler into a small girl with a pointed chin and a mop of black curls. Perhaps, thought Lila, the child wouldn't remember her. After all, a year was a long time, when you'd only lived four. But Ren straightened, and looked up, and her face bloomed in delight.

"Hello, Delilah Bard!"

"Hello, Ren Maresh," she said evenly.

Lila did not like children, and she had decided long ago that Rhy's daughter would be no exception. She would not coddle the girl, would not fawn, would not make her words small and lace her voice with syrup and indulge the child's every whim. Unfortunately, Ren Maresh didn't just *like* Lila—she adored her, and nothing Lila did seemed to dampen that joy. The child was always so damned happy to see her.

"We talked about this, Ren," said Alucard, holding out the rabbit. "Put him away."

Ren took the pet, and then turned and promptly set it down again facing the other direction, watching as it bounced away down the hall. Alucard tipped his head back and sighed, the long-suffering sound of a parent who couldn't be bothered.

Esa had wandered into the hall at some point, too, and the cat sat on a cushion, white tail flicking as the rabbit passed, its lavender eyes hanging on the captain who'd usurped its ship. Lila stared back at the beast until a small voice sang her name again.

"Delilahhh," said Ren, beckoning. Lila sighed, and knelt so she was eye to eye with the little girl. Those eyes, like Rhy's, burned gold inside their halo of black lashes. Ren simply stared at her, waiting. Lila got impatient.

"What do you want?" she asked.

Ren leaned in and cupped her hands around her mouth and whispered, "Do the trick." Lila arched a brow. That was the problem with children. If you did a thing once, you had to be willing to do it again. And again. And again.

"Please," added the princess as an afterthought.

Lila folded her arms. "What will you give me?"

"Come on, Bard," chided Alucard.

228

"What?" she said as the girl patted her pajama pockets. "Nothing is free. And your child is a little hoarder."

Sure enough, Ren shoved a little hand deep into one pocket, and came out with a lin, a ruby earring, a figurine of a palace guard, and single black feather. Lila studied the haul as a greying woman appeared, the rabbit thrust under one arm.

"There you are," she said, addressing Ren. She shot an apologetic glance at Alucard. "I turned my back for just a moment." She was coming forward, empty arm out as if she meant to sweep the child up as she had the pet.

But Lila held out her hand. "Wait," she said. "We're in the middle of a deal." She considered the contents of the child's pocket. "Which is your favorite?"

Ren pointed to the onyx feather.

"It fell off," she explained, very somber, in case anyone thought she'd come into possession of it by less moral means. Lila took the feather, and slipped it into her coat.

Then she looked around the hall, searching for a flower vase or a pitcher or some other source of water. Finding none, her attention drifted to Alucard's hands. She'd left her own glass of wine behind, but he'd brought his along, topping it up on his way out. A healthy pour still sloshed inside.

"May I?" she asked, and by the time he said, "No," the contents were already drawing up into the air, a liquid ribbon of silver wine that coiled around her palm. It twitched, and spasmed, and drew itself into a rabbit.

Ren stared up, delighted, and Lila glanced at Alucard, only to see a strange sadness sweep across his face, the far-off look of someone thrown into a memory. But then he blinked, and looked at her, and it was gone.

The child clapped, delighted, and reached for the watery shape, but it leapt away, escaping from Lila's right hand into her left, a few wayward drops of wine dripping to the carpet in its wake. It was hard to shape an element, harder still to make it move like this, with any semblance of life.

"You know," she said, as the rabbit bounded through the air over her head, "I learned this from Alucard." Seven years ago, in the belly of the *Barron*, when it was still the *Spire*, and he was the captain, Alucard Emery had agreed to teach her magic. Taught her to focus her mind, to latch her will on to words.

Tyger, Tyger, burning bright.

Of course, he'd known then what Lila had only suspected—that there was more to her than flesh and blood and grit, more to her missing eye. He had that strange gift of sight, had seen the silver in the air around her the day they met, threads glowing with *Antari* magic. But he'd taught her all the same. How to hold an element. How to hone it. How to make it hers.

Ren's eyes widened, her attention swiveling from the watery rabbit to her father. "Luca?"

"Yes, Luca," said Lila, shifting the animal from hand to hand like a hot stone. "And he can do this trick, *any time you like.*"

Alucard shot Lila a look over his daughter's head. *Thanks,* he mouthed, clearly annoyed, but she just shrugged. It served him right, for having a kid. She could have stopped there, should have stopped there, handed off the trick and freed herself from Ren's attention.

But for some reason, she didn't.

For some reason, she knelt, so they were eye to eye again, and cupped her hand beneath the magic. Lila's fingers twitched, and the rabbit froze midair, crystals of frost tracing its silver skin. It fell into her waiting palm. But she wasn't done.

"You know," she said, dropping her voice to a conspiratorial whisper. "Luca can do many things. But he can't do this."

Her grip tightened; not enough to break the little sculpture, just enough to prick her thumb on the frozen tip of the rabbit's ear. She whispered, "*As Staro,*" and the animal in her hand turned from ice to polished stone.

Ren's eyes widened, her mouth cracking into a buoyant smile, as someone gasped.

"*Mas aven,*" said the nursemaid, dropping the real-life rabbit in her arms, and sinking into a bow as she realized what Lila had done. What Lila *was.* The look on the nursemaid's face wasn't fear, but awe. She was clearly one of those people who believed *Antari* were more than gifted magicians; they were the true avatars of magic. Chosen. Blessed.

Lila knew that Kell hated such displays of worship, that they made his skin crawl, but she found it nice, now and then, to be seen as more instead of less. In another London, the woman might have crossed herself. Here, she touched her lips, whispered something against her fingertips.

"Sasha," said Alucard gently. "Would you be so kind . . ."

The nursemaid came back to herself. "Right," she said. "Of course."

Lila set the figurine in Ren's outstretched hands, and Sasha hurried forward and lifted the child into her arms. She touched the stone rabbit, running a finger reverently down its back. "Right," she said again. "Your mother will want to say goodnight."

"And that's my cue," said Lila, turning on her heel, and heading for the palace doors. "Night night, Princess."

"Night night!" Ren called back, as Sasha hauled her off to bed.

"She's never bowed that deep to me," mused Alucard, trailing Lila to the doors.

Two guards stood waiting there. They each pressed their hands to the wood, and Lila heard the hum of spellwork come to life, the bolts sliding deep within the wood. And then the doors fell open, and the cool night air rushed in. She stepped out, then glanced back and saw Alucard framed by the golden light of the hall.

"You could join me for a drink," she said, knowing the answer before he shook his head. Lila clicked her tongue. "Fatherhood has made you a bore."

He didn't even pretend to act wounded. His gaze flicked past her to the night-swept city. "You're welcome to a carriage."

Lila snorted. "How generous! I'll take a brace of guards and a trumpeter, too." She spread her arms. "After all, why blend in when you can stand out?"

He offered her a lopsided grin. "You get into so much trouble that I sometimes forget, you don't like being noticed."

She let her arms fall back to her sides. "Hard to pick a pocket when they're already staring at your hands."

She smiled as she said it, but Alucard picked up on the meaning. His mood darkened. "Be careful."

"I'm always careful," she said.

But as she strode down the palace stairs, she found herself humming Ren's little tune.

Careful, careful, purred the cat.

Right before it pounced.

V

Rhy hung his crown on an apple branch.

The lovely brightness of the silver wine had thinned, leaving only a weary cotton in its wake. He knew better than to drink like this; it always tipped his spirits from cheerful to morose. Oddly, Kell swung the other way. He had gone to his rooms singing a sea shanty. Rhy should have gone to bed, too, but his bed was empty, save for the sleeping tonic waiting on the table, and he knew what would happen when he drank it. Knew the way the drug would settle over him, his body, his mind—less like a blanket and more like a pair of hands, holding him down until his limbs went heavy and his mind stopped fighting. And then in the morning, his mouth would taste like stale sugar, and Rhy would have the unshakable sense that he had forgotten something, even if all he'd forgotten was a dream.

He knew, and he wasn't ready, and so he'd swept the crown from the bed, and kept walking, let his feet carry him past his rooms, and down the stairs, and out into the palace courtyard.

The guards had fallen in behind him, churned up like dust in his wake. But at the doors, he bade them stay.

"Your Majesty," they said.

"It is not safe," they said.

"The courtyard is beyond the palace wards," they said, as if he did not know. He did—he simply did not *care*. Let his queen bristle. Let his lover chide. He did not need to be protected. He was the safest man in all the world. He was the Unkillable King.

And he wanted to be alone.

So he commanded them to stay put, and they obeyed, stood there bound by the light of the doorway, as if the warding were a cage, and Rhy, for once, the only one set free.

He moved between the trees of the royal orchard, touched an apple, testing to see if it would yield. But the fruit wasn't ready. It clung to the branches, the skin just beginning to turn pink.

"Patience," Tieren used to say. "Patience is what makes it sweet."

Rhy closed his eyes, and then it was no longer fall, but spring, three years before, and he was no longer alone because the *Aven Essen* walked beside him. There was a drag to Tieren's steps, even in the memory, as if the white robe weighed more than he did.

Death was coming for him slowly, but coming all the same, winnowing the old priest down a little more with every day. When he spoke, his voice was thin, like wind through a reed.

"Some people have a talent for hiding their thoughts, Rhy Maresh. You do not." His laugh was soft, an airy whisper. Only his blue eyes retained their sharpness. "I can see them hanging like a cloud over your head."

Rhy tried to speak, only to find his throat going tight. He looked away.

A moment later, Tieren stopped walking, and rested his hand against a tree, weariness visible in every line of his face.

"Do you need to sit?" asked Rhy, but the *Aven Essen* brushed aside the offer.

"I fear that if I do, I won't get up." And then, at the look of horror in his eyes, that whispering laugh. "I'm speaking of my legs, not my life, Rhy. My joints get stiff."

They walked on, and then Tieren said, "It is not a bad word, death."

And yet, it was heavy enough to stop the king's legs, to pin him to the path. He swallowed, and looked up. The first green buds dotted the trees, and it seemed unfair that Tieren should be withering, when the rest of the world was beginning to bloom.

"Are you afraid?" asked Rhy.

"Afraid?" echoed Tieren. "No. I am *sad,* I suppose, that it is almost over. And there is so much I will miss . . ." And for just a moment, Rhy saw the old man's throat bob, his eyes go misty, before he pressed ahead, ". . . but all things end. That is the nature of the world. Death is essential. A laying down. And I admit, I am looking forward to the rest."

"Rest," echoed Rhy. "Is that all there is?"

"We are borrowed things," said the priest. "Our bodies decay, and our essence—well, magic is the stream that waters all things. It lends itself to us in life, and in death calls it back, and so the stream appears to rise and fall, but it never loses a single drop."

"But what of our minds?" pressed Rhy. "Our memories? What of *us*?"

"We are a moment, Your Majesty. And moments pass."

It was not enough. Not after all he'd seen. Not after everyone he'd lost. "So in death we simply cease to be? We come and go, and then are nothing?"

Rhy could hear his voice rising, but Tieren only sighed. Over the years, those sighs had become their own language, and Rhy was fluent in them. A single exhale could be exasperated, tired, infinitely patient. This sigh had something of all three.

"Just because we do not carry on," said the priest, "doesn't mean we haven't been. We live a life, we leave a legacy. But the river runs one way, and we are carried on it."

Rhy shook his head. "If that were true, I would not be here. You forget, I *died*," he said. He did not say that in that brief but solid stretch of death, he had felt nothing. "I died, and you say that should have been the end, but I came back. Which means I was still there. I did not cease to be."

"Your death was brief," ventured the priest. "Perhaps you were not yet gone. There is a time, after all, when the flame has gone out but the fire is not cold."

Rhy threw up his hands. "You speak as if you do not know."

Tieren sighed, and this time there was impatience in it. "I have never pretended to be *wise*. Only old. So no, I do not *know*. But I *believe*. I believe we do not linger, nice as that would be. I believe that if we do live on, it is in those we love."

There was a word he left unsaid.

Only.

But if there was nothing beyond the dark, then what of his mother and father? Rhy couldn't form the words. What of Tieren himself? What of those he'd lost, and those he would still lose? Alucard and Nadiya and Ren? What would become of all they'd seen and felt and known and

234

loved? How could he carry their hearts in his, when he knew he would forget the sound of their voices, the weight of their hands? And one day when Kell died, and so did he, what then? After all that bound them, would there truly be no tie beyond the dark?

These were the fears that followed him to bed each night, and Tieren looked at him, as if every one was written in a cloud around Rhy's head.

"Love and loss," recited the dying priest.

But Rhy rounded on him then. "Have I not lost enough?" he snapped.

Tieren looked back, a gentle sadness in his eyes. And then he turned and brought his hand to a low branch, running his fingers over the blossom. "How lucky we are," he said softly, "that after every winter, we are rewarded with a spring."

Rhy opened his eyes.

The orchard was dark.

Tieren was gone.

He was alone again.

And yet, something had drawn him out of the reverie. He held his breath, and listened, until it came again.

Footsteps.

Not the heavy tread of soldiers' boots, but the lightest whisper, the caress of leather on stone. Someone trying to be quiet. The king's hand drifted to his pocket and retrieved the small blade he kept there, its surface freshly spelled to incapacitate. He had only to draw blood.

Rhy pressed his back into the nearest tree and waited, ready to drive the blade into the attacker's side, to cut swift and deep, waited as the steps drew near, until the body was close enough for him to hear its breath, and then he rounded the tree, and swung the knife—

And stopped, the blade an inch from the priest's white robes. And for a moment, even now, his heart quickened, and he thought that if he looked up, he would see Tieren's face.

But then he did, and there was no white hair, no blue eyes, no patient smile. They had been replaced by smooth skin and a heart-shaped face, black hair carving a faint widow's peak before running like an ink stain over the pristine robes.

The tenth *Aven Essen* stared at him, amusement spreading like frost across her face. She glanced down at the weapon. "Were you expecting someone else?"

"Ezril," he said, the blade falling back to his side. "What are you doing here?"

She spread her hands, white sleeves fluttering. "I am the *Aven Essen*. I know your heart, *mas res*. I can feel your mood when it darkens, like the wind turning cold."

She kept a straight face as she said it, but Rhy had learned, over the last three years, that where Tieren had been unrelentingly earnest, Ezril rarely said what she meant. And sure enough, a moment later her mouth twitched and she nodded back toward the palace. "One of the guards sent for me. They seem to think you have a death wish."

"Is it possible to have a death wish," he mused, "when you know you cannot die?"

Her smile wavered. "It is," she said, "if you insist on testing that protection every chance you get."

Rhy shot a dark look back at the palace doors. He could see the outline of his guards, within the light. "They shouldn't have summoned you."

"And yet, they did. And I am here. Awake, in all my finery. The least you can do is pretend to need my counsel." And so, they strolled together beneath the branches until the copse of trees gave way to the stone walk that circled the courtyard. To his right, the shining palace. To his left, the glowing Isle. And Ezril at his side.

What a strange replacement she had been, the young *Aven Essen*.

Ezril was raven-haired, with brown eyes that changed shade like tea, shifting from pale to dark depending on how long it steeped. She had the air of a girl playing dress-up in someone else's clothes. There was a mischief to her. A coyness to her voice that belonged to the pleasure gardens more than the priesthood. And on top of that, she couldn't be much older than Kell.

"You are a very young priest," he'd said the day she strode into the Rose Hall.

But she had simply shrugged and met his gaze. "You are a very young king. Perhaps they didn't want to keep replacing your counsel."

Have I not lost enough?

Perhaps this was a parting gift from Tieren.

If so, it was a welcome one. For even though Rhy's heart would always stutter at the sight of those white robes, and there would always be a moment when he longed to look up and see Tieren's face, it would have been unbearable to find one that held its similar age and likeness.

Ezril tipped her head back and sighed, smiling when her breath came out in a thin plume. "The season's turning," she said. "A nice reminder, isn't it? That all things change." Her gaze dropped back to him. "What were you thinking of, before I interrupted?"

"What happens when we die."

"Ah."

Rhy waited for her to say what Tieren had said, to feed him the Sanctuary lines, of currents, and streams, and sleep. Instead, she said, "You want to know what happens after." And then, reading his surprise, "Oh, I know what I'm supposed to say. That we live and die and that is it. That is what the Sanctuary teaches, after all, and perhaps it is the truth. But the Veskans have priests who claim to speak the language of the dead, and in Faro, they make altars to those they've lost. They leave offerings, and seek their council. They lay out extra plates, and leave doors open, even in winter, so that their dead can find shelter."

She stopped walking, white robes settling as she turned to face him. "Who is to say what is truth, and what is superstition? We choose the stories that bring us comfort. Believe what you want."

"What do you believe?" he asked.

"Well, the Sanctuary says—"

"That isn't what I asked."

Ezril's mouth twitched, in a way that said she clearly knew. "I believe there are things we know, and things we don't. We know that magic flows through everything, that the elements can be wielded and made into spells. We know that the world is guided by a natural order, and that it demands balance. But beyond that . . ." She shrugged. "You yourself are proof that magic still holds mystery. After all"—she tapped a finger on his shirtfront, right over his heart, and the spellwork that bound his life to Kell's—"we are taught the river flows one way, and yet, here you are." Her hand vanished back into her robes. "A nice reminder, that we are only guessing."

After that, they walked together, side by side, strolling the moonlit orchard until the clouds cleared from his head, and though Rhy hadn't called for Ezril, he was glad that she had come.

VI

Tes couldn't remember the last time she'd slept.

A headache had crept through her skull halfway through the first night, fueled by sugar buns and bitter black tea. It thudded in time with her pulse, but she didn't care. She was lost in the work.

The next day, she kept the shop locked tight, ignored the occasional knock at the door, the rattle of the handle, ignored the hunger mounting behind her ribs, and the snarl of her curls, ignored Vares until even the little owl stopped clicking his beak, stopped shifting his talons, trying to get her attention. Only his head swiveled now and then, mismatched pebble eyes watching as she rose, and circled the piece, studying it from every side.

"*Kers ten?*" she whispered to the broken object as she worked.

What are you?

It was like trying to assemble a puzzle when you didn't know the image. At first, you simply tried to find the pieces that went together, but at some point, you started to see it, the picture that existed somewhere between what you had and what you didn't.

"*Kers ten?*" she said, the words becoming a chant.

Halfway through the second day, she'd glimpsed the shape, if not the spell. It was a kind of box. Or at least, it was contained in one. But as she put it back together, the magic lined up, too, until she could finally make out the places it had tangled and torn, and how to mend them.

"*Kers ten?*" she asked, over and over.

Until, at last, her work answered back. Told her what it was. What it was meant to be.

Her hands froze in midair as she finally understood. A thread twisted between her fingers, waiting to be woven through, but Tes sat perfectly still, only her eyes darting over the spellwork, reading it again and again to be sure.

And she was.

Not a box at all, though it was made to look like one. No, this was a *door*. Or rather, a door*maker.*

A shortcut, basically, something designed to collapse distance, to allow a person to move across an unlimited amount of space in a single step, regardless of walls, or locks, or space. Which wasn't forbidden. But it was impossible.

Or at least, it should be.

Tes knew that the *Antari* could create doors like this, so that meant the magic was there, it *existed,* but it was a talent only they could use. This device took that power, and handed it to anyone. Tes tried to imagine a spell that would give everyone the ability to see and change the threads of power, and shivered at the thought. Some gifts were rare for a reason.

And yet.

Someone had found a way to take the rarest magic in the world and put it in a wooden box. A box that sat, almost fixed, on her table. And Tes couldn't walk away, not now. Her heart began to race, but her hands were steady. Her fingers moved, quickly now, darting like fish between the final threads of the spell as she paired and mended the last strings, the work going faster and faster until it was done.

Tes tugged off the blotters and tossed them aside, rubbing the bruised skin around her eyes as she took in the device. It looked so *ordinary*. Or it would have, to an ordinary pair of eyes. But to her, it was *incredible*. A piece of *Antari* magic translated into an articulated spell. It was an extraordinary piece of craft, unlike anything she'd ever seen. Tes shoved up from the stool, limbs stiff and aching, body calling out for food and sleep, but she had to know if she'd done it. Had to know if it *worked*.

She took up the box and rounded the counter, knelt as she set it gingerly on an empty stretch of floor. Spellwork like this needed a trigger, but the original commands had been damaged beyond use, so she'd written her own, using Arnesian, and kept it simple: *Erro,* and *Ferro.*

Open, and *Close.*

The word sat waiting on her tongue, growing heavier with every passing second until her mouth fell open, and the sound tumbled out.

"Erro."

The box shivered, and strained, and for a second Tes thought it would shatter, thought she had made a mistake, bound two threads wrong among the hundred there—but then it drew itself in, like a breath, and the spell took hold. The box *unfolded,* the inside limned with light, threads that shot out beyond its wooden borders, vaulted up through the air, tracing the outline of a door.

The air inside the outline rippled and darkened until the shop vanished, replaced by a curtain of shadow. Beyond the veil, a scene rippled and took shape, insubstantial. The blurred outline of an empty road. Motionless. Colorless. Still.

Tes rose, and walked around the door, waiting for something to come out. Nothing did. She reached out, and brought her fingers to the door, let them hover there above the darkness. There was a draft. A metallic smell, like rust, or blood. The bitter edge of frost.

"How strange," she said, and she must have leaned forward, just a little, as she spoke, because her fingers touched the veil and the veil wrapped around her hand, and dragged her through.

VII

SOMEWHERE ELSE

Tes stumbled.

She threw out a hand, intending to steady herself on the table she knew was there in Haskin's shop, but it was gone. The shop was gone, too.

Tes caught her balance, just barely, and saw that she was now standing on the street outside. She looked up, expecting to see the stores that faced her own, but they were all gone, replaced by an unfamiliar stretch of pale stone wall. She shivered, suddenly noticing how cold she was, and remembered—

The *door.*

Tes spun around, afraid it would be gone—but it was still there, thin as a pane of darkened glass propped upright in the road. Through the doorframe, she could just make out a pale shadow of the shop she'd left behind. The box-that-was-not-a-box sat on the ground, in the center of the threshold. Its magic traced a burning line around its edge. Tes knelt and reached out to touch the device. She tried to lift it, but it wouldn't budge, weighed down as it was by the activated spell. She stood again.

Where was she?

An alley, one she didn't recognize, though she knew every one of the routes through the *shal.* Looking around, Tes noticed thin threads of magic that wove through the stone of the wall, and shimmered in the sky above, but the light was different than usual. A deep sound echoed around her, steady as a heartbeat, and it took her a moment to realize what it was: a drum.

She cocked her head, trying to figure out where the sound was coming from. To her right, something *moved.*

Tes jerked around to see an old woman peering out from an alcove. She was dressed strangely, in layers of tattered cloth, her face gaunt, her weathered skin traced with thick black marks. Tattoos. She spoke in a voice as dry and brittle as paper. A question in a language Tes didn't know, which itself was odd—as a child, her father had forced her to learn all the dialects they spoke in Arnes.

She shook her head in reply, and as the woman shuffled forward, into the light, Tes recoiled. The threads of the old woman's magic hung in the air around her like blackened roots, withered and lightless. This wasn't a curse, poisoning the flow of power. There was no flow, no movement at all.

The magic was ruined.

Dead.

The woman spoke again in that strange tongue, and this time her eyes darted from Tes to the doorway—she clearly saw it too—and back again, her hand drifting up, palm open, gnarled fingers flexing toward the veil. Whatever she was saying, it was no longer a question. The edges were flat, her tone sharpening as she began to repeat the same words over and over again like a demand, or a curse.

And then she shot forward, a sudden, feral burst of speed, and caught Tes's wrist with a bandaged hand, her fingers vising, tight and cold as iron. Tes tore free and scrambled backward, catching her heel on the box and falling back through the open door, into the repair shop.

The box didn't move, but as soon as Tes hit the familiar ground, the world beyond the curtain vanished behind its shroud, taking the strange alley and the ravaged woman with it. And yet her hoarse voice was still audible, getting louder, and closer, and Tes's mind tripped after her body, trying to catch up as the withered, inky hand pierced the veil, reaching toward her.

"*Ferro!*" shouted Tes, and the door came down, fast as a falling blade.

Something fell with it, bouncing across the floor before coming to a stop several feet away. Tes crept forward, her hand halfway outstretched before she saw what the object was.

A single tattooed finger.

She yelped, and kicked it away, watching in horror as the woman's severed digit rolled beneath a table. Tes sat, chest heaving, for several seconds, every foul word she knew in any language now pouring from her lips. Finally she calmed, her attention going to the place where she'd conjured the door. It was gone, back into its box, but the air where it had been still looked *wrong*.

The burning edge of the doorway lingered, and Tes squeezed her eyes shut, thinking it must be an echo—she saw them, sometimes, after working too long, the tendrils of magic branded against her eyelids—but no matter how many times she blinked, the lines in the air remained, like a scar.

Her gaze dropped to the doormaker, which now sat, unassuming and closed, on the floor. Something had gone wrong. The magic in the device was meant to create shortcuts, to collapse the distance between two places—and then Tes realized her mistake.

"Stupid, stupid, stupid," she hissed aloud.

A door was only a door if it went somewhere, and how would it know where to *go*? There should have been a terminus, a key, a piece of the device that marked the destination. But there hadn't been.

"Is this everything?" she'd asked, as the man with the dying magic had stared at her, then said, "Everything you need."

Everything she needed, perhaps, to *repair* the doormaker, but not to *use* it.

He'd obviously kept the terminus—and Tes, not understanding what she was fixing, hadn't thought to leave space for it in her repair, or shape a new one. She had just put the spellwork back together without that vital part, mended it as if it were whole, and so instead of creating a door that led somewhere else *within* this world, she'd made one that carved right through it.

Into another world entirely.

Tes drove her fingers into her hair as the force of the error hit her.

She knew the history, of course, though it was old enough to have the taste of legend.

There had been a pair of drawings in her father's store, the four worlds depicted as books stacked one atop another. In the first drawing, the books burned, as if on fire, the bottom one engulfed in a light that stretched up and curled around the pages of the next, and the next, its blaze dimming faintly the farther it reached. In the second image, the bottom book was charred and black, the light replaced by lines of smoke. A single word was printed on the frame below the drawings.

Ruin.

When Tes was little, she used to run her fingers through the air over those drawings, counting up one, two, three, to the book that stood for her world. She'd never bothered giving the other three much thought. What was the point, when she would never see them? Worlds you could not touch became ones that lived in stories, and nowhere else.

But Tes knew—there had been a time when anyone with enough magic could step from one world into the next. There had been a time, but it had ended centuries ago, with the fall of Black London, with the worlds being severed, and the doors locked shut, to keep the poisoned magic out. After that, unless you were *Antari*—and by the time Tes was born, there were so few left—there was no way to move between those different worlds.

Until now.

She had just made one.

Tes rushed over to the doormaker. No longer held down by the force of the active spell, it weighed nothing more than what it seemed: a small wooden box. She carried it to the counter.

Sometimes Tes fixed things.

Now and then, she even made them better.

But she knew, better than most: anything that could be fixed could be broken again.

V

THE QUEEN, THE SAINT, AND THE SOUND OF DRUMS

I

WHITE LONDON

The drums began at dawn.

Duh-dum. Duh-dum. Duh-dum, they sounded across the air, strong and steady as a heartbeat, as if to remind the entire city it was *alive, alive, alive.* The sound spread from each of the nine walls that ran like arteries through the body of London. Once those walls had cleaved the city, carved it up. These days, the pale stone was studded with archways, hundreds of open channels that let life flow, uninterrupted, through the city.

Kosika stood at her bedroom window, eyes closed, and listened to the pulse of the drums while Nasi and the servants flocked around, braiding her hair into a crown and binding her body into layer after layer of ritual white.

She had refused to wear a dress, opting instead for a tunic and a pair of fitted trousers, but she let them settle the long white cloak over her shoulders, and pin it with the Saint's seal. Kosika brought her fingers to the silver sigil, touching it lightly, as she always did. A reminder that she was not alone. That every step she took was in a legend's wake.

The servants stepped back, and Kosika swayed a little side to side, watching the white cloak pool and swish across the floor.

By the end of the day, she knew, it would be red.

Kosika started to smile, but then Nasi poked a pin too hard into her scalp, and she hissed, a small feral sound that the other girl simply ignored.

"You know," muttered Kosika, "it is a crime to hurt the queen."

Nasi plucked another gem-tipped pin from between her teeth. "Then the queen should stand still."

Kosika scowled, and Nasi scowled back, the only one bold enough to meet her gaze and hold it. The servants kept their heads bowed. The Vir did, too. Even Lark would look away first. But Nasi didn't even blink, and soon Kosika gave up the contest, and turned her attention back to the window.

She could feel the city coming to life. Could see the streets rippling with motion as every citizen answered the call of the drums.

It was a tithing day.

The ritual had been her idea, a chance for the city to give thanks—thanks for the seasons, for their blessing, and their cost. And as needs of the city rose, so did the need for the citizens to make their offerings.

Now, the drums rang four times a year—when winter gave way to spring, and spring to summer, and summer to fall, and fall to winter. Four times a year, but secretly, Kosika loved this one the most—the third tithe. The day when summer gave way to fall. She loved it for the color of the leaves on the trees, a blushing red, a golden yellow, shades she'd only dreamed of when she was small. She loved it for the changing skies, and the way they reflected on the Sijlt each morning and each night.

And she loved it—selfishly—because it was her birthday (a bad omen, her mother had said, to come into the world when the life was going out, but standing in her castle chamber, Kosika hardly felt that she'd been cursed). And while she would never let the occasion of her birth overshadow the importance of the tithe, she still took some secret pleasure in it.

This year more than most.

Today, Kosika turned fourteen. An age that mattered to her in one way and one alone. She'd been on the throne for seven years—seven years marked by peace, and power—which meant she'd now spent half her life as queen.

And every day from this one forward, she could say she'd ruled longer than she hadn't.

Nasi slid the last pin into her hair, and Kosika moved away from the window, and toward the silver ash tree that grew in the center of her room. Its roots drove down between the stones, its branches up toward the vaulted ceiling. Kosika stopped before it, and touched the bark as if for luck.

Then, only then, did she feel ready.

Nasi held out the silver blade, and Kosika fastened it at her hip as the drums echoed on through the city, calling everyone to bleed.

The castle doors swung open onto a waiting world.

Dozens of royal guards flanked the pale steps, and halfway down, Kosika saw Lark. He stood out—he always did. Only seventeen, but already taller than most, his silver-blond head tipped back, dark eyes on the sky instead of the ground, the scar that wrapped like a chain around his throat on full display, as it always was. He wore it with such pride.

At the base of the stairs, the Vir stood waiting. All twelve members of her council, adorned in their silver half-cloaks, Serak at the front, his dark head bowed, his gauze-wrapped hand resting on the Saint's seal at his shoulder.

Beyond them, the courtyard brimmed with citizens and soldiers, and all those who lingered hoping to catch a glimpse of their queen as she set out on the tithing road.

And yet, for a moment, Kosika didn't move. She stood at the top of the castle steps, and felt the sigh of morning on her skin, felt the crispness on the air, one season tipping into the next, the balance of it all, and the change, the rise and fall of her breath, in time with the drums, and she felt small and vast at once, a single drop in the Sijlt, and all the water in the world coursing through her veins. She felt beyond the edges of her narrow frame, and knew that she stood in the blessed place, in the center of the current, and let it draw her forward, over the edge and down the stairs.

Kosika descended, the white cloak rippling around her, as to every side, the heads bowed and the voices rose to greet their queen.

Seven years ago

The day the world changed, Kosika was trying to take a nap.

She and Lark were sitting on top of the Votkas Mar, the Fifth Wall, which was her favorite one because it was the highest, and from there she could see the river snaking through the center of the city, and the castle, jutting up like a piece of shattered slate. Usually she'd make a game out of counting market stalls or passing carts, but today, she was stretched out along the top of the wall, one arm thrown across her eyes. She was tired, but that was probably because she hadn't gone home, not since the incident with the collectors in her mother's kitchen the day before.

And then Lark poked her in the side.

"Have you heard the news?" he said. "The king is dead."

And as soon as she heard the words, she just knew.

Knew that the body she'd found in the Silver Wood the day before, the man slumped against the tree as if asleep, the one with the grass growing beneath his hands, was the king. She knew it in her bones, and in her fingertips where they had touched his, and behind her ribs, an ache like sadness.

She'd gone back to the Silver Wood first thing that morning. By then, the man's body was gone, but she could still find the right spot because the grass was still there. More than that, it had spread, like a puddle, overnight, and she had lain down on it, in it, the tender blades brushing her cheek. She thought of the soldier sobbing.

"What happened?" she asked, surprised to find her eyes burning, her voice tight.

Lark shrugged. "What always happens to kings, I guess. Someone must have killed him."

But Kosika knew that wasn't true. She'd seen him, in those fine-cut clothes, that silver half-cloak, and there had been no blood, no wound. He didn't look as if he'd been struck down. He'd looked peaceful. A tired body searching for a moment's rest.

"It's going to get bad again," Lark mused, watching as a pair of soldiers passed by below their perch. And he was probably right. It was always bad, after someone killed a king. Even if he hadn't been killed, and no one came forward to claim they'd done it, there was now an empty throne, and who knew how many people would try to take it. In the end, it would go to the strongest, or the most brutal, and either way, it could take a while.

Kosika closed her eyes, sadness pooling in her chest.

Life had just started to get better. There was warmth in the air. She imagined the cold seeping back in, the magic slipping away again, and shivered.

She dug her fingers into the wall, and it was strange, but she swore the stone was humming faintly beneath her hands. She frowned, pressing her palms flat.

"Do you feel that?" she asked, but Lark wasn't listening. He was counting out coins on the wall between them, the profit from the amulets she'd found yesterday morning. The sound of the metal *clink clink clink*ing made her stomach turn, but as soon as he was done, Kosika grabbed them—five silver tols. Enough to buy bread and cheese and meat for a week. Enough to feed her mother as well, Kosika thought, before she remembered *why* she'd been in the Silver Wood. She hadn't told Lark about that. She knew she'd been lucky to start out with a mother, even a bad one—he didn't have anyone, and he'd gotten by. She would, too.

Kosika shoved the coins in her pocket, frowning at the way the metal sang against her skin, the silver going warm, almost soft, as if it might melt. She felt a little dizzy, and when Lark hopped down from the wall, and reached back up to help her, she shook her head, and said she'd stay a little longer.

"*Oste*," he called over his shoulder, jogging away.

"*Oste*," she called back.

They never planned when or where they would meet again. They didn't have to. He'd come find her, or she'd go find him. Kosika's gaze drifted over the city, and she started counting the boats on the Sijlt. She'd gotten up to nine before she heard the scream.

Her head whipped around. The sound was close, close enough to make the hair prickle on the back of her neck, to make her skin tighten and her

251

blood tell her to run—not toward the trouble, never toward—but as Kosika hopped down from the wall, another scream split the air, and she knew that voice, even though she'd never heard it in that shape, never heard it so full of pain or terror.

Lark.

She took off in the direction he'd just gone, the same direction of the scream, rounded the corner, the road splitting into three, and even though the voice bounced off the walls, she knew where it was coming from, could feel it, like a string drawn taut between them. She took a sharp right, and there was Lark, fighting with all his strength, even though a chain was wrapped around his wrists. He'd always seemed so big to Kosika, so tall, but he was so much shorter than the two men attacking him, so much smaller than the fist that crashed against his cheek.

"No!" she shouted as his body buckled to the street. One of the men turned toward her, and her heart lurched in her chest as she recognized him from her mother's house, the rope tattoo on his left hand, his body all gristle and grease.

The collector smiled.

"Well, well," he said, a second length of metal hanging from one hand.

Behind him, Lark was trying to summon fire, but the chain around his wrists must be cutting it off, because his fingers splayed and nothing happened. He tried to get to his feet, but the man shoved Lark back down as the one who'd paid her mother started toward Kosika.

"Run!" shouted Lark, and she wasn't proud of it, but Kosika took a single step back before arms came down around her, a third man crushing the air from her lungs and hauling her off her feet. The first was still coming toward her with that chain, and the world was humming and she didn't so much *think* as *reach* for the stone wall and pull it toward her.

And to her surprise, it came.

A massive piece of the wall listed, leaned, and tore free, crashing down like a wave onto the gristle man, burying him beneath the stone. The arms around her tightened, and she slammed her head back, felt the satisfying crunch of teeth, even as it sent a lancing pain through her own skull,

252

her vision going black-and-white for a second before the captor cussed, and dropped her. She hit the ground hard, skinning her hands and knees. When she touched the back of her head, her fingers came away red. She was hurt, and scared, but there was no time for fear.

"You little bitch," said a voice, paired with the scrape of steel, and Kosika twisted toward the man who'd grabbed her, blood spilling from his broken mouth as he slashed the sword through the air and she flung her hands out in a useless plea for him to stop.

And he did.

His whole body jerked to a halt, limbs trembling, like a bug stuck in a spider's web. She could feel the bones shivering beneath his skin, could feel the metal in his sword as it turned, tip driving back into his chest, could feel the life leave his body as he fell to the ground.

She stared, shaking as she got to her feet.

"Kosika."

Lark's voice was a hoarse whisper, and she turned and saw him, past the pile of rubble, on his knees, his head wrenched back and a blade against his throat. He made a signal with his bound hands. *Run*. But this time her legs didn't betray her. This time, they carried her *forward*.

"You stay right there," ordered the man, his fingers tangled in Lark's silver hair. The blade kissed the boy's throat, drawing a thin line of blood. Lark winced, and there was fear in his eyes, but his hands were moving again, not signaling now but reaching, and she realized too late, that Lark was reaching for the knife he kept in his boot.

It happened so fast.

Lark pulled the blade, and drove it down into the man's foot. He howled, and jerked back, drawing his knife across Lark's throat.

"NO!" screamed Kosika, running as fast as she could, not for the man, who was already fleeing, but for her best friend as he slumped and toppled to the dirty street. She'd always been fast, but the wind was at her back, and it pushed her, carrying her toward him with impossible speed. She fell to her knees beside Lark's body as his mouth opened and closed, as his eyelids fluttered and his life spilled out, too much, too bright.

Kosika tore the chain from his wrists, and pressed her hands to his wounded throat.

"*Nas aric,*" she pleaded, as the blood slipped between her fingers. *Don't die.*

"*Nas aric,*" she whispered, again and again, but as she did, the words changed in her mouth, the *n* to a softer *h,* the end open, a new plea welling up. A word Kosika didn't know, had never said before.

Hasari.

Another sound rose up to join it, like a hitching breath. *As.*

"*As Hasari. As Hasari. As Hasari.*"

The strange words spilled out like a chant, and as they did, the blood stopped pouring from Lark's throat. There was so much of it, on him, and on her, and on the road beneath, but his skin was no longer grey. His body went slack but it was the kind of relief that came with sleep, not death. Lark's chest rose and fell, and when she dared to lift her hands from his throat, she saw the gaping wound had closed, leaving only a raised line, like a welt, running from edge to edge across his neck.

Kosika let out a sob. Lark's eyelids fluttered, and drifted open. He swallowed, and the first thing he said wasn't a question. It was only two words, whispered in a tone of wonder.

"Your eyes."

And before she could ask what he meant, she heard the heavy tread of armored boots, and looked up to see two soldiers, a man and a woman, marching toward them in dark grey plate.

"What happened here?" demanded the man, and only then was Kosika aware of her surroundings: the city wall, half-collapsed, a tattooed hand sticking out from the rubble; the body with the sword jutting out from his chest; Lark on the ground, still covered in blood, but not bleeding; her own hands stained red, her body still humming with fear and relief. Other faces were starting to appear, in windows and doorways, studying the scene.

"On your feet," ordered the woman, and Kosika rose, stepping in front of Lark as she did. She wanted to run, but he couldn't even stand, not yet, and she wouldn't leave him. Besides, she was starting to feel dizzy, as if she was the one who'd lost all that blood.

Kosika was still trying to decide what to do when horse hooves thundered on the stones, and a third soldier arrived, dressed differently from the other two, clad in silver armor and riding a dark horse. A royal guard. He dismounted, and removed his helmet as he took in the scene.

"*Kot err,*" he muttered. *King's breath.* And then, louder, "Who did this?"

"I did," said Kosika, defiantly meeting the royal guard's eyes. His breath caught, surprise sweeping across his face.

She didn't realize one of the previous soldiers had gone away until he returned, hauling the collector who'd slit Lark's throat—the one who'd gotten away. The man was limping, the little knife still stuck in his foot, and babbling on incoherently until the royal guard made a sign and the grey soldier struck the man hard, so hard he fell to his knees, and stayed there. *Good,* thought Kosika, and she might have gone and kicked him for good measure, but the royal guard turned and knelt in front of her so they were face-to-face.

The silver armor on his chest was so polished that Kosika could *almost* make out her reflection in the gleaming metal. Almost, but not quite.

"Whose blood is that?" asked the royal guard, gesturing to her hands. Kosika flexed her fingers, the red drying brown on her palms. Most of it was Lark's, but she had touched the back of her head, before, hadn't she, which meant a little must be hers, too. She didn't say any of that, only glared at the man on his knees.

"He cut my friend's throat."

The royal guard didn't look at the collector. Didn't look at anyone but Kosika. His hair was pale, his eyes the color of the sky, a watery blue.

"Good thing you were there to fix it," he said, and there was something in his voice; not anger, or kindness—it was *wonder.* She heard the hiss of steel being released, and then the man on his knees toppled forward, his throat open and blood spilling out onto the street, the way Lark's had minutes before. But no one rushed forward to fix *him,* and so Kosika watched, satisfied, as he died.

One of the grey soldiers—the woman—was kneeling next to Lark now, helping him sit up, and Kosika wanted to go to her friend, to make sure he was all right, but the royal guard held her still with his gaze.

"How long have you had magic?" he asked, and she was about to say that she didn't, that it hadn't arrived yet—but obviously that wasn't true, not anymore. When she didn't answer, he tried again.

"Where is your home?"

Kosika chewed her lip, wasn't about to tell the guard that she no longer had one, that last night she'd slept in an attic with a loose window latch, hoping there weren't mice. She just shook her head, and the royal guard seemed to understand, because instead of pressing her, he said, "My name is Patjoric. What is yours?"

That, at least, she could answer. "Kosika."

"Kosika," he repeated, his face breaking into a smile. "Do you know what it means?"

She shook her head. She hadn't known a name could *mean* anything— her mother told her she was named for the jagged stretch of the Kosik itself, which ran along the city's edge like a wound that wouldn't heal. But the royal guard looked her in the eyes.

"It means *little queen*." He straightened, and held out his hand. "You must be tired and hungry, Kosika. Why don't you come with us to the palace?"

She tensed, suspecting a trap, wondered if the guard was just another kind of child thief. And Lark must have thought so, too, because he was on his feet now, lurching toward them.

"Don't go," he shouted hoarsely. But the female soldier grabbed him by his arms and hauled him back, and anger rose in Kosika like a wave as Lark tried, weakly, to pull free.

"*Don't hurt him,*" she said in a feral growl, and the world seemed to echo with her voice. The stones beneath her feet began to tremble, and what was left of the wall began to lean, and a gust of wind whipped against her skin, and the whole alley groaned and splintered, and she didn't hear the bootsteps or see the hilt of the sword until it crashed into the side of her head.

And everything stopped.

II

Now

Kosika would be the last to make her offering.

She made her way down the castle steps, and the royal guards fell in stride, trailing like shadows in her wake. She passed the silver-clad Vir at the bottom of the stairs, and then the crowd that lined the path. Merchants and sailors, tailors and bakers, parents with children in their arms, all of them bound together not by their age or dress, but by the bandage wrapped around their palms.

Servants stood waiting at the castle gates, their trays piled high with sugar buns for those who had already made their offering. The first of three rewards for the first of three tithes.

A reminder that this was not just a day of sacrifice, but celebration.

As Kosika neared the altar on the path, the air took on the copper scent of blood, and the crowd cleared to reveal a statue of a man, poised above a shallow basin, the surface shimmering red.

The stone figure was larger than life, though folded beneath its weight, depicted on his hands and knees. The man's head was bowed beneath an unseen force, his shoulders hunched, his shirtfront torn askew, revealing the binding spell once burned into his chest by Athos Dane. Holland's carved stone hands pressed into the bottom of the basin, so that as it filled, the blood rose over his shins and wrists, and made it look as if he were sinking, inch by inch, into the pool.

Kosika approached, stopping only when she was close enough to look up into Holland Vosijk's face. To see the pain in his jaw, the furrow of his brow, the eyes, cast in different shades, one pale, the other black.

Just like her own.

"First you were a servant," she said softly to herself. The words were not for the crowd. They were private as a prayer.

She pulled the silver blade from her hip and drew it across the meat of her forearm, one swift, deep cut. Blood welled, and spilled into the waiting pool, rippling the surface. Kosika ran her fingers over the weeping cut, and touched them to the collar of the basin. Unlike the rest, this part was made of frosted glass instead of stone.

"As *Steno*," she said, and the *Antari* spell took shape in the world, breathed into life by her power. The surface of the basin rippled like a pulse, and the glass walls *shattered*.

Blood spilled like rain over an awning. It splashed, and pooled around Kosika, staining her white clothes. It poured out until the basin, which was no longer a bowl but a plane of flat stone, was empty, and Holland's hands revealed themselves, stone fingers splayed against the rock.

Kosika stood there, as blood leached up the hem of her white cloak, and soaked into the soil of the courtyard, turning it the black of loam.

The first tithe was done.

Seven years ago

Sunlight danced across the ceiling.

That was the first thing Kosika saw when she woke up—at least, she guessed it was a ceiling, but it was so far away. The stone walls surged up, and vaulted overhead, but the ground beneath her was too soft to be ground, and too soft to be a bed, even though that's what it was. A bed so big she could lie in the center, her arms and legs thrown wide, and not come close to reaching the sides. And for a moment, that's what she did, her mind blissfully blank as she looked up at the light on the ceiling, and tried to remember—where had she been? On top of the wall with Lark, staring up at the sky, and then—

She heard a sound.

It was quiet, the soft *tap* of a pebble hitting stone, and Kosika sat up, wincing at the sudden pain in her head. She touched her temple and it all came rushing back, the thieves and the struggle and Lark and the soldiers, and then she was scrambling across the pillowed ground, trying to reach the edge of the bed.

"Oh good," said a voice, "you're awake."

Kosika jerked around, and found a girl sitting cross-legged in a nearby chair, elbows balanced on her knees. She had fair hair drawn back in a braid, and a narrow face covered in scars, as thin and white as seams.

On a low table in front of her was a game board, half the figures black and gold, the rest silver and white. They mingled on the board, and a few lay cast aside, as if in the middle of a game, but if she'd been playing, it must have been against herself.

"Who are you?" asked Kosika. The sound of her voice made her temple throb, and she reached up and touched her head.

"I'm Nasi," said the girl. "If it's any consolation, the soldier who hit you has been arrested."

Kosika didn't understand. She'd been struck a dozen times by a dozen people, and no one had so much as said that they were sorry.

"If you ask," continued Nasi, "they might even kill him."

Kosika winced. She didn't want to kill anyone. "Why did he hit me?"

Nasi nodded to the window, as if there was an answer there. Kosika hopped down from the bed—the jolt of landing sent another spike of pain through her skull—went to the sill, and gasped. She wasn't in a house. She was in a castle. *The* castle. This high up, she could see the grounds and the high stone wall that ringed it, could trace the nine smaller walls of the city as if they were chalk lines, could count every block and square. The carriages were the size of raindrops, the people grains of rice. The Silver Wood sat, the size of her palm, at the city's edge, and all of London sprawled beneath her like a toy set or a tapestry.

It took her a moment to see it, but then she did. From here, it was small, little more than a patch of shadow, a broken line, a pool of dark. When she brought her hand up, she could cover the whole mark with the tip of one finger. But she knew that up close, it was bad. Part of the Votkas Mar was missing, and deep cracks ran down the street. It looked like a large hand—like the one she held up now—had crushed the spot beneath their thumb.

Kosika felt a little dizzy, a little sick.

"They were scared," explained Nasi. "Of what you might do if you kept going."

Kosika turned. "I didn't mean to."

259

The other girl only shrugged, and moved another piece on the board. "But you did."

Kosika's heart began to race, and at the same time a breeze kicked up in the room, even though the windows were closed. What about Lark? What if they'd hurt him? What if *she* had? She had to go, had to find her friend. She went to the massive door, and pushed, and pulled, with all her strength, but it didn't move.

"It's locked," said Nasi, as if that wasn't obvious.

Kosika looked around at the chamber, at the lush tapestries that covered the floor and hung from the walls. The room was big, bigger than her whole house, and made entirely of stone. "Are we prisoners?"

The girl studied the board. "I'm not," she said. "As for you, maybe." Kosika would learn that Nasi didn't bother with gentle lies. She believed it was always better to know the truth. "But," she went on, "there are far worse places to be kept."

Nasi held out the bowl of fruit, and Kosika's hand darted forward, quick-fingered, before the other girl could pull it away. But Nasi only held it, and waited, and Kosika's hand slowed, her eyes searching. She took a plum, and bit down, shocked by the sweetness.

Nasi took one, too.

"If you *want* to leave," she said, studying the fruit, "I'm really not sure they could stop you."

Kosika thought of the destruction in the street below, and wondered if the other girl was right. She was about to find out. Turning back to the door, she pressed her hands flat against it, and focused. She could feel the wood, and the metal, the place where they met. She began to pull and—

"What are you doing?" asked Nasi.

"I have to find Lark."

"Blond boy?" ventured the other girl. "Dark eyes? Covered in blood?"

Kosika rounded on her. "You've seen him? Where is he?"

"Last time I checked, he was in the kitchens, eating the Vir out of bread and cheese and everything else."

"Vir?"

"The royal guard. That's what they call themselves. Very proud, dressed all in silver."

Kosika remembered the pale man who knelt before her. Patjoric.

Nasi waved her over to the board. Kosika came. Up close, she saw the pieces were not all the same. There were knights. And cloaked figures. Children. And kings.

"It's called kol-kot," explained the girl, clearing the pieces from the board until there was only a white-and-silver king. "When Holland Vosijk took the throne," she said, "the Vir were the first to bend their knee. The first to believe that he was the Someday King."

As she spoke, she added white-and-silver knights to the board, one by one, until they formed a circle around the king. Kosika counted them: thirteen.

"Now the king is dead." Nasi lifted the figure from the center of the circle, and set it, almost gently, to the side. "And the Vir are trying to hold the peace, but it's only a matter of time before someone comes along to claim the empty throne by force. But they're hoping it won't come to that, not if *you* take Holland's place."

Kosika reeled. "Why me?"

"Well," said Nasi, setting another piece—a child—in the circle, "because you are like him. *Antari*."

Antari. Kosika didn't know that word, and it must have shown on her face, because Nasi rose, unfolding her narrow limbs from the chair. She was clearly older than Kosika, but still half-grown. Closer to Lark's age, maybe nine or ten, her cheeks full, but her arms and legs thin, as if she were sprouting up at different rates.

Nasi went to a shelf by the bed and lifted a small mirror. She came over and held it up for her to see. Kosika studied her reflection.

She was still an in-between girl, with in-between skin and in-between hair. But only one of her eyes was its usual in-between shade. The other was now black from edge to edge and lid to lid, like someone had poured ink into the socket. Kosika recoiled at the sight, scrubbing furiously as if she could clear the stain. But when she pulled her hand away, it was still there.

"Eyes like that are rare," said Nasi. "It's a mark of magic. The last king had an eye like yours, and he woke up the world. Now you have one, and they think maybe it's a sign. Maybe the magic will keep coming back, so

261

long as an *Antari* stays on the throne. Maybe you can keep the city from plunging into war. Maybe they will look at you and see a good omen, a beacon of change. Or maybe," she went on, "they will see a helpless child standing in their way, and cut your throat."

Kosika swallowed, but she couldn't take her eyes from the mirror. She reached out and touched the glass, even as her heart thrilled in her chest.

"What do I have to do?"

"Nothing," said Nasi. "Just stay. And stay alive." She handed the mirror off to Kosika. "And try not to destroy any more of the city."

With that, she went toward the door, and knocked three times.

"What are you doing?"

"Letting them know you're awake."

A heavy bolt slid free, and the door swung open onto a hallway, and a silver guard—a Vir. He looked past Nasi to her, and then sank to one knee, head bowed.

"Kosika," he said softly, and it took her a moment to realize he was not addressing her by name, but title.

Little queen.

III
Now

The sun was high by the time Kosika reached the second station on the pier.

Her fingers were sticky with sugar, and stained red. She'd eaten the bun on the walk from the castle to the plaza at the river's edge, dusting the last traces of pastry from her palms along with flecks of drying blood.

The crowd along the Sijlt was twice as large as that in front of the castle, and twice as boisterous, the mood made bright by the second tithe's reward: a steaming cup of cider wine. The drums played on, counting out the city's pulse, but here they were joined by other music. Nearby a woman sat on a rooftop, singing a song about the Someday King, and merchants sold food to go with the gifted drink, and Kosika's arrival was heralded with cheers, and bows, the crowd parting to allow their queen and her guard, then folding closed again, as if she were a fire, and they hoped to feel her heat.

Nasi and two of the Vir had yet to make their second tithe, so Kosika stopped to watch and wait. Lark caught her gaze, lifted a cup of wine, and winked, and she fought the urge to roll her eyes, even as her cheeks warmed. She wasn't sure why his smile did that to her. She didn't want his attention, not like that. And yet, when he turned that smile on a pretty girl in the crowd, she felt the warmth curdle.

"I don't blame you," observed Nasi, wrapping the strip of white cloth around her hand. "He *is* pleasing to look at."

"Then you may have him," said Kosika, too fast.

"How kind," said Nasi, "but I prefer your company."

Kosika ducked her head to hide her smile.

The truth was, she loved them both, always had, but these days, Kosika loved Nasi and Lark with a need that frightened her, a hunger that climbed into her bones and burned there, and made her want to hold them close, to bind them to her. She thought of the Danes, binding Holland, and wondered if it had been an act of hate, or necessity—a need to keep him close, to feel them linked. Not that she would ever follow in their footsteps.

Then the way was clear, and it was time.

Kosika approached the pier, and the second altar.

This Holland Vosijk stood waiting for her, no longer on his knees, but standing upright on a plinth over the water. A polished black crown circled his stone temples, and his two-toned gaze looked straight ahead, at his city, at her. A carved cloak lifted behind him, caught in a permanent breeze, and his boots vanished into the basin at his feet, his reflection rippling in red.

"First, you were a servant," Kosika said under her breath. "Then, you were a king."

Beyond, and below, the river glowed. The Sijlt had thawed with Holland's reign, but it still ran pale. Mist clung to the surface, and the water itself emitted a soft silvery light, not unlike frost, that Kosika finally understood was not a sign of sickness, but strength. A place where magic gathered. Where it flowed. It was the first place to suffer, and the first to heal.

Her eyes dropped to the waiting basin.

So much sacrifice. And yet, in truth, it was only a few drops. A few drops from each and every soul in London. *We all must bleed a little . . .* she thought, drawing the blade across her skin a second time.

A second time Kosika touched the side of the basin, and said the ritual words, and a second time the walls of the altar shattered, and the blood cascaded down into the river below, a moment of deep blooming red before it dissolved in the tide. People stood downstream, and watched as the ribbons vanished in the current, but her gaze lingered on the statue, the bottom hem of its cloak dripping blood, just like hers.

Kosika turned back to the plaza, where Nasi stood waiting with a cup of cider wine and—

She felt the blade sing toward her.

The whistle of metal, the glint of steel, but Kosika was already drawing the air tight on instinct, the way someone else might suck in a breath, wrapping it into a shield the moment before the dagger struck, and clattered, useless, at her feet.

Shouts went up, a strangled cry, and then Nasi was there beside her, her own weapons ready. The Vir drew in like a wall, and then the guards were on the would-be killer, forcing him out of the crowd and onto his knees. He fought, until a gauntlet collided with his face, a sword slicing toward his throat.

"Wait."

The excitement had bled out of the plaza, taking the sounds of celebration with it. Only the distant drums beat on, unaware of the incident, so Kosika's voice rang out through the square.

The guards stilled. The man fought like a mouse in the grip of a snake.

Kosika looked down at the weapon on the pier.

It was not the first time someone had tried to kill her. And on a Saint's Day—but she supposed that was the point. There were those who wanted her dead because she was queen, and those who wanted her dead because she was *Antari*. Because they believed the power of Holland's life lay only in his sacrifice.

And sure enough, the man was ranting on under his breath.

"*Och vil nach rest,*" he said, again and again, as soft and swiftly as a prayer. *In death, you set us free.*

264

Kosika stepped over the blade, and crossed the square to the four soldiers, and the man on his knees, his face swelling from the gauntlet blow. And as she neared, she saw that his hands were unwrapped. Unmarked.

"You have not tithed," she said.

The man looked up at her with venom in his eyes. "The world does not want *our* blood," he hissed. "Only yours."

The queen considered her fingers, stained with her offering. "Is that so?" She brought her hand to his shoulder. "Shall we ask the world what it wants from you?"

He tried to recoil from her touch, but the guards held him fast. Kosika closed her eyes and waited for the words. That was the way of the *Antari* spells. They came as she needed them, whispered through her head, and shaped themselves on her lips.

So she waited, and the guards waited, and the citizens and soldiers in the square all waited, and the moment drew long and still, and in that stillness, a new word rose to meet her, and she gave it voice.

"*As Orense,*" she said, and the spell's meaning echoed through her as she spoke it.

Open.

A strange spell, and not the one she would have chosen, but it had been chosen for her, and as she said it, the man's eyes went wide and his mouth yawned, and his skin *split,* as if held together by a hundred invisible seams that all gave way at once, and his blood poured forth—not the drops he would have given in the tithe, but all of it, every crimson ounce, came spilling out into the pier.

He did not scream.

No one did.

It was London, after all. They had seen horrors.

And it *was* horrible.

But it was also right. It was the world's answer to the man's claim that only she should bleed.

The guards let go, and what was left of the man's body fell like wet rocks into the spreading pool that had been his life. But Kosika would not waste it. She reached out, and the blood rose and flowed in a ribbon across the square and over the river's edge, before vanishing into the Sijlt with the rest of the sacrifice.

And with that, the second tithe was done.

Six years ago

Kosika held a hand over Nasi's face, to make sure she was breathing. She could see the steady rise and fall of the other girl's chest, but it still amazed her, the way Nasi slept—as if there was no danger in it.

Kosika didn't know how to sleep like that.

Her mother used to sleep like a star, her limbs flung out to every side, so if Kosika wanted to join her in the narrow bed, she had to fold herself into the empty spaces, and even then, she only skimmed the surface of sleep. Her skin had always been awake, her ears pricked for trouble. Now and then, she'd sink deep enough to dream, but even those crumbled as soon as her mother stirred.

Now Kosika sat up, eight years old and wide awake in the massive bed, marveling at Nasi's steady breath, how lost she was to the world. She gave a testing bounce, but the other girl didn't so much as murmur.

She huffed. The least Nasi could do was keep her company. She considered shaking the girl awake, forcing her to play a game of kol-kot, or tell her a story, but Nasi would probably punish her by telling a scary one, full of shadows and teeth, and then she'd have the nerve to fall right back asleep.

Instead, Kosika slipped down from the bed.

Her nightgown whispered around her ankles, silver and white. Her feet were cold, and she eyed a pair of slippered boots, almost left them—it was easier to sneak around without the shuffle of shoes—before remembering she didn't have to be quiet anymore. This was her castle. This was her home. She could be as loud as she liked.

Kosika stepped into the shoes and padded to the window.

Beyond, the moon was a white hangnail in the sky, and the river had taken on a pearly glow. At midday, you might not notice, but when the sun went down, it gave off a silvery shine, like starlight.

The first year, the whole castle had seemed to hold its breath, the soldiers waiting, hands on weapons, for the inevitable fight. But there hadn't been any fighting. Kosika was presented to the city, and the city accepted her like a gift. Their Little Queen. No one had come forward to challenge her claim. At least, not that she knew of. If there had been stealthy attempts, they hadn't gotten very far.

People accepted her, she knew, because London was changing faster now, magic rushing back. Nasi could conjure water, and did so every chance she got (Kosika hoped magic wasn't the kind of thing that could run out, or Nasi wouldn't have any left by the time she turned twelve). And it wasn't just the children.

Some of the grown-ups were getting magic, too.

Every day, there were more of them, adults now able to conjure fire or wind, water or earth. And they all said it was connected, to the old king, and to her. And it had to be, didn't it? After all, she was the one who'd found him in the Silver Wood, even if nobody knew it. She was the one with the black eye, the mark of magic.

Now people came to the castle every day, wanting to see her, to touch her, to be blessed. They came, and sometimes the Vir let them through, and sometimes they didn't. One day, even her mother came, suddenly full of want. Her mother, who'd tried to sell her. She came, and for a moment, Kosika thought it was because she missed her daughter, wanted her back. But she didn't. She only wanted to be *paid*. The Vir kept her away after that. Sometimes, when she was falling asleep, she could still hear the coins on their kitchen table going *clink clink clink*.

Kosika turned away from the window, surprised by how dark the room seemed now with the thin light of the moon at her back. She curled her fingers, and fire ignited in her hand.

It was so easy—as easy as wanting, and she knew how to want. Other people struggled to conjure a flame. She struggled only to contain its size. The fire bloomed, hot and bright, swallowing her fingers, and she held her breath and focused until it shrank back to candlelight, hovering just above her palm. Nasi slept on as she shuffled past the bed, heading for the doors. Most of the floor stones were smooth but a few were patterned, and she liked to play a game, hopping between the marked ones until she reached the other side.

She pressed her ear to the carved surface of the door, listened, and heard nothing, save for the hum of the wood against her palm, inviting her to take it, to bend it, to make it grow. She imagined it coming apart beneath her fingers, braiding itself into tendrils, into limbs, a tree, but she must have imagined it too hard, because the door let out a splintering crack. Kosika jerked her hands away and squeezed her eyes shut and imagined the door as a door and nothing more. And when she opened her eyes again, it was still there.

She pushed it open.

A pair of soldiers stood on the landing beyond, dressed in armor so dark it seemed to swallow the light, making them blend right into the walls. She knew they were there, even if they didn't move, knew they weren't going to lurch forward and grab her. She knew—but she still walked a little faster until she was safely past them, and on the stairs.

Almost a year she'd lived in the castle, and Kosika still hadn't learned the whole shape of the place. She knew there were four towers, and that she was in one. She knew her stairs led down and down and down, three landings, and three floors. She knew that on every floor below, there was a four-sided hall that went all the way around, touching the towers and studded with narrow windows that looked out onto the city. She knew the thirteen Vir stayed on the two floors beneath her, and that the bottom floor held the castle proper, with the throne room and half a dozen other halls, and also some of the guards. She knew there was another floor underground, for the kitchens and the castle servants.

She knew, but in the dark sometimes, she still got turned around, so she kept to the halls that bordered each floor, counted to make sure she touched all four sides and ended up back at her own tower. Tonight, she miscounted. Or perhaps she didn't miscount. Perhaps she heard the whisper, or saw the light ghosting on the stairwell wall, and simply followed it up the tower steps.

When she reached the top, she saw a Vir.

In her mind, the thirteen Vir were like the little kol-kot statues Nasi had used, all of them more or less the same. Some were tall and others short, some dark-skinned and others pale, but in their silver armor and their half-cloaks, the ring pin at their shoulders, they blurred together in her mind, these chosen few, the members of the old king's original guard.

This Vir stood before a kind of altar, a shrine placed before a door like the one that led to her own rooms. At first, she thought there was a second Vir in front of him, but then she realized it was a statue.

A statue of the old king.

His head was bowed, just like when she found him in the Silver Wood. But here, he was on his feet, a crown resting on his stone temples.

Kosika crept closer and saw that the altar in front of the statue had been draped in a silver cloak, just like the ones the Vir all wore, the same silver ring pin lying at its center. Candles stood around the ring, and she watched as the Vir lit them one by one, then knelt.

She thought of the soldiers in the Silver Wood. The way one of them fell to their knees before the old king's body. This Vir didn't fall, but he sank slowly down, and whispered, so softly she couldn't hear the words, only the breathy sound they made.

When he spoke again, it was to her.

"*Os,* Kosika," he said, and she jumped, fingers tensing around the little light in her palm, which went out. The Vir rose and looked at her. His hair was thick and dark, taking over his face like a thicket, from the heavy eyebrows that looked like soot smudged across his brow to the beard that shadowed his jaw.

"What are you doing?" she asked.

"Making devotions."

Kosika drifted forward, and studied the statue of the old king. From this angle, she could see the shine of two polished gems set into the stone face, one green, the other black. They stood together for several moments, and the Vir didn't talk. Kosika felt she shouldn't either, but questions had always made her tongue itch.

"Who was he?"

"His name," said the Vir, "was Holland Vosijk."

"Holland Vosijk," she echoed. When she said it, she tasted the sugar cube melting on her tongue. Felt grass tickling her fingers. She didn't know much about the man she'd found in the Silver Wood, only that he had gone to sleep, and something in her had woken up.

"Tell me about him," she said, and even though she was queen, she added, "please."

The Vir smiled, his gaze still on the statue.

"Have you heard the story of the Someday King?"

"Once there was magic," she told herself. "And it was everywhere . . ."

Kosika's fingers trailed along the castle wall as she spoke, reciting the story to the stones, and the grass, and the sky. She could feel the rocks singing beneath her fingers, feel the ground humming under her bare feet, which she knew wasn't fitting for a queen, but she didn't care.

She was alone—but of course, she was not alone. She was never alone. A handful of Vir studied her from a balcony. The soldiers watched from atop the wall. Nasi glanced down, now and then, from the nearby tree where she was perched, reading a book on strategy and war.

"Once there was magic," she began again, "and it was everywhere. But it was not equal . . ."

Every night for the last month, she'd met Serak—for that was the Vir's name—at the top of the stairs, and every night, he told her the stories, and every day, she told them to herself, until she knew them all, inside and out. Stories of the time before, and the time after. Of the other three worlds, and what happened when they disappeared behind their doors. Of the way magic was bound, and the way it withdrew. Of the way the world began to wither.

Of the many kings and queens who tried to force it back into the world, and failed, because they did not understand: a thing taken by force would always be a pale shadow of something given freely.

Of the challengers who rose, all claiming to be the Someday King, the legendary figure who would call the magic home, and how the magic refused them one by one, because they gave nothing of themselves.

And then, of Holland Vosijk.

Holland, who did not want the throne, but helped his friend Vortalis to it, Vortalis who was slain one night by Astrid and Athos Dane, who captured

Holland, and branded him with magic and bound him into service, and made him wear the mark of his own capture on his cloak.

Serak told her of the Danes, how they held the throne for seven years, before they too were killed, and Holland had disappeared, and when he returned it was not as a servant, but as a claimant to the empty throne. How the few who stood against Holland fell like wheat beneath the scythe of his most devoted, Ojka, who was a Vir before they were called Vir, and when he took the throne, how he did not try to force the magic, to bind it to him, it simply came. The river thawed, and the color flooded into the world like a blush into cold cheeks, and all knew, then, that Holland was the Someday King.

Up in her nearby tree, Nasi turned the page. She had heard all the stories by now. Kosika told them to her every night, and when she learned that Nasi had *been* there, in the castle, that she had met Holland, first as the servant and then as the Someday King himself, well, she had wanted to know *everything*.

"What was he like?" Kosika asked again now, and Nasi looked up from her book.

"I didn't *know* him any better than you."

"But you saw him . . ." And Kosika wanted to say *alive*, but she hadn't told anyone, even Nasi, of that day in the Silver Wood.

She'd almost told Serak once—for all the stories he'd given her, she didn't have any of her own. She knew he'd believe her, it wasn't that, but that encounter felt like something that lived only between her and the dead king. A light cupped in their hands. She wanted to keep it there.

"How did he seem?" she pressed.

Nasi looked off into the distance, as if trying to remember. At last, she offered up a single word. "Lonely."

She waited for the older girl to say more, but Nasi went back to her book, and Kosika drifted away from the wall and the tree, and took up her story again, reciting it like a prayer, tracing the words as if they were as string, a ribbon, a road. And at some point, Kosika looked up, and realized she had wandered around the side of the castle and was standing at the edge of the statue court.

It was a gruesome sight, a stretch filled by the bound and twisted forms of the kings and queens who'd climbed to the throne, and fallen from it. Serak told her they were only sculpted tributes, but Nasi insisted that they were real people, turned to stone. That the Danes had started the awful court, to make an example of anyone who tried to stand against them. Kosika didn't know if Nasi was being truthful or just teasing, but she stopped before the twins, Astrid bound on her knees, Athos on his feet, being eaten by a massive snake. She leaned in and wondered if they were in there, caught forever at the edge of death.

There was no statue of Holland in the courtyard yet, but the space had been made, the path changed so that anyone who came through the gate and crossed the court to the palace stairs would be confronted by him.

She looked around. She'd heard some call the statue court a garden, but there were no flowers anywhere. The London air had warmed, and the river no longer froze, but the castle grounds were still sparse, the ground unyielding. Kosika had never seen a garden, not in real life. Only in books, pictures of thick grass and wild blooms, and once, in a painting Serak showed her, a painting of the city, the way it must have been in the times before.

Kosika knelt and pressed her palm to the dark soil, remembering how the ground had felt beneath the old king's body. Lush as velvet. She knew, now, that Holland's magic ran through her veins.

She was his heir.

And she wanted a garden.

Kosika had no knife on her, but she searched and found a bit of broken stone around the turned-up earth, brushed away the dirt, and brought it to the inside of her arm. She pushed down, dragged the jagged edge across her skin until blood welled.

It hurt, but it was supposed to hurt. Give, and take—that was the nature of *Antari* magic.

All she needed was the word. The spells had come to her strangely, not all at once, but one by one, appearing only as she needed them. So far, she had learned the words to *open,* and to *close,* to *light,* and to *heal.*

To *heal*—the first *Antari* spell she'd ever needed. It had spilled out of

272

her as Lark's blood poured through her fingers. To heal—that must be the one she wanted now. After all, what was she trying to do, if not heal the ground itself?

Something moved at the edge of her sight. Nasi had followed her into the courtyard, her voice drifting between the statues.

"What are you doing?" she called out, but Kosika was focused on the task at hand. She swiped her fingertips along her bleeding arm, and drove both hands deep into the damp, dark soil.

"*As Hasari.*"

She held her breath, and waited for the spell to work, for the grass to grow, for the flowers to bloom, for the barren earth to change beneath her hands. But nothing happened. And yet, Kosika could feel the pull of magic, feel it being drawn out of her, down into the soil. Her head began to pound.

Something was wrong.

She tried to pull her hands free but her body wouldn't move, her bones locked in place and her pulse roared in her ears as the world reached up—not the ground but something deeper—and drove a hundred hooks into her—not skin but something deeper—and was too big, it was too big, it felt like being crushed, like her breath and her blood and her life was being squeezed out of her and eaten up and she tried to scream too but nothing came out, and the last thing she saw was the flash of silver armor and the flutter of a half-cloak and a crown of dark hair as Serak put his hands over hers and pulled them from the ground and something tore inside her and everything went black.

Kosika was back in the Silver Wood.

She had been running, from someone, something, it didn't matter who, or what, because the moment she plunged between the trees, she knew they wouldn't chase her here. Knew that she was safe. And yet, her legs kept moving, drawing her deeper into the trees, heart pounding until she realized the pulse she felt wasn't in her chest. It was beneath her feet. She stopped then, knelt, and sank her hands into the soil, and began to dig, and dig, and dig, until her fingers closed around the beating heart, and Kosika woke up.

She was alone in bed.

It was too big without Nasi in it, even with the pillows piled around her, and she didn't even remember lying down, but daylight was streaming through the windows, high and bright, and every part of her ached, from her skin down to her bones and deeper still. Ached as if she'd been scooped out of her own flesh and put back, like the soup they made and served in gourds. Her stomach growled at the thought, and even that hurt, and she wondered why.

Kosika tried to sit up, but her limbs felt pinned down beneath the sheets, and a strange fear began to steal across her then, that she was still dreaming, or worse, that she was dead. She pushed at the blankets, desperate to be rid of the weight, and then Vir Serak was there, at her bedside, silver half-cloak swaying.

"Gently, my queen."

His beard was longer than it had been that morning, and dark shadows pooled beneath his eyes, as if he hadn't slept in days. That was odd.

"What's wrong?" she croaked.

Her throat was dry, and it took two tries to shape the question, and when she did, the Vir's dark eyes took on a shine. But when he spoke, it wasn't to her. She didn't realize there was anyone else in the room until he turned and said, to someone she couldn't see, "Tell them she is awake."

A door opened, and then closed, and then Serak explained, in his storyteller's voice, what had happened, and that was how she learned that she had been asleep for more than a week. That they didn't know if she would die, or wake, or be forever trapped between the two. And there was more that Serak wasn't saying. She could see it in his eyes, or in the lack of them, the way he wouldn't meet her gaze when he said that the city did not know about her illness, that the Vir had been holding council, trying to decide what to do.

They'd been planning for her death.

And then the door flung open, and Nasi was there, and she wasn't crying, but Kosika could see she had been, the way her eyes were ringed with red when she flung herself against the bed, and the first thing she said was, "What were you *thinking*?"

And only then did Kosika remember sinking her hands into the barren earth, remember the horrible pull as the hungry soil ate up everything she had to give.

"I thought I could heal it," she said, feeling small and foolish as the words came out.

Kosika should have known, when the world didn't offer up a spell, should have known that its silence was a kind of warning.

"Your power is strong," said Vir Serak. "But even you have limits."

"I had to do something," she said. "We have roused the magic from its sleep, but it is weak. I felt its need. I felt its thirst."

"That may be," said Serak, "but there is not enough blood in your veins to water this world."

Kosika sat up a little straighter.

"Then perhaps," she said, "we can water it together."

IV

Now

The tithe road ended at the Silver Wood.

Around the grove, the people of London stood gathered and waiting, their final bounty in their bandaged hands. It was a bag of seeds, the pouch spelled so that when planted with the rest, no matter the season, the seeds inside would grow. Another reminder of why they made this trek each season, of why they had been asked to bleed.

The crowd seemed somber, and she wondered if word had reached them of the would-be killer in the square, if that was why they bowed their heads so low when their queen went by.

Kosika walked into the waiting woods, and paused, smiling up at the pale trees. Overnight, it seemed, their leaves had turned from green to gold, begun falling in haloes on the ground below.

She made her way to where the third and final altar stood, not deep within the trees, but just inside the forest's edge, nestled among the silver trunks so that pale wood bled right into pale stone.

The third and final statue of Holland Vosijk stood on a raised block flush with the basin, so that when the bowl was full, as it was now, he seemed to walk atop the blood instead of wading through it. He no longer wore his crown but held it in his hands, his head tipped back, his gaze turned to the canopy, and the waiting sky. A thicket of branches tangled around his cloak, so that he seemed part of the Silver Wood, or it a part of him.

"Once, a servant," said Kosika, standing before the altar, "then a king." She drew her knife. "At last, a saint."

She made a third cut on the inside of her arm, the deepest yet, and watched her blood join the pool until it brimmed, threatening to overtake the edge. She stared down into the surface, waiting for it to smooth, then touched the basin's glass side and said the words. The altar walls gave way, soaking into the roots of the Silver Wood, the dark stain spreading farther up her once-white cloak.

The third tithe done, the citizens began to turn away, retreating down the path and into the streets, making their way home.

But Kosika lingered, her gaze trained on the trees ahead. A thousand eyes stared back, unblinking, from the narrow trunks, and it was hard to think that she had ever been afraid of this place.

She moved past the statue. Into the woods.

Four years ago

"Once, there was magic," Serak began, "and it was everywhere."

Normally, the alcove burned with candles, but that night, only one was lit, its small, unsteady flame casting jagged shadows onto the walls, and the statue, and the Vir.

"Magic was everywhere, but it was not equal."

As he spoke, his hand drifted, as it always did, to the seal at his shoulder, the silver cloak clasp, a ring driven through by a bar. It was the same seal that lay on the altar, and she knew now, it was the same one Holland had worn when he served the Danes, the same one Athos burned into his skin to bind him. The Vir wore it to show that they had bound themselves to Holland's legacy.

"It burned like a hearth fire set in the center of a house, heating one room first, and then the next one, and so on, its warmth and light growing weaker the farther that it must reach. Black London was the first room, the one closest to the flame. And we were the next. And then two more followed after, farther from the heat, but still within the house."

Serak took a candle and set it on the altar.

"But the flame became too strong, and Black London began to burn." He took up a lantern. "And instead of standing near a hearth, our world now stood beside a conflagration. And so the worlds decided to close their doors to stop the fire's spread." He set a lantern over the candle. "But even after the fire was contained again, the people here were still afraid."

The lantern had four thin glass walls, all of them open, but as Serak spoke, he began to close the sides.

"We looked out at our magic, and feared it would grow too hot, too hungry."

He closed the first side.

"And so we trapped it."

He closed the second.

"We built cages."

He closed the third.

"We bound it to us."

He closed the fourth and final wall, trapping the flame within the airless glass.

"But do you know what happens to a fire when it's trapped?"

Kosika watched the light shiver and shrink.

"It goes out," she whispered.

"It goes out," echoed Serak, sadness heavy in his throat. Kosika could not take her eyes from the flame. She watched as the light began to thin, retreating from a tall flame to a short one, from gold to blue, felt a twist of panic as the life retreated down the wick, until it met the pool of wax and—

—died.

A thin tendril of smoke rose from the candle, clouding the lantern. For a moment, they stood in silence in the full dark, and she held her breath, and wondered if the lesson was done. But then, Serak spoke again.

"Here is the difference, Kosika. Magic does not die."

Serak lifted the lantern off the candle, setting it aside.

"Magic withdraws. It resists."

He held his own hands out to either side of the extinguished candle, brows furrowing with the effort.

"It grows harder and harder to kindle again, but—"

A small spark. A tiny flash of blue, and then flame slowly returned, small and fragile, but burning. And Serak smiled.

"That is what Holland did for us," he said, lowering his hands. "What will *you* do?"

Kosika studied the solitary candle, its light barely reaching the walls.

What will I do? she wondered, and then held out her hand, not toward the single, burning flame, but the hundred darkened candles lining the alcove. She flexed her fingers, and the tapers burst to life, fire spreading in a wave until the entire space blazed with light.

Now

No one followed Kosika into the woods.

Not her soldiers, or her Vir. Not Serak, or Lark. Not even Nasi. The Silver Wood was now a sacred site, and no one else was allowed to pass within. Her cloak dragged in her wake, snagging on new growth until her fingers found the clasp. It came free, and the heavy cloth slid from her shoulders, and pooled in her wake, and she continued on, until she found the place where Holland had died.

She knelt, and ran her fingers through the grass that grew, as it always did, beneath the tree, as soft and green as the day she found him.

Even after all these years, she'd never told anyone that she'd been there. The first to find the dead king's body. Perhaps the Vir would welcome the knowledge, see it as further proof of her claim to magic and the throne. Or perhaps they would say that she'd taken his strength, stolen it from his cooling skin. Kosika didn't know, and didn't care. The truth of that day, like the power in her veins, did not belong to them.

Kosika drew her blade, and made a fourth cut along the inside of her arm. A private tithe. Let the red drops fall like rain onto the patch of grass below the tree.

She knew the right spell now. The *Antari* word she'd wanted in the courtyard the day she nearly died.

As Athera.

To grow.

But she didn't say it. Didn't need to. The golden leaves shimmered overhead. The roots ran strong and deep below. They had been watered well.

She rose, and hauled the heavy cloak back over her shoulders as, beyond the woods, the drums finally stopped beating. They didn't end all at once, but trailed off like a slowing pulse, as word spread through the city that the ritual was done.

VI

THE
STRANDS
CONVERGE

I

RED LONDON

There were plenty of things that set Delilah Bard apart.

But perhaps the most important, at least here, in this London, was this.

She didn't *need* magic.

Sure, it made things interesting, but she'd been raised in a world without spells, without shortcuts. And despite her eye, or perhaps because of it, she'd learned the importance of close study. Of observation, exploration, boots on pavement.

Lila had no doubt the palace was doing everything it could to find the Hand. And yet. The fact was, Alucard may have played at pirate, but he'd never stopped being noble, Rhy was the literal king as well as the target, and Kell could practice being a swashbuckling sailor all he liked, could shed his coat and call himself Kay, but he had been the best magician in the world for the first twenty-two years of his life, and he was still, and would always be, a prince. All three men had been born and raised in power. That was how they saw the world. That was how they saw their city—from the stronghold of the *soner rast*.

But a city was so much more than that.

It didn't have one face, one mood. It could call itself one name, but in truth, it was made up of a hundred smaller worlds, private and communal, domestic and wild. A handful were dazzling bright spots and a few were lightless corners, but the vast majority fell somewhere between.

There was the night market, for instance, the shimmering, magic-filled tents that bloomed in the shadow of the palace, and thrived in the Isle's light. And there was the Narrow Way, an alley south of the *shal* that catered to darker tastes. But there were dozens of other markets on dozens of other streets, less flashy, perhaps, but just as full.

Every city street had its own rhythm, its own color, its own pulse. And the best way to learn them—the only way, really—was by walking.

So that's what Lila did.

She walked. Not the way Kell did, with the purposeful strides of a man always on a mission. No, she walked like a body with nowhere else to be. She strolled, her head tipped back, and her hands in her pockets, fingers grazing the tokens. The same ones Kell still insisted on wearing around his neck.

A shilling, for Grey London.

A lin, for Red.

And a tol, for White.

As she felt the tol's shape—an eight-edged coin, struck in silver—she thought of her first visit to the city after Holland's death, how relieved she'd been to hear they'd crowned a child queen. That was, until she saw a painting of that child's face. Lila had looked into those two-toned eyes— one hazel and the other black—and muttered, "Fuck."

She had returned to Red London, and a waiting Kell, had told him about the healing city and the child queen and, at some point, had decided to leave out the fact she was *Antari*. Kell had enough problems, so Lila had resolved to handle it herself.

She'd gone back, again and again, and every time she thought about killing the young queen, and every time she decided to wait another month, another year. It wasn't mercy that stayed her hand, not really, only the knowledge that White London was a power-hungry place, and whoever came next might well be worse.

So Lila had waited, and watched as, over the years, the city took on color like a pale body in the sun, watched as it raised monuments to Holland Vosijk, watched as the *Antari* grew from a child into a lanky teen, watched, and waited for those two-color eyes to turn and look to other worlds. So far, at least, they hadn't.

And one day, if they did—well, she would handle it.

Lila turned her attention back to the city around her, the street unspooling beneath her boots. She remembered the first day she'd come to Red London, hitching a ride on the back of Kell's magic. They'd been dragged apart by the force of the spell, and the first thing she'd come across was a parade. A vast spectacle of magic, strange and wondrous. The sight of it had made her hungry, and she felt that hunger now—not in the pit of her own stomach, but the city itself. In the gaps left between wealth and want, and how they'd spread.

As she moved away from the shelter of the palace, she felt the city change. It was a subtle thing, like the slow rise of a tide, or the air in the hours before a storm, but there all the same.

It only took her an hour to find the first sigil.

She stopped before the wall and ran her fingers over the stone. The paint was long dry, beginning to flake, but she could tell that it had been a hand.

"Where are you?" she murmured, laying her own palm flat in the center of the mark.

It was then she noticed that the hand was tipped off-center, turned faintly on the axis of an invisible wrist, as if mid-wave. She tipped her head the same direction, to the left, looked down the road. Into the *shal*.

Lila frowned. It felt too obvious. The roughest corner of the city was surely the first the royal soldiers would have searched. But the night was dragging on, and she had no other leads, so she took a deep breath, and plunged into the warren of streets as if the darkness were a curtain, one that parted to let her through, and swung shut again in her wake.

She found the second handprint one street down.

And then a third.

But the tilt of the hand always went to the left, which was as good as leading nowhere. Or, she realized, in a circle. Lila closed her eyes and called up a map inside her head, and laid the marks like pins, until the picture formed.

The hands made a loose ring around the block, a circle of three shuttered storefronts, a stable, a brothel called the Merry Way, and—

Lila froze. She turned her thoughts a different way, calling Verose back to her, along with the tavern, and Tanis.

If you find yourself in London, she had said, *I hear the gardens are lovely.*

Lila swore under her breath. The city had plenty of greenery, but Tanis hadn't been talking about flowers. Red Londoners had a special term for brothels. They called them *pleasure gardens.*

She doubled back down the road until she found the canopied entrance of the Merry Way, and went in.

In retrospect, calling the Merry Way a pleasure garden was . . . generous.

It was more a rowdy tavern offering a collection of dark corners and rooms overhead, and you didn't have to listen hard to hear the sound of bedposts scraping on the floor. Lila leaned against the wall beside a belching fire, nursing a pint and watching as hosts drifted through with painted red lips, and let their hands graze the shoulders of any patrons whose affections they'd accept.

More than once, Lila sensed a host coming toward her, and sent them on their way with a pointed look, flattered though she was. She took a sip of her ale, and winced. It was black, and bitter, thick enough to leave a trail on the inside of the glass. And like all brothel drinks, it was brutally strong.

That's what she was counting on. It was common knowledge that liquor made tongues loose. It also made them loud. Whispers quickly became shouts, and secrets had a way of spilling out as patrons leaned further into their cups.

And yet, so far, she'd learned nothing.

Oh, she'd heard the usual mutterings of discontent, but not a single mention of the Hand. No one even had the decency to look as though they were conspiring. One man did spit the king's name, but it had all the force of a mumbled oath. Other than that, it was raucous laughter and slurred stories and a sailor passed out by the fire. Either the patrons were good at holding their tongues. Or, she suspected, they weren't involved.

This wasn't the right garden.

And now, her own head was beginning to fuzz in that warning way, and she knew that when she stood, she'd feel the swell and sway of the floorboards underfoot. But she had sea legs, and knew how far she could go before they failed her.

So Lila stayed long enough to finish her drink.

When it was gone, she went to leave the glass on the bar, and for the first time noticed it was cracked.

She traced the line, her thoughts skating like a pebble off the shore. What was it Maris had said, about the *persalis*? That it had been damaged in the fight. Maybe it still worked, and maybe it didn't. Say it was broken. Needed to be fixed. An object that dangerous, maybe they'd try to repair it themselves. But if they hadn't—if they *couldn't*—

Lila flagged the brothel's barkeep, a stocky woman with a hard jaw, but when she went to fill the glass, Lila put her hand over the rim.

"Let me ask you something," she said, softening her words to sound a little drunker than she was. She made sure to pair the words with a lin on the counter. "Let's say you got lucky, had a fine piece of magic fall into your lap." The barkeep raised a brow, waiting for the question. "But it got a little banged up on the way there. Where would you take it?"

"Me?" said the barkeep, putting her hand over the coin. "I'd save the cost and the trouble, and fix it myself." She slid the coin into her pocket. "But if I weren't so clever, I'd go to Haskin."

Lila's gaze flicked up. She turned the name over on her tongue. "Haskin?"

The barkeep nodded. "He can fix *anything*. Or so I've heard."

Lila smiled and sat back. "Good to know."

A shout went up across the room, and the barkeep drifted away. Lila looked down into the dregs of ale as if it were a scrying glass. *Haskin,* she thought. In the morning, she'd start there.

She nudged the glass away and shoved a hand in her coat, only to find she'd given the barkeep her last lin. She switched pockets and found the handful of coins Maris had given her, the ones lifted from the Hand who'd died on the ship.

Lila weighed the three lins, letting them spill from one palm into the other. She had come all this way because of them, she reasoned. The least they could do was pay for her drink.

She put two back in her pocket, set the third on the table, and rose. A little too fast, it turned out, thanks to the last pint. She paused, steadying herself a moment. And frowned. Perhaps it was the angle of the light on the edge of the coin, the way it hit the ridges in the crimson metal. Or perhaps it was something else, something harder to define, some gut sense that made her take the lin back up. Lila ran her thumb along the edge and saw that she was right—it wasn't entirely even.

"Son of a bitch," she muttered as she turned it, trying to make out the pattern, but it was too small, the metal of the coin too dark.

Lila sank back down into her chair.

She drew the other two coins from her pocket, and studied their edges, but they were even all the way around. This one alone was different. Embossed with a code. Or a message. Lila only needed a way to read it. Of course, she had no paper on her. No ink. She rapped her fingers on the table, mind racing.

Her gaze dropped to the wood beneath her hand, pocked and scarred. Lila smiled.

She drew a kerchief from her coat with one hand, and placed the other flat on the wood. The surface was a tapestry of stains, and she doubted anyone would notice one more flaw. Still, she kept her eye on the barkeep as she called on the fire. Heat bloomed beneath her palm, a tendril of smoke curling up between her fingers, and when she took her hand away, the wood beneath had been singed black. She tipped the last drops of ale onto the scorched wood, and mixed it with the tip of her finger.

She kept the gestures slow, almost bored—a tipsy patron simply humoring herself—even though her heart was beginning to quicken the way it did right before she drew her knife, fast with the promise of action. When her fingertip came away black, she rolled the coin through the makeshift ink and then, carefully, across the kerchief.

"Son of a bitch," she said again as the words revealed themselves in tiny strokes.

SON HELARIN RAS ● NONIS ORA

288

It wasn't just a message. It was an address. And a time.

Six Helarin Way. Eleventh Hour.

Lila was already on her feet and out the door before she realized she'd forgotten to pay for her drink.

II

The dead owl perched, his pebble eyes watching, as Tes tore the spell apart.

Days and nights of hard work ruined, and she'd be lying if she said it didn't hurt. But she knew she'd put her power to the worst kind of use, gone and done something impossible. Something *forbidden*. The worlds had been cleaved apart for a reason, and then she'd gone and made a bridge, crossed a boundary that had been put up centuries ago, one that was meant to keep her whole world safe.

Tes thought of the ruined magic around the old woman's head, the dead threads hanging on the air, thought of the man who'd brought this cursed thing into her shop, the way his own magic seemed to rot, and her hands moved faster, ripping at the knots she'd so carefully made, dismantling the magic she'd worked so hard to mend.

The shop door rattled.

Tes ignored it—Haskin's had been closed since she took the job of fixing the doormaker, and in that time, a dozen customers had tried the handle, found it locked, and gone away. She expected this one to do the same.

Only they didn't. They rattled the handle a second time, and Tes stopped working. She looked up. The rattling stopped. She held her breath, and waited, but it didn't start again. Instead, the lock in the door began to *groan,* like metal bending out of shape, and Tes had just enough sense and just enough time to sweep the remains of the cursed doormaker into a sack, and shove it beneath the counter, before the shop door swung open and a man and a woman strolled in as if they'd been invited.

"We're closed," said Tes, but the words had no effect. The two continued forward.

They were a mismatched pair.

She was short and sinewy, her black hair braided up into a crest. Her skin was the color of wet sand, her eyes a cold, flat grey. A metal cuff ran the length of her forearm, and her magic twisted around her, the glowing orange of molten steel. That explained the lock.

He was pale—pale hair, pale skin—and built like a butcher's block. He had a face like one, too, the surface deeply scarred. It looked like someone had tried to hack off his nose at some point, but the blade had gotten stuck on the bridge. His magic was a dark green, by far the brightest thing about him. *An earth mover,* Tes thought, right before he flicked his fingers, and the door slammed shut behind them.

Working in a shop like this, she'd learned to read her customers. It wasn't just written in their threads, but in their eyes, their gait. Tes knew bad people when she saw them.

These were bad people.

"We're looking for Haskin," said the woman, ambling toward the counter.

"He isn't here."

"But you are," said the man, running his hand over a table.

"I'm just his apprentice," she said.

He stopped, pausing right beside the place she'd made the door, the scar hanging in the air barely a foot from his face, though he didn't seem to notice. She forced her gaze back to the woman, who was now standing right across the counter.

Tes watched as she produced a black ticket, the gold *H* stamped onto the front. She flipped it around, so the number was showing. It was, of course, the same ticket Tes had given to the sick man. The one who'd brought her the doormaker.

Tes reached for the ticket, but as soon as the slip of paper grazed her fingers, the woman caught her wrist, and slammed it down against the counter. She yelped, tried to pull free, but the woman flexed, and a sliver of metal unraveled from the cuff on her forearm and drove into the wood around each of Tes's fingers, her hand, her wrist, pinning her there.

It happened so fast, Tes didn't feel the pain until it welled, thin lines of blood where the bands of steel cut into her skin. Panic rolled through her,

her free hand already reaching out, intending to undo the threads inside the steel.

"I wouldn't," said the woman, who clearly assumed that Tes intended to pry herself free the usual way. "There is a lot of metal in this shop."

Tes's free hand stopped, hovered, withdrew. It was true—she could get herself loose, and expose her power in the process, but in a test of speed, she would still lose.

"What do you want?" she asked.

"We'll get to that," said the woman, leaning an elbow on the counter. "But first . . ."

Suddenly she had a knife in one hand and a lock of Tes's hair in the other. With a flick of her wrist, the curls came free, dropping like a dark ribbon into the woman's palm. As Tes watched, the knife vanished, and the woman tied the lock of hair into a knot, and slid it in her pocket. Panic wormed through her; not at the loss of the curls—she had a mountain of them—but at how they could be used. Just as names had value, so did anything that came from a person's body. That was meant to belong only to them.

The woman rapped her fingers on the counter, drawing Tes's attention back to the metal pinning her hand.

"Now," said the woman, "before I begin, you should know, for every lie you tell, you'll lose a finger." She looked around. "I imagine those are important, in this line of work."

Tes fought to steady her heart. She had never been a good liar, which was why she'd always opted for omission. Better to say nothing and avoid the traps, the tells. But she had a feeling silence wouldn't buy her much.

"Where is Haskin?" asked the woman.

"There is no Haskin," she said. "It's just me."

"Could have told you that," said the man, hefting a sword from a shelf. He held it up to check his teeth. The woman let out a low sigh, halfway to a hiss, but kept her attention on Tes.

"What's a girl your age doing with a shop all her own?"

Tes swallowed. "I'm good at what I do."

"So am I," said the woman, and Tes sucked in a breath as the metal pinning her hand tightened a fraction, cutting into her skin. "Our friend brought in something to be fixed. Where is it?"

"You'll have to be more specific," said Tes. "After all, this is a repair shop."

The man chuckled, the sound like a blade on a whetstone. The woman didn't smile. She nudged the ticket forward. Tes made a show of staring at the number.

"I remember him," she said after a moment. "He was sick."

"Not anymore," said the man, in a way that made it clear he hadn't gotten *better*.

The woman clenched her teeth. She didn't like this man, thought Tes. That was good. That was something.

The woman's cold eyes swiveled back to her. "What's your name?"

A name was often a valuable thing, but only if you were alive to use it. "Tes."

"Well, Tes. Our friend made a mistake. He should have brought that piece to us, not you. We're here to take it off your *hands*." As she said that last word, she tapped the metal pinning Tes's fingers to the table. "Did he tell you what it was?"

"No," said Tes, glad it was the truth. "He practically shoved it at me, never even said what it was meant to do. Do you know how hard it is to fix a spelled object without knowing its purpose?"

The woman's eyes narrowed. "Did you? Fix it?"

"No," she said, the word coming out too fast. The metal tightened suddenly, white-hot pain as the steel sliced into the base of her thumb. "I mean, not yet," she gasped out. "I'm still working on it."

"But it *can* be fixed?"

Tes nodded, frantic, and after a moment, the metal loosened. Blood dotted the counter between her fingers.

"Where is it now?" asked the woman, gaze drifting over the shelves, and Tes gritted her teeth to hide her surprise. Something in the bland way she scanned the shop made Tes suspect she'd never *seen* the doormaker before, at least, not when it was whole. If they didn't know what they were looking for—

Tes twisted, gesturing with her free hand to the wall of shelves behind her. The *stash*, as Nero called it.

292

"Third shelf," she lied, the words coming out too fast as she wracked her brain for the contents of each basket, something that was roughly the right shape. "Second bin from the left."

It was a dangerous gamble, and as the woman rounded the counter and pulled out the bin, Tes watched for signs of suspicion, or anger, braced for the feeling of steel slicing through skin. But all the woman did was lift the contents from the bin.

A box.

Roughly the same size and shape as the one bundled beneath the counter between her feet. Only *this* box would never open doors to other worlds. It was a simpler thing, meant to capture and play sounds, like the one she kept beside her bed to help her sleep.

She'd salvaged it from a market a week before, wanted to see if she could modify the spell to hold a voice, thought it might be nice if Vares could talk as well as listen.

"Doesn't look very broken," said the woman.

"The box is just a container," said Tes. "That part was easy to fix." The same had been true for the doormaker. "It's the spellwork inside that's hard."

"Well then," said the woman, placing the box on the counter. "I suggest you get to work."

Tes took a deep breath. "I need both hands."

The woman tipped her head, as if considering. Then the metal released, withdrew, returning to the cuff on her arm. Tes rubbed her hand, flexed her fingers, tried to hide how badly they were shaking. Her thoughts spun as she looked down at the box on the table in front of her.

"This will take time," she said.

Please go, please go, please go, thudded her heart, loud as the drums she'd heard in that other London.

The woman turned, as if to leave, then grabbed a chair and dragged it across the shop floor to the counter. She spun it around and sat, arms crossed along the back.

"We'll wait."

III

L ila Bard should have listened to her gut.
      After all, it had gotten her this far.

Six Helarin Way wasn't in the *shal*. Far from it. Helarin Way lay on the city's northern bank, nearer the *ostra* and *vestra* than the dregs of London. It was an affluent borough, with elegant, well-appointed shops, all of which sat dark at this hour, though the streets were still well lit, lanterns burning with warm, enchanted light.

There was no date etched into the coin, no way to know if the time printed on the edge had come and gone, or lay ahead. But the *Ferase Stras* had been attacked less than a week before, and one of the thieves had been carrying this coin. She had to hope it wasn't a keepsake, but an invitation— one that hadn't yet expired.

SON HELARIN RAS ● NONIS ORA

Eleventh hour. According to the clock on the corner and the watch in her pocket, it was half past eleven now. She quickened her step, boots sounding first on stone, and then on wood as she crossed the bridge onto the northern bank.

This part of London moved at its own pace, time turned to honey by the moneyed elite. It played home to performance halls and smoking parlors, dinner clubs and grand estates, places where the city's wealth and power were both on full display. She saw no painted hands, and yet, the coin rolled in her fingers, letters pressed against her skin.

As she neared Helarin Way, Lila forced her steps to slow and lengthen into a more casual stride, turned up her collar and straightened her spine, carrying herself with a confidence she always felt, but rarely showed, taking on the airs of the people she'd passed as she made her way to the address.

With any luck, it would be the pleasure garden Tanis spoke of, the Hand all gathered neat within, her hunt begun and ended in a single night. But when she got there, she found only a darkened house.

Not a *vestran* estate, with grounds and a gate, though hardly a hovel. Three stories, with dark iron ringing its doorway and trimming the balconies above, the roof a series of gold-tipped peaks.

She kept walking, past the house to the corner, where she paused beneath an awning, and considered the façade, waited to see if anyone else came or went. Lanterns burned in other windows, but 6 Helarin Way was dark, and not the shallow dark that fell when a house's tenants had simply gone to bed. It had the hollow dark peculiar to abandoned places.

Lila chewed the inside of her cheek.

Perhaps she was too late. But she didn't think so. No, she thought, whatever was meant to happen here, it wasn't happening tonight.

She turned down the road, toward the river, and the inn, and the narrow bed that waited, when she felt a body moving in her wake.

Lila slowed, craning to hear footsteps, but they must have been timing their strides to hers, because she heard only her own boots, the far-off canter of hooves, and the murmur of voices drawn high and thin on the breeze.

And that was what made them stand out. The silence of them was too heavy, too solid, like stuffing in a pillow. Kell had told her once that if she tried, she could feel the magic present in another body, and she didn't tell him that she'd been able to feel that long before she knew it was magic.

Lila rolled her wrist, and the blade whispered against her palm.

She stepped into the road, as if to cross, and in a shopfront window, she saw it, the flicker of movement at her back. A hooded figure, blending almost perfectly into the dark.

She turned, the blade already singing through the air.

The shadow lunged out of the way just in time, but Lila twitched her fingers, and the dagger followed, dropping an inch at the last second so that it buried itself in the fabric of their cloak, and the wooden door behind.

The figure gasped in surprise, pinned like a moth to the wood.

"Well, hello," she said, as if stumbling across a friend, and not a Hand. Perhaps this had not been a wasted night at all. Beneath the hood, the shadow wore a mask, featureless and black. Even their hands were hidden beneath black gloves, which reached not for Lila or for magic, but the dagger, the metal scraping against the wood as they dragged it free an inch.

"Not so fast." Lila flexed, and the metal drove back in to the hilt. "I have some questions—"

That was as far as she got before a small object tumbled from the figure's hand, hit the street between them, and exploded. There was no force to the blast, and barely any sound, only a flash of blinding light, followed by clouds of choking black smoke. Lila's arm flew up to shield her eye from the flash, and then the smoke was everywhere, swallowing the lanterns and the street and every other source of light.

She braced herself for an attack, a weapon or a body surging out of the dark, but nothing came. The smoke hung, unmoving, and she sliced her arm through the air. A gust of wind sliced with it, cutting through the wall of black, revealing the door, and the place where the figure had been pinned against it. But they were gone.

Her dagger lay on the ground, abandoned, and she swept it up, and turned, surveying the street as it came back in pieces. She caught the edge of a black cloak as it vanished down another road.

Lila ran.

The shadow was fast, and as her boots thudded over stone, she cursed them for fleeing, and making her chase, when they could have just stayed put and fought and lost.

By the time she reached the corner, and turned onto an alley, they were nearly to the other end.

She missed her flintlock then. Her lovely gun, which had run out of bullets years before and been relegated to the bottom of her trunk. Aim, and fire, and down they would go. Instead, she was about to make a mess.

Lila took a deep breath.

Tyger, Tyger, she thought, and even though she didn't need the words, she felt the magic rise to meet them, folded into hard steel by the sounds they made, if only in her head. Lila turned her hand, palm up, and the street beyond the figure buckled, and rose.

The night shook, and the world beneath her trembled with the force of earth and stone scraping together as they were hauled up to block the road.

A dead end.

The figure spun, looking for another way out, and perhaps they would have found one, but she was tired of running. She clenched her hand, and the street grew up over their boots, binding them in place.

"Now," she said, ambling down the road as if she had all the time in the world. "Let's try this again." In one hand, she held her knife. In the other, fire bloomed.

But as she neared the figure, they fell forward, collapsing to their hands and knees, and for a moment, she assumed they were injured. The truth was much worse. They were *bowing*.

She reached the kneeling figure, and used the tip of her knife to push back their hood. When it fell back, so did the mask, revealing a young face, dark skin and wide brown eyes and cheeks that looked like they couldn't even grow hair.

Her gaze dropped to his front. His cloak had fallen open, and in the firelight she saw the armor, and the symbol pressed into its surface, black on black, so the sigil barely showed. But she knew it. Of course she knew it. It was a chalice and sun.

Lila's breath hissed through her gritted teeth. No wonder he hadn't fought back. He wasn't a Hand. He was a member of the *res in cal*. The crows that spied for the crown. For the *queen*.

"Apologies, *mas aven*," he said, folding English and Arnesian together as so many of the guards did among the palace royals.

Lila let go of the magic, and the earth crumbled from his boots.

"Get up," she ordered, and he rose, eyes flickering up to her chin. "What were you doing at that house?"

The confusion on his face said enough. There were people who knew how to school their expressions, hide whatever they were thinking behind a placid mask of calm. This boy wasn't one of them. She was willing to bet he'd never won a game of Sanct.

He hadn't been waiting at Helarin Way. That was just when she'd finally noticed him. She put out the flame, and brought her hand to her face, rubbing her eyes. "How long were you following me?"

"From the palace," he answered, an obedient servant now. "You crossed the southern walk, then circled the *shal* before going into the Merry Way, then—"

"Enough." Lila prickled in annoyance. She hadn't heard him coming. It was the queen's damned work, the cloak absorbing light, the armor spelled for stealth, even the boots warded so they made no sound on the paving stones. Still, she thought, she should have sensed him sooner. She wouldn't make the same mistake again.

Lila rested the tip of her blade against the chalice on his chest.

"Take a message to the queen. Next time she sends a crow to follow me, I'll cut off its wings."

The boy—and he really was a boy—looked about to speak, then thought better of it. He nodded once, but didn't move. Lila stepped aside with a flourish, but he still hesitated, as if waiting for her to leave first. Not a chance.

"Fly away," she ordered, and as she said it, a gust of wind rolled through and pushed him in the right direction. She watched him leave, watched until her eye couldn't split him from the other shadows, until he melted away into the dark.

On the way back, she took her time.

It was almost midnight, and the city had quieted, taken on the weariness of a body needing sleep. She retraced her steps across the Copper Bridge, which despite its name was mostly wood and stone, the green-tinged metal reserved for rail and arch and filigreed post.

Lila stopped halfway across.

Despite the hour, she wasn't the only one on the bridge. A carriage rattled past, and a few nobles were making their way back to the northern bank on foot. One stopped to admire the palace, the way it vaulted over the Isle and doubled there, golden edges reflected against the watery sky. But Lila put her back to the spires, and looked out at London. Stood there, halfway between the banks, the city cleaved in two by the crimson river.

They'd been looking in the wrong place.

She had no doubt that Alucard and his guards were searching for the Hand, but she was willing to bet they'd focused their efforts on the city's darkest corners.

298

She thought of the handprints circling the *shal*, how obvious they seemed. A bull's-eye in red paint. The X on a treasure map. Her hand slipped into her pocket, fingers tightening around the coin, its uneven edge digging into her palm as her gaze skated back to the northern banks, home to the city's elite.

They cannot hide, said Alucard.

But what if the real danger wasn't hiding at all?

What if it was standing in plain sight?

Back at the Setting Sun, the tavern was dark, the shutters drawn. Lila climbed the stairs, limbs growing heavier with every step, but when she reached her room, it was empty. Crimson spilled in through the window, caught on the edge of the trunk, cast pale red fingers across the unused bed.

Kell hadn't come back.

No matter, Lila told herself as she slumped onto the cot. More room for her. She tucked her hands beneath her head, let the quiet settle like a sheet, waited for sleep. It didn't come. At last, Lila heaved herself up, an oath on her lips, the knife already in her hand. The brief prick of pain, the well of blood against her fingers. She drew the mark, and whispered the words to the wall, felt the wood drop away as she stepped through.

The narrow room vanished, replaced by the grand palace chamber, as if the world had drawn in a very deep breath, and pushed outward, the low ceiling thrust into a vaulted one, decked in gossamer clouds, the weathered wood turned to marble. The only common tie, that crimson light, spilling now through etched glass doors, glancing off the gold threads in the rug, and the body sprawled atop the royal bed.

Kell lay half-dressed and facedown, his coat and shoes cast off in a breadcrumb trail from the door to the foot of the mattress. His back rose and fell. His copper hair fanned out like a dying fire over his cheek and onto the pillow.

Too many years of safety had made him a heavy sleeper.

He didn't stir when she kicked off her boots. Or when she shed her coat, and the more cumbersome blades. Or when she climbed onto the bed. Or

299

when she reached out and ran her fingers with all the lightness of a thief over the pale streak that glinted in his hair. Or when she curled in, close enough to hear the soft tide of his breath, and let it pull her down to sleep.

IV

WHITE LONDON

It was dark by the time Kosika mounted the castle steps, her clothes stiff with blood.

With every stop on the procession, she had shed more and more of her guard. Now, returning from the Silver Wood, only four soldiers flanked her, Lark among them. And only one Vir—Serak. And Nasi, of course.

The drums had ceased, but she could still feel them echoing in her skull. Kosika told herself it was not a headache; it was the pulse of the city growing stronger. Still, it had been a long day. Her arm ached where she had cut it in the ritual, and her legs were sore from crossing the city on foot, and she wanted nothing more than to rinse the blood from her skin, and sleep.

But the castle doors swung open onto celebration, the great hall brimming with life.

Lanterns hung like orbs of silver light, a dozen pale suns casting the shadows from the stone, and the scent of a banquet wafted through the air like steam. It was the Vir who insisted on throwing these extravagant feasts. As if the tithes and gifts were only a preface, as if they weren't the entire *point* of the day.

The city's highborns gathered, their hands neatly bandaged in silk instead of gauze, the only signs that there had been a tithe at all. The royal guard had cast off their helms, and now moved about the room, mingling with the guests, and the Vir stood around, resplendent in their silver mantles.

The sight of it all rankled Kosika.

This was meant to be a day of prayer. Of sacrifice. Devotion. And instead—

"Our queen!" said Vir Talik lifting his glass, and across the hall, the drinks all rose, their contents crimson.

Nasi came up behind her, reaching to peel the bloodied cloak from Kosika's shoulders.

"Leave it," she snapped, striding out of her friend's reach. She walked into the gathered crowd, the sea of people parting like water, burbling their praise. But Kosika didn't linger to be fêted. She continued past them, to the stairs. She wasn't in the mood to entertain, to be paraded through the halls. Vir Reska, a keen-eyed woman with greying hair, tried to cut her off.

"Your Majesty, the feast."

"I'm tired," said Kosika, and that should have been reason enough to make her step aside, but the Vir gestured at the crowd of nobles.

"But you must—"

Kosika's gaze swung toward the Vir like a blade as she realized her mistake. She took a step back, and dropped to one knee, her silver half-cloak skimming the floor. Kosika reached out, and brought her hand to the Vir's shoulder, just as she had earlier that day. She could feel the woman tense beneath the touch. They both knew that of all the blood that stained Kosika's skin, some of it was her own. Knew that it would only take a word, and the Vir would come apart, just as her attacker had. His bones were still heaped in the street, the rest of him churned into the river.

The sounds of the party faltered around them, and Kosika lowered her voice, the words meant only for the silvered servant.

"Tell me, Vir Reska," she said, "what *must* I do?"

"Nothing, my queen," answered the Vir, her voice tight as bowstrings. "You have done more than enough. If you are tired, you must rest. The Vir will host this evening in your stead, and in your honor."

Kosika lifted her hand from the Vir's shoulder.

"You do that," she said, turning again toward the stairs.

The time, everyone had the sense to let her go.

Four years ago

The doors to the throne room were heavy things.

It took four guards to guide them open and closed. Or one annoyed *Antari*.

It was Nasi who had come to find her that afternoon, to warn her of the Vir.

"What of them?" Kosika had asked, distracted until she saw the look on Nasi's face.

Just as the other girl had never held her tongue, she could not hide her emotions, either. When she smiled, her whole face seemed to be splintering with joy. But when she was mad, her scarred face took on the stiffness of a mask.

"They're meeting," she'd said. "Without you."

The throne room doors groaned open on their hinges as they swung wide, announcing Kosika's arrival. She had seen drawings of a whale, a sea creature large enough to stand within. The throne room reminded her of that, the bone-white pillars, the vaulted ceiling arched like ribs far overhead.

The queen's Vir had the decency to look surprised, their voices dropping away mid-sentence as she strode into the vast hall, her small shoes sounding on the floor. That floor. It was rumored that once upon a time, it had been laced with bits of bone. The enemies of Astrid Dane, bleached white and studded in the marble. It was only a rumor, and even if it weren't, those stones had long since been replaced.

Right now, she wished they hadn't been. She would have liked to add some more.

Kosika's throne sat in the center of the room, the council's chairs curved in a loose circle, like hands cupped around the queen. That throne alone sat empty.

"Your Majesty," said Vir Patjoric, rising to his feet.

"Don't get up," she said, but they did anyway. She knew it was a sign of deference, but all it did was make Kosika feel even shorter than she was. "It's my fault for being late." She took her seat, tucked her legs beneath her to hide the fact they didn't reach the floor. "Of course, I wouldn't have been

302

late if someone had told me we were meeting."

The Vir exchanged looks, their faces lined with everything from annoyance to discomfort. Thirteen of them, and honestly, aside from Serak, most of the others still bled together in her mind. It wasn't just the silver half-cloaks they all wore. It was the way they held themselves, the way they sat in their chairs, the way they spoke to her, as if she were a child and not a queen.

Now, twelve of them looked at each other. Only Serak had the decency to look at *her*, and seemed about to speak when Vir Patjoric cut in. Patjoric she would always know—after all, he was the one who'd found her.

"We didn't want to bother you," he said, bowing his pale head.

"Matters of state can be quite boring," added Vir Reska, who was easy to remember because she had eyes the same shade as the Sijlt, so light they were nearly colorless.

"I assure you," said Kosika, "nothing about my city bores me. Now," she added, sitting back in her throne. "What have I missed?"

Another Vir cleared his throat. "We were discussing what to do about the other worlds."

Kosika frowned. She knew of them, of course. The other rooms in the house, as Serak would say. "What of them?" she asked.

"Well, there has always been . . . communication in the past, and—"

"Has a messenger come to us?"

"No," said another Vir. "Not yet. But we think we should go to them."

"We," echoed Kosika. But there was no *we*. The doors between worlds were closed, and only an *Antari* could open them again. Only an *Antari* could step through.

"I do not see the point," she said. A murmur went through the Vir like wind through leaves. "You want me to go to this other London? And do what? Deliver mail?"

"Holland did it." That, from Vir Patjoric.

"As a servant," said Kosika through gritted teeth, "not a king. And only then because the Danes coveted that other world. I think it's time to focus on our own."

Serak met her gaze, and she saw the faintest smile at the corner of his mouth. He approved.

"It is not worth the risk." This from Vir Reska. "If Kosika was taken, we would have no *Antari and* no queen."

Kosika did not fail to notice the order Reska had given to those titles.

"One day," said a dark-haired Vir named Lastos, "the walls will fall. We should be ready."

"All the more reason to focus on *our* strength instead of theirs," countered Kosika.

Vir Lastos sat forward, fingers gripping his chair. "We should know our enemies before we meet them on the field."

"Why must they be our enemies?" asked Vir Serak. "Why must they be anything at all?"

"*We* are closer to the original seat of power," said Kosika, "and every day, *our* world revives a little more."

"And what if theirs does, too?" pressed Vir Lastos. "We have no other way of knowing."

But Kosika's attention was no longer on his words. He was the type of man who gestured as he spoke, and she saw that both his hands were bare.

"Knowledge is always better," he was saying, but she cut him off.

"You didn't tithe, Vir Lastos."

He gave a cursory glance down at his hand. "I was busy with affairs of state." The Vir drew breath, about to dive back into his argument, but Kosika did not let him.

"For this, you will make time."

He waved the words away as if they were a fly. "Very well," he said. "If it humors the queen. Now back to the matter of the other London—"

"Do it now."

Kosika had drawn the blade from her hip, and was holding it out to Vir Lastos. He looked at the weapon's edge, repulsed. "Your Highness?"

"The ground does not stand on ceremony. It will welcome your tithe a day late."

She waited, but the Vir did not take the offered blade.

"Then let it wait," he said, "until the next tithing day. They are becoming rather frequent."

304

"Lastos," warned Patjoric, but the Vir pressed on.

"No. First, it was once, then one time a year, now two. At this rate, soon we will be too weak to do anything *but* bleed."

"You say weak," chided Kosika, "but our London grows stronger every day."

"Do you know why?" he snapped. "Because we have banned binding spells, and scrubbed the worst offenders from our streets. Because we have guilds that bring their goods up and down the Sijlt, now it has thawed, and collect taxes relative to wealth." He shook his head. "*You* can choose to tithe in blood and worship men as saints, my queen, but rituals do not sustain this city."

"You too served Holland," said Vir Serak scornfully. "You too believed—"

"I believed he was the best we had at hand," said Vir Lastos. "Not some mythic king."

"You have seen the trees blooming in the courtyard," said Vir Talik. "The amount of grain arriving on those barges from up north."

"Why do you think the Sijlt flows so swiftly now?" interjected Kosika.

Lastos gazed at her with cold, flat eyes. "All that freezes thaws in time. Perhaps it is simply nature."

"And yet," she said. "It has yet to thaw in you."

The Vir's hands closed into fists, the gesture only half-hidden beneath his cloak. He was not the only one, of course, to still lack magic. Most children these days had elements blooming in them, but a fair number of adults were proving barren soil. Among the Vir, there were still three—Lastos, Reska, and Patjoric—who could not conjure so much as a candle flame.

"Perhaps you are afraid," Kosika went on. "Perhaps you don't want to believe that magic has a will, that it is choosing, because that would mean it isn't choosing *you*."

"I would not be so arrogant, *little queen*." Those last words, name and title, spat as if they were a seed stuck between his teeth.

Kosika looked down at the blade still in her hand, studying her reflection in the steel. "This castle is made of stone," she said. "And stone carries sound. I have heard what you call me, when I am not there, *Kojsinka*."

Little tyrant.

Vir Lastos blanched, but she could not tell if it was fear or anger that made him pale.

"Do you deny it?" she pressed.

He shook his head. "You are a child. With a child's knowledge of the world."

The other Vir stirred, uneasy. Patjoric reached for Lastos's arm, but he shook it off.

"A little girl content to play at being queen."

Kosika didn't stand. It would feel too much like rising to the bait. But she couldn't stop the air from churning through the hall around her. The stones crunched like grinding teeth. She sat forward on her throne.

"Then you should not have put me here," she said.

"No," he said slowly. "We shouldn't have."

Lastos looked around the room, waiting for the other Vir to stand with him. Or at least, against *her.* Kosika thought of the kol-kot board in her room. Nasi had shown her all the ways to lay the pieces out. In more than one arrangement, the priests were strong enough to rule without their king. But that was only a game. And Kosika was not only a queen. She was *Antari.* The heir to Holland's power. And the other Vir knew it, even if they did not wish it so.

Patjoric shook his head, and sighed, and Reska kept her eyes on the floor. Talik looked at Lastos as if he'd doomed himself. And slowly, Lastos realized that he had.

"I am called to rule," said Kosika. "But you are not bound to serve." She gestured to the throne room doors, still open wide.

He tore the silver mantle from his shoulders with so much force that the circle pin came free and fell, ringing like a bell as it bounced across the floor.

He should have turned and left. Instead, he glared at Kosika and said, "Patjoric should have put you down when he first found you in the street. After all, the best thing Holland Vosijk ever did for us was di—"

He cut off, his voice replaced by the sick crunch of blade on bone. Lastos let out a ragged gasp and looked down to find a length of steel protruding from his chest.

306

"That is blasphemy," hissed Serak, who stood like a shadow behind him, his dark eyes black with rage.

The other Vir were on their feet, hands on their swords, and for a moment, the air in the hall felt solid as glass, about to break. But the moment passed, and none came forward. They only watched as Serak withdrew his sword, and Lastos crumpled to the pale stone floor. His mouth opened and closed, but all that escaped was a rattle, and a gasp, and then nothing.

Kosika watched his blood spread across the stones and thought, *What a waste.* She looked up, and saw Serak's eyes on her.

An understanding passed between them, and then Serak spoke, loud and clear.

"Kos och var."

The words were taken up and carried through the hall.

Kos och var. Kos och var. Kos och var.

All hail the queen.

V

RED LONDON, *now*

"How long is this going to take?"

It was after midnight. Tes's eyes burned and her head ached, and for the last hour she'd been harboring the fragile hope that if she took long enough, the killers might get bored enough to let down their guard and give her a chance to escape.

But the man with the butcher's block face was still pacing the shop, palming half-fixed pieces of magic, and the woman with the crested braid hadn't moved from her chair, those flat grey eyes hanging on Tes.

Until Vares twitched.

The owl had been still as—well, a normal skeleton—as if he could sense the danger in the room, but the question had stirred the spellwork in him. He ruffled his bone wings, swiveled his head.

The woman's eyes flicked sideways. The edge of her mouth quirked into something like a smile. *"Kers la?"* she asked, reaching toward the owl. He responded by pecking her fingers. Her smile sharpened. "What a clever bit of magic."

She flexed her hand as she said it, and the metal wire running through the owl shivered.

"*Don't*," said Tes, a single pleading word. And maybe it was the way she said it, or simply the fact that her hands stopped moving, that made the woman let go of the little owl, her gaze dropping back to the box sitting disemboweled on the counter. It was a tangle of magic, a snarl of strings, made messier by the chaos of the surrounding shop, but Tes didn't dare put on her blotters. She couldn't afford to narrow her gaze, couldn't afford to forget the other bodies in the room, even as the headache bloomed.

Despite the audience, Tes didn't bother masking her power, or pretending to use tools, didn't bother with anything but her eyes and her hands as she drew her fingers through the air, shaped the spellwork around the box into something she could use.

The man slumped against the door, looking bored. The woman leaned forward in the chair, her fingers rapping on the metal cuff, the only sound in the shop.

"What's your name?" asked Tes, when she couldn't bear the quiet. The woman raised a dark brow. "I told you mine," she added weakly.

The woman's mouth twitched again. "Bex," she said, the sound sliding through her teeth. "That walking lump of shit over there is Calin."

Tes kept her hands moving. "You don't like him."

"What gave it away?"

"But you're here as partners."

The scarred man—Calin—snorted. "Wouldn't say that."

Bex considered her words. "At the moment, we share an employer."

"I thought assassins worked alone."

Bex's eyes narrowed. "You're a little too sharp," she mused. "If you're not careful, it'll get you cut." She stood, and stretched, the bones in her neck cracking audibly. "Now do your job, or I'll do mine."

Tes surprised herself by bristling at the threat. "Why should I? You'll kill me either way."

"Sure," said Calin, "but if you make it quick, so will we."

Her boldness cracked, and fear got in.

"Look at it this way," said Bex, resting her elbows on the counter. "I wasn't *hired* to kill you, and I don't make a habit of doing work for free."

Tes wanted to believe her—might have, if Bex were there alone—but Calin had the look of a man who'd killed plenty of people, just because he could.

"Don't worry about *him*," said Bex, as if reading her mind. "Worry about me. Worry about that," she added, pointing to the box on the counter.

So that's what Tes did.

What, in truth, she'd been doing for hours.

Tes kept her eyes on her hands, forced herself not to glance at the echo of the door that still hovered in the air to Calin's left, its edges burning. She wondered if they couldn't see it at all, or simply weren't looking.

At least they couldn't see what *she* was doing.

If they'd been able to see the threads of magic, they would have noticed that she had braided pale gold lines of air upon air upon air together inside the wooden frame. It was a blunt but effective piece of work—one she almost ruined when Calin, having abandoned his place by the door, knocked a giant metal box of scrap to the floor.

Tes's hands jumped, and she held her breath, afraid the spell would trigger then and there, but mercifully it didn't.

"Fucking saints," muttered Bex. "If only someone would hire me to kill *you*."

"Don't act like you haven't tried for free," said Calin, kicking the metal box aside. "I'm as hard to kill as the king himself."

"I heard he has a spell on him," said Tes, gingerly attaching the final thread and doing her best impression of someone with plenty of work still to do.

"I guess we'll find out," said Bex.

Another box went crashing to the floor, and the woman closed her eyes and clenched her teeth. "If you drop one more fucking thing . . ." she snarled, but Calin wasn't listening.

He was staring at the space in front of the shelves, head cocked to one side. *"Kers la?"*

Tes followed his gaze, and went cold. He was staring straight at the remains of the door she'd made. He made a cautious circle, squinting at the spot, and though he couldn't see it fully, not the way she could, he had clearly noticed *something*—a shimmer in the air, a wrongness.

"Hey Bex," he said, large hand drifting toward the echo of the spell. "Come see this."

Tes's heart pounded as the other killer sighed, rising from her chair. She was out of time, and as soon as Bex turned away from the table, Tes made her move.

She hefted the object she'd been working on, the one that was not, and would never be, a doormaker, and lobbed it into the center of the room. As it fell, Tes grabbed the owl and ducked beneath the counter, curling into a ball around Vares and the bundle of disassembled parts left over from the real doormaker.

The wooden box—which, as she had told the killers, was really only a container for magic—hit the workshop floor of Haskin's shop and shattered, and as it did, it triggered the wind spell she'd coiled within.

Which exploded out with sudden, violent force.

Tes had never made an elemental bomb before, had no idea if she'd given the magic enough kick, not until the air slammed out, splintering wood and shattering glass and shaking the entire building.

Even the counter, bolted to the floor, groaned beneath the percussive force of the explosion, and in the ringing aftermath she couldn't hear the assassins, didn't know where they were, if they'd been killed by the blast or merely rattled.

But Tes knew better than to wait.

She grabbed the bundled doormaker and the dead owl and hurled herself out from behind the counter, toward the back of the room and the curtained doorway that led to her quarters. There she stopped, and looked back, saw the woman, Bex, tangled in the limbs of a buckled metal shelf, the man, Calin, slumped against a far stone wall. But they were both still alive, and already starting to recover.

Tes slammed her hand against the doorframe, and the spell she'd woven there. The first thing she'd ever built in Haskin's shop, and it wasn't for a customer, it was for herself, in case she had to run again.

Tes loved the shop, but it was just wood and stone and a painted door, and she didn't hesitate. She laced her fingers through the threads and *pulled,* as hard as she could.

Cracks ran out from her hand, shooting across the walls and over the ceiling and through the floor. As they did, Tes turned and bolted through the curtain and the narrow quarters at the back of the shop, past the little table and the lofted bed and the life she'd made there, and out the back door, just as the entire building sagged, and the roof caved in, and the whole place came crashing down.

VI

Over the years, a great number of people had tried to kill Calin Trell.

His body was a map of failed attempts, times he'd been stabbed and burned, hacked at and cursed. He'd broken most of his bones, lost a good deal of blood, and been buried more times than he could count.

Which was to say, it would take more than a fallen house to keep him down.

The girl had been quick, he'd give her that. The blast of wind had slammed his head into the wall, rattling his skull, and in that ringing second, he'd almost missed the follow-up assault—almost, but not quite. He'd had just enough time to throw his power out and up, blocking most of the stone and wood and metal as it came crashing down.

Now Calin stood among the settling debris, a mountain of rubble to every side. Blood ran into one eye where something sharp had found the skin over his brow, but otherwise, he was unscathed. Let Bex Galevans keep her steel, with all its flourishes, he thought. Earth work was blunt, but effective.

Speaking of Bex—he hauled himself up out of the makeshift hole, stood atop the heap that used to be Haskin's shop, before the little bitch had brought the whole thing down on top of them. He shifted his feet, and the rocks and timber groaned beneath him. He paid no mind to the spectators now pouring into the street, some shocked, others merely curious. This was, after all, the *shal,* whose unofficial motto was: *Mind your own business.*

He looked around. No sign of Bex.

With any luck, she was dead beneath the wreckage.

Not that Calin ever had much luck.

He turned, scanning the buildings to either side, the alley and the road, and caught a twitch of movement, a girl-shaped shadow, sprinting away into the dark.

Calin smiled, blood and dust in his teeth.

He'd always been fond of the hunt.

He leapt down from his perch atop the ruins and landed hard, boots hitting the stone road. More blood dripped into his vision, and he wiped it away. The cut in his brow was deep—it would scar. One more mark to add to the tally.

Calin drew a blade from his belt, and started down the road.

Tes wove between the buildings in the dark.

She knew the *shal* better than the rest of London, knew it as well as anyone could when they weren't born and raised among these narrow streets, knew it was a different place at night. The roads were always narrow, a warren of alleys, few wide enough for a carriage or a cart, but in the dark, those winding streets blocked out the light as well. Here and there, the Isle's red glow tinted rooftops crimson, but no river or lantern could truly push the shadows back.

Luckily for Tes, and her strange eyes, the threads of power shone so bright that no place in the world was ever truly dark. But her feet were clumsy with panic, and unlike the rest of the city, the *shal* didn't sleep at night; it came alive as the sun went down, despite the heavy dark, or perhaps because of it. Tes twisted her way through a midnight market, avoiding half a dozen low-lit stalls, only to collide with a group of bodies as they spilled out of a tavern, apologies tumbling out as she pushed past, Vares still shoved in her pocket, and the broken doormaker bundled against her chest.

The roads in the *shal* weren't straight lines so much as circles, funneling you deeper in instead of out, as if the warren didn't want to let you go, and while her head filled with the single, pressing need to run, her feet could only carry her so fast, so far, and she needed to get away, not just out of the *shal,* or even London, but somewhere no one could follow, and that was how she ended up kneeling in a darkened dead-end alley, the bundle open on the damp ground, the disassembled doormaker filling her vision.

"Come on, come on, come on," she whispered as her hands flew over the threads.

She suddenly wished she hadn't done such a thorough job taking it apart, but she'd always had a good memory for patterns once she'd made them work, and it was much easier to repeat a thing a second time than do it for the first.

The dead owl twitched and fluttered nervously in her pocket as if to say, *Hurry, hurry.*

"I know, Vares. I know."

Her fingers moved quickly, reconstructing the pattern, tying off the knots she'd torn.

"Almost there."

Something crashed behind her, and she jerked around, but it was just a drunkard, knocking a planter from a sill as he stumbled home. A few seconds later, a window slammed closed overhead. This time, she didn't jump. Nor did she look up when she heard the footsteps trudging past the alley.

Not until they slowed. And stopped.

"Well, well," said a voice like a mouth full of rocks.

Tes's hands slid from the box as she turned to face him. Calin stood at the mouth of the alley, the green of his magic lighting him better than a streetlamp, glancing off the dagger in his hand, the lank hair plastered to his face. Dust and debris clung to his shoulders, and blood dripped from his temple to the corner of his mouth. His tongue swept across his lip, and found it.

"Bex was right," she said, trying to keep her voice steady. "You are hard to kill."

His gaze flicked to the alley behind her, which ended in a wall. "Nowhere to run," he pointed out.

"You'd be surprised," she said, meeting his gaze. *"Erro."*

She heard the little box unfold, felt the door rise up behind her. Saw, out of the corner of her eye, the edge of the doorway carve itself across the air, felt the veil, and the draft coming through, carrying the scent of smoke and damp stone.

Calin's eyes widened, his mouth twisting into a snarl as Tes stepped back, over the threshold. The world shuddered, and blurred, and through the veil, she saw the shape of him surging forward, his arm flung out.

"FERRO."

The door obediently slammed shut, erasing Calin, and the *shal,* and the rest of London.

Tes stood, gasping for breath, not in an alley but on a lamplit street.

It was raining; not a heavy rain, but a light and steady drizzle, and the doormaker sat on the cobblestones at her feet. The night looked strange, and dim, but that made sense, it was a different night, a different world.

She'd done it. She was safe.

Tes let out a small, startled laugh that quickly died because it *hurt.*

She winced as a strange ache rolled through her stomach, warmth blooming across her front before sharpening into heat, and at first she thought it was just the aftermath of the blast, the chase, but when she looked down, she saw the strangest thing: a dagger's hilt jutting out above her hip. But that was silly, she'd know if she'd been stabbed. She reached out, and touched the hilt, and as she did, the blade moved and the pain caught up, a blinding, burning thing beneath her ribs.

She acted on reflex—wrapped her hand around the blade, and pulled it out.

That, it turned out, was a horrible idea.

The pain turned white-hot, and Tes sagged to her knees in the street, stifling a scream.

Blood spilled between her fingers. She pressed down hard, even though it made her heart pound and another cry rise up her throat.

"Get up," she hissed between clenched teeth, saying the words aloud to give them strength. Her body didn't listen.

"Get up, get up, get up," Tes chanted, as if it were a spell, and at the same time another voice called out, the words foreign, but almost familiar.

How strange, she thought, head spinning, it sounded like they were speaking High Royal. She and her sisters had all been taught, but it had been years now, language had gone stiff, unused, and she tried to translate now, but the pain made it hard to think. The voice shouted again, and this time, she swore she could make out the last word.

Street.

And then another sound, much closer; this one she recognized as the clatter of hooves, and Tes looked up just in time to see a horse and cart barreling toward her in the dark.

The driver yanked on the reins and the horse reared, turning hard, and the cart wheel broke, and the whole thing began to fall toward Tes and the doormaker on the ground. Her limbs came to life, and she swept up the box and dove out of the way just before the cart crashed down, splintering wood and spilling crates into the street where she'd just been.

Somehow, Tes kept moving. She half stumbled, half ran, trying to put distance between herself and the crash, made it half a block before the pain in her side dragged her to a stop. She sagged to the curb beneath an awning, one hand on the doormaker and the other on her wounded side. She squeezed her eyes shut, trying to think, but her thoughts were sluggish, slow to answer. She opened her eyes. Her vision was slipping, darkness creeping in, or so she thought, until she realized why the night light looked so strange.

There were no threads.

Not in the rain, which should have shimmered with strands of pale blue light.

Not in the lamps, which should have been shot through with tendrils of yellow.

Not in the road itself, which should have been woven with strands of earthy green.

In fact, the only threads she *could* see were the ones coiled around the doormaker, or spilling down her front, each drop burning with a filament of crimson light that faded moments after it fell.

315

A world without magic.

It might have been a nice reprieve, if she weren't dying.

No, she told herself. Not dying. Not yet. She could fix this. Tes was very good at fixing broken things. Admittedly, she did it using magic, and there was no magic here, and she was a person, not a thing, but she was hurt, and hurt was a kind of broken, and she could fix it. She had to.

The owl in her pocket was fluttering nervously, and she was glad, at least, that he still worked. Glad she wasn't alone. Even if the movement of skeletal wings against her wounded front hurt enough to make her stifle a sob.

She needed to stop the blood, she knew that much. Close the wound. Quiet the pain. The streets were lined with shops. Perhaps one had something she could use. It seemed like a lot of work.

Tes wanted to close her eyes again. To rest. Just for a moment.

Instead, she took a deep breath, and got to her feet.

Calin leaned against the alley wall, picking his nails.

"Why the fuck are you just standing there?" said a grating voice.

Still alive, then, he thought, as Bex stormed down the alley toward him. And they said *he* was hard to kill. She was bleeding from two or three places, and favoring one leg. It wasn't as good as dead, but he'd take what he could get.

"We have a problem," said Calin.

"Where is she?" demanded Bex.

"Gone."

"And you didn't go after her?"

"Couldn't," he said. "She closed the *door.*" He nodded at the faint scar in the air as he said it. He might not have even noticed the echo of it in the dark, if he hadn't seen the door with his own eyes, the place where it had come—and gone.

"So she *did* have it." Bex tried to hide her surprise, but Calin saw it, memorized the arch of her eyebrow, the slight part of her lips. *One day when I kill you, you'll make that face for me.* His mouth twisted at the thought, but Bex was already kneeling on the alley floor, unrolling a city map.

"What are you doing?"

"That lying little bitch owes me a finger," she said, drawing a series of marks on the map. Calin had never bothered much with spells. The way he saw it, you could be decent at a lot of things, but only great at a few. He'd rather spend his energy on killing. Plus, a spell like this took the fun out of the hunt. And yet, as he stood in the alley, waiting for Bex or a better idea, he admitted, if only to himself, that a finding spell came in handy at a time like this.

He watched her pull the knotted lock of hair from her pocket, the one she'd cut from the girl's head, and tug free a strand, dropping it into the center of the map. She said a few words and the marks and the hair caught fire, turned to cinder. This was the part, he guessed, where the cinders were supposed to point the way, to draw a line from them to the girl.

But they didn't. They just sat there, waiting for a light breeze to blow them away.

"*Anesh?*" he asked, impatient.

Bex kept her eyes on the map, but he saw her shoulders tighten, hackles raising the way they did whenever she was mad. Normally he would have savored it, but his head was beginning to ache where it had met the shop wall, and he'd lost a perfectly good knife.

Bex was muttering to herself.

"*Well?*" he asked again.

Bex sighed. "For once in your life, you're right about something," she said. "We do have a problem." She looked up. "According to this map, the girl's not here."

"Obviously," he said, gesturing at the empty alley, but Bex was already shaking her head.

"She's not just *not here*, you mindless lump of coal." Bex swept the ash from the map. "She's *nowhere*. It's like she doesn't exist."

"Maybe you're just shit at spells," offered Calin. "Or maybe I killed her."

He had seen the knife go in, right before the door slammed shut.

Bex shot him a dark look. "Let's hope, for both our sakes, you aren't *that* stupid." She stood, staring down at the blank map for a long moment.

317

"Fuck this," she muttered, shoving past him. As she did, she made a half-hearted attempt to slide a dagger between his ribs.

Calin knocked the blade away.

"Where are you going?" he asked, trailing her out of the alley.

"*We're* going," she said, "to tell the boss."

VII

WHITE LONDON

Everyone had the sense to let the queen go, except, of course, for Nasi, who trailed her up the spiral stone stairs until the hall below was out of sight.

Kosika wasn't in the mood. "Go back," she said as she passed the first landing. "I'd hate for you to miss the party."

"You did not have to scare Reska like that," said Nasi. "It was petulant, and small."

Kosika rounded on her friend, the air tightening around them both. She hadn't even meant to conjure it—lately things had begun to follow the shape of her mood, the curve of her temper. Nasi stiffened, sensing the change, but unlike the Vir, she didn't retreat. Instead she continued up the steps, stopping on the one just below so they stood eye to eye. She studied the queen's face. "Why are you so mad?"

Kosika's gaze dropped to the stairs, the sounds of revelry rising from below. "The people down there are opportunists, following the current. Half of them knelt to the Danes before they knelt to me."

Nasi shrugged. "If you punished every soul who bent their head as evil passed, there would be no one left to follow you. But there is a difference between fear and devotion."

"Devotion," muttered Kosika, sagging against the wall. "Forgive me if I'm in no mood to be paraded through the castle like a puppet."

Nasi quirked a brow. "Last I checked, you had no strings. You cut them all away."

"Then why do they still treat me like a doll?"

"They treat you like a *queen*," countered Nasi, huffing in exasperation. "That is what you are. The symbol of their strength. The power that restored the world."

"It is Holland Vosijk's power. They should pray to him."

"Holland Vosijk is dead," said Nasi grimly. "And you are not." She stepped close, laid a hand on the shoulder of Kosika's bloodstained cloak. "You resent them because they do not live and breathe the stories of the Summer Saint, as you do. But they do not follow the Saint. They follow *you*. As far as they're concerned, *you* are the reason the crops grow in their fields. *You* are the reason they can summon wind into their sails." Nasi rolled her free hand, and a flame bloomed in the air. "*You* are the reason they can call fire to their hearths." Her fingers closed, and the flame went out. "You are their queen, and tonight they celebrate, but today they bled, because you willed it."

"They bled because it serves them."

"It serves us all. Isn't that the point?"

Kosika looked down at her own hands, crusted in blood. "And if the magic dried up again? If the power bled out of the world? Would they still follow me?"

"Oh, no," said Nasi cheerfully, "then they would surely turn on you." Only she could say such a thing with lightness in her voice. "This is London, after all. But you and I both know they will not need to. Because you would open your veins into the Sijlt before anyone tried to cut your throat."

Kosika tried to manage a smile, but it fell short. "Go back down," she told Nasi, nodding at the stairs. "Enjoy the feast. Make sure the Vir don't go mad with power in my absence."

"You should eat," said her friend, and Kosika bristled, even as her stomach growled in protest, full of nothing but sugared buns and cider.

"Fine," she said. "Send something up."

She turned, only to feel Nasi's hand catch hers, then the weight of something pressing into her palm.

"Happy birthday," said Nasi, leaning in to kiss her cheek, and Kosika let herself blush, only a little, before she looked down and saw what the gift was: a marble figure, like the ones on the kol-kot board in the corner

319

of her room. Kosika knew the rules now, had even beat Nasi half a dozen times. The figure was modeled on the game's most important piece. The single faceless king.

Only this wasn't a faceless king.

It was a queen.

It was her.

From the white cloak to the braided crown to the eyes cast in gemstone, one light brown, the other solid black. Her spirits lightened as her fingers curled over the token. She looked up to thank Nasi, but the girl was already vanishing down the spiral steps, toward the noise and revel of the feast.

Kosika turned the talisman in her hands as she continued up to her room, past the second landing and the third to the royal tower, past the two guards posted outside her door.

At last, in the quiet, she shrugged off the bloodstained cloak and pulled the jeweled pins from her hair, leaving the finery laid out like a ghost on the bed. She passed the silver ash tree that grew in the center of her room, brushed her fingers against the bark on her way to the game board that waited as it always did on its low, round table.

She sank onto a cushioned stool. The game was set, each king with a wall of soldiers in front, a set of priests behind. Kosika took up the silver-and-white king, faceless beneath his crown, then dropped it in the drawer, and set her own piece in its place. Her fingertips were tracing her stone features when something—someone—moved in the room behind her.

"Kosika," said a voice, low and smooth.

She turned, and there he was, dressed in charcoal, one hand on the post of her bed and the other on the stained cloak, his long fingers as graceful as they'd been when she curled them around the single sugar cube in the Silver Wood.

"Hello, Holland."

VII

THE HAND THAT HOLDS THE BLADE

I
RED LONDON

The city was full of pleasure gardens.

Some made the most of the long summer nights, and others burned away the winter chill, some were intimate and others grand, and all were dazzling in their own way.

But few held a candle to the Veil.

Like the rest, it catered to a wealthy clientele, and was known not only for its luxury but also its discretion, welcoming patrons with a wall of polished masks, to don as they came in. But *unlike* the others, it had no grounds, no walls, no roof, no roots. Instead, the Veil descended on a different house each night, and only its most devoted members knew where it would bloom.

Thus, its size and shape varied with the nature of its grounds—that was indeed part of its appeal. Sometimes the venue was large enough to host a ball, other times it was little more than a network of narrow rooms and curtained alcoves. It was a traveling circus, a fluid festival of fine wine and scented smoke, and every day, by dawn, it was gone.

The staging changed, but the rules stayed the same.

The servants of the Veil were set apart by golden masks, while the patrons wore ones that were either solid black, or solid white. It was a sea of faceless faces, and while most were engaged in one form of debauchery or another, some stood apart, choosing to watch without the fear of being watched, while others enjoyed the privacy the Veil afforded.

It wasn't strange to pass a set of figures on the stairs, their covered faces bowed close in talk instead of want. Or a handful seated around a table, discussing forbidden magic or foreign trade. Or a room reserved not for plotting one's enjoyment, but the downfall of a king.

A gold mask was hung on the door to show that it was being used, and in the space beyond, two guests sat waiting for the third. One's mask was black, the other's white.

"He's late," said the first, his features hidden behind the onyx guise, his scarred knuckles shining as they tightened on a pipe. There was a pale mark around his thumb, where a piece of jewelry had been removed. He was a large man, and when he reclined, his broad shoulders filled the high-backed chair.

The mouth of the pipe vanished beneath his black mask and a moment later, smoke plumed around its edges. "Remind me again why we bother with him?"

The second guest, her own face hidden behind a bone-white mask, inclined her head. She was slight, her body curving with the contours of the chair in which she lounged. "All tools have their uses." She crossed her legs. "Speaking of, where is this *persalis* of yours?"

"On its way."

Behind the white mask, she pursed her lips. "The next meeting is tomorrow night. If you don't have it by then, the Hand won't be able to—"

"I'm aware of how time works," he warned. He had the kind of voice that pressed down, made most flinch, or look away. The woman did neither, only shrugged.

"It is your plan," she said. "If you're not ready, we can move on to mine."

He shook his head. "The Long Dark Night is weeks away."

"Too much time is always better than too little." She always spoke like that, it seemed, in sculpted phrases, her tone as smooth as river stone.

The man said nothing. His gaze flicked to the clock against the wall. It would make no sound until the Veil drew shut at dawn, which was still hours off, but time's hands were slipping silently down the right side of its face.

"Insolent brat," he muttered, drawing on the pipe, only to find the fire had gone out. The woman held out her hand, producing a delicate tendril of flame, but he ignored it, rising to his feet to approach a lamp instead.

As he inhaled, the door flung open on its hinges, and the third member of their party strolled in, more a tumble than a stride, though it was hard to tell if he was drunk, or simply in good spirits. His gold mask shone, from the pointed chin to the spokes that curled into his burnished hair, but his clothing was rumbled and askew, as if it had been abandoned for some time, and only recently resumed.

"Apologies," he said, a bottle in one hand and three glasses in the other. "I was detained a moment on the stairs. Business, you understand," he added, gesturing to the room, and the Veil, which both belonged to him.

The Master of the Veil filled the glasses and handed them to his guests. The man in the black mask took the drink. The woman in the white waved it away. The Master shrugged, and poured the contents into his own. Then he drew the golden mask up just enough to tip it back, exposing a strong jaw, the line of his cheek. They knew each other's faces well by now, and yet, the first and second kept their own masks down.

"Are we all set," asked the third, refilling his glass, "for tomorrow night?"

"No," said the second, as the first answered, "Yes."

The host's eyes danced behind his golden mask. "Dissent already? What did I miss?"

"He doesn't have it," said the woman.

"I will," growled the man, in a tone as dark as his mask.

The Master of the Veil took his seat. "Let's pretend for a moment that you do." He turned his attention to the woman. "And *you* are able to put the key inside the palace."

"The king trusts me," she assured him, unsmiling behind the white mask.

"And look at what that trust will get him."

She considered her hands and said, "All that lives must die."

"*I* heard the king cannot be killed," goaded the man in gold.

"Then he will be removed," she said.

"We can say he fled, and left his family to the wolves." The humor in his voice was clear. "I do wish I could be there. It is only so much fun to watch." He rolled his empty glass. "I take it no one should be spared."

At that, the man in the black mask spoke up again. "Let them do what they want with the queen and heir, but the consort is mine."

325

"It would be cleaner," began the woman, "to let them—"

"I don't care," he cut in, fist clenching. "The *persalis* will carry them beyond the palace wards. They will slaughter the household, incapacitate the king, and bring Alucard to *me*." He turned on the last member of their group. "Are we clear, *boy*?"

The Master of the Veil sat back in his chair, his eyes hidden behind the glinting gold mask. "You mistake your host for a servant."

"A servant would be *useful*."

The man in the gold mask rose, and as he did, the spritely humor melted like candle wax, revealing something hard beneath.

"Do not forget, old man, the *persalis* might be your idea, but the Hand were *my* invention. You make plans that crumble under weight, but I make weapons that will hold. And they may be blunt, but they are ours to wield. They will cause their havoc. They will take the credit, and the blame. And when the Maresh are all dead, and the throne is empty, and the city is reeling, looking for guidance—" Their host spread his arms. "—*we* will be there to guide them. *We* will hunt down the vile servants of the Hand, deliver them in the name of justice. And then we will not have to *take* the throne. It will be *given* to us. And when that happens, I want you to remember which of us was most useful."

He tossed a coin onto the table, like a patron paying for a drink. It was an ordinary lin, or so it seemed, but on its edge, an address was etched—the following night's address. "In case you forget where you are going."

He gave a sweeping bow.

"In the meantime, enjoy the Veil."

And with that, their host was gone, out into the hall, vanishing into the cloud of music and laughter that spilled through the house. The man in the black mask watched the door as it swung shut. In his scarred hand, the glass splintered, the contents leaking through the cracks.

"I will not sit on a throne beside him," he said under his breath.

The woman in the white mask sighed and rose from her chair. She went to him, resting her hand on his sleeve. On someone else, the gesture might have read as gentle, even warm. But her touch was a passing breeze, meant only to get his attention.

"Fight over the corpse when it is dead," she said, and then she, too, was gone.

The man in the black mask stood, silent and still, until the door swung shut, until he knew he was alone. Then he cast the broken glass aside, shards littering the plush rug of the borrowed house. He tore off his mask, and flung it onto the table, scraping a hand through his dark hair. He went to the lamp, and lit his pipe a final time, smoking until there was nothing left, and he trusted his temper to hold. Then he tucked the pipe back into his coat, and went to the table.

He plucked up the coin, and held it to the light, though he knew the words printed on its edge: *6 Helarin Way—Eleventh Hour.* Still, he pocketed the altered lin, swept up the black mask, and settled it back over his face before leaving the room.

He descended the stairs, into the foyer of black and white masks, and returned his to the wall like any other patron, then stepped out into the night. A handful of carriages dotted the street, their patrons still inside. He walked past them to his own, a block away, and as he neared, he drew a silver ring from his pocket and slid it back over his thumb. Two horses stood lashed before his carriage, pale as cream. He ran a hand along one's side, and as he did, the lamplight caught on the grooves in his ring. The edge was uneven, the band not a band at all but the impression of a feather.

The driver stepped down and opened the carriage door.

The interior was a lush and midnight blue.

"Where to, my lord?" asked the driver, and Berras Emery's hand fell from the horse's flank.

"Home," he said, climbing up into the dark.

Seventeen years before

Everything hurt.

As the carriage rolled along, every rattle and bump made his body tense, his muscles cringe. Berras Emery sucked in a breath, let it out through his teeth. He could feel the bruises blooming across his chest, along his ribs, the ache taking shape at his jaw, in his skull.

The worst of it, at least, was hidden beneath the tunic, with its high collar and long sleeves. A noble's garments hiding a fighter's form. Only his hands showed the damage. His knuckles were raw, blood seeping through the bandages that wrapped them. He had won the fight.

These days, he won them all.

Nineteen, and they roared his name when he entered the ring. Of course, there were no arenas constructed for matches like these, no tournaments attended by *vestra* and kings. Not in Arnes, where the greatest insult one could show a fellow man was to strike him, not with fire or ice, but one's own hand.

It was base, they said. Brutal.

And they were right.

These were not element games, graceful bouts adorned with magic. The very *use* of magic was forbidden, the buildings warded to keep it out. As it should be. A man did not choose his magic. It was a gift, a luck-made thing. But a man chose what to do in its absence, when they were nothing but flesh and bone and brute force. The will to get back up, to keep going.

That was a different kind of strength.

The carriage pulled through the gates of the Emery estate, and Berras took a last, low breath, steeling himself. A servant opened the door and he stepped down and crossed the stone drive, his back straight and his head up.

He would not let the pain show.

And he didn't, not as he climbed the steps, not as he slipped inside, not as he peeled off his coat and tossed it to a servant and strode down the hall. There were tonics and balms, he knew, to smooth the cuts and ease the ache, but they would soften the skin as they healed it, and the next time he struck, or was struck, it would hurt just as much. No, better to let the skin harden, the tissue scar.

The study door stood open, a handful of voices spilling out. His father, clearly holding court. Berras didn't dare stop, but he slowed enough to pick up pieces as he neared.

". . . eight years old, and not a drop of magic . . ."

". . . the *Antari* follows him like a pet . . ."

". . . Maxim should be ashamed . . ."

". . . a son so weak . . ."

And then Berras was passing the door. He saw three men with their backs to him, but his father sat as he always did, facing out. Reson Emery didn't pause his speech, but his eyes latched onto Berras. They dropped to his hands, before cutting away, his attention returning to his guests.

Berras kept walking, the pain replaced by something worse.

He was tall and broad, the picture of strength, while his father was old, sinew on a shrinking frame, and yet, Reson could still make him feel small with a single blue-eyed glare. In that moment, he missed his mother, dead six years, missed her cool touch, her gentle voice. It was a weak thought, small and soft, and he clenched his fists until the injured knuckles wept, and continued down the hall.

Quiet laughter trickled out of the sitting room.

There was a fire in the hearth, and before it sat Alucard, his back against the sofa and an empty pitcher at his side. He was holding out one hand, upturned, and in the air above, a tendril of water twisted and curled into the shape of a dragon. It coiled and danced, the water catching the firelight.

Berras watched, his mood darkening.

He was not *without* magic, like the prince, but his power lacked refinement. He could draw up a wall of earth, or bring it down, but the gestures had all the nuance of a butcher's cleaver, while his younger brother had been handed a surgeon's blade. It did not matter how much Berras tried, how much he trained, he still ended up with a pile of dirt.

Alucard's lips moved, his fingers twitched, but otherwise, he didn't even seem to be trying. It came so easily to him, and he treated it like nothing but a parlor trick.

Their little sister, Anisa, knelt on the cushions behind him, braiding his hair as she called out different things for him to conjure.

"A boat . . . a cat . . . a bird!"

"Alucard." Berras's voice cut through the room. The water, now a hawk, faltered in the air, a few beads dripping from its feathers as he turned his head.

329

"Yes, brother?" he said without rising.

"Come here."

The water hung suspended, then reversed its curl, returning to the pitcher as Alucard stood and came toward him. He looked ridiculous, two half-finished braids in his shoulder-length hair. At fourteen, he was a full head shorter than Berras, and had to look up to meet his brother's gaze. When he did, Berras saw that Anisa had painted his eyes, gold dust smudging his lids.

Berras scowled. "Have some dignity."

Alucard flashed an impish grin. "Sounds dull."

"You look like a fool."

"Yes, well, you look like you got your ass kicked—"

Berras's fist slammed into Alucard's stomach. He heard the ribs crack, felt them splinter as his brother sank to his hands and knees, retching.

Anisa screamed, and rushed forward, throwing her small body over Alucard's, saying "No, no, no," the table and chairs rattling with the force of her displeasure. Six years old, and already flush with magic. The sight of it made Berras bristle.

Alucard dragged in a breath of air and said, "It's all right. I'm all right." He put a shaky hand on her small shoulder. "Go upstairs now."

Anisa's wide eyes flicked between her brothers.

"*Go,*" barked Berras, and Anisa fled the room, bare feet pounding down the hall.

Alucard was still on his hands and knees, trying to catch his breath. Berras waited, watching as he dug his fingers into the floor and rose, slowly, blood slicking his teeth. He swallowed. "Do you hate me so much?"

Yes, thought Berras, the word rising like bile in his throat. He hated Alucard for having so much magic. He hated Alucard for being soft. There were tears in his eyes when he looked up, and Berras hated him for that, too, the way he let them roll down his cheeks, the emotion that flooded his face. He hated Alucard for not hating himself.

Berras's sore knuckles cracked as he clenched his fists. Someone had to teach him. It was *his* job, their father said. He was the oldest. The example. If Alucard was weak, it was because Berras had failed to make him strong.

"Our father says—" he started.

"Our father is cruel," snapped Alucard, wiping his mouth with the back of his sleeve. "He was mean before Mother died, and he is meaner now. Why must you follow at his heels?"

"That is what it means, to be a son."

"No," said Alucard, "that is what it means to be a shadow."

Berras towered over him. "Do you know what it means to be an Emery?"

"I thought it stood for pride and honor," said Alucard, scrubbing at his tears, "but apparently, it means one is a raging dic—"

Berras struck him again. This time, Alucard at least put up a fight. His hand flew out, and the water in the pitcher surged to him, froze around his forearm as he brought it up to block the blow. The ice shattered with the force of Berras's fist, and knocked Alucard to the floor again.

Anisa reappeared, tugging on their father's arm, trying to pull him into the room, to make him intercede. But if she wanted help, she should have called a servant. Reson Emery only stood there, watching. His eyes skated over Alucard as if he were invisible, and went to Berras, landing on the blood that wept from his ruined knuckles.

"Well," he sneered, "did you at least win?"

Berras met his father's gaze. "I always do."

II

Now

Moonlight spilled into the royal chamber, mixing with the Isle's glow. It cast thin fingers over the bed, over Rhy's shoulder, as it rose and fell, the rest of him weighted down by sleep; over Alucard Emery as he sat up, gasping for breath.

It was just a dream, he told himself, over the angry hammer of his heart.

Just a dream. But that was, of course, a lie. It was a tangle of memories, of brutal moments wound together into nightmare. It was his sister burning from the inside out. It was iron chains in the belly of a ship. It was Berras breaking his bones while their father watched.

Alucard looked down at his hands where they gripped the sheet, forced his fingers to release their hold, frowned when he saw that they were shaking. He flung off the covers, and rose, reaching for his robe, shivering as the silk kissed his bare skin.

The nightmares left him feeling raw, old wounds reopened, nerves exposed. He could feel sleep retreating like a tide, and knew he would have to swim to meet it.

He padded barefoot to the gilded tray against the wall, with its stoppered bottles, and short glass cups waiting to be filled. He could have lit a lamp, but the truth was, he had made the tincture for Rhy so many times that he could do it by feel, even without the glow of the river and the moon. He ran his fingertips over the bottles until he felt the sharp edge of the diamond-shaped stopper, and drew it out. As he did, he should have heard as much as felt the liquid slosh within. Instead, there was only absence. The bottle was empty.

Alucard swore under his breath.

In the bed, Rhy rolled over, murmured something to himself before sinking deeper into sleep. Alucard went to his side, bowed just long enough to kiss his brow, then slipped the empty vial into the pocket of his robe, and left.

The queen's workshop was empty.

It was strange, thought Alucard, given the hour. Nadiya always said the darkest part of the night was the best for getting anything of value done. Those long, black hours before dawn, when she could cast off the mantles of mother and queen and be what she wanted most: a Loreni. An inventor.

Another time, Alucard might have lingered to explore. But tonight, he wanted only to find his way back to sleep. The kind that fell like a curtain, and brought neither dreams nor memories.

He went to the chest on the far side of the room, its surface covered in cut-glass vials, jars of herbs, a stone mortar and pestle. The vessels were all marked, and he studied their labels, trying to remember the exact

332

portions of dreamsquick and hallowsroot as he drew the empty bottle from his pocket. He'd just taken up the first vial, was trying to decide between three drops and four, when a voice behind him cut in.

"There's a fine line between medicine and poison."

He turned, and saw Nadiya at the base of the stairs, a tray balanced on her hip.

"I thought you might be asleep," he said.

"At this hour?" she asked, as if that were absurd. "I wanted tea." She set the tray down. It held a steaming pot, a cup, and a stack of small spiced cookies.

"I'm sure the servants would have obliged."

"I'm sure," she said, striding toward him. "But I have two legs and a passing ability to boil water." She plucked the empty bottle from his hand and shooed him away from the chest.

"You know," she went on, drawing the dropper from the hallowsroot, "there are times in life when it serves one to guess, and times when it does not." Two small beads of liquid disappeared into the bottle. "This is one of the latter. Unless, of course, you like not knowing if you'll wake."

"I would prefer it," he said as she returned the hallowsroot, and reached past the dreamsquick for a bundle of widowswork instead, dropping a leaf into the mortar.

"The king is going through this batch quite quickly."

"It's not for him," admitted Alucard.

Nadiya met his gaze but said nothing, only returned to preparing the tonic. He decided to make himself useful; drifted toward the tray and poured the tea, swiping a spiced cookie from the top of the stack. He placed the cup at her elbow.

"Did you know that the *Antari* are in residence?" she asked, as if making pleasant conversation.

"Mhmm," he said around the cookie. Swallowed. Offered nothing else. The queen was brilliant, but her eyes took on a different light when Kell and Lila were around. She called it curiosity. He called it hunger.

"What brings them to London after all this time?" she pressed.

"The Hand," he said, then continued to wander about the queen's workshop as he explained about the raid on Maris Patrol's floating market, and the stolen *persalis*, and Bard's certainty that it had been smuggled here to use against the crown. He trailed off as he reached the worktable in the middle of the room.

"What's this?" he asked, studying the counter.

"You'll have to be more specific," the queen called without turning to see. But Alucard was busy trying to make sense of the sight himself.

The three Antari rings were out of their glass box. The wide silver bands sat like weights, pinning the corners of a large black cloth, its surface covered in Nadiya's slanted hand, the white chalk markings of a spell. The marks were connected, a vast, intricate web of lines, and at their center sat two lengths of chain, both wrought in gold. One was thinner and shorter than the other.

"Oh, that," said the queen, appearing at his side. She set her tea down on a nearby stack of books, and handed him the sleeping tonic. He slipped it absently into his robe, unable to take his eyes from the work laid out before him.

"What is it?" he asked again.

"Right now? It is a work in progress. One day, perhaps, it will change everything." Unease prickled beneath his skin as Nadiya took up the thicker chain, held it between her hands as if it were a priestly relic.

"It's one thing," she said, "to devise an object that magnifies a user's magic, as long as that magic is confined to a single element. Two water mages. Two fire workers. Two—or even three—*Antari*. Something that functions only as an amplifier, allowing one magician to borrow another's strength. But it is quite another for that magician to borrow a *different* power. Imagine being able to pair a water worker and an earth mage, or a fire maker and a wind one. Or"—her eyes flicked up to his—"a person without magic, and one who has plenty."

A dark feeling coiled in his stomach. "Nadiya—"

"Those rings allowed the *Antari* to do it once," she went on. "Unfortunately, as far as I can tell, they respond *only* to *Antari*. Which severely limits their application. I couldn't modify them, so I had to start from scratch. Here," she said. "I'll show you."

And before he could say no, she wound the gold chain around his wrist. Alucard shivered at the cold weight of the metal on his skin, the way it wrapped against itself, the echo of old chains. He waited, but felt nothing else change.

"How does it work?" he asked, as Nadiya took up the smaller length of chain and wrapped it around her index finger, where it bound to itself, becoming a gold ring.

She said nothing to activate the spell, only flexed her hand, as if admiring the bauble. But as she did, Alucard felt the gold chain tighten around his wrist, and become a cuff, flush with his skin, a band with no beginning and no end.

Nadiya flashed him a performer's smile. "Let me show you."

She crooked her fingers, and as she did, Alucard felt something come loose inside him. It was the strangest sensation, a collapsing inward, a weight dropping, if the weight were his lungs, his heart, everything that took up space beneath his skin. A dizzy lightness, a sudden, shocking hollow. And he didn't know what was missing, what was gone, until the air around Nadiya's hand began to ripple. Until the teacup rose and the contents spun out and the three elements churned together above her palm—wind, and earth, and water.

Even though Nadiya had only ever been a fire worker.

Those were *his* elements, *his* magic, or they had been. Alucard caught his own reflection in a mirrored surface, and saw the air around him bare of color, the blue and green and amber threads of his magic now twining through the air around Nadiya instead, braiding with the red of her power.

He tried to pull the magic back, only to find he couldn't reach it. There was nothing to grab on to. It simply . . . wasn't there.

"Give it back," he demanded, clawing uselessly at the gold around his wrist.

"That's the trouble," she said, eyes trained on the twisting elements above her palm. "It is much easier to take a thing than share it."

Alucard felt sick. The way he had his first days at sea, when the deck tipped and bobbed beneath his feet. He threw out a hand to steady himself. "Nadiya."

But she went on, as if she weren't holding his stolen magic in her hand. "Ideally, the power would go both ways. Shared equally between its users. As you can tell, right now, it's one-directional." She looked around the workshop. "Interesting," she said. "I still can't see the way you do."

"Nadiya, *stop*." The words came out soft and hoarse, and her attention flicked back to Alucard, as if she'd forgotten him entirely.

"Oh, sorry," she said, touching the ring, and it unraveled again, the short gold chain dropping into her palm; the elements she'd controlled a moment before now crumbled and fell away. The cuff went slack around Alucard's wrist, and violently he shook off the adornment, as if it were a snake, the gold rope chiming faintly when it hit the floor.

He could feel his magic pour back in as if he were a vessel, emptied and refilled. It churned with his shock and anger and for a second he was torn between charging the queen, and getting as far away from her as he could.

"What were you *thinking*?" he demanded as she knelt to retrieve the fallen length of gold.

The queen looked at him, perplexed. "Come now, Alucard," she said, returning both pieces to the table. "It was only a test."

"You weren't the one chained." He straightened, flexing his fingers, studying the threads of magic in the air above his skin. "You had no right to do that."

Nadiya sighed, impatient. "I thought it would be easier to demonstrate than to explain." She took up a narrow piece of chalk and began to make notes on the edge of the cloth. "As I said, it isn't finished. When I'm done, the spell will always go both ways, to ensure consent."

"There is a reason power has limits," he said.

The queen clicked her tongue. "You sound like the *Aven Essen*. Ezril is always coming down here, lecturing me about the balance of magic, the flow of power. As if all we're capable of is floating down the stream. Sometimes you have to bend the rules—"

"This isn't bending, Nadiya. This is *binding*. And in the wrong hands—"

She waved him off. "In the wrong hands a paring knife can end a man's life. Shall we ban them from the kitchen?"

Alucard stared at her, aghast. Nadiya Loreni was a brilliant inventor, but she had a kind of tunnel vision when it came to her work. She never seemed to see the danger in it, only the potential. In her mind, power was a neutral force. Alucard wished he could agree.

"This is dangerous."

"This is *progress*," she shot back. "Magic chooses, that's what the priests say. Do you believe that you've been *chosen*? That the forces guiding the world decided *you* should be able to wield not one element but *three*? What makes you so deserving?" He said nothing, then. He had no answer. "Why should some arbitrary force decide who wields water or fire or stone? Who has magic and who does not?"

Alucard stilled—this was not some pursuit followed for the sake of curiosity. This was a weapon against scrutiny, a way to protect their family and their throne. He did not blame her for it. And yet.

"Nadiya," he said, the anger slipping from his voice.

But it only mounted in hers. "Think of Rhy. Of how many people claim he should not be allowed to rule simply because he has no magic."

"Those people are fools," he said.

"Of course they are," she said, "but fools have voices, and voices carry. They want to punish Rhy, Alucard, all because magic did not *choose* him. But we can. We can give him power."

"By taking it from someone else."

"It isn't *done*," she said, exasperated.

"Yes, it is." It had to be. Because Alucard understood. Understood that if Nadiya offered Rhy power, he might take it, and if he did, those people—the ones who called him weak—wouldn't stop, they'd simply have another, better reason to hate him. They would find out his magic was borrowed, or stolen, the balance of the world tipped unrightly in his favor, and then, when they called for his head, they would be right.

He stepped toward Nadiya, set his hands on the queen's shoulders, and met her eyes.

"Destroy it," warned Alucard, "or I will."

III

WHITE LONDON

Holland Vosijk stood beside the tree in the center of Kosika's room.

It had grown over the last year, from a knee-high sapling to a tree half as tall as the room was high, a hundred eyes staring out from its pale trunk, and its leaves the color of amber. But unlike the ones in the Silver Wood, those leaves never fell. They colored, and withered, curled in only to fan wide again when the seasons changed.

The servants whispered of the tree that had taken root overnight. Spoke of signs and miracles. They had no idea how right they were.

"How was the tithe?" asked Holland now.

"You should have come with me," said Kosika, rising from the kol-kot board, where she'd left Nasi's present.

His eyes found hers. "I am always with you."

She felt warmth flood beneath her skin as he said it, turned to hide the blush and made her way to the basin. It stood waiting on a marble shelf, a bottle of salve and a length of clean cloth beside it. A castle of servants at the ready, but she preferred to tend the tithing cuts herself. They thought it was a part of the ritual, when in truth, it was privacy, so that she and her saint could speak.

Kosika rolled up her sleeve. Her head was bowed over her work, but she could feel Holland's shadow fall over her as she cleaned the four fresh cuts that scored her forearm.

"You are troubled."

She looked down into the basin, the water tinted with her blood. "I feel the city's magic getting stronger. I do." She swallowed. "But some days it feels like the soil will never be sated."

Holland rested his hand on her head. She could feel it—no longer just the shadow of a touch, but something closer to flesh and bone. "Magic can speed the work of many things, Kosika. But change itself will always take time."

His words were steady, but she was sure that if she turned her gaze to his, she'd see disappointment in his eyes. She was disappointing him. Her king. Her saint.

The weight of his fingers fell away. "We are working a vast and complicated spell. You must be patient."

Kosika shook her head as she smoothed the cold salve across the inside of her arm. *Patience* was a word for ordinary souls. She was *Antari*. If *she* could not summon enough magic—she tried to silence the fears, knew she shouldn't give voice to them, lest he take her thoughts as a lack of faith. But of course, he heard them anyway.

Holland sighed, soft, almost soundless. "Perhaps you are expecting too much."

Kosika turned toward him. "What do you mean?"

He was quiet for several moments, and though one eye was black and one green, somehow, they both seemed to darken. "Only that you are young, and I am . . . a shadow of myself. We have done much, and if the city grows no stronger—"

"No," she snapped.

"It is better than it was."

"A candle is better than the dark," she said. "But it is not enough to warm your hands by. Not enough to banish the cold from your hearth. And not enough to light a city."

Holland considered her. A ghost of a smile flickered across his face. "So stubborn, little queen. But you cannot build a fire like that from will alone."

Kosika brought the bandage to her arm but paused, considering the three lines. "The other worlds . . ."

Holland's mouth tightened. "Do not think of them."

"You wanted me to, once."

"I was wrong," he said simply. "Those worlds have brought ours nothing but strife. Besides, power is not a parcel to be carried home, and so long as the walls stand, and the doors are shut fast, magic will not flow between." He touched her arm, fingers ghosting hers as they tied the clean bandage around the fresh cuts. "What good does it do, to covet what you cannot have? I have watched kings and queens ruin themselves for less.

339

No," he said softly. "Let us tend our own flame, and trust that in time, the heat will be enough."

She studied the place where his hand hovered on her skin, and swore she could feel its weight.

One year ago

There was a room behind the altar.

Kosika had spent so many nights in the alcove, studying the statue of Holland Vosijk while Serak told her tales, and yet she'd forgotten that the recess stood in a tower identical to hers, and that, behind it, there was a door. She'd forgotten—until one night the candlelight caught on the wood behind the statue, and ever since it was all Kosika could think of, that door, and where it led.

But she knew, of course.

Even before Kosika stole up the tower steps one stormy afternoon, as rain battered the castle walls. Even before she ducked into the alcove, slipped into the narrow gap between the altar and the door. She knew there was only one place it could lead.

To the last king's chamber.

Holland's room.

She held her breath, and turned the handle, but the door held firm, didn't so much as jostle in a lock. Which meant it had been *sealed* somehow. Like a tomb. Kosika shoved her hand in her pocket, felt the triangle of steel she kept there, the size and shape of an arrowhead. She pressed her thumb to the tip until it broke the skin, blood welling as she pressed her hand to the wood.

The words hummed in her head before she said them.

"As Orense."

Open.

The door groaned under her hand like a tree in a storm, the splinter of wood and drag of metal. The sound echoed down the tower stairs, and she hissed, waiting a moment to see if anyone would come (there were still times she felt like a child stealing through someone else's house), but no one did, and this time, when Kosika pushed against the door, it swung open. She glanced back once over her shoulder, and stepped into the dark.

The windows were shuttered, and only weak light spilled in from the alcove behind her, not enough to see by. But it glanced off the dark metal of a candelabra at the far side of the chamber. Kosika flexed her hand, and the tapers lit.

She looked around.

Holland Vosijk's room appeared untouched. The space itself was a mirror of her own, the same curved walls, the same vaulted ceiling, the same vast bed, but a film of dust lay over everything, an echo of the pale patina that had clung to London for so many years like frost.

Kosika tugged on the air, conjuring a gentle breeze, just strong enough to skim the dust away.

She held her breath as she moved through the chamber, aware that she was stepping where he had stepped. Touching surfaces that he had touched. She pried open a set of shutters. This had been his view. She wanted to linger there, but rain was already dappling the windowsill, so she pushed the shutters closed again, as if the contents of the room might melt.

Her fingers skimmed the bed where Holland had slept, the chair where he had sat, her eyes scavenging the room for clues. A grey cloak still hung on the wall. There, on the desk, a note in his own hand, the writing falling sharp and slanted as the storm.

Vortalis once said there are no happy kings.
That the worthy ruler is the one who understands the price of power,
    and is willing to pay, not with his people's lives, but with his own.
The greater the power, the higher the price.
To take the throne is meager. To mend the world is dear.
Here is what I know.
I would bind myself again to see this place restored.
I would bend a knee to any king.

The entry ended there. Kosika turned through the stack, finding another.

What have I done? Only what I must.
Carried a spark out of the darkness to light my candle.
Sheltered it with my body.
Knowing I would burn.

And then, on another scrap of paper, a single word.

OSARON.

The letters sent a strange chill over Kosika's skin. It was familiar, the way *Antari* magic was familiar, the spells already there beneath her skin, nested in her mind before she knew their shape.

"Osaron," she whispered. An odd word. Not her native Maktahn. It had the air of magic. She said it again, and this time, the word changed on the way up her throat, twisting into a spell.

"As Osaro."

The power surged up out of her hands. Shadow billowed through the room, pluming into a sudden, solid darkness that doused the candles and choked the light. Panic gripped Kosika. She conjured wind to banish it, but it was not smoke, and it did not so much as ripple. She conjured fire, felt the heat of it tickling her palm, but she couldn't *see* the flame, couldn't see anything. She felt like she was drowning in this darkness, wanted it gone, but there was no way to end *Antari* spells, only to counter them, so she searched her mind, desperate for light.

Light.

Light.

Light.

"As *Illumae*." The word spilled out, and so did the stark white glow, blooming around her as swiftly as the shadows had, and driving the darkness back. The room returned, the candle flames wavering.

Kosika let out a ragged breath, and fled the chamber, sealing the door in her wake.

But that night, when she stood again with Serak in the alcove, her eyes drifted back to the wood at the statue's back.

"Tell me of the ten days," she said.

Ten days—that's how long had passed between the death of the Danes and Holland's return to claim the throne. Ten days, and in that time, no one knew where he had gone.

Vir Serak said there were a dozen different myths. Some claimed that he was simply waiting, biding his time. Others said he was wounded in the fight, and needed time to heal, that he'd dragged his body to the Silver Wood, and the roots had wound around his limbs, and magic had seeped back into his veins.

Others still said that he had *died*.

What have I done?

Kosika chewed her lip. She didn't understand. She felt she *should,* but it was like a riddle.

Carried a spark out of the darkness to light my candle.

She thought of Serak's demonstration with the lantern, the flame snuffed out, and then rekindled.

". . . in Black London."

Kosika's head snapped back to Serak. "What was that?"

"I said, there is even a version of the tale where Holland went to the burned-out world, and culled an ember from the ashes." His heavy brow furrowed as he spoke, his eyes thrown into shadow. "But that is blasphemy. Holland Vosijk would never taint our world with such black magic."

"Of course not," said Kosika, even as her mind spun over his words.

The greater the power, the higher the price.

I would bend a knee to any king.

Knowing I would burn.

The next day, she returned to Holland's room.

Stole up the stairs and slipped behind the altar, into his chambers. She returned to his desk, and the papers strewn across it, but this time she looked past them, to a small wooden box. At least, she guessed it was some kind of box. There was no lock, no clasp, only a stained circle on the wood and a thin line showing where a lid might join a base. When she tried to lift

343

it, she could tell it was hollow, could hear the rattle of something inside, but the two halves held firm. Sealed, like the chamber door.

Kosika's hand went to her pocket. The prick of steel, a bead of blood on the pad of her thumb before she touched the small, stained circle on the wood, as Holland must have done.

"*As Orense*," she said, the words rising as they had the day before. Within the circle, the line became a seam, and then it opened.

Inside, she found three coins.

One was silver and stamped with a man's face, and marks she didn't know. GEOR:III. D.G BRITT.REX. F.D. 1820.

The second was red with a gold star cut into its front.

The third was black, and made of stone as slick as glass.

Her fingers hovered for a moment before she reached in, fingers closing around the third, startled by how smooth it was to the touch. She held it to the meager light, could see the candle flicker through it. A new spell rose to her lips, spilled out before she thought to keep it in.

"*As Travars.*"

And then the room came apart, and she was falling.

First through nothing, and then through the empty space where the castle should have been, the air rushing past her and the ground coming up fast, fast, fast. Kosika threw out her hands, and a wind rose up, the air twisting beneath her, around her. It caught her limbs and slowed her fall—slowed, but didn't stop—and she landed hard, knees buckling with the impact, hands slamming into packed earth.

One palm stung worse than the other, and when she pulled back she saw why. The black glass token had shattered between her palm and the ground, shards slicing into skin. And yet, her first thought was not the pain, it was that she'd broken something that had once belonged to Holland Vosijk.

She scooped the largest shards back into her pocket, dug out a kerchief and wrapped it around her wounded palm as she got to her feet. And frowned.

The castle was *gone*.

Instead, she was standing on a road she didn't know, surrounded by ruined buildings, their corpses slouched, crumbling.

Her heart pounded in her ears, louder than any other sound until she

344

realized, there was no other sound. A horrible quiet hung over everything. The road was empty. No horses, no carts, no signs of life.

"*Os?*" she called.

There was no answer, not even the echo of her own voice.

It had been raining beyond her castle walls, but the ground here was dry and the air tasted wrong, like cinders on her tongue, and if there was a sun somewhere, it was well hidden, buried behind clouds that hung low and dark as smoke.

Too late, Kosika realized what she'd done, what she'd said, given voice to the spell that let *Antari* travel between worlds.

She was no longer in London.

Or at least, no longer in *hers*.

This other London looked wrong. No, not just wrong. *Burned.* And she knew, then, exactly where she was. Kosika scrambled backward, as if she could simply step out of the city's reach, brought her sleeve to her mouth, not wanting to breathe in the ashes that hung on the air, stirred up when she broke her fall.

She was in Black London.

The world that burned so bright it ate up all its tinder and burned itself out.

But if it had ever been a hearth, it seemed long cold, reduced to nothing but cinders. And yet, what had Serak said? Magic does not die. It waits. For what? A spark?

Her gaze flew back to the bloody handprint she'd left on the street. She half expected it to start smoking, to kindle itself into a flame. But nothing happened. The road stretched, silent and empty. It felt like a tomb. Like Holland's hand when she'd touched it in the Silver Wood that day. Cold and dry and dead.

Kosika shivered and fetched the shard of black glass from her pocket, its edge dotted red.

"*As Travars,*" she said again.

The world rippled around her, the air tensing.

But then it settled, and she was still standing there, in the unfamiliar road. Fear coiled inside Kosika, then, the sudden, horrible certainty that

345

she was stuck, that whatever magic had brought her here was not strong enough to take her home, that Black London had her now, and would never let her go.

The air hung heavy with ash. It left her dizzy, made it hard to breathe. Kosika fought down another swell of panic.

Either her magic was not strong enough.

Or she wasn't using it right.

There was no other spell, it would have come to her, but she studied the splintered token in her hand, and thought of the other two coins in the box in Holland's room. She could guess where they led.

Three worlds.

Three keys.

But there were four, including hers. There had been no key to her own London, but obviously he'd needed one. Kosika turned out her pockets, finding no tokens, only the other shards of the Black London glass, and her arrow-point knife. It had been a gift from Vir Serak, its small handle carved from a branch in the Silver Wood. It already had her blood on it, but she unraveled the kerchief from her wounded palm and swept the blade lightly through the welling red for good measure.

This will work, she assured herself. And then, aloud, "This will work." She said it as if it were a spell, something willed into being. And then she closed her fingers over the narrow blade and forced that will into the words.

"*As Travars,*" she said again, and this time, Black London shivered, and came apart like smoke. She didn't fall so much as lurch, the sudden off-balance sensation of a missed step, and then her feet were on the ground again, not a crumbling road but a polished stone floor.

She was back in the castle, not up in Holland's tower but the great hall below.

And the great hall wasn't empty. Far from it: a dozen members of the guard lined the walls, and servants dotted the space where three Vir were holding court with a handful of nobles. And maybe the room had been bustling with motion before her sudden, unexpected arrival, but now it lurched to a stop. A servant dropped their tray. Glass shattered. The three Vir turned, and the four nearest soldiers lunged forward, hands going to their hilts before they realized the ashen figure in the center of the hall was in fact their queen.

Kosika couldn't blame them.

A small cloud of soot swirled up around her, and a few drops of blood fell from her hand where she had gripped the blade, and for a single, horrible moment, she thought she might faint. But the moment passed, and Kosika stayed on her feet.

The soldiers dropped into a bow, but the Vir started toward her, and she could see the questions in their eyes as they went from her face to the blood dripping from her hand. And Kosika knew she could not tell them where she'd been.

But then she remembered that she did not have to. She was not some child, in need of scolding. She was an *Antari*. She was their *queen*. She owed them no explanation, so she turned in silence, and headed for the stairs, leaving a trail of ash and blood in her wake.

IV

RED LONDON, *now*

Berras Emery sat forward as the carriage rolled through the gates.

The horses slowed, drawing to a stop before the house.

Once upon a time, it had belonged to a reclusive nobleman named Astel, but Astel had perished in his bed during the Tide seven years before. Not that anyone save Berras seemed to care—though, admittedly, his concern was more for the property than its previous owner.

He had descended on the house one night, much the way the Veil did now, but unlike the pleasure garden, Berras hadn't disappeared at dawn. If anyone had noticed his arrival, perhaps they assumed he was a distant nephew come to see to his uncle's affairs, a man as private and unfriendly as Astel had been. The Emery heir brought nothing from his old life, and hired only one servant, the driver, who was paid well to be incurious.

The same driver now opened the carriage door, bowing deeply as Berras stepped out. He looked up at the house. He hadn't just chosen it because it

347

was empty, with no apparent heir. It was also tall—three stories—and from the study windows on the top floor, he had a view not only of this street, but the one directly to the north, and the Emery estate.

What was left of it.

For months it had sat, little more than a ruin, but then, from those study windows, he'd seen movement. Berras had watched as it was painstakingly restored, as if by a loving hand. Only to then sit dark, neglected. Waiting.

It taunted Berras, a brazen baited trap. For he was sure that if he stepped back into that house—by right, *his* house—he would wake to a knife at his throat, to guards dragging him from his bed and into a palace cell, forcing him to kneel on the cold stone and beg forgiveness from his brother, or mercy from his king.

Berras Emery had no intention of doing either.

Inside the stolen house, the lamps had been lit. Their pale glow spilled out of his office, along with the soft crackle of a fire he hadn't started.

Berras sighed, rolling his neck as he crossed the hall. He could see Bex in his chair, her legs up on his desk, and Calin sprawled on the sofa, arms stretched along its back. Berras paused only to brush his fingers down the doorframe before he entered.

"Get your feet off my table," he said, shrugging out of his coat.

Bex sat up, her boots thudding as they hit the floor. Calin's pale eyes drifted open. He looked tired, or bored.

"*Tac?*" Berras gave a cursory look around the room. "I take it your presence here means you have it."

Bex glanced at Calin. Calin didn't look back. She shifted her weight, and Berras knew before she had the nerve to say the words.

"We don't."

He closed his eyes. The Hand was gathering in less than a day. The bitch in the white mask was right. Without the *persalis*, this plan—*his* plan—wouldn't work.

"I hope you mean *not yet*," he said through clenched teeth. Judging by their faces, they did not. "What happened?"

"It's not our fault," offered Calin, chewing on the words before he spat them out.

"One of your thieves fucked up," said Bex. "He broke the *persalis* getting it off the ship, and then, instead of bringing it to *us*, he took it to a repair shop in the *shal,* gave it to some girl to fix. A tinkerer."

Berras felt his muscles tighten. It happened that way. A stiffening, like frost, that spread over his skin. Other people went hot. Berras went cold. "Where is this girl?"

"Dead," answered Bex, and he might have believed her—after all, she didn't flinch, or give herself away. But *Calin* did. His expression twitched, snagging on the word a second after she said it.

"You're lying."

"She couldn't fix it," said Bex. As if that was that.

As if Berras Emery didn't *need* the *persalis.* As if it were some trinket he'd sent them to fetch on a whim, and not the key to his strategy. He looked down at his hands, at the net of lines, fine as lace, that crossed his knuckles. For years, his father had ordered him to wear gloves, but Berras relished the scars. He had earned them.

"We tried," said Bex. "Trust me. Calin may be an incompetent shit, but I'm not . . ."

She went on making excuses, but Berras had stopped listening. He began to roll up his sleeves. The skin on his forearms was tan, and tough, the veins faint shadows beneath. He had survived the Tide and bore no silver scars, because when the dark god poured itself into his blood, he did not fight. Instead, he let it rage. Let it burn through him, unchecked, and as it did, it spoke. It told him what could be. It showed him that change was not a gift, it was a prize, something to be *taken.*

Across the room, Bex was still talking. Still making excuses. He cut her off. "Why are you here?"

Bex crossed her arms. Shifted her weight. "Well, the way I see it, we did our part."

Berras stared at her, nonplussed. "You want me to pay you for a job you didn't do."

"It was a fair amount of work," said Calin.

349

"I didn't realize I was paying for the effort." Berras took a step forward. "Your *part* was to meet the three thieves, dispose of them, and deliver the *persalis* to *me*. You failed. And yet, you have the nerve to show your face. To come to me for recompense. Get out before I break your necks."

Calin stood. Bex straightened. But neither so much as looked toward the door. For a moment, no one spoke. In the end, it was Bex who broke the tension. Bex who rolled her shoulders and spread her hands.

"One way or another," she said, "we'll be needing our *cut* . . ."

As she spoke, her fingers twitched toward the metal wrapped around her forearm. She clearly expected the steel to answer, perhaps provide some dramatic flourish to the word *cut*—but the metal didn't so much as twitch. It hung there, useless as a bangle on her wrist.

The mark he'd touched glowed faintly on the doorway. A sigil. A *ward*.

Berras watched, savoring the way Bex faltered, the confusion that spread like shadow on her face, her eyes widening, just a little, as she realized her magic wouldn't answer. Too late she went for her nearest weapon, but Berras was already there. His fist crashed into her cheek, and he heard the satisfying crunch of bone as she staggered back, dropping to a knee. One hand went to her face, trying to stem the blood now pouring from her nose.

Her other hand managed to draw a dagger, but Berras's boot came down, crushing her fingers under his heel as Calin finally caught on, and flung himself into the fight. Or tried. He threw a punch, and he was a large enough man that the blow would have hurt, if he'd known how to land it. But he didn't. The gesture was sloppy, and Berras turned out of its path, palmed the side of Calin's skull, and slammed it into the wall. The man dropped like a brick, but Berras kicked him once in the head, to keep him down.

Bex was up again by then, and came at Berras with the dagger, but she was half-blinded by tears and he caught her wrist, and snapped it cleanly. She gasped, her grip loosening on the blade, which he took, and drove down through the meat of her hand, pinning it to his desk.

Bex let out a feral sound. "You fucking *pilse*—" she got out, before Berras leaned on the blade, sinking it another inch, and she cut off, stifling a scream.

Calin was still on the floor nearby, clutching his head and groaning.

"My father taught me many things," said Berras Emery, "but this one most. *If a man does not know how to bow, you show him how to kneel.*"

With that, he pulled the blade out of the desk, and Bex scrambled back out of his reach, cradling her bleeding hand and broken wrist, her eyes full of hatred. Hatred, and fear. Calin got to his feet, swayed violently, braced himself against the wall, and retched. Bex used her less injured hand to snap her nose back into place.

Berras studied the blood-soaked knife. "You want payment?" His dark eyes flicked up, the color of a storm at dusk. With his bare hands, he broke the blade in two, and flung the pieces at her feet.

"Bring me something worth paying for."

V

GREY LONDON

Rain dripped from the signs that hung over the darkened shops.

Tes squinted, trying to make out the words, and wishing she had kept up with her lessons. They were not *ostra*, her family, but her father still insisted all his daughters knew the tongue they spoke at court, in hopes that they would make it there. Make him proud. Now she struggled to make sense of the signs.

Dressmaker. Butcher. Spirits. Baker.

Of course, he'd lost his fervor halfway through her lessons, when it was clear she wouldn't bring him glory. Her father—Tes tried to push the thought of him from her thoughts, as she always did, but she'd lost too much blood to fight her body *and* her mind, and soon his voice crept in.

What are you worth?

Four words, and there he was, standing at the counter of his shop, a rare and precious purchase hefted in one palm, his dark eyes sliding from the talisman to her.

Tes stumbled, gasped as she caught her balance, the jolt tugging at the stab wound in her side.

A small, frustrated sob escaped. The rain had stopped, but it was the middle of the night, and everything was closed. The streets were empty, and even with the lampposts, it was impossibly, unnaturally dark, and her head was spinning, and the pain had grown less sharp, which should have been a relief, but she knew enough to know it wasn't a good thing, when wounds this bad stopped hurting.

She was beginning to lose hope when she saw it.

Not a shop window or a sign.

A *thread*.

It crept down the street, a single tendril of light, so faint she would have missed if it not for the glaring absence of any other magic. Even still, she blinked, sure it was a phantom, her eyes finally beginning to fail.

But when she looked again, it was still there—a filament, unlike any she'd seen before. It had no color, nothing to define its element, was rendered instead in black-and-white, a core of darkness limned in light. Tes followed it to a break in the road. For a moment, the thread vanished, and she stumbled as she turned, desperate to catch sight of it again, then—there. At the corner, it flickered, returned a little brighter.

She followed it, until the river came into sight.

The Isle—though of course, it was not the Isle, only carved the same path. She thought the thread must stem from there, but when she neared the river, it was an oily black, lightless in the dark. It was eerie, to see the water at the heart of the city without a pulse.

Tes shivered, her shirtfront long soaked through with blood. She closed her eyes, swayed, forced them open again. Found the thread. It ran along a nearby wall, brighter still, until it dove between the bricks of a house and disappeared. The windows of the house were shuttered, but light seeped beneath the door, and Tes used the last of her strength to pound against the wood.

No one answered.

She kept knocking, but the sound seemed far away. She was so tired. Her forehead came to rest against the door. Her fist slipped. She closed her eyes, felt her legs begin to buckle. She heard a voice, a set of footsteps, the scrape of an iron lock. And then the door swung open, and she was falling.

"She's been stabbed."

"I can see that, Beth."

"Girl shows up half-dead at your door, leaving bloody handprints on the wood and leaking on the floor, and you don't think to call someone."

"I called *you*."

Tes dragged her eyes open, and saw that what she'd taken for a house was in fact a tavern. Low wooden beams drew tallies overhead, and the scent of ale wafted through the room. Her fingers twitched against the slats of wood beneath her. She was lying on a hard, raised surface. A table.

There were two voices, somewhere beyond her sight, talking loudly, as if she were not there. A man, his voice not deep but even. A woman, her tone drawn taut as she said, "If she dies, you'll have a bigger mess."

Tes tried to move, but her limbs felt like sacks of sand. She closed her eyes again and strained to catch the words as they rushed past in High Royal.

"It's my tavern."

"Aye, and last I checked, I'm a barmaid, not a surgeon."

"I've seen you truss a roast."

"Ned Tuttle, if you don't know the difference between a side of beef and a young woman, it's no wonder you're still single."

The slosh of hands in water, the twisting of a rag, and then—the soft, bony click of a dead owl's beak. Vares. Tes dragged her eyes open. She turned her head toward the man's voice. He was thin, and younger than she would have guessed, with a narrow nose and floppy brown hair. He leaned back against the counter, and there, laid out on display, were her coat, a short stack of red lin, and her owl. In his hands was the repaired doormaker.

Tes lunged up—or meant to. She made it halfway onto one elbow when a white-hot pain shot through her side and she half tumbled, half fell back with a gasp, knocking her head against the table as she did.

"Oh great," said the woman, "she's awake."

The man swept forward, leaving the doormaker behind as he gently pressed Tes's shoulder back against the wood.

"Lie still," he said. "We're trying to help." And then, to her surprise he held up a single red lin, between his face and hers, and whispered, "You're safe here."

And before she could wonder who he was, and how he knew about her world, he pressed a cloth over her nose and mouth. It smelled sweet, and cloying. But the pain began to dim, and the edges of the world went soft. Tes looked up into the man's face, and then past it, at the faint tendril of magic coiling through the air around him. Her fingers twitched, and she reached out, as if to catch it—but then her hand fell, and the room faded, and everything went black.

VIII

THE GIRL, THE BIRD, AND THE GOOD LUCK SHIP

I

HANAS, *nine years ago*

Tesali Ranek had a wind-blown heart.

That's what her mother always said. That her youngest daughter had been born with a breeze inside her. It was why she couldn't sit still, why she was always escaping out of open doors, why she was always in motion, churning through the halls of the house, playing in the shop below until her father couldn't stand her restless limbs, how near they got to the precious things on his fragile shelves, and he inevitably swept her from the shop, and set her free until dark.

That day, six-year-old Tesali had blown even farther from home, climbed up the cliff path, which was not a path so much as a ribbon of grass worn bare, a slippery road of shifting rock.

But it was worth it, for the view.

A breeze was picking up, carrying the scent of a storm, but when she scanned the bay, she saw the clouds sitting like distant ships. *Plenty of time,* she thought, clambering up the last jagged slope.

Hanas was a sea city, built along a series of rocky outcrops, big as giant's stairs, that led up from the coast. The port sat in the bowl of the bay below, and the cliffs rose above, peaks trimmed with mossy soil. No one built along those cliffs—they said the rock was too fickle, too loose, prone to flaking off like pastry crust—but if that was true, she didn't see why they'd gone and put all the buildings right below. The cliffs would

357

stay put, they insisted, as long as they were left alone. But little girls were lighter than houses, so Tesali climbed, careful to avoid any stones that looked even a little loose, and when she reached the top, she stood, hands on her hips, and beamed in triumph, as if she'd conquered the city as well as the cliff, as if everything below belonged to her.

"I am the queen of Hanas!" she shouted, but the wind stole the words, plucked them away like a ribbon from her hair, and she flopped down, breathless, in the weedy grass, and watched the ships come and go, their sails reduced to tiny white pennants.

Tesali settled back, and stared up at the vast and open day until the air just above her eyes began to shimmer, and move, like fingers rustling a curtain. It was happening again. She squinted, trying to refocus her vision, but the shimmer only sharpened, drawing lines until it looked less like a sky and more like a tapestry. She waited for it to disappear, and when it didn't, she squeezed her eyes shut, letting the wind pick up in her ears, in her bones, in her heart, and carry her away.

Drip.

A drop of water landed right between her eyes.

Tesali blinked.

She didn't remember dozing, but the day smelled different now, and when she sat up, she saw that the storm had swept in, no longer a shadow on the horizon but a roiling darkness overhead, threatening to—

Drip. Drip. Drip.

Like a pipe about to burst, and sure enough, seconds later, the drizzle became a downpour, and she was up, half running, half sliding down the slope, as dirt turned to mud and the pebbles skittered beneath her shoes and the rain crashed down, her vision blurring in the storm until it didn't look like drops at all but a thousand tiny filaments of light. She shook her head, tried to make her eyes work right as she raced home.

By the time the path became a street again, and the ground turned from packed dirt back to cobblestone, she was soaked through, her curls slicked against her face and neck, her dress clinging to her legs. Tesali passed a shop window, caught her reflection in the glass. She looked wild, and wind-made, and mad, and the sight made her smile.

She ran on, slowing only when she saw the sign.

That sign, stamped in metal instead of wood, so it shone, even now in the middle of the storm. ON IR ALES, it announced in glinting gold. *One of a Kind.*

Their housemaid, Esna, was standing on the steps, her face blooming red with anger, and she caught Tesali's arm and hauled her past the entrance to her father's shop and through the second door, the one that led up into the house above.

"Of all the foolish things . . ." she muttered, and Tesali knew from experience that it was better to just let the woman fume like a kettle until she ran out of steam.

She was forced to strip right there, at the top of the stairs, leaving her soiled clothes beyond the entry to the house, and then Esna carried her through, past glass cases and dark wood cabinets and closed doors.

"Four daughters," ranted Esna, "and each with less sense."

And with that, she dumped her unceremoniously into the bath.

Her fork scraped softly against the dinner plate.

Tesali fought the urge to fidget. Esna had put her in a stiff dress, which felt like a punishment, and her curls had been wrestled back into a plait, the braid so tight she was getting a headache. She'd caught her reflection in the hall glass. She looked like a doll.

"Like your mother," Esna sometimes said. Which was supposed to be a compliment, she knew. Her mother was pretty, in a fine-boned way. Refined. The picture of an *ostra,* a noblewoman of Arnes.

Her father, on the other hand, had a face like a crow. A pointed nose and small, sharp eyes, and a head that swiveled, neckless, on his shoulders. When her sisters were still at home, Mirin would do an uncanny impression, and Rosana would dissolve into laughter, and only Serival, who resembled him the most, would scowl and say it wasn't funny.

Tesali missed her older sisters.

She hadn't always gotten along with them, but the house felt hollow without them in it. Funny, how a place could feel empty when it was so full of *things*. Her father's collection grew up out of the shop below, climbed like weeds into every corner of their house, which wouldn't be so bad, except she wasn't allowed to *touch* any of it.

Not because the things he owned were fragile—half were already broken in some way—but because they were *valuable*. And according to her father, valuable things had to be protected, kept behind glass, so their worth could grow.

Not that any of it was *forbidden*.

Everyone knew Forten Ranek didn't deal in forbidden magic. He was too proud. He had no interest in the dangerous and the obscene.

"Leave that to Sasenroche," he'd say. No. He was a *curator,* one who specialized in the precious and the rare.

Now and then, Tesali's father would give her an appraising look, the same one he leveled at a piece brought in to be sold. She knew he was waiting to see what she was worth.

To find her value, and make use of it, as he had done for his other daughters.

Her sisters.

There was Mirin, made rare by her beauty. The Diamond of Hanas, they called her. Eighteen, and so striking, men came from all three empires to bid for her hand. Carried off by an Arnesian old enough to have grey hair, and installed in a manor up north.

Then Rosana, made rare by her powers. By ten, she could wield not only fire, but ice. By fourteen, she was gone, the star of a performing troupe, though Tesali knew she dreamed of winning the *Essen Tasch*.

And Serival, the oldest, made rare by her cunning. Not sold off, but sent away, all the same, to be her father's eyes out in the world, and find new things for his collection.

Three sisters gone.

Three chairs sitting empty at the table.

Her parents talked as if there were already four, and Tesali thought she might die of boredom. Her plate was clean, but she couldn't leave, not until she was excused. A taper burned in front of her, and as her parents spoke, she let her vision slip, gaze sliding in and out of focus until the little flame seemed to peel itself apart, dividing into strands as thin as hairs.

She was certain that if she reached out, she could catch one. So she did, forgetting that it was a trick of the eye, that the light only *looked* like threads, that it was in fact still fire. Her hand went into the flame, and a searing heat tore through her fingers. Tesali yelped, and pulled back, and for the first time that night, she had her parents' attention.

"I didn't mean to," she said quickly, clutching her burned fingers. "I was reaching for the salt." Her father shook his head, but her mother only stared, an odd expression on her face. She'd seen Tesali do it, knew she hadn't reached past the taper, but straight into it.

Her mother put her knife down, and rose. "Come," she said briskly. "Let's put some salve on that." She took Tesali by her unburned hand and marched her into the kitchen. She didn't say anything else, not as she found the pot of salve, not as she sat Tesali down, not as she rubbed some of the cold mixture into Tesali's fingers. But when it was done, she caught Tesali's eyes—they had the same eyes, the brown flecked with bits of green and gold—and asked, "Why did you do that?"

Tesali chewed her cheek. "I thought I could touch it."

"The fire?"

She shook her head. "The threads."

Confusion traced itself across her mother's face. "What threads?"

Tesali nodded at the hearth, the fire there shot through with strands of light, though the truth was, she'd seen them in the surface of the table, too. And in the basin of water. And in the pot of salve.

"Don't you see them?" she asked, and when her mother shook her head, Tesali felt a small triumphant flare—at last, she had something of worth. At last, she would matter.

But the look in her mother's eyes wasn't pride. It was fear. And that's when Tesali realized: whatever was happening with her eyes, it wasn't a common ability, an ordinary gift. It was rare, just like the things her father traded in, and Tesali knew he didn't keep the best things for himself.

He sold them off to the highest bidder.

Her mother knelt before her and grabbed her hands hard, ignoring the burns.

"When?" she demanded. "When did this start?"

Tesali shook her head. She didn't *know*. It was less like a fire being lit, and more like the sun coming up, a brightening so gradual that she hadn't noticed, not at first. And then, one day, she couldn't *not,* because every object seemed to have an aura, a faint glow, like the lanterns on the docks when the fog hug low at night. Only it wasn't night, and it wasn't just the lanterns that glowed. It was *everything.*

And then, of course, she hadn't realized it was strange. After all, how was she supposed to know what others saw? But the look in her mother's eyes said enough, and the fear in her voice said the rest.

"You mustn't tell," she whispered, her face so close their foreheads almost touched. And then Tesali's mother dragged her to her feet, and marched her back into the dining room, with its empty chairs.

"Silly girl," she said, smiling at Tesali's father. "Always dreaming."

Tesali took her seat, and said nothing.

But that night in her room, she sat on the floor, legs crossed, and studied the taper she'd brought with her to bed. Watched as tendrils pulled away from the fire, and twisted through the air.

The pain in her fingers had cooled, but now she reached out again, felt the warning heat against her palm as she grazed the flame, careful not to touch it. Instead, she waited for the thread to waver and ripple, bend away from the fire, and when it did, she caught it. It pulsed, hot, between her finger and her thumb, but didn't burn.

She pulled, just a little, expecting resistance. Instead, the flame unraveled, and went out. For a moment, the thread lingered, glowing like an ember in her hand, and then dissolved.

She smiled in the dark.

Then relit the candle.

And tried again.

II

Seven years ago

Her father's shop was full of wonders.

Books so old, she couldn't read the spines. A letter to a king in another world. A head sculpted in marble from an artisan in Vesk. A painting made of a hundred separate panes of layered glass. A map to the *Ferase Stras*. A scrying bowl, its polished surface spelled to show not the future but the past. A frosted glass orb that could hold a person's voice.

It was a maze of cabinets, a winding corridor of glass cases and wooden chests, easy to get turned around when you couldn't see over the tops, but whenever Tes got lost, she stood on her toes—or on a table—and searched for the glorious bird.

The bird sat on a pedestal at the heart of the shop, like the center of a compass, its vivid green feathers catching the light, gold crown visible over the chests and shelves. Tes found it, and hopped down, heading in the right direction.

On her way, she passed a narrow chest, its contents shrouded despite the angle of the nearest light. But Tesali had memorized the contents: a scrap of paper written in the true language of magic; the broken hand of a small sculpture; a piece of stone that once made up the gate between worlds, when the doors were open. Relics from Black London.

Tesali didn't like the items in that case. They had no threads, but the air around them wasn't empty: a thin rim of shadow surrounded each object, the opposite of the haloes that formed around the lanterns at night. Once, and only once, she'd opened the cabinet, reached in to touch them—not the objects themselves, but the darkness that fuzzed the space to every side.

At the time, she'd felt nothing. But it was a bad kind of nothing, a wrong kind of nothing, and she found herself rubbing her hands together for hours after, unable to get them warm.

363

Her father claimed they weren't forbidden, these objects, that they were pieces of history, and history had worth—and yet, he never sold them. Never even showed them. She wondered if he forgot they were there, buried in the maze of the shop. She tried to forget, but she always seemed to find the darkened case. She turned her back on it now, and focused on finding the glorious bird.

It had been in the shop as long as she could remember.

Once it had been as large as Tesali, but then she kept growing and it did not, and now, she was the larger. Still, it was magnificent, too big to fit in any of the cabinets, and so it perched on top, watching over the precious contents of her father's shop.

It was, according to him, extinct. The last of its kind, and so, the perfect emblem for On Ir Ales.

But it wasn't the bird itself that captivated her.

It was the way it *moved*.

As she stepped into its line of sight, the bird ruffled its feathers and stretched its wings. Its head twitched, eyes craning down at her, its beak clicking softly. It moved through these small, predestined motions, guided by a delicate network of magic that wove through the air above its wings, around its feathered body, between its taloned toes.

It had disappointed her once, to learn it was only imitating life. But that was before she could see the threads that animated it. Now, Tesali marveled at the sheer complexity of the magic. She reached up and plucked one of the glowing strings that coiled in the air, as if it were an instrument, and the bird answered by lifting slightly, as if about to lurch into flight. This was not one of its set motions. This was something only *she* could make it do.

"Tesali!"

Her father's voice should have gotten tangled in the maze, bent around the cabinets and cases in the way, but it didn't. It had a way of cutting straight through space.

Her hand dropped from the bird, and she remembered her errand. She crouched, opening the cabinet that formed its perch, and pulled out the coin chest, hurrying back to the front of the shop. The maze never seemed to catch her on the way out, the way it did on the way in, and in moments, she was there.

Her father stood waiting with his customer, an older man, his silver hair pulled back in an elegant braid. They were talking about London—everyone was—and the tide of cursed magic that had spilled through the streets the week before. Some thought it was a spell gone wrong, others, an assault. After all, the king and queen were dead. But that wasn't what her father cared about.

". . . will soon have one of Maxim Maresh's swords," he was saying, "and Kisimyr's tournament mask. I have a collector in the city."

She knew he meant Serival.

Tesali's attention went to the counter between the two men, where something thin and sharp-edged waited beneath a sheet. She tried to guess at what it was as her father plucked the coin box from her hands.

"My youngest," he said to the customer. "She has a way of getting lost inside her head."

The other man offered her a smile. "The world needs dreamers."

"Does it?" asked her father dryly, his eyes landing on her as the bird's had, shrewd and dark and searching.

"Indeed," continued the customer. "You have dreamers to thank for half the wonders in your shop." Her father smiled tightly, but as he began counting out coins, she knew what he was thinking: What use was a dreamer without magic?

Tesali retreated to the table where she'd been when the customer came in. She climbed back onto the stool, and stared down at the element set that sat open, waiting, as it did every day, because every day, her father ordered her to practice.

The night before, she had heard him talking with her mother.

Powerless, he'd called his youngest daughter, spat the word like a curse.

Her mother had soothed him and said that the new king had no magic, reminded him that he had been blessed three times already with powerful children, and that the world sought balance. As if Tesali were a tithe to be paid, the cost of other blessings.

She heard the shop bell chime as the customer left, but she didn't look up. She squinted at the pieces, and moved her lips, and pretended to have no power over any of them, even though that wasn't strictly true. As far as she could tell, she had no *elemental* magic. She couldn't make something from nothing, couldn't conjure flame from the bead of oil, or whip up wind to move the pile of sand, or control the bit of bone. But if someone had lit the oil, she could have pulled the burning drop into any shape, transformed it into a raging fire, or a delicate ribbon of flame. She could have turned the water to ice by tugging on its threads, or shaped the earth into a ring. She could have pulled on the strings of the wooden box itself, and turned it into a bracelet, a mug, a sapling. She could see the very fabric of the world, and all the magic in it, and touch each and every string, unravel the patterns, and remake them, and—

"You're not even trying," scolded her father.

Tesali bristled, and in that moment she wanted to tell him everything, to show him just what she *could* do. Maybe then he would look at her the way he did Serival, or Rosana, or Mirin. With pride instead of expectation. But every time she felt the urge well up, she remembered the fear in her mother's face, remembered that her sisters were all gone, that if she told the truth, her father would not love her.

He would sell her.

"Come here," he ordered, and Tesali abandoned the set and the stool and returned to the counter as her father pulled the sheet from the newest piece of his collection.

It was a mirror.

Of course, it was not an ordinary mirror. Her father did not bother with ordinary things, and she could see the magic twining around the frame, tracing a second pattern over the silver edging. But before she could read the meaning in it, he told her.

"Some mirrors show the future," he said. "Some mirrors show the past. Some can show you what you want, others what you fear. A few will even show your death."

Tesali shivered, and hoped this was not one of those.

"But this mirror," he went on, running a hand down the silver side.

366

"This mirror reveals what you are capable of. It shows your true potential."

Tesali saw her eyes widen in the glass, and her father mistook her expression for eagerness, and smiled. He did not often smile, and it looked wrong, unnatural.

"Now, my little dreamer," he said, "what are you worth?"

It was a question he posed to every item in his shop, to each piece as it joined his collection. A question he asked softly, almost reverently, speaking not to the seller but to the object itself as he took it in hand, and set it on his shelf.

What are you worth?

Fear prickled across Tesali's skin as he took her wrist and dragged her closer to the glass.

Fear—but also relief. She was tired of hiding who she was, what she could do. Now, she had no choice. The mirror would expose her, and he would know the truth, and it would not be her fault.

Her father pressed her hand to the surface of the glass.

It was cold to the touch, steam instantly forming around her small fingertips, but as she watched, the steam grew and spread, fogging over the entire pane of glass, erasing the shop, and her father, but not her.

Tesali stood there, in the center of the silver frame. And then the frame disappeared, and she stood alone, no longer in her father's shop but on a street she didn't know, in a bustling city. She tried to look around, but before she could take it in, the street and the buildings around her began to *unravel,* became a thousand threads. She moved, and the threads moved in answer, rippling away, and then drawing in.

She reached out and ran a hand along them, as if they were harp strings. And they did sing. They sang in color. They sang in light. She could feel the power in each and every one of them. The potential. She flexed her fingers, and they splayed, pulled and they came, gathering between her hands. She looked down and in the space between her outstretched palms, the threads coiled, faster and tighter until they became shapes.

There, between her hands, a box, a bird, a blade. There a house, a tower, a palace, a road. There a city crumbled, dissolving like a castle made of sand. There a dead man rose, like a puppet, drawn back to life. There a river of light overflowed its banks, and drowned a world. After this last, the threads spilled out, past the bounds of her hands, arced around her, until she was standing in another frame. No, not a frame. A doorway.

And then the threads turned black.

They recoiled, turned back on her like a wave, cresting up over her head. She held her breath as they came crashing down over her, into her, coiling around her limbs, her body, her face, until they swallowed her up, and she was gone.

Tesali recoiled from the glass, and as she did, the visions dissolved, and she was back in the shop, heart pounding in her chest as the mirror became a mirror again. Her father stood behind her, gripping her shoulders, and she could feel the greed in his touch.

But then he said, "What did you see?" and Tesali realized that the reflection had been hers, and hers alone. Her secret was her secret, still. To share, or to keep. But how could she tell him what she had seen? What *had* she seen? What did it mean?

"Well?" he pressed, and so she told him.

"I see myself here," she said, "with you."

It was the truth—a kind of truth, at least. After all, it was what she saw right then. She mustered a smile as she said it. As if she would be happy with that future. As if either of them would. Her father let go of her shoulders. He took up the sheet, and cast it back over the mirror, but she was still looking at the glass, so she saw the disappointment scrawled across his face right before the cloth came down.

III

Three years ago

Tesali ran, cursing the slippers as they slipped and skidded on the pebbled road.

Her mother made her wear them, since she insisted on acting *like a chicken out of its pen and not a girl of twelve.* She thought the cursed shoes would discourage her from running.

They didn't.

Whenever her parents sent her on an errand, she ran, getting to the butcher or the baker or the bank in half the time, just so she could cut through the dock market on her way home.

Tesali *lived* for the dock market, the makeshift stalls that popped up overnight like mushroom caps along the port, tables made of crates, tents conjured out of tarp, manned by sailors who came to sell whatever wares and trinkets they'd come by on their travels. Not the meat of their work, but the trimmings. Of course, her father scorned the market, insisted there was nothing there of any worth, but she marveled at the array, gathered from the far corners of the empire, and sometimes even farther. It was easy to forget how large the world really was, living in Hanas.

She had only been outside the port city once, a half-day's trip by carriage south to see Rosana perform, the youngest member of her troupe, and so clearly destined for great things. A future victor of the *Essen Tasch*, her father used to preen, before the Veskan prince killed the Arnesian queen, carving a trench in the treaty between the three empires, and ending the tournament for good.

Most days Tesali just came to look at the wares, and imagine the places from which they came. But today, as she surveyed the stalls, a large roast in the satchel slung over her arm (the purpose of her trip) and a month's petty change in her pocket, she was on the hunt for a prize.

A gift.

It was her father's birthday, and though he was by no means a sentimental man, he had decided that fifty years was a number worth marking, and her mother saw it as a chance to call her daughters home. Mirin and Rosana were already there, unpacking their gifts, and Serival was bound to arrive any minute—Tesali gave a quick, nervous scan of the docks, unsure if she would come by land or sea—and would no doubt bring something grand. She always did. It was the nature of her work, to find precious things.

And Tesali was determined to find something, too.

She moved along the line of stalls, eyes skimming here, grazing there, unsure what she was looking for but sure that she would find it. And then she did.

Most of the stalls had at least one bit of faulty magic among their wares, the spellwork fraying, or fractured in ways they couldn't see. But on one table, *everything* seemed to be broken. From the glass balls, which should have been able to capture a season, to the heating stones, which should have boiled the water they were sitting in, to the ship prisms, which would have turned colors to warn of coming weather, if they had worked at all.

A man sat on a crate behind the table, whittling something with a blade the size of his thumb. He had dark skin, and black hair twisted into ropes, each one ornamented by a bit of silver, and a thin tendril of blue magic that twined in the air around his shoulders.

As she watched, he cut a notch too deep, and the piece of wood split in his hand.

"Never been good at whittling," he muttered, tossing the stick into the surf. And yet, he took up another bit of wood, and started again, cut three slices before he looked up, and saw her studying the wares.

"Something you want?" he asked, his voice full of salt.

The table was cluttered, but she nodded, picking up one of the orbs. He had three for winter and two each for fall and spring, but the one she chose was a summer glass.

"How much?" she asked, then held her breath. She only had six lin, and a working seasons-glass would have cost twice that, and even if it wasn't the kind of thing her father would put in his shop, he was always complaining of the cold, and she thought he'd like it. This palmful of warmth.

"Two," said the sailor, and she had to bite down to hide the smile. Her father was always saying she should never let her feelings reach her face. She reached in her pocket, pulling out two lin.

"Just so you know," he added, "it's broken."

That was very honest of him, she thought, when most of the sailors would tell you a plank of wood was a golden sword if it would make you buy the block.

She put the two coins on the table and said, "I know." She did *not* say that she could see the exact spot the threads had frayed. It wouldn't be hard to fix.

As she was slipping the broken orb gingerly into her satchel, the sailor did a series of odd things. First, he finished whittling the bit of wood into a

370

tiny pipe. Then he produced the small, articulated skeleton of an owl from somewhere around his feet, set it on top of the table, and put the pipe in its beak. The sailor smiled, amused. Tesali stared in wonder.

"How much for that?" she asked.

"The pipe?"

"The owl."

He glanced up, studying her. "S'not magic," he said. And it wasn't. There were no threads of spellwork, broken or whole, no signs of any craft running through the little bird, only silver wire, holding the bundle of bones together.

He gave the owl a long, appraising look. "Five," he said.

"Four," countered Tesali, but he must have seen the want in her eyes, and shook his head. Her heart sank. "I don't have five."

He shrugged, as if that wasn't his problem. She chewed her lip, searching her pockets, as if the coins might multiply. Then her hands went to her hair. It was pulled up, as it always was, wrangled and pinned with a clasp. She freed the clasp, and her hair with it, a cloud of brown curls spilling down around her shoulders. The clasp itself was nothing much, but there was a silver bauble on it. She pried it free, and added it to the four coins in her palm.

The sailor considered. She held her breath.

Then he reached for the little bird, and plucked the wooden stick from its beak.

"That will buy you the owl," he said. "But no pipe."

She could have thrown her arms around the sailor then, but she didn't. Instead she handed him the payment, and swept up the dead little bird into her arms before he changed his mind. She watched him pocket the coins and slip the bit of silver into his own hair.

And then she turned and ran all the way home.

For the first time in years, there were no empty chairs at dinner.

Forten Ranek's four daughters were all home, and sat arranged around his birthday table, as fine as prizes in their best clothes, done up like dolls. One day at the dock market Tesali had seen a set of nesting wooden figures.

The sailor showed her how they fit, one inside the other, each painted with a different face. Ever since, that was how she thought of her sisters. It didn't help that there were exactly four years between each, a set of descending stairs, from twenty-four to twelve.

The four Ranek girls were different in almost every way. They ranged in age and height, in beauty and in mood, even their eyes, which spanned from amethyst (Rosana) to hazel (Serival) to brown (Tesali) to almost black (Mirin).

The only thing they had in common were their curls, and even those didn't grow the same on all four heads.

Serival's grew in loose dark waves, and were somehow always wrested back into a plait, sleek and groomed.

Mirin's were sun-kissed rings, never bound up, but left to fall in a shining mane.

Rosana's curls were cut short, a halo of warm brown wisps that fit beneath her many performer's wigs.

And then there was Tesali, whose curls were wild, unruly, a thicket of ever-escaping weeds. She had done her best, tonight, to tie up the stubborn mass, wrangle it into a pleasing shape, but by the time the roast was cooked and served at midday, the glasses filled with strong southern wine (of which even Tesali was allowed a pour, though she didn't like the taste, or the way it made her head feel large and small at once), she could feel the tendrils coming free.

Her mother beamed at them, glad to have her family home and whole.

Her father smiled, too, glad to see the sum of his work.

Then Esna cleared the plates, and it was time for gifts.

Tesali clutched hers beneath the table, waiting her turn. It was wrapped in a gauzy scarf and bound with ribbon. It had taken her all afternoon, from the second she'd come home to the time she'd been called downstairs for dinner, but she'd done it.

Her knees bobbed anxiously as Rosana went first, holding out an envelope, sealed with dark wax. Their father reached for it, but before he could, she conjured a delicate flame that burned away the envelope in a flash of red sparks, and melted the wax, revealing the contents.

An invitation.

"To a performance," she said, "in your honor."

Their father smiled, lips pressed tight as he took the slip. It was a fine gift, but he clearly expected more. Rosana saw it, too, and looked down, her face reddening. If only the *Essen Tasch* hadn't been canceled, thought Tesali. Rosana would have to find another way to shine.

Mirin stepped into the silence, a cat's smirk on her lovely face.

"My gift," she said, holding no obvious present—until her delicate fingers dropped to the front of her dress. "Though you will have to wait to hold it."

Their mother gave a cry of delight, and their father's smile split open, showing teeth, and as Mirin rambled on about birth dates and names, happiness turning her cheeks pink, Rosana and Tesali shared an exasperated look, knowing that neither could compete with a grandchild.

For it was, as always, a competition.

Only Serival seemed untroubled, clearly confident in her own gift, and that made Tesali nervous—and bold—enough to throw herself in front of her oldest sister, not wanting to be in her wake.

"Father," she said, offering the bundle, "my gift, to you."

Tesali held her breath as he took the parcel, peeled apart the makeshift wrapping to reveal the summer-glass. When the surface of the orb met his skin, it came to life, a small tree in the fullness of bloom at its center.

Tesali smiled, knowing she hadn't just fixed the summer-glass.

She'd made it better.

When she was mending the broken threads, she saw a way to twist them, change their path, so that when her father held the glass, he not only saw the taste of summer trapped within, but felt it. Felt the warmth of the sun on his skin as if he were standing beneath that tree. Her father, who was always complaining of the chill that autumn brought. Whose hands ached with the encroaching cold.

Something crossed her father's face then, an expression she'd so rarely seen, shadowing him in the shop. Surprise. And with it, an almost childish delight.

"Marvelous," he murmured, and Tesali felt like she was standing beside him in the glass, soaking up the summer sun. Mirin and Rosana chirped their approval.

But Serival's expression had gone shrewd.

"Where did you get that?" she asked, and the question drew their father out of his reverie, his attention narrowing, too.

Tesali knew when to lie, and when to shield herself in truth.

"From the dock market," she said.

"How did you pay for it?" demanded her sister.

"It was damaged," she said, "so the sailor sold it cheap. But I am rather good at fixing things." She registered the weight of her mother's gaze, but she looked only at her father as she said it. "I have learned from watching *you*."

It was the right thing to say. She watched as the flattery smoothed her father's feathers. Serival's gaze lingered, but it was her turn now.

"Father," she said, producing a small wooden box, and sliding it toward him. Her hands, as always, were hidden beneath a pair of black gloves. An affect, Mirin called it. To make her seem imposing.

The table went quiet as Forten Ranek set the summer-glass aside, the sunlit tree vanishing with his touch, and lifted the lid of the box, withdrawing a narrow vial, not glass, but gold.

His brow furrowed.

"What is this?" he asked. And that itself should have been a warning, for their father was a collector, and knew most treasures by sight, his keen eyes registering worth the way hers did magic. But Tesali saw what he could not. She saw the tendril of light that twisted not around the narrow vial, but inside it, coiled like a small snake. Pitch black, and yet glowing. It made her shiver.

"What do you give the man who has everything?" asked Serival, as if it were a riddle. And then, when no one answered, she did. "Time."

She pointed to the vial. "That is five years."

"Five years?" he echoed, a question in his voice.

Serival smiled then. "Of life."

If a wind had blown through and doused every candle, the room would not have felt darker.

"What have you done?" demanded their father.

Serival actually laughed. It had all the warmth of hail on glass.

"I have not killed anyone, if that's what you're asking." She took up her goblet, gloved fingers pinching the stem. "I have yet to board the *Ferase Stras*," she said, "but I have heard the captain deals in years instead of coin. Time is such a treasured currency." She quirked a brow. "Are you not happy with your gift?"

He put the vial back in the box. "That is forbidden magic."

"It is only forbidden if taken by force, and that was not. It was made in payment."

"For what?"

The air in the room had drawn taut as rope. Serival met her father's gaze. "That is my business, not yours."

Her mother's chair scraped back as she stood. "This isn't a topic fit for dinner."

"Is it not?" said Serival, amused. "It is your birthday, Father. Fifty years, who knows how many more?"

Rosana sucked in a breath. Mirin bit the inside of her cheek. Tesali looked on in horror. All waited for something to break. Instead Forten Ranek rose, and ordered Serival into his office, taking the vial in its box as he stormed out of the room. She followed, and their mother vanished into the kitchen to help Esna, leaving the three remaining sisters at the table, dotted by empty chairs.

Tesali stared at the summer-glass, which sat, abandoned, by her father's place.

"*Anesh*," said Rosana, taking up her wine. She was only sixteen, but she had the airs of someone twice her age.

"Why does she do it?" asked Mirin, rubbing her stomach, as if to soothe the life within.

"Bait our father, or deal in dangerous things?"

"Both."

"Does she?" asked Tesali. The sisters noticed her, which they rarely did, so she went on. "Does she actually trade in forbidden magic?"

"No," said Rosana at the same time Mirin said, "Yes." The two shot each other a look, but Mirin leaned forward with a grin.

"I heard she has a compass that points toward powerful things. Father gave it to her himself."

"Don't be silly," said Rosana. "If Father had a compass like that, he'd keep it for himself." A sigh. Then, as if she couldn't help herself, "Serival doesn't need a compass. She has a gift for finding things."

"A gift?" asked Tesali, as her sisters' magic swirled in the air. Could Serival have her own kind of sight?

"Why do you think she wears those gloves?" asked Rosana.

"Because it's pretentious?" offered Mirin with a snort.

Rosana pursed her lips. "She told me once, she could know a thing's worth just by touching it."

"What a crock of shit," said Mirin, turning to Tesali. "What I know is, there's rare, and there's forbidden, and there's whatever Serival deals in. Sacrificial magic, possession—"

"Father wouldn't let her," said Rosana.

"Father couldn't *stop* her," countered Mirin. "I heard she auctioned an *Antari* eye at Sasenroche. They don't rot when the person dies," she added, plucking a grape from the center of the table, "just turn to stone. And if you have one, no one can kill you."

"You sound like a child telling tales," chided Rosana.

"The point is," Mirin went on, "our sister is a *hunter*. She enjoys the chase as much as—" But she cut off as their mother appeared in the doorway, wiping her hands, a look of warning in her eyes.

"If you're determined to gossip like hens, do it somewhere else."

"Sorry, Mother," said Rosana.

"We were just going out," said Mirin, "to get some air."

Tesali stood with them, but they shot her a look that said wherever they were going, she wasn't invited. That was fine. For once she didn't even feel left out. She slipped away down the hall and into her room, shutting the door behind her.

The small bone owl sat waiting on her bed.

"Hello," she said, running her finger down the curve of its skull. It didn't move, of course. There was no magic threaded through the bones.

Not yet.

IV

Tesali was good at mending a thing when the pieces of the spell were there, but she had never created one from scratch before. And yet, she told herself, she was not so much creating as *re*-creating. She'd called to mind every thread that wove through the glorious bird in her father's shop below, the way they twined, the pattern and the flow.

A shelf ran along one wall of her room, and it was home to her own small collection: a dozen different charms, some gifts from her parents and siblings, others tokens bought for spare change at the dock market. Now she inspected them, plucking away the threads she needed one by one, sacrificing the spellwork for the raw material. The threads sang faintly in her hands, shuddering like moth wings, delicate, brittle, but she managed to wrap each one around the owl's small skeleton, anchoring the magic to its skull, its wings, its feet.

And there, sitting cross-legged on her bedroom floor, Tesali began to weave.

Even as the spell took shape beneath her hands, she feared it wouldn't work, certain there must be more to magic, a threshold she couldn't cross. She told herself she was just a girl playing a game, imitating the real thing.

But then, as she knotted off one of the threads, the owl lurched, a ripple of motion that ran through its bones, and made her heart leap into her throat. She worked faster then, as if the spell were a fragile candle flame, one that might gutter and die if she let out a breath.

It didn't.

In fact, it came together, settling over the owl like a net. Soon it ruffled its bone wings. It clicked its bone beak. It lifted its bone skull, and seemed to stare at her through empty sockets.

Time fell away as Tesali worked.

Her senses narrowed to the little owl, and nothing else. Not the murmurs of the house. Not the motion of the door swinging open.

"Kers la?"

Tesali jerked, pulling her hands away as if burned. Serival was leaning in the doorway, arms crossed, eyes narrowed to hawkish points.

"Kers la, ri sal?"

Ri sal. Little rabbit. She hated that nickname—and her sisters knew it, so of course, Serival refused to call her anything else. When she didn't answer, her sister took a step into the room. Her feet were bare, but her heels still managed to click against the wood.

"What do you have there?" she asked, and in that moment, Tesali made a terrible mistake. She should have stared blandly up, made nothing of it. Instead she flung her skirts over the little owl. It was an instinct, born of being the youngest sibling, but she might as well have confessed to a crime.

Serival didn't rush forward. She simply *continued,* three slow steps until she was there, standing over Tesali. And then she knelt. Serival wore trousers, not skirts, so nothing but her shadow pooled around her feet.

"Show me," she said, the words like a hand on the back of her neck, and Tesali knew that if she refused, there would be a struggle, and she would lose. She knew because she was stubborn and had done it a hundred times, and it had never gone her way. Still, she was tempted, the denial on her lips, but what scared her off was the wicked smile on her sister's face, which seemed to say, *Go on, little rabbit, try and run.*

Tesali drew the skirts away from the owl.

"What a morbid little pet," tutted Serival, amused. She reached out and tapped a gloved finger on the bird's beak. Tesali held her breath. So long as the owl didn't move, she could pass it off as just a piece of fancy, another ornament for her cluttered room.

But then Serival said, "Are you that lonely, little rabbit?" and the owl twitched to life, and looked up, because of course, she had made it that way, designed it to react to the uptick in a voice, the sense of being asked a question. So she could talk to it. It had been a novel idea. Now she cursed it.

Serival's eyes narrowed, the humor vanishing from her face, replaced by something sharp and shrewd. They had all grown up with the glorious bird, of course, and knew how rare the spellwork was.

"Now *that,*" she said, reaching for the owl, "is a pretty piece of magic."

Tesali lunged, but her sister was faster. She plucked up the little bird in one gloved hand, and turned it over, studying the bones and the silver thread that joined them. Tesali knew she was searching for the marks of a spell, the articulation of magic, knew she wouldn't find them. The owl ruffled and twitched in Serival's fingers, as if trying to get free.

"Give it back," she said, but her sister's grip only tightened.

"You could never afford a thing like this," she said. "Which means you stole it. The summer-glass, too."

"I *didn't*," gasped Tesali, insulted.

"Don't lie," warned Serival, squeezing the owl. She would crush it, and all her hard work with it—and in that moment Tesali didn't care about the magic—that she could redo—but the dead little owl seemed so alive— she had brought it to a kind of life—and it writhed and opened its beak in a silent plea and—

"I made it!"

The words were out, and for the briefest moment, she was proud of the surprise they triggered on her sister's face. And then Serival's eyes narrowed, just like their father's, and she wished she could take it back.

"What do you mean?" she asked calmly, but Tesali had recovered her senses enough to hold her tongue. Serival looked down at the owl.

"Perhaps if I smash it," she ventured, as if to herself. "You did say you had a knack for fixing broken things." Serival raised the little owl over her head. "I'd like to see how you—"

"*Don't*," pleaded Tesali, as another voice cut through the house, unencumbered by walls and doors.

"Serival!" called their father.

Her sister hesitated, but even she knew better than to ignore a summons. Slowly, almost gently, she returned the owl to the floor between them, and rose to her feet.

"We'll talk about this in the morning," she said, as if *this* were just a bedtime story or a bit of gossip, something that would keep. "Sleep well, little rabbit."

Tesali swept the owl into her arms, and pressed it to her front. She sat, shaking, on her bedroom floor as the door swung shut. "I'm sorry," she whispered to the little owl. "I'm sorry."

379

She knelt there, mind spinning over what she'd done, what she'd said, as she listened to the sound of her sister's retreating steps, heard her father's join them, followed by the creak of stairs as they went down into the shop below.

And then she was on her feet, sprinting into the hall.

Tesali had always been mature for her age. Independent to a fault. But in that moment, she wanted her mother. Wanted to feel her soothing touch, and hear her say that it would be all right. That it was bound to come out sooner or later, that she had only needed to hide the talent when she was little.

But as she stood in her mother's room, and showed her the owl, and told her what Serival had seen, her mother's face lost all its color. And when Tesali was done, she did not tell her daughter it would be all right, did not say they'd find a way, that Serival would never do her youngest sister harm. No, she turned, and went to her dresser.

"Where is Serival now?"

"In the shop, with Father."

Her mother nodded and pulled out a pouch. "Good," she said, pressing the pouch into her hands. It was heavy with coins. "You must go."

Tesali stared down at the money. She didn't understand. *Go?* She was twelve years old. This was her home. A cloak settled over her shoulders. Quick fingers tied the laces at her throat. She found herself saying all the things she'd come to hear.

"It will be all right."

"I'll say I stole the bird."

"We will think of something."

"Look at me," said her mother, gripping her arms, and when she did, there was fear in her mother's eyes. Her mother, who mourned each daughter's absence like a death, who longed to have them all home. Her mother, who often joked that at least she had Tesali. Would always have Tesali.

"I won't do it again," she said, but it was a lie, and they both knew it. When you had a power, not using it was like trying to hold your breath underwater. Sooner or later, something made you come up for air.

Tesali didn't know she'd been crying until her mother smoothed the tears from her cheeks.

There was pain in her mother's face, but not surprise, and Tesali realized she'd been waiting for this day, had known it would come. Her mother kissed her forehead, and pulled her close, and whispered into the wild of her hair.

"Your power is yours. Let no one else claim it."

And then she pulled back, taking the warmth with her. "Now go."

For once, Tesali did as she was told.

The house was quiet, save for Esna, humming softly in the kitchen. Tesali crept past, down the stairs to the front door, where the shoes were left.

She started for her soft-soled slippers, then stopped, and changed course. She *almost* took Serival's—they were leather with laces that wound like corset bindings up the front, and toes capped in silver—but didn't, in case her sister might use the boots to track her. In the end, Tesali reached for Esna's sturdy boots instead, peeled off her socks and pushed them down into the toes to make them fit.

Then she opened the door and crept out, past the house, and the windows of her father's shop, before taking off down the street.

V

Go, her mother had said.

Perhaps she should have asked, *How far?*

Perhaps she should have asked, *How long should I hide?* But she hadn't, afraid the answers would be like rocks in her pockets, weighing her down until she couldn't move.

Tesali kept the owl pressed to her chest as her stolen boots sounded on the stone road.

It was almost dark when she reached the docks. The sun was gone, but not gone out, the waning light hugging the horizon, turning the ships there to shadows. But in Tesali's eyes, the world was always bright.

The dock market was shuttered for the day, the stalls collapsed, sailors now loading whatever they'd failed to sell back onto their ships. The vessels looked like birds, some readying for flight, others pulling in their wings, bedding down for the night.

She found the sailor at the far end of the docks, hefting a crate of unsold things toward a narrow ship. The silver tokens in his hair caught the last of the sun. The pale blue of his magic shone on the air.

"You again," he said as she ran up, dragging to a breathless stop. Her cheeks were flushed, her curls escaping. She must have looked as wild as she felt, because he glanced over her shoulder to see if she was being chased. "Are you in some trouble?"

"Yes."

"Then take it somewhere else," he said, turning away.

Her eyes darted to the ship. "Is that yours?"

He grunted, a sound that could have been either yes or no, save for the fact he was in the process of carrying a crate up the ramp. She followed in his wake, but he stopped at the top and turned, blocking her way. "Go on. Don't need you tracking mud on my deck." She looked down at her boots before realizing it was a turn of phrase.

"Please—" she started.

"—is a nice word for fine company," he said, jerking his head toward Hanas. "Now go home. It's past your bedtime, little lady."

Tesali bristled. "I can pay," she said, feeling the weight of the coins in her pocket.

"Not enough for the trouble," said the sailor.

Her eyes dropped to the crate in his arms. "You won't get much for broken magic."

He cocked a brow. "Insulting my wares now?"

"But you could," she continued, "if it was fixed."

What are you worth? her father asked.

She was about to find out.

"I can fix broken things," she said. "Sometimes, I can even make them better."

She opened her cloak, revealing the little owl he'd sold her earlier that day.

"What do you think?" she asked, and before he could say that it looked the same, the owl twitched in answer to the question, and tucked its head under one wing, and began to preen the place where its feathers would be.

The sailor jumped, and then let out a barking laugh that caught her off guard. It was rich and full, and delighted. "I'll be a priest," he swore.

She tucked the skeleton away. "I have a knack," she said.

"I can see that."

"If you take me wherever you're going, I'll fix everything you couldn't sell."

He studied her. "What is your name?" he asked, and she almost told him. But then she stopped. Names had value. And her father taught her never to give a thing away for less than it was worth. Especially something you couldn't buy back. She thought of giving him Serival's name, but the idea left a bitter taste in her mouth, and she knew it would make her jump, every time he said it. So in the end, she bit off the first part of her own, and gave him that.

"It's Tes."

"Well, Tes," he said, setting down the crate and holding out his hand. "You have a deal." They shook on it, her hand swallowed up in his as he drew her aboard the ship.

His name, she soon learned, was Elrick. His ship was the *Fal Chas*.

The *Good Luck*.

"Where's the crew?" she asked, and he spread his arms, as if to say *me*, but also, perhaps, to say *us*.

"She is light, and sweet," he said, patting the hull. "And she gets jealous easily. But you're small enough, I hope she won't be cross and try to drown you."

He had a way of flattening his tone when he spoke, which made it impossible to tell if he was joking. (She would learn that while Elrick was a sailor now, he'd been a soldier, first, which had given him a very dry humor.)

Soon the ship was free of its mooring. It pulled away from the dock. Away from Hanas. Tes stood on the bow and watched the port city drift out of reach. Elrick stood on the other side of the narrow ship, his magic bright as he guided the *Good Luck* forward through the current, one hand held over the water.

In his other hand, he held a small stone. It wasn't spelled, she could tell, not to amplify his magic or focus his mind, but he turned it over and over, its surface long worn smooth, and when he caught her looking, he said, "It's always good, to have a bit of land on hand when you're out at sea. Keeps you grounded."

Tes thought about that as she turned her gaze back to the retreating coast. Night fell like a shroud, and soon only the lanterns and the lights in the houses traced the shape of the place she had lived all her life. She held up her hand, and the whole port city seemed to fit there, in her palm. Then, on the tip of her finger. Then, gone.

As Hanas disappeared, and the sea stretched out like a sheet in every direction, the world felt suddenly very, very large. Her heart began to race, and she sucked in, filling her lungs with air.

She was alone. And though she was frightened, for the first time in years, she was also free. That night, when the *Good Luck* found its current, Elrick gave her a blanket and a corner of the cabin floor, and she curled up with the little owl, and let the ship rock her to sleep.

The water below the boat had come alive.

The currents on the open sea had shone a low and steady blue, but since they'd passed the port, trading the ocean for the waterway that would carry them inland, the water had been changing colors. Now it glowed an eerie *red,* shot through with threads of crimson light.

"Amazing, isn't it?"

Tes's head jerked up. Elrick was leaning over the side now, too, staring down into the current. "You can see it?"

"Well, I'm not blind, so yes, I can see the light of the Isle. As can everyone, from Tanek on."

Tes marveled at the idea of a magic others could see. Elrick was no longer watching the water. He stared at her, turning a question over in his cheek. This time he seemed about to give it voice, but at the last, he swallowed it, turned his gaze back to the river.

Since picking her up in Hanas two nights before, he hadn't asked a single question. Not about who she'd been, or what she was running from. Not when she fixed each and every object in his crate. Not even when he came into the cabin once and caught her adjusting the threads around the little owl, her fingers hooking through what must have looked like empty air.

"Your business," he'd said, turning on his heel, and walking out again.

Now they stood side by side, leaning over the rail as the color deepened in the water below.

"They say it is a source," explained Elrick. "A place where magic runs so strong the naked eye can see it." *The naked eye,* she thought as he nodded at the prow. "It will only get brighter as we near London."

London.

She knew of the Arnesian capital, of course, but back in Hanas, it had felt like the stuff of stories. A city so big you couldn't see its edges. The jewel of the empire, overflowing with magic. Rosana had once gifted their mother an illustration of the royal palace, which had supposedly been built on a bridge over the Isle, though that seemed a ridiculous place to put a castle.

Or so she thought, until she saw it.

Soon the river widened into a crimson thoroughfare, crowded with ships, and on either bank the buildings rose, so many and so close she couldn't see the streets between, and Tes finally had to close her eyes against the shine and tangle of so many burning strings. Beyond her lids, a shadow, as she felt them pass beneath a bridge, the brief dark like a cool compress. And then, the light was there again, and Elrick telling her to look.

When she opened her eyes, she saw the *soner rast,* the city's beating heart. The palace vaulted over the crimson river, its spires pricking the sky, the sun turning them to flame.

The docks were crowded with all manner of boats, from small skiffs to massive ships with more masts than the *Good Luck* had sails. Boats with spellwork carved into their hulls, and streaked like paint along their prows. Everywhere she looked, she saw the lines of magic. An almost blinding tapestry of threads.

Her spirits sank a little when she scanned the docks, and saw no market, no makeshift stalls.

"This city has a hundred markets," said Elrick, at her side. "You will find them all."

She threw a mooring rope down to a waiting dockhand.

Elrick laid the ramp.

"There you are," he said, as if he'd simply given her a lift from one port to another. As if he hadn't saved her, set her free. Her borrowed boots sounded as she crossed the deck, the coin pouch in one pocket and the owl tucked beneath her arm. She felt too light, as if she'd forgotten something instead of leaving it behind on purpose. She set off down the ramp, but Elrick caught her arm.

"Wait."

If, in that moment, the sailor had invited her to stay aboard, she might have said yes. But he didn't. Instead he took her hand, and placed the small dark stone inside it, the one he held on to as he guided the ship. He curled her fingers around the rock.

"To ground you," he said, "whenever you're at sea."

She held fast to the little stone as she descended the ramp, and crossed the dock. Held fast as she reached the steps that led up to the street, and into the vast and vibrant city. Held fast as she plunged into the rippling current of light and motion, and knew that no matter what, she would find her way.

IX

THE
THREADS
THAT
BIND

I

WHITE LONDON, *now*

A knock sounded on the bedroom door.

Holland's hand dropped from Kosika's shoulder. He drifted past her to the window as she said, "Come in."

She expected a servant, or perhaps Nasi, but instead it was Lark who entered, holding a tray.

"My queen," he said. There was a quirk to his mouth when he said it, not mocking, but playful. A reminder that he had known her back when she was a street rat, and he a scrawny thief. Before she'd gained a black eye and a crown. Before he'd gained that scar at his throat. Before his shoulders had grown wide and his bearing tall and his voice had taken on that rich honey lilt.

His eyes scanned the room, passed right through Holland before lingering on the blood-soaked cloak she'd thrown off on her way in. "Good thing you're not squeamish."

Kosika shrugged. "Never have been."

She didn't realize how hungry she was until he set the tray down and she saw the food piled high on the plates. Thick-sliced meat, and roast carrots, a loaf of bread and a bowl of stone fruit and a pitcher of cider—easily enough for two.

In the beginning, she had been unnerved whenever anyone else stood in the presence of her saint, unnerved by their inability to see him as she could. But now, it gave her a kind of thrill.

389

"Do you wish they could see me?" asked Holland, and Kosika surprised herself by thinking *no*. She should want it, she knew, but she *liked* that he had chosen *her*. Only her.

Holland's mouth twitched, a ghost of a smile.

And she forced her attention back to her friend.

"Eat with me."

"A soldier, taking from the queen's plate?" he said, aghast. But she rolled her eyes and split the food between them. She sank into a chair. He perched on a footstool.

"You're missing quite a feast," he said.

"And now you're missing it, too. A servant could have brought this tray."

"I'm glad for the excuse," he said, meeting her gaze. "I hardly see you anymore."

"You see me every day."

"I see the queen."

Are we not the same? she wanted to ask. But she knew they weren't. She would never be a proper queen—a proper queen would be downstairs, smiling and nodding at nobles—but she could not be the reckless, feral girl she had once been.

She looked to the bloody cape. "I wish she were a cloak or crown," she mused. "Something I could shed."

"I don't," said Lark. "You are changing the world, Kosika."

The words surprised her. So did the light in his eyes.

"He is loyal to you," mused Holland. She had almost forgotten he was there until he spoke. She half expected Lark to flinch, to jerk at the sound of the voice. But of course, he didn't hear it. Didn't see Holland drift forward, fingers gliding along the trunk of the silver tree.

It took all her effort not to shift her attention, let her gaze follow him across the room, so she was grateful when he passed behind Lark, and stopped there, so she was looking at them both.

"Tell me about it. This feast I'm missing."

"Well," said Lark, swiping a plum from the tray. "Half the nobles are drunk, and the other half are fools. Two of the Vir are having an affair and terrible at hiding it, and Nasi is flirting with this soldier—Gael, do you know him? Handsome enough but hollow-skulled."

"Jealous?"

"Well," he said, rolling the plum between his hands. "I have heard Gael's a talented lover."

Kosika snorted into her cider. Lark rambled on, and as he did, she imagined the castle falling away, imagined them sitting on the edge of a city wall, legs swinging over the side as they shared a stolen meal. And then she yawned, and the room snapped back into shape, and Lark rose, and said he should be going.

"My queen," he said with a bow.

She rose, following him toward the door. He pulled it open, the sounds of celebration wafting up from below. But he stopped on the threshold.

"Almost forgot," he said, digging in his pocket. He turned, and held out a small black pouch. "Happy birthday."

She blushed as she took the pouch, turning the contents out into her palm. Dusty white blocks rattled into her hand. Sugar cubes.

"Stole them from the kitchen."

"The castle kitchen," she pointed out. "Which belongs to me. You could have simply asked for them."

"Yes, well, a little girl told me that stolen things taste twice as sweet."

"I'm not a little girl anymore," she said, and Lark laughed as if it were a joke.

He left, after that. The door swung shut behind him, silencing the sounds of the party below, and she was alone again with her king.

Kosika looked down at the sugar cubes in her palm, felt Holland's shadow fall over her.

"Do you remember?" she said.

Holland's brow furrowed. "Remember what?"

"The day I found you lying in the Silver Wood. I put a sugar cube in your hand."

He shook his head. "You found my body. But I was no longer there."

Kosika frowned. "If you weren't there, how did you choose me?"

His green eye briefly darkened. Silence stretched between them, growing heavier with each passing second until Holland reached out, and brought his hand to rest on her head.

"What matters is that I did."

She nodded beneath the weight of his palm, and told herself he was right. Of course, he was right. Who was she to question the Summer Saint?

But that night, when he was gone, Kosika lay awake in bed, and turned the sugar cube between her fingers, trying to decipher the shape of the shadow that had crossed his face, until the image bled and she forced the thought from her mind, and gave in, at last, to sleep.

One year ago

Kosika needed a bath. Needed to scrub every trace of that other world from her skin.

She wanted to be alone, but word had a way of traveling through the castle. (More than once, Kosika had wondered if it was magic, some spell that allowed gossip to go through walls, to move faster than feet.) By the time she reached her chambers, Nasi was there with a pair of servants, perching on the edge of the stone tub in the corner of the room, which brimmed with hot water.

The servants came forward to undress their queen, the way they had a thousand times, but as their fingers reached for the laces at her wrist and throat, Kosika recoiled.

"Don't touch me," she said, her voice too loud, too sharp.

The servants flinched, but Nasi scowled. "What's gotten into you?"

Kosika only shook her head, undoing the laces herself, and Nasi must have motioned for the servants to leave, because a moment later the door sighed closed, and they were alone.

"Where did you go?"

Kosika said nothing as she wrestled with her clothes. Cinders had settled on the shoulders of her white tunic and the tops of her shoes, staining them grey. She felt contaminated. At last she was free, and climbed into the scalding tub, hissing at the heat, plunging even her wounded hand into the bath.

In seconds, the water was no longer clear, but cloudy, stained pink and grey. Nasi watched as Kosika pulled the pins from her hair and flung them aside. Watched as she took up soap and scrubbed her skin raw. Watched, and waited for Kosika to explain, and when she didn't, Nasi took up a bar of the sweet-smelling soap, and began to wash her hair.

As long as Kosika could remember, she had loved the feeling.

In the months after becoming queen, when the castle was too big and too quiet and she couldn't sleep, she would lie with her back to Nasi, and the girl would run her fingers through her roots.

She remembered her mother doing it when she was very, very young. But it was such a gentle memory, it must have been a dream.

Now she leaned back, and fell beneath the spell of Nasi's hand, and when the girl said, "Tell me," Kosika did.

She told her of Holland's room behind the altar, of the box and the tokens in it, of the words that came to her, and the world where they led. She expected Nasi to recoil at the mention of Black London, but she didn't. Her hands never stopped moving.

"What was it like?" she asked quietly.

Kosika stared up at the bones of her ceiling and said the only word that came to mind. "Dead." She rolled her head, looking to the soiled clothes that lay piled on the floor. "Burn them. To be safe."

Nasi's hands disappeared from her hair as she knelt to collect the clothes. She stood, holding them out like an offering. Her eyes narrowed in focus, and her lips moved, and a moment later, the fabric in her hands began to burn. Fire swallowed the beautiful stitching, the silk and leather and laces, filling the room with an acrid smell and a plume of smoke.

But not all of it burned.

As the bundle in her hands collapsed, four shards of blackened glass slipped out, ringing faintly as they hit the stone floor.

Nasi knelt to pick them up, fingers hovering over the tokens.

"Don't," said Kosika, but for once, Nasi didn't listen. She took the largest shard gingerly between her fingers and held it up, peering through the darkened glass at Kosika. And for a moment, only a moment, the eerie black shine, the way it filled her eye, made Nasi look like an *Antari* herself.

393

And then her hand fell, and she piled the four pieces in her palm, and set them on the low table beside the kol-kot board, and slipped away.

Kosika stayed in the bath until the water went cold.

Then she climbed out, leaving wet footprints on the floor as she fetched a robe, and pulled it tight around her. The window was latched, but she could tell that it was night. The air always felt different in the dark. She dressed herself again, and took up the shards Nasi had stacked on the table, and then she slipped out, down one tower, and up another, back to the alcove at the top of those stairs, and the door beyond. She took a burning candle from the altar, and slipped behind the statue. She would not linger in the old king's room, would go straight to the desk, return the pieces of the token to the box.

But when the door opened beneath her touch, Kosika gasped.

The room was neither dark nor empty. The candelabra burned, and Holland Vosijk sat at his desk, the box open in his hands. Kosika froze, but his head jerked up as if she'd moved, his white hair rising in a crown, and he looked at her with those eyes, one green, one black, and his face, which she had only seen in death or stone, which had always been a mask of quiet pain, was now contorted into rage, his voice a roll of thunder when his mouth opened.

"What have you *done*?"

Kosika lurched back, felt herself stumble and fall, and—

She landed with a splash in the tub.

Chest heaving, water spilling over the sides of the stone bath with the force of her waking. The water was tepid, not yet cold, but she shivered as she climbed out, and fetched her robe, each step like an eerie echo of the ones she'd already made, so that by the time she dressed and climbed the stairs to Holland's tower, by the time she ducked past the altar and into the chamber beyond, she was sure he would be there, waiting at the desk.

But the room was empty, the candles unlit.

The wooden box sat open on the table, just as she'd left it.

Kosika hurried forward, and dumped the broken shards of the third token back inside before closing the lid. But she didn't seal it. She told herself it was because the wounds on her hand had finally stopped weeping. She told herself she simply didn't want to bleed again. She told herself there was no point, when she was the only one who could use the tokens. Whether the things she told herself were true, she left the box unlocked and fled, past the altar and down the stairs and up to the safety of her room.

Nasi had returned, and was laying out the pieces on the kol-kot board, dinner steaming on a nearby tray. If she noticed that the shards were gone, or that Kosika's hair was still wet, she said nothing, only asked if she wanted to play. Kosika tried, but her heart and mind kept skittering away, until she flung her pieces down in a fit of pique, and went to bed.

As she lay there, in the dark, she waited, sure that Holland was waiting for her, just beyond the door of sleep. All night, she tossed and turned, trapped in her tangled sheets, until Nasi abandoned her bed, muttering about the need for peace. Sometime before dawn, sleep finally came for Kosika, but it was shallow and empty, shadows that refused to coalesce into shapes, and she was about to give up and fling herself out of bed, irritable and achy, when she turned over one last time, and sank through the sheets, and dreamed.

This time, the alcove was dark, the altar candles all snuffed out.

Behind the statue, the door stood open, and Kosika's bare feet carried her silently across the stones, and into the room beyond, no longer pitch black, but bathed in morning light. She knew he would be there, but something inside her still lurched at the sight of the Someday King, the Summer Saint, standing by the desk, one hand resting thoughtfully on the now-closed box.

This time, as Holland's gaze flicked toward her, Kosika dropped into a bow, one knee touching the cold stone and her eyes on the floor.

"My king."

At first, nothing. Then, the slow tread of boots crossing the floor, a shadow falling over her. She did not look up, but she could see the toe of his boot, the edge of his half-cloak skimming the stones as he knelt before her. She felt the weight of his hand as it came to rest beneath her chin, and guided her face up to meet his.

Kosika caught her breath.

She had dreamt of Holland Vosijk before, of course, but in those dreams, he was either the body in the woods, or the altar come to life, a shape more than a man.

This Holland was different. This Holland had a flush of color in his cheeks, blood running beneath his skin, a chest that rose and fell with his breath. Up close, his white hair—for years she thought it had always been white, until Serak showed her a portrait, and she learned it had in fact been black until the day he died—rose off his cheeks, as if caught in a breeze.

This Holland's eyes were not made of gemstones or glass. Up close, the green one was not solid emerald but paler green, shot through with filaments of silver. The black was as smooth and dark and lightless as her own.

As she studied her king, he studied her, his brow furrowed, but his expression drained of the rage she had imagined, something cautious in its stead.

"Interesting," he said, his voice smooth and low.

His fingers dropped from her chin, and he rose again to his full height. She didn't, not until he held out his hand, and beckoned her to her feet.

"Who are you?" he asked, the words curling around her.

"Kosika," she said.

Holland inclined his head. "Kosika," he echoed. The name had been nothing in her mouth, sounds she'd made a thousand times, but the way *he* said it, as if it were a spell, made her feel dizzy. She stole another glance at his face, and saw something soften, the line between his brow smooth and the corner of his mouth tense, ever so slightly, as if he were about to smile.

"I have been waiting for you."

He turned, expecting her to follow, but as she took the first step, the room began to thin around them. The edges faded. Her vision narrowed. The last thing she saw was the king glancing back over his shoulder before the dream crumbled.

She was back in her bed, sunlight spilling in through the open windows, and Nasi bouncing on the edge of the cushions.

"I let you sleep as long as I could."

Kosika closed her eyes again, trying to hold on to the dregs of her dream, to find her way back, but it was gone, and so was Holland.

"What a monster you were last night," Nasi was saying. "I think it's time you slept alone."

She said it gently, clearly expecting some resistance, but Kosika instantly agreed.

II

RED LONDON, *now*

The first thing Lila noticed was that the world wasn't moving.

She'd learned to distrust the absence of motion, the lack of bob and sway that accompanied life aboard a ship. Stillness was not only strange, but dire. It meant something had gone wrong. Before she could even place the wrongness, she was reaching beneath her pillow for the knife she kept there. But the space was empty, and the pillow was silk, and the bed beneath her was too soft, and as her mind finally caught up, it supplied a single word: *palace*.

Lila groaned, and rolled over.

Pale morning light spilled across the bed, and the place where Kell had been lying, dead to the world, the night before. Only now, there was nothing but a tangle of rumpled sheets. Bad enough she'd followed him into the palace. Worse, that he had left her here.

Lila threw off the covers and got up, wishing she'd barred the door the night before.

Her jacket lay cast onto a chair, along with her boots, and the handful of blades she'd bothered to shed before collapsing into bed. But the boots had been cleaned, and someone had arranged the knives left to right in descending order of size. She unsheathed one, and checked its edge. Of course. It had been sharpened. And even though no one would be foolish enough, she still found herself touching the knives she kept on even while sleeping—the ones strapped to her thigh, her hip, the small of her back— just to be sure they were still there.

Lila sighed, and crossed the massive chamber.

A marble basin sat on a shelf on the far wall, a pitcher beside and a mirror mounted overhead. She poured the water into the bowl, and even though the pitcher had likely been sitting for hours, waiting to be used, the water came out hot. Lila stared at the steam rising from the basin.

Seven years, and the casual magic of this world still took her by surprise.

Despite everything, she'd forget, and then she'd see a lantern light itself, a man breathe wind into sails, hot water spill out from a cold pitcher, and her mind would lurch, like a boot catching a crooked cobblestone. Hell, sometimes when she called on her own magic, she was still shocked that it answered.

She leaned forward, crinkled her nose as the scent of blossoms rose from the basin. *Fucking royals,* she thought, as she splashed the scented water onto her face, the back of her neck, ran a damp hand through her blunt-edge hair.

A glint of metal caught her eye, and she glanced up into the mirror over the bowl. Her collar was unlaced, and Kell's ring had slipped out, and hung swinging on the end of its leather cord, the ship winking in the light. She tucked the black band back inside her tunic, but her gaze lingered on her reflection.

Two eyes stared back at her, both of them brown, one real, the other glass.

Unlike the eye she'd traded to Maris, a relic from her life back in Grey London, this one was a perfect match. As far as Lila could tell, she was the only one unsettled by the sight of it. The eerie sameness, the symmetry forged by magic, a glimpse at how she would have looked, if her real eye had not been taken as a child. Back when—as she knew now—Lila had awakened as an *Antari.*

She held her own gaze, inclined her head until the light caught on the surface of the glass, interrupting the illusion. The brown eye had a purpose—it helped Lila to blend in, to move unnoticed. But when she was alone, or on the safety of her ship, she never wore it, opting for the black one Maris had given her, the one she would have had if she'd slept aboard the ship, the one that made her smile whenever she caught her reflection in a puddle or a pane of glass.

She was not smiling now.

She pushed off the basin, reclaimed her blades, and her boots, and her coat, and set out to find Kell and a cup of strong black tea, not necessarily in that order.

Word had obviously spread that the *Antari* were in residence.

None of the guards drew their weapons as Lila emerged from the royal suite, made her way down the hall, descended the stairs. Below, the palace was unfurling, like some giant flower, its petals turning to the sun. Servants bustled, opening doors, adjusting rugs, trading out yesterday's bouquets before they even began to droop.

Where, she wondered, did the day-old flowers go?

Probably into the bath water.

As Lila moved through the palace, servants stopped, and bowed, frozen like statues in the middle of their work. Two brown eyes or otherwise, they knew what she was, and they looked at her the way they had looked at Kell, their expressions ranging from respect, to reverence, to fear. But unlike Kell, Delilah Bard welcomed their trepidation.

She was halfway down a branching hall when a servant rounded the corner, facing her. There was plenty of room, yet he sidestepped and pressed his back into the wall as if it were a sin to take up space while she did.

"Have you seen the prince?" she asked.

The servant didn't answer, not at first, as if she were addressing someone else. There was no one else, at least, not in earshot, and when he finally seemed to realize that, his gaze twitched up, stopping somewhere near her chin. Lila sighed. If there was a protocol for this, she'd never learned it.

"Well?" she pressed.

"*Mas arna*," he said, bowing deeply again. *My lady*. Lila grimaced. She hated being called that, as if she were some *ostra* mingling at court.

"Call me Captain," she said.

The servant hesitated. "Apologies," he said. "But your rank here outweighs that title."

"My rank?" she ventured, assuming he meant *Antari*. She was wrong.

399

"Your rank, as someone promised to the prince."

Lila stared at the servant, and felt the sudden urge to break something. The air curdled around her, and he must have sensed it, because he shrank back.

"Tell me," she said slowly. "What do you call *Kell*?"

"*Mas vares*," said the servant.

My prince.

"And if he were a commoner?"

The servant ducked his head. "As *Antari*, he would still be *mas aven*."

My blessed.

"Excellent," said Lila. "Then call me that. Now," she went on, scanning the hall. "Where is your *blessed* prince?"

The servant pointed her toward the breakfast room, and she set off again. She found the glass-walled chamber overlooking the courtyard, its long table laden with sweet buns, and pies, and fruit. She was about to go in when she heard a sound across the hall.

A small, joyous laugh that could only belong to Ren Maresh.

There, at the far end of a sun-drenched gallery, Lila found the child sitting on a step, and at her side, light glancing off his copper hair, was Kell.

Ren was chattering softly, and cupping something small and white in both her hands, and Kell was nodding soberly, his coat cast off beside him on the floor, and his sleeves rolled up, his face turned just enough for her to see his blue eye, and the way his lips moved as he spoke.

He didn't see Lila, and perhaps that was why she lingered, studying the gentle incline of his head, her fingers drifting almost absently to the ring beneath her shirt. Until she heard the sound of footsteps drifting toward her, not the hushed and hurried steps of a servant, or the tread of a soldier, but the slow, even glide of a body at home.

Fuck, thought Lila as her hand dropped to her side.

"Your Majesty," she said aloud, turning toward the queen. Lila knew she should bow, but she couldn't bring herself to do it. Instead, she offered the barest incline of her head, more a nod than an attempt at deference. The queen either didn't notice, or didn't care.

"Please," she said, "call me Nadiya. We are family, after all."

Family. The word scratched at Lila's skin like rough wool. As far as she was concerned, family had nothing to do with proximity or blood. Family was a chosen thing. A label earned. Barron had been family. Kell was family. Alucard, and Stross, and Vasry, and Tav, and Rhy. But Nadiya had yet to gain purchase. Lila doubted she ever would.

She raked her gaze over the queen.

Facing each other, they looked like two sides of a warped mirror. They were the same age, and nearly the same height, and ever since Nadiya had hacked away the heavy mane she'd brought to court, their hair fell in the same way, skimming their shoulders. Their coloring was where they differed—the queen's skin was olive where Lila's was pale, her hair jet black where Lila's was dark brown, her eyes the same shade where Lila's were not, and her body curved in ways Lila's never had, filling her dress while Lila's shirt ran uninterrupted from her shoulders to her waist.

But it wasn't the ways they were different that bothered her.

It was the ways they were alike.

It was the way Nadiya looked at her, as if she were a prize. It was a look Lila herself had leveled at plenty of things. Things she had stolen, or killed for.

Now the queen's hungry eyes slid past her. To the gallery, and Ren, who was now holding the little white shape aloft, so Lila could see what it was: an egg.

"She took it from the kitchen months ago," mused Nadiya. "Rescued from a skillet. She's convinced if she is kind enough, the egg will hatch. I cannot seem to convince Ren there is nothing there to rescue." She inclined her head. "Children can be marvelous."

"You could just crack it open," offered Lila. "I'm surprised it hasn't spoiled."

"Oh, it would have," said the queen. "But once a week, I trade it for a new one while she's sleeping." A smile twitched at the corner of her mouth. "What harm is there, in hoping?"

"And when the hope runs out?"

"She's four. I think it can last a little longer."

Ren laughed, and the queen and Lila both turned toward the sound. Kell was now holding the egg to the light, and tracing a shape along its shell.

"He is a good uncle," said the queen. "He'll be a good father." Lila snorted. Nadiya frowned. "Haven't you ever wanted a child?"

The question had a strange effect, like a corset cinched around her ribs, but the answer was easy, automatic. "No."

She half expected Nadiya to tut, to say that one day she would, but the queen only nodded thoughtfully, and said, "I always wanted one. I don't know why. It wasn't ego. Some women just want to see their own reflection. I wanted to know what it felt like. To make another person. And then, when she was here, I wanted to see what she would do. Who she would be. Every day, she is different. Every day, she is new."

"You talk of her like she's an experiment."

"I suppose she is," said Nadiya, though there was a dreamy quality to her voice when she said it. "A grand experiment." She tore her attention away from her daughter. "I know you don't like me."

Lila cocked a brow. "I don't *like* most people, Your Majesty. You, I don't *trust*."

"Why is that?"

"It might have something to do with you expressing a desire to dissect me over dinner."

"I did say, after you were dead."

A servant appeared, a pot of tea and two cups balanced on a gilded tray.

The queen poured, and handed one to Lila, and tempted as she was by the rich, dark liquid, the curls of steam, Delilah Bard still wasn't about to drink *anything* offered by the queen. Oh, she took the cup, and turned it in her hand as if studying the pattern stamped into the porcelain's side. Then, as she held Nadiya's eye, Lila exerted her will, and the steam vanished, giving way to frost that cracked across the surface as the contents froze.

The queen's mouth twitched. "What a waste," she mused, lifting her own tea to her lips. "I'm not your enemy, Lila." Her gaze returned to Ren, and Kell. "Everything I do, I do for my family. For their future. For our world. If you would only help me, let me study your magic while—"

402

"No."

"I know it's not ideal. But there aren't exactly a wealth of *Antari* subjects, and I'm not about to risk Rhy's safety by testing Kell. Especially not in his diminished state."

"Your Majesty," said Lila through gritted teeth, "I mean this with the most respect." She turned to face Nadiya and said, "Go fuck yourself."

The queen pursed her lips. "You are an extraordinary person, Delilah Bard. I'm surprised you are not more . . . progressive. Your magic holds the keys to countless doors. And yet, you choose to hoard it."

"What can I say? I like being the strongest in the room."

Nadiya shook her head. "It is not just about magic, though. Think of the knowledge locked inside your blood. Who knows what it could do? It could heal the kingdom." Her eyes brightened. "Perhaps it could even heal *Kell*."

In a step, the cup was gone from Lila's hand, replaced by one of many blades, the edge pressed against the queen's long neck.

"Do not lie to me," she hissed, and then the guards were storming forward, weapons drawn, and Lila didn't want to make a mess. She backed away, sheathed the dagger at her hip. The queen held out her hand to stay them, then touched her fingers to her throat, as if expecting blood. As if Lila's hand weren't steadier than that.

"I don't know how to heal him *yet*," said the queen, fingers falling, "but that doesn't mean I'm lying. Progress takes time. And sacrifice."

Lila had never liked Nadiya, but she *hated* her then, hated that there was a chance—even a *sliver* of a chance—that she was right, which made her hate herself as well. Lila drew her blade again, and the guards twitched in warning, armor scraping as they took a half step forward, but instead of turning the blade on the queen, much as she longed to, Lila dragged the steel across the delicate skin on the inside of her wrist. She tipped the ice out of her tea cup, and held her bleeding arm over the empty vessel, crimson painting the delicate porcelain. And when it was half-full, she wrapped a kerchief around the cut, and tied it tight enough to hurt.

"Happy?" she asked.

The queen nodded, and took up the bloody cup. "It's a start."

And because Lila had resolved not to make a mess, she walked away, turning her back on the queen, and the princess, and Kell, who still sat beside the little girl, his back to them and his head bowed forward on the steps.

III

A lucard hadn't always been a morning person.

Growing up, he'd savored sleep, but life at sea had taught him to get up with the sun, and ever since trading the *Night Spire* for the *soner rast*, he'd kept the habit, rising at dawn to train the royal guards.

By the time he strolled into the breakfast hall at nine, he was wide awake, and sore from sparring. Perhaps Lila was right, and he was out of fighting shape. Or perhaps he was just getting old. Thirty-one. It didn't sound like many years, but he swore, he felt each and every one of them.

He kissed the top of Rhy's head before drawing out a chair, murmured thanks to a servant as they poured a stream of hot black tea into his cup.

The queen sat across the table, turning through papers, her pen flicking in the margins. She glanced up as he came in, but if she was thinking of his warning in the workshop, it didn't show.

Kell was there, too, much to Alucard's chagrin. The prince didn't sit, but instead stood drinking his tea, as if to emphasize the fact he wasn't staying. Ren, on the other hand, was busy looking at a book of birds and ignoring the toast that Sasha was trying to put in her hand. The nursemaid shot Alucard a weary look.

Just wait, he thought, *until she can use magic.* Ren was still too young, of course, to have an element, but she moved like his old friend Jinnar, a whirlwind, leaving chaos in her wake. Every day, Alucard expected to see colored threads unfurl around his daughter, to watch her magic bloom. But so far, the air around her was filled only with a halo of black curls and the occasional crow feather.

"Morning, Luca!" she said brightly.

Kell and Rhy both winced at the volume of the child's voice.

Rhy had *never* been a morning person; he rarely found his stride before noon, but today, he looked positively miserable, his head in his hand. "The bubbles," he muttered. "The cursed bubbles."

"A little too much wine?" asked Alucard, leveling a heavy look at Kell. The prince said nothing, but Rhy dragged his head back up, the gold of his eyes foggy, tarnished.

"Why do we keep that silver stuff?" he asked.

"Because it's wonderful in moderation," said Alucard.

"And better than a tonic at drawing out the truth," added the queen, turning a page.

"Burn it all," hissed the king, indignant. "Tell me why I can heal from a knife to the chest faster than a bottle of spirits."

No one had an answer for that.

Alucard swept an orange from the center of the table, and sat back, noting the empty place at their table. "Where's the captain?"

"She left," said the queen.

At which point Kell sighed and put down his cup.

"Better go fetch," muttered Alucard into his tea, and Kell made a rude gesture with his hand as he left. Alucard looked to Nadiya. "When did you see her?" The captain and the queen were oil and flame, safe so long as they didn't get close enough to mix.

Nadiya shrugged. "A passing moment in the hall."

Her green eyes were half-lidded as her pen flicked across her work. If he didn't know better, he might think she was just waking up, instead of winding down, making notes before retiring to her rooms at last to sleep.

"*Kers la?*" asked Ren, cheerfully slipping into the common tongue as she climbed the side of her mother's chair, and jabbed a jammy finger at the papers by her plate.

"This?" said the queen, her voice softening as it only did for Ren. "It's a design for an amplifier."

Alucard tensed at the mention of the work, but he could see the page on the table, and it bore no resemblance to the *Antari* rings, or the golden chains.

"Amplifier?" asked Ren, sounding out the word.

"A way to make a person's magic stronger."

405

Her tone was gentle, patient, but her speech didn't change. Since the girl had been born, Nadiya had spoken to her as if she were a grown adult, bound inconveniently but temporarily in a child's form. If she said a word Ren didn't know, the girl would ask its meaning.

Ren squinted at the page. "Why don't I have magic yet?"

Rhy looked up. It was his greatest fear, he knew, that his daughter would be like him. And he always told Rhy the same thing that Nadiya now told Ren.

"You are young," she said. "It will come."

"Daddy's didn't."

Alucard stiffened. Only a child could say something like that, stating the obvious without meaning or malice. Rhy met his wife's eyes, waiting to see what she would say to that.

Nadiya only smiled. "Your father is powerful in other ways."

Ren took this in, rocking heel to toe on the side of the chair. "If I don't get magic," she said, "can I still have my animals?"

A smile caught the edge of Rhy's mouth.

"Of course you can," said Nadiya.

Ren nodded thoughtfully, and said, "That would be okay." With that she hopped down, made to flee the table, but Sasha caught the child, guiding her back to her chair.

"You don't need magic," said the nursemaid, "but you do need breakfast."

An easy quiet fell over the room as they ate.

Alucard took it in. When he was young, a set table was a dangerous thing. His father looming at the head. His brother across. His sister beside. No chair for their mother—no space for sentiment. Those scenes, a reminder that looking like a family was more important than being one.

That table was full of traps he could not see, ones just waiting to be triggered.

Sit straighter. Speak up. Do not use that tone with me.

There was no joy in those meals, only expectation, and Alucard could not wait to be excused, the air rushing back into his lungs only when he was free of that room.

But as he looked around the table now, his chest grew tight for other reasons.

This, he thought, *this* was a family. An odd one, perhaps, a strange and different shape, and despite Rhy's moaning and the queen's distraction and Ren's restless squirming as if she were a pet trying to escape, while Sasha tried first to goad and then to bribe her into eating, there was nowhere else Alucard would rather be.

Everyone he loved most was seated within reach. He laced his fingers through Rhy's, and gave a gentle squeeze. And Rhy looked down as if Alucard's hand there was a gift, some unexpected but wholly welcome surprise. He brought it to his mouth, and kissed his knuckles.

Alucard smiled, and sipped his tea, and did his best to savor the moment, knowing it wouldn't last.

And it didn't.

Ren was the first to break away. Having been coaxed to eat an egg, and some toast, and half an apple, the child finally escaped, and flung herself toward the courtyard doors, Sasha on her heels.

Their daughter's presence was a clasp, holding them together. Without her, Nadiya rose, and made her excuses, collecting her papers and a sugared roll as she drifted up to bed.

Their family peeled away like petals until it was just the two of them at the laden table. Even that didn't last long. Before the tea had time to cool, Isra arrived, her short gray hair scraped back and her guard's helm under one arm.

"Your Majesty," she said, bowing her head. "The merchants are here, to discuss the import rules for the Long Dark Night."

Alucard frowned. "*Sel Fera Noche?* You can't intend to go ahead with that—"

"Oh, not you, too," said Rhy, dragging himself to his feet. Before Alucard could point out what a monumentally stupid idea that was, the king had snatched a sweet bun and followed Isra out.

Alucard sighed, alone now, save the four servants posted like pillars around the edges of the room. Waiting to be summoned with a look, or simply an empty cup.

"You can go," he said, dismissing them all.

He told himself it would be nice, to have a moment's peace. But in the silence, his thoughts took hold. Alucard sat back, eyeing the mountain of food before him, as his appetite dissolved. His mind tried to latch on to *Sel Fera Noche,* but the festival was weeks away, and at the moment, they had a far more pressing problem. His conversation with Lila replayed through his mind, the threat of the Hand now amplified by their possession of a *persalis.*

He bowed his head, resting it on his laced fingers as he tried to think.

They could remove the royal family from the palace, but what message would that send?

Footsteps shuffled into the room.

"Sir," said a voice. Alucard glanced up, expecting a servant. Instead, he found a young soldier, with hair long enough to be braided, and bright brown eyes, and a coil of earthy magic in the air around him.

He searched his memory for the young man's name. "Velastro."

The soldier blushed, and ducked his head. "That's right, sir," he said in Arnesian. "Apologies for intruding on your breakfast."

Alucard looked around at the empty chairs. "You're forgiven. What brings you to me?"

"You gave orders to report any activity by the Hand."

His stomach sank. "And?"

"Four more marks were found last night, tacked across the city." The soldier produced a map, the symbols crimson dots scattered across the south half of the city. Another mark, this one an X, marked the map not far from the palace.

"And this?"

"A dead body was found propped against a wall, a crown drawn in blood over his head."

Alucard swallowed. "Not exactly subtle." He rolled the map back up. "Anything else?"

Velastro hesitated. "I'm—not sure." He shifted his weight. "You asked for news of anything *strange.* Well, I was on patrol this morning, in the *shal,* and it seems a building collapsed overnight."

Alucard waited, unsure where he was going.

"Well, it's just . . ." Velastro searched for the words. "The houses on either side were perfectly intact."

"Could be a fight gone wrong," said Alucard. "A drunk magician out of hand?"

"Right, right," said the soldier. "But the thing is, I've got a knack for earth and stone, and when I was a kid, well, I didn't have the best control. I'm not saying I knocked over any buildings, but . . ."

"You know what a building looks like when it happens to fall down?"

Velastro flashed a nervous smile. "Right. And the way the building fell, it's like it fell *in,* right? Like someone dragged it down on top of them."

"A spell gone sideways?"

"That's what I thought!" he said brightly, adding quickly, "*Mas arno.* Or a targeted attack. But if that's true, there should be bodies. And there aren't. We've cleared the rubble enough to search, and there's no one inside, and it just doesn't feel right, and I heard you can see things that others can't, and I don't have that gift but my gut says there's more to it, and I told my squad leader and she told me it was nothing. And maybe it is nothing, or maybe it's not nothing, but it's not the kind of something you need to hear about either. . . ." The longer the soldier talked, the more he stumbled. "But it's probably nothing."

It probably *was* nothing, but Alucard didn't have any other leads, so he swallowed the last of his tea, and got to his feet.

"Show me."

IV

Kell's boots sounded on the Sanctuary floor.

It was the kind of place where noises echoed, every rustle of fabric and heeled step bouncing off the cool stone walls. Kell changed his stride, tried to walk as Lila had taught him, with the quiet of a thief. The sound vanished, as if drawn into the rock, and he smiled, imagining the quirk of her own mouth, her pride parading as amusement.

As for where she was at present, he had no idea.

He'd gone to the inn, first, hoping to find her waiting in their room; hoping, but knowing better—Lila Bard waited for no one. Sure enough, she wasn't there, and he tried not to feel left behind, knew that she could move through this city in a way he could not, so he had decided to go to the one place he knew she would not. He'd changed his coat, trading royal red for common grey, and put on a cap, smothering the flame of his hair, and if he did not become Kay, well, at least he was not entirely Kell Maresh as he set out for the Sanctuary.

The city of London was always changing.

Magic made it easy. Buildings rose and fell, as fickle as the season's taste in fashion. Pleasure gardens became theatres, and theatres became arcades, and arcades became plazas, and so on, and so on.

Only two things ever seemed to hold their shape.

The first was the royal palace.

The second was the Sanctuary.

Kell had spent his entire youth between those two buildings. Raised in one, trained in the other, the second as solid and simple as the first was grand. In these stone halls, Tieren had taught Kell to control his power, to quiet his mind, and focus his magic when it was a torrent, spilling out with every burst of temper.

After—after the battle with Osaron, after the shadow king was bound, after Kell accepted that his bond to magic was broken—he had gone to see the *Aven Essen*.

"What am I now?" he'd asked, angry, and frightened, and in pain.

And Tieren had cupped his cheek and said, "You are alive. Isn't that enough?"

Now Kell passed beneath an arch, and out into a walled courtyard, and felt the air go solid in his chest. The space had the stillness of a Grey London cemetery, the paths made of white marble, but in the place of tombstones were several dozen trees, spaced as evenly as pillars, each a different size, or age, or season.

Each one grown and tended by a priest, using only the balance of their power.

It seemed an easy enough feat, to grow a tree. But it was not—it required a mastery of all the elements. Aside from *Antari*, priests were the only magicians who could do that, but their talent lay not in the scope of that power, but in its restraint. A priest held no affinity for any one element, but an ability to wield them all in some small measure. They were the living embodiment of their mandate.

Priste ir essen. Essen ir priste.

Power in balance. Balance in power.

Such was the nature of magic, they said, that all scales must find their level. They could not move mountains or conjure rain. They could not burn ships to cinders or shatter walls with the force of their wind. Theirs was a gentle magic. The sea that eroded stone.

The tree was the embodiment of this restraint.

Too much power would kill it as surely as too little, and it must live within the bounds of the courtyard, without stealing more than its share of soil, or water, or sun.

When a priest died, so did their tree, not all at once, but slowly, left to wither without their care. And when it was dead, it was dragged out, and burned, and its ashes tilled into the dirt for the next priest, the next planting.

Tieren's plot should have been empty now, but the tree remained, or what was left of it. A grey husk, leafless and dry, its roots lifting like gnarled fingers, slowly letting go of the ground beneath.

"I told them to wait," said a voice. "I had a feeling you'd want to say goodbye."

He turned, and saw Ezril standing in the archway. No, not standing, *leaning*, arms crossed and hip cocked to one side. Kell did not think he'd ever seen a priest lean before—when they were children, Rhy was convinced that he could balance a tea cup on Tieren's head all day, and it would never spill.

Ezril padded down the steps, and he saw that beneath her white robes, she was barefoot. Her black hair hung loose, straight and sharp as glass from the widow's peak to the ends, but it was her eyes he found most striking. Fringed in black lashes, her eyes were brown, and yet, somehow pale, like paint on a pane of glass shot through with light. Indeed, they even seemed to glow.

When Rhy had first met his new *Aven Essen,* he'd said, "What a waste." She was radiant. Undeniably beautiful. But Kell's first impression had been only that she wasn't Tieren. He told himself that was the reason he did not like her.

411

Rhy said he was being unfair, and perhaps he was—after all, it was hardly Ezril's fault that Tieren was gone. A man he'd known all his life, replaced by a woman young enough to be the priest's granddaughter.

Perhaps Kell resented her for more than taking Tieren's place. After all, she had been there for Rhy when he himself had not. Rhy said he would like Ezril, if he only spent time with her. His brother knew her better than he did. Perhaps he resented her for that as well.

"*Aven Essen,*" Kell said now, by way of greeting.

"Master Kell," answered the priest. "Or is it Kay?" Those eyes glittered with mischief.

Kell stiffened. "Rhy has been telling tales, I see."

She gave a careful shrug, a studied smile. "That coat of yours has many sides. So, I suspect, do you."

"Indeed," said Kell carefully. "And what else has my brother told you?"

She sobered. "I am the king's priest, and his counsel. His burdens become mine, if and when he shares them. But I do not hand them off to others."

It was not, he noted, an answer. She held his gaze, as if daring him to ask again. Kell did not like the way she looked at him, eyes flicking between his, from the black to the blue and back again, a constant reminder of their difference.

Some priests worshipped the *Antari,* saw them as an incarnation of Magic itself. But others saw them as a warning, a reminder of what happened when power existed in extremes. The opposite of balance.

Kell wondered which he was in Ezril's eyes. He didn't ask, instead turned his attention back to the tree—and the last traces of Tieren's magic.

"Thank you for waiting," he said. "I know it is just a tree. And yet . . ."

"Of course it is just a tree," said Ezril. "This is just a building. The Isle is just water."

He studied her. "Spoken like a true priest."

"What gave me away?" she asked wryly, smoothing her white robe. "You think me an odd choice, for *Aven Essen,*" she went on. It wasn't a question, so he wasn't forced to answer. She looked past him, to Tieren's tree. "Sometimes change is easier to stomach. Have you ever had a beautiful meal? You try to repeat it, you make the dish the same way over and over and it is never as good. Better to try something new." She smiled, and shook her head. "Apologies, I must be hungry. You did not come to talk of meals, or trees."

He had not. Indeed, he'd asked the priests at the door to send for Ezril when he first arrived.

"The Hand," he said. "Do you have news?"

Ezril's good humor faltered. "I told you, Master Kell, the Sanctuary is not the crown's crows. The priests witness. We serve. We do not *spy*."

"And yet," said Kell, "you do not confine yourselves to the Sanctuary. You walk among the people. You know the city's power, its pulse."

"Priests answer to the balance of magic. Not to the thrones of kings."

"You are the *Aven Essen*," he persisted. "You serve the king, you are *his* counsel and *his* priest. If you know something—anything—if you have any love for Rhy—"

"Enough," said Ezril, with the simple force of fingers snapping.

She looked past him, past the trees, and the walls of the courtyard. For several moments, she said nothing. Then, "They keep their voices low, but we have heard whispers." Her tea-stained eyes flicked back to him. "Whispers of a device that can bend space. Cut through wards."

Kell's heart sank. The *persalis*. So it was here.

"What is their plan?" he demanded. "Do you know?"

Ezril only shook her head. "No, but it is a complicated piece of magic. It had to come from somewhere. Or someone." Her voice dipped lower. "I have wondered if the queen—"

"No," cut in Kell. "Nadiya Loreni did not make it."

Ezril frowned. "You are sure?"

"It was stolen from a ship, and smuggled into the city."

One brow lifted. "Then you know as much as I do."

"I know *nothing* of any use," hissed Kell. "Only that it must be found before the Hand use it against the royal family. Have you learned nothing of the Hand itself? Who is behind them?"

Ezril's head swept side to side, and Kell felt his chest tighten in exasperation.

"Someone must know *something*," he snapped, head spinning. He was no closer to finding the *persalis*, to stopping the plot, to uncovering the power behind the Hand. His fingers curled into fists, magic rising with his temper. A wind kicked up, whipping through the courtyard, and on its heels, the wave of pain rolled beneath his skin. He let go, quickly, but not quick enough.

The air settled, but he was left fighting for breath.

Ezril was staring at him, but her expression held no surprise. "It must be frightening," she said, "to be at war with your own magic."

Kell stiffened. *He* had never told her about the rift. "My brother should learn to hold his tongue," he said, forcing the air back into his lungs. He straightened, steadied. He needed to find Lila. "If you have nothing else to tell me—"

But as he moved to pass her, the *Aven Essen* caught his arm.

"It's not the pain that frightens you. It's what you are. And what you're not. A priest removes their robes, and they are still a priest. But what is an *Antari* without their magic?"

"A prince," said Kell curtly as he moved to pull away, but her fingers were solid, unyielding. The impishness was gone, replaced by an intensity, as hard and clear as glass.

"You must wonder why," she said. "Why the power you've had all your life has turned against you now. Was it a spell gone wrong? Or have you broken the laws of magic one too many times?" Her words were a sharp knife in a steady hand, cutting straight through him. "All power has its limits. You are still a servant of magic, and magic demands balance. When that balance is upset, it demands a recompense. Perhaps you are being punished."

Her hand drifted up, came to rest on his right cheek. Just beneath his black eye. Her expression rippled, priestly anger dissolving into something soft, almost sad.

"Or perhaps," she said gently, "you are punishing yourself."

Her hand dropped away from his skin.

"If you ever wish to tell me why, I will be here. After all," she said, that playful light returning to her eyes, "I am your *Aven Essen*, too."

But this time, Kell wasn't fooled by the impish grin, the easy air.

"You never told me how you came to be named *Aven Essen*."

414

"Trial by combat," she said blithely. "I'm stronger than I look."

That he did not doubt. Kell started away, stopping only when he reached the archway. He turned back. "You're wrong about one thing."

"Oh?"

"If *you* shed those robes, you would not be a priest. You'd be a noble. Ezril Nasaro."

If she was surprised that he knew her family name, it didn't show. "Neither the name nor the station are mine anymore. I shed my royal claim when I joined the Sanctuary."

"Your family must have felt the loss. Their only daughter. Why did you choose to be a priest?"

She tipped her head, as if considering. "Why did you choose to be *Antari*?"

The answer, of course, was that he hadn't. It had chosen him.

"All my life," said Ezril, "I've felt the current of Magic. In the air, beneath my feet. I choose to walk in the stream, Master Kell, but Magic led me to it. There is a reason I am standing there. There is a reason you are, too. We are both a part of something larger than ourselves."

The words hung like a weight around his shoulders, but the *Aven Essen* seemed lighter, buoyed by them. He turned, and left her in the courtyard, her white robes floating in the breeze.

V

Lila's stomach growled.

She'd left the palace without breakfast, another thing for which she blamed the queen as she cut through the night market.

Despite its name, and the hour, a handful of stalls were beginning to stir and throw off sleep, unfolding tents and assembling their wares, while others still were open for business. A thin crowd trickled between the stalls, preferring the scenic path to the busier streets, or drawn by the scent of spice and sugar on the air.

She stopped at a baker with a tray of steaming sweet buns, bought a sack of four, eating as she walked. She ambled past a charm-maker, already hawking vials of glowing red drops from the Isle (an obvious forgery, since the water remained neither red nor incandescent once drawn from the river), and a handful of emerald and yellow and crimson tents, their flaps down, their contents hidden from view.

The glint of steel caught her eye, and she came to a stop before a stall of blades.

They were laid out by length. The shortest, meant to disappear into a palm. The longest, a sword that looked as though it took two hands to lift, let alone wield. Her fingers danced across the weapons, pausing over one the length of her forearm. It was a work of art, the metal thin as glass.

"You can test it, if you like," said a lilting voice.

Lila looked up at the merchant. She was young, younger than most of the sellers in the market, and the point of her nose and chin reminded Lila of a fox. So did her hair, the brown curls threaded here and there with streaks of red.

Lila lifted the weapon. It was beautifully light, and perfectly balanced, and she could hear Kell asking how many knives could one person possibly need. She searched the metal for sigils, signs of spellwork. The last time she'd used a strange blade, it had murdered a man with his own magic.

"Any tricks?"

The merchant shook her head. "In the right hand," she said, "a good blade needs no tricks."

Lila smiled. "Is it wise," she wondered, "to lay out your wares like this?"

The merchant looked down at the table, as if she'd only just noticed that the weapons weren't sheathed, and the hilts and grips all faced out in invitation, the tips pointed in to the stall, and to her. "I haven't been robbed yet."

"Then you're very lucky."

The girl laughed. "I'm many things. Lucky has never been one." She reached out and ran her finger thoughtfully along one of the swords. "It takes sweat and blood to make a blade like this. Use the two right, and the steel can't be used against you."

"So they *are* spelled," said Lila.

The merchant shrugged. "A precaution."

"A handy one," mused Lila. "Don't suppose you could apply the spell to an existing blade?"

The merchant shook her head. "No," she said, "but I could make you a new one. I'd need a few days, and some of your blood. . . ."

The girl's eyes had brightened when she said it.

Perhaps it was just the promise of a deal, or the challenge of the work, but Lila thought she caught a glint of steel in that gaze, just like the one that had drawn her to the stall. Her grip tightened on the knife, the cut along her hand still aching from the sacrifice she'd made to the queen.

Blood was a valuable thing. It anchored spells and strengthened curses. It made all magic stronger. According to Nadiya Loreni, it held countless secrets. And Lila had made her way through enough black markets in the past few years to know the value of that blood if it came from an *Antari*. Lila was glad she'd left the black eye back on the ship. She pretended to consider the merchant's offer before returning the knife to the table.

"On second thought," she said, "what fun is there, without a little risk?"

The merchant shrugged, but held her gaze. "If you change your mind . . ."

But Lila was already moving away from the stall, and the blades, and the fox-faced girl. She reached the far edge of the market, and turned right, away from the river and toward the *shal,* and Haskin's.

Now all she needed was a pretense for visiting the shop. She patted her pockets, felt the familiar weight of her watch. Not *her* watch—the one Holland had found in her old rooms, along with Berras, the one he'd returned to her stained with blood, the one she'd given to Maris as payment years before—but a gift from her crew one summer festival, the surface engraved with a C. For *Casero.*

Captain.

She drew it out, ran a thumb over the silver shell before she clicked it open, listened to the steady, almost silent tick of seconds passing. And even though the hands inside were driven by a spell instead of cogs, it was easy to forget. Perhaps harder to break, she mused, but she was sure she could do it, was about to pry away the face when she saw the time, the minute hand slipping past the hour, both of them a breath off straight.

"*Nonis ora,*" she murmured.

Eleventh hour.

Her steps dragged to a stop. She'd assumed the time on the edge of the coin referred to night, but what if she'd been wrong? After all, the surest crimes were those done in daylight, right under the mark's nose.

Lila turned, and headed for the nearest bridge.

VI

WHITE LONDON

Kosika leaned her elbows on the castle terrace.

Below, a hundred soldiers were going through their morning practice, the motions of battle broken down and ordered into movements. They reminded her of leaves, the way they bent and moved, the way they rose up and turned together, guided by an invisible wind, their charcoal armor turning them to shadows on the training ground.

As she watched, Kosika plucked at a strip of linen wrapped tight around her forearm, her skin still raw from yesterday's tithe. And perhaps it was just her imagination, or the nature of the season—and there were *seasons* now, four of them, instead of the pale breath of change that used to mark the passing of the year—but today, the sky looked bluer, the leaves a more vivid shade of green. The sun was burning off the morning chill, and Kosika savored the warmth of it against her skin as a shout rose up from the training ground below.

The soldiers had finished their movements, and broken off to spar, those who could conjure paired with those who couldn't, so each could learn how to best the other.

Kosika spotted Lark among them. He had grown a foot or more in the last few months, his narrow shoulders banded with new muscle. And while there were other fair-haired soldiers, his curls alone shone silver-white in the sun, making him look less like a boy of nearly eighteen and more like a struck match.

She watched him circle his partner, turning the sword in a lazy arc, fire licking down the blunted practice blade. The other man was twice his size, but Lark darted and dodged like flame itself, and in moments, the other soldier was stamping out a lick of fire on his forearm. As he did, Lark twisted around his sparring partner and came up behind him, resting the blade against his throat.

And then he looked up at Kosika, and flashed her a wicked, toothy grin. An infectious smile that made her smile, too. As if they had a secret—the only secret being that they had lived a life before this one. That they were thieves, had stolen their way into this castle.

"You've got a crush."

Kosika jumped, fingers tensing on the terrace wall. Nasi had come up behind her.

"Are you sure you cannot bend the air?" asked the young queen. "I never hear you coming."

Nasi shrugged. "It comes in handy, being quiet. The better to watch you swoon."

Kosika crinkled her nose, even as she felt her cheeks burn. She was *not* swooning. She looked down, but he was gone again, a blur of motion.

"Don't be silly," she said, turning her back to the soldiers. "Lark is like a brother."

Nasi's mouth twitched into a smile. "Just as I am like a sister?"

"Exactly."

The other girl drew closer then, until their fronts were pressed together. She ran teasing fingers down Kosika's ribs, her waist, still flat and narrow as a child's. "One day you will want more than the company of siblings."

Kosika hissed between her teeth, and swatted Nasi's hand away.

"I just don't want you to be alone," said Nasi, and Kosika wished that she could tell her friend she wasn't.

She was never alone anymore.

Holland stood beside her, as he had all morning, as he had every day for nearly a year. Her constant shadow. Her blessed saint. The hand that guided everything.

One year ago

After Holland appeared to her in that first dream, she lived for sleep. Kosika sat through the council meetings, and entertained the parade of citizens who came to ask her favor, and walked the castle grounds, and dined with the Vir, and waited for night, when she could fall into bed and go in search of Holland.

Sometimes she found him in his room.

Other times, she found him sitting on the throne, or in the courtyard, or on the steps.

Some nights they walked the castle, side by side, and some they stood before his own altar, and he told her the stories of his life as Serak had so many times—only he also told her things that Serak hadn't, details of his life before he came to serve Vortalis.

And if it was strange that a dream could know things that she did not, well then, Kosika assumed it was her own imagination. But every night she dreamt of him, Holland seemed to grow more real. Until one night, as they stood before his altar, she found herself saying, "I wish you were here."

Holland had been studying the statue. Now he looked down at her, perplexed. "I am."

"But this is only a dream," said Kosika.

He surveyed the alcove where they stood. "It may be a dream for you," he said. "It is something else for me. A shadow world. A waiting place. I was here, long before you found me."

The words rattled through her, shook loose a vicious hope that he was not merely a figment after all. That he and this were somehow *real*. That Kosika was in the presence not of a conjuring, but the Someday King. An impossible hope, and yet, what was impossible, in a world where magic rekindled and power passed like a sugar cube between hands, and her eye turned black, and she was queen?

"What are you then?" she asked.

The question elicited the faintest twitch at the edge of his mouth. In all the works of art, in all the statues and sketches and reliefs, Holland Vosijk

420

never smiled. His brows drew together, his mouth always a firm line, his jaw clenched, as if biting back words. Or pain. Even this could hardly be called a smile—it was only the barest curve at the corner of his lips—but she felt bathed in light.

"Do you believe in ghosts?" he asked, and Kosika shook her head. She never had, even when Lark tried to scare her with tales when they were young. She knew that magic came and went, and so did people. Here was here and gone was gone—but what, then, did that make Holland Vosijk?

He seemed to consider the question, though she didn't ask aloud.

"I know what I *was*," he said. "But not what I *am*. I bound myself to the magic of this world. And so, it seems, I am still here." He studied his hands. "In a way. I have been here in this place between. And then you found me. The question is . . ." His gaze flicked back to her. "How did you find me *now*?"

Kosika said nothing, even as his eyes weighed down on her.

"Your power was mine once," he ventured. "Perhaps it grows. Or perhaps you have done something . . ."

She flinched, and knew he saw the truth, in her face, or her mind. Of the day she had used his token to travel, the day her dreams of him had started. And it was as if he himself had forgotten, and now remembered, suddenly, the open box, the missing piece.

What have you done?

His anger rekindled, then, and all the altar candles with it.

"You should not have gone there, Kosika." She took a step back, but he caught her by the shoulders. "Tell me you took nothing out." His fingers tightened, until it hurt. The pain felt real. "Tell me."

She shook her head. "Nothing. I swear."

Holland let go as quickly as he'd grabbed her, the sudden absence of weight leaving her off-balance. He turned away from her, and the circle of altar lights, and leaned against the alcove wall, shadows washing over his weary face.

"There was nothing to take," Kosika went on. "No signs of magic. Everything I saw was dead." But as she said the word, she thought of Serak's lantern, the wick hissing with smoke as the fire went out.

421

Magic does not die.

Fear sparked inside her then, fear that she had carried some piece of cursed magic from that place, like mud on the bottom of her shoes.

But Holland shook his head. "You would know." His mouth was a small, bitter line. "The magic in that place is not subtle. It has a mind and a will of its own." He studied the altar. "Trust me," he muttered, and her mind went to the writings in his room.

"The ten days," she said. "The ten days you vanished from the world. That is where you went."

Holland did not look at her. "I would have done anything, to see our world restored. And so I did."

The worthy ruler is the one who understands the price. . . .

"Black London is the source of all magic," he said. "It is a wellspring. But every drop comes at a cost."

He told her, then, what happened in the ten days after the Danes fell, and before he took the throne. How he'd been mortally wounded, forced into Black London. How he'd lain there, lifeblood leeching into the ruined soil. How he would have died, had he not met Osaron—Osaron, the shadow king, the center of the flame that burned the world to ash, now reduced to an ember in an empty world. How he carried that ember out in his own form, to rekindle the magic of their world.

What have I done? Only what I must. Carried a spark out of the darkness to light my candle. Sheltered it with my body. Knowing I would burn.

"In the end," he said, "it cost me everything." He looked to the window, open onto the summer night. "But it worked."

"And Osaron?" she asked, hating the way the word snaked across her tongue.

Holland clenched his teeth. "Osaron wanted what all flames want. To spread unchecked. To burn." He met her gaze. "But that fire, at least, has been put out. Extinguished with my own."

And yet, thought Kosika, *you* are still here.

But she said nothing.

•

One night, Holland told her of the other Londons.

Not of the fallen world—he did not like to speak of it—but of the other two, whose tokens she'd seen in the box. The first, and farthest, where magic was forgotten, and the other, closer, where it burned so much brighter than their own. That world, which the Danes had coveted, and so many kings and queens before them, as if its magic was a prize that could be taken back.

He told her of Kell Maresh, the *Antari* who called that world home. Told her of Delilah Bard, the *Antari* from the world beyond, who thrived despite its absent magic.

He explained how to travel between the four worlds, spoke of them as if they were doors, not lining the same hall, but set one before another, so that to reach the farthest, she would have to pass through the one that sat between. He taught her these things, as if she had *any* desire to set foot beyond the boundaries of her own world. But she did not.

"I don't see the point," she told him. "Why should I care about the other worlds?"

And for the first time, she saw a shadow of displeasure cross Holland's face. She flinched from it, afraid that she had angered him. But then the shadow passed, and he only sighed and said, "Perhaps you will not have to."

But he told her no more stories that night.

And the next, he wasn't there.

Kosika dreamed of the castle as usual, searched the halls, the throne room, and the tower altar, even traipsed barefoot across the courtyard. But she couldn't find Holland. Panic bloomed behind her ribs as she called out for her saint, her king, voice echoing through the empty halls, and she began to fear that he was gone, gone for good, that whatever had possessed this past week had been nothing but a strange and fleeting vision. The waiting place, he'd called this space, and it felt empty now, hollow in a way it had never been, and as she searched, the panic grew, and grew, and by the time she woke, it had wound itself around her ribs, made it hard to breathe.

He was gone, she thought. Gone.

Grief wrapped itself around her as she sat up, flinging off the sheets, and—

There he was.

Holland stood at the window of her chamber. It was the first time she had dreamed of him in daylight, and he looked different. The sun caught the white of his hair, and the silver of his cloak and pin, light tracing his edges even as it poured through his body, as if he were a curtain.

"There you are," she said, relief overcoming the strange sensation of waking from one dream into another. "I have been looking everywhere."

Holland glanced over his shoulder. "I am right here." He turned his attention back to the window. "Come and see."

She rose, surprised by how cold the stone floor felt on her bare feet, her senses keen even though she was still dreaming. She joined Holland at the window, felt the almost weight of his hand as it came to rest on her shoulder, the other gesturing out and down to the courtyard below. The leaves were changing on the trees, the red and gold so bright it looked like they were burning.

A moment later the door flew open behind them, and Kosika turned, Holland's touch falling away as Nasi barreled in. There was a sweet bun in her mouth, another on a plate.

"Oh good, you're up," she said.

Kosika realized, with some surprise, that she was indeed awake.

Nasi flopped down on the nearest chair. "What are you doing at the window?"

She looked back, sure that she would find the room behind her empty. But Holland was still there, one hand resting on the sill.

Not a dream.

"I have never been a dream," he said evenly, and Kosika expected Nasi to startle at the sound of his voice, but the other girl didn't seem to notice, sprawling across the sheets in the presence of the Summer Saint.

"She cannot see me."

His voice rang so clearly, not in Kosika's mind but through the room itself. As if he were standing there. As if—

"Again you doubt me," said Holland, his voice taking on a darker note.

Kosika pressed her palms against her eyes. It was one thing to see someone in your dreams, in the in-between, the shadow realm of sleep, and quite another to see them standing in the living world, especially when no

424

one else could. She was afraid then, of what he was, and wasn't, afraid that she wasn't blessed, but mad.

"What's wrong?" asked Nasi. A moment later Kosika felt cool fingers brush her forehead, and looked up into her friend's scarred face. She wanted to tell her—but what would she say? That she was seeing phantoms? That her dreams were following her out of sleep?

Holland stepped behind Nasi, his eyes dark, impatient.

"Is your faith in me so fragile? That it bows and breaks under the slightest breeze?"

"*No,*" said Kosika, quickly, only to realize she'd spoken aloud. Nasi was staring at her, confused. "I don't feel well," she said. "Could you fetch some tea?"

Nasi searched her face another moment, then kissed her temple, and said of course. The moment she was gone, Kosika turned to face the king.

"Why can't she see you?"

"Because I did not *choose* Nasi," he said. "I chose you." Those words, like a hand smoothing rumpled sheets. Followed too quickly by the disappointment on his face. "Tell me, Kosika, did I choose wrong?"

"No," she said, her voice tinged with desperation.

She wanted him to be real. She wanted to believe. And as if he knew her mind, Holland stepped closer.

"Hold out your hands," he said, and she did, cupping them before her. To her surprise, he held out his own, and brought them to rest around hers, and she could *almost* feel them, like a breeze brushing her knuckles, grazing her skin.

"I chose you in the Silver Wood," he said, and as he spoke, she felt a sudden flush of heat, a warmth that kindled at her very core, spreading through her chest and down her arms to the place where Holland's fingers swallowed hers.

"I chose you," he said, "to be my hands."

Something began to happen in the room around them. Crumbs of dirt rose from the floor, where they had lodged between stones, and beads of moisture squeezed themselves out of the air, and warmth dragged itself from the sunlight in the window and all these fragments gathered in the space between her palms, and began to grow. Out of everything, and out of nothing, a seed, a sprout, a sapling that threw roots down between her fingers—and his fingers—and reached its narrow limbs to the ceiling and sky as it grew in the space between their bodies. It was a silver tree, its bark tender and pale.

Holland's palms fell from hers.

But the sapling remained, heavy in her outstretched hands. Kosika marveled at it, felt her eyes prick with tears. She knelt, and set the sapling on the floor. Holland's voice spilled over her.

"We are bound together," he said. "Your magic was once mine. My legacy is yours. I will guide your hands, if you let me."

Her head rose, and this time, there was no hesitation. No doubt. "I am your servant."

"Then I will be your saint," he answered, green eye bright, and black eye infinite. "And together, we will do wondrous things."

VII

RED LONDON, *now*

Rock shifted beneath Alucard's boots.

"Careful, sir," said Velastro. "It's not exactly stable."

The soldiers had carved a makeshift path through the building's wreckage, heaping the splintered wood and broken stone into piles and shifting the bulk of the debris out to the edges, where the walls had been before they fell.

Two soldiers had cordoned off the ruins, and were still searching the debris, while a third was making the rounds for information, which was a harder task—this was the *shal*, after all, a place known both for its dislike of the crown and its desire to keep its business to itself. But good coin spent in every quarter, and Alucard had supplied a bag of it in the hopes that bribery would do what civic duty wouldn't.

"*Anesh?*" asked Velastro, trailing in his wake. "What do you think?"

"You were right to come to me," said Alucard. Whether or not this had been the work of the Hand, there was nothing normal about the building's fall. The damage had been total, the tearing down so complete it couldn't have been accidental. There were no lingering roofbeams, no fragments of wall left standing.

This had been a demolition—the work of someone burying their tracks.

Velastro beamed at the praise, and Alucard resisted the urge to pat the eager young soldier on the head. Instead, he turned, and squinted, the debris a tangle of threads in his sight.

His eyes were accustomed to seeing too much, but usually there was an order to it. As he stepped over a broken beam, around the warped remains of shelves, it all blurred together, so much he almost missed it.

It—whatever *it* was—was lodged in one of the head-high piles, only a thin piece poking out the top. At first he thought it was a sliver of metal, catching the sun, but as he stepped closer he realized there was no object, only a line of light, burned onto the air itself.

"Stand back," he ordered.

As soon as the soldiers were clear, Alucard swept his hand, felt the familiar rush of magic rising to his fingers as they dragged through the air, and the pile of earth and rock answered, emitting a dull scrape as it was pushed sideways, revealing bare floor. And a shape, carved into the air. A set of perfect lines, squared off into a frame.

Alucard swore under his breath. No, not a random act at all.

"What *is* that?" asked Velastro.

Alucard tore his gaze from the mark. "You can see it, too?" he asked, surprised.

Velastro's head wobbled a little, as if it couldn't decide between a yes and a no. "I can see it, and I can't." And then he used a word Alucard hadn't heard in years, not since his time at sea.

Trosa.

Ghost.

Sailors had all kinds of stories. Of the Sarows, who stole over ships like fog, and the *garost,* who reached up from the deep and scraped its nails along the hull, and the *trosa,* spectral vessels that followed in a ship's wake, lurking at dawn and dusk on the horizon but never drawing closer.

427

But Velastro wasn't a sailor, and to him the word meant something else.

"That's what we used to call them," he explained, "when we were kids. The echoes you see when you stare too long at a bright light and then close your eyes, and it's still there. No matter how many times you blink."

Alucard reached out, fingers grazing the air over the mark. He half expected to feel some resistance when he touched it, but whatever magic had been in play, it was spent, leaving only this scar, its vivid lines carved into the air, the edges burned white.

"A remnant," he murmured.

Just then, another soldier rode up on a royal mount. Alucard's fingers fell away from the mark as she dismounted, tucking her helmet beneath her arm.

"Well," he said, "what have you managed to buy with our coin?"

"More than you'd think," said the soldier, "and less than you'd like." She surveyed the wreckage, contained as it was to only one house, and explained that before this place fell down, it had been a repair shop, run by a man named Haskin.

"Any sign of him?"

"That's the thing," said the soldier. "When I asked for a description, no one could oblige. According to everyone I met, he never left the shop. Never even handled customers. He was, by all accounts, a recluse."

"But there was no body found in the wreckage," observed Alucard.

"Maybe he doesn't exist," said Velastro.

Alucard looked at the young soldier. Perhaps he was sharper than he looked. "You think it was a front?"

It was the older soldier who answered.

"Oh no," she said, shaking her head, "as far as I can tell, Haskin's shop did plenty of repairs. Not sure how much was legal. But all business was handled by his apprentice. A girl. Fifteen years, give or take. Lanky. Lots of hair. One described her as a feral cat."

"Name?"

The soldier shook her head. Alucard sighed. Of course not. That would have been too helpful. He kept listening, but his gaze drifted over the wreckage toward the front of the shop—what was left of it—which was when he noticed the young man lingering across the street.

If he was trying to hide, he was doing a pretty bad job.

He stood on the curb, a paper bundle clutched in both hands, and stared straight at the ruined shop, his face slack-jawed as he took in the damage. The first thing Alucard thought was that he must have been either a customer or a friend. The second thing Alucard thought was that they'd met before. It was in the shape of his face, the way his black hair carved a widow's peak into his brow, the way his eyes widened when he noticed Alucard staring back at him.

The man froze.

Froze the way Ren's rabbit, Miros, did sometimes when it was being chased by servants, as if it thought it might be able to blend right into a chair leg, or the carpet, or the tapestry against the wall. And then, once it realized it couldn't, it did what rabbits do.

It ran.

"Wait—" started Alucard, but the man was already turning on his heel. Sprinting away down the street.

"*Sanct,*" he swore, grabbing the reins of the soldier's mount and swinging himself up. He dug his heels in, and the horse surged into motion, leaping a low pile of debris as its hooves pounded down the street.

The young man was quick but he was also clumsy, long limbs tangling as he ran. He half skidded, half slid around a tight corner, dropping the bundle as he did, spilling what looked like *dumplings* across the paving stones as he scrambled back to his feet, started to run, then changed his mind, and turned to face his pursuer.

The horse reared to a stop, and Alucard dismounted, holding up a hand in peace.

"I just want to talk," he said, which was true. He knew not everyone ran because they'd done something wrong, and even if he had, Alucard only cared about the young man's crimes if they would shed light on the ruined shop and its missing apprentice.

"What happened to Haskin's shop?"

"I don't know," said the man, breathless. "I was just going to visit Tes, to pay her back, you know? For the dumplings, and— Is she all right? Was she inside?"

"Tes—that's the apprentice at Haskin's shop?"

His head bobbed. He looked around again, as if the alley walls might be narrowing.

"What's *your* name?" asked Alucard, thought it was innocuous enough, but the man's eyes—a pale brown, like weak tea—narrowed. His face snapped shut. And Alucard realized why he'd stopped running.

Before, he'd been too busy to notice the color of the young man's magic. But now, Alucard saw the threads, bruising the air around his opponent's shoulders. It was a color he almost never saw: a dark and warning violet.

"It doesn't matter," said Alucard, waving his own question away. "Right now, we need to find your friend, Tes. Make sure she's safe." He regretted the words as soon as they were out. He'd just tipped his hand, admitted she wasn't in the shop. The man's brown eyes flicked up. Alucard pressed on. "If you come back with me, maybe you'll see something—"

"Tes can look after herself." He took a step back as he said it, shaking his head.

"I can't let you go," warned Alucard.

The man flashed him a pitying grin. "I don't think you have a choice."

They moved at the same time, each reaching for their magic, Alucard for the street stones, and the younger man for *him*. Alucard was fast—but for once, not fast enough. The ground beneath them shuddered, but before it could rise up, the other man slammed his hand down, and Alucard felt his own body buckle, fold.

Bone magic.

That was the power turning the air around him such a vivid shade.

Alucard's limbs were forced to the ground, his head bowed so he couldn't see anything but the street, his hands splayed on the stones. He gasped, trying to wrest his body back from the man's hold, felt his jaw grind shut so he couldn't call for help.

"I'm sorry," said the man, and if Alucard weren't being held against his will, he might have stopped to think how strange it was, that apology, stranger still that it sounded sincere. He heard the man's boots skirt around him, careful to stay beyond Alucard's line of sight.

"I'm sorry," he said again. "I just wanted to bring her dumplings."

His steps retreated down the alley, and the last thing Alucard heard was him pausing by the horse to pat its flank and say, "Good boy," before slipping away.

As soon as he was gone, Alucard's body was his again. Not gradually, like feeling coming back into numb fingers, but all at once, control slamming back into his limbs with all the force of a wave on the rocks.

Alucard rose to his feet, shaking out the unsettling sensation of having been a puppet on someone else's strings. The horse stood, waiting patiently at the mouth of the alley.

"You could have stopped him," he muttered, mounting the beast. But neither he nor the horse were going after the bone magician.

Not while the ghosted mark still burned behind his eyes, hanging there as it had in the ruined shop. A scar the size and shape of exactly one thing.

A *door*.

VIII

The house sat still and dark, exactly as it had the night before.

Lila leaned at the mouth of the alley across the street, and searched the edge of the coin again for some clue she might have missed, some hint or mention of a day to go with the blasted hour. But the words hadn't changed.

SON HELARIN RAS ● NONIS ORA

The street around the house had come alive—carriages went up and down the road, and customers spilled in and out of shops, and the houses to either side showed signs of life—but the eleventh hour came and went, and no one approached the doors of 6 Helarin Way.

This was beginning to feel like a riddle, and as far as Lila was concerned, riddles could go hang themselves.

She was about to go, then stopped. If she was going to be standing vigil twice a day, at least she could save herself the walk. She unwound the bandage from her hand, the cut still fresh; a little pressure and it welled.

431

She touched her fingers to the blood and made a small mark on the nearest wall. A vertical line, and two small crosses. A shortcut.

She wrapped her hand, and scowled at the empty house one last time. Six Helarin Way stared grimly back, its windows dark, its gate locked tight as teeth, its façade taking on a rictus grin.

The longer she looked at it, the more she felt like it was mocking her.

Fire sparked in her palm. She briefly considered burning it down. The urge passed, until she felt the body in the shadows at her back.

Lila sighed, and drew a blade. "I warned you what would happen," she said, "if you followed me again."

She was about to throw the knife when a familiar voice replied, "Well, that sounds menacing."

Lila decided to throw it anyway. To Alucard's credit, he sidestepped the blade, and caught the metal edge between his fingers.

"I'm going to pretend," he said, "that you didn't know it was me, and were merely acting on instinct."

"You do that," said Lila, flicking her wrist. The blade plucked itself from Alucard's hand and returned to hers. He joined her at the mouth of the alley.

"I admit, I was surprised to find you here."

She could ask how he did, but she could guess. Those bloody crows.

Alucard was studying the houses on the road, and she caught a flicker of discomfort cross his face. The Emery estate wasn't far from here. This had been his neighborhood, the streets where he was raised.

A couple passed by, startling a little when they saw the prince's consort. He flashed a smile, but she could see the strain behind it.

Served him right, she thought, for following her.

He looked past her at the row of houses across the street.

"So," he said casually. "What are we doing here?"

She resented the use of "we" and considered telling him to fuck off, but she was sick of looking at the stupid house. Perhaps a pair of fresh eyes would help.

"That one there," she said, jerking her chin at it. "I don't suppose it's spelled somehow. Something you can see that I cannot."

She didn't often envy Alucard's sight—in a world saturated with magic, it seemed to cause him headaches more than help—but she'd been glaring at the stone façade for nearly an hour to no avail, and if it turned out the meeting had been happening all along, she really might just burn it down.

Alucard looked at the building, his eyes taking on a far-off focus as they scraped across its front. "There's no veil," he said. "Why?"

Lila dug the coin from her pocket and tossed it to him.

"A tip, for my fine company?" he asked, weighing the lin in his palm. "Believe it or not, Bard, I am not pressed for pocket change."

She rolled her eyes. "That coin was found on one of the dead thieves, on Maris's ship. Look at the edge."

Alucard held it to the light. The metal was still faintly stained from the night before, soot gathered in the tiny grooves. "A message?" he ventured, squinting as he tried to make it out.

"I'll save you the trouble," she said. "It's very small. And backwards."

She pulled the kerchief from her pocket, the words printed in the right direction. He noticed the bandage wrapped around her wrist, and frowned. "Cut yourself?"

"The price of playing with knives," she said dismissively. "Now look." She tapped the writing. "It's a *meeting*. And I'm willing to bet more than that coin it's for the Hand."

Alucard blew out a breath. "This must be how we haven't caught on. You must admit," he said, "it's rather clever."

"I'd appreciate it more if they'd bothered to give the day as well."

"But they did." He pointed to the little mark that separated the two halves of the message. On the kerchief, it registered as a small black circle.

"That," said Lila, "is a dot."

"Only for someone with no imagination. Or no education in Arnesian shorthand. In which case, that little dot, as you call it, is a moon."

Lila's stomach dropped.

"Or perhaps a moon-*less*," he added. "It's hard to know which school they're using."

Lila cursed herself. How had she missed it? On a surface that small, no space or symbol would be wasted. She searched her memory—the moon had been waning the last few nights, the sky growing darker. If it was a full moon, that could be weeks away, but if it meant moonless that could be as early as—

"In any case," said Alucard, handing back both coin and kerchief, "it isn't happening right now. Good thing, too," he added, turning to go, and expecting her to follow. "There's something else you need to see."

Half an hour later, Lila had traded the broad avenues of the northern bank for the narrow corridors of the *shal,* and found herself no longer standing *outside* a house, but in the ruins of one.

It seemed to have been torn down—no, torn *apart,* from the inside out. As she trailed Alucard through the remains, Lila noted that the act lacked the air of accident, felt more like a demolition. Which didn't explain why she was here.

"This way," said Alucard, leading her through the wreckage. Lila kicked a broken bit of stone out of her path. Amid the debris, she noticed pieces of metal, too small to be structure, a crumpled tea tin, spilling wire and twine. The splintered remains of a sign, the words *once broken, soon repaired* still legible.

Dread coiled in Lila's gut. "This place," she said. "What was it called?"

She knew the answer before he said the name, but it still landed like a dull blow. "Haskin's."

Lila groaned. She had been so close.

"And what of the man himself?"

"Doesn't exist." Lila cocked a brow. That was a surprise. "Shop seems to have been run by an apprentice—or that's what they called her. A girl, goes only by Tes. No sign of her, but—just wait—where is it? Ah, here." Alucard stopped walking suddenly, and Lila drew up short to keep from running into him. He gestured at the space ahead, where the rubble had been cleared. Lila looked. There was nothing there.

"Is this something only you can see?" she ventured.

But Alucard shook his head. "I don't think so. Just focus. Or, rather, unfocus."

Lila didn't understand. She stepped past him, raking her gaze down the air. Still, she didn't see anything unusual. And then Alucard carefully rounded the space and turned to face her. He looked wrong, like he was standing behind a pane of warping glass.

"What is that?" she murmured, half to herself.

Alucard's hand flexed, and a breeze kicked up in answer, a current of dust that caught the light, and drew the shape of the mark. She frowned, following its outline to the ground.

"I have a theory," said Alucard. "I think it's—"

"A *door*," she said.

He actually looked a little disappointed, like he wanted to be the one to say it. "Well, yes. Exactly."

Lila stared at the echo of the door. She'd been right. The *persalis* had been damaged. The thief must have brought it here, to be repaired. And either it had been fixed, or someone made a mess while trying. She reached out, as if she could lay her hand against the mark, but her fingers met with no resistance. It was only an echo, a scar left by a spell.

"When did this happen?" she asked grimly.

"Last night, we think," said Alucard, "or early this morning."

Lila swore under her breath. If only she had come here, instead of Helarin Way. She'd been so close, and now, she had nothing. The *persalis* was in the wind now, and whatever clues she might have found destroyed, and whatever happened here in the hours before dawn, whatever answers she might have found—

Lila straightened suddenly.

For a moment, the wreckage disappeared, and she was back on Maris's ship, the old woman handing her a small glass card. A *backward glance,* she'd called it.

In case, like me, you find yourself a step behind.

Lila's hand went to her pocket, before she remembered she'd stashed it in the captain's quarters. She turned on her heel, and strode out of the rubble.

"Where are you going, Bard?" asked Alucard.

"To fetch something from my ship."

X

OUT OF THE FRYING PAN, INTO THE FIRE

I
GREY LONDON

Dead people didn't hurt this much.

That's how Tes knew she was alive.

The tavern was dark, the candles all burned out, but the weak dawn light leaked between the shutters, tracing the room in shades of grey instead of black.

She was no longer on a table in the center of the unfamiliar room, but on a makeshift pallet, made from a cushion and a couple benches pushed against the wall. Tes ached from her fingertips to the place she'd been stabbed, and far deeper, in the center of her chest. Like her heart had worked too hard, pumping all that blood, only to lose it.

When she tried to sit up, she felt the pull of stitches down one side, the tender skin drawn taut against the thread. She hissed through her teeth, then eased herself up, closing her eyes against the dizziness until it passed.

Tes tugged up her shirt—which was no longer her own, but a fresh one (and judging by the length of the sleeves and the way the hem skimmed her thighs, it belonged to the man who'd found her)—and studied the wound over her hip. The blade had gone in straight but deep, and must have missed the important parts, but it would definitely leave a scar. Nero was always telling her that scars were sexy (usually right after he came in with a split brow or a fresh scrape) but Tes thought of Calin's ruined face, and grimaced.

439

Her curls were loose, falling in her face, but when she tried to pull them back, the movement tugged the stitches, and sent a fresh stab of pain through her side, so she left the wild mass and padded over to the counter, where the contents of her coat had been laid out: the stack of coins, and the doormaker, and Vares.

Only, the owl wasn't there.

Panic fluttered through her, until she turned and saw the dead bird sitting on a table, in front of the man who'd saved her. He sat slumped forward in a chair, his head resting on his folded arms, and the little owl at his elbow. Tes took a cautious step forward.

Ned Tuttle, that's what the woman had called him.

It was a weird name, but then, this was a weird place. The farthest world, the one whose magic had been lost. That's what she'd been told, and yet, here it was, curling quietly around the shoulders of a skinny sleeping man.

The thread wasn't bright—it emitted only a soft, golden glow—but it was *there*.

Stranger still, it wasn't the same thread that had led her here, to this oddly familiar tavern and its odd proprietor. The one she'd seen in the dark had held no color, only a hollow black-and-white glow. The barmaid had had no magic, so it wasn't hers, but Tes was certain the thread had come from here.

Her gaze drifted, searching the tavern. There was the front door, as well as a set of narrow stairs that led up, perhaps to rooms overhead. But there was a third, one that didn't lead out onto the street. Tes padded toward it. Tried the handle. Locked. Back home, she could have simply pulled the threads inside the bolt to free it. But she wasn't home, and things didn't work by magic here. They were stubborn, and solid, and it was maddening.

Her hand fell from the knob just as something twitched between the wood and the surrounding wall.

A thread. Black-and-white, emitting that impossible glow.

Just like the one she'd seen the night before.

Now that Tes wasn't bleeding to death, the sight of it tickled her memory. She'd seen its like before, that lightless shine that seemed to eat itself. It reminded her of the shadow that clung to the cabinet in her father's shop, the one that held the relics of Black London. Even if it wasn't, she knew better than to handle things she didn't understand.

She retreated from the floating strand, when suddenly it reached for *her*. The magic itself twitched forward, shooting toward her with such sudden speed and force that Tes recoiled, staggered back away from the questing thread.

Her heel caught on a chair leg, which scraped against the floor, and Ned's head shot up, his head swiveling around until he saw her.

He sighed in relief. "Oh good," he said. "You're alive."

Tes glanced back to the door, half expecting the tendril to surge out into the room. But it was gone. She turned her attention to Ned, and cobbled together her rusty High Royal.

"Thanks to you," she said, the words strange in her mouth.

He rose to his feet and began to talk very fast, the words blurring together.

"Please," she said. "Slow down. This isn't . . . my language."

Ned cocked his head to one side. "Oh, huh, I never thought of that. It makes sense, I suppose. Other worlds, and such. But Kell always spoke the King's English."

Tes started at the name. "Kell *Maresh*?"

But of course, it had to be. There was only one Kell who could move between worlds.

Ned nodded enthusiastically. "Do you know him?"

Tes snorted. People didn't *know* the crimson *Antari*, Kell Maresh, adopted brother to King Rhy. Most never even met him. The closest she had ever come was when she named the owl Vares after him. But Ned was staring at her expectantly, as if it were a perfectly fair question.

"No," she said. "I've never met the prince."

"*Prince?*" Ned's eyes went wide. "As in, heir to a throne?"

Tes nodded. Ned whistled softly. "He never told me." He began to pace. "You sure we're talking about the same Kell? Red hair? One fully black eye? And there's his companion, Lila Bard—but she's no princess. Have you met *her*?"

In fact, Tes *had* met the other *Antari,* once, when she first got to London. It hadn't gone well.

441

"Speaking of," said the man, rambling on. "You don't have one—a black eye, I mean—but you're still here—how did you do that? I thought only those magicians with the black eyes could cross the threshold. Of course Lila doesn't have one either, but then, that's because one of hers is glass, not that you'd ever know. . . ."

The room was spinning and he was talking too fast again. Tes sank into his vacant chair and pressed her fingers to her temples. What she really needed was a very large, very hot, very strong cup of—

"Tea?" offered Ned.

She looked up. "You have *tea*?"

He bobbed his head. "Can't get by without the stuff. You look like you could use some. I could, too. Long night. Of course, not quite so long as yours . . ."

He swept across the room, his long legs carrying him quickly behind the counter, and into an alcove. She heard the rattle of a kettle, a match being struck, a stove.

Vares sat on the table, the threads of the owl's magic bright against the backdrop of the empty room. Tes reached out and ran her finger lightly down one string and the bird fluttered happily, as if she'd stroked the feathers he didn't have.

Ned reappeared with a rattling tray. "How do you take it?" he asked.

She didn't understand the question. "In a cup?"

He laughed—it was a gentle sound—then set a pot and two cups on the table, as well as a saucer of milk and a bowl of sugar. It had never occurred to Tes to foul the beautiful bitter strength of her tea with cream and sweetness, but maybe the tea here needed it. She watched as he put three cubes of sugar and a splash of milk in his cup. She put nothing in hers.

If the tea was bad enough, she decided, she would try it.

But the tea wasn't bad enough. It wasn't bad at all.

It was . . . different, of course. Different, but just as strong as she liked it. It was nice to know, that worlds might change, but this, at least, was constant. She wrapped her fingers around the steaming cup, and drank, and for the first time since she'd fixed the doormaker, and stepped into another world, and killers had come and threatened to cut off her hands,

442

and her shop was destroyed and she was stabbed and forced to flee into another world, Tes felt her eyes burn with tears.

A few dripped to the table before she scrubbed them away.

Ned pretended not to notice. She was grateful for that. He nudged a small plate toward her. On it, a stack of pale disks, little bigger than coins.

"Biscuits," he explained.

Tes considered them. They looked like *kashen,* a spiced cookie she'd eaten as a child. She took one, and sniffed it, but couldn't detect any spice. She bit down, or tried, but it was hard, and bland, and resisted in her teeth, and she was wondering how—and why—a person would eat it when Ned took one and dunked it in his tea.

Skeptically, she followed his lead, placing the moistened biscuit in her mouth. This time, it was warm, and soft, and sugary. Not kashen by any stretch, but nice.

Vares clicked his beak, and Ned stared at the owl with a kind of childlike wonder.

"Amazing," he murmured, and Tes felt herself preen a little—it *was* an elegant bit of magic. She finished her cup, and he poured her another, this one even stronger for how long it had steeped.

"Did you and Kell have tea often?" she asked.

Ned started to laugh, and choked on half a biscuit. "No. His visits have always been strictly business. He's never even taken off his coat."

"I've heard it's magic," she said. "That coat."

"I wouldn't be surprised," he said. "Isn't everything magic where you come from?"

Tes started to shake her head, then stopped. Not everything was *spelled,* of course, but there was magic in it. That's where the threads came from.

"You have magic," she said, glancing at the tendril in the air around him. "You shouldn't. But you do."

It was like she'd lit a lamp inside Ned's face. "You can tell? I mean, I know it's not much, but I've been practicing, every day, and I feel like I'm getting better . . ."

There he went again, talking too fast in High Royal, his hands moving in his enthusiasm. In fact, this man never seemed to stop moving. He reminded Tes of Vares. All those little twitches and shifts. She waited until he lost enough steam that she could catch the words—something about candles and element kits—and then her gaze drifted back to the locked wooden door on the other side of the room.

"There's magic in there, too."

Ned's brow furrowed. The joy dropped out of his face. "Oh."

"What's behind the door?"

"Nothing," he said, swift as a window slamming shut. The kind of lie that made it clear she wouldn't get the truth.

Tes wanted to tell him that whatever it was, it wasn't safe.

But there was a look on Ned's face that said he already knew. He knew it was bad. He knew it was wrong. He knew, and here it was, and here he was with it. So she simply said, "Be careful."

And then she finished her cup of tea, and stood, wincing as the stitches pulled.

"Where are you going?" he asked.

It was a good question. She didn't have a good answer. But she couldn't stay here. She went to the counter, and gingerly pulled on her coat, shoved her feet into her boots, tucked the doormaker under her arm, and slipped all of the coins save one into her pocket. She put the last on Ned's table. As payment, for the help, and the tunic, and the tea.

He did a strange thing then. He took up the coin and brought it to his nose, murmuring what sounded like *flowers*.

"You're very odd," she said.

He smiled. "So I've been told. If you see Kell or Lila, tell them Ned Tuttle says hello."

Tes laughed a little at that, even though it hurt. She couldn't imagine running into the two *Antari*, but he seemed hopeful, so she said, "I will."

Ned stood, following her to the door. "You can come back, you know. Anytime," he said, throwing the latch. "You don't have to be bleeding to death. I mean, obviously, if you *are* hurt, do come, but if you just want to swing by for a tea and a chat, that's fine, too."

The door swung open, revealing a pale grey morning.

"Oh," he said, "I never got your name."

And perhaps it was because of all he'd done to save her life, or perhaps it was because she never thought she'd see him again—perhaps it was just her tired mind giving way—but she found herself telling him the truth.

"It's Tesali Ranek," she said, adding, "but friends call me Tes." Even though the truth was only Nero called her that.

Ned smiled. "Well, Tes. You know where to find me."

And she did.

Outside, the streets were full of carts and people and voices, the morning cluttered with movement, but without the many layered threads of magic, there was a flatness to it. Was this how her world looked to everyone else? It was so . . . quiet, and while it was certainly unnerving, to see only the material, mundane world, Tes also felt a strange relief. Like a cold hand on a fevered cheek.

She looked back, reading the sign over the tavern door.

"The Five Points," she murmured to herself, committing the High Royal words to memory.

And then she set off down the street.

II

A few heads turned at the sight of the girl in a too-long tunic and tight britches, a mane of wild curls and a slight hitch in her step, talking to herself under her breath in a foreign tongue.

But of course, Tes wasn't talking to herself.

She was talking to Vares. Not that anyone else could see the dead owl tucked inside the pocket of her coat.

"I'm not stalling," she muttered. "I just need a *plan*."

She stopped on a street corner. Looked up and down the road.

What a strange city.

The buildings were a mix of wood and brick and stone, mismatched, a mixture of new and old. They ranged from narrow houses squeezed in like sandwich meat between hefty chunks of bread, to vaulting structures with pointed peaks. She wondered how they did it, built all this without a drop of magic. If they really had to fell every tree, lift and set every stone.

It was impressive.

But it was also dirty. Every time she breathed, she caught a foul taste, like food gone off, and smoke belched into the sky, sending up clouds as black as coal.

She walked along the riverbank. In daylight, it turned out, the water wasn't black, or blue, but grey. The pale grey of puddles in the street, of soot and storm clouds. It made her shiver, to see the Isle stripped of color, a source reduced to a simple stream. She walked on until she reached a bridge, stopped to orient herself again.

"Yes," she told the owl. "I know where I'm going."

That wasn't strictly true. But she had a hunch.

It wasn't just that she'd heard of the other cities called London. The river, though it lacked its crimson glow, seemed to occupy the same space, and though the buildings and bridges were all different, the city had the same rough shape. As if the same bones were there, just inside a different body. So, as Tes walked, she drew a map in her head, not of this city, but her own, grateful that she'd spent the last few years learning the ins and outs of the capital.

When she'd gone through the door, Tes had and *hadn't* moved through space. A different world, yes, but the same physical place. She thought it was a decent bet, then, that walking a step in one world would carry her a step in the other.

"If Calin survived," she went on, "I'm betting Bex did, too."

Which was why she was now putting a healthy distance between herself and the shop ruins and the *shal*—or at least, where she guessed they were— before going back into her London.

"No, I can't stay *here*," she muttered, as if Vares had been the one to offer the option. She shuddered even as she said it. Nice as it was to rest her eyes a little while, the thought of a life in a place like this, a world without magic, was enough to turn her stomach. No, she had to go back. Even if it was dangerous. Even if they were looking for her.

The world—her *own* world—was a big place. She had run once.

She could run again.

Tes paused and closed her eyes, drew the map in her head one last time to be sure she was in roughly the right spot. Then she knelt, and set the little wooden box on the ground. She glanced around, saw a pair of women strolling by, lost in chatter, a vendor setting up a cart, an old man on a bench, reading a paper, but none of them had noticed her.

Tes turned her attention back to the box, and whispered, "*Erro.*"

For a second, nothing happened, and she was scared the lack of magic in this world would somehow keep the box from working, that the spell would have nothing to grab on to and she would be stuck here in this powerless world. And in that second, she realized how badly she wanted to go home.

Then the second passed, and the spell sprang to life, the box unfolding and the door rising up, carving itself against the empty air in a single burning thread of light.

The old man looked up from his paper, and she wondered what he would think, when she was gone. If he'd convince himself it was magic. Or convince himself it wasn't.

Strange world, she thought again, as the space inside the doorway darkened, the curtain rippling as one London was replaced by another, and Tes flung herself through.

In her mind, the door had led to an alley across from the docks. But her mind must have been off by half a dozen strides, because instead of stepping into the street, she walked straight into a kitchen. Which might not have been so bad, if the kitchen had been empty.

But it wasn't.

A woman stood at the stove making breakfast, and Tes had just enough time to notice the tendrils of magic in the flame beneath her pan before the woman turned, and shrieked, and flung out her hand. Tes saw the gust of wind the instant before it slammed her back, through the conjured door and onto the damp cobblestone street she'd left seconds before.

Tes gasped, pain rippling through her side. She pressed her hand against the stitches, hoping they hadn't torn.

"*Ferro,*" she hissed, and the door collapsed. Tes sat up, noticed the old man staring, wide-eyed, his paper forgotten, as she took up the doormaker. Counted off a handful of paces, and tried again.

447

This time, she waited for the door to resolve, waited until the world beyond took on a blurry kind of shape, enough to at least be certain that it would not dump her into someone else's house.

Then Tes looked at the man, and flicked her fingers in a wave, before she disappeared, taking the door and the magic with her.

RED LONDON

It was blinding, at first, the sudden return of so much light.

The vibrant, overlapping patterns of the world, dizzying and dazzling at once. But even as Tes fought to steady her gaze, she felt a flush of visceral relief. Home. She never thought the word could encompass an entire world, but there it was.

And then, on its heels, the reminder of why she'd left. And where she had to go.

The docks.

The owl twitched in her coat pocket, pecked at her ribs.

"I don't *want* to leave London," she muttered, and it was true. She'd been in the city three years, and in that time, she had made a place for herself in the *shal*, a home in Haskin's shop.

"And then you tore it down," she said bitterly, even though she knew she didn't have a choice. It was just rock and timber. Houses, like lives, could be rebuilt. But only if you were still alive to do the building.

Tes joined the bustle of morning crowds and market stalls, the doormaker bundled under one arm as if it were a loaf of bread. Nero had told her once to never act like you're running from something, or people will notice, and wonder what. So she resisted the urge to glance around, to scan the faces, search for trouble, or quicken her pace. Even as she crossed the crowded road and descended the wide stone steps to the London docks.

Her steps slowed at the sight of all those ships.

Some big, some small, trading vessels and members of the royal fleet, merchant skiffs and a Faroan strider, and a handful of boats that flew no flag. She had grown up in a port city, and whenever she felt trapped, she'd sit and watch the ships coming and going, and know there was a way out.

She'd taken it once. And here she was again.

She studied the ships, entertained the brief but dazzling hope that she'd find Elrick's little boat tethered to a berth, see the man waiting for her, unchanged by time, silver baubles shining in his twisted hair, one hand raised in welcome. But of course, he wasn't there.

She considered the ships that were, trying to find the right one. Could she buy passage, or would she have to stow away? Either way, the merchant vessels were best, because they came and went, and always had room for unexpected cargo. One caught her eye. A fast-looking ship with a dark grey hull and white sails, a bird's head carved into the prow.

But when she tried to move toward it, her feet felt pinned to the wooden slats. Not by magic, only doubt. Was running really the right answer? How far would she have to go, to feel safe again?

Sailors swept past, calling orders and unloading crates, and she might as well have been one of the figureheads, mounted to the prow of a ship.

Tes couldn't bring herself to move. To go, and leave London behind.

Problems were meant to be fixed.

There had to be a way to fix this.

It wasn't even *her* the killers wanted. It was the doormaker. She thought about chucking the device into the Isle, but she knew it wouldn't help. If Bex and Calin came for her, and she told them what she'd done, they'd think she was lying, that she'd stashed it somewhere, would proceed to break every bone in her hands and then the rest for good measure, and once they figured out she *was* telling the truth, they'd probably just kill her. So no, ditching the blasted thing wasn't a way out.

But there was another option.

She could stay, and try to fight.

The owl shuddered in her pocket, and Tes amended the thought. She could find someone else to fight *for* her. Bex and Calin were sellswords. Someone had hired them. But the city was full of strong magicians with loose morals. Maybe she could hire one of her own. Of course, the *shal* was the place to do that, and she couldn't go back *there*. It was the first place they'd be looking for her.

Tes buried her fingers in her curls.

She wanted to scream. Instead, she turned and kicked the nearest crate, as hard as she could, and then she did scream, a little, in pain if not frustration. She was still rubbing her foot when she heard a voice nearby say, "Well, if it isn't our illustrious captain."

Tes turned, and saw the telltale shine of *Antari* magic.

It twined through the air, the color of moonlight but twice as bright, so bright it almost blurred the figure at its center. But as the threads shifted and danced, Tes saw the tall woman approaching a ship, whip thin, dark hair cut knife-sharp along a pointed chin. She knew her, at once.

Delilah Bard.

One of the strongest magicians in the world.

And unlike the crimson prince for which Vares had been named, Lila Bard was *known* for using her power, as if hungry for an excuse to put it on display. There was a rumor she'd even fought in the last *Essen Tasch,* disguised as Stasion Elsor. The *real* Stasion Elsor was from a port town near Hanas and spent the next year telling anyone who would listen that a strange woman had stolen his identity, and his spot in the final games. Whether or not it was true, everyone said that she was just as good with a blade as blood, or any of the elements. And she was always spoiling for a fight.

And Tes knew then, she'd found her champion.

Delilah Bard stood in her silver shine, one boot lifted on a crate and her head tipped back, chatting with an older man on the deck of the dark-hulled ship. Tes retreated a few steps, into the shadow between boxes.

"Aw, poor Stross, drew the short stick, did you?"

"*Nas,*" the deckhand grunted. "I volunteered. Let the newlyweds wander off. What about you? Food in the palace not to your taste?"

"Bed's too soft," said Bard, rolling her neck. "But Alucard sends his regards." She kicked the hull. "What have you done to the *Barron?*"

"Took off a month of salt and grit. You're welcome."

"I didn't say I liked it. She looks despicably decent."

"Are we leaving port?" asked the deckhand, sounding hopeful.

"Not yet," she said. "Just came to fetch something."

"Hey Captain," said a second, younger man, as Bard started up the ramp, "how long are we stuck here?"

"Till the job's done. What's wrong, Tav, not enough brothels in our fair capital?"

"I get dock-sick," said the younger. "A ship's not meant to be tied up like this. . . ."

"Funny," said Bard. "I thought I hired sailors. . . ."

With that, she vanished aboard the ship. Tes chewed her nails, and waited several painful minutes, hoping Bard would reemerge. She did, tucking something into an inside pocket of her coat. She strolled down the ramp again, silver threads dragging like star trails in her wake, and Tes followed.

It was a perfect plan, really. Delilah Bard didn't even have to know. If Bex and Calin were out there, they'd come for Tes. She just had to make sure she was standing close to Lila when they did.

"How many times are you going to do that fucking spell?"

Bex didn't look up as another dark curl burned to nothing over the map. "Until I find the girl."

It was morning, and the Saint of Knives was almost empty at this hour, save for a man who was either sleeping, or dead, and a trio playing a rather subdued game of Sanct. Calin slumped in a nearby chair, nursing his headache with a bottle of spirits. That was the worst of his injuries—the upside to having such a thick skull.

A bowl of stew sat at Bex's elbow, the contents long cold beneath a film of grease. She was grateful she couldn't smell them. She'd set her broken nose, bound her wrist, and stitched up her hand where Berras's blade had gone straight through. It was hardly the first time she'd had to sew herself back together, but she needed both hands to do the spell, and every time, the stitches pulled and the splintered bones in her wrist sent white-hot sparks of pain up her arm.

Calin grunted, and offered her the bottle of strong spirits.

Any other time, she would have thought it poisoned. Today she knew it wasn't, but still, the gesture rankled her. Let him dull his pain. She preferred to sharpen hers into a point. She waved the spirits away.

"Suit yourself," he mumbled, drinking deeply. He leaned back in his chair and closed his eyes. "You're going to run out of hair."

Fucking useless sack of meat, thought Bex. But he was right—she had been going all night, was down to nine strands, and still the spell had turned up nothing, even when she tried maps that showed not just London but the entire empire.

"People don't just disappear," she muttered, half to herself. "She shouldn't have been able to use the fucking door without the keymark."

"Must have made a new one," said Calin, the words half swallowed by encroaching sleep. "While she was fixing it."

"Maybe," said Bex, bitter that he'd made a good point.

She shoved up from the table, taking her empty glass and stretching out her stiff neck and throbbing knee—it had been a long night, and unlike Calin, she didn't take well to having a building dropped on top of her.

Bex made her way over to the bar as dawn began to leak through the windows.

Despite the unwholesome hour, the Saint of Knives never truly closed. After all, it catered to sellswords. Death didn't sleep, and neither did the hands that ferried it. The owner, Hannis, however, did go to bed, with the strict warning that anyone who tried to leave without paying would be cursed upon exit.

Bex doubted there was actually a spell on the threshold, but decided not to chance it, so she dropped a coin on the counter as she filled her own pint, and strolled the long way back to the table, passing the wooden sculpture of the saint as she did. Every wooden inch was a patchwork of divots and scars from the years the patrons spent throwing knives at his arms, his chest, his head. One hand looked like it was a single solid blow from breaking off.

Calin fancied himself a modern Saint of Knives, she knew. But her fellow sellsword was an idiot, one who didn't seem to realize that the wooden effigy wasn't a faithful depiction of the saint. That in the stories—which Bex had actually read one night, whiling away the hours before a job—the Saint of Knives was not in fact scarred by enemy blades. He had made the cuts himself, one for every life he took. If a patron got close enough to the statue, they'd see those faint lines, methodically carved, beneath the hundreds of hacking marks left by drunken fools.

That was the problem, thought Bex. People didn't even know what they were worshipping.

Take the fucking Hand.

Ask any three members of the Hand why they believed in the cause, and you'd get three different answers.

The king has no power.

The king has too much.

There shouldn't be a king at all.

Sure, there was the general through line about magic's *disappearance*, the myth of this world's power waning and all that, but it was a crock of shit, as far as Bex could tell, and even if it wasn't, no one actually cared about sweeping tides and grand patterns, as long as here and now, magic still served *them*.

No, at the end of the day, what the Hand wanted was *change*.

And change was an easy thing to want. It was a malleable idea, like molten metal, fluid enough to take on whatever shape the people *controlling* the Hand deemed most useful. A key. A knife. A crown.

So the Hand would kill the royal family, and for a while, they would be glad, would claim that they had won, until they realized all they'd done was swap the colors flying in the palace halls.

Not that Bex cared.

At the end of the day, the coins they paid her would still spend.

Back at the table, Calin was snoring. His head had fallen back in his sleep, his throat exposed, and her fingers twitched as she entertained the idea of drawing a pretty red line across his neck. But then she'd have to tell the good lord Berras, and the thought was just enough reason to let Calin live.

She kicked his chair, jostling him just enough to make sure he was breathing, then sat back down, cracked her knuckles, and began the finding spell again.

And again.

And again.

Until finally, the spell crackled, and instead of charring black, the burning lock of hair became a single, perfect cinder, and it fell in an X onto the map, leaving a scorched mark at the river's edge, right where it met the docks. A thin tendril of smoke rose up where the mark burned the parchment.

Bex was on her feet and out the tavern door before it stopped.

Calin could sleep all he pleased.

She had a job to do.

III

It was easy to keep track of Lila Bard.

Tes could simply let the rest of the world blur together and fall away, leaving only the glaring light of the *Antari*'s power as it burned like a torch against the tapestry of other threads.

Tes followed her from the docks, and along the riverbank, trailing half a block behind, and as she did, she marveled, not at the way Bard moved, slicing easily through the street, but at the way no one seemed to notice an *Antari* walking in their midst. To them, Lila Bard was just another body, a little odd, perhaps, dressed as she was in men's clothes, but they were fine enough, and she wore them with an ease that made them come across as commonplace.

Tes followed, half expecting the *Antari* to stop and look over her shoulder at any moment, check her surroundings, to sense the weight of the girl in her wake, but she never did. Bard walked on, in the general direction of the royal palace, and for a panicked instant, Tes feared she was headed there, to the one place she had no way to follow. But then the *Antari* continued past, into a crowded square.

She strolled across the square, past vendors selling loaves of bread, and fruit, and tea—Tes resisted the urge to stop and purchase a cup from the whistling pot, the steam strong and black—before continuing on.

Bard seemed to be heading, of all places, toward the *shal*.

Tes's pulse quickened as she trailed in the magician's wake—half hoping and half fearing that she was being led back there, but soon the *Antari* turned again, this time up a narrow road.

At last, two blocks later, Bard stopped, and slipped inside a tavern inn. THE SETTING SUN, announced the sign over the door. Tes paused on the step. She counted to ten, pulled her hair back and up, even though it sent a wave of pain through her injured side, adjusted the box under her arm.

And went in.

The room was almost empty, only a handful of bodies scattered among the tavern tables, coils of blue and green and golden magic lighting the air around their shoulders.

No silver.

She scanned the tavern, and caught the hem of Lila Bard's black coat just as her boots vanished up a narrow set of stairs.

Tes drifted toward them as the innkeeper—a narrow-faced woman with a shock of white hair and threads the color of wet grass—looked up from behind the counter.

"You lost?"

Tes hesitated, then put a lin on the bar. "Just thirsty."

The innkeeper swept the coin into her pocket, and eyed Tes, clearly trying—and failing—to guess her age. "Ale or water?"

Tes bit her lip. "Do you have tea?"

The woman nodded, and shuffled away, and Tes's gaze flicked back to the stairs. No sign of the *Antari*, but there was only one set of steps, so she had to hope that this was close enough, if trouble came to call. She crouched and set the doormaker on the wooden floor beneath her feet, in the shadow of the counter. The innkeeper returned and set a steaming mug of tea on the bar, and Tes was just about to reach for it when another hand came down on top of the cup.

"You know," said a dry voice. "It's rude to follow people."

Tes looked up at the figure now sitting on the stool beside her, ringed in silver light. Lila Bard lifted the mug of tea, took a long sip, humming thoughtfully. "I told someone recently that the next time I was followed,

I would send them back in pieces. Obviously, you didn't get the message. Though I must admit, you don't look like a crow—"

Tes blinked. "A what?"

"And yet here you are, shadowing me." She studied Tes a moment longer. Her eyes were the same shade of brown, but this close, Tes had time to see that one had the faintest glassy shine, before both narrowed and the *Antari* said, "I *know* you."

Tes cringed.

It was true, they had met once, three years before. Tes had been new to freedom, to London, to need, and so perplexed by the sight of the *Antari* as she passed her in the street, she couldn't help herself.

"You tried to pick my pocket."

That wasn't strictly true. It wasn't the contents of her pocket Tes had wanted. It was the silver-bright light of the magic itself, the way it pulsed and twined, but more than that, it was the closeness of it.

Until that moment, she'd thought there was only one *Antari* in the world, Kell Maresh, the crimson prince, and even then, she'd only seen him once, and at a distance, his silver threads so bright they blurred the shape of him within. But here was another, and her hand seemed to move before her thoughts, reaching for the *Antari*'s magic, hoping to steal a thread, just one.

She hadn't been quick enough.

Or perhaps, the *Antari* had just been quicker.

Lila Bard's hand had caught her wrist, grabbed it with such force she thought the bones inside would break.

"Please," she'd said. "I need my hand."

"Then you better find another way to use it," Bard had said. But a moment later, her fingers had loosened, just a little. "How old are you?" she'd asked, and Tes had lied and said fourteen though she was barely twelve. She'd lifted her chin as she said it, because she wasn't a coward, even if she was afraid.

"Look at me," said the *Antari,* and Tes had done it, even though it hurt her eyes. Bard had leaned in, close. "Never steal something unless you're *sure* you'll get away with it."

With that, she'd flung Tes's hand away and carried on down the street. The whole interaction had lasted less than a minute, but Tes had never forgotten. Apparently, neither had Lila Bard.

The *Antari* finished Tes's tea, and stared into the dregs at the bottom of the cup. "Why are you following me?"

"I'm not."

"Don't lie," she warned, and as she said it, the magic around her twitched, and Tes felt the bones of her rib cage *constrict*, a strange and horrible sensation, one she'd never felt before, because it was forbidden. Bone magic.

"You're not—supposed to—do that," she said, gasping for air.

"Really?" said Lila, feigning surprise. The invisible hold only tightened. "Let's see if anyone notices . . ."

Tes couldn't breathe, couldn't break free, so she did the only thing she could—she reached out and grasped the nearest silver thread, felt it hum against her palm before she *pulled*. In truth, she wasn't sure what it would do, if it would do anything at all.

But the *Antari* recoiled, as if burned. The hold on Tes's rib cage vanished, and she sucked air into her aching lungs as Bard's face darkened. "What did you just do?"

Tes dragged in a ragged breath and winced, trying not to think about the feel of stitches tearing, the dampness at her side.

"Please," she said. "I'm being hunted. I need help."

Lila raised a brow. "So find a guard."

"I need *your* help."

She cocked a brow. "And why is that?"

"You're the strongest magician in London."

"Flattery will get you nowhere." Lila rose from her stool and turned to go.

"I know you're an *Antari*."

Lila Bard paused then, cocking her head, studying her with those two brown eyes. "And how do you know that?"

Tes hesitated. "I can see it. Your magic."

She seemed to consider, then shrugged. "Bully for you," she said, walking away. "Don't follow me again."

Tes got to her feet. "They're going to kill me."

"Sounds like a *you* problem."

"I have something they want. A doormaker."

"I don't—" Whatever Lila Bard had been about to say, the words died. She stopped. And when she turned back, the anger and annoyance had both been replaced by true surprise. "*You* have the *persalis*?"

Tes hesitated. So it had a name. "If a *persalis* is a device that makes doors to other places . . ."

Lila did something shocking then. She *laughed*. Not loud, but softly, to herself. "Once in a while," she murmured, "the world does provide. Now," she said, grabbing Tes by the shoulder and hauling her onto her feet. "Who's coming to kill you?"

"Assassins. They came to my shop last night and—"

"I saw. How many are there?"

"Two."

"That's all?"

"They're strong."

"I'm sure," said Lila blandly, steering Tes toward the stairs.

"Wait," she said, trying to twist around. "Where are we going?"

"Somewhere safer." The *Antari* pushed her up the stairs. "To talk."

"I have to go back. I left the box—" But the words fell away as they reached the narrow landing at the top of the stairs. Three doors led to three rooms, and one stood open, but not empty. Tes saw the ripple of crimson light as Bex strode through, palm up, the metal buttons already peeling away from Lila's coat, shooting toward the molten ball of metal in the assassin's hand.

"Look out!" shouted Tes right as the metal divided itself into nails and the nails shot toward them. Lila Bard shoved Tes down to the floor, but the slivers of metal only changed course and followed, falling like sharpened rain. Tes curled in, braced for the impact, the piercing pain, but the nails missed skin, found cloth instead, pinning her cuffs, her collar, the hem of her coat to the wooden floor of the landing.

She twisted, trying to get free, but Lila was already on her feet, a dagger in one hand. She slashed at Bex, but as she did, the blade simply dissolved, and the killer slammed her boot into Lila's chest and sent her crashing down the stairs into the tavern below.

Shouts went up, and Tes heard the *Antari* ordering *everyone out,* and then the shape of the assassin filled her vision as Bex knelt before Tes, watching as she fought to free one of her hands. The fabric at her cuff tore a little, but didn't give. And if there had been amusement in the killer's face the night before, it was long gone. Her eyes were flat and grey and dangerous, and a vicious bruise was blooming beneath both, as if her nose had been recently broken. She flicked her wrist, and a short, sharp blade took shape in her palm.

"Where is it?" demanded Bex.

Tes swallowed, and shook her head. "I don't have it."

It was the truth. She'd left it sitting on the floor next to the bar below.

"Wrong answer," said Bex, and then, before Tes could tear free, she drove the knife down through the back of Tes's trapped hand.

Her mind went white with pain as the blade sank through to the hilt, the tip lodging in the wood below.

"Hurts, doesn't it?" hissed Bex, and Tes felt a scream rise up her throat, but when it came spilling out, she couldn't hear it, not over the sudden howl of white noise in her ears.

A wall of wind slammed past her, and into Bex, sending her back across the landing and into the far wall, hard enough to splinter wood.

Tes gritted her teeth and yanked the knife out, choking back a sob as the steel came free. She thought she might be sick, turned her head and saw a swish of coat, and a pair of black boots as Lila Bard strode past her, blood dripping down her cheek.

Across the landing, Bex pushed off the wall and straightened, rolling her shoulders with an audible crack.

"Ice or stone?" asked the *Antari,* and when Bex only cocked her head in question, Lila touched the cut at her temple and said, "Never mind. I'll choose."

She moved fast, faster than a body should. A blur of limbs, her bloodstained hand thrust out as she shot across the landing, and Tes saw the silver of her magic twitch and brighten as the words spilled out.

"As Isera."

The spell took shape just as her fingers grabbed at Bex's front, but somehow, the killer twisted free at the last moment. The *Antari*'s hand found cloak instead of skin, and frost shot across the fabric—through it—turning the cloth to ice in the time it took to say the spell. Bex ducked and spun out of the cloak and it fell, and shattered on the landing floor between them.

The killer stared down at the frozen shards, and for the first time since she strode into Tes's shop, the bland arrogance was gone, replaced by surprise, and perhaps, even, a touch of fear.

"Not fair, *Antari*," she said as the metal bracer on her forearm unspooled, forming into blades.

Lila Bard only shrugged. "Fair has no place in a fight."

Bex's blades came singing through the air, but this time, the *Antari* was ready. She didn't duck or dodge. Instead, she flung her own hands out, and the metal shivered to a stop.

"Just the one trick, then?" she asked. "Fine. But I can play it, too."

The blades twitched, and then began to turn back toward Bex. The killer clenched her teeth, and they stopped, hovered, caught between them. In the air, Tes saw the strands of magic drawn taut as rope.

"When two magicians wield the same element," said Lila Bard, "it becomes a battle of wills. Let's see, then, which of us folds first."

Her face was smooth, one eyebrow cocked as if it were all just a game, but Tes could see the strain in the air around her—she was using all her strength. So was Bex. The blades shivered, and the landing began to tremble as the two wills drew not just on the knives, but the surrounding metal. The hinges groaned and the nails pinning her down drew free, and Tes did what she should have done the moment the fight started.

She got out of the fucking way.

Tes scrambled down the stairs. She didn't look back, not when halfway down she felt the tension break, the shudder of air and hiss of steel and the thunk of metal as sharpened points found wood.

She hit the ground floor and staggered, pain shooting through her bloody hand and wounded side, but she kept going, across the empty tavern to the door, which she flung open, only to collide with a man coming in.

She stumbled back, felt a hand on her shoulder, but there was no malice in it, only a gentle firmness as he steadied her. She looked up and saw silver light, saw red hair, parted by a streak of white, saw two eyes, one blue, the other black.

Kell Maresh, the *Antari* prince.

Tes was pretty sure she was supposed to bow, but her side hurt too much and he was still holding her up so she managed only a weak "*Mas vares.*"

Like Lila Bard, he stood at the center of a silver net, but something was wrong with the threads. Where the other *Antari*'s shone bright and steady, his flickered and frayed.

Broken. His magic was broken.

Kell Maresh looked down at her and frowned. "You're hurt."

And Tesali Ranek looked up at him and said, "So are you."

His frown deepened, a question forming on his lips. But he never got a chance to ask, because in that moment, the building rumbled and shook from the battle upstairs, and Kell looked up, over Tes's head, and Tes looked past him into the street and screamed, "Look out!"

Kell was already turning. Already drawing a sword from his hip as he did, the blade singing as it clashed against Calin's ax with ringing force.

"Get back," he warned, and it took Tes an instant to realize he was speaking to her. She retreated into the tavern, and so did the *Antari* prince, Calin on their heels. The second killer was just as tall as Kell Maresh, and twice as wide, his body blocking out the light of the street beyond as surely as a door.

"Now this is a treat," he said in that broken-stone voice. "I've killed a lot of people, but never one like you."

"An *Antari*? Or a prince?"

His face split in a wretched grin. "You know, they say you're hard to kill. I think they're just not trying hard enough."

The ax swung again, and Kell Maresh produced a second sword, crossed the two in time to stop the weapon's force.

461

"You'll need more than swords," said the killer.

"I doubt it," said Kell. "You look like you've lost a lot of fights."

Calin's smile widened. "No," he said. "The losers are all dead."

He surged at the prince, who twisted, and blocked, and Tes saw her chance, and bolted for the open door. She was nearly there when it slammed shut in her face.

"Don't let her leave!" shouted Lila from the top of the stairs. "She has the *persalis*."

The *Antari* prince glanced at Tes, eyes wide in surprise, and in that instant, Calin spun his ax and slammed its handle into the prince's cheek.

Kell Maresh staggered, lip splitting from the blow. His fingers went to the cut, and came away red.

"Come on, princeling," goaded Calin. "Don't tell me that eye is just for show."

Kell's hand clenched, and Tes saw his magic twitch, the way Lila's had before she called forth the freezing spell. But then he spit the blood onto the floor.

"You're not worth it," he said, and as Calin roared, and came again, Kell swept his arm across a table, sending an abandoned pint into the killer's face. The glass didn't shatter, but the spirit splashed the killer's front. Kell scraped his blades, and a spark leapt off, and onto Calin. It caught, fire racing over the killer's front.

He flailed, struggling to douse the flames, and Tes knew what she had to do.

She pushed off the door, launched herself back across the tavern. She fell to her knees beneath the bar, searching with her hands until she found the hidden parcel, and pulled it out. The doormaker—the *persalis,* Lila had called it—the source of all this strife.

She began to tug at the threads, pulling them apart, but this time, she wasn't just disassembling the spell. Her fingers flew across the magic, as across the room, Calin had put himself out, smoke rising from his singed dishwater hair. He surged toward the *Antari* prince, as the ceiling above them gave way, and Bex came crashing down. She landed in a crouch atop a table and rolled out of the way just as Lila dropped through, blood running into one eye and a wicked smile on her face.

The stories about Delilah Bard were true.

Despite the violence, and the chaos, she was clearly having *fun*.

She held in her hands a pair of blades now; not steel, but conjured out of stone and ice.

"Some people," she mused, "just don't know how to die."

Blood darkened the cloth on Bex's arm and thigh, and stained her cheek, and there was a feral light in her eyes, her magic burning crimson on the air around her as she called her metal home into a shield, then a sword, then a molten whip.

Tes worked faster, blood slicking her wounded hand as her shaking fingers frantically tied off a knot. The building groaned, and Tes wondered how much longer it would hold. She didn't want to find out.

Calin swung his ax, only to find that the metal edge had disappeared, drawn into Bex's fight, while Kell's sword held firm, its edge gleaming with spellwork. He brought the blade to the killer's throat, but Calin only smiled.

"I'll get that magic out of you," he said, "one way or another." The floor rumbled as he spoke, and earth shot up between the slats, turned to tendrils. Kell Maresh slashed through them, but they simply parted and re-formed. One found his wrist, and clamped down, dragging his sword out of the way, exposing the prince's chest, and throat.

"*Stop!*"

Four heads turned toward Tes.

She was on her feet, holding the *persalis* out in both hands.

"This is what you came for, right?" she said. "Then take it."

Lila Bard looked at her in horror. Bex smiled grimly, and took a step toward her, and as she did, Tes's fingers twitched, pulling on the strings at the edge of the spell. A light flickered through them like a lit fuse, a spark only she could see. It skated, bright and fast across the surface of the box.

And then, the *persalis burned*.

IV

"No!" shouted Bex, surging forward, but Lila blocked her path as the object in Tes's hands went up in flame. It burned fast, far faster than it should—days of work, erased by a single spell—and then the *persalis* crumbled, like ash, between her fingers.

"Shouldn't have done that, little girl," growled Calin.

Bex stared, face going from scarlet to grey.

"You're dead," she snarled, metal coiling back around her forearm, but Lila Bard stepped between the killer and the girl.

"So keen to go again?" she asked, a sharp thrill in her voice. "You should know, I've been holding back." The air whipped around her as she said it. The whole inn groaned. The light in the lanterns peeled into ribbons. "And Kell here, well, he hasn't even gotten started." Those ribbons of flame circled his shoulders. The wind caught his copper hair. If Tes didn't know better, if she couldn't see better, she might have thought the magic was his own.

The two killers finally seemed to take stock of their situation. Blood stained Bex's skin from a dozen weeping cuts. Smoke wafted off Calin's half-burned shirt. Two of the strongest magicians in the world stood between them and Tes, and the *persalis* they'd come for was nothing but a smear of soot on the splintered floor.

Calin flashed Kell a smile that felt like a threat, but said nothing.

Bex's eyes slid past the *Antari*, and landed on Tes.

"You and I," she said coldly, "are not done."

Lila flicked her wrist, and the tavern door swung wide.

"Run along now," she said. "Unless you'd like to stay and tell us who hired you. We can pour a pint and talk about the Hand."

Bex's mouth twitched, but whatever she was about to say was cut off by Calin throwing his arms wide. His power flared, and every one of the tables and chairs came flying toward them.

Tes flinched, but Kell and Lila moved at once, their hands outstretched, silver magic flaring bright as the torrent of wood splintered and broke apart against a wall of will. By the time the debris collapsed to the ground, the room beyond was empty.

The killers were gone.

Lila Bard sighed, and dropped her hand, but Kell Maresh buckled forward, heaving, sweat shining on his brow. The threads around him spasmed and sparked. Tes was right—something was very wrong with the *Antari*'s magic.

She watched, expecting Bard to hurry to the prince's side, to help him up, but she just shook her head and said, "Honestly, Kell." And then she turned, and grabbed Tes's arm, fingers vising as she dragged her toward the stairs.

"Can't stay here" was all she said by way of explanation. Kell straightened, and made his way to the bar, where the innkeeper had risen to her feet.

"What's wrong with him?" she asked as Lila Bard hauled her up the stairs.

"He's an idiot," answered the *Antari*, glancing back over her shoulder.

"The palace will pay for everything," the prince was saying to the frazzled innkeeper. "And I'll send magicians round to fix the damage."

They reached the landing—what was left of it, the walls cracked, the rug rucked up, one corner quietly burning—and the *Antari* steered them past a pool of blood on the landing that was definitely hers, and several more that weren't. She pushed Tes into a bedroom. A chest sat open at the foot of the bed, black clothes spilling out, a ghoulish face jutted up, and Tes recoiled before realizing it was a horned mask.

"Let me go," she protested, but Lila only snorted, pushing her toward the wall where a small stain darkened the wood.

She reached up and touched her cheek, where blood leaked from a deep cut, and then used that blood to draw the symbol fresh. Tes watched as a single silver thread drew away from the net and laid itself over the mark.

"Kell?" she called over her shoulder, and moments later the prince appeared, looking weary as he brought his hand to Tes's shoulder.

"Hold on," he said gently, and then Lila was saying something, and the room was tumbling away, and Tes was falling, not down, but *apart*, the whole world unraveling around her, thread by thread and all

465

at once. And when it wove itself together again, she was no longer in the ruined tavern, but standing in a massive marble-floored room, with gilded curtains and an ornate bed. She looked up, and saw the night sky, only it wasn't a sky, but hundreds of gossamer lengths that stretched and billowed to form the illusion.

A pair of glass doors gave way onto a balcony, the crimson ribbon of the Isle shining far below, and Tes realized that she was in the royal palace. A wave of dizziness swept through her, and she reached out to steady herself, but the instant her hand met the cloth edge of a sofa, she recoiled, half in pain, and half in horror. Her hand. She'd tied a kerchief around it at some point, but the cloth had long soaked through, and a stain now darkened the ornate fabric.

"Don't worry," said the prince, sinking heavily into a chair. "The servants are well versed in removing blood."

The silver threads around him twitched. Tes found herself following the path they made, as if he were an object open on her desk, her fingers tracing their way to find the breaks.

Kell Maresh saw her staring. "What is it?"

Tes ducked her head, and said nothing.

Lila Bard had stopped before a full-length mirror, and seemed to be taking note of her own injuries, examining the cut on her brow, the tear in her shirt. Her gaze met Tes's in the reflection.

"That was a clever ruse," she said, turning from the glass. "Now where is it?"

Tes stared at the *Antari*. "Where is what?"

"The *persalis*."

Tes's head was spinning. She didn't understand. "I destroyed it. In the tavern. You saw me."

"I saw what you wanted them to see. But it was obviously a decoy."

Tes said nothing, and the amusement died on Lila's face, replaced by a slow but vivid horror.

Her boots echoed sharply as they crossed the floor. "You mean to tell me," she said, enunciating every word, "that what you destroyed back there was the *real persalis*."

466

Tes's silence spoke for itself.

Lila shook her head. "Empty your pockets."

When Tes did not, Lila grabbed her roughly by the arm.

"Gently," warned Kell. "She's clearly injured."

But Lila began to search them for her. When her hand grazed Tes's injured side, she hissed in pain, the whole room threatening to disappear. When it steadied, the *Antari* was holding, of all things, the dead owl. It stared up at her, one eye blue, the other black.

"What the hell is this?" she asked.

In response to the question, the owl cocked his skull, and fluttered his bone wings.

Lila yelped, and dropped the bird. Tes lunged to catch it before it struck the floor. Her side screamed at the movement, and sweat broke out along her brow, but the little owl was safe.

"His name," she said, breathless, "is Vares."

Kell Maresh looked up at the mention. So did the bird. Tes had to resist the urge to laugh. It wasn't funny. Nothing was funny. She had lost a lot of blood.

Lila crossed her arms. "How do we know that was the real *persalis*? Maybe you've stashed it somewhere."

"Why would I? I never wanted anything to do with it! I run a repair shop. Someone brought it in to me, to be fixed. I didn't even know what it *did*."

Lila's eyes narrowed, and even though one was glass, they both seemed to look through her. "If you didn't know, how could you fix it?"

Tes hesitated. "I'm good at my job."

The *Antari* came closer. "The world is full of good liars," she said. "You're not one of them."

"Lila," warned Kell, but the *Antari*'s focus hung entirely on Tes.

"In my experience," the woman said, "it takes one of two things to survive in the world. Talent. Or cunning. And a cunning person would have found a way to save the *persalis*. You must have quite the talent."

Tes swallowed, the truth rising in her throat. Her breath shuddered. At some point, she had begun to shake. She wondered if she was going into shock, thought it rude, that after everything she'd been through, her body was choosing now to fall apart.

She reached to steady herself on a table, but her balance was off, or else the table had moved, because she missed it, stumbled, gasped in pain as the movement tore at her side.

"She's injured," said Kell, getting to his feet.

"Hands bleed," said Lila with a dismissive wave.

But the prince was staring at Tes's stomach. "Not that much."

She followed his gaze. A dark stain was spreading across her shirtfront. "Oh," she said slowly. "That." Her teeth were chattering.

"Lila, she's *hurt*," said Kell. "You should heal her."

But the *Antari* wasn't listening. Her thin fingers found Tes's chin, and forced it up to meet her gaze.

"How did you fix the *persalis*?" Her face slid in and out of focus. Tes was so tired. Tired of running. Tired of keeping secrets. And if anyone would understand how it felt, to have a rare and wanted power, surely it was an *Antari*.

"I can see it," she said, the words sliding between her teeth. "I can see the threads of magic that run through spells. That's how I knew what it was. And how to fix it."

For a moment, after she said it, all Tes felt was relief. Heavy as a blanket.

The prince made a sound that might have been a laugh. Lila and Tes both turned to him.

"Alucard will be devastated," he said, "to learn he's not the only one gifted with such sight."

Tes stiffened. "There are others?"

"It would appear that way," said Lila.

"I didn't know." Tes looked down at Vares, the little strings of light wound like wire through his bones. "I've never met anyone else who could manipulate the threads of magic."

It was a very large room, but in that moment, all the air seemed to go out of it. Tes looked up, and found both *Antari* staring at her.

She felt as if she'd said something wrong.

"You're a tinkerer," said Lila slowly, as if understanding the words for the first time. "You see broken magic, and you fix it." Tes nodded slowly. Lila looked to Kell Maresh. "Can you fix him?"

The words hung in the air. Tes's mind struggled to wrap itself around them. "I don't tinker with living things."

"That isn't what I asked," said Lila. "You have just said you can not only see magic, but lay your hands on it. You can mend it when it's broken."

"I repair broken *objects*," said Tes. "I've never fixed a person."

"But *can* you do it?" she demanded.

"I don't know!" answered Tes. "To even try would be against the laws of magic—"

"Hang the laws," said Lila Bard, "if they are all that's in your way." She ran a hand through her dark hair. "If it can be done, then you will do it." There it was. The order. Her power reduced to a tool, wielded by another hand.

Tes stood as tall as her injuries would allow. "And if I refuse?"

She didn't see Lila draw a knife, but suddenly one was pressed against her throat. "Then so help me god, I will cut off pieces until you change your mind."

Kell was on his feet, at Lila's side, his hand tight on her arm.

"*Enough*," he said, sliding into the royal tongue.

Lila shook him off. "You want me to *heal* her?" she snapped in the same language, gesturing with the tip of her knife as she spoke. "Fine. I will. As soon as she agrees to heal *you*."

Tes shook her head. "There is a difference between an object and a human being," she said to the prince, switching back to Arnesian. "If I make a mistake—"

"Then do not make one," warned Lila.

But Tes held Kell Maresh's two-toned gaze. She saw the strain in the set of his jaw, in the crease between his eyes, in the way he held himself, even now. Could it be done? She did not know. She felt herself wanting to reach for those broken threads, wanting to help. But this *Antari* was not an object in her shop. Repair was often trial and error. Half the time she fastened the threads wrong inside a spell, and had to undo the work and start again. But the vessel did not care when it was made of wood, or clay. A living body could fail under that strain.

469

"Your Highness . . ." she began.

He looked at her, tired, but resigned. "It's all right," he said, "I understand."

"I don't," snapped Lila. "I have watched you suffer for seven years. Seven years I have searched high and low for a cure, some way to fix what was broken. Here she is, and you refuse to even make her *try*."

Kell sighed, and rubbed his eyes. "She says she can't—"

"Can't and won't are different things."

Kell gave the other *Antari* a heavy look. "It is not worth the risk. Just heal her, Lila. Please."

Tes saw Lila's anger waver on that last word, a door cracking to reveal something ragged, pained, before it slammed shut. She flung her blade at Kell's feet. It skidded over the marble floor, came to rest against his boot.

"Do it yourself," she snapped, "since you don't want any help."

Kell sighed. And then he knelt and retrieved the blade.

"It's all right," said Tes, the room swaying in her sight. "You don't have to."

"I know," he said gently, bringing the knife to his thumb. A muscle ticced in Lila's jaw. Her shoulders twitched, as if willing the rest of her to intervene.

Tes watched the skin part, dark blood welling as he reached to touch her and—

"Oh for fuck's sake, stop," said Lila, pulling the prince away. Her other hand was already bleeding, her fingers vising around Tes's wrist.

"*As Hasari,*" growled the *Antari,* and as the spell rolled over Tes, the pain dropped like a stone in a deep well.

Healing was a gradual thing, pain lessening from a sharpened point to a dull ache before it faded. Now, it simply fell away. Tes could see the silver magic twining with her own, see it flare around her as her side knit itself beneath her shirt. Her hand closed beneath the kerchief. The weakness washed away, and left her pulse strong and steady in its wake.

Tes sighed in relief as Lila's fingers dropped from her wrist, leaving a smear of red behind. "That was the first and only time I bleed for you."

"Thank you," she said.

"Yes, thank you," echoed Kell.

470

"Oh, shut up," snapped Lila, turning on him.

Tes, meanwhile, started for the gilded door, hoping it led out, out of the room, out of the palace. She went to pull it open, but a hand slammed into the wood, forcing it closed.

"Going somewhere?" demanded Lila, her tone full of menace, and Tes realized how wrong she'd been, to seek out the *Antari*'s aid. Lila Bard wanted the same thing as Bex and Calin—to use her.

"I'm grateful you healed me," said Tes. "But I can't help you, with the *persalis,* or the prince. You have no reason to keep me here."

"We are doing you a *favor,*" said Lila. "It isn't safe out there. Not with the Hand."

"She's right," said the prince. "The two we met today will still be looking for you."

Tes shook her head. She'd wanted a champion. Now all she wanted was to get as far away as possible.

"I'll take my chances," she said, tugging on the door, but Lila must have been using magic to hold it fast, because it did not so much as give.

"This is the safest place in the city," said the *Antari,* a grim smile tugging at her mouth. "Here, I'll show you." With that, she wrenched the door open, and shouted, "Guards!"

"Lila," said Kell wearily, as two soldiers appeared in the doorway.

"Put her in a cell."

Tes tried to retreat into the room, but Lila put a hand in the center of her back.

"We're not done talking, you and I," she hissed in Tes's ear, before forcing her forward, into the hall, and the waiting arms of the palace guards.

Tes fought, for whatever it was worth, which wasn't much. Lila had healed her wounds, but she was still half the soldiers' size, and before she could so much as reach to pluck a thread of their magic, her arms were forced behind her.

The last thing she saw was Kell Maresh sinking into a chair behind Lila Bard, who smiled at Tes before she flicked her wrist, and the door slammed shut, and the guards hauled her away.

V

Tes should have gotten on a ship.

She'd been right there, could have stolen away aboard one of the many vessels crowding the London docks, and dropped the doormaker over the side when they were safely out to sea, and started again in another city, on another shore. There would always be work for a man like Haskin, which meant there would always be work for a girl like her.

And if Bex and Calin had followed?

Better to be free and on the run than sitting safely in a cell.

What's the difference between a gamble and a good purchase? her father had quizzed her more than once. *Retrospect.*

Two soldiers stood a short distance beyond the cell, their heads bent together, their voices little more than murmurs. She looked past them to the stairs they'd brought her down. The bedroom had been on the third floor. She was somewhere beneath the first now. She'd counted the steps down, reached thirty before they hit the cells, guessed that meant they were housed in one of the pillars that made up the palace base, held the *soner rast* aloft over the Isle. She wondered if that meant she was underwater. She looked around. There were three other cells, but all were empty.

There was no cot, so Tes sat cross-legged on the cool stone floor. A pair of manacles hung around her wrists. They weren't spelled to dampen magic. They didn't need to be. The entire cell was warded. The air had a leaden weight that reminded her of that other London, the one without magic, but that had been an almost pleasant absence—this felt like a wet blanket dousing flames.

She could see the spellwork of the ward—it was an odd, confusing magic required to negate itself. The lines of power hung suspended in the air, shivering in place, and when she pulled Vares from her pocket and set him on the ground, he sat there, lifeless, his skull drooping forward, the many tiny filaments that wove between his bones gone dark. Tes rose, and perched his little body between the bars, to see how far the wards reached.

"Vares?" she whispered, her tone rising in question.

He didn't move.

She left him on the ledge, and sank back to the ground, and waited.

Tes studied her right hand, where Bex's knife had gone through. Ran her fingers along her palm, the back of her hand. Nothing but a thin silver scar, painless and smooth. She knew the same was true for the wound in her side. It no longer hurt to breathe.

Behind her eyes, Kell Maresh buckled to one knee.

You could fix him, said a voice in her head. It sounded an awful lot like Lila Bard's. Tes let her hands fall back into her lap.

"*Kers la?*" said a voice.

She looked up in time to see one of the soldiers pluck Vares from between the bars.

"Don't—" she said, feigning protest, but the guard was already retreating with the owl. One stride, that was all it took for Vares to come back to life, his little bone wings flapping in the soldier's hand. That told Tes something. Only the cell itself was warded.

The soldier gave a small, delighted laugh. "Hey, Hel," he said. "It moves."

As if on cue, Vares gave another flutter, and clicked his beak.

Traitor, thought Tes.

"Let me see," said the second, holding out his hand.

The first shook his head. "*Nas,* you're always breaking things."

"Come on, then."

"You have to be gentle. . . ."

At least the soldiers were occupied.

"Look at its eyes," said the first. "One blue, one black. Just like the prince."

"Doesn't have red feathers, though."

"Well, it might have, once. You never know."

Tes rolled her eyes, and slumped onto her back, staring up at the barred ceiling.

"Think," she whispered to herself.

This was just another kind of puzzle. A problem to be solved. The entire prison wasn't warded, only the cell, but unfortunately, the cell was where she was currently housed. Which made things tricky, but not impossible.

She studied the lines of the ward that ran overhead, traced the lines of it down the bars.

Wards were a kind of paradox. After all, they muted magic, but at their core, they were still *active spells*. That meant, even when they blocked power from being used, they had to make an exception for their own. And if there was a source of working magic, she could take it apart.

Tes sat up.

She glanced at the soldiers, who were now sitting on a bench, Vares perched between them, their attention wholly on the occasional movements of the dead owl. Tes turned around, putting her back to them, her attention on the bars at the other side of the cell. She rose and approached the bars, got close enough to study the iron-colored threads that wound around the cell. Sure enough, unlike her magic, which was pinned in place, the power here was flowing.

Tes reached out her cuffed hands, and rested them against the bars, as if bored. But as her fingers met the steel, she hooked one of those iron threads, and pulled and—

A spasm tore through her body, the air forced from her lungs as the world went white. The next thing she knew, she was lying on her back on the cell floor, ears ringing. Tes coughed, and curled in against the pain as she tried to breathe.

"Shouldn't do that," said one of the soldiers blandly.

Tes groaned and sat up. The two men were now feeding Vares bites of sweetcake.

"Are you hungry, little Kell?" cooed one as the owl clacked its beak, and the crumbs tumbled through.

Her stomach growled.

"Excuse me," she called out to the soldiers. "Could the *human* get something to eat?"

They ignored her.

"Assholes," muttered Tes.

She sagged, letting her head rest on her folded arms as she wracked her mind, trying to think of a way out. She was still trying when a pair of boots echoed on the prison stairs.

Tes looked up, expecting to find Lila Bard, come to continue her interrogation. But when the woman stepped out of the shadows, the lanterns caught on a different face.

The two soldiers shot to their feet.

"*Mas res,*" they said, and Tes realized she was staring at the queen.

VI

Kell lay on the sofa, his coat cast off, and a cold cloth over his eyes. The pain was receding like a tide, leaving only a weary ache in its wake. He didn't need to see the king's chamber to paint the picture in his mind. The slosh of spirits and scrape of glass as Rhy poured a drink from a decanter. Lila's irritated steps as she paced the floor, each clipped stride a rebuke, the brief muffling of her boots when they crossed from stone to silk and back again.

"Judging by the soreness in my jaw," said Rhy, "I'm guessing you've had a busy day."

"Indeed," said Kell. "There's an inn that will need some reconstruction."

The doors swung open, and Alucard swept in. "You left me waiting in that ruined shop," he said. "Gone to fetch something, you said. If a crow hadn't told me you were here, I'd still be standing around, kicking stones."

"Apologies," said Lila blandly. "I was busy getting my hands on the apprentice from Haskin's. And the *persalis,* too."

Alucard's boots stopped abruptly. "You succeeded?"

"Don't sound so surprised."

"Where are they, then?"

"Lila threw the apprentice in a prison cell," offered Kell.

"For safekeeping," she cut in. "As for the *persalis,* it was, regrettably, destroyed."

"Are you sure?" asked Rhy.

"I watched it burn," said Lila.

"A decoy?" asked Alucard.

Kell could practically hear Lila grind her teeth. "Apparently not. I searched her, to be sure. Found nothing but a dead owl."

"Excuse me?" said Rhy and Alucard at the same time.

"Apparently it's a pet. It has a blue eye and a black eye and she calls it Vares."

"I can't decide," said Rhy, "whether that's charming or creepy."

"Both," said Kell and Lila at the same time.

"There's more," she went on. "She's like you, Alucard."

"Devastatingly handsome?" he asked, pouring a drink. "Utterly charming?"

"Humble?" added Rhy.

"She can see magic."

Kell heard the glass stop halfway to Alucard's mouth. "Really?"

"And unlike you," he added, "she can *touch* it."

Kell didn't *need* to see Alucard's face, but he found he *wanted* to. He dragged the cold cloth from his eyes, and flinched. The sun was sinking beyond the windows, shards of light knifing through the room.

"How does it feel?" he asked. "To know you're not the best at something? That there's someone out there who can actually put that power to good *use?*"

Alucard glared at Kell. It was worth opening his eyes for that. It made him feel just the slightest bit better. Until Lila ruined it by saying, "She can heal Kell's magic."

Rhy's head jerked up.

Kell sighed, running a hand through his hair. "She didn't say that."

"She didn't have to. She's a fixer. She can fix this." Lila gestured at Kell. "Fix you."

"Let it go," he said wearily.

"No. You may be content to live like this, but I won't watch you—"

"You think I relish my condition?"

"I think you are resigned to it," said Lila. "I think you have been burned by magic so badly that now you shy away from any source of heat."

"It is not the magic that stops me." He felt his throat tighten around the words. "I would give anything to be severed from this pain, one way or another. Every day, I pray it will hurt less, that there will come a day when I no longer reach for magic, even though the thought of living without it makes me wish that I were dead."

476

"Then let the girl try and *fix* it."

"I *cannot!*" he shouted, the words splintering his voice. "I cannot, Lila. Don't you understand? If it were just my life at stake—but it is *not*. You seem to forget, I am bound to my brother. If the girl's work failed, if it went wrong, my life is not the only one that would be forfeit."

Lila, at last, said nothing.

Across the room, Rhy cleared his throat. "If that is what's stopping you, Kell," he said, "you have my permission."

Alucard looked horrified. He opened his mouth to speak, but Kell cut in first.

"It's not *permission*," he seethed. "It's a weight. One you do not wish to hold, so you force it onto me. You might be willing to gamble with your life, but I am not."

Alucard crossed his arms. "For once, Kell and I are in agreement. It is not worth the risk."

Lila's gaze raked across the room. He could feel her anger, in the tensing air, in the pressure on the glass, in the flare of the candles.

"Hang you all," she muttered, turning on her heel.

"Don't leave the palace," warned Kell.

Lila raised one hand in a rude gesture, and stormed out.

The doors banged shut behind her. Kell folded forward in his chair, head falling into his hands.

He was so very tired.

The sofa dipped beneath the weight of a new body. Kell didn't need to lift his head to know it was his brother. A lifetime of sharing space, and he knew the way the air bent around Rhy's shoulders, long before the ringed fingers settled on his sleeve.

"We should talk about this."

"There is nothing to discuss," said Kell.

"If there's a chance to free you from this—"

"No."

"You would do anything to spare me, Kell," pressed Rhy. "Why can't I do the same for you?"

He dragged his head up, met his brother's golden eyes. "Because I am not the king."

"You are my family. Surely that matters more than any crown."

"The two of you," muttered Alucard, "always competing for the role of martyr. And you," he snapped at Rhy, "you would do the Hand's work for them."

"At least I know that if I die," said Rhy, "you will make a handsome king."

"And what of Ren?" asked Alucard.

Rhy's expression faltered. It was one thing, to be a brother, or a king, another to be a father. Pain flashed like a current beneath his skin. Kell saw it, and squeezed his brother's knee.

"There is no need to speak like this. It is my choice, and I have made it. Besides," he said, pushing himself to his feet, "I am getting quite good with a sword."

Rhy blinked, and tried to smile. It didn't reach his eyes.

Alucard reached out to the nearest lantern, as if grazing the threads that only he could see. But he frowned as his fingers went straight through. He set down his glass, and started for the door.

"Where are you going?" asked Rhy.

"To the prison," he said, straightening his coat. "I for one would like to see this girl, whose power is so much greater than my own." He stepped out into the hall, but held the door. "Well?" he asked. "Are you coming?"

VII

WHITE LONDON

Kosika woke to laughter.

It rose like tendrils of smoke through the floor of her room, thin, but impossible to ignore. She tried tossing and turning for several moments before finally flinging off her sheets. It was the middle of the night, but she pulled on a robe and followed the sounds out into the hall. There were no guards. That was odd. She padded barefoot down the tower stairs, the sound growing with each descending step. By the time she reached the third floor, she heard music. By the second, voices. By the first, the chime of glasses and the shuffle of feet.

The feast day was long over. The celebration should have dimmed by now.

Instead, it had grown, bloomed into something raucous and bright.

A hundred lanterns filled the castle hall, which brimmed with bodies, a sea of jewel-toned dresses and capes studded by the silver-clad Vir.

Kosika strode across the room. Or tried. The crowd should have parted for her, should have bowed, but they did not move. In fact, they seemed to close ranks, and jostle, so that she had to force her way between their limbs like an intruding child.

A fountain stood in the center of the hall, the sound of its spilling water lost beneath the burble of voices and the tinkling laughter, a statue of Holland looming over the pool, but as Kosika got close, she realized it wasn't Holland the Servant, or the King, or the Saint. It was Holland, *her* Holland, and he was not made of stone, though he might as well have been. He did not move, did not look at her, only stood, white hair rising in a crown, and head bowed over a large bowl in his hands. A bowl that spilled wine into the basin below.

Only it wasn't wine, of course. It was blood. His blood. It ran in rivers down his arms into the pool, and as she watched, the people dipped their empty glasses in the basin, and drank, drank it all up in single gulping swallows, their mouths stained red.

"Stop," she said, but no one listened.

"*STOP*," she shouted, in a voice that should have shattered the glasses in their hands, should have snuffed the lanterns and split the marble floor. But nothing happened. No one seemed to hear. The party continued.

Kosika staggered back, away from the horrible fountain. Away from the bodies, which parted now, to let her go. Only the Vir turned their heads to watch as she fled the hall, and flung open the castle doors, and surged out into the night.

She stumbled, body lurching as she missed a step, because the step wasn't there. The castle was gone. So were the voices and music and laughter. Instead, she stood in the center of the Silver Wood, bare feet sinking into mossy earth.

It was so quiet. So still. Only the whisper of her breathing, the steady thud of her heart. Only, it wasn't *her* heart thudding. The beat came from

479

somewhere beneath her feet. The eye-shaped knots in the trees watched, unblinking, as she sank to her knees and began to dig, fingers clawing at the soft, dark soil.

She dug and dug and dug, the beating below as steady as a fist against a wooden door, until at last, her fingers found the heart. She swept away the dirt, until it lay exposed in the bed of earth.

It was soft, and human-sized, and yet, it wasn't the tender meat of flesh, but something else, not red but silver-white, glowing with the milky shine of the Sijlt. And when it pulsed beneath her hands, she knew it was the heart of the city, of the world. Roots coursed and ran like veins deep into the soil to every side, but they were loose enough to let her lift the heart.

It beat in time with hers, and as it did, she began to pour her own power into it, felt the magic leave her, and not leave her, because it was still there, in her hands, in the heart that grew brighter and brighter, brighter than the river, brighter than the sun in the sky, and the trees bloomed and the sky grew blue and the ground became a tangle of grass and flower and sapling and fruit.

And for a moment, she saw her London as it must have been once, as it could be again, if she could feed the heart enough.

But even as she thought it, the light faltered in her hand, began to dim again.

"No," she whispered, tried to pour more power in, but she had nothing left to give, and still, the glow faded, the light ebbed, weakening until it was not a blazing sun but a lantern, a candle, a small and fragile flame. And as it faded, so did the other version of her world.

The flowers died and the sky went grey and the leaves fell from the trees and the earth turned hard and cold beneath her knees and everything took on a pale and frosted glaze.

"No," she pleaded, as the light died in her hands, and the heart stopped beating, and everything fell apart.

Kosika woke with dirt in her hands.

She blinked for a moment, disoriented by the absence of a bed, the dappled sunlight where a ceiling should have been. She wasn't in her chamber at all, but lying beneath a tree, its branches dotted by clusters of unripe fruit, and even though the ground beneath her back was hard, she could feel slivers of grass tickling her neck.

Kosika held up a hand, and saw dark soil sticking to her fingers, where she must have gripped the ground in sleep. Voices wafted toward her, and she sat up and saw Nasi and Lark sitting a few feet away, their heads bowed together over a book. He said something in her ear, the words too soft to reach, but she was close enough to see the way Nasi smiled, the twitch of her lips tugging on her scarred cheek, setting off the tracery of silver lines.

"It's rude to whisper," announced Kosika, brushing the dirt from her palms.

Nasi cocked her head. "Ruder than it is to wake a sleeping queen?"

The dream rose up, brushing against her mind, and Kosika wished they *had* woken her sooner. Besides, she didn't like the idea of sleeping so exposed—but she hadn't been able to help herself. She remembered drifting off, feeling full and tired and sun-warmed as a peach.

A picnic sat between them on a wool blanket, a bowl of cherries and a tray of sandwiches, a paring knife in a block of cheese, and three cups half-filled from a pitcher of tea.

It had been Lark's idea, the picnic.

He'd shown up at her chamber door that morning, while Nasi was somehow beating her at kol-kot, a basket swinging from one hand, and announced it was too fine a day to be inside. Sure enough, sun was streaming in the open window. The weather was always nicer after a tithe. As for the picnic, he'd even dressed the part, trading his soldier's armor for a fitted tunic and trousers and a pair of polished boots, a violet kerchief tied over the scar at his throat. She wondered if the clothes were his, and when he'd grown into them. He'd caught her looking, and smiled, and Kosika felt herself smiling back, caught herself halfway and rolled her eyes.

"Shouldn't you be guarding something?" she'd asked, to which he said that, obviously, he would be guarding *her*.

"Is that why you're dressed like a noble?"

"I'm in disguise," he said with a wink.

And on the short trek from the tower to the castle grounds, he'd told Nasi about the picnics he and Kosika had had when they were kids whenever the sun was out, most of them on rooftops or city walls, the meals cobbled together from stale bread and bruised fruit. Kosika remembered, of course, but these days, those memories felt like they belonged to another girl, another life. One she was all too happy to leave behind.

The only part she'd wanted to keep, she had.

Lark lounged in the grass, his long legs crossed at the ankle as he listened to Nasi read from her book. His silver-blond hair was swept off his face, a neat little braid was woven behind his ear. It hadn't been there when she fell asleep.

As Nasi read—it wasn't her book of war, but a poem, and Kosika hated poems, they talked in circles instead of lines, and the cadence always distracted her from the words, and in fact, the poetry was probably what had lured her to sleep in the first place—as Nasi read, Kosika looked up, at the tree, and the sky beyond, the blue interrupted by crisp white clouds.

The tithe had cast a blush over the city, but how long would it last? She swore she could already *feel* it fading. It wasn't enough, nothing she did seemed to last, and she was trying to decide what to do when something hit her on the side of the head.

It was small, and hard, and it bounced off and landed in the grass. It was, in fact, a cherry.

Kosika stared at it a moment, and then looked up at her friends, the bowl of fruit clearly in arm's reach. Nasi, for her part, looked just as stunned by the attack, while Lark was looking pointedly away, as if something incredibly interesting was suddenly happening somewhere beyond the trees.

Kosika flicked her fingers, and the paring knife rose out of the block of cheese, and drifted almost lazily into her hand.

"Lark," she said casually. "Did you just throw a cherry at me?"

He glanced back, as if noticing her for the first time.

"What? No. Of course not." Her friend was many things—a good actor had never been one of them. He feigned shock, pointedly ignoring the

482

weapon as he looked up at the branches overhead. "Must have fallen from one of the trees."

Kosika followed his gaze up, confirming what she already knew. "There are no cherry trees in this orchard."

"Huh." He shifted his weight as he said it, inching away from the bowl.

"That really is an oversight," said Nasi. "Can't have a good orchard without a cherry tree."

Kosika looked down at the blade in her hand. "You're right," she said, with a wicked smile that made her friends—rightfully—more nervous than the knife did. She turned the blade, and made a quick, clean slice across her thumb. Then she took up the offending cherry, its skin the color of a deep bruise, and popped it into her mouth, savoring the brief, bright sweetness before she spit the pit back into her palm, and pushed it down into the soil.

She knew the words she wanted now.

"As Athera."

The world shivered, like a plucked string, and beneath the dirt, she felt the pit split open, felt the line of magic plunging down into the soil, becoming roots as the first green growth sprang up between her fingers. In seconds it was a sapling, the earth mottling under her palm as the tree spread, and the trunk rose and the branches twisted overhead, and blossomed, and bore fruit.

Her friends stared up at the tree, their faces lit with awe, and Kosika didn't blame them.

It was one thing to light a hearth, or conjure a breeze. It was another to push a bloodstained pit into the ground and grow it into a tree in seconds, its limbs heavy with a hundred ripened cherries.

Nasi smiled in childish delight, and Lark opened his mouth to say something, but before he could speak, Kosika flicked her fingers, and every cherry on the tree came raining down onto their heads.

VIII
RED LONDON

It turned out that the quickest way to escape a warded cell was simply to be let out.

"Come," the queen had said to the girl in the dungeon, "I want to show you something."

Something turned out to be the grandest workshop Tes had ever seen.

Chambers connected by high stone archways, every room full of tables and counters and every surface covered in a dazzling array of magic. Spells laid bare like bodies, their skin peeled back, their inner workings open to the light. She would have been tempted to reach out, run her fingers over the magic, but her wrists were still bound.

The queen stood across from her, appraising, and Tes knew that she should do something to show her deference, but the truth was, in that moment, she wasn't feeling very deferential. And she was hungry.

At the thought of food, her stomach growled again, and the queen turned to the two soldiers who'd escorted Tes.

"I was so lost in work," she said, "I forgot to eat. Please go and fetch me something."

Only one of the soldiers turned to go. She nodded at the other. "Go with him."

"*Mas res,*" said the soldier, "surely I should stay and guard the prisoner."

The queen looked at Tes, bedraggled, manacled, stained with blood though she was no longer bleeding.

"Somehow," she said, "I think we'll manage."

Tes should have felt insulted. She would have, but the queen had not said *I,* but *we,* as if they were conspiring.

When the soldier still hesitated, the queen straightened, her eyes going sharp.

"Don't mistake my tone," she said. "It wasn't a request."

At that, the soldier bowed deeper, and withdrew.

The queen waited until they were alone, then lifted the dead owl to the light, and studied it as if it were a precious jewel.

"Few people in this world would appreciate how elegant this magic is," she said. "Fewer still could create it." She held Vares out, but when Tes reached out her shackled hands, the queen pulled back. "Tell me, what is your name?"

When Tes hesitated, the queen laughed. "Is it so hard to give?"

"It is," said Tes, "when you don't have many things to call your own."

The queen considered. She offered the owl again, and this time let her take it. "There. Now you have more."

She returned Vares to her coat. Then said, "It's Tes, Your Majesty."

The soldier reappeared, carrying a tray. The queen pointed to a metal table, one of the few with space, and the soldier deposited his burden. This time, there was no protest. He melted away, leaving them alone again.

The queen gestured to a stool. "Sit," she said. And then, softening the command, "Please."

Tes did, sinking gratefully onto the perch. She watched as the queen lifted a frosted glass cover to reveal an array of sliced meat, a fine cheese, and wafer-thin pieces of toast, along with two cups and a steaming pot of tea. Tes's mouth began to water, but when the queen said, "Help yourself," Tes shook her head and laced her fingers to keep from reaching for the food. The manacles clinked in her lap.

"Apologies, Your Majesty," she said. "I am running short on trust today."

The queen surprised her with a smile. "I hardly blame you." She considered the spread, and began assembling a small sandwich.

"Ever since the Hand," she said, cutting it in two, "I have worried about poison." She took a bite of one half, and chewed thoughtfully. "Perhaps it's just their name, but I swear I dream of fingers reaching for me in the dark." She set the food down. "Half the spells I devise these days are to keep my family safe."

As she said this, she touched a pendant at her neck, but when her hand dropped, Tes saw it was actually a gold ring, and a spelled one at that, though the spellwork was so small and delicate, she would have had to hold it to her eye to see the pattern.

The queen poured the tea—it was black, and blissfully strong, Tes could tell by the scent when she brought it to her nose. Still, she waited for the queen to take a drink first.

"Rest assured, I have no desire to poison or drug you, or do anything to dull your senses." She took a sip from her own cup, then offered it to Tes. "I want them sharp."

Tes took it and drank, her head filling with spice and heady warmth. She sighed, feeling more herself than she had in days. She reached for the other half of the sandwich, cuffs dragging on the metal table. The first bite was relief. The second, pleasure. The third, and she felt tears threaten to spill down her cheeks.

As she ate, her attention drifted again, dancing over the many workshop surfaces, the room bright with so much magic. Tes couldn't help but marvel at it all, her fingers itching to reach the magic in the threads.

On one, a mirror faced a scrying board. On another, a spell was drawn in what looked like iron filings. Against one wall a column of water ran in a constant cycle, though no magician held it up. There were other things too, their purpose hidden from her. She longed to take them up, take them apart.

She had heard stories about the queen of Arnes. No one could decide if she was a prisoner or a recluse, a brilliant mind or raving mad. Truth be told, Tes had never taken much interest in royal gossip. What she did know was that before the queen became a Maresh, she was a Loreni. And the Loreni were known for their inventions.

"I suppose we are both tinkerers," observed the queen, following her gaze. "Though I do not have your gift."

Tes flinched at the mention, wishing she had never told Delilah Bard about her power, and wondering how word had spread so fast. The queen seemed to read the question in her face.

"Places this large tend to echo." As she spoke, she crossed to a nearby counter. "To lay hands on the very fabric of the world." She lifted a closed black box, returning with it. "What I would do," she said, opening the box, "with a gift like yours . . ."

486

She trailed off as she looked down. So did Tes. The box was empty. A shadow crossed the queen's face, and Tes swore she heard a name cross the queen's lips, little more than a whispered oath—*Alucard*—before she snapped it shut.

"Tell me, Tes. Do you create, as well as repair?"

"Sometimes," she said. Then, "I like to improve things. Make good magic better."

The queen nodded in understanding. "And tell me," she went on. "How did you come to serve the Hand?"

The food went tasteless in her mouth. She fought to swallow. "I swear, I didn't know. I would never have taken on the job."

"They did not recruit you, then?"

"No," she said emphatically. "A man came to my shop. He was sick, I think. Or wounded. He brought me something broken, and wanted it fixed. I didn't know what it was. And now it's gone. They can't use it against you."

"A fact for which I'm very grateful," said the queen. "You have protected my family, Tes. For that, I owe you a debt. Still," she added, sipped her tea, "it is a shame, that it was lost."

"Your Majesty?" she said, confused.

"We are creators. It is always a pity, is it not? To destroy a piece of work."

Tes nodded, though in truth, she was glad to see it gone. The *persalis* had cost her the shop she loved, and the life she'd built in London. She'd been threatened, taken hostage, stabbed—twice—and thrown in prison. All because she'd done her job.

"Would you show me, how you do it?"

Tes blinked. She hadn't noticed the queen rising, but she had stepped away and returned, carrying a small box. She cleared a space, and set it on the metal table.

"Perhaps there is a place for you here. A place for your gifts." She gestured at the massive workshop. "I could use an apprentice. Particularly one as skilled as you."

Tes looked down. It was a music box, its cover gone, revealing the pattern of its insides. Tes's fingers twitched automatically; she saw at once what was wrong with the magic, the place where a few of the threads had unraveled. The repair was so simple, she knew it was a test.

"Oh, wait."

The queen touched something to the shackles, and the lock inside them turned. The weight of iron fell away, the cuffs landing open on the table. Tes rubbed at her wrists.

"There," said the queen. "Now show me."

Tes stared at the box, but didn't move. Until Bex and Calin, no one had ever seen her work. She had been so careful, for so long, disguising every gesture, every movement. It was exhausting, to keep it secret. But there was a reason for it.

"Show me," said the queen again, but her voice was different now, the careful softness peeled back, revealing something cold and hungry. She stared at Tes, studying her, and the eyes were another color, a different shape, but the look in them was too familiar. It belonged to Serival. Serival, who looked at everything of worth like it was something to be used, or sold, or taken apart. It belonged to her father, who watched, arms crossed, inside his shop, for Tes to show him what she was worth.

The vast workshop suddenly felt smaller than the cell.

Run. The word raced through her blood, the way it had three years before, when she looked up and saw her oldest sister watching from the doorway, eyes trained on Tesali's hands where they hovered over threads she could not see.

Her gaze scraped over the metal table, the music box open on its surface, the unfastened cuffs halfway between Tes and the queen.

"Show me," pressed the queen, leaning forward, and so Tes did.

She reached inside the broken music box, and took hold of a broken amber thread, a piece designed to amplify the sound. But instead of mending it, she rolled the thread between her fingers, then drew it long, tracing a loop around the wooden frame.

The queen watched, as if entranced. So entranced that she leaned closer, and as she did, her elbow knocked the cup of tea, and sent it off the table's edge. The queen jerked, turning as the cup fell and shattered on the workshop floor. She frowned.

The crash had made no sound. Those piercing hazel eyes flew up to Tes.

"What have you done?" she asked, or at least, that is what Tes guessed she said. Her mouth formed the words. But nothing came out. Every sound in the workshop had suddenly been doused.

The queen's gaze dropped to the music box on the table. She lunged for it, and as she did, Tes went for the cast-off manacles, grabbing them with one hand, the other pulling on the strings. The iron went soft as putty in her hands, and before the queen could reach the music box, Tes slammed the softened metal down over her wrists. The queen recoiled, but Tes had already let go, and the iron was iron again, fused to the metal surface.

Tes scrambled back, away from the table and the queen's shocked expression.

"*Solase,*" she said, but the apology was nothing but a shape on her lips as she turned, and fled.

Tes ran, sound returning as she sprinted up the stairs. When the queen had come to fetch her, she'd been led up out of the prison, across a gallery, and down into another pillar. She'd seen two doors, the first, leading up into the palace above. The second, subtle as a crack in stone, and set into the pillar's landing halfway up.

She reached it, and pulled—but it was locked.

Tes ran her hands over the iron. With time, she could have picked the lock, but she didn't have time. Instead, she wrenched on the magic as hard as she could. The door crumpled, like paper, and tore free with a groan. Tes flung herself out, expecting to find steps, only to find nothing but air. She had just enough time to panic, to grasp that she was falling, about to plunge straight down into the river, before her boots landed on the soft earth a few feet below.

She stumbled forward, hands sinking into wet grass, the blades tinted red by the Isle's glow. The riverbank. The sun had gone down, the sky above darkening from blue to black, casting the southern bank in deep shadow. Tes scrambled up the slope, crested the rise to find the lanterns

489

of the night market glowing in the distance, the paths full and the tents alive with people.

Relief flooded through her.

She pulled her coat close, and started forward, intending to slip into the crowd and disappear. But as she crossed the lawn, a shadow stepped into her path. Even in the dark, Tes could see the black braid that rose like a crest over the woman's head, the metal wrapped around her forearm. Her blood went cold.

"Well, hello there," said Bex, strolling forward. "I told you we weren't done."

"I already destroyed the *persalis*," said Tes, inching backward. Her heels slipped on the wet grass, only the slope and the river at her back. Or so she thought. Until Calin's large, scarred arm swept around her shoulders, and hauled her up, off her feet.

"I can't give you what I don't have," Tes gasped.

Bex inclined her head. "Let's hope, for your sake, that isn't true."

Calin forced a cloth over her nose and mouth. She tried not to breathe, but soon her aching lungs betrayed her, dragging in the tainted air. Something sickly sweet coated her tongue, her throat, filled her head. The last thing she saw was the blurring lanterns of the market beyond Bex's shoulder. And then they blinked out, one by one, and she was left in darkness.

XI

IN
THE
WRONG
HANDS

I

Lila Bard was in a foul fucking mood.

Seven years, she'd watched Kell suffer. Seven years, without a way to make it stop. And now here one was, and he was saying no. Because there was a risk. Of *course* there was a risk, but that was the problem with these people born to magic, it made their lives too easy, it made things too sure. They did not seem to understand that sometimes living came with risks.

She cared for Rhy, of course, but she was tired of watching Kell sacrifice himself on his brother's altar, as if his own life and pain meant nothing.

Fucking martyrs.

"Don't leave the palace," Kell had said, and for some reason she'd listened, at least at first, gone to the training grounds in the hopes of finding soldiers, guards, new recruits—anyone willing to spar. But the grounds had been empty.

So Lila walked—stomped, really, as if she could force her frustration down out of her body through the heels of her boots. She felt like a bottle of sparkling wine after it's been shaken and before the cork bursts free. Her power churned beneath her skin, spilling into the air around her. Lanterns brightened as she passed. Pebbles shivered and skidded down the street.

She wanted a fucking fight, but clearly no one at the palace was willing, or able, so Lila did what she did best.

She went looking for trouble.

Her cuts hadn't healed from the brawl in the tavern, but Lila didn't care. She wondered if she could find the woman with the black braid, and finish what they'd started. She'd been a good enough opponent. Plenty of knives. What was her name?

Bex.

"Bex, Bex, Bex," Lila mused aloud, as if she could be summoned. No Bex appeared, but that was fine—she'd had the look of a hired hand, and Lila knew where to go looking for those.

The *shal.*

The sun had gone down as she walked, and perhaps it was the thinning light behind her, or just a gut sense that she was going in the wrong direction, but Lila noticed how dark the sky was getting.

Her boots dragged to a stop. She scanned the horizon opposite the sun, and the faint light of emerging stars, and realized—

There was no moon rising.

No smudge of white, or hangnail sliver. The image on the coin's edge came back to her. Full moon. Or moon*less.*

Lila checked her watch. It was early, just after nine, but she had nowhere else to go. She turned to the nearest wall, fist clenching, nails biting into the cut she'd made to heal the girl. Pain lanced through her palm as the cut reopened. She touched the blood, and drew the mark on the stone—a vertical line and two small crosses—before splaying her hand flat against the mark.

"*As Tascen.*"

The city dropped away, and shuddered back into shape a moment later, her hand pressed to a different wall, on a different street, the same mark humming faintly beneath her skin. Lila pushed off the wall, and turned to face the house at 6 Helarin Way, prepared to wait all night if she had to.

It turned out, she wouldn't have to wait at all.

The house, which had been dark that morning, and the night before, had already undergone a transformation. Carriages now lined the street out front, and lanterns dripped from every window, and the grim smile of the gate had broken wide.

And Lila knew exactly what it was.

A pleasure garden. Just like Tanis had told her.

Clusters of men and women strode up the walk. A few were dressed as if attending a royal ball, and Lila briefly considered relieving someone of their fine clothes, the better to blend in, but decided against it when she saw others dressed more plainly.

She crossed the street, slowing as a pair of gentlemen stepped down out of a nearby carriage. One wore a velvet, high-collared coat, the other, a black vest over a tunic, but both spoke with the clear tones of *ostra*.

". . . called the Veil," said the one in velvet. "It changes venue every time. Took me a month to track it down, but I've heard it's worth the work."

"How did you find out where it would be?" asked the vest.

"It's a secret," said the velvet.

"Pretty crowded secret," said the vest.

And he was right.

When Lila first found the message on the coin, she had imagined a far more clandestine arrangement, held in the hidden chambers of a darkened house, far away from prying ears and searching eyes. After all, the Hand had been at work for months, and never been caught.

But the best crime was the one you pulled off in plain sight.

Lila had no doubt that half the guests streaming into this place were simply patrons of the pleasure garden. They were providing perfect cover for the rest.

She fell in step behind the men, trailed them toward the door, which hung open ahead, though any glimpse of the house beyond was concealed behind a curtain. A host stood waiting to greet each guest as they arrived. He was dressed head to toe in white: a fitted suit beneath a pale, pearl cloak. Over his face, he wore a golden mask.

If the host noticed that Lila was dressed in men's clothes—and underdressed at that, her tunic and trousers smudged beneath her coat, the remains of dust and blood from the tavern brawl, though she had buttoned the coat to hide the worst—he made no comment. And if his smile faltered, thanks to the mask there was no way to tell.

"Welcome to the Veil," said the host, extending a gloved hand. "Do you have an invitation?"

Lila's fingers twitched toward her nearest knife, a habit whenever the choice was either lie, or fight, but instead she reached into her pocket and produced the coin she'd discovered in the tavern. She checked its edge with the pad of her thumb to ensure it was the right one, then dropped the altered lin into the host's waiting hand. For a moment, he simply stared down at it, as if surprised to see it there. Then his gloved fingers closed over the coin.

"There will be a toast," he said, "in the library. At the appointed time."

Lila didn't have to ask when that would be.

Nonis ora.

Eleven.

Lila passed through the curtain, and stepped into a foyer full of faces. Masks. Dozens of them hung mounted to the walls—not gold, like the one worn by the host, but black, and white, and featureless—and dozens more were missing, their absence marked by golden hooks. Lila selected a black one, and settled it over her face, and though it lacked the horns that adorned her own, Lila still felt herself humming as she made her way to the back of the foyer, and the second curtain there.

How do you know the Sarows is coming, is coming, is coming aboard?

She pushed the curtain aside, and entered the Veil.

II

Alucard ran his hand over the stone wall as they descended the prison steps.

He could see the threads that danced over the rock, just as he could see the ones that carried on the draft that wafted from below, and the ones that bound Kell and Rhy together, the way that only Kell's looked frayed, while his brother's were mercifully unbroken. He studied the web of tendrils, the places they crossed, and tried to imagine having the gift that this girl supposedly did, being able to reach into the threads, take hold, and change them.

How many nights had he lain awake beside Rhy, studying the silver threads, watching the way they flowed out from the king's heart? Now he tried to imagine his fingers between the narrow gaps, how careful his touch would have to be to land on only the right ones, let alone to sever and retie them without causing some catastrophic failure. The complexity was terrifying, the potential for error so great, and Alucard was left to wonder, if he *could* do it, would he trust himself?

He was secretly relieved he didn't have the choice.

Kell's shoulders tensed as they neared the royal cells, and Alucard remembered that the prince had spent time behind the bars once, for defying the late king.

"Where are the guards?" Rhy asked now as they reached the row of cells. And it was true—there should have been someone guarding the girl. But there was no one stationed, and when they reached the last cell, he saw why.

The girl was gone.

The cell stood empty, the door wide open. For a single, lurching moment, he thought she must have escaped. But the wards in the cell were still active, and there was no sign of tampering. No, someone had taken her out.

"Lila," hissed Kell, a single, damning word as he doubled back down the row, and surged up the stairs, and Alucard found himself hoping Kell was wrong—Lila had been in a dark mood, convinced the girl was holding back. He didn't want to know what she would do, left to her own devices.

Rhy and Alucard followed Kell back up the stairs, into the palace hall where he'd approached the nearest guard.

"Have you seen Lila?" he demanded.

"She took the girl from the prison," said Rhy.

"Why was the cell unguarded?" asked Alucard.

The guard bowed deeply. "Your Majesties," he said, glancing between the three as if unsure which to address, before deciding, at last, on the king. "Lila Bard did not take the prisoner."

"How do you know?" demanded Kell.

He hesitated only a moment. "Because it was the queen."

•

The night, it turned out, was full of surprises.

The three of them arrived at the queen's workshop to find, again, no girl, and Nadiya Loreni leaning over a table. She looked at her husband and his consort and the prince as they came in, but made no motion toward them.

As Alucard moved closer, he could see why—her wrists were cuffed, and bound to the table, the metals literally fused together. She opened her mouth to speak, but nothing came out, and Alucard realized how oppressively quiet it was in the workshop, as if the ambient sound had been sucked out.

She nodded at something on the table. It looked like a music box, though the threads had been pulled out and tied around it.

Ingenious, he thought, right before he smashed it.

Sound whooshed back into the room as it broke, and Nadiya sighed audibly.

"What happened?" demanded Rhy.

"She got away," said Nadiya, as if that explained everything. "Can one of you fetch Sasha? She's a metalworker."

Five minutes later, the nursemaid was there, and the queen was free, rubbing her wrists.

Kell, meanwhile, had gone in search of Lila.

Alucard's attention remained on the queen. She didn't seem terribly upset by the assault, and he trailed her across the workshop to another surface, watching as she unrolled a length of parchment, and uncorked a bottle of black sand, which she upended into the center. He watched her make an indent in the sand, and then, watched her produce a small white bone and put it in the groove.

She murmured a few words, and the black sand began to move, tracing itself outward in thin lines across the parchment until it began to resemble a map.

A cold feeling rolled across him. "You let her go on purpose."

Nadiya said nothing, her lips moving with the spell, attention trained on the sand as it hissed and skittered, drawing the city.

He grabbed her shoulder, and pointed to the bit of bone. "Where did that come from?"

Nadiya stopped talking. The sand stopped moving. She gave him an impatient look. "Her pet owl."

Understanding landed like a weight on Alucard's shoulders. "You *wanted* her to escape."

He hadn't noticed Rhy joining them, but the king sucked in a breath. "Why?"

"Because," explained Alucard, "the queen is using her as bait."

Rhy stared at his wife in horror, but she'd already turned her attention back to the spell. She began again, the sand continuing until the king slammed his hand down on the parchment. Nadiya stopped, and met her husband's gaze.

"This is going to take time," she said, "and focus. So if you don't mind—"

"I mind," snapped Rhy. "What have you done?"

"What I thought best," said Nadiya. "We need to find the Hand. They want to find the girl. It made sense." She looked to Alucard. "You would have done the same."

It wasn't a question. Rhy stared at Alucard, waiting for him to deny it.

Alucard sighed. "I'm not sure I agree with the method. . . ."

"Speaking of methods," she said, eyes narrowing, "you may disagree with mine, but don't you *ever* steal from my workshop again."

Alucard flinched as if struck. "What are you talking about?"

"The chains," she said. "The transfer spell."

His stomach dropped. "What about it?"

"Don't pretend."

"Nadiya," he said, voice hardening. "What about it?"

Her expression slipped, accusation cracking into confusion as she said, "It's gone."

Just then, Kell returned, breathless. "Lila's not in the palace."

"No," said the queen. "She left an hour ago, on foot."

Kell swore. "Of all nights . . ." And Alucard closed his eyes. Of all nights.

"Is there a moon?" he asked.

"What does that have to do with anything?" demanded Kell, but Alucard wasn't asking him. He was asking the queen. The queen, who

499

worked in a windowless hold beneath the water, and yet, always seemed to know exactly what was happening above it.

"Is there?" he asked again.

"No," said the queen. "It's a moonless night."

Alucard let out a heavy breath, and turned to Kell.

"I know where Lila is."

"How long will this take?" asked Rhy, pacing the queen's workshop.

"Longer, every time you make me stop," said Nadiya. In truth, it was taking longer than it should because the map had changed. Twice now, it had rewritten itself, sand lines finishing, only to crumble and re-form, drawing new streets, which she took to mean the girl—Tes—had been moving. Or was being moved.

Now Nadiya finished the commands a third time, waiting for the lines to settle.

Rhy stood across the table from her, glaring. She had seen the king grieve, and laugh. Seen him forlorn, and happy, frustrated, and in pain, but she had rarely seen him *mad*. His gold eyes burned into her, not with passion, but anger, disdain. His mouth crushed into a line, as if he were biting back words.

"If you have something to say," she said, "then say it."

"How could you do it?"

"Do what?"

"Put this girl in danger. Treat her life as if it is disposable. As if it matters so much less than mine or yours."

"It *does*." There was no malice in her voice, only a grim resolve, but Rhy looked at her as if she were a monster. Her gentle husband, so kind, and so naïve. Nadiya knew Alucard made a habit of indulging him, but right now, she could not.

"Lives are not equal, Rhy. It is folly to think they are. It makes you a good person, yes, but it will doom you as a king." He flinched. "And it will be the death of the Maresh," she went on. "Perhaps you cannot die. But you forget, *I* can. *Alucard* can. Your *daughter* can. So if you want to play the part of saint, go right ahead, but I have no such delusions. I have worked too hard to keep this family safe. Let's hope a single girl is all we have to sacrifice tonight."

Rhy said nothing.

Nadiya looked down.

On the table between them, the sand had finally stopped whispering over the paper. It fell still, turning to solid black lines around the piece of bone as it drew the map. A bank. A street. A house. One stroke at a time, the city unraveled. Rhy's breath caught in his chest. Nadiya frowned. There were no names, no numbers, but they were not necessary. Both of them knew exactly where Tes had been taken.

The Emery estate.

III

Tes woke to the violence of cold water.

She sat up, heaving as icy rivers ran into her eyes and down her neck, soaking into her curls. Bex stood over her, holding a now empty bucket.

"Rise and shine," she said, setting it aside.

Tes's heart was pounding her chest, the taste of dreamsquick heavy on her tongue. She was lying on the floor of a well-appointed room, a puddle forming on the wooden boards. She wasn't tied down, at least. That should have made her feel better. It didn't. There were no windows, and only one door, and Calin was leaning against it, a dark bruise blooming like a shadow on one side of his face. Bex only watched as Tes rose, unsteady, to her feet, and wrung the water from her hair.

Something had changed.

In her shop, the two assassins had an easy swagger, the confidence unique to sellswords. There had been a looseness to their shoulders, an ease to their gait. Now both of them stood quiet, tense as harp strings.

She wondered why—until a voice behind her cleared its throat.

"I asked for a *persalis,* and you brought me a girl."

Tes turned, and found a large man, cloaked in navy and silver. The threads that wove the air around him were an earthy green, but they were

501

thin, and dim. His brown hair was trimmed short, his eyes a blue so dark she might have taken them for black if the light hadn't caught their edges. His accent was pure *vestra,* and he had the bearing of a noble, but his knuckles were traced with pale white scars. Tes took a reflexive step back, even if it meant stepping closer to the assassins.

"Best we could do," muttered Calin.

"My lord," added Bex, and Tes caught the slightest mocking lilt in the words. "But in the absence of a fish, I thought you'd want the fisherman."

The nobleman ignored the killers. He studied Tes, and as he did, she realized this must be him: the leader of the Hand.

"You've caused me quite a bit of trouble," he said. "Let's hope you can fix it."

He stepped aside, revealing a large desk. Piled atop and around it were a myriad of spelled objects, many household, but not all, and half of them in disrepair. The kinds of things that had filled the shelves at Haskin's, before she'd torn it down.

"Everything we could find," offered Calin, "on such short notice."

"And everything you should need," said the nobleman. "To make another *persalis.*"

Tes recoiled, and said what she should have when the dying thief had first walked into her shop with the broken doormaker in tow.

"No."

In her head, it had been booming, but when it crossed her lips, it came out hoarse and small, barely a whisper. And yet, it seemed to fill the room. Out of the corner of her eye, she saw Bex flinch, but the nobleman nodded, as if he understood. And then he began to unfasten his cuffs. The clasps, she saw, were silver feathers. Her mind spun. She wished she'd paid more attention to the royal houses, back when her father had insisted on her taking lessons.

"I'm afraid," he said, rolling up his sleeves, "I do not have time to be persuasive." He drew a small bottle from his pocket, its contents the color of oil. When he tipped the bottle, it left viscous stains against the glass. "Hold her."

Tes stumbled back, shoes sliding in the puddle, only to find hands grabbing her arms, forcing her down against the wet wood floor. She fought, and screamed as they held her there, kicked out as the large man loomed. She landed a blow to his stomach, but it was like kicking stone; he didn't even wince. And then he was kneeling beside her, uncorking the noxious vial, and Bex's fist was tangled in her hair, forcing her head back.

The pain made her cry out, and as she did, the glass was forced between her teeth. Bitter liquid hit her tongue. She choked, throat closing against it, but the nobleman's massive palm came down over her mouth, fingers clamping it shut until, at last, she swallowed.

The hands holding her disappeared, and Tes rolled onto her side, heaving. She curled small, as if to shield herself. As if the damage was not already done. A shadow fell over her, darkening the room. The nobleman, smoothing down his sleeves.

"That was widowswork," he said, buttoning his cuffs. "Perhaps you've heard of it. It slows the heart, thickens the blood, shuts down the vital organs one by one. Most people use it to poison slowly, in which case a drop or two will do, spread out over weeks, or months." He held the bottle to the light. It was empty. "I'd say you have an hour. If you're lucky."

It wasn't enough time. Even if Tes were in her shop, with her black tea and her blotters. Even if she hadn't just been poisoned. And if she were already dead, what was the point?

But then the nobleman produced a second bottle, its contents a milky white.

"An antidote," he said, striding for the door. Calin got out of the way, and the nobleman tossed him the bottle, as if it were a tip, as he vanished into the hall.

Bex and Calin watched him go. Their bodies loosened, just a little, when they could no longer hear his steps. Calin closed the door, and Bex looked down at Tes.

"Well," she said, "I'd get to work, if I were you."

Truth be told, Lila had never spent much time in pleasure gardens.

Not that she scorned pleasure—she enjoyed a fine wine, a sharp knife, the things Kell could do with his mouth when he put it to good use—but once a thief, always a thief. She didn't trust the kindness, the closeness. Someone placed a glass into her hand. Someone grazed their fingers down her arm. Someone's body whispered against hers, and every time, her muscles stiffened, and her nerves told her she was being robbed.

Music spilled out of a large chamber, a quartet of instruments perched on a stand, spelled to play without players, but the rest of the room was full of people, some playing cards, and others smoking, and most enjoying the company provided by the Veil. The light was low, and it fell on the masks, picking out the occasional gold of a host drifting among the tapestry of black and white, and making all of them glow.

A woman's hand grazed Lila's back, and she had to resist the urge to stop the bones, or check her pockets as a voice purred with feline grace. *"Avan, res naster."*

Lila turned, and found another white-dressed figure, albeit wearing far, far less of it, her face hidden behind its own gold mask.

"Avan," answered Lila. "Can you point me toward the library?"

"Why go there," she teased, "when you can stay with me?"

"What can I say?" said Lila. "I have a love of books."

She could almost *see* the woman pouting behind her mask, but then she wrapped her arms around Lila, and turned her around, pointing down a hall.

"That way," she said, giving Lila a playful nudge, her embrace retreating like a tide.

She made her way down the hall, which was lined with doors, all of them closed, gold masks hanging on the wood. The first two turned out to be locked. The next opened onto a pair of men playing cards. Someone had just lost a hand, and was stripping off his shoes. The other seemed to have lost several—he was barely clothed. Neither seemed to notice Lila as she let the door fall shut. She continued, searching room after room, discovered all the markings of a pleasure house, and none of a rebel group. She reached the end of the hall, only to discover it did not end, but turned onto an alcove, and a final door, unmarked by mask, or glass, or sign.

She put her ear to the wood, and heard nothing from the other side. She tested the handle, and found it unlocked. The door swung open onto a large and well-appointed library, the walls lined with books, a large wooden desk in the corner, a pair of chairs set before an unlit fire.

Lila stepped inside, and closed the door behind her.

A clock on the wall chimed, and she took in the time. *Ten.*

Lila studied the books on the wall, then went to the desk, and opened drawer after drawer, searching for something, anything, to tie this place to the Hand. She was still searching when the library door groaned open, carrying the ghost of music and voices from the house. Lila turned, and saw a man.

He was tall, and broad enough to fill the doorway. His brown hair was cut short on the sides, but it rose over the top of his black mask. He was dressed in a navy coat with silver buttons. Her gaze went to his hands. They were scarred.

"You're early," he said. His voice held the rumble of thunder.

"Better than late," said Lila lightly.

"Indeed." He did an odd thing then. He was still standing in the open door. Now, as she watched, he reached up and ran one hand down the side of the frame, as if testing the wood, before stepping forward into the library. He pulled the door shut behind him. And locked it.

The small sound of the bolt turning might as well have been a warning shot.

"You know," he went on, "I hoped you would come."

Lila frowned. "You'll have to forgive me," she said. "I never forget a face, but since I can't see yours . . . have we met?"

The man continued his slow advance. "No," he said. "We have not been introduced. But you're no longer as anonymous as you once were, Delilah Bard."

He flexed his hands, scarred knuckles going white as he said her name, and Lila reflexively reached for her power. Not the air in the room, or the candles on the wall, but the bones inside his body, to halt his progress, to make him stop.

She pulled on that magic—and felt nothing.

No flutter, no promise, no sense of a will warring with her own. She reached then for the wooden floor, for the air, tried to spark a flame inside her hand. Nothing.

Warded. The room was warded.

"I hope you weren't planning to rely on magic."

She imagined the man's mouth drawing into a grim smile behind his onyx mask as he said it. Lila forced herself to match that imagined smirk.

"Believe it or not," she said, drawing a blade, "I have other tricks."

"Is that so?" He continued forward, close enough now that Lila would have to either attack, or step back. And she wasn't about to step back. "Show me," he said, but Lila was already moving.

She leapt onto the desk and over it, slicing down toward the man's mask. He raised his arm, and the blade came down on that instead, steel ringing against steel as it cut the coat, only to hit an armored plate. His other fist swung toward her head, but Lila was already twisting out of the way, slicing the blade along his side.

She felt it bite through cloth and skin, but the man didn't recoil. He didn't even flinch. He simply turned, with shocking speed, and, before Lila could lunge back out of his reach again, he struck her, hard, across the face. Hard enough to crack the mask, which fell away. Hard enough to fill her mouth with blood. She rolled back and rose again, but her ears were ringing and her good eye blurred, and for a terrible second, she couldn't see, her attacker nothing but a vague shape coming toward her.

It didn't escape her notice that he hadn't drawn a weapon, and that he held his hands as if they were the only ones he needed. This was a man experienced in hurting others.

"Well?" he asked. "Already out of tricks?"

Lila's fingers tightened on the knives, searching his clothes, the way they fell, trying to find the points that weren't armored. The man, meanwhile, turned his head, and studied the clock on the wall instead of her.

As if she weren't even a threat.

Lila was offended, but the disrespect gave her the opening she needed, and she took it, springing toward him, angling the dagger toward his throat.

At the last moment, the masked face turned back toward her. At the same time, his hand came up, and caught the knife by the blade, wrenching it forward.

Lila should have let go.

Afterward, she would play the fight back in her head, over and over, and every time, she would regret that moment. She should have let go, but she didn't, and when the man pulled the blade forward, he pulled her too, off-balance, and as he did, his other palm came to rest against the side of her head, and slammed it down into the wooden desk.

And everything went black.

IV

Two horses tore across the bridge.

They bore no royal markings, but anyone with a passing knowledge could tell they were bred well. Their coats were lush—one grey, the other white—and their hooves glinted as they galloped, as if they had been shod in gold.

Of course, Alucard had not bothered to tell Kell where they were *going*, only that it was on the coin.

"What coin?" Kell had demanded, swinging his leg over the grey mount the guards had brought him.

Alucard had let out an exasperated sigh. "From the dead thief, on Maris's ship," he'd said, as if that answered everything. "It gave the time and place, where the Hand would meet."

Kell bristled—he did not know which bothered him more, that Lila had not told him about the coin, or that she had told *Alucard* instead.

"You knew she would go," he'd snapped as Alucard had mounted the white horse and taken the reins. "You knew, and you said nothing."

"I was distracted," answered Alucard. "And I haven't been a sailor for seven years. I have bigger concerns than the phase of the moon."

With that, he'd kicked his mount into motion, and Kell had had no choice but to follow, or be left behind.

Now the bridge disappeared beneath them as they reached the northern bank, and the avenues filled by *ostra*-favored shops and houses. Alucard urged the horse on, slowing only as he turned at last onto a wide street.

Helarin Way.

He drew to a stop, and Kell stopped with him, the two dismounting as a carriage rattled past, and slowed, pulling up before the open gates of a well-lit house. It didn't strike Kell as the kind of place rebels would meet—it had all the subtlety of a parade—but perhaps that was the idea.

"Mind the horses," said Alucard.

Kell glared. "If you think you're going in without me . . ." But he trailed off as Alucard shot him a long-suffering look, and held his reins out in the opposite direction. A shadow peeled away from the walls and took the ropes, first from the royal consort, then from Kell.

He shrugged out of his coat, and turned it, abandoning the grey exterior that he'd been wearing since his trip to the Sanctuary, and exchanging it for the lightless black of Kay's mantle. He donned it again, exhaling as the new coat settled over his shoulders with a comfortable weight.

He slicked back his hair, and then pulled up the hood to hide the copper.

"Oh yes," said Alucard blandly. "They'll never recognize you now."

Kell gave him a dark look, then reached into the coat's pocket and withdrew a black mask, settling it over his cheeks. His two-toned eyes vanished.

"What are you supposed to— No, you know what, I don't care," said Alucard as he turned up his collar, and strode across the street, clearly unconcerned with blending in.

A man in white stood waiting on the front steps, his own face concealed behind a golden mask. The door was open behind him, but any view of the house beyond was hidden by the crisp black curtain that filled the doorway.

"Welcome to the Veil," he said, extending a gloved hand. "Do you have an invitation?"

"Yes, of course," said Alucard, patting his pockets. "Hm," he said after a moment. "I must have left it in my other coat." He smiled as he said it— the kind of smile that must have charmed others, but made Kell want to kick his teeth in. "But surely, you can make an exception."

The host inclined his head. "I'm afraid," he said, "I cannot."

"Oh, wait," said Kell, stepping closer and reaching into his coat. "You gave it to me."

Alucard cocked a brow. "I did?"

"Yes, here it is. . . ." He looked down, and so did the host, only to go very still as the tip of a blade came to rest beneath his chin.

"Walk away," said Kell softly, and perhaps the host caught the glint of his black eye, and guessed at the identity of Alucard's companion, or perhaps he simply did not think it was worth dying for, because as soon as Kell withdrew the point of the knife, the host turned, and strode down the stairs, tearing off his mask and casting it into the bushes as he went.

"You know," mused Alucard as Kell slid the knife back into his coat. "I think you've been spending too much time with Lila Bard."

"So it seems," said Kell, stepping past him and through the curtained door.

Inside, a wall of black and white masks lined the entry hall, more than half of them now claimed. Kell opted to hold on to his own, but Alucard selected a white mask, fastening it over his face. And together, they entered the Veil.

V

Pain.

Ringing, black-edged pain rolled through Lila's head.

She couldn't *see*. Her vision was gone, replaced by a flat, black *nothing* that made her chest tight, panic rising like bile in her throat. She had never been afraid of the dark, because the dark wasn't *really* dark. There were always shades to it, layers of shapes and shadows. But this was different. This was *impenetrable*. This was blindness. This was the thing Lila had been afraid of since she lost her eye. But as her skull stopped rattling, and the pain quieted enough to let her other senses speak, she blinked, and felt her lashes scrape cloth.

Not blind.

Blind*folded*.

She rolled her neck, which sent a fresh wave of pain through her skull. She flexed, tried to move, but her shoulders strained, and rope scratched rough over her wrists, along with something else—cold metal? Either way, it seemed her hands were bound behind her.

Once again, Lila reached for her magic.

And once again, it didn't answer.

At last, her senses cleared enough to reach beyond her own limbs, and she picked up the weight of a body shifting on the wooden floor nearby. She wasn't alone.

Lila swallowed, made her voice as bland as she could.

"Is this your idea of a good time?" she asked. "Because I have notes."

She half expected no one to answer. But for better or worse, the body stepped closer, and the blindfold came away, showering the room in merciful light.

Lila blinked, and looked around, surprised to discover she was no longer in the library. No longer in the Veil at all, judging by the lack of music whispering through the walls, the darker floors and grim décor, the window looking out not onto Helarin, but another street. The air was stale with dust. The room felt neglected. Unlived in. Abandoned. She was sitting in a wooden chair.

She dragged her attention to the shadow looming over her, who was now wrapping the black blindfold casually around his fist. His cuff links were silver, modeled into feathers. Her mind flickered, but her attention was already being pulled up, to his face.

The man who'd attacked her was no longer wearing a mask. A trimmed beard shadowed the bottom half of his face. His eyes were the dark blue-grey of storms at sea. She had the uncanny sensation that she knew him, and, at the same time, the certainty they'd never met.

"The host at the Veil was told to keep an eye out for certain people," he said. "The *Antari* prince, for one. My brother. And you."

Brother.

The knowledge lurched through her. The features fell into place, laid over a different face.

Her memory stuttered, and she was standing on a familiar ship, back when it was still named the *Spire,* as Alucard leaned his elbows on the rail, and spoke of the night his brother Berras beat him unconscious while their father watched. Of how he woke the next day, arm broken and ribs bruised, chained in the bottom of a ship.

This, then, was Berras Emery.

"Well," said Lila, "it looks like your brother got the manners *and* the looks in the family."

Berras sneered, and stepped closer, hand raised to strike, but as he did, Lila swung her legs up and kicked him, as hard as she could, in the stomach. It would have been a paltry move, if she'd been going for any damage, but luckily she wasn't. As her boots connected with his front, she pushed backward. The force of it was enough to make the chair tip, and it went crashing to the floor, taking Lila with it. She rolled, and when she rose, her hands were no longer bound behind her, but in front, which was an improvement. She'd reached for a blade as she fell, but she'd been divested of them all, so her hands came up empty.

That was when she saw the gold.

Her hands were bound with rope, but beneath the rough cord, a gold cuff circled her left wrist. It had no beginning and no end, and was pressed flush with her skin, and before she could wonder at its meaning, Berras Emery raised his own hand, and a wall of wind slammed into Lila. The floor disappeared beneath her feet as she was flung back across the room and into the stone mantle of the hearth, all the air knocked from her lungs as she was pinned by the sheer force. A moment later, the wind died, and she stumbled forward, fighting to stay on her feet.

She didn't understand.

Alucard had told her once that his brother was a weak magician, that he could barely cobble together a wall from rock and earth. Rock and earth, he'd said. Not *wind*.

If the room was warded, how was he using magic? And if it wasn't warded, where was hers?

"Clever, isn't it?"

An arc of flame curled through the air around Berras, unruly but bright.

First wind, thought Lila, *now fire?* How was he doing it?

"The queen should keep a closer eye over her tools. Or at least, over her company."

Berras flexed his hand, and Lila had just enough time to see a glint of gold before Berras made a fist, and her entire body buckled under an unseen force. She hit the floor hard, but this time, there was no wind. She tried to move, but her limbs refused, her whole skeleton groaning as she pushed back against the hold.

Bone magic.

"I was planning to use the bind on my brother."

She tried to will her body, to make it hers again, but this wasn't one will at war against another. It was something else.

"I thought it would be fitting," he went on, "to kill Alucard with his own power. But I could hardly pass up yours. After all, why have a piece of magic when you can have it all?"

Horror swept through Lila.

The gold cuff. The gold ring. Berras wasn't using his magic. He was using *hers*. Channeling it.

"Of course, I'm not versed in *Antari* spells," he said, "but that's all right. You'll teach them to me."

"Here's one for free," offered Lila through gritted teeth, dragging her head up as far as the working would allow. "Go fuck yourself."

Berras smiled, tight and humorless. "You know, of all the elements, bone really is the most useful."

There was an audible crack as he said it, and one of Lila's lower ribs snapped in two. Her jaw was locked shut, but a scream still tore between her teeth.

"The ability to control another person's body."

A second rib snapped.

"Even *break* it."

And a third.

Lila cried out, gasping as a splintered edge dug into her lungs.

"Oh," she hissed, her breath uneven. "I can see why Alucard hates you."

In answer, an invisible hand cupped the back of her head and forced it down, pinning her gaze to the floor.

Something swung there, like a pendulum. A black ring on a leather cord. Her ring. Kell's ring. She cursed herself for not wearing it like he'd wanted her to.

She strained, fingers twitching feebly on the wood.

Lila focused all her strength into one hand. If she could just reach . . .

She heard the chair scrape against the floor as Berras righted it, and then she was being dragged upright, and shoved roughly back into it, her ribs screaming as they hit the wood. But the weight on her bones disappeared, and in that stolen moment, Lila grasped for the necklace, her bound hands halfway to her chest before the wood of the chair reached out and caught her fingers.

"So much power," said Berras as branches of wood grew around her arms, forcing them down. "Wasted on you." The wood wrapped her shoulders, pinning them back to the chair.

"Fuck," she hissed, clawing uselessly at the air. At the ring swinging just out of reach.

Berras noticed. "What's this?" he asked, fingers closing around the blackened band.

And for the first time, Lila was glad Rhy had married such a clever queen. Glad she'd designed the rings so that they worked no matter whose hand was holding them.

Lila knew the spell, of course. Kell had told her the words, the day he'd given her the ring. She'd pretended not to listen, but she'd still committed them to memory. Now, for the first time, she said them aloud.

"As vera tan."

I need you.

The words came out, barely a whisper, and Berras leaned in, those eyes—a mocking shadow of her Alucard's—stopping inches from her own.

"What did you say?" he asked.

Lila drew in a breath, ignoring the scrape of bone on lung. "I said, all the magic in the world won't make you less of an ass."

Berras Emery frowned, and tore the ring from her throat. The cord snapped, coming away in his hand. He straightened, and walked away, taking her magic with him. He flung open the door, and vanished into the house beyond. As he did, she heard him cast the ring away. Heard it bounce, and roll down the hall.

Lila closed her eyes, and smiled to herself, even though it hurt.

513

Alucard Emery was well versed in the city's many sources of debauchery.

He visited the brothels for their information, but he'd always favored the drink and entertainment of the London pleasure gardens. In his younger years, he'd prided himself on his knowledge of them all, but Lila was right.

Marriage had clearly made Alucard a bore.

He'd heard of the Veil, of course—a traveling garden, one that descended on a different place every time it opened—but he'd never visited, and had to admit, he was impressed. Not just by the décor, the offerings, the discretion, but by the idea.

It was the perfect place to hide the Hand. He cursed himself for not thinking of it sooner.

Alucard held a long-stemmed pipe in one hand, an untouched drink in the other as he drifted through a crowded chamber, trying to hear something, anything of use. Kell had hovered at his arm until he'd sent him off, insisting they'd have more luck if they split up. It wasn't a lie. Not entirely.

He checked his watch. It was half past ten. He knew that Lila was here—she had to be—but he'd skimmed the rooms, and so far, found no sign of her. Or the Hand. Which meant they were either hiding somewhere else, or right here, mingling in the sea of masked faces.

Kell returned to his side. "Nothing," he growled, and Alucard threw an arm around the prince's shoulders as if they were the best of friends, enjoying a night on the town. Kell, idiot that he was, recoiled. Alucard tightened his grip, leaning his weight onto Kell, as if steadying himself.

"Have you been drinking?" hissed the prince, and despite the black mask that covered his face, Alucard could perfectly picture the way Kell's features were twisting, his brows drawn together, his mouth turned down in that perpetual scowl.

"Believe it or not," said Alucard, careful to keep his voice lower than the music, "I'm trying to blend in. You act as if you've never enjoyed a pleasure garden, when I know for a fact Rhy dragged you to more than one. According to him, you are at least *capable* of having fun."

Alucard reached up and embraced the side of Kell's hood, the way he'd cup a close friend's cheek. This time, Kell did not recoil, but his body was stiff as stone under his touch.

"Have you found anything or not?" he muttered.

Alucard shook his head. "Not yet. Perhaps we should—"

But at that moment, Kell stiffened, and pulled away. He turned, sweeping out of the room into the hall, and Alucard had no choice but to follow. He caught up in time to see Kell ducking into an unclaimed room, holding his hand as if burned.

Alucard shut the door behind them. "What's wrong?"

"My ring."

Two bands circled Kell's right hand, one red, the other black. This second had taken on a faint glow, and Alucard knew, from the times Rhy had called on him, that it was hot to the touch, just shy of burning.

"I thought she refused to wear it," said Alucard.

Kell shook his head. "She told me she didn't."

"Yes, well, good thing she lies," said Alucard, looking around for a scrying table as Kell pulled off the ring.

"She'd never use it, unless she was in trouble."

Alucard didn't see the blade until it was already against Kell's palm, a line of red welling up beneath the steel. Lila would kill him if he let the *Antari* use his broken magic.

"Wait," he said, grabbing Kell's shoulder, but he was too late, because Kell closed his bloody hand over the ring and said, "*As Tascen,*" and the room was ripped away, the whole world subsumed by a sudden, infinite dark.

It lasted only a moment.

Less than that.

And then it was back, Alucard's boots no longer on a rug, but a stretch of paneled floor. The Veil was gone, replaced by a different house, cavernous and still. There was no sign of Lila, but Kell buckled to his knees with a gasp, as the threads around him sparked and frayed. He tore the mask off, dragged in shuddering lungfuls of air, pain scrawled across his face as he struggled up to one knee.

"Where are we?" he gasped.

515

Alucard was about to say he didn't know, but the words died in his throat as he looked around. His heart fell down, through his chest, and his feet, and the floor. He knew exactly where he was.

He was *home*.

VI

Tes worked as fast as she could, trying to ignore the grim truth.

An hour wasn't enough time.

It wasn't enough time to make a *persalis* from scratch—especially since her hands had already begun to shake. She'd cleared the desk, separating the objects by use, and which elements she'd find threaded through each spell. The container itself didn't matter, so she'd chosen a clock, pried open the back, and studied the inner workings, the twisted ribbons of amber and green. She drew them out, moved them quickly to another box and tied them there, before the light went out.

She wished that she'd put Vares on the desk, so she could at least pretend—pretend that she was back in her own shop, getting lost in the work. But she didn't trust Calin not to crush the bird for sport, so she kept him in her pocket as she tried, frantically, to reconstruct the spell.

Not enough time, pounded her heart, even as her hands kept moving, weaving threads, holding them aloft.

It had taken so many hours to fix the first doormaker.

But you didn't know then what it was, she countered to herself. *Now you do.* It was true, she had learned the pattern of the spell, the warp and weft of the threads that made it up. All she had to do was repeat it.

And if you do? said another voice. *What then?*

This wasn't just a piece of magic. It was a weapon, one the Hand planned to use to kill the royal family, and cause a rebellion, throwing the empire into chaos.

If Tes failed, she would die. But if she succeeded, others would instead. And she might still perish anyway. Or worse, the nobleman would keep her. Put her talents to other use, or sell them to the highest bidder. Like Serival.

516

Tes wouldn't let that happen, and she couldn't do nothing, so for the moment, she focused on the work.

She scanned the medley of parts, her vision blurring as the magic tangled in her sight. Across the room, Bex was slumped in a chair, but Calin was still doing his best impression of a doorstopper. On the wall to his right was a shelf with a pitcher.

"I need a glass of water," she said to him.

Calin didn't move. Tes nodded at the open spellwork in her hands, even though they couldn't see it. "It's for the *persalis*."

Calin huffed, and straightened. "Since when am I a fucking babysitter?" he said, grabbing the jug of water.

"Go and say that to the lord," said Bex. "No, on second thought, wait until he's here, I'd like to see his face. And yours, after he breaks it. Oh, wait," she added, "he already did."

"And you?" he grumbled, slamming the pitcher onto the edge of Tes's worktop. "How's your hand, Bex? Can you still see right through it?"

Bex rose from her chair. "Calin. I mean this with absolute sincerity— fuck off and die."

"Will you both shut up?" snapped Tes, trying to hold the spell with one hand while drawing a tendril of light from the water with the other.

"Oh, look," said Bex, "the pup has teeth."

She drifted to the table. Tes could feel her watching, but she didn't look up, couldn't afford to drag her attention from the work. But the crimson lines of Bex's power danced at the edges of her sight.

"Back up," she said. "Your magic is distracting."

The clock's hands lay cast aside like used matchsticks on the table. Bex took one up and waggled it, clicking her tongue. "Tick tick tick," she said. "I'd hurry up, if I were you."

"I'd work faster," she muttered, "if I wasn't dying."

"Perhaps you should have thought of that," mused Calin, "before you refused his lordship."

At that, Tes paused. There was an edge to his tone, and it wasn't directed solely at *her*. She looked up, meeting Calin's watery gaze.

"If I fail," she said, "what happens to the two of you? Will that *vestra*

517

let you walk away?"

The killers said nothing, but she could tell she'd struck a nerve.

"You have the antidote," Tes went on. "You could give it to me now, and give us all a better chance of living through the night."

For a moment, she thought they'd do it. Calin's hand even twitched toward his pocket. A muscle ticced in Bex's jaw. They shared a silent look. But then the bootsteps sounded in the hall, and they flinched, and she knew they were more afraid of defying the nobleman than dying at his hands.

Tes dropped her head and went back to work as the *vestra* reappeared.

"Bex," he said. "We have a guest downstairs. Go and keep her entertained."

The mention of someone else in the house made Tes look up, and when she did, the air lodged in her throat.

The nobleman was *burning*.

Before, his magic had been only a dim coil. Now, the air around him shone with iridescent light—as if he'd gone out a man with little power, and returned an *Antari*.

It made no sense.

Until she saw that he was wearing a new ring. Before, his only jewelry had been a polished silver ring, sculpted to resemble a feather. Now, on his thumb he wore a golden band and every strand of his new power stemmed from there, blooming out, and winding up around his limbs like silver-white weeds.

Bex disappeared into the hall, as if grateful for the excuse to get away, as the nobleman looked to Tes, and the box open on the table. "Is it done?"

"Almost," she lied. He seemed about to speak when the silver in the air around him gave a little pulse, and his eyes cut to the open door. The *vestra* cocked his head, as if listening to a music only he could hear, and then he smiled, if anyone could call it a smile. The faintest tic at the corner of his mouth.

"It appears," he said, "I have another guest."

With that he turned, and swept out, pulling the door shut behind him, leaving Tes alone with the half-finished *persalis*—and Calin.

"The antidote," she tried again, but the assassin crossed his arms.

"First, you finish the work."

Tes swallowed, and forced herself on. A pain had started somewhere in her chest. She tried to ignore it. She had gotten good, over the years, at working through the hurt. But moments later, a shiver ran through her and she slipped, nearly dropping several threads. She bit back a frustrated sob. One wrong move, and she could ruin the entire spell. One wrong knot, or missing string, and the doormaker wouldn't work at all. Or worse, it—

Tes's hands stopped moving. Her fingers hovered over the delicate web, waiting for her mind to catch up. And then it did.

There were different kinds of doors. Ones that led to different places in the same world. Ones that led to different worlds. But there was a third kind of door, wasn't there?

One that led to the place between worlds.

One that led *nowhere*.

Her hands started moving again, fingers racing to finish the spell.

The house hadn't changed.

Alucard had stood outside the Emery estate countless times on countless nights, but hadn't been inside, not since it was rebuilt. Hadn't been able to cross that threshold. He'd wondered, of course, if it would look the same, or if only the shell had been reconstructed, the inside a blank slate, a crypt for a dead life.

But it had been resurrected.

Every pillar, every door. Works of art hung on the walls. Even the furniture had been replaced. Rhy must have thought it a kindness, an act of love, but standing inside the house now, Alucard felt haunted.

What was Lila doing here? How had she gotten from the Veil to his own abandoned estate?

Alucard looked around. They were standing in the front great room, just beyond the foyer. A corridor vanished to the right, and straight ahead a staircase led up to the second floor. If they continued past those stairs, deeper into the house, on the right would be his father's office. On the left, a sitting room with a large stone hearth.

Alucard pulled off his own mask, casting it aside as he helped Kell the rest of the way to his feet.

"Get up," he said. "Something is wrong."

Kell fought to steady his breathing. He stared down at the black ring, still clutched in his hand.

"It should have taken me to her," he said. "Or at least, to the other band."

He looked around, then turned, and started down the hall.

"Wait," hissed Alucard, as if afraid the slightest motion would wake the sleeping house. Kell didn't go far, only a few strides, then knelt, and when he stood again, Alucard saw what he was holding: the other ring, hanging from a broken leather cord.

At that moment, a figure appeared at the top of the stairs.

Alucard went very still. He wanted to believe it was a shadow. A demon. A specter, haunting his dreams. But Berras Emery was none of those things.

He was a man, and he was coming down the stairs.

"Well, well, well," he said, punctuating each word with the thud of his boots. "Look who finally decided to come home."

He hadn't noticed Kell, and for once the *Antari* had the sense to keep his mouth shut. Alucard glanced toward him, a look that said *Go*. A look that said *Find her*. A look that said, *This is my fight*.

Kell retreated into the shadows.

And Alucard stepped forward, into the light, to face his brother.

VII

Few things could knock Alucard off guard, but Berras Emery was one of them. He was so thrown by his brother's appearance on the stairs that it took him a moment to notice the air around him, the way it shone, not with Berras's dull green threads, but a web of blazing silver, bursting from the golden ring on his right hand. The one that had vanished from the queen's workshop. The one that now granted Berras *Antari* magic.

Lila's magic.

"I've been waiting for this, little brother."

"You knew where I was," said Alucard. "You could have come to visit."

Berras reached the bottom of the stairs. "Hiding behind your palace walls."

"Is that why you wanted the *persalis*?" asked Alucard.

Berras didn't deny it. Didn't feign ignorance about the doormaker, or the Hand, or the plot to kill the royal family. *Alucard's* family. He just looked down at the golden ring on his thumb, and smiled.

"I wonder which element I'll use."

Alucard took a small step back, the groan of the floorboards concealing the way they shuddered as he pulled against them, drawing not on the wood but the packed earth below.

"I thought you favored your fists?" he said, dragging the soil up between the planks of wood as Berras flexed, and the silver magic brightened in warning.

"Oh, don't worry," said Berras. "When I end your life, it will be with my own hands. But first—"

Alucard felt the brush of someone else's will, a fist that tried to close around his bones, but he moved, just in time, threw up his hand, and the dirt came with it, a cloud of dust that blocked Berras's view.

The grip fell away and he lunged, intending to circle his brother. To attack him from behind. If he couldn't see him—a massive hand shot through the cloud, and closed around Alucard's throat, slamming him back into the nearest wall. The cloud crumbled, blown away, revealing Berras, the silver threads dancing in his slate-blue eyes.

"Amazing," he said. "I can *feel* your magic. It's racing, with your panicked heart." His fingers tightened, a crushing force. "You're scared." He leaned closer. "You should be scared. You—"

Alucard grabbed the air in Berras's lungs, and squeezed, choking off the words.

In response, his brother slammed him against the wall again, but Alucard didn't let go. Even though he couldn't breathe, even though his own head was beginning to spin—he crushed the air from the other man's lungs, until, at last, he felt Berras's fingers weaken a little around his throat. He would

521

have to let go, thought Alucard. He would—but then Berras grinned, a feral thing full of teeth, and reared back, and threw Alucard into the wall hard enough that it crumbled, and he went crashing back, into the dark.

The door swung open, and Lila dragged her head up, hoping to see Kell.

She was disappointed.

The hired killer—the one with the black braid, *Bex*—ambled in, looking at Lila like she was a gift, wrapped and set beneath a Christmas tree. "Bad night?"

Lila tried to laugh, but it hurt too much. "Not sure if you've heard," she said, "but you have shit taste in friends."

"Who said they were my friends?"

Lila rolled her neck. "Then the company you keep." The wood cut into her arms. She couldn't move. She knew—she'd been trying for the last few minutes.

"I'm curious," she said, trying to hide how hard it was to breathe. "What do you have against the crown?"

"Me? Nothing," said Bex. "But a job is a job, and in my world, coin is king. Now," she added, running her hand over the bracer on her forearm. The metal peeled away into a blade. "I guess it's time we finish what we started."

"Sure," said Lila. "Just let me up."

Bex chuckled. She brought her boot up to the chair, and leaned in. "I don't think so."

"Then it's hardly a fair fight."

Bex shrugged, and said, "No fight is truly fair." And Lila thought, under different circumstances, they might have gotten along quite well. Hell, they might even have been friends. Or at least, the kind of acquaintances that didn't try to kill each other.

But Bex's blade came to rest against her cheek. It bit, the pain a whisper compared to everything else, but she felt the bead run like a tear down her face.

"*Antari* blood is worth a lot," she said. "Do you really want to waste it?"

A smile twitched at the corner of Bex's mouth. "You're right." The blade vanished from Lila's cheek as she turned, moving toward a pitcher on the wall. She lifted the vessel, dumping the contents onto the floor.

"This will do," she said. Her back was to the door, so she didn't see what Lila did.

She sighed in relief. "You came."

Kell stepped into the room, the black ring's cord swinging from his fingers. "You called." He smiled a little as he said it. That smile felt nice. Even if it faded as he noticed Bex against the wall.

"How sweet," said the assassin, setting the pitcher down again. "But I'm afraid you're interrupting."

Kell looked to Lila, as if wondering why she was bound to a chair, or rather, why she was *still* bound, why she hadn't used her ample magic to get herself free. And since there was no time to explain, she simply said, "This one's all yours."

Mercifully, Kell didn't ask. He just drew his sword, and shifted, putting himself between Lila and Bex.

"Again, the blades," said Bex with a smirk. "Careful, *Antari*, someone will wonder what's happened to your magic."

Lila saw Kell's shoulders stiffen, and in that moment, Bex attacked.

She lunged toward his chest, only to drop her knife at the last instant, into her other hand, intending to drive it up from below, but Lila had taught Kell that move, one of a hundred in their sparring sessions, and so he was there, cutting downward before the blade could slice his front.

The swords clashed, and scraped, searching for skin and finding only steel.

She'd taught him well. All those months aboard the *Barron,* in sunshine and in rain, training the *Antari* out of Kell, stripping him of everything but sword, and speed. He moved as fast as Bex, even as her metal became molten, changing form, multiplying. He moved with all the grace of a born fighter.

And then, he made a mistake.

One of Bex's blades gashed his arm, and the sword fell from his grip, and skated across the floor, out of Kell's reach, and into Bex's.

He clutched his injured arm as she grinned.

"The beauty of my power," she said, kneeling to pick up the fallen sword. "Sooner or later, all steel becomes mine."

Her hand curled over the hilt, and Lila could almost hear Kell's voice, in the captain's cabin, when he'd introduced her to Kay. When she'd tried to claim one of his swords. He'd warned her not to, and still she'd grabbed the hilt, only to feel the sear of heat, the scalding pain as it burned.

Bex must have felt it now, because she gasped, and let go, dropping the blade as Kell unsheathed another, and she looked up just in time to see him drive it through her chest.

"Not every blade belongs to you," he said, as Bex let out a wet rasp.

He drew the sword free, and she collapsed.

Lila tried to laugh, but the pain cut her off short, and then it turned into a cough, which hurt ten times worse. She gasped, tasting blood as Kell rushed toward her, hacking at the wood of the chair until she was free.

"Fucking . . . bracelet," she managed, clawing at the band of gold that pressed into her skin. There was no clasp, no give. "Can't . . . get it . . . off."

"We'll find a way," he said. "But first, let's get you up."

He wrapped his arm around her ribs, and a pained cry tore free of her throat.

His eyes widened. "You're hurt."

"No shit, Kell," she said through gritted teeth.

His fingers were already going to the tear in his sleeve. "Let me heal you."

Lila shot him a venomous look and said, "Don't you fucking dare." Berras was out there somewhere, beyond the door, with Lila's magic, and she could barely breathe, and the last thing they needed was for Kell to be crippled by the pain of mending a few ribs. After a moment, he seemed to understand, or at least, to accept that *one* of them had to be able to fight.

"All right," he said. "Then lean on me."

"I can walk," she insisted, taking a step, only to feel her legs threaten to buckle as her broken ribs moved, and scraped inside her chest. Kell's hand was there, gentle but firm.

"Lean on me, Lila," he said again.

This time, grudgingly, she did.

VIII

Tes put her hands down on the table. "It's done."

She closed her eyes, tried to ignore the sluggish pounding of her heart, the way each pulse seemed to drag its feet.

Calin trudged across the room and stared down at the object on the desk. He cocked his head to one side in a way that reminded her of Vares. Under different circumstances, she might have found it funny. But right now, she focused all her strength on staying upright.

"Looks like a clock," he said.

Her lungs felt heavy, but after a moment, she convinced them to inhale.

"It doesn't matter what it looks like," she said, the effort causing sweat to break on her skin. "Only what it *is*."

She'd scribbled the spell words on a slip of paper—*Erro,* to open. *Ferro,* to close—and pushed it toward him. "The commands." His pale gaze raked over the paper as he lifted the object. It was smaller than the last doormaker. The whole thing fit into one hand, and any other time, she would have felt proud of the work.

"Where's the other piece?"

The words rolled over Tes, followed by a sickening horror. The other piece. The *key*. The final part, the one the man in the shop had never given her, the one that marked the destination. She hadn't known about it, not when she first repaired the *persalis,* which was why *her* doormaker had cut between worlds instead of through them. She'd forgotten. She'd forgotten because she was copying her own work. She'd forgotten because this new doormaker didn't *need* one.

Her gaze dropped to the cluttered table.

"Oh, that," she said, eyes landing on one of the cogs she'd pried out of the clock. She took it up with shaking fingers, trying to pass the gesture off as careful instead of random as she held it out. "Here."

Tes had never been a good liar, but if Calin caught the tremble in her voice, he must have assumed it was the poison. He snatched the cog, and turned away.

"Wait." Tes rose, her legs nearly buckling beneath her. She caught herself against the table as the world tipped. "The antidote." It was getting hard to breathe.

"Not so fast," he said, crossing the room. "Got to make sure it works."

He tossed the cog into the far corner, and set the clock on the floor against the wall. Tes followed, pulse flickering like a dying light inside her chest. The room swayed, and she braced herself against a chair as Calin said the word.

"*Erro.*"

The clock shivered on the ground.

And then it fell apart. Its wooden sides split open, and its face tipped forward, as if hinged, and out of the gaps spilled two lines of crisp white light. They burned, like fuses, spreading out to either side, and then up, tracing twin cracks through the air, until they were as tall as Calin, taller still, and then they turned again, and joined together overhead, carving the outline of the door.

The space within the doorway darkened, the wall behind the *persalis* blotted out, replaced by a curtain, a veil. But this time, she could see no place waiting beyond the curtain, no ghostly shimmer of another world. Only a solid, inky black.

"There," gasped Tes. "You see? It works."

Calin grunted, and dug a hand into his pocket, producing the antidote, the milky contents shining in the vial. But then his eyes cut to the corner, where he'd flung the cog, the cog that wasn't a key, just a piece of metal.

"Does it?" he asked, right before he cast the antidote through the doorway.

A sob tore from Tes's throat as the bottle disappeared into the dark. It didn't reappear in the corner by the cog. It didn't reappear at all. Because the door was not a door to any room, or any world. It was a door to nowhere.

And now, the antidote was gone. Her life, gone with it.

Calin rounded on her, his eyes flat with disappointment.

And in that instant, Tes did the only thing she could. She pushed him.

She was not strong enough, of course. The full force of her slamming into Calin was only enough to make him stumble half a step, more in surprise

526

than pain. But in that half a step, his elbow met the blackened surface of the door, and the door did a strange thing. It grabbed hold of Calin.

And dragged him through.

It happened so fast. A moment's struggle, boots sliding on wood, hands clawing for purchase, and then he was gone, voice swallowed up halfway through a shout, words cut off as cleanly as fingers beneath a sharpened knife.

Tes's legs folded. She sank to her knees on the damp wood floor. She should have been devastated. Perhaps it was the poison's work, but in that moment, she felt only grim resolve. She'd done the right thing.

"*Ferro*," she said to the door.

Close.

But the door did not.

Tes stared at the veil of darkness inside the glowing frame. The line of light that traced its edges should have split. The veil should have fallen away as the spell retreated back into the clock.

"*Ferro*," she said again, pushing the last of her strength into the word, making it solid, making it strong.

The door to nowhere stared defiantly back.

And then, she noticed the breeze.

There were no windows in this room, and yet, a gentle wind had started. It was not flowing out from the door. It was going *toward* it, dragging at the air, and the room, and everything in it. The scraps she'd tossed aside while she was working began to shudder and drift across the floor like leaves, vanishing into the open black mouth of the void.

Tes crawled forward to the open clock, wrapped her fingers against the front, careful not to let her hands touch the wall of black that had swallowed Calin as she tried to pry the shell away, to reach the threads inside. But as she did, the clock did a horrible thing. It broke. The frame crumbled, and was sucked into the darkness.

And still, the door didn't close.

In fact, it opened further, splintered past the edges of the frame. As it did, it made a sound, like a hammer against stone.

BOOM.

527

Tes scrambled backward, tried to get to her feet, but her legs buckled, the last strength going out of her limbs.

BOOM came the sound again, rattling through her as the doorway cracked, and threw out jagged black lines into the air to every side.

Get up, she pleaded with her body. It didn't listen. *Get up,* she tried to say aloud, but her lungs were out of air. Her heart skipped a beat, and then the world flickered, and she was on the floor, her cheek resting against the wood. She didn't feel scared.

The boom came again, but it sounded far away, or maybe she was.

Tes reached her hands into her coat, and folded her fingers over the little bone owl, felt him nestle against her palm.

She closed her eyes, and told herself the sound was the waves, crashing against the rocks back in Hanas. Told herself it was the sound of home as she drifted off to sleep.

IX

Alucard's ears were ringing as he got to his hands and knees, brick debris curling around his shoulders. The room was dark, but he knew, even by the contours, where he was.

His father's study.

Growing up, he was never allowed in here. Berras either. They only ever went as far as the doorway, and then, only when their father summoned them. But from that doorway, Alucard had learned every detail of the chamber. His father's dark wood desk. The glass windows that rose behind it, their panes stained midnight blue and traced with silver.

Now, the door hung shut, but the wall was open.

Alucard rose, and turned toward the ragged tear. Berras stood, waiting, on the other side. As if even now, he were loath to enter. But then he splayed his fingers, and the rest of the wall between them crumbled.

He stepped into the room.

Alucard had already drawn his blade, and as Berras crossed the threshold, he sliced through the air, but as the metal cut toward his brother, it melted, falling to the floor in molten silver drops, and Berras's fist connected with Alucard's jaw.

His head snapped to the side and he staggered. His lip split open, blood dripping down his chin.

"Any other night," he said, as Alucard wiped his mouth, "I'd take my time, but tonight, I'm in a hurry."

This time he saw the way the silver flashed in the air, just before his brother struck. As the broken bricks rose around Berras, his own hand shot toward his father's desk, and it scraped over the floor as its massive weight turned on its end, and came soaring into the space between the brothers the instant before Berras's rocks hurled themselves into Alucard, smashing against the desk instead. Alucard didn't wait—he shoved against the upright desk with all his strength, sent it slamming forward into Berras.

Heard it splinter as it struck—

And broke, with all the force of waves crashing against cliffs, and exactly as much use. Berras stood, unmoved, as the desk, reduced to slivers, crumbled around him.

"Why?" asked Alucard. "Why did you create the Hand?"

Berras flexed and the lamps burst to life on every wall, showering the study in light. "You have forgotten what it means," he said, "to be an Emery."

But as he spoke, the lamps he'd lit caught fire, consumed by the sudden force of too much magic. They began to burn, scorching up the walls, filling the room with acrid smoke. Something occurred to Alucard. Berras wasn't used to having this much magic. He wielded it like a mallet, clumsy and blunt.

"If it means being a traitor," he said, eyes cutting across the study, "I'm glad I gave it up."

Berras came toward him and Alucard retreated half a step for every one his brother took, letting the distance shrink between them.

"An Emery deserves to sit on the throne," said Berras. "Not kneel behind it."

Alucard reached to draw his second blade, only to feel Berras's will slam down around his bones with sudden, crushing force. His gasped as his ribs cinched, and his jaw locked shut, and his limbs froze. His brother stepped toward him, cracking his knuckles.

"Admit it," said Alucard, through gritted teeth. "You're jealous."

Berras's hand tightened, and so did the force on Alucard's body. "I'd rather be a traitor than the king's whore."

Alucard met his brother's eyes, and smiled. "Well, that makes one of us."

He couldn't move, but he could still *see*, and as the gold ring glinted on Berras's right fist and he drew it back to land a blow that surely would have shattered bone, Alucard cut his gaze toward the stained-glass window, and it shattered, as if he'd slammed his hand against it instead of his will.

Having magic was a gift.

But using it took practice.

Every element Alucard had gained was another one he had to juggle. It was one thing to have access to wind, and water, and earth—it was another thing to use them at the same time. There was a reason most magicians could only focus on a single one.

The window caved in, shards of blue and silver glass flying forward, and Berras did what any inexperienced magician would. He flung out his right hand to stop the shards of glass, dropping his hold on Alucard's body as he did.

The shards dragged to a stop, easily rebuffed by Berras's stolen power, and hung suspended, but Alucard was already moving, drawing that second sword and slashing the blade up, through Berras's right hand.

He roared in pain as a hundred shards of broken glass rained down onto the floor, Berras's severed fingers landing dully among the shine. The golden ring sloughed off, became a thin chain again. He screamed, and lunged for his brother with his other fist, but Alucard was ready, the wind at his back, and it met Berras with more force than a body—even his—could muster.

It should have been enough to knock his brother back a dozen feet.

But Berras had always seemed made of more than flesh and bone. Hatred was a heavy thing, and it kept his boots on the ground, though they slid as he struggled to stay upright, mouth yawning wide in a pained and furious growl.

Alucard crooked his fingers, and the wooden fragments of their father's broken desk rose up, and flung themselves into Berras, pummeling his brother until at last, he lost his footing and crashed backward, out of their father's study and into the ghost of the house where they had lived, slamming into the far wall with so much force the building shook.

Berras fell forward to his hands and knees, chest heaving, ruined right hand bleeding. Alucard stepped over the glass, and the ring, and the fingers he'd cleaved away, Berras's blood a slick red smear on the edge of his blade as he went to meet his brother.

It was time to end the Emery line, once and for all.

Bodies were too fucking fragile.

One damaged piece, thought Lila, and suddenly, the whole thing fell apart. It hurt to breathe, hurt to walk, hurt to speak, hurt to lean on Kell, and hurt to stand without him, but one thing kept Lila going and that was the knowledge of what she'd do to Berras Emery when she found him. A fantasy greatly aided when, halfway down the hall, the golden manacle around her wrist suddenly let go, falling to the floor in a pile of delicate chain.

As it did, Lila felt her magic come rushing back, into her lungs, her blood, the marrow of her bones. It didn't unbreak her ribs, but it was a salve, quieting the pain.

She flicked her fingers, and the chain rose up into her waiting hand as somewhere, nearby, a roar tore through the air, an animal howl.

"What is that?" asked Kell, but a crash went up and she pulled away, quickening her pace, the pain receding in her body and her mind.

The howl had sounded like Berras, which meant he was suffering without her. And that wouldn't do.

Lila reached the main room, Kell on her heels. It looked like a violent storm had slammed into the house. One wall had been destroyed, the floor littered with wood, and brick, and blood.

Berras Emery was on his hands and knees, trying and failing to rise to his feet. One of his hands was soaked in blood, the other clutching his ribs—Lila hoped at least three of them were broken—and Alucard was walking toward him, blade in hand.

"You think I'm the only one," Berras growled. "You are a fool." He looked up, and smiled, blood staining his teeth. "Go ahead and kill me."

Alucard's fingers tensed on the sword.

Lila had plenty of blood on her hands, but as far as she knew, Alucard Emery had never ended a life. Perhaps that made him a good person. Or a bad pirate. But in that moment, she knew, he was going to kill his brother.

She stepped forward, in part because *she* would be glad to put an end to Berras, and in part because she wanted to spare her old captain, because he was, for all his airs, too kind, too caring, because it would haunt him.

"You won't stop the Hand," Berras was saying. "We are coming for your crown. We are coming for your king."

Alucard raised the sword, but Lila reached out and caught his wrist. As she did, the estate doors burst open, bodies in. She turned, expecting another assault, only to see a dozen royal soldiers spilling into the house, their weapons drawn and ready for a fight. They slowed as they looked around and realized they had missed it.

They took in the two *Antari*, and the king's consort, and the man on his knees.

"A little late," snapped Lila, dropping Alucard's arm as the soldiers came forward and fanned out around him, swords leveled on Berras.

She pushed past them, following the trail of blood, picking her way through the wreckage until she found the study, the severed fingers, and there among them, what she guessed were the remains of the golden ring, though like the cuff, it was now a chain. She pocketed it, then stepped through the debris of the ruined wall in time to see Berras make one last attempt.

As Alucard turned to face the soldiers, Berras lunged up, tried to seize the blade from his brother's hand. But Alucard stepped back, and slashed his arm through the air, and Berras was thrown backward, into the wall. This time, when the older Emery hit the ground, he did not get up again. Lila hoped for a moment he was dead, but then she saw the rise and fall of his chest. Too bad.

Alucard turned toward the soldiers. "Arrest the leader of the Hand."

As he spoke, a crash echoed overhead. It was more than a sound—it ran through the bones of the house, shook the air as if they were standing inside of a bell. Everyone looked up. It wasn't the kind of thing you wanted move *toward,* but Lila did, taking the stairs as fast as her wounded body would allow.

"Lila, wait," called Kell, but his voice was drowned out as the crash came again, a deep, rattling *BOOM.*

At the top of the stairs, another hall, and Lila followed the sound into a room, and saw—

A door.

Or rather, a *doorway.* It stood in the middle of the room, open onto black, onto nothing. There was no sign of a *persalis,* and the door's edges were uneven, tattered. A breeze blew toward the open door, dragging at Lila's tunic, and as she watched, the frame seemed to splinter, and spread, throwing cracks out through the air itself.

"You can see it too, right?" she asked as Kell arrived beside her. He nodded, gaze scraping over the door. He approached it, hand grazing the air, the wind tugging on his hair, his sleeves. Kell circled the doorway, vanishing for a moment behind the blackness as if it were a curtain before appearing again on the other side.

Only one person—and one supposedly ruined object—could have *made* this door. Lila searched, and found Tes on the floor behind the desk. She was curled on her side in a pool of dark hair, as if she'd fallen asleep. But her skin was grey, and she didn't move, even when the sound shook the room again.

Lila knelt and grabbed the girl's shoulders. "Tes. Tes, wake up."

At first, nothing. Then, the girl opened her eyes. They were glassy, and Lila could feel her pulse flutter, unsteady beneath her skin, even as she smiled.

"I didn't help them," she said softly, as if she were drugged, or dreaming. "I didn't—" Her eyes widened sharply. "Look out."

Lila rose and turned in time to see Bex lurch into the room, blood-soaked and breath rattling in her chest even as she flung the blade at Lila's heart.

She reached out, and the knife shuddered to a stop, inches from her skin, Bex's will too weak to counter as her blood pumped onto the floor.

"You just don't want to die," said Lila, plucking the knife out of the air. "Let me help you." She swept her hand sideways, and the wind in the room turned sharp, slamming Bex into the waiting black embrace of the open door. She fought, boots sliding, but as her arm met the surface, it seemed to grab her, dragging her limb by limb into the dark.

Lila turned back to Tes. "Where does that door lead?"

Tes gave her a weak smile. "I have no idea." And then a shadow swept over the girl's face, and her limbs folded. Her head hit the floor. Lila shook her, but this time she didn't wake.

"Kell," called Lila, and he was there beside her. "Get her out of here."

He took the girl into his arms—she looked too young, too small, too still—but didn't leave. He looked past Lila to the door.

"We have a problem," he said. Lila saw it. The door was still spreading, those cracking tendrils growing wide and deep as they split the air.

"You get her out," she said, "I'll close it."

Kell nodded, and was gone, leaving Lila to face the door. She touched her fingers to her cheek, where Bex had sliced her. The cut was still weeping. Her hand came away red. She touched her palms together, staining both as she approached the door.

The wind was getting stronger by the second, a sucking force. The whole thing reminded her of an open mouth, a devouring dark. But mouths were like doors. They could be closed.

She wrapped her fingers around the frame, careful not to touch the black inside, felt the door's edges beneath her hands as she took a deep breath.

"As Staro."

Seal.

The wind weakened as she said it, the edges of the frame narrowing beneath her hands as the door began to close. The two sides drew together, the space between them shrinking. But halfway there, they stopped. The sides of the door trembled under her grip. As if pushing back against it.

Lila scowled, and clutched the frame.

"As Staro," she said again, but as her will slammed into the door, the door slammed back, shoving her arms apart as it sprang outward again, yawning wide. Lila staggered back as the cracks deepened and the horrible, earth-shaking sound came again.

BOOM.

Lila stared in horror at the door. It hadn't worked. She was *Antari*. The strongest magician in the world. And the spell just—hadn't worked.

The door cracked and spread, the wind whistling in her ears.

Lila didn't know what to do.

She didn't hear Kell return to her side until he laid a hand on her shoulder.

"You have to get out," she called over the rushing air. He shook his head. "I can't stop it."

"Put on the ring!" he shouted over the tearing world. And for a single, confused second she thought he meant the black band, the one she'd been too proud to wear, until she saw the heavy gold chain in his hands. The magical device that had just torn away her power, and given it to Berras. Kell was already wrapping the chain around his wrist.

Lila shook her head. "You can't use your magic."

"No," he said. "But you can."

She didn't fully understand the chains, but she knew enough to know that the one wearing the cuff was bound to the one with the ring, that the first's power became the second's. She pulled the thin length of gold from her pocket, its edge stained red with Berras's blood. She hesitated, long enough that Kell took it from her and wrapped the gold around her finger. As he did, the chain around his own wrist changed, became a solid cuff. Hers became a ring.

She'd been on the other side. Felt the utter absence of her magic. Now, she felt it double, as Kell's power poured in on top of hers. The whole world hummed with the force of it.

At the same time, Kell sighed, his shoulders sagging, as if a massive weight had suddenly been lifted. He closed his eyes, hand wrapped around the cuff as if to keep it there.

There was no time to ask if he was sure.

535

Lila turned back to the open door.

The wind was a torrent now, dragging at her clothes, but her very bones felt grounded with power. She touched the cut on her cheek, only to find it healed. The pain in her chest had faded too, the surge of Kell's power enough to mend her wounds. She drew her knife, and cut deep, painting both hands red as she approached the chasm.

It was so large now, she had to spread her arms wide just to touch the sides. Her fingertips curled around its edges. She filled her lungs, and forced the magic down into her hands as she called the spell.

"AS STARO."

The wind was a howling force, and yet, the words rang out, through her skin, through the room, as loud as that crashing bell. She felt them, clamping like giant hands against the splintered doorway, felt the frame shudder, and cave in, the darkness shrinking as the door was finally forced closed.

Then it was gone, leaving nothing but a ragged scar, like a badly stitched wound, on the air in its wake.

The wind died with it.

The room was still.

Lila sagged with relief, and turned toward Kell, hoping to see her own triumph mirrored on his face. But he wasn't standing there beside her. He was on the floor, his entire body rigid, muscles seizing.

"Kell."

Lila dropped to the ground beside him, tearing the ring from her finger. As soon as it was gone, the gold chain sloughed off his wrist, the connection between them broken. He should have been okay then, but he wasn't.

"Talk to me," she pleaded, but his teeth were clamped. His muscles clenched. His eyes were open, but he didn't seem to see her, tears sliding into his hair.

"God dammit, Kell," she said, gripping his face.

But as she touched him, something finally came loose inside his jaw, and he opened his mouth, and began to scream.

X

WHITE LONDON

The greater the power, the higher the price.

Kosika thought of Holland's words as she stood beneath the cherry tree. The one she'd grown with only blood and want.

It was an intruder, taller than the others in the orchard, in full summer bloom instead of giving way to fall. But that was not what troubled her. It was the trees to either side. They looked sickly now, their own leaves curling as if parched, their color leached away. As if, without realizing, she'd stolen from them to feed her silly spell.

What have I done?

"Magic is not infinite."

She jumped a little at the sound of Holland's voice. He was standing on the grass beside her, white hair lifting off his cheeks as it had in her dream. He followed her gaze. She thought of the Silver Wood, the heart of the world in her hands.

Footsteps sounded behind her on the path, and she turned to find Serak coming toward her. The Vir had always been a somber man, his dark brows often creased in thought. But she had seen him in the halls that morning, and he had seemed in good spirits. Now, he had the look of a messenger carrying bad news.

"My queen," he said. "You are needed."

"What is it?" she asked, but he would not say, only gestured for her to follow; not back to the castle, but toward the outer gates.

Kosika sighed, and started after him, casting a last look back at the tree. Flowers bloomed, but to its left and right, the branches withered.

"All spells have a cost," said Holland.

Kosika rubbed her injured thumb against her finger. "I thought I paid it."

"What did you say?" This, from Serak, who had stopped a few strides down the path.

Kosika looked from the Vir to her king, and for a moment, considered telling him the truth, that she was speaking to the Saint himself. But Holland cast her a heavy look, and in the end she shook her head, and said nothing.

The carriage rattled through the city streets. Serak's mouth was a grim line, his eyes cast down, and when Kosika asked where they were going, he shook his head and said only, "Better if you see."

If it had been anyone but Serak, she might have suspected malice, might have wondered if this was some attempt at a coup. If the Vir meant to lead her into danger, even death (she wondered briefly if any of the Vir were strong enough to kill her, but she doubted it). But this was Serak, loyal Serak, who looked at her and saw the incarnation of power, the heir of a saint.

Still, as the carriage trundled on, she kept her hands folded beneath her cloak, one nail grazing the shallow cut she'd made to grow the cherry tree.

At last, the carriage stopped, and Serak stepped out first, holding the door for her. As Kosika stepped down, she saw they were at the edge of an alley, the city walls rising high to either side. Ahead, the narrow road was interrupted by a white tent.

It struck her as an odd place to pitch a market stall, until she realized, of course, it had been erected to hide something else from view.

A soldier stood waiting for them, and as she followed Serak forward, he drew back the flap, and ushered her inside.

Holland had not followed her into the carriage, but she felt him now, at her side as she stepped into the tent. She blinked, eyes adjusting as sunlight was traded for soft lanterns. She looked down, expecting to see something on the ground—a body, perhaps, or the remains of a spell, something worth hiding from view—but the stones beneath her feet were bare, unstained. Kosika frowned, gaze flicking up to Serak, lips already forming the protest that there was nothing here—when she saw it.

What it *was* she saw, she couldn't say. It hung in the air between her and the Vir, rippling his image slightly like a pane of imperfect glass. At her back, Holland drew in a short, sharp breath, and she nearly glanced back, over her shoulder. Instead she reached out, sure her fingers would land on something solid, but they passed through the mark without resistance, as if there was nothing there.

Kosika's frown deepened. "What is it?" she asked, speaking both to Serak and the Saint.

"We are not sure," said the Vir. "It was discovered this morning by a soldier's wife, who told her husband, who came straight to us. Which was fortunate. It's not in a very public place, and we were able to erect the tent before rumors spread—"

"Rumors?" she asked.

Serak cleared his throat. "The nature of the mark, the way it is and isn't here. There is a chance—a small chance—that it could be a sign of damage to . . ."

"The walls." Holland's voice was low, and yet it filled the tent, heavy as smoke.

"—the walls," finished Serak a moment later.

Kosika didn't understand. And then, suddenly, she did.

The walls. The ones erected between worlds. As she stared at the warping in the air, it took on a different shape, seemed less like a ripple, and more like a crack.

"You think the walls are weakening?"

Serak said nothing, and that was answer enough. Panic pinged through her, tight and sudden as a plucked string. "There must be a way to reinforce them," she said. "Make them stronger."

"Perhaps," said Serak, sounding unconvinced. After all, it had taken dozens of *Antari* to create the walls that sealed the worlds off from each other. That kept the magic of Black London from spilling out. If the dam was breaking—

"I have soldiers scouring the city," said Serak. "Searching for other marks."

Kosika studied the crack in the air. "Leave me," she said. The words came out tight, and sharp, and so she cleared her throat and added, "For a moment. Please."

Serak bowed his head, and stepped out of the tent. As the flap fell, Holland took the Vir's place, his image warping slightly through the mark.

Kosika studied the ripple. Perhaps it was nothing, but the longer she stared, the more it resembled a door. A way out. A way in.

She had resolved, long ago, not to dwell on the existence of those other worlds. And yet here they were, pressing in on hers.

"There was a time before the walls," said Holland. "There will be a time after." His two-toned eyes scraped over the mark. "If it is a crack, it is the first. Perhaps the walls themselves will hold another hundred years."

"And if they don't?"

Holland frowned, one pale hand drifting up, grazing the air around the mark. "Nothing made can last forever."

But she was looking at his hand, the crack, the way his fingers leaned against it, as if it were solid. Kosika started forward, blood already staining her fingertips. Cracks could be mended, she told herself. Wounds could be healed.

"Kosika," said Holland, wearily, but she was already reaching up, her hand to the mark and the spell spilling out.

"*As Hasari.*"

The air shivered. Her pulse filled her ears, and Kosika braced herself for the wrench of her magic being poured into the world, the hollowing she'd felt when her power had been forced down into the soil, but she didn't care what it took, not if it fixed the wall, not if it kept her world safe, and—

Nothing happened.

The blood found no purchase. A single red bead slid down her palm, and maybe her eyes had simply adjusted to the light inside the tent, but the mark on the air seemed, if anything, more real.

XI

RED LONDON

Tes woke to a gossamer sky.

Twilight stretched over her head in wide swaths of blue, and violet, cut through with narrow lines of gold. The ground beneath her was soft as down.

If this was death, she thought, it didn't feel so bad.

But then she remembered, she had seen this sky before.

In Kell Maresh's room.

Tes shot upright, realizing she was alive, alive, and lying in the prince's bed.

Vares—*her* Vares—sat on the table just beside her. She knew it was just clever magic, she'd designed it herself, but when she moved, he fluttered his bone wings, as if he for one was glad she was alive, and awake. That first one, she didn't understand, but as she leaned over to stroke the little owl's skull, and said, "I'm glad to see you too," she saw the figure by the balcony doors, staring out at the river, and the city.

Lila Bard stood, arms crossed, her coat cast off and her chin lifted, as if savoring the sunlight that poured in through the glass. But her face was drawn, her jaw tight.

"Oh good," she said without turning, and Tes realized the *Antari* could see the bed in the door's reflection. "You're finally awake." She turned and came toward the bed, stopping at the ornate wooden frame, one shoulder tipped against the gilded post. "That was a close call."

"The door—" started Tes.

"It's closed." Lila's mouth was a grim line. "You made quite a mess."

Tes bristled. "I was just trying to stop them."

Lila studied her. "Why?" Tes balked, but the *Antari* only shrugged, as if it were a fair question. "They wanted you to make a *persalis*. You know how. So why didn't you give them what they wanted?"

"Because they'd use it to hurt people. To kill them."

"But *you* would have lived."

"They wanted me to make a weapon."

"Surely you've done that before."

"I didn't want to *be* a weapon," snapped Tes, exasperated. "You're an *Antari*, you should understand. People want power and if they can't have it themselves, they want to have the ones who do. If I'd made that *persalis*, it wouldn't have stopped. They would have found other things for me to fix, to make. So I didn't."

Lila nodded, finally satisfied by the answer.

"You lied, you know," said Tes. The *Antari* cocked a brow. "When you healed me before, you said that was the first and only time you'd bleed for me."

A smirk tugged at the corner of Lila's mouth. She shrugged. "I changed my mind," she said. "It happens sometimes."

"Thank you," said Tes.

Lila's expression hardened. "I didn't do it from the kindness of my heart. You owe me a favor. Now get up," she said. "I'm calling it in."

The last time Tes had left the prince's chamber, it had been under guard. Now the soldiers stood against the walls, staring past her as if she were not there, though they did bow their heads to Lila as she led Tes down the hall, toward a pair of ornate doors that stood waiting at the end.

A little girl sat on a cushioned bench outside those doors, a white-haired woman at her side. The woman was holding a children's book, and the girl was holding a rabbit, its fur the color of honey. Her black curls tumbled into her face as she whispered to it in a soft but constant stream, the way Tes sometimes did with the owl. She was young—four, maybe five, too young for her magic to come in, but Tes thought she could just make out the ghostly glow of light on the air around her, though it was too faint to have a color yet.

A white cat sat beneath the bench, amethyst eyes glaring out at Lila, as if personally offended by the *Antari*'s presence. But it shrank back into the shadow of the seat as Lila paused, and brought her hand to the child's black curls, in a gesture that was *almost* gentle.

"Hello, Ren," she said. "Are you guarding the room?"

The little girl looked up, revealing eyes that were a burnished gold. She nodded. "We have to be quiet, though," she said in a whisper. "The prince is sleeping."

Pain lanced across Lila's face, carved a furrow between her eyes.

"But it's okay," continued the child. "I brought him Miros, and Sasha said that when he wakes, I can go in and read him a story from my book."

Lila's hand fell away from the girl's head. "That sounds like a very good idea."

542

The child's gold eyes went past her, landing on Tes. Or more specifically, the skeleton bird in Tes's hand. Her mouth turned down. "Is your owl dead?"

In answer to the question, Vares fluttered his bone wings, and the girl's face opened in delight. Tes found herself holding out the bird for her to see. "Would you look after him for me? For a little while."

The child reached out and accepted him carefully, as if he were made of glass instead of bone and spell. She balanced him on the rabbit's back—the creature didn't seem to mind—and stroked his beak. "What's his name?"

"Vares."

The girl's gold eyes widened. "Like me!" she said, for a moment forgetting the need to whisper, and Tes startled, eyes widening. The word *vares* could mean *prince*—or *princess*. Which meant this little girl was in fact Tieren Maresh, the heir to the throne.

She flinched from the sound of her own voice, glanced at the doors, then scooted closer, and gestured for Tes lean in. "Are you the one who's going to wake him up?" she asked.

Tes's stomach sank. She'd known, somehow, this was the favor. But before she could answer, Lila laid a hand against the doors and said, "She's going to try."

The pattern on the doors was the chalice and sun, a massive *M* carved into the center, the lines filled with gold, and still, Tes was surprised when she followed Lila into the room, and found herself standing in front of the king.

Rhy Maresh slumped forward in a chair, looking twice his age.

His black curls tumbled into his gold eyes, his crown tossed onto a nearby cushion, chin resting on his laced fingers. The king was said to have no magic, but she could see the silver threads that bloomed outward from his chest and wound through the air around him.

There was no sign of the queen, at least. That was a mercy, but another man, one whose magic coursed in three different-colored strands, stood at the king's side, his hair drawn back, revealing storm-drenched eyes. Tes flinched at the sight of him, a sudden, visceral memory of the nobleman in the house. But this man was slighter, and his knuckles bore no scars, though there were delicate lines along his wrists, and up his throat—but she'd seen those marks before, on those who had survived the plague. When he met Tes's eyes, she saw the jagged lines that coiled in them, like bolts of lightning, and guessed that he was the one who shared her strange gift of sight.

The king cleared his throat. "I see our surgeon has arrived." He rose, only to sway a little. He closed his eyes, and steadied himself against the back of the chair.

"Apologies," he said. "We've had to kept him drugged, and I fear, what he feels, so do I."

That was when Tes rounded the sofa, and saw Kell.

The prince was sedated, but not deeply, the strain still showing in his hands, his jaw, his throat.

"Every time he woke," said the king, his own voice hoarse, "he started screaming."

Tes could see why. The threads around Kell Maresh were no longer simply frayed, but shattered, torn in places, in others held by a single brittle filament, and as the magic tried to course, it sparked.

Tes drew closer. Copper hair fell across Kell's face, interrupted by a streak of silver. His coat was gone, his shirt open at the collar, revealing the edge of a blackened brand over his heart—a spell she didn't recognize—but threads of silver coiled there, flowing in, instead of out, and Tes realized it was the echo of the magic that circled the king, the other half of the silver pattern that bloomed from Rhy Maresh's chest. Their lives were somehow tethered.

"Can you heal him?" asked the king.

The same question Lila had asked the day before, and Tes felt the same protests rising to her lips. But this time, she bit them back. She had built a *persalis* from scratch, her hands shaking with poison. Now they hung steady at her sides. If anyone in the empire could do this, it was Tes.

"In theory, yes," she said. "But you're bound together, aren't you?"

The king was said to be unkillable, but he wasn't. Not really. Every spell had a weakness, and Tes had just uncovered his.

"If Kell dies," she said, "then so will you."

The king managed a weary smile. "That is a risk I'm willing to take."

He glanced at the other man as he said it. The other man grimaced, seemed about to speak, then changed his mind, and looked away.

"Do it," he said under his breath.

"Will you help me?" asked Tes. The man's head jerked up, and she explained, "I could use a second pair of eyes."

"There, Alucard," said the king, sounding oddly cheerful. "Now if I die, it will be at least in part your fault." Then, to Tes, "What else do you need?"

She pulled her hair up into a pile on her head, and rolled her sleeves. "A cup of tea," she said, "as strong as you can make it. A pair of blotters," she went on, "I saw a pair in the queen's workshop. And last of all"—she turned to Lila Bard—"a thread. From your magic. I need something to mend him with."

She expected the *Antari* to protest, but Lila only held out her hand, and said, "Take it."

Three years ago, Tes had tried to steal a strand of that silver magic, thought she'd be able to pinch a thread and slip away. Now she realized she'd never have been able to. It turned out, it wasn't like plucking a hair from a passing head. As Tes pulled a thread from the coil in the air around the *Antari*, it came free, but Lila hissed, and swore in a flourish of High Royal, and even if Tes didn't understand the words, she got their meaning.

When it was done, Tes took a deep breath, and drew the thread out long between her hands, a single silver wire, bright as moonlight. "Ready?"

Rhy Maresh lowered himself into his chair.

Alucard brought a hand to rest against the king's shoulder.

But Lila went to Kell's side. She knelt beside his sleeping body, and whispered something in his ear, and if Tes had been standing farther back, she'd never have heard it. But she did.

"There is nowhere you go," said the *Antari* to her prince, "that I cannot follow."

And then Lila was on her feet, sweeping past them, to the far side of the room. Tes approached. She looked at Kell Maresh, tried to imagine he was not a man, but a vessel, an object brought into her shop.

Once broken, soon repaired, she thought.

And then, she got to work.

XII

UNRAVELING

I

WHITE LONDON

Everywhere Kosika looked, she saw disaster.

In a cloud of steam, the fall of her castle. In a cup of tea, the ruin of her city.

"All hail the queen," said a Vir.

But she wasn't there. Oh, technically she sat in a gilded chair at the center of the table, Nasi to one side and Serak to the other, as the toast was made, and the food heaped onto her plate, but her throne might as well have been absent.

Voices rose and fell, but Kosika did not hear them. Just as she did not feel the wood of the chair beneath her arm, the weight of the crown on her head, or the damp slick on the stone table, where a reckless pour had left a pool of water, even though she'd been dragging her fingers through it for several minutes.

No, as the others ate and drank and spoke of nothing, Kosika was back in the white tent, staring at the crack that scored the air. A weakness in the walls of the world. *Her* world. The only one she had ever cared about. The only one that mattered, so long as the walls held. But—

"One day the walls will fall," Vir Lastos had said. "We should know our enemies."

"Every day, *our* world revives a little more."

"And what if theirs does, too?"

Lastos had been cut down that day, for his insolence. But his warning lingered.

Kosika looked down, and saw that she had not been drawing aimless patterns in the water. Her fingertip had made a door. Not just any door— the sides were straight but the top arched into a peak. The door to her own room. And to Holland's.

Her chair scraped back. It wasn't a loud sound, but it might as well have been a whip, for how it cut through the hall, silence ringing in its wake.

"My queen," said Serak, rising with her. "Are you unwell?"

Kosika murmured some excuse, her own voice sounding far away in her ears. Nasi looked to her, was halfway to her feet to follow when Kosika shook her head. Nasi frowned, but sank back into her seat as Kosika escaped the dinner, and the hall.

As she climbed the stairs, she dug her nail into the cut along her thumb, felt the dull lance of pain as it reopened. She went up, and up, and up, to the alcove and the altar. She expected to feel her king fall in step beside her, but she reached the top alone. She took a candle from the table, slipped behind the statue of the Saint, whispered the word into the door, and went inside, the candle in her hand casting unsteady light across the darkened chamber.

She went to the desk, to the small wooden box that sat on top, expecting Holland's voice to waft toward her as she took it up. But there was only her heart, and her own voice hissing in her head.

Had she been naïve, to ignore the other worlds so long?

She had no desire to venture out into them.

But what if the walls failed, and they came in?

What if they came for her magic?

How could she fight what she did not know?

She tucked the box under her arm, and turned away, flinching as she caught sight of her reflection. Her crown shone like a band of molten light in her braided hair, as did the silver buttons that trailed down her front, the polished gemstones at her collar. She tugged the crown free, and then the braids. Loose, her hair rippled and fell into her eyes, hiding the *Antari* mark behind a brown-blond curl.

Holland's grey cloak hung from the wall, and she pulled it around her shoulders, shivered as the weight settled on her like a hand. And then she knelt on the stone floor, and drew an X.

Holland himself had shown her this spell. Guided her through it one summer day, when she longed for a way to get out of the castle unnoticed. He almost smiled as he told her how, and she tried to imagine her king, her saint, as a boy her age, slipping through the city, as if he'd taken a map and folded it up, and used a pair of scissors to cut straight through.

As far as she knew, no one had noticed the square of bark she'd peeled away from a courtyard tree, the matching mark she'd carved into the trunk beneath, the lines darkened faintly with blood. The X had long dried to a faint and fading brown, but it was still there, and as Kosika pressed her palm to the mark on Holland's floor and whispered the spell—"*As Tascen*"—the king's chamber fell away, and so did she.

When they both came back, she was no longer kneeling on stone, but grass, her hand pressed to the base of the tree. In the distance, the castle rose, its windows glowing like milky eyes. The grounds were dark, but the night was clear, and the moon was nearly full, so there was enough light to see by.

Kosika pressed her bloody fingers to the box, and said the words to open it.

Her head spun a little with the sudden use of so much magic, and she thought of the cherry tree—another reminder that she was drawing from a finite well.

She lifted the lid of the box, and moonlight fell on the coins inside. Three tokens to three other worlds. One silver. One crimson. One black. Kosika waited, and at last, she felt his presence.

Like a sliver of sun on a cold day, a sudden, welcome patch of warmth.

"Where have you been?" she asked softly as Holland emerged from the shadow of the trees, his white hair shining like moonlight.

"I was here. I am always here."

"You have not been with me since we saw the crack."

He reached her side, and stopped, a pale shadow looming over her. "I did not want you to feel my hand at your back." His gaze dropped to the box in her hands. "I know your mind. I will not push you."

His brow was furrowed, his eyes taking on a mournful cast. But there was resignation in it, as if he'd known it would always come to this.

Kosika dragged her own gaze back to the open box. The waiting coins. Her hands drifted to the crimson one, but as her fingers grazed the metal, Holland spoke.

"Wait."

He knelt, laying his hand over hers.

"I mean it, when I say that I am always with you. I am bound to you, Kosika. I go where you go. I cannot go where you don't. But there is something I must see." She looked up and found those two-toned eyes—green and black—searching hers. "Do you trust me?"

"Of course," she said, the words spilling out without resistance.

Holland's hand moved from the crimson coin to the shard of black glass. "Then take me here."

Kosika hesitated. She had been to Black London only once, the year before, and had never wished to go back. The hollow dread of that place had lingered on her skin like cobwebs. But Holland was her king, her saint, and she would deny him nothing, so she drew the token from the box, felt the cold weight of it in her palm before closing her fingers over the shard.

"As Travars."

The darkness around her went solid. The world came apart.

But this time, she did not fall.

There was no terror, no rush of air, no body plunging down from a tower that was not there. And yet, she seemed to *land,* the ground around her sending up a plume of ash that hovered, and began to sink, windless, to the ground.

She rose, and looked around, gripped by the sudden fear that Holland had not followed, that she was alone again in this cursed world. But then the ashes around her settled, and he was there. He stood several feet away, his back to her, staring out at the wasted landscape, and despite the stillness of this place, the strange breeze that always surrounded Holland's image was still there. His pale cloak rippled, and the white hair rose off his cheeks, and somehow, he seemed even more the saint.

Until he sighed.

The breath came out ragged, so undeniably human, as if he were steeling himself against this place, and Kosika remembered the stories he told, of being cast into this place, near death, drawn back from the edge by a demon who promised to resurrect his world, in exchange for his body, his life.

"Holland." Her voice carried like a shout in a hollow hall.

He turned his head, exposing the line of his jaw, his cheek, his black eye. She wanted to ask why they were here, but he held a finger to his lips. The black eye fell shut, his head tipped faintly to one side as if listening.

Kosika fell silent too, and looked around. They were standing in what once might have been a market square, the stones splintered beneath their feet. The buildings to every side had once been spiked and spired, but most of the points had broken off, and crumbled, taking rooftops with them.

"Hard to believe, isn't it?" said Holland softly. "That once, this place was the source of all power."

It *was* hard to believe, looking at it now, as cold and dark as an abandoned hearth.

But Kosika knew that it was true—that once, all the magic in the worlds had come from here. That it had emanated, rolled across the worlds like heat, cooling the farther it got from the source. Then it was poisoned, and that had carried, too.

A twitch of movement—she turned to find Holland walking away, stride by careful stride, though his own steps made no sound, and never stirred the ash as hers did.

He reached the center of the square, and knelt, placed one palm flat against the broken stones, fingers splayed as if he were flesh and blood instead of ghost. After a moment, his lips moved, his voice barely a whisper, though the words still reached her.

"Do you feel it?"

She knelt, and touched the ground as he did, expecting a shiver, a dread, a prickle of rotten magic. Instead, she felt only the surface of the stone. No magic, and for a moment she was a child again, before she found Holland's body in the Silver Wood, before she woke the next day with the world humming inside her skin. And even that was not quite right, since before she had magic of her own, she could still feel it in the world, a strained and straining force, leaning out of reach. This was different. This was like when Kosika was nine, and she had stepped into a warding spell.

The kind designed to sever a body from its magic.

It had been one of the first—but certainly not the last—times someone had tried to take the young queen's life, and Nasi had been there, blade in hand, to cut the killer's throat, and pull her from the trap, but in the moments after she'd been trapped, and before she'd been saved, she'd been overcome by the strangeness of the spell.

The warding hadn't *hurt*. It had felt like this. *She* had felt like this—a vessel emptied out.

An empty thing.

Holland was on his feet again, moving toward her.

"Do you feel it?" he asked again.

Kosika shook her head. "I feel nothing."

"Exactly," said her king, the word rushing out with his breath, his shoulders sloping in relief. "When I saw the crack in the world, I wondered. I did not dare to hope. But now, I know."

"Know what?"

"It's over." He stopped before her. His eyes had a glassy shine, his voice tight with feeling. "Osaron's fire has at last gone out."

Osaron.

The shadow king. The piece of magic that became a god, and ruined everything.

"Gone out?" It was true, she felt no power in this place. But the mark of Osaron's ruin was on everything. She found herself holding her breath, unwilling to inhale the ash, lest it have traces of corrupted magic.

"Do you know what this means?" he said, dragging his fingers through the air. "We can rekindle the fire now. We can restart the source."

Kosika recoiled, as if struck. "The magic here is cursed. If we rekindle the fire, we rekindle the blight and—"

"No," said Holland, shaking his head. "Raze a forest, and the rot goes with it. Before this became the source of poisoned magic, it was the source of *everything*. All the power in the worlds began *here*. It can again." He brought his hand to rest on Kosika's shoulder. "The walls were made to shield the other worlds. But they were also a dam. From the moment they went up, no power could flow between. From that moment, the magic became finite. Each place, left to nurture its own store. We had the most, at first, close as we were, but we used it wrong, carved it up into smaller and smaller fires, smothered each until they began to go out. My death was a breath on the embers of a dying world. Your reign, too. Together, we have kept our flame from going out. But, I fear, we have reached the limits."

Kosika's stomach turned as he spoke her fears aloud.

"There isn't enough power left," he said.

"I know," she whispered. But Holland did not look defeated. Far from it. There was a light behind his eyes, a power to his voice.

"Do not despair. If we light the fire here, if we restart this source, our world will burn again, brighter than it ever has. You will not have to choose which tree to water. Our people will not need to bleed to thaw the winter chill. Everything I suffered. Everything I lost—it will have been worth it."

In that moment, Kosika saw Holland as he must have been, before the Danes had bound him. She saw the boy who dreamed of healing a dying world. She saw the king, who gave everything to see the power restored. Saw the saint, who even in death could not rest, could not leave his task unfinished.

"What about the walls?" she asked.

Holland's hand fell from her shoulder. "Let them crumble. Or tear one down, and forge the other fresh. Let the other Londons tend their embers, while we enjoy the heat."

And then her king did something he had never done before.

Holland knelt before Kosika. Folded, gracefully, one knee resting on the splintered stones.

"My queen," he said. "We can do this. Together."

She wanted it. And she saw how badly he wanted it. Holland Vosijk had given so much. Had given everything. And it hadn't been enough. But it could be. With her help.

Kosika looked around at the dead world. "How do you rekindle a fire this large?"

"The same way you do in any hearth," he said. "Enough kindling, and a well-placed spark."

As Holland said it, his face lit with a dazzling thing: *hope*. If he had asked Kosika, in that moment, to open her veins, and spill every drop of blood onto the dead soil then and there, she would have done it.

Instead, she simply nodded and said the words that would set the world ablaze.

"Show me how."

II

RED LONDON

Kell remembered everything.

If anyone asked, he would tell them he didn't, that the last thing he recalled was winding the golden chain around his wrist as he told Lila to use his magic, to close the door. That after that was only darkness.

But it would be a lie.

For a merciful moment, after the chain turned to a cuff around his wrist, he had felt nothing at all. The magic blinked out like a candle at the end of its wick, and he was left hollow, an empty vessel, and there was some mercy in that.

But then, it had started.

He had thought that maybe, if the magic were in someone else's hands, it couldn't hurt him, but as Lila called the spell, he felt it, that wrenching, bone-deep pain, and every second she had poured her power and his into the words it had gotten worse, and worse, and he would have let go, but he couldn't, because he wasn't in control.

The blowback had always been agony, but it had always been brief, only this time, it wasn't, because it never ended. The pain simply mounted and mounted until he could not breathe, could not speak, and by the time the door was finally closed and the spell was done, and the shackle fell away, he was trapped inside that pain. Inside his skin.

The world outside his body went away, but he was still there, still screaming.

And then—finally—it stopped.

It stopped, and he knew that death had come at last, and it felt wonderful. It felt like his brother's arms, like Lila's voice, like floating off to sea.

Then Kell opened his eyes.

And saw a rabbit.

Miros hopped along the foot of his bed. A small face peered over the top of the blankets just beyond it, black curls and gold eyes staring at him.

"Ren," said Rhy, crossing the room. "What did I tell you about bothering your uncle?"

"But he's awake."

Rhy turned, and saw Kell, and several emotions flickered across his face before he hauled the princess into his arms.

"Go find Alucard," he said, kissing her hair. "Tell him I said you could have *three* stories."

He set Ren down, and she bounded away, the rabbit hopping in her wake.

"That should buy us a little time," he said, watching her go.

"What happened?" asked Kell. His voice felt raw, as if he'd been screaming.

"What do you remember?"

"Nothing," said Kell, but the way his brother looked at him said they both knew it was a lie.

"How do you feel now?" asked Rhy.

Kell shifted, and sat up. His muscles were stiff, but nothing hurt. "What did you do?"

"*I* didn't do anything. Tes did all the work."

Kell's head shot up. "No."

Rhy held up his hands. "We're both alive. So that is something."

"You shouldn't have risked it."

"It wasn't a choice," said Rhy darkly. "It was that, or keep you drugged forever. Not that I didn't enjoy the high, but I do have a country to run."

Kell's hands tightened on the sheets. "Rhy—"

"Don't thank me yet," he said, lifting a candlestick from the table. "We don't know if it worked."

He held out the unlit taper.

Kell stared at the candle, but made no move, and for a terrible moment the years fell away and he was standing before the ice house game in the lightless fair, terrified to test his power only to find it broken. He was in his narrow cabin aboard the *Barron,* tearing himself apart, certain if he only tried hard enough, he would break through the pain. He was fighting beside Lila, swords in hand, determined not to reach for that ruined magic, trying to convince himself it wasn't there. He was right here, right now, sitting in his royal bed, afraid of what would happen if he reached for the power and it did not come. Afraid of the pain he'd feel if it did.

But Rhy had risked his life for this. A chance to be restored.

Kell knew he had to try.

He reached out, and cupped his hand over the unlit taper. Called the warmth to the wick.

The candle sparked.

It wasn't *effortless,* the way it had been once, when he was young. There was a resistance, the difference between drawing an arm through water instead of air. But it worked.

The fire bloomed under his fingers, and then, all around, as every taper in the chamber lit at once, bathing the room in flickering light. Rhy sucked in a breath, but Kell's attention hung on the candle between them, the fragile flame growing hot beneath his palm. He stared at the fire until the pain finally came, not a wave rolling through him, only the burn of a candle against bare skin.

Kell heard Rhy hiss and he pulled back, shaking the sting out of his own hand. He looked down at his singed palm, the skin pink from the heat, and broke into a smile.

Tears slid down his face.

It was the most welcome pain Kell had ever felt.

Over the years, Lila had explored most of the *soner rast,* from the five ballrooms to the secret halls that ran between the royal chambers, the sunken baths and the training grounds, and the courtyard. But there was one place she always went out of her way to avoid.

The queen sat at a table in the middle of her workshop, her back to Lila and her head bowed over a notebook, and yet, as Lila slipped, silent as a thief, between the counters piled high with papers and pieces of half-formed spells, Nadiya Loreni cleared her throat.

"Delilah Bard," she said without looking up. "What brings you to my chambers?"

"Well," said Lila, running her hand over half a dozen stoppered jars. "You keep inviting me. I thought it was time to take you up on the offer."

The queen stopped whatever she was doing, and rose to her feet, turning as she did to face her. "Is that so?" Her voice hovered on the line between distrust and curiosity.

Lila shrugged, continuing toward her. As she did, her hand slipped into the pocket of her coat.

"I heard Tes's work on Kell was a success," said the queen. "I would have liked to see the process for myself."

Lila's fingers closed around the metal pooling in her pocket. "Yes, well," she said, drawing out the two gold chains, "it turns out she and I have something in common."

Nadiya's eyes dropped to the glinting metal. "And what is that?"

"We don't like you very much," said Lila, letting the chains pour from one hand to the other. "And we trust you even less."

She held out the gold chains, but as Nadiya reached to take them, Lila's hand closed over the top, and they glowed, and then melted, dripping between her fingers.

"No," yelped the queen, lunging forward, too late, but instead of stepping out of her path, Lila stepped in to meet her, free hand vising around Nadiya's throat.

The queen tensed beneath the grip, tried to pull back, pull free, but Lila took hold of Nadiya's bones and forced them still.

"How does it feel?" she growled. "To be helpless? To be bound? At the mercy of someone else's will?"

"I'm sorry," gasped Nadiya.

"You're sorry?"

"Alucard told me," rasped the queen, struggling for breath. "About Berras. What he did."

"Someone *gave* those chains to Berras Emery." Lila's grip tightened on the queen's throat. "Was it you?"

Something flashed in Nadiya's eyes, then. Not guilt, but righteous anger. "I would *never*." Lila scowled, but didn't let go. Nadiya's face colored. Her pulse raged beneath Lila's hand. A heart, like a candle, so easy to snuff out.

And then the queen met her gaze. "So keen to do—" she gasped, "—the Hand's work—for them?"

Lila sighed and flung the queen away. She crashed back into the table, caught herself there. She lifted a hand to her throat. Her fingertips were shaking.

"You and I may not see eye to eye," said Nadiya, "but I am not your enemy. The chains were stolen."

"By who?"

"I don't know."

"Bullshit," hissed Lila. "Nothing happens in this place without your knowing."

Nadiya scowled. "Someone betrayed my trust. Believe me," she said. "I want to find out who."

"That's the problem, Your Majesty," said Lila, the wind picking up around her as she spoke, sweeping clear the tables and emptying the shelves. "I don't believe you. I don't trust you. And the next time you even *think* of creating something like those chains, I will turn you to stone and use your lifeless statue as a coatrack."

With that, Lila turned and left the workshop, the wind dying in her wake as the remnants of paper and spell fluttered down like ash around the queen.

Alucard forced himself down the prison steps, one by one by one, steeling himself for what he'd face when he reached the bottom.

Of the four cells that composed the royal jail, three again were empty. There, in the last, where Tes had briefly been, was Berras. He sat on the stone floor, his back against the wall, his face in shadow. A heavy bandage was wound tight around one hand, where the fingers were missing. The cloth was red where the blood had wept, a patch of wall stained too, as if he had been hitting the same place, over and over, wondering which of them would crack first.

There were no soldiers standing guard. Alucard had sent them all away. His brother had already poisoned enough minds against the palace. He would not get the chance to ruin more.

The first thing Alucard had done last night, upon leaving the Emery estate, was order it torn down. He'd gone that very morning, to make sure it was done. And as he stood on the bare spot where the house had once been, he'd felt an overwhelming peace. A burden finally set down. A weight released.

Staring at his brother now, he felt no such relief, but the same grim resolve. Alucard straightened his coat as he crossed to the cell. He had chosen to dress in red and gold that day. Not a hint of Emery blue. His hair was pinned back with a chalice and sun, and at the sight of it, Berras sneered.

"I thought it would please you," said Alucard, "that I wear these colors instead of yours."

"No matter what you wear," said Berras, rising to his feet, "it won't change what you *are*, little brother."

"And what is that?" asked Alucard blandly.

His brother approached the bars. "A disgrace."

Alucard smiled. "Once upon a time, those words would have cut, as surely as a blade. Now I see them for what they are. The last punches of a man who's lost his fight. What would Father say, if he could see you now? His oldest son, arrested for treason. Would he be proud, that you tried to overthrow the empire? Or simply disappointed that you *failed*?"

Berras's good hand gripped the bars, squeezing until his scarred knuckles went pink, then white.

"What do you think will happen to your followers," mused Alucard, "now that you're gone? Cut off the head, and the body quickly crumbles."

Berras's mouth twitched. "But I am not a head," he said. "I am a hand." His eyes darkened. "Do you know why we call ourselves the Hand?"

"Because you clutch at other people's power?" ventured Alucard.

Berras grinned. It was cold, and hateful, and mocking. "Because even if you lose one," he said, releasing the bar, "there is another."

Alucard wasn't sure if the words were a bluff, or truth, but they sat ill. Not that he would give Berras the satisfaction.

"So you weren't the leader, then?" he asked. "Just a pawn? A tool being used by smarter people? A blunt weapon, to be wielded, and then got rid of? If that is true, why?"

"I already told you."

"That's right. To take the throne. To show me what a real Emery is. But the thing is, Berras, I don't believe you. I think you did it because you are small, and petty, and cannot bear a world where I am stronger."

His brother's smile slid, becoming a feral, humorless grin. "Come into this cell and face me. Let's see how strong you are with nothing but your fists."

"Tempting, but I'll pass." He turned, and started for the stairs.

"How dare you turn your back on me, little brother."

Alucard stopped. "Oh, I'll come back," he said. "It's not like you're going anywhere. But I have places to be. My husband is waiting for me. My daughter, too." He looked up at the ceiling. Through it. "You see, it's dinnertime. I want to know which animal Ren has tried to sneak under the table. She's been very into rabbits lately, but really, there's not a single living thing she does not love. She's like Anisa that way." He swallowed, their little sister's name scraping his throat. "Before bed, she'll need a bath, which is always an adventure, and Rhy and I will read her a story, and the queen will shine a lantern into every corner of her room, to show her that every shadow is nothing but a lack of light. You see why I must leave you? There is so much love up there."

His eyes fell back to his brother.

"I sometimes wonder if you would have been so hateful, had we lived in a kinder house." He shrugged. "I suppose it doesn't matter now."

Berras glared out between the bars. The anger rolled off him in waves. Once, they would have crashed over Alucard, too. Would have pinned him down, and drowned him. Now, he simply stepped back, out of its reach.

"Alucard," growled Berras as he turned, and left.

"Alucard!" His brother's voice clawed at the air, but came no closer as he climbed the stairs, out of the dungeon and the darkness, and up, up, up, to the light.

III
SOMEWHERE AT SEA

The *Grey Barron* sliced its way through the open water.

Its captain stood at the prow, black coat billowing like a pirate flag, her eyes—one brown, the other black—turned to the bare horizon.

Now and then Lila's fingers drifted to the ring she wore on her right hand, one thumb running absently over the ship carved into its scorched black surface. The owner of its twin was back in London, but she knew that if she called Kell, he would come. And for the first time in seven years, he could cross the distance between them, no matter how great, and it would cost him nothing but a drop of blood and a whispered spell.

The night before she'd left, they'd lain in bed, and Lila had run her hand across his brow, and down his cheeks, trying to smooth each and every line the pain had carved in and out of Kell Maresh, until he had taken her wrist, and pinned her to the bed, *Kay* glinting like mischief in his eyes, as he convinced her not every change needed to be erased.

Now, Lila Bard rapped her fingers on the rail of her ship. Waves crashed up against the hull, spraying a cool mist that seemed to curl around her as she scanned the line where sea met sky, searching for the *Ferase Stras*.

After all, she had a parcel to deliver.

At the back of the ship, Tes folded her arms on the wooden rail, and watched the water ripple in the *Barron*'s wake. She'd sewn a pocket on the outside of her coat, and Vares poked out from the top flap, his small head bobbing, wings pinned down over her heart. Now and then, when the breeze picked up, the dead bird nipped his beak at the buttons and fluttered, as if he was flying.

She already missed London.

Missed her shop in the *shal,* and the dumplings she got from the market stall on Heras Vas, and Nero, to whom there'd been no chance to say goodbye. It had been two days since the crimson glow of the Isle vanished from the water beneath the ship, replaced by tendrils of ordinary light. More than a day since she'd seen land.

Not just any land, but Hanas.

She'd known it, of course, the lines of the cliffs she'd climbed when she was young standing out like a jagged stitch on the horizon.

She imagined her father preening over the rare objects in his shop.

Imagined Serival standing on the docks, the wind tugging at her plaited hair, one hand lifted to shield her eyes as they scanned the water for something of worth. For Tesali.

Where are you, little rabbit?

She'd held her breath as the ship sailed on, and the cliffs shrank from sight.

That first night on the *Barron,* when the hull rocked her to sleep, Tes had dreamed of another life. One where she'd asked to stay on Elrick's boat, and the two of them had sailed away from London the same day they'd docked. One where she'd spent the last three years skimming from port to port, fixing any trinkets that came their way, and nothing bad ever happened.

That's how, even before she woke up, she knew it was a dream.

The ship began to slow, the wind falling out of the sails, and Vares twitched, a small restless spasm of his bone wings.

"It'll be all right," Tes told the dead owl as she pushed off the rail and made her way to the front of the *Barron.* In her brief time aboard, she'd mended the spell in Stross's watch, and added a hidden compartment to Vasry's trunk, and tweaked Raya's galley kettle so its water was always hot. She kept her hands busy, and tried to forget that she wasn't there by choice. That she was, in fact, Lila Bard's prisoner aboard this ship.

Soon enough, her future cell came into sight.

The *Ferase Stras* rose out of nothing, looking less like a vessel fit for open water and more like a stack of parts, as if several smaller boats had been broken up, and then pieced together, level upon level, a tapestry of wood, and cloth, and spell.

Tes had heard stories about the floating market.

Some said the *Ferase Stras* was the blackest market in the world, others that it was not a market at all, but a vault, housing the world's most wanted and forbidden magic. Heard that even if you were invited aboard the ship, there were rooms you'd never be allowed to enter, things that weren't for sale, to any bidder. She'd heard that the captain was a hundred, three hundred, five hundred years old, that she took payment not in coin, but life. Heard that the floating market was a myth, and that it was very real, but impossible to find without the right map.

She'd heard, too, that the *Ferase Stras* could not be robbed, though that was obviously a lie, since according to Lila Bard, the *persalis* had been housed there, safe until it wasn't.

Still, as the ship drew near, and the lines of magic glimmered in Tes's sight, she wondered what else about the *Ferase Stras* was false. And what was true.

She was about to find out.

The *Grey Barron* pulled up beside the market, drifting close until there was only a stride between the rail of one and the covered awning over the other, a threshold marked by a single wooden door. Lila leapt nimbly across the gap, and gestured for Tes to follow.

Vares clacked his beak. Tes's heart quickened. She fought the urge to back away. They had told her she could not stay in London. Told her it wasn't safe. Not until the Hand was gone for sure. It was too dangerous, they said, but Tes had a feeling they meant her. She was too dangerous. Her power wasn't just a gift, or a curse, it was a weapon, one that could do unspeakable things if it fell into the wrong hands.

The king said she would be safe here.

Tes tried to believe him.

Lila Bard cleared her throat, and gave her a look that said she would be getting onto the *Ferase Stras* that day, one way or another. Her silver threads twitched in the air, and Tes felt an invisible hand against her back, warning her to move. She swallowed, and stepped onto the threshold.

Lila knocked, and a few moments later, the door opened, revealing a tall and handsome man, broad-shouldered and dark-skinned and dressed all in white. His magic was a tendril of amber light around his shoulders.

"Back so soon?" he asked Lila.

"What can I say, Katros? I'm good at my job."

His brows went up. "So you have the *persalis*?"

"Well. Not that good." Lila gripped Tes's shoulder. "But I don't come empty-handed."

He looked from the *Antari* to Tes and back again. "Well," he said. "This should be interesting."

He led them through the door, into the cabin, which turned out to be an office, carefully treading the line between full and cluttered. Tes's eyes took in everything—cabinets full of objects that might have passed for trinkets if she couldn't see the complex spellwork threaded through them. A massive desk sat in the center of the room, behind which sat a well-worn chair, and a large black sphere in a gold stand, its threads an eerie, warning shade.

Tes's fingers twitched, and she felt herself drifting forward to examine it closer when Lila grabbed her arm.

"This way," said Katros, leading them out of the cabin, and down a flight of steps, into the maze that was the floating market. It reminded Tes of her father's shop, the way there was always something to look at, and always the promise of more around the corner, or down the hall. Lila's hand remained firmly on Tes's sleeve as she steered her past curtains and ladders and doors until they reached the main deck, where another man, younger, leaner, but close enough in face he must have been related, stood over a table, inking a map with a minuscule brush, his white sleeves tied out of the way.

And there, sitting on a chair in the sun, a grey sack on the boards beside her, was Maris Patrol. The captain of the floating market.

She was reading a book, and at first, she didn't look up.

Her skin was dark, and deeply wrinkled, her hair a shocking silver, but what struck Tes most was that the air around her was empty. No threads, bright or dim, no dancing lines of light. It seemed the captain of the *Ferase Stras,* home to so much power, had no magic of her own.

She looked old, very old, but not frail, and when she spoke, her voice rang like a bell.

"So few gentle days at sea," she said, closing the book, "you learn to enjoy them when they come."

Maris rose, and as she did, the grey pile on the deck twitched, and resolved itself into a large and ancient dog. Maris stared at Tes, and despite the fact she knew the woman had no magic, she couldn't shake the sense that she was being read. Her eyes never left Tes, but when she spoke, it was to the *Antari.*

"That is not a *persalis,* Delilah Bard. That is, if I had to guess, a teenage girl."

"No," admitted Lila. "The *persalis* was, regrettably, destroyed. But I think you'll find Tes is an . . . improvement."

"Is that so?" asked the old woman.

Lila leaned in, and whispered something in the other captain's ear. Her eyes sharpened. "I see." There it was again, the hungry flash, as she realized she'd come into possession of something rare. "Perhaps we have a place for her."

"I'm not a prize for your vault," snapped Tes.

Maris gave her a long, appraising look. "What are you then?"

She straightened. "I'm a tinkerer."

Maris raised a brow.

"I mean, I fix things," explained Tes. "I make them better. And I'm good at it. And yes, I can see magic. And yes, I can change it. And yes, I know that is a strange and valuable gift, but it doesn't make me a thing instead of a person. I'm not a piece of magic to be put away, and taken out, whenever you have use, and I'm not going to be put in a cage or buried in the bowels of the ship."

It came spilling out, and left her breathless.

Maris crossed her arms. "Have you finished?"

Tes swallowed. And nodded. Maris smiled. "Good. Now, here is what *I* know. There is a great deal of magic on this ship. So much that sometimes,

567

I cannot keep track of it all. There are things that have been aboard longer than I have—yes, it's true—and others whose function I have never been able to discern. Now, it seems you have a talent, one that might make you useful, if you choose to be. And if you stay, as my apprentice, you will be free to use your gift, without being used for it, and maybe even learn a thing or two along the way.

"But," said Maris, stepping closer. "I have never kept a living person on this ship against their will, and I certainly won't be starting now. So if you do not wish to stay, then by all means, return to the *Barron*, and go back to being Lila's problem. It's your choice."

The *Antari* scowled at that, and seemed about to speak, but Maris shot her a heavy look, and for once, she held her tongue while Tes stood on the deck, and looked around at the floating market, the light spilling through every curtain and doorway, the whole place rich with the promise of magic.

And so she made a choice.

Tes watched as the *Barron* drifted away from the *Ferase Stras,* and turned, setting a course she couldn't follow. A hand came to rest on her shoulder, the fingers old, but strong. Tes glanced toward Maris.

"I heard your ship was supposed to be impenetrable," she said.

"That's right."

"Then how were you robbed?"

Maris smiled thinly. "It seems my wards could use improving."

Tes's fingers twitched at the challenge, her eyes already tracing the lines of light that wove across the ship, her mind racing ahead to all the ways they could be fixed. "I can help with that."

"Excellent," said Maris. "Just tell me what you need."

Tes glanced around at the floating market, with all its levels, its rooms, its secrets. "I don't suppose you have any tea?"

IV

The palace rose over the Isle, the crimson water lapping at the stone pedestals that held it up. But from the prison deep inside, there was no sound of water, no tinted light. Only the dull echo of footsteps for the second time that day.

They seemed to run ahead, warning the man in the cell below that someone was coming.

Berras was on his feet by the time his visitor arrived. He took in her pale brown eyes and her widow's peak, the long black hair that fell in a curtain behind her crisp white robes, and for the first time in days, he smiled.

"Ezril."

The *Aven Essen* stood beyond the bars, her priestly garments shining like a moon against the dim stone confines. He was used to seeing her in ordinary clothes, her face obscured by her white mask, but she had the kind of voice that conveyed expression, even with her features hidden. Now, her annoyance was on full display.

"Berras Emery," she said with a long-suffering sigh. "What a mess you made."

His brow furrowed. "It can be fixed."

Ezril inclined her head. "Can it?" she mused in her airy way. "I think not. Your plan was rushed. And you, too eager. I warned you of that, didn't I? Change may seem sudden when it comes, Berras Emery. A tree, split by a bolt of lightning. A flood overrunning the banks. But it's easy to forget, the storm must gather first."

He gripped the bars. "Must you always speak in riddles like a priest?"

"I *am* a priest," she pointed out, "and they are not riddles, just because you fail to understand them." She folded her hands inside the sleeves of her robes. "Nature provides an analog to every human problem. An answer to every question."

"I don't need answers," he muttered. "I need you to open the cell, so I can finish what I started."

"What you started . . ." she echoed, looking up, not at the prison ceiling, but the palace overhead. "You worked so hard to get within the walls, and here you are. So far, and yet, so close."

Berras grimaced, but said nothing.

"But you are alone," she went on. "No *persalis,* no borrowed magic, no contingent of willing *hands*." Her gaze flicked to his bandaged fist. "Just you."

"If you help me—"

She pressed on, as if he hadn't spoken. "Oh, you might kill one of them, before you're caught. But I fear we both know which one you would choose."

He opened his mouth, but she cut him off. "Do not lie," she warned. "I know we each have our own reasons, but you promised me when we first met that this wasn't for revenge."

"It's not."

Ezril clicked her tongue. "The problem with venom, Berras, is that if you're not careful, it can also poison you." She shook her head. "No, you had your chance, and failed." She unfolded her arms, reached out, and trailed her thin fingers over the bars. "Obviously, this requires a more delicate touch."

Berras lunged at her through the bars, but she was already out of reach. She tutted, lips twitching in a smile. As if it were a game.

"Fine," he growled. "We'll do it your way. *Sel Fera Noche.* Just get me out of here."

But Ezril had stopped listening. The ring on her hand, carved from pale marble, had begun to glow, warming as it did with a pleasant heat. "I have to go," she said. "It appears I'm being summoned by the king."

She turned toward the stairs.

"Ezril," he called after her. "I will tell them. If you leave me in this cell, I will tell them *everything*."

The priest stopped, and sighed. "Well," she said, "in that case . . ."

She turned back to the cell, one hand reaching out, not for Berras, but the stone wall at his back. People often forgot that priests had magic. They assumed that because they held the world in balance, their power must be weak. That they could not fell a tree as easily as grow one.

But as Ezril flexed her hand, the stone wall splintered, shearing off a sharpened edge. It sang through the air, changing tune only when it slid across the skin at Berras Emery's throat. Skin that parted like a piece of summer fruit. His good hand went to the wound, and he opened his mouth to speak, but the stone blade had cut deep enough to silence as well as kill.

Berras Emery staggered, and then sank to his knees on the cell floor, as life ran between his fingers, pooling at his feet. It always surprised Ezril how much blood a body held. He toppled sideways, those storm-dark eyes clouding over as he did, and she watched as the pool spread like fingers, reaching toward her, then stepped back, careful to keep her white robes clear from the spreading crimson stain.

The ring's warmth had turned to heat on her hand, a reminder that she was being called to serve. And so the *Aven Essen* turned her back on the dead man in the cell, and went upstairs to greet the king.

END OF BOOK ONE

ACKNOWLEDGMENTS

People ask me how it felt to write this book, and the truth is, it felt like coming home.

In *A Conjuring of Light,* when Lila makes the deal with Maris, that black eye in exchange for a favor, I saw a way to prop the door to this world open, to let myself back in. All I had to do was hold space for the stories I still wanted to tell.

It doesn't sound that hard, holding space, but it is. It's heavier than it looks.

We talk of how it takes a village (some days it feels more like a city), and in the case of *Fragile Threads,* it wasn't simply a matter of spreading the work over so many hands, wasn't simply about ensuring the success of this book when it finally hit shelves.

The truth is, telling a *new* story in this world means first keeping the world alive, helping it thrive in the space between the arcs of Shades and Threads, preserving the demand and ensuring the support over the intervening years.

It is an act of generosity, and care, to hold space in that way, and here are the people who've kept Shades of Magic shining bright, laid the way for Threads of Power, and made this entire ongoing journey of ours possible:

My agent, Holly Root. My editor, Miriam Weinberg. My PR rep, Kristin Dwyer. You three are the strings holding me together, with your unwavering faith and constant support. I could not ask for a better team of incredible humans and friends.

My parents, Kent and Linda Schwab. You put up with me, even when I'm six hundred pages into a first draft and so full of doubt and dread that it comes spilling out my mouth at every "how are you?"

My big sister, Jenna Maurice. You are my family in all ways but blood, a stellar tour partner, a great photographer, and an even better friend. Thank you for always looking for ways to help me take better care of myself.

My found family, Cat and Caro Clarke. You are cheerleaders, colleagues, partners in crime, dreamers, and damn good humans. You feed my heart.

My friends Jordan Bartlett, Zoraida Córdova, Dhonielle Clayton, Sarah Maria Griffin, Laura Stevens. You make sure I never feel alone on this long and winding journey.

My incredible team at Tor—Devi Pillai, Eileen Lawrence, Lucille Rettino, Sarah Reidy, Giselle Gonzalez, Emily Mlynek, Tessa Villanueva, Alex Cameron, Michelle Foytek, Rachel Taylor, Peter Lutjen, and more— the most extraordinary champions. You keep my books in print, and work tirelessly to ensure they have the greatest chance of finding readers, new and old.

Eyden's, the coffee shop in Edinburgh I call my office, my living room, my second home. Adonis, Eyden, Connor, and the rest of the lovely team. Thank you for always making sure Riley and I have a fresh pot of tea, a snack, and a corner in which to write.

Kip and Giada, the dazzling chefs of Via Aemelia. You've supplied me week in and week out with fresh pasta so after long days of writing, I could have a lovely home-cooked meal.

And last, and *most*, you.

My lovely readers.

Never doubt your importance or your power.

Your love for this world and its characters is what made it possible for me to reopen the door, and come home.

ABOUT THE AUTHOR

V.E. Schwab is the No.1 *New York Times* bestselling author of *Vicious*, *The Near Witch* and the Shades of Magic series, which was described as "a classic work of fantasy" by Deborah Harkness. It was one of Waterstones' Best Fantasy Books of 2015, *The Guardian*'s Best Science Fiction novels, and a *Telegraph* choice for the Best Young Adult Books of 2015. *The Independent* has called her "The natural successor to Diana Wynne Jones." She lives between Nashville, France and Edinburgh.